SKULLENIA COLLECTION

BOOKS 1-3

TONY LEWIS

CONTENTS

WHEREWOLF 1

CUP AND SORCERY 185

WUTHERING FRIGHTS 371

About the Author 555

WHEREWOLF

SKULLENIA BOOK 1

For James
Maybe you'll read this book
Love, Dad

WHEREWOLF

The woods were as silent and still as a fresh corpse with only the faint rustling of small woodland creatures and the predators hunting them registering any sound at all as they waged their nocturnal battles. Majestic in its frigidity, the moon was full and high in the ebony sky, but the dense foliage of the lofty, ancient trees was enough to ensure that only a meagre amount of its light filtered through to illuminate the loamy forest floor below.

It was then that an almost imperceptible footfall disturbed the pristine calm, and a quiet whisper floated across the gloomy air.

"Do we have to do this now?"

"Well, when else do you suggest we do it? You could try coming out at lunchtime I suppose but I don't think you'll find many werewolves strolling about trying to work on their tan."

"Okay, fine, but just remember what happened to the last two chaps who got this job."

"And what would that be?"

"Coming out here totally unprepared without having done any research. They even brought silver bullets, for goodness sake, and everyone knows they don't work."

"Well, don't keep me in suspense by blathering on all night. What happened to them?"

"One was never found, and all they found of the other one was his hat."

"And?"

"His head was still in it!"

"So, on the strength of that, you're just *presuming that* he was eaten by a wolf," came the sarcastic reply.

"Well, what else could have done that out here? A Boy Scout gone postal? Finally tied one too many reef knots and completely unravelled?"

"Maybe Cowan got fed up with his constant whining and cut his head off to shut him up."

"Don't wind me up, I'm nervous enough as it is." "I didn't know you were afraid of the dark."

"It's not the dark that bothers me. It's what's hiding *in it* that gives me the willies. Especially out here."

A quiet snort impinged upon the funereal hush.

"Look, there's really nothing to worry about. You know I've brought along everything we need. I've got Wolf's Bane, chains and padlocks, a dog whistle... "

"Yeah, and half a sheep festering away in that bag. I can smell it from here, it's disgusting. It's so strong there's more chance of us getting attacked by a shark. Look, even the maggots are running away."

"I didn't know maggots could run." "Shut up."

"I really don't know why you came out here, Alf," said the first figure, dropping the meat laden sack to the ground where it landed with a glutinous squelch. "All you've done is moan and jump at your own shadow."

"It's too dark for a shadow. It's like being down the bottom of a bloody well."

"Look all... " "Sssshhhh." "What?"

A hushed, almost indiscernible noise had punctured the abyssal silence. In reality it was no louder than a freshly laundered towel caressing a baby's cheek, but it resounded like a gunshot because the forest was so still.

Both men reacted instantly, hunching over, straining their ears for all they were worth, trying not only to figure out what they had heard but where it had come from, and from what.

Alf was now way beyond his initial fears about the venture. He'd arrived at St. Panic Station and was on the verge of becoming a full blown gibbering wreck. He wanted to flee but his feet were glued to the floor, his knees were trembling, and his bowels were quickly turning to water.

"Hey!" he whispered, "what is it?"

"I don't know for sure," replied his companion, "but I think it might be behind us."

Whatever *it* was emitted a rich, bass growl that the two men felt way down deep in their chests.

"We're in trouble."

The snarl grew louder and more menacing. "We're definitely in tro..."

All Alf saw was a large, vague shape launch itself at his friend's back, and when it hit a second later, it had enough force to carry him to the forest floor. He felt a chilled rush of air sweep past his cheek and detected the unmistakable odour of damp dog.

His stricken partner screamed once and was then silenced, his cry replaced by a sickeningly liquid crunch. Alf gazed in fascinated horror as a head the size of a horse's turned towards him and two intense red eyes fixed him with a wicked glare. Thick dark fluid dripped from teeth the length of an index finger as the creatures' breath formed a miasmal cloud before it. An instant later the massive beast launched itself at the now lone hunter, hell bent on rending him to shredded chunks so that it could continue its grizzly feast.

Alf reacted instinctively, his adrenal gland pumping for all it was worth in order to fuel his taught muscles, and before he was consciously aware of what he was doing, he was turning to flee.

Sadly though, his instantaneous attempt at flight was brought to a sudden and dramatic halt. As his right foot pivoted, the toe of his boot caught on something wooden and, even though every fibre and sinew in his body fought to keep him upright, he lost his balance and crashed heavily to the leaf strewn forest floor. Time seemed to slow and as he fell, he turned his head. The werewolf was nearly on him. It was in full flight, all four legs off the ground, slavering jaws wide open and ready to strike. Realising that without further action he was about to be torn to pieces, Alf brought his left arm round, intent on finding purchase in an effort to spur him to his feet and away from what was going to be the most certain of certain deaths. His grasping fingers, however, did not hit the soil. They touched and unconsciously closed around a piece of frigid wood that was much too uniform to be a part of any tree.

With time now seemingly at a stand still, he brought the object closer to him. At the very least he could make use of it as a club. Then, with a flash of intense relief that actually made him shudder, Alf realised it was the high powered rifle that he and his recently deceased acquaintance had brought with them.

The wolf was now close enough that he could see the small red capillaries in its eyes and smell its foetid, meaty breath. Without a second thought, Alf brought the barrel of the weapon to bear on the creature and pulled the trigger, sending a hollow point bullet straight at it. He didn't see where the bullet penetrated, but the sudden silence and the fact that he wasn't being torn limb from flailing limb told him all that he needed to know. He collapsed back onto the forest floor and let out the breath that he'd been holding for what had seemed like an eternity.

"Never again," he muttered to himself.

———

"Dinner time, Ollie!"

"Oh, good grief, do I have to?"

"I fink you do yes, uverwise you put your, umm, immortal soul in, drier, uh dire peril, decci, dicec, mess up your very flush and, um, bones, and den 'ave to spend all 'ternity wandring about da efereal neverworld."

Ollie Splint closed his eyes and sighed, trying to push the thought of dinner from his mind. Actually, and by way of introduction (never let it be said that us authors are rude types) it might help you to know that Ollie was a vampire. Well, he was half vampire anyway. His father, Glut the Bodyripper, was a most infamous bloodsucker and was renowned throughout the undead world as one of the most gruesome and malevolent creatures ever to don the black cape and pointy fangs.

His mother, however, wasn't such a denizen of the dark, occupier of the otherworld or inhabitant of any evil environs of any description whatsoever. Her name was Sharon Goldsmith and she was, to this day, an assistant in a small library in Cardiff (she worked in the Welsh language section so spent most of her time wiping phlegm off the books and telling English tourists that 'heaty hottio' didn't mean microwave oven).

His father had met her during one of his many night time hunting expeditions (or to put it another way, he was out to kill as many living things as possible before the sun came up and turned him into a Cornish Pasty).

Sharon, on the other hand, being slightly more academically inclined and not really that interested in slaughter on a scale not seen since the Spanish Flu epidemic, had been on a college gap year and was hiking through Eastern Europe to broaden her mind and expand on her life experience.

As was traditional (and who am I to tamper with that) they'd met in a secluded, pseudo medieval village that was populated by dribbling simpletons, world class idiots and a mad woman who spent her days wandering about yelling 'WHOOOOO!" at passers by. You know the sort of place don't you? If not, imagine Southend but just a tad friendlier and with a higher collective IQ.

Anyway, their meeting had been something of a revelation to them both. In all his centuries of existence Glut had never been so affected by a human female (in that he didn't have the urge to tear her throat out and drink her blood. Well, he did for a bit but then he wouldn't have been a proper vampire if he didn't would he), and as impossible as it may seem, he'd actually fallen in love with the demure Welsh lass.

And so, stricken as he was by Cupids fateful arrow, he realised that if he wanted to forge any sort of meaningful relationship with Sharon he needed to be truthful with her, so he took a risk and told her about his, how shall we put it, colourfully alternative lifestyle. Surprisingly she took it all on board without batting an eyelid and dealt with the vampires surreal tale in an amazingly level headed fashion because, if the truth be known, she was as smitten with the giant blood sucker as he was with her. They'd never married of course, because vampires simply don't do that by tradition, and what with traditions being

9

somewhat traditional, and vampires being very traditional in their keeping of traditions there was no way that Glut could break that particular tradition because it was so traditional, and as you can imagine there are certain traditions that simply can't be trifled with. She had, however, been afforded the greatest honour that a male vampire can bestow upon a human female. He'd chosen her to bear his child and since then they'd enjoyed a very happy romance thank you very much. Even to this day he still visited with her several times a year (it's in all the papers whenever he does. Well, almost. The last headline was 'Another 34 unexplained deaths in Wales' capital city.' No doubt they'll figure it out one day but by then there'll be no one left except Sharon, that statue of Sir Gareth Edwards and the bloke who polishes the Millennium Stadium).

So Ollie, thanks to his mixed parentage, had been blessed with some very distinct and somewhat odd character traits. He could mesmerise anyone he liked (as long as they had the brain of an over the hill heavyweight boxer and the IQ of a boiled turnip that is), he needed to avoid direct sunlight, but could go out in it if he wrapped up like an Eskimo who really hated the cold, he slept in a coffin the size of a piano crate and, for some strange reason, he could make his left foot invisible. On a good night, if he'd had plenty of sleep and concentrated really hard, he could turn himself into a decently sized bat. Well, he'd managed it once, but had gotten fed up with the entire process and vowed never to do it again after spending three hours hanging upside down from a branch, passing water all over his own face, passing out and falling to the floor. And trying to shave when you didn't have a reflection was a constant pain in the chin.

On the flip side of all these black, vaguely evil and some might say, outrageously nefarious talents (and let's face it, it's nice to have some balance. It doesn't pay to be completely rotten all the time does it, not unless you're a serial killer, an evil dictator or an estate agent anyway), he was fond of a cup of Earl Grey tea (decaffeinated of course. Vampires can be stroppy enough even when they've had a good day's sleep), Marmite sandwiches with the crusts cut off, a nice drop of wine and a good cry at anything remotely sentimental.

His heritage was also the reason for his rather peculiar moniker (not the one from Friends. She was just weird). In true vampire tradition where the male's title was meant to be something as vile as possible, his given name was actually Gore the Spinesplitter, but once he'd reached an age where these things mattered, he'd decided that it would be next to impossible trying to go through eternity with such a ghastly title, especially after he'd tried booking a meal in a restaurant one evening. He'd barely finished getting his name out when the maître d' gave him a rather peculiar look, went deathly pale and asked him to leave otherwise he'd call the authorities. Obviously a squad of policemen wouldn't have posed the young vampire any problems at all, but it wasn't quite how he'd planned the evening to go, and having to kill several officers of the law would probably have put him off his trifle.

Ollie did, however, love his old Dad, so as a sign of respect rather than changing his name completely, he'd contracted it to the reasonably more user friendly Splint. Ollie was the name of a pet cat that he'd had as a boy. A cat that had mysteriously disappeared one weekend when his cousin, Grind the Felinekiller, aged nine and a half, had come for a sleepover.

The main bugbear in Ollie's life though, was a total and utter loathing of the sight, smell, taste, feel and look of blood. It made him shudder every time he thought about the revolting liquid, which was twice a day in fact, a pint at a time. And as you can imagine it was no fun being a creature of the night when blood-letting and everything else related to the vile substance made you retch. The twice yearly meeting of the Vampire Union, V.L.A.D (Vampires Love a Drop) was a complete nightmare from beginning to end. The other members, happily throwing gallons of AB negative down their necks, would quite happily pull his fangs out if they discovered he'd smuggled in a couple of bottles of strawberry flavoured Ribena. And the buffet, well, that was beyond words (it was putrid, nauseating, horrific, nasty, noisome and downright yucky. There you go, not quite as beyond words as I thought. Hurrah for a bit of hyperbole, overstatement, exaggeration, over-embellishment and the like).

As Flug placed the tray on Ollie's desk and backed off slightly, Ollie thought about what Flug had just said. It sounded wooden and stilted, almost rehearsed. He could never have come up with anything like that on his own.

"Have you been looking at the pretty pictures in your vampire comics again, Flug?"

"Yeah. Me like da hunters. Dey cool," he rumbled. "I'm sure they are."

"And good cooks." "Cooks?" asked Ollie.

"Dey do good stuff wiv steaks, me like steaks." Ollie gazed despondently at the hulk before him.

"S-T-A-K-E-S. Not S-T-E-A-K-S, you bonehead," said Ollie breaking down and spelling the words as if he were addressing a particularly stupid child, or an adult from Chatham. He chose to gloss over the fact that Flugs apparent hero spent the majority of his time nailing vampires to the floor, yanking out their teeth for souvenirs and, to top it all off, hammering bits of wood into their chests, which, if nothing else, was rather unhygienic quite frankly. And what if you got a splinter? You could end up with a really nasty infection.

A dry, rasping laugh came from a shadowy figure lurking in the doorway.

"It's no good spelling it out, Ollie mate. You know he has trouble stringing sentences together. And understanding them for that matter, let alone a whole word."

"He'd have trouble stringing two beads together. So, what can I do for you?"

Phillip "Stitches" Meeup ambled over towards Ollie's desk. He had a rolling, lopsided gait and a dusty, grey, sort of thrown together look about him, which he virtually was if the truth be known. In the one hundred and sixty years since his reanimation, wear and tear had taken its toll on the zombie's joints, muscles and tissues and trying to turn the clock back was an ongoing battle that he would never win. Parts of him were forever falling off and no amount of cod liver oil, skin cream or WD40 was going to keep the extreme ageing process at bay. He carried around a small sewing kit at all times in case of any mishaps, hence his apt, if not very imaginative, nickname (but let's face it, is there any such thing as an imaginative nickname? Um... no. If your names Jones, it's Jonesy. Smith.. . Smiffy etc. If you're a tad large, it's Tiny and if you're tall it's Shorty. The most popular of course is reserved for contestants on Celebrity Big Brother. Every one of them is known as Who the hell is that?)

Stitches sat in an old, leather chair facing Ollie.

"I was just wondering if we've had any work come in. Shouldn't you be drinking that, by the way? You don't want it to clot," he said, pointing to the blood filled tankard.

Ollie grimaced and reached for the revolting refreshment. "Thank you sooooo much for reminding me," he growled.

Stitches sat back in his chair and crossed his legs, eliciting a loud crack and a worrying puff of dust.

"No problem, sunshine. You know me, always glad to help," he said. Ollie paused with the tankard a few inches from his mouth.

"How many times have I told you it's not funny to call a vampire sunshine?"

"Makes me laugh," said Stitches, sporting a cheeky smirk. "That's no guarantee of comedic quality. Excuse me."

Ollie clamped his eyes shut and pinched his nose before taking a deep breath, dry swallowing, sniffing loudly, clearing his throat, sniffing again and, if it were possible, pinching his nose even tighter, before drinking the warm liquid straight down.

"Yuck," choked Ollie, as he slammed the empty tankard back down, sending microscopic droplets of blood onto the wooden surface of his desk in the process, a mess that he wouldn't notice until he tried to pick up a sheet of sticky paper. He belched massively and what felt like half a strapping six footers lifeblood bubbled up into his throat. It wasn't pleasant.

"Wot matter, Ollie. You no like?" inquired Flug, a look of concern on his face (or it could have been wind. Flug's facial expressions could be a little bit hard to determine what with him having the appearance of a haphazardly sewn together car crash, so how he was feeling was a matter of guess work most of the time. To keep things simple it was best to assume that Flug was confused. You'd usually be right).

"No, it was bloody awful," offered Stitches.

Ollie wiped his mouth with a silk hanky then threw it in the bin. It could have been washed in sulphuric acid and hung out to dry on the sun and he wouldn't have used it again.

"I'm sorry, Flug. I still don't like it," he said. "Do me a favour will you and get rid of that rancid thing." Ollie gestured towards the empty tankard.

"Okay, Ollie," replied Flug. He picked up the empty vessel and thudded out of the office.

Stitches sniggered once the befuddled behemoth had departed. "Of all the luck," he said.

"What do you mean?" said Ollie.

"Well, most monsters you come across are made by a disturbed genius or a mad scientist aren't they? Or at the very least a biology student with a grudge, but not our Flug."

"True, true," replied Ollie, shuffling some papers in the vain hope of looking efficient. Some very sticky papers. "You wouldn't think an accountant would have that much spare time would you. And come on, bolts through the neck. Yes, we all expect that, but one through the forehead? Methinks someone came bottom in monster building class."

"He can pick up radio on that thing, you know," said the zombie. "Really!"

"Yeah. On a clear night with no wind, face him north on the roof, clip an aerial to his bolt and drop his trousers, the shipping forecast comes out lovely."

Ollie frowned.

"Seems like a lot of hassle to go to just to listen to boat news. And why drop his trousers, does that help with the reception?"

"I'm not sure," pondered Stitches, "but the first time we did it they fell down, so I suppose it's become a sort of tradition."

"Traditions," said Ollie, with a hint of sarcasm in his voice so heavy that it needed to go on a diet, "are time honoured practices, passed down through the ages that take on revered significance. Pulling down poor Flug's trousers on the roof does not come under that particular umbrella I'm afraid. So, how often do you perform this ancient and hallowed rite then?"

"We started last Friday."

"How noble, how holy. This has the potential to become legendary, you know."

Stitches lowered his gaze and concentrated on his lap. "Just a bit of fun is all," he murmured.

"Just one more thing", Ollie continued. "Why the shipping forecast? We live two hundred miles from the coast."

"It's all we can pick up apart from Radio Moscow. We tried to get The Postmortem Review but the reception was terrible."

Ollie rubbed a hand over his face and let out a sigh. 'I'm losing the will to unlive' he thought.

"Changing the subject ever so slightly," he said, "where's Ronnie?" "I haven't seen him," said Stitches.

Ollie shook his head. "Do you know, if I had a penny for every time that joke about him being invisible was funny I'd have precisely no pennies. I meant do you know where he is?"

"Nope."

Ollie got up from behind his desk and walked around in front of it, to stretch his legs.

"What was it you came in here for anyway?" he said. "It seems like decades ago."

Stitches stuck a finger in his ear and waggled it about to try and dislodge an errant particle of dust that was annoying him.

"Oh, yeah. I was just wondering if we'd had any work come in."

"Not at the mome... uhh, your finger." "What about it?"

"You need to take it out of your head. It looks like you're either growing a tusk or you're one of those sad acts who can't go five steps outside their house without attaching an antenna to their skull in case they miss a really important phone call."

Stitches reached up with his now four fingered hand and retrieved his disembodied digit.

"I thought it'd gone quiet," he said, getting his sewing kit from an inside pocket.

Legs suitably exercised, Ollie returned to his chair.

"Anyway, as I was saying, no. We don't have any work at the moment."

"What, none at all? Not even a sniff?" asked the zombie, dexterously threading a needle, or as dextrously as he could anyway. It wasn't easy when you had fingers like dessicated carrots.

"Nope, I'm afraid not so we'll have to continue basking in the glory of solving the cryptic and enigmatic Case of The Cracked Mirror. Remember that?"

"How could I forget?" said Stitches. "A fiendish, nay heinous crime involving irreparable damage to the mirror in the upstairs bathroom."

"Indeed," agreed Ollie.

"The mirror that Flug head-butted because he thought someone was staring at him?"

Ollie nodded. "The very same."

"Mind you, a broken mirror and a screaming monster with a three inch shard of glass in his face didn't take much working out did it? Even Constable Gullett could have gotten to the bottom of that one."

Ollie didn't respond as he was lost in thought. He was mulling over the decision to take over his uncles' detective agency. Not that he'd had much choice in the matter of course. It was stated in the will of his dad's brother, Gorge The Corpsegrinder (1376-2015), that Ollie should head the business for a period of no less than six months, with the option to stay on for longer if he fancied it. Yeah right. As if that was going to happen. If he was honest he couldn't wait to get out of this godforsaken place and then have a little chat with his dad about his less than subtle interference in his sons life choices. Ollie was convinced that the old boy had had a taloned hand in the affair.

His Uncle Gorge had lived and worked his whole life in Skullenia and its strange surroundings (population: some living, some dead, most undead, and the rest, who knew? It was a rather drab and dreary place that had once ranked eleventh in top ten list of 'Places I would rather go on holiday if Iraq was fully booked'. It was nearly twinned with Chernobyl at one point but the Russian town had withdrawn from the agreement because their council leaders had felt that its image would have been irreparably tarnished, and it was also the only place on record that Kentucky Fried Chicken had refused to open a branch in. McDonald's had tried, but the Skullenians had said no), so apparently there was no better place for Ollie to spend some time than in the birthplace of his family and immersed in their unholy practices and traditions.

The decision had probably been made after Glut realised that his son wasn't the body ripping, blood drinking, heart devouring fiend that he himself was. And let's face it, you always want the best for your kids. Ollie's reticence had, to say the least, left Glut a tad miffed, and when he found out that Ollie had developed a passing interest in astronomy and wanted to go to night school, he'd almost burst.

"No offspring of mine is going to spend his evenings gazing up at the sky comet watching," Glut had spat whilst looming over his son from his full height of seven feet four. "The only heavenly bodies you should be concerning yourself with are the ones that you're about to sink your teeth into."

"But, dad... "

"Don't interrupt me when I'm speaking, boy," Glut had snarled, his piercing eyes seeming to bore into Ollie's soul with a look that could stop a heartbeat in an instant. "It's unseemly for you act like a normal person. You'll be telling me you want to buy some designer trainers and get a job in WH Smith next. You're a vampire for heavens sake."

"Half vampire."

"Well, you're mostly vampire."

"Mum's human and you fell for her, or had you forgotten that little detail?."

"No, I hadn't forgotten that, but it doesn't mean you have to become slave to a few inferior genes wandering about your system."

"Perhaps you should have called me Wrangler then."

"Don't be flippant. It doesn't suit you. The fact is that you have many of the qualities associated with the Wamphyri that you can't escape from and I want you to start acting like it. Your heritage spans thousands of years and I won't have it sullied because you've developed a bit of a conscience. Now, go to your cellar and think about what I've said."

"Dad." "What now."

"I'm twenty seven." "Bugger."

So all the evidence said to him that Glut had pushed Gorge into putting the caveat in his will, forcing him to spend some time in Skullenia.

But what Ollie still failed to understand was how running a hugely unsuccessful detective agency would give him an insight into the life of a vampire. All he'd learned so far was how to get incredibly bored. He didn't go out much at night because it was terrifying, and according to Stitches the chances of him finding a virgin to sink his teeth into in this neck of the woods were virtually nil. There was Fragrant Fiona of course, but she was about as attractive as a Rottweiler in a tutu, only with a worse temper and more teeth. And as her name suggested, she smelled so bad that the woodland scavengers regularly bypassed the local rubbish dump and headed straight for her.

All in all, the next few months were looking pretty grim.

———

The assembled gathering numbered about a dozen. Males and females ranging in age from early twenties to mid-fifties sat on various chairs, sofas and the floor. Despite the disparity in their ages though they were all magnificent specimens, each and every one of them in tremendous physical condition. The only person standing was a female who was pacing the floor.

"Has he returned yet?" she asked.

"No, he hasn't," came the reply from one of the males who had just entered the room, "and he should have been back well before now. I hate to say it but I think. . . "

"I know," the female responded, a pensive edge colouring her words. "So what do we do now? Suggestions anyone?"

A chorus of voices rang out, ideas and thoughts flowing from the concerned group.

"Let's get together and find out for ourselves what's going on," said one.

"They'll come back eventually, let's wait and see what happens," said another.

"I'm for trying to find them right now," said someone else.

The lady stopped her pacing and stood in the midst of the group. She folded her arms but raised a hand to her mouth, an index finger gently tapping on her cheek as she considered what she'd heard.

"I can appreciate what you're all saying," she said, "but I think the best course of action would be to let the Master know. As capable as we are he's going to be in the best position to get to the bottom of it."

Though slightly muted and not entirely enthusiastic, murmurs of begrudging agreement issued forth from the other members.

"Right," she announced, detecting their reticence. "Whilst I can understand your willingness to plunge in feet first, the last thing I want is for all of us to go charging round the forest like headless demons stirring up a lot of trouble and putting ourselves at further risk. And besides, if the Master found out that this had been kept from him I think you'll agree that he'd be more than a little annoyed, and people going missing would be the least of our concerns."

"Who's going to tell him?" someone asked.

"I'll do it," said Obsidia, facing the group once more. "But in person. This isn't the sort of news to be passed on via a message. I'll leave now."

———

Stitches shuffled out of Ollie's office and made his way along the hallway to the kitchen. He wasn't hungry or thirsty but he needed to drink some water every now and again to keep his dusty innards lubricated. He'd tried three in one oil but it had just sunk to his feet and leaked out. He found Flug sitting on a chair staring intently at a bottle of washing up liquid over by the sink.

"What you doing, mate?" he asked, getting himself a glass. "Sssshhhh," muttered Flug.

"Why, what's going on?" "Don't bovver me." "Why?"

Flug wouldn't take his eyes off the bottle. "You make me miss it." "WHAT?"

"Me watchin' my faverit soap like Mrs. Ladle do."

Stitches burst out laughing and dropped the glass to the floor, smashing it to pieces and making Flug jump.

As he wasn't the most intelligent of beings, a lot of what Flug did was accomplished by learned behaviour, the way children do when they watch their parents. The problem was, Flug wasn't as clever as your average toddler and also tended to be a bit more literal than was good for his health. For those very reasons he needed to be kept an eye on when he was in 'learning mode'. Or, to put it another way, locked in his bedroom until the moment had passed and he was safe to rejoin society. Ollie had discovered this not long after his arrival in Skullenia when he found the giant reanimate in his office, using his desk as a make shift bonfire and eating a hot buttered shoe because he'd watched Ronnie make some toast.

"You total doughnut," gasped the zombie, very much in danger of literally laughing his head off. It had happened before. He considered pointing out the tiny misunderstanding to his friend but decided against it. There was no point whatsoever in trying to explain much of anything to a creature with the intellectual capacity of a brontosaurus with severe learning difficulties.

Stitches went to get a broom when Flug let out a gasp. The bottle that he'd been watching levitated off the side and hovered a foot in the air gently swaying to and fro. Flug stared goggle eyed at the floating object and watched in horror as it moved slowly towards him.

"Wot goin' on, Stitches?" he whimpered in a voice far too high for a creature that could knock down a semi-detached house with one punch. Stitches clapped a hand over his mouth, attempting to stifle the giggle that was trying to escape.

"Me scared. ME SCARED!" wailed Flug.

The plastic bottle was now positioned directly over Flug's head. He looked upwards, the terror evident on his face, but he was unable to look away. Then, with a resounding THWACK, the object suddenly lost its aeronautical ability and fell onto Flug's forehead.

"Ow!" he said, rubbing the sore spot as Stitches slapped him on the shoulder.

"You fall for it every time, don't you, matey?" he said sympathetically.

"Wot?"

"Show him, Ron."

The air in the kitchen began to writhe and undulate, as if the temperature and humidity had suddenly increased, and a high pitched whine, like a badly played harmonica, cut through the quiet. A small static charge buzzed the atmosphere, and a shimmering waterfall of colours appeared and slowly coalesced into a human form. Finally, with all of his atoms reconfigured, Ronnie Smalls ran a hand through his hair and grinned at his colleagues.

"Surprise!" he said, winking at Flug.

"You a big naughty. Me fought it was ghost," said Flug.

"A ghost in Skullenia? Who'd have thought," said Ronnie.

Stitches went to the sink and finally got his drink. "What have you been up to then?" he asked Ronnie after downing a pint of the clear stuff.

"Nothing much," answered Ronnie, pulling up a chair and sitting next to a now calmed down Flug. "Just been wandering round town trying to find something interesting to poke my nose into. You know, listening at doors, peeking through windows, that sort of thing. All in the interests of the agency, of course!"

Stitches raised a doubtful eyebrow. "Oh, of course. But why do you have to sneak about everywhere?" he asked. "No one can see you when you're invisible, which is one of the major benefits of being invisible, so you might as well be invisible seeing as you have the ability to go invisible. That's kind of the point of being invisible isn't it?"

Ronnie took a black leather pouch from a pocket and rolled himself a cigarette. Once lit, he took a deep, and obviously satisfying, drag on it. Stitches was thankful that he could see Ronnie at this point, because when he smoked whilst invisible, the sight of the carcinogenic fog circulating through Ronnie's unseen system was quite disconcerting. "Sneaking around is half the fun, especially when there's a chance I might be seen," said Ronnie. "Being out there snooping about is far more exciting if there's a possibility of getting caught."

"If you say so. I take it there's not much happening out there then?" said Stitches after looking at the clock on the wall. It was still relatively early.

"Not really," said Ronnie. "Old Sweaty's flying about trying to spook people as usual, Mrs Ladle's having trouble with her broomstick again, and it's talent night at The Bolt and Jugular."

"Dazzling," said Stitches sarcastically. He'd only experienced talent night at the local pub on one occasion, and whilst a lot of people might find the sight of an ogre juggling dwarves entertaining, it wasn't really for him. The acts were even worse.

"Isn't it. I've seen a lot of strange things but five minutes of Blind Arnold singing 'I Can See Clearly Now' is enough for anyone," said Ronnie.

"You've got that right. That bloke's got a sander in his throat, not vocal chords. Still, it can't be as bad as that Egyptian mummy's fire eating act. Probably lasted longer too."

Flug heaved himself out of his chair and made to leave the kitchen. "Where you off to, big guy?" asked Ronnie, shrouded in a pall of pale smoke.

21

"Put cat out," came the reply from the departing monster. Ronnie cast a puzzled look at Stitches. "We haven't got a cat."

"I know. He puts a saucer of milk outside and keeps a litter tray in the pantry. Apparently it's to do with dormant subconscious memories resurfacing and manifesting themselves physically."

Ronnie stubbed out his cigarette and flicked the butt into the bin. "Maybe. Or it could be because he's got less brain cells than I've got gills."

"That's true," laughed Stitches. "He couldn't pour water out of a glass if the instructions were on the bottom."

Ronnie rolled himself another smoke. "I'll tell you who I did see," he said, the fag dangling from his bottom lip. "Dr Jekyll."

"Oh yeah, what's he up to these days?" asked the zombie.

"He's gone into partnership with Mr Singh from the corner shop." "Doing what?"

"Bounty hunting of all things."

"Mmmm. Could be useful if we ever need to track someone down. What're they called? I'll let Ollie know." "Hyde and Sikh."

The zombie snorted. "Catchy."

"I thought so. Fancy a game of crib?"

Stitches pulled up a chair and joined Ronnie at the table. "Might as well. Nothing else to do."

———

Alfred Resco sat in an outer office, perched on the edge of a burgundy leather sofa, tapping his fingers on his knees, his eyes darting in all directions. Due to the success of last night's venture, he knew that he'd end up here again, but it didn't mean he wanted to be. All he wanted was his money. He also needed a smoke, but a large sign on the opposite wall portraying a cigarette with a dagger through it put pay to that.

The room was sparse and unwelcoming to say the least. Alf thought he'd feel more comfortable sitting in a Second World War bunker whilst it was being bombed. Strangely there was an aquarium sat in the middle of the floor, an out of place looking item if ever there was one. On inspection Alf saw that it contained some of the most evil looking fish that he'd ever seen. Small bones and pieces of matted fur lay on the bottom of the tank, and the water was tinted with a subtle hint of red. They were the sort of fish that, if you had one of them on your plate, it would get to your chips before you did. He was about to go and have closer a look when a voice boomed from an intercom, making him jump.

"You can come in now."

Alf crossed the room, feeling like a prisoner on Death Row called to take his last walk, and if he was honest he thought it might be good to trade places with them, because a nagging worry at the back of his mind was telling him that said prisoner had better prospects for a long and happy life than he did. Stay calm, deep breaths he silently told himself. In through the nose, out through the mouth and keep cool. Yeah right!

He opened the door and entered. "Ah, Mr Resco. Sit down won't you."

The man was huge. He was standing by the window, looking at the view, but it was lost on Alf because the guy blocked it out. He was obviously a soldier, the uniform was a dead giveaway, but that and his American accent were the only things that Alf knew about him.

The man turned to face his guest. A chin carved from granite supported chiselled, hardened features, and cruel, steely grey eyes stared out from above a badly broken nose. His hair was cropped into a severe crew cut that looked sharp enough to cut paper. He looked like something out of a Marvel comic.

"Why are you still standing, Mr Resco? I asked you to sit."

It was clear from the tone of his voice that asking wasn't what he meant. It wasn't an order as such, but the implication was definitely there.

Alf sat down.

The military man let him sit in silence for a couple of minutes before perching on the edge of his desk, not eighteen inches from Alf. He sat with his hands on his lap, fingers interlaced and twiddling his thumbs, an action that seemed entirely out of character for some reason. Maybe he's a bit nervous too, thought Alf, but instantly dismissed the notion as nonsensical.

Alf looked for a name tag on the uniform but couldn't see one. All there was were ribbons, lots of them. He'd obviously seen a lot of action.

The soldier leaned backwards and opened a drawer that Alf couldn't see but heard, and took out a white envelope which he placed onto the table in front of Alf. "Good work last night, Mr Resco. I trust we can expect the same results tonight?"

Alf froze in position, mid-stretch, his hand hovering over the money laden package.

"T. . . tonight? I thought it was a one off job. I wasn't expecting to go out again," he said.

The other man grinned. A cracked face leer that held not a trace of emotion.

"Come now, Mr. Resco. You know full well that the wolves only hunt a couple of nights a month," said the soldier. "So we need as many specimens as we can gather in that short time frame." He leaned in closer. "Or should I say you can gather."

"But I was nearly killed last night!"

"But you weren't. And you won't be tonight."

Alf decided to be bold. Last night had been terrifying enough, and he didn't want to go through it again.

"I won't do it," he said with as much authority as he could muster. "The deal was for a werewolf and that's what you got."

He went to take the money but a fist like a club pounded the envelope back down onto the desktop.

The big soldier leaned even further forward, crowding Alf's personal space to the point that he moved backwards ever so slightly. Not much, but enough to signal that he'd acquiesced.

"Let me make this very easy for you, Mr Resco, and put it in a way that you'll understand. You have two choices. You can do as I ask or you can leave now with your payment. The problem is I can't vouch for your safety or that of your family's if you take the second option." Alf knew he was cornered, and that he had no choice in the matter.

There was no doubt that this chillingly polite psychopath meant what he'd said. And as much as he didn't particularly like his wife, a taciturn and unpleasant woman if ever there was one, he'd rather go through a divorce than have to explain her sudden and, no doubt, very messy disappearance. The smile on his face would be a dead giveaway. His children of course were a different matter entirely.

"Do we understand each other?" growled the soldier. Alf pocketed the money and stood up. "We do." "Excellent! Good day, Mr Resco."

Once Alf had left, a door to the right of the one he'd used opened and another soldier entered the room.

"What do you think, sir?" asked Lieutenant Travis Tyler as he approached the desk. "Is he going to do it?"

Major Buddy "Ironheart" Cowan opened an ornately carved wooden box and took out a fat cigar which he rolled under his nose, enjoying its rich aroma.

"Of course he will. What choice does he have? But I don't trust him. He's now the only local that knows we're here, and I think he's close to spilling his guts," said Cowan.

Tyler held his superiors' gaze. "The usual procedure, sir?" he asked, a glimmer of anticipation in his voice.

Cowan lit the cigar and took a long draw, holding the toxin filled vapour in his lungs for a few seconds before slowly blowing it out in a thin, grey stream towards the ceiling, where it formed an undulating, spectral cloud. "I think so, but let him finish the job first. No sense in letting any of our guys get hurt, agreed?"

"Yes, sir."

"Dismissed, Lieutenant."

———

Alf was successful that night. He managed to capture a fine specimen in an old bear pit after a brief chase through the forest. He didn't get to spend his hard earned money though. In fact no one ever saw Alfred Resco again. They didn't even find his hat.

———

Ollie paced around his office, willing the phone to ring or for a letter to arrive or for someone to at least drop by with a problem that had a passing resemblance to. . . well anything really. At this precise moment he'd have even invited Dusty Spuds in for a cup of tea and a chat, and he couldn't go for more than five minutes without removing his trousers, putting them on his head and trying to sell you timeshares in his allotment (a dusty, barren, fly ridden piece of land in his bathroom. Or as you and I would call it, the garden. Dusty's toilet had broken years ago and he'd never gotten round to getting it fixed, ergo, his calls of nature were answered outside. This, though, did explain his rather distinct aroma, the state of his shoes and why he always won the vegetable growing competition at the fayre in Scapula. Last year he'd entered a parsnip so large that two children got lost walking round it). Ollie hadn't slept much the last few days, tossing and turning in his coffin, worrying that his Uncle's centuries old business was going to fold within a couple of weeks of him taking over. There was also Stitches and the rest of them to think about. They'd worked for Gorge for years. What would become of them if he couldn't make his time at the helm a success?

So at a loose end and sick to the back fangs with doing nothing, Ollie decided to pay a visit to the laboratory (I'm using the word laboratory in its loosest possible sense, however, because nothing remotely sensible, useful or indeed laboratory like went on down there. Madcap, distinctly worrying and virtually genocidal was more like it but more of that in a bit).

Ollie didn't really know the full story as to why or how the lab came to be buried in the bowels of the building, but he was sure that his uncle had watched too many James Bond films. The only problem though, was whereas James Bond could call upon the genius inventor, Q to come up with incredible and, let's face it, unerringly handy gadgets, Ollie had been saddled with Rufus Barber Crumble. Known as Rhubarb to his friends, he was the one time owner of Professor Crumbles Emporium of Jokes, Jollies and Japeries, a short lived venture that had collapsed faster than a bouncy castle at a Weight Watchers picnic. The problem with the business was that nobody in Skullenia was much into practical jokes (unless walking up to someone, murdering them in cold blood, eating their internal organs and leaving their corpse on the pavement was funny. Still that depends on who does the murdering of course. If it happened to be a ravening, gore soaked ghoul wearing a silly hat I'd certainly find it amusing. They normally wear spinning bow-ties), so the need for whoopee cushions, sneezing powder and fake blood was virtually non-existent, and what with Halloween type creatures being in abundance every night of the year, more or less everyone had their own costume. By some quirk though, the unemployed Crumble had ended up on Gorge's doorstep, where he'd been taken in. Gorge must have liked him a lot, because he left Crumble human, unusual behaviour for a vampire, especially one as bloodthirsty as his uncle.

Ollie opened the secret door at the rear of his office and descended the stairs to the basement. At the bottom was a short hallway that led to an ancient, rusty door that bore the sign 'My other corridor has a

Porch'. He opened said door and was met by the overpowering and somewhat farty smell of sulphur, and a grinning Professor Crumble clad in a filthy lab coat and wearing a pair of safety goggles that were so thick, if the glass had cracked, his head would have de-pressurised. "Ah, Ollie, my boy," he said, beckoning Ollie into the dingy interior. "I've got a couple of new things to show you, if you have a few moments."

"Oh right," replied Ollie, trying his best to sound upbeat.

Rhubarb led him to a cluttered bench that had so many dishes, test tubes and beakers on it that it was difficult to see what was going on. It was obvious that this was the source of the stink though, because a putrid, vaporous shroud of yellow smoke was hanging over a large container. It looked like a small nuclear explosion had gone off. Ollie tried to breathe through his mouth, but a tiny tendril of stench still stole up his nose.

"What the Devil have you been up to, Rhubarb, it smells like a morgue down here?" he said.

"My latest creation," he replied proudly, indicating the offending glassware. "A cunning fusion of explosive gel and toothpaste."

"And where would I use such a concoction?" Ollie asked sarcastically. "Because I can't envisage any dangerous bathroom situations coming up in the near future. Not unless I'm actually using the stuff, that is."

Rhubarb smiled the smile of the totally deranged and the eternally optimistic. Never mind the glass being half full, Crumble's was always full to the brim, laced with Malibu and had a little pink umbrella in it.

"Well, you never know. It could come in handy."

"Only if a blue whale has a problem with plaque," said Ollie. "So what's it called then?"

The Professor grinned. "Gumpowder."

Ollie chuckled and patted the little man on the back. "If nothing else it's worth it just for the name. What else have you got, you said a couple of things?"

"I'm really pleased with this," said Crumble, indicating a wooden box attached to the wall.

As they approached the box, Ollie began to hear a distinct fluttering noise coming from inside it, and only when he was really close did he notice a small light bulb on top that was struggling to give off a faint glimmer of light.

"And what do we have here?" he asked, genuinely interested this time.

Rhubarb unhooked a latch and opened the box, revealing the cause of the noise. There was a wheel inside and attached to that, at six equally spaced intervals by tiny leather harnesses, were half a dozen small bats, each furiously flapping its wings. For all their efforts though, the wheel was turning incredibly slowly, which explained the pathetic glow.

"The Pipistrel Dynamo!" announced Rhubarb triumphantly.

Ollie inwardly sighed, not wanting to cause offence, but at the same time wanting to give the Professor a hearty slap across the chops.

"It's a bit weak, isn't it?" he said. "It would take thousands of them to make a decent amount of light. And aren't you worried about the animal rights people finding out?"

"Mmmm, still it's not like I mistreat them. They're very pampered little creatures, and I always let them have a nice rest when they get tired."

"Ah, their *bat*teries keep running out, do they?" said Ollie. "Excuse me?"

"Never mind. Well, keep working on it. You never know. Bats in a box might be the next big thing. As well as a few too many 'roos loose in the paddock," he added under his breath.

Ollie was just about to make his excuses and leave when the lab door flew open and Stitches, as much as he could, rushed in.

"We've got a phone call," he said, stopping to retrieve his hand which, in his urgency to get in, he'd left gripping the door handle. "Well, you have anyway."

"Who?" asked Ollie, watching as the zombie put his right hand into his left hand coat pocket for safekeeping.

"You," said Stitches. "I already told you that." "I meant who's on the phone?" said Ollie. "You'll never guess."

"No I probably won't." "Go on, have a go."

Ollie sighed and folded his arms. "Elvis Presley?" "Nope."

"The Pope?"

"He called yesterday." "Eh!" exclaimed Ollie.

"Gotcha!" said Stitches pointing, well, stumping, and laughing. "Try again."

"I give up."

"Aww, go on. One more," pleaded Stitches.

Ollie was now on the verge of plunging a stake into his own chest just for a bit of peace and quiet. "Stitches! For the love of a supreme being, just shut up and tell me."

The zombie looked puzzled. "How can I shut up and tell you, Ollie?" "JUST. TELL. ME. NOW!"

Stitches pouted and looked at his feet, swaying back and forth like a scolded child.

"Count Jocular."

Ollie's breath caught in his chest and his eyes nearly burst from their sockets. He tried to speak, but his mouth had suddenly turned into a desert. After a moment he regained a modicum of composure. "Why the hell didn't you say so in the first place, you useless column of dust?"

"I've got a bag for that," interjected Crumble.

"Shut up," growled Ollie, pushing past Stitches and heading quickly for the stairs.

"Sorry, Ollie! But there's no need to get your cape in a twist!" He followed Ollie up the stairs back to the office.

Ollie lowered his voice as he neared his desk, lest the noise carried to the phone.

"Don't get my cape in a twist? Look, as far as vampires go he's God. Well, the Devil at least, or. . . put it this way, he's number one round here, and anyone who doesn't treat him as such had better watch out. Now sit there, be quiet and sew your hand back on."

"Okay," mumbled the zombie and dropped into a chair.

Without realising what he was doing, Ollie straightened his jacket and smoothed his hair before picking up the phone.

"Hello."

"Ah, Ollie my fine fellow. Vot kept you?"

The voice was deep and menacing and sent a shiver down Ollie's spine. It was as if all the evil in the world had been collected and turned into a horror based audio transmission (or an episode of Eastenders, that's equally as terrifying).

A thousand clawed hands tapped their gnarled fingers on his flesh. The vampire lord sounded like someone who'd failed an audition for the next Saw movie because he was too scary.

"Sorry, Sir," Ollie squeaked, "bit of trouble with the staff, but you know how it is with underlings."

"Try hanging a few. It vorks for me."

"I'll consider it, sir," he replied, casting a glance at Stitches.

The phone felt cold and clammy in his hand, as if the creature on the other end of the line were sucking all the heat from it. Ollie was sure he could see tendrils of ice beginning to form on the dial, clouding the numbers.

"What can I do for you, sir?" asked Ollie trying not to sound like a schoolboy up in front of the Headmaster.

"I vont you to come up to ze castle. I haff some business to discuss viz you."

"Ah, right you are. What time would you like me to be there?" "Come tonight at tvelve. And bring your friend along, ze vun who keeps falling apart." "Stitches?"

"Zat's him. And now I must fly."

"Very good, sir," Ollie said, trying to suppress a giggle. "Vot is very good?" replied Jocular, sounding perplexed.

"Vampire, I must fl. . . until tonight, sir." Ollie hung up the phone. "What did he want then?" asked Stitches whilst in the midst of reattaching his hand.

"He wants me to go and see him up at the castle. I reckon he's got some business for us by the sound of things."

"Such as?"

"He didn't say, but he asked for you to come with me." Stitches dropped a stitch.

"As long as it's not another fancy dress party. Last time I went as a zombie and came third."

Ollie laughed. "That's not bad."

"Indeed it isn't, but that Frankenstein clone that we live with went as Dorothy from the Wizard of Oz and won! How's that fair?"

"Well, I can imagine he must have looked the part."

"He ate two munchkins!" the zombie protested incredulously, "and their little dog too."

Ollie gazed at Stitches. "Trying not to laugh at Jocular is the hardest part."

"What do you mean? He's never struck me as being overly amusing." "Oh, you know. Those mispronunciations and funny sounding phrases that he drops into a conversation every now and again. It wouldn't be so bad but he doesn't realise he's doing it. The last time I was there he said to me, 'Don't forget zat viz ze upcoming vinter ze little voodland creatures vill need ze sustenance."

"That sounds perfectly normal," said Stitches. "He does love his flora and fauna."

"Not when he added, 'zo don't forget to hang your fatty balls in ze garden so ze bats can haff a nibble.' "

Stitches gave a barely noticeable, derisory chuckle, the sort reserved for desperately unfunny people, who think they're hilarious when they are, in fact, about as funny as a power cut in an intensive care ward.

"I wish I'd reacted like that but I burst out laughing," said Ollie. "Oh dear. What did he say?"

"Well, after glaring at me, which quite frankly scared me half to undeath, he said, 'vot are you laughing at, Ollie?' "

"How did you get out of that?" said the zombie.

Ollie raised an eyebrow. "I told him that joke about the dwarf, the chainsaw and the nun. I said I'd heard it earlier that day."

"And?"

"He didn't get it. He said the undead community was no place for levity."

Stitches tied off a loop of cotton on his wrist. "He obviously hasn't been to a summer season show in Eastbourne, then," he said around the pin clamped between his teeth.

"Exactly. Right, meet me back here at eleven, okay? And don't be late."

"Gotcha."

———

"I hate this, everybody stares. Why can't we use a bus like everyone else?" said Stitches.

Ollie looked at the disgruntled zombie. They were standing in the street outside the office, waiting for their ride.

"Because firstly, buses are for tourists, old people, and undercover monster hunters and their talking dog. Secondly, there aren't any buses to Jocular's Castle anyway, you should know that by now, and thirdly, even if there were, His Royal Darkness can be a bit of an old traditionalist and he wouldn't allow it. He likes certain things done the old fashioned way. Personally I think he's gone one station too far on the crazy train but there it is. Don't tell him I said that though."

At that moment, the thunderous clatter of horses' hooves pounding on cobble stones assaulted their ears, and a black carriage emerged from the mist (obviously there was mist. It wouldn't be a supernatural village without mist. That's what living in a supernatural village is all about, having mist. If it didn't have mist it would out of place, very unsupernatural like and considerably less misty and supernatural. How weird would that be).

The carriage was being pulled by four massive beasts who were all sinewy of muscle and evil of glare. As they powered along, the wheels bounced and juddered atop the uneven stone, making the cab sway from side to side so much that it looked like it was going to tip over. Up in front sat the driver, a mysterious hooded figure who was perched aloft like a monstrous vulture.

As the horses neared their destination he reined them in, his white skeletal hands gripping the leather straps and pulling them back, bringing the vehicle to a standstill. The creature turned to face them, regarding them with a pair of deep red eyes that glowed from the depths of the hood. He was malevolence personified, the arbiter of perversity and conduit to the sinister beast who awaited them in his exalted aerie. A bony, bleached finger pointed to the cab, indicating that they should get on board.

"Awright, Ollie me ol' doodah. 'Ow's ya flange for walnuts?"

"Evening, Bill," said Ollie, "how's business?"

"'Ansome," came the reply, "bin really busy lately, rushed off me planks , know wot I mean an all 'at?"

"I wish I did," Ollie said wistfully. "Haven't had so much as a nibble for ages."

"Never mind me ol' monkfish, sumfink'll turn up you mark my words and no mistake, cor blimey, guvnor, apples 'n' pylons, rub a dub deckchair an all 'at 'n' evryfin.'"

Ollie and Stitches clambered into the carriage.

"Where the hell did Jocular get him from?" asked the zombie, casting a glance at Bill as he got in. "I'm thinking either The Artful Dodger's really let himself go or Cockney Stereotypes R Us have got a sale on?" "I don't know," said Ollie in reply, as Bill got the horses moving. "I think he's new. I've only met him once before. He's no doubt some poor, hapless traveller who wandered innocently into this begotten realm and fell prey to the clutches of the evil. . . "

"Whoa there!" said Stitches. "I got the message."

The carriage suddenly came to a shrieking halt, the wheels skidding on the slick cobble stone surface. Bill pulled back a small hatch situated in the roof panel of the carriage and peered down at them.

"Awright, who's the comedian who said whoa?"

Stitches raised a guilty hand. "Sorry, mate. won't happen again." "Fanx, guv. Don't wanna go flyin' orf them bends now, do we, mutton pants?"

The hatch slid shut and they resumed their journey.

———

The laboratory, for that is now where we are, looked a bit like the one Professor Crumble pottered around in, except that this one was more modern, considerably cleaner, had state of the art equipment in it and trained staff that were capable of using it for its intended purpose. It was also studiously quiet, with no Hiroshima sized blasts going off for no apparent reason every ten minutes, something that happened in Crumble's lab on a regular, and very noisy basis (and that was just if he was making toast. You should see the mess when he tries splitting atoms. It ruins the carpets).

It was into this serene area of research that Major Cowan entered, interested to see what, if any, progress had been made.

"How goes it, Meredith, you got anything for me?" he asked.

Dr Paul Meredith smiled weakly at the soldier and shrugged his thin shoulders.

"Slowly. We can isolate and remove the specific gene we're after, but once it's free of the host organism it immediately begins to break down. Within thirty seconds it's totally corrupted and useless to us."

Cowan looked pensive, annoyed at the apparent delay. Those above him wanted results and he'd been chosen specially to lead the mission to deliver them. This wouldn't look good, and Cowan was not a man to tolerate failure of any description, no matter what the excuse.

"So what do you suggest, Doctor?" he said.

Meredith took off his glasses and began to polish them with a handkerchief. "I need to retrieve the gene sample from living tissue. That's the only way we're going to obtain any tangible results. You'll have to capture me a live specimen, Major."

Cowan bristled at this arrogant display of disrespect. "That sounded like an order to me, Doctor," he growled.

"Take it as you will, but if this experiment has any chance of success, that's what I need."

"You do realise what you're asking me to do, don't you?"

Meredith finished cleaning his glasses before wiping a thin sheen of sweat from his brow and popping them back on. He wasn't accustomed to confrontation, but he couldn't afford to let this uniformed dictator rattle him. He needed to project an image of control.

"I'm sure you'll manage to give the orders to your men without coming to too much harm. I mean, what possible dangers could there be lurking in that plush office of yours?" he said.

Cowan was starting to boil. He needed to remove himself from this situation fast, otherwise this upstart scientist was going to push him too far. Cowan could take many things, but sarcasm and disrespect from his subordinates was guaranteed to rile him.

"And don't try and pull rank on me, Major," Meredith continued, undaunted by Cowan's obvious displeasure at his attitude. "I'm not connected to the military. I work for the Government. Basically, you'll do what I ask."

Cowan swallowed hard and counted to ten. He leaned in toward the diminutive doctor and spoke in a hushed voice. "You'll get your specimen and then, when we're finished here, I'll feed you to it. Good day, Doctor."

———

The carriage bumped, shuddered, jostled and wobbled its way along the mountain track, all the while with the wooden wheels flirting with the edge of the precipice as if the cab itself were engaged in a deadly game of dare with the abyssal depths below. With just a touch of over enthusiasm, Coachman Bill was whipping the horses into a frenzy, urging them ever faster as if their very lives depended on reaching their destination as quickly as possible. At some point in the journey Bill opened the hatch again and peered inside.

"Won't be long na, Guv. We've made good time t'night don't ya know."

Stitches looked up nervously at the skeletal cabbie whilst pointing at what he thought was forward, although such was their velocity and apparent lack of direction they could well have been in orbit by now. "We won't make it at all if you don't pay attention to the road."

Bill grinned, seemingly impossible for a skull due to its physical restrictions, but he grinned nonetheless. "Darn't worry yaself me ole china rugmuffin. I've got eyes in the back of me ed so I 'ave."

"Mmmm, I'm sure," said the zombie.

With that, Bill whipped down his hood and turned back to face the front and there, in two recesses at the base of his bony bonce, was another pair of eyes as red and fearsome as the ones above his cheek bones.

Stitches rolled his eyes skywards and let out a sigh. "I should have known. That's weird, even for these parts."

Ollie smirked. "Well, it takes all sorts I suppose."

"So does British Immigration, but I bet even they wouldn't let a four eyed walking Yoric into the country."

Ollie reached into a pocket and pulled out a small foil wrapped bundle. He carefully opened it and took out one of the Marmite sandwiches he'd made for the trip.

"Wonderful," he said around a mouthful of sticky bread.

"I don't know how you can eat that stuff," said Stitches. "It looks like it belongs in a pathology lab."

"Mmmmph," and a sneer was the only reply Stitches got.

"Still," the dusty one continued, "if we ever need to get rid of anyone we'll just get some of those revolting things, lace them with strychnine and voilà!"

"What?"

"A suicide pact lunch."

Ollie swallowed his mouthful and glared at his companion with a wry, somewhat tortured grin on his face. "Stitches, you are without a shadow of a doubt the funniest zombie I know."

"But I'm the only zombie you know." "I know."

Despite the light hearted exchanges going on inside the cab they both noticed the air had suddenly become heavier, almost tangible, making it harder to draw a breath. You could feel the oppressive atmosphere bearing down on your shoulders and squeezing your chest. Although it didn't bother Stitches, on account of his being rather dead and his lungs being about as much use as a garlic trifle at a vampire buffet, it made Ollie feel decidedly uncomfortable physically, and it was a feeling he would never get used to no matter how many times he visited Jocular's Castle. He opened the window, not to let in the fresh air, but to let the air that they had move about a bit. A stiff, dewy branch caught him on the chin as he leaned further out.

"Ouch," he whined, rubbing the sore spot. "Nearly there now, though."

"Tremendous. Just do me a favour and make sure you keep that malignant dwarf of Jocular's away from me this time."

"What, old Egon?"

"Yes, old Egon. He doesn't half give me the willies, always staring at me in that weird way he's got."

"He's harmless enough," said Ollie who knew full well that Stitches was terrified of the little creature.

"If you say so," said the zombie doubtfully, "but who knows what's going on inside that weird head of his and what he's thinking about. Actually, forget I said that. As a matter of fact I've got a pretty good idea about what's going on inside that weird head of his and what he's thinking about. On the other hand if I've got it all wrong and I don't know what's going on inside that weird head of his and what he's thinking about, I don't *want* to know what's going on inside that weird head of his and what he's thinking about."

Ollie squinted and tried to make sense of the verbal tango that had just danced into his ears. "And what exactly do you think he's thinking then?"

" 'I wonder how he works, and would I be able to put him back together again?' "

"So he thinks you're some kind of Humpty Dumpty themed jigsaw then?"

Ollie received a rather rude two fingered reply.

"You won't be making jokes when I'm scattered all over the castle grounds and my head's on a jesters stick next to his bed," said Stitches.

"Don't worry. Jocular keeps him on a tight rein." "Round his neck, hopefully."

The door slid back once more as Bill announced their arrival. "There ya go gents, safe an sarnd, luvly jubbly, would you Adam and Eve it, rub a dub dub an all at type 'o' colloquially based flim flammery."

"I didn't get a word of that," said Stitches. "He said we're here."

"Oh, right. Tell you what, he's the only English bloke I've ever met that needs an English interpreter." As he stepped from the cab Stitches, a mischievous look in his eyes, turned to Bill and said, "Cheers cakey me ole sock, catch the muffin penguin side about half past pants. Wibble?"

"Righto, John," Bill replied jovially as he turned the cab round. "I'll be lookin' forward to it an no fabrics." With that he waved and drove off.

Stitches was too dumbfounded to be coherent. "Did he..? I mean, did I..?"

Ollie clapped him on the shoulder. "Come on you top hat. Let's go and find out why we're here."

————

Flug threw a counter down onto the kitchen table. "Snap," he bellowed with all the unalloyed joy of an excited camel.

Ronnie gazed at him dejectedly through the cloud of cigarette smoke that was ever present around his head. "That's very good, Flug mate, but this is draughts, remember. You take your opponents pieces by jumping over them."

"Ah, me get it," said the reanimate.

That being the case, Flug picked up all of Ronnie's black counters and placed them into a neat pile on the floor.

"Oh, he's not," Ronnie muttered to himself.

Oh, but he was. Flug carefully gauged his position, nodded approvingly, smiled at his friend and then leaped over the stack with all the grace of a new born rhino with a hip problem. He landed with a bone jarring thud on the other side of the now spilt pile of discs. He stood there, grinning proudly. "Mine now. Me win."

Ronnie put his hands over his face and shook his head. "Yes, mate. A bit too literal to be honest, but you win. Just remind me never to play Murder in the Dark with you."

Flug picked up the pieces and returned them to the board. "What we do now?" he asked.

"Dunno, really. Ollie and Stitches are up at the castle, and all the pubs and clubs are shut. Well, the decent ones anyway." (He might have considered taking Flug to The Bolt and Jugular but ruled it out in case his friend got into another fight, as had happened the last time. After binging on half a pint of shandy so weak that a confirmed teetotaller would have happily drunk it, Flug had punched a wall because it wouldn't get out of his way. The landlord had been okay about it but he'd politely requested that Ronnie keep Flug away for a while. As he'd eloquently pointed out, the last thing he needed was to be breaking up a bout of fisticuffs between a stack of immobile bits that had all the sentience of a tangerine and parts of his building). "Fancy going out for a walk?"

"Yeah, we go sing Christmas Carols ay, Ron?"

"If you like. It'll make a nice change to hear them in April. Come on, then."

———

Cowan sat behind his desk, studying the four Marines before him. They were stood rigidly to attention, so much so that a rugby scrum would have had trouble shifting them. Heavily made up for covert night-time operations, each carried night vision goggles and an impressive array of weapons, including tranquilliser guns. They were his best men. They needed to be.

"I cannot stress enough the importance of you men bringing me back a live specimen," said the major. "I know it's a tough assignment, but you can handle it. You've got enough tranq between you to floor an elephant, so there's no need for any of you to take any risks and get hurt."

"Don't worry, sir," said one. "It's just a simple seek and trap exercise. We'll have one cornered and put to sleep before it knows what's going on."

The others nodded in agreement.

Cowan stood up and methodically approached the squad.

"That may be, private but these monsters take victims all the time. Forget everything you might have heard or seen in a stupid movie or read in some book. Full moons don't seem to matter, they transform when they get the urge to hunt and silver bullets don't work because we've tried them. These things are more dangerous than anything you've ever come across before, so watch yourselves. They're not wild animals or some rabid dog that needs putting down. They're agile, super-efficient killing machines with the strength of five men and the intelligence to match, so don't play games out there. Get the job done and we can all get out of this godforsaken place. Understood, marines?"

"Sir, yes sir."

———

Some time after the marines headed out on their perilous mission, Mrs. Ladle was wandering around the town square cursing, muttering to herself and generally using language that is far too bawdy to be repeated here (I'm sure you wouldn't really mind to be fair but my mum will read this as well and I don't want to get told off for being rude. I'm forty nine now and I'd look rather silly sitting on the naughty stair, especially when dad's already there because mum's caught him smoking in the greenhouse again. It wouldn't have been so bad but they were visiting Kew Gardens at the time and he burnt an orchid that bloomed so rarely, the last person to see it's petals had been King Henry VIII and maps still had 'here be monsters' written on them, although that still holds true today for some villages in the north of England.)

She was having trouble with the Aeronautical Dynamics of her PreIndustrial Revolution Floatation Device. To the layman and those of you who don't understand management speak, in that you're not a manager and therefore quite sensible, her broomstick wouldn't fly. She'd tried everything from white magic to black magic, all colours of the rainbow magic, colours that hadn't been invented yet magic and everything in between. She'd even attempted a little bit of beige magic, which was usually so weak that it would normally struggle to turn a newly retired couple into members of the Caravan Club. She'd tried casting various spells, drawn elaborate runes and pentagrams on every available surface, mixed various potions and finally resorted to chucking the damn thing into the air in the vain hope that it would stay there. Lastly, and somewhat desperately, she'd dived off the Town Hall roof in an attempt to jump start it, but this had only resulted in an unfortunate head-on meeting with Bill the Coachman's horses. Disheartened, she unscrewed the cap at the top of the handle and checked inside. As she thought there was plenty of flight powder in there and it was nice and dry. She had to admit to being at a bit of a loss. It was at that moment that Ronnie and Flug came round the corner and saw her predicament.

"Still having trouble, Mrs. Ladle?" Ronnie asked pleasantly. "Anything we can do to help?"

Mrs. Ladle smiled, hawked loudly and spat on the floor in the traditional witches greeting. Well, it was traditional for her as it would be for anyone who smoked eighty fags a day that had enough tar in them to surface a dual carriageway. She rested her defunct mode of transport against a wall and pulled out her cigarettes, which she kindly offered to the two night time wanderers. Ronnie lit his and took a long drag. Flug ate his and took a long swallow.

"Unless you know how to get that stupid thing into the air, then I'm afraid not," she said, pointing at her broom.

Ronnie blew a smoke ring the size of a steering wheel into the still night air and shook his head. "I think I might be a bit out of my depth tinkering with that thing of yours, but I know a man who might be able to help."

"Who's that?"

"Professor Crumble. I bet he'd have a few ideas."

"Rhubarb Crumble?" she said. "The worst scientist and inventor that ever entered a lab?"

Ronnie smiled and nodded. "That's the one."

"The man who invented a teapot with the spout on the inside to avoid spills."

"Even he."

"The dimwit who owns the patent on the world's first paper submarine."

"Yup."

Mrs. Ladle dragged some fluid up from the depths of her lungs and launched it at the Town Hall wall, where it hung like a crucified jellyfish.

"So what makes you think that pot plant can help me then? I've known him for a long time and the only useful thing he's ever done is sit down."

"I didn't say he could," said Ronnie, squashing his spent smoke under his boot, "but it seems to me that you're having so much grief with that thing that you've got nothing to lose."

"That's a very valid point and well presented," said Mrs. Ladle begrudgingly. "Will he still be awake at this time of night?"

"Crumble always awake, Mrs. L," rumbled Flug, "he a maniac."
"Insomniac," corrected Ronnie, "and yes, he is. Go and see him, Mrs. Ladle. You might be surprised."

"That's a given. The last time I went in there I got assaulted by three tea bags. It wouldn't have been so bad but they weighed fifteen stone each and had teeth. I think he said it was something to do with making a strong cup of tea that had bite. Well, I'm more than likely going to end up wishing that I hadn't, but okay, I'll give it a shot. Thanks boys."

With that she retrieved her broomstick and sauntered off. Ronnie waved her goodbye. "She's rather pleasant for a witch." "A what?" replied Flug.

"Not a what, a witch." "Which what?"

"Not which what, that witch." "Which witch?"

"That witch, the one we've just been talking to."

Flug slapped his head in sudden and unexpected comprehension. "Ah, me not know which witch you mean."

Ronnie looked puzzled. "What do you mean which witch. There was only one."

Flug grabbed Ronnie's arm and pulled him into a dark recess in the wall. He peered round the side and bade Ronnie do the same. "There, look. More witches."

Ronnie allowed his gaze to follow in the direction that Flug was pointing. On the other side of the Town Square was a row of houses and shops and behind that, separated from the properties by a wide, overgrown path, was the forest, and it was into this forest, through an alleyway between two houses, that Flug was indicating.

"Dere, Ron," he whispered, "far away in da trees."

Ronnie leaned further forward and squinted, trying to block out the extraneous light, forcing his eyes to penetrate the darkness.

"Whoever put you together gave you good vision, Flug mate. I can't see a thing."

"Dere," repeated Flug, pointing as hard as he could. "Witches carrying dere sticks."

Ronnie definitely had qualms about believing the monster, but he was being so insistent that he had to give the big dope the benefit of the doubt.

"Look, I really can't see a thing. Tell you what, you stay here, nice and quiet, and I'll go and have a look, okay?"

"Okay, Ron. Be careful."

"Hey, don't worry. They won't see me coming. Stand back."

Flug pressed himself to the wall and made himself as

inconspicuous as possible, which was no mean feat for something eight feet tall with the body mass index of a Volvo.

Ronnie stood still and relaxed, allowing his respiration to slow until a good breath in and out was taking nearly thirty seconds. Then, he quite simply, imagined himself fading away to nothing. A tingling started in his fingers and toes, and his stomach churned with a nervous cramp, the type you'd get on a first date, not unpleasant, but enough to keep you within dashing distance of the nearest toilet just in case. The more he concentrated, the more intense the feeling became, until POW. The shock was like an ice cold shower and he was never ready for it.

"My goodness, I'll never get used to that if I live to be six hundred. How do I look, mate?"

"Me dunno, me can't see you," Flug replied, staring into the space that his friend had previously occupied.

"Perfect, that's the idea. Now you wait for me here okay? I'm just going to have a nose around, see if I can see what you see, alright?"

"Kay," stuttered Flug. "But don't be long, me get scared."

"Try counting to ten, that'll take your mind off things for a bit. Won't be long."

"One, fr. . . ummm."

"Can't I wait here?"

"Why?"

Stitches gave Ollie his best 'do I have to state the bleeding obvious' look and sighed sarcastically.

"Oh, don't worry about it. Here, take these." Ollie reached into a pocket and pulled out a brightly coloured cardboard tube which he handed to Stitches.

"Jelly Bodybits!" said the indignant zombie.

"Egon loves them. Just slip him one every few minutes and he'll be putty in your hands. The red ones are his favourite."

"It's not him being putty in my hands that's the concern; it's me being dismembered, squidgy chunks in his that's ever such a tiny niggle. And if I start giving him sweeties he'll just think I really like him. And to be perfectly frank, I'm not really comfortable with the idea of *slipping* him anything so please don't ever say that again."

"But it'll distract him I'm telling you. Trust me." "Well, if you say so."

"I do."

"But if I end up on all fours in the downstairs cloakroom as an umbrella stand, I'll tell His Lordship that you like watching moths fly round the garden of an evening with a mug of Ovaltine and a big stack of Bob's Nobs." (Obviously it was Ollie who had the Ovaltine and the dunkable snacks not the moths for that would be ever so slightly silly. As everyone knows moths prefer hot chocolate and a ginger biccie).

Ollie did a reasonably good impression of a goldfish. "Well that's just childish."

"I thought so, but I'll still do it."

Ollie reached up and grabbed the enormous door knocker in both hands and gave it a mighty swing. It boomed against the massive oak door like a thunderclap and made the ground tremble beneath their feet. It echoed around the valley like a volley of cannon fire.

"Bit over the top," murmured Stitches.

From the other side of the six inch thick door they could hear bolts being thrown, keys being turned and chains being released.

"He's rather security conscious for a vampire, isn't he?" observed Stitches. "You'd have to be the most desperate burglar in the world to try and break into here."

Ollie just stood patiently with his hands clasped firmly behind his back. He was as nervous as a postman at Crufts, but he didn't show it. "He's just a bit funny about some of his possessions that's all," said Ollie. "The last time I was here he asked me to find out if there's a local Crime-stoppers Group."

"What on earth for?" said Stitches. "Don't the children of the night and his retinue of imps, thralls and flunkies look after him?"

"Well, yes," replied Ollie. "But they don't work weekends."

"Oh, right. Well, I suppose you can't be too careful. Fangs ain't what they used to be."

"Keep that up and I'll *let* Egon have his way with you. I'll even give him the umbrella."

The iron handle turned and the door began to open slowly and painfully, groaning like an arthritic hip and creaking like an MFI wardrobe. A small hand crept around the edge about two feet off the ground and gripped the wood. Then they heard puffs and pants as the, whatever it was, and it could be literally anything, strained to let them

44

in. Moaning and complaining emanated from within as the gap widened.

"Bloody stupid thing. . . far too heavy... ruining my hands.. . get a nice UPVC double glazed one. . . but oh no. . . tight as a virgin's. . . Ah. Welcome, Sir, and welcome to you, Mr. Stitches. What a delight it is to see you both again."

I wish I could say the same, thought Stitches as he gazed at the abstract creature standing before him.

Egon was four feet tall, bow legged, had splayed feet, arms that hung down to his knees, skin that an elderly pachyderm would have considered moisturising, an interesting aroma that defied description and the traditional hump, the prerequisite appendage for any servant of the dark arts and their weird ways. Uniquely, and somewhat disturbingly, however, the hump wasn't in the traditional place. It was on a lead by his feet and it followed him everywhere. Facially, he looked like he'd been set on fire and put out with a speeding train, and had a comb over that beggared belief. It could easily have covered two bald heads. Interesting was the kindest way to describe Egon's appearance. Melted was more appropriate. He resembled a candle that had been left too close to an open fire.

"Come in come in," said the diminutive servant, ushering the two visitors into the dimly lit innards of the castle. "The Master is already aware of your arrival and awaits you in The Sketching Room."

"The Sketching Room?" enquired Stitches.

"It's similar to a drawing room, just a tad smaller," said Egon. "I had to ask."

"Indeed. If you'll allow me, gentlemen," said Egon, indicating a long corridor leading off the hall they were standing in. "Walk this way."

"Don't you dare," warned Ollie, pointing a prohibitive finger at his colleague.

"No. Wasn't going to."

Above them was a magnificent vaulted ceiling that was at least thirty feet high. Dark wooden beams criss-crossed the stonework, meeting in the middle, where ornately carved centre pieces supported grand candelabras every few yards. There were so many candles burning that the heat they gave off could be felt at floor level. It must have been a hell of a job lighting them all. The walls of the corridor were adorned with fine old paintings and tapestries depicting wars, sieges, skirmishes and just about every other form of conflict you could think of. Suits of armour that no human form could ever have fit into stood sentinel at regular intervals along the passageway. Two headed, multi limbed, no limbed, web footed, they were all there.

"Looks like we've wandered onto the set of Star Wars," observed Stitches as they passed a suit of armour that looked like a four car pile-up.

"Very droll, Mr. Stitches," said Egon without turning or stopping. "Obviously you've noticed the eclectic nature of the displays."

Stitches was rather taken aback at being overheard. He thought he'd spoken quietly enough to get away with the quip. "Well, um, yes. I was wondering what sort of creatures would have fit into them."

"None, actually. His Lordship created them. Well, he conceived them. I built them. The Master fancies himself as a bit of an interior designer you see."

"You don't say. So how did that come about then?" asked Ollie, who after a couple of visits to the castle realised that he actually knew very little about Jocular.

Egon stopped and turned to face them. His face paled, if that were possible, and his gaze dropped to the floor, a sad look on his face.

"It happened over the course of one terrible weekend. His Lordship became sick. Blood poisoning. Or poisoned blood to be more accurate. He was vomiting everywhere and believe me, you haven't smelt anything until you've had a whiff of several pints of partially digested blood."

"Oh, I don't know, "interjected Stitches. "When Flug's had a few bags of Rotten Fingers, the stench of his po. . . "

"Thank you, Stitches, we get the picture," Ollie interrupted. "Do go on, Egon."

"Thank you, Sir. Well, as I said, the Master was confined to his room and of course even vampires get bored if they can't get out, so he asked me to install satellite television for him."

"Oh dear," said Stitches.

"Quite. Unfortunately all he could tune into was UK Unliving and he spent the entire two days watching back to back episodes of that awful make over show." Egon waved his hands in an effort to get his memory to function. "Oh, you know the one I mean. It's got that interfering Scottish witch and her foppish posse in it. They visit the homes of the undead and completely ruin them."

"Ah, Changing Tombs," said Ollie.

"Ouch, that is bad," added Stitches. "I mean, who's ever heard of a ghoul having satin throw pillows and a pink coffee table made of driftwood?"

Egon raised an eyebrow, which was a weird sight because it was on his cheek. "Well, exactly," he said. "Unfortunately the Master loved it, and ever since he's been fiddling with the place like there's no tomorrow. Some parts of the castle look like they belong in a fairground now." The little chap edged closer to the two visitors, looked around surreptitiously and lowered his voice, putting it level with the top of Ollie's socks. "So a word of warning. You'll notice strange things dotted around the place, even stranger than you've already seen, so if you're with His Lordship, either say something complimentary or wait for him to point it out to you and then say something complimentary." Stitches scratched an ear and inadvertently moved it an inch lower down his head. "I imagine it wouldn't be wise to constructively criticise anything then."

"Best not. One of his thralls did last week, and found himself walled up in a dungeon for all eternity. There's a beautiful pair of silk curtains covering the brick work though so it's not all bad."

"Right, well we'd better extol the virtues of everything we clap our eyes on then. Thanks for the tip, Egon. Shall we continue?" suggested Ollie.

"Indeed we shall. This way."

Twenty feet into the next lengthy corridor, Ollie stopped in front of something. It left him staring wide eyed, mouth agape, shaking his head and muttering to himself in disbelief, amazed and very confused about the thing before him. "What," asked the incredulous half vampire, "the hell is that?"

Stitches put a hand over his mouth and closed his eyes. If he'd had any moisture in his system, you would have heard a loud gulp.

"Ah, one of the Master's more conceptual works. Rather original, don't you think?" said Egon.

"That's not quite the word I'd use," said Stitches, remembering Egon's warning.

In front of them was a large arched window ten feet tall and five feet wide. What they could see of it was made up of the most beautiful stained glass. The remainder was hidden by the obviously dead figure of a man who was nailed to an ebony frame, which was itself attached to the window surround. Two puncture wounds on his neck indicated the nature of his demise, but it was the other aspects of the display that puzzled Ollie.

"Um, why is he wearing dark glasses and holding a white stick, Egon?" he asked.

"How very astute of you to notice, Sir," said Egon fawningly. He could grovel with the best of them and then tell the best of them how good they were at grovelling. "You've observed the most important parts of the piece. The deceased gentleman was a gondolier in his former life, so his Lordship thought it would be pleasant to have him permanently on show up here at the window."

"But what is it supposed to be?" said Ollie.

Egon cracked a grin that would have put the willies up Broadmoor's most deserving guest. "A Venetian Blind."

Ollie suppressed a shudder that was almost violent enough to qualify as a fit, and indicated that they should proceed. "Good grief, can you believe that?" he asked Stitches, very quietly.

"I know. I think we should find out what Jocular wants and get out of here before we end up as soft furnishings."

Four turns, five hallways and various cringe-inducing decorative disasters later they arrived at the sketching room. Egon was about to knock on the door when a voice from inside said, "Enter." Egon opened it up, entered and stood to attention to announce the visitors. "Mr. Ollie Splint and Mr. Stitches to see you, my lord."

Count Jocular, Skullenia's lord and master, was standing at the window, gazing contemplatively into the night. He truly was a colossal being. He was the best part of seven feet tall and built like the top three contenders of the world's strongest man competition combined. His every movement, no matter how subtle, caused taut muscles to ripple, and hands that could have popped a basketball like a balloon hung at his sides (sounds like my Auntie Blodwyn, but then she is from North Wales so goes relatively unnoticed).

As you may have noted, Jocular's appearance belies one of the great misconceptions from literature and film that full blood vampires are slim, elegant, caddish characters that beguile ladies by making them go weak at the knees, and who easily blend into mainstream society by simply changing clothes, popping on a pair of sunglasses and effecting a charming accent. That, of course, is absolute rot. They're powerfully built, killing machines that rip through flesh and bone like a meat grinder on speed, so the next time you're watching Interview With The Vampire don't go all gooey and start wishing for some pale faced dandy to float gracefully through your bedroom window and give your neck a bit of a nibble. You'll end up gooey alright and not in a good way.

Jocular's only concession to popular myth was a cape that he wore over a very nice two piece suit. Turning to face his guests a slight smile passed across his face, but it couldn't hide the sadness that was lurking beneath.

"Sank you, Egon," he said. "You can leaf us."

Now that they were alone with Jocular, hopefully they would finally find out what they were doing here.

"Ollie, sank you for coming."

"No problem, sir. Always glad to help. What can we do for you?"

Jocular glided across the floor towards them, making Stitches think that he must have a skateboard under his cape, he moved so smoothly. He spoke in a hushed voice, as if he didn't want anyone to overhear what he had to say.

"Vell, it is all rarzer upsetting really. Normally, ven any problems arise on my property, I, or von of my employees deals vis it. Zis, however, is most perplexing. My children, and more specifically my verevolves, are going missing."

Ollie frowned. "As in running away?"

Jocular raised a long, manicured index finger and waggled it in front of Ollie's face.

"No! My children are supremely loyal to me, and me alone. I sink zat somevon, or somesing is kidnapping zem, but no matter vot I do to try and find out vot is going on, I cannot seem to get to ze heart of ze mystery. Maybe I'm too close to ze issue to make any headvay and my judgement is clouded. I do haff one of my most trusted followers conducting her own enqviries, zough she seems to haff come to a dead end."

"Why on earth would anyone want to steal a werewolf?" asked Stitches. "And what about feeding it, and where the hell would you keep it?"

"In a verehouse," replied Jocular with no hint of humour whatsoever.

Unfortunately Stitches did see the funny side of it and he clamped a hand over his mouth, but an errant giggle escaped nonetheless.

"Vhy do you snigger, Mr. Stitches. My volves, ven zey are in human form, liff in a large house on my estate."

"Sorry, My Lord, touch of dust in the old windpipe. It's the plague of a zombie. Dust."

"I see. Vell, ze accommodation is about a mile from here. Perhaps it vould be prudent for you to start your infestigation zere."

Ollie offered up silent thanks that Stitches' little indiscretion had gone unnoticed.

"That's all very well, Sir," he said, "but is it safe for us to go tramping through the woods at this time of night? With all due respect, I don't relish the thought of ending up on tonight's menu."

"It's all right for you," protested Stitches. "I'll end up being buried somewhere."

"Don't vorry yourselves, gentlemen. You von't be molested or harmed in any vay. Trust me."

Trust you, thought Stitches. That was the equivalent of Adolf Hitler saying 'I've only come to Poland sightseeing. I'm not staying. Honest.'

"Find my children, Ollie. Ze nights are too qviet vizout zem. And ven you discover who is responsible, bring zem to me. I should fery much like to speak vith zem."

"We'll get right on it, my lord. How shall we find the house?"

"Egon vill show you ze vay. And now I must get on. I'm sinking of turning sub-dungeon number four into a games area viz an African theme. Vot do you sink?"

"Lovely idea, sir," offered Stitches. "Very tribal, should work well."

"I sought so. It also takes my mind off vot's been happening," Jocular replied, turning back to the window.

"Well that's perfectly understandable. At a time like this you need something to get our teeth intoooooof!"

Stitches rubbed the spot where Ollie's elbow had connected sharply with his ribs.

"I'm sorry?" questioned the Lord of Darkness.

"Oh, nothing," said Ollie. "We were just leaving. We'll get back to you when we've got some answers."

"Very vell. Good luck, Ollie, and sank you."

The door opened and they saw Egon waiting in the corridor for them.

"This way, gentlemen. Actually, would you like to partake of some refreshment before we depart? It's not a long trek to the werehouse, but it can be heavy going through some dense woodland."

"I wouldn't mind a glass of water," said Stitches.

"Very well." Egon looked at Ollie. "And I have something rather special in the fridge that you'll appreciate. Follow me please, gentlemen." Ollie inclined his head towards his zombie companion and hissed quietly into his ear. "Thanks, mate. He's going to get me a glass of blood to drink, you know that don't you?"

"Oops. Sorry, Ollie. Look, just tell him you've not long got up, and it's too early for you."

"I can't. A visiting vampire can't turn down the offer of fresh virgin's blood in Jocular's own home. One, it's rude and two, it's me. If I say no he'll get all offended and the next thing you know I'll be staked out and barbecuing at dawn because he's found out I hate the stuff. You can be such a dimwit sometimes. Now put your ear back where it should be and shut up."

"Bu. . . "

"Shhhhh."

They made the rest of the trip to the kitchen in silence.

———

Ronnie crossed the Town Square and waited quietly at the top of the alley between Mrs. Strudel's Café and Hector Lozenge's house. Being invisible was all well and good, but it didn't preclude you from making noise, so Ronnie still needed to be stealthy and vigilant about where he was treading and whom he was near. As if to highlight this point, Hector came wobbling up behind him and almost knocked him clean off his feet.

"Where are you? I know you're in there somewhere," he slurred, rummaging around in his pockets. "Ah, there you are, my beauty." Recovered key in hand, he staggered to his front door and got it open on the third attempt before falling inside and slamming it shut.

"Drunken old bugger," Ronnie muttered under his breath.

Hector Lozenge was the town cleaner, and he spent all of his days collecting and removing all manner of filthy detritus from the streets of Skullenia, and as you can imagine it wasn't just scraps of paper and the odd food container that went into his sack, unless you're the sort of creature who classifies an empty rib cage as a food container of course, in which case please don't ever come to one of my book signings. Use Amazon instead.

Hector had been a promising warlock back in his youth, but his weakness for a bottle of anything vaguely alcoholic, and a dalliance with his tutor's lady-friend had seen him expelled from university and stripped of all his flourishing new powers. He'd wandered aimlessly for a few years, trying to come to terms with being restored to merely human status, until he'd finally ended up in Skullenia. Now he was just a pathetic, lonely old man who picked it up all day and poured it down all night.

Ronnie waited until the coast was clear before stepping into the alley. Try as he might, he still couldn't make out what Flug had seen. He gradually made his way to the back of the buildings, narrowly avoiding stepping on a sleeping cat, and stood in the lane itself. Ah, there it was, in the pitch black about two hundred feet into the trees, some vague shapes huddled together. Ronnie stayed where he was to allow his eyes to adjust to the dark void that he was concentrating on. After a couple of minutes and even with the fact that whatever it was was moving deeper into the forest, the forms coalesced into more recognisable figures. They were definitely men; well, they had heads and appeared to be in possession of the correct number of limbs anyway, so he decided that his conclusion was a fair one. As his vision grew more accustomed to the intense darkness, he was able to make out more and more details. They seemed to be wearing uniforms of some description, and each had on a back pack, and what Flug had thought were witches' broomsticks were, in fact, weapons of some sort. The distant click of a round being chambered into a gun barrel made him certain of that. He could only conclude that the mysterious figures were soldiers, but what on earth they were doing in the middle of the Skullenian forest in the dead of night was anyone's guess. The area had had its fair share of visitors of one sort or another down the centuries, but what seemed to be a highly professional, heavily armed fighting force was a tad unusual. Still watching intently, Ronnie could see that the figures, whilst virtually silent, were very animated and gesticulating at an object that was being held between them. It was only when one of them moved slightly that Ronnie could see that they were studying what had to be a map. One of them would look at it, then point in a certain direction, and the others would nod in agreement and make various hand signals as if they were using sign language. Whatever this was it was no ordinary group of squaddies out on a mundane route march. They were in a dense, dangerous forest that he knew from experience wasn't the safest place in the world. To be out doing whatever it was they were doing you either had to be as mad as the maddest of hatters or, and the second option Ronnie considered the most likely, focused on a mission of some description and determined to carry it out no matter where it took you.

One of the figures folded up the map and tucked it away into the thigh pocket of his fatigues. With a gesture that indicated a bearing that would take them even deeper into the forest, he led them off.

This was too good an opportunity to miss. After weeks of hanging around with nothing better to do than play asinine invisible jokes on his colleagues, something interesting seemed to be unfolding right in front of him. Ronnie crossed the lane, and when he was sure he had a safe enough distance between himself and his quarry, he entered the forest.

————

"How far did he say this place was?" asked Stitches, swatting yet another branch away from his face.

Ollie wiped an arm across his sweaty forehead and let out a long, out of breath breath. Despite the chill of the night, the hike was taking its toll on the unfit undead.

"He said about a mile, but it feels like ten already. And he could have told us it was mostly uphill," said the half vampire.

Egon halted and turned to face them. "If you're finding the pace too tough, gentlemen, we can always stop for a rest. I make the journey once a week, so I'm more than used to it."

"No thanks, we're fine," protested Ollie. "Let's just keep going."

"I could give you a piggy back if you like, Mr. Stitches," Egon proposed, a horribly lascivious sneer gracing his squashed features. "All you have to do is climb on board, wrap your legs around my middle and hang on."

Stitches took a large step backwards and tried to hide behind Ollie, whilst trying to make it look like he wasn't trying to hide behind Ollie when he was, in fact, trying to hide behind Ollie.

"Oh, ummm, no thanks. I've got dodgy hips don't you know, I never know when they're going to pop out. Next thing, leg falls off and I'm a walking pogo stick, not that a pogo stick can walk of course, it sort of pogoes, doesn't it. Then it's round and round in circles like a mad round and roundy thing, and I'm wondering can I buy half a pair of shoes, which is one isn't it, and would it be half price. . . "

"Stitches," said Ollie. "Uh huh?" said Stitches.

"You're babbling," said Ollie. "Am I?" said Stitches.

"Oh yes," said Ollie.

"Sorry, don't know what came over me," said Stitches.

Egon stepped towards the shaking zombie and put a hand on his shoulder. "Not to worry, but if you change your mind, let me know, okay? I'm always at your disposal." He gave a squeeze and returned to his lead position.

"He winked at me just then," said a rather disturbed Stitches. "No he didn't, it was a trick of the light."

"What light? It's gone midnight and we're in the middle of a herbaceous black hole. I'm telling you he winked at me."

"Well, possibly. Look, maybe he was just being friendly. And if you were that bothered why didn't you get the Jelly Bodybits out like I told you?"

"I forgot about the sweets because I was in a hurry to get away from the drooling weirdo that you wanted me to give sweets to. And friendly I can put up with, but he makes Mad Derek look normal. Just keep him away from me. Please!"

Ollie gave him a reassuring pat on the back. "Okay, but hey, give it time. You two might hit it off."

"Mmmmph. I'd rather wash Flug's underwear."

Ollie winced. "There's a thought to make a strong man weep." "Too right. I could have murdered Ronnie for showing him how to use the toilet. Flug was perfectly happy wandering around outside until nature took its course but now, wow. You want to go in after him, you better think about sending in a canary first. The last time I saw anything like that I was at the zoo."

"Why do you need to use the bathroom?" asked Ollie with a puzzled frown. "You haven't got any bodily functions to speak of. You don't even breathe."

"I need a soak every now and again to blow, well, wash the cobwebs away, and moisten everything up. And believe me, repairs are a damn sight easier when I'm wet. It's like trying to sew a suitcase shut otherwise."

"Urrrgggh. The bath must look like a bowl of muesli by the time you've finished. No wonder it takes a day and a half to empty it. I dread to think what it's doing to the pipes."

"That's a little terse isn't it," replied Stitches, a hurt look on his face. "At least I don't use a little pink toothbrush."

"Look, it's the only one that gets in behind my fangs. They're hell for getting food stuck."

"If you say so."

"If you two have quite finished, we're here." Egon indicated a light source emanating from a clearing about twenty yards ahead. "It's through there, gentlemen. I'll be waiting here for you when you're done."

"You're not coming in?" asked Ollie.

"No," said Egon. "They don't seem to like me. I don't know why, but I seem to make them a little edgy."

You make me feel positively precipitous, thought Stitches.

"So, if it's okay with yourselves, I'll stay out here and await your return." Egon picked up his hump and went and sat on a large rock.

"Fine by me. Anyone in particular we should ask for? I don't want to go barging in and upsetting someone," said Ollie.

"Wouldn't want to tread on anyone's paws," added Stitches.

"Ask for Obsidia. She's what you might consider to be the leader of the pack," said Egon.

"The top dog, eh?" said Stitches.

Ollie turned and headed for the house, followed by his companion. "Thanks Egon, see you later."

––––––

Mrs. Ladle arrived at the office and walked straight in. Say what you like about life, death or even undeath, in Skullenia, there was a certain community spirit amongst the populous that rivalled anything that went on in most other villages, towns and cities across the globe. You could leave your door open and not worry at all about who or what was going to sneak in and steal your coffin, pop next door at the drop of a body and ask to borrow a pint of bile or a cup of maggots, or whatever other food items you'd run out of, and the local branch of the Neighbourhood Witch was second to none. Simply put it boiled down to good old fashioned friendliness and every resident to a creature would attest to that (it was either that or it had something to do with the fact that, if you got caught in some beings house nicking stuff, there was a very good chance that you'd be given a stern telling off, relieved of a limb or three, and the juicier of your internal organs).

"Anyone home?" she bellowed. Mrs. Ladle was met by stony silence. "Mmmm, must be a boys' night out," she mumbled to herself. She made her way to Ollie's private office and went directly to the secret door. She knew about it on account of the fact that she'd been quite close to Ollie's Uncle Gorge. They'd wiled away many cold winter nights shooting the breeze, shooting the locals, and talking about anything and everything until the sun was due to rise. That, however, was as far the relationship went of course. They'd never taken it any further because the vampire/witch divide was just too great. It would have been 'spooktacularly inappropriate' as Gorge would often say in a rare moment of levity (if he'd had said something funny it would have been even rarer). Nevertheless, they had always been great friends.

She wandered down the stairs and along the passageway and slipped quietly into the lab lest she disturb the resident scientist. Unless you knew what he was doing it was best not to make him jump as he could be handling anything from a piece of paper to the eddying strands of an event horizon. And trust me, you didn't want him dropping one of those. The last one had his shopping list on and it took them ages to find it.

Upon seeing that Rhubarb was hunched over a bench and doing something nondescript with a pair of tweezers, Mrs. Ladle crept up silently behind him and let out an almighty "BOO!"

Professor Crumble carried on his work, not paying a blind bit of notice to the rather loud and sudden interruption.

"I SAID BOO!"

Nothing. Determined to get some sort of a reaction, Mrs. Ladle used the non-sweeping end of her broomstick and gave the Prof a sharp poke in the kidneys. That did the trick. He jumped yards and a pair of tiny headphones fell from his ears.

"Thundering goitres woman, you nearly gave me a coronary." "I obviously wasn't trying hard enough then, was I?"

"Well, that's charming," said Rhubarb, returning to his intricate tweezering.

"Aw, I was only joking," said the witch, peering over his shoulder, trying to see what he was doing. Whatever it was it involved a punnet of raspberries, a bowl of sugar, a jug of cream and the aforementioned tweezers.

"New invention, Rhubarb?" "No."

"What are you up to then?"

"I don't like the hair that grows on fruit, and raspberries happen to be my favourite so. . . " he trailed off as if embarrassed to say anymore.

"So what?" prompted the intrigued witch.

"I'm plucking them," he said, going as red as the berry in his hand. Mrs. Ladle chuckled to herself and ruffled the Prof's hair playfully.

"Have you tried shaving them?" she asked.

"Yes, but they come out in an awful rash. Not very appetizing as you can imagine."

"I suppose not."

Mrs. Ladle found a spare stool, dragged it to the bench and sat opposite Crumble.

"Well, as much as I enjoy talking about hirsute fruit, I did actually come here for a reason," she said.

Professor Crumble put his tweezers and half plucked raspberry back into a bowl and gave the witch his best slightly miffed look, which did no good at all due to the fact that Rhubarb had the complete inability to get annoyed at anything. He would be quite happy to tip the taxman, get friendly with a debt collector and thank a traffic warden for giving him a ticket. He made the Pope look like a serial killer.

"Speak then, dear lady. I am a field of corn." "Field of corn?"

"All ears."

"Ah. Well, it's my stick. I can't seem to get it up."

"Mmmm. It is getting on a bit though, isn't it? Actually, Mr. Doom came in last week with the very same problem. He's been having trouble with his for months and it had got to the point that he was almost too embarrassed to come out of the house. Poor Mrs. Doom didn't know what to do with herself and had a miserable look on her face for ages. She's smiling now though."

"Are you sure we're talking about the same thing?" said Mrs. Ladle, suspiciously.

"Absolutely. It's all a question of gravity, physics and giving the working parts a bit of a jolt by putting something into the system that'll straighten things out as it were."

"So what do I do?" said the witch, now slightly less suspicious but wary enough to run away at a moments notice.

Crumble reached behind him and took a small glass jar off a shelf. He unscrewed the lid and tipped out a half dozen small blue pills onto the bench.

"And what do I do with them?" asked Mrs. Ladle.

"That couldn't be easier. The next time you want to get the old chap airborne, pop one of these into the tank, give it a shake and he'll be up for hours. Satisfaction guaranteed."

She took the pills and tucked them away into the depths of her shawl. "Thanks, Prof, that's a weight off my mind. Oh, by the way, have you got any more of those candles? They're much better than the shop ones."

"I most surely do, dear lady," said the Prof, moving over to a cupboard on the far side of the lab. "Same ones as before?"

Mrs. Ladle pondered for a moment. "Actually, can I have a dozen of the sixty watt ones? They'll be better now the nights are drawing in."

"No problem." Rhubarb put the candles in a bag and handed them over. "Anything else I can help you with?"

"No, that's it. I've got to get home now and bake some biscuits for tomorrow night's coven meeting. They won't cook themselves, you know. Well, they will, but it's much more fun to make them myself. Thanks, Professor. Bye now."

"Goodnight, dear lady," said Rhubarb, shuddering at the thought of what might be going into those biscuits. A witches cooking was something to behold. Mrs. Ladle's cooking was something to be avoided. Alone once more, he turned back to the bench, replaced the headphones and continued working on his raspberries.

———

Ronnie stepped into the forest and immediately felt as if the world had disappeared. He'd become enveloped by a total and utter blackness that was so total and so utterly black that it put all the other total and utter blacknesses in the shade, and if it wasn't for the dim glow of a torch that one of the soldiers was wielding, he would have had to call off his little jaunt because he wouldn't have been able to see his hand in front of his face. Obviously he wouldn't have been able to see his hand in front of his face even if his hand was in front of his face anyway, what with his being invisible and all, but you get the point. It was dark on it.

One good thing though, was that he wasn't going to have to be too careful about the amount of noise he was making. He reckoned that the group were about seventy five feet away now and what with their equipment, weapons and size fourteen boots, although not being overly noisy, they were making enough of a disturbance to cover the sound of any stepped on twigs or slapped out of the way branches that Ronnie inadvertently encountered.

Looking on he could see that the soldiers had spread themselves out into a sort of skirmish line. They were all level with each other, but had spaced themselves about fifteen feet apart, and it was in this formation that they were slowly and painstakingly advancing. Clearly expecting something to happen, each of them now had their weapon at the ready, held securely at hip level so that if required they could engage in an instant.

At that point the figure carrying the torch flicked it off and Ronnie went instantly blind again. Damn it, he thought. All that he could see now was the dim and flickering green glow from the night vision goggles that they obviously had attached to their helmets. It made them look like something out of a science fiction movie, the only question was, what were they hunting?

Ronnie stood with his hands on his hips, cursing his rotten luck but then, casting his gaze upwards he noticed a small gap in the tree canopy. Through it he noticed that a dense bank of clouds was dispersing and an eerie luminescence was beginning to pervade the heavens. "Excellent, a full moon," he whispered to himself, a wide, invisible grin spreading across his face. Thirty seconds later the wispy formation had moved on, leaving the huge, beaming disc of the satellite alone in the sky, free to cast its aged glow down into the forest beneath it.

The trees took on a malevolent, phantom-like quality and the whole forest looked like it had been completely drained of colour and painted in varying shades of grey, not dissimilar to the effect that occurred when a solar eclipse was at the point of totality. In the meagre light time seemed to slow down and everything around him, including the figures up ahead, appeared to be moving at half speed, as if the atmosphere itself had become thicker.

The light, although not brilliant, was good enough for Ronnie's needs, however. He now had a clear view of the path ahead that he needed to take, and his quarry was now in full view, which was perfect. He decided that now would be a good time to try and close the distance between himself and the four men, not only to decrease the chances of losing them but also to be able to sneak close enough and pick up any stray bits of information that they might let slip.

Still mindful of extraneous noise, he waited until they moved off before continuing his pursuit. They were being extremely stealthy and cautious, there was no doubt about that, but for the life of him he still couldn't postulate a theory as to what a squad of highly trained soldiers were doing in a Skullenian forest in the middle of the night. It was possible, he supposed, that they were on manoeuvres, except that those sorts of operations were usually conducted in the Scottish Highlands or the rolling, unpronounceable hills of North Wales. No, this was something very different, and Ronnie was now more determined than ever to find out what it was.

Within a quarter of an hour he'd managed to get within twenty feet of the squad, and thus far he'd remained undetected by using their combined footfalls and intermittent chatter to cover any sounds that he may have inadvertently made.

They were steadily making their way deeper and deeper into the trees when, without warning, the figure second from the right suddenly raised his right arm and, with a deliberate slowness, brought it back down until it nestled once again on the trigger of his weapon. This was obviously the command to halt, because the other three came to an abrupt stop and regrouped in a tight huddle. This was what Ronnie had been waiting for, he just needed to be a few feet closer and he might be able to ascertain what was occurring.

Silently, he got to within ten feet, stepped over an ancient algae encrusted log and put his boot down on possibly the oldest, driest and consequently noisiest branch the world has ever known. CRRRACCCCKKKK!

Ronnie instantly panicked and froze in position, as, to a man, the squad turned in the direction of the sound, raised their weapons and flooded the area with a torch-beam so powerful that it could have warned ships away from treacherous rocks. Ronnie recoiled as the light hit his retinas and he very nearly dived behind the nearest tree for cover until, in the midst of his literally blind stupor, he remembered that he couldn't be seen by the gun toting men. Quickly regaining control over his erratic breathing he stayed still, stayed quiet and listened. The light from ahead had destroyed his night vision, so now he couldn't see the figures at all, but, in the dead forest air he could make out some snippets from a whispered conversation.

"... was that?" "Don't know."

"...came... where... 'er there." "Urrrgggh what... stood in?" "Do... think... looking for?"

"Could... but... made more noise... "

"...straight at us... mess around... creeping about." "Mmmm... eleven."

"May... squirrel."

"... off. Let's... and move out."

The light snapped off and Ronnie was once again plunged into an all-encompassing darkness that somehow seemed denser than before and it took him a good few seconds to readjust. Even though he'd managed to close his eyes (a pure reflex action of no use whatsoever) the microsecond after the torch had come on, it had been freakishly bright and the sudden change from coffin dark to supernova light and then to dark again had been too much for his poor optic nerves to deal with all at once, particularly in view of the fact that his eyelids were about as much use as the Spanish edition of How to Speak Spanish. Within a couple of minutes, however, his vision had settled down and he was able to locate the squad up ahead once more. Ronnie quickly got back up to them determined that he wasn't going to let them go without getting some answers. They were hunting something that was clear, but as to what it was and why, he was unsure. Time would tell, he was certain.

———

Thick black hairs bristled and twitched, undulating in waves that travelled backwards along a prominent spine. Bulky muscles clustered under the flesh, writhed and rippled with a sinewy grace, loose and relaxed but ever ready to burst into frenzied action in a split second. The werewolf was huge. On its hind legs it stood eight feet tall and had paws like dinner plates, each one tipped with five four inch claws that could tear through skin and bone as if it was so much tissue paper. It was a pure hunting machine, bred to kill, perfectly designed, intent on its goal and in search of prey.

A faint odour caught its hypersensitive nose, so it stopped and raised its massive head in order to catch more of the scent as it travelled on the night air. Coloured images flooded the beasts' consciousness. At first they were haphazard, as if an artist had decided to experiment with his entire paint collection and a single sheet of canvas, but as the scent increased, they began to separate and become more structured, forming shapes and tantalising patterns before finally coalescing into a recognisable representation. It was manflesh, and plenty of it. The animal's keen senses detected five individual entities a few hundred yards ahead, a group of four together and one on its own, but all within relatively close proximity.

Its target acquired the lycanthrope continued on its way, a plan of attack already beginning to form. It would take out the loner first, and while the rest were still running around in panic it would pick them off one by one. A low growl of satisfaction rumbled deep in its throat as it slowly paced onwards.

———

"I've got a bad feeling about this," said Stitches, as he and Ollie stood on the porch.

Ollie cocked an eyebrow. "What's the matter now?"

"This." Stitches indicated their surroundings with a wave of his hand to let his friend know that 'this this' was the 'this' he was referring to when he mentioned a 'this' in his original comment and not just any this 'this', which out here could be any old this or that. Or something like that anyway. Or is it something like this? Mmm, I think we'll leave this/that here because I'm all confused now and this/that won't do at all. The zombie continued. "We've been sent all the way out here by a psychotic vampire lord in company with his idiotic and retarded servant to a great big house in the middle of a forest that werewolves live in. This is not my idea of a fun evening. Call me Mr. Pessimistic, and I dare say that many have, but I can't see it ending on a high note." (And apologies for the use of the phrase 'retarded servant'. I know it's not strictly PC but I felt the use of the word was necessary in this particular instance to convey Stitches' feelings about their predicament. Retard, on the other hand, is a perfectly acceptable word and should be used as often as possible. No one's telling me what I can and can't say, right kids, hurrah!).

Ollie's hand paused on its way to connecting to the door. "That was quite an outburst," he said. "I'm sure your little friend over there enjoyed it."

Stitches cast a worried glance over his shoulder and scanned the front yard. "Where's, Egon?" he said.

"I don't know," replied Ollie. "Maybe he took the hump for a walk to do its business."

Stitches smirked. "The hump needs a dump, huh. Come on, knock the door and let's get this over with."

Before Ollie's clenched fist could connect with the wood, it was opened from within, and what they saw caused both of their jaws to hit the floor.

"Stitches." "Huh."

"Do you want to pick that up?"

The zombie looked down and, without any indication that anything remotely unusual had happened, bent down, picked up his chin and nonchalantly popped it back into place. The figure in the doorway stifled a giggle. "That must be handy for shaving."

She was by far and away and without a shadow of a doubt, the most gorgeous creature that either of them had ever seen in their entire lives, deaths, or indeed, undeaths, and on the plus side at least it was blatantly obvious she was female, which in Skullenia was a bit of a boon. Such was the diversity of Skullenia's population that it wasn't always apparent what exactly you were looking at so it paid to be cautious. A drunken Ronnie had been caught out like that more than once, including three times in one night with the same creature.

The lady made catwalk models look like pre-pubescent schoolboys. She had curves in all the right places, and all of her places were right curvy. A petite waist flared out to shapely hips and long, slender, welldefined legs. Her height, which was about five feet nine, was accentuated by four inch stiletto heeled shoes and she carried herself with a natural grace and elegance. She was voluptuous in every way, from her perfect heaving bosom to her full pouting red lips which, when parted, revealed a dazzling white smile that was devastating. This was matched only by seductive, steely grey eyes that were framed by sweeping lashes. Her perfectly symmetrical features were surrounded by lustrous deep brown, almost black hair that tumbled to just below her square, muscular shoulders.

"Y... yes it is," stuttered Stitches. "At least it would be if I shaved, which I don't, but if I did it would be handy."

When she smiled the whole world seemed like a better place, as if nothing was wrong and nothing bad could ever happen.

"Well that's that cleared up then." Her voice was as smooth as silk. You wouldn't mind hanging around at King's Cross all day if the train announcer sounded like that. In fact, you'd miss your train on purpose just to keep on listening. "My name's Obsidia. You must be the two investigators we've been expecting."

"Indeed we are, Miss. I'm Ollie Splint and this is my colleague, Stitches," Ollie extended a hand, which she took.

"How did you know we were coming?" asked the zombie. "Are you psychic?"

"No," replied Obsidia, "we could hear you coming from about three hundred yards away. And I must say it's a very pleasing turn of phrase you have, Mr. Stitches. You've been keeping us entertained for quite a while."

Stitches would have blushed if he'd had any blood in his system. "It's my nerves," he said. "I use humour as a defence mechanism." "I see. Won't you step inside, gentlemen."

They entered the building and had a look around. It was more of a converted barn than anything else. High beamed ceilings gave way to slatted walls, recessed into which were cubby holes, each of which contained a mattress and a blanket. Other than that there were very few homelike items. The floor area was basically open plan and had a large communal space in the centre, comprising half a dozen sofas, two coffee tables, a couple of chairs and a large chest of drawers. Two of the sofas were presently occupied.

"Excuse me for saying so," said Ollie, "but isn't this whole set up rather basic? I would have expected a few more home comforts if I'm honest."

Obsidia closed the front door and sashayed across the floor to stand next to the two investigators.

"I suppose it would look like that to an outsider, but for us this house contains everything we need. You'll find that once the lycanthrope gene is in the blood, materialism and all the frivolities and trappings of a modern existence no longer seem quite as important. Even in human form we tend to prefer things rustic. We are quite a countrified ensemble I suppose, but at its most basic we're ordinary folk who have all responded to the call of the wild."

"No creature comforts then?" said Stitches, and then immediately wished he hadn't.

Ollie shook his head and rolled his eyes. "Excuse my friend's sledgehammer wit. In his former life he was an idiot."

Obsidia laughed provocatively and placed a beautifully manicured hand on Ollie's arm. "Don't worry, Mr. Splint. I have a liking for men that can make me laugh." She looked over at Stitches and raised an eyebrow. "I think we're going to get on just fine."

"Get on your nerves, more like," muttered Ollie under his breath.

"Now now, Mr. Splint. Tolerance is a virtue you know," said Obsidia. "Call me Ollie, please. And if I may say, you try working with him for a couple of weeks and we'll see how long your tolerance lasts."

Obsidia coyly nibbled on a nail and gazed at Stitches with a look of seductive innocence. "Well, on first impression I think I would be quite happy to spend a few weeks collaborating with him. It could be an interesting experience."

Stitches stared back at her in wonder. It was obvious, even to the most brain dead of entities, that their hostess was quite taken with the zombie. Stitches had noticed and couldn't believe his luck. Ollie had noticed and just couldn't believe it, and Obsidia was just, well, you can figure it out for yourself.

"Well, that's all fine and dandy," Ollie cut in, "but perhaps we should be dealing with the matter at hand. Your missing pack members."

"Of course. Won't you sit down?" she said.

As the three of them sat on one of the empty sofas, Ollie glanced around the large room. Obsidia included they were in the company of about a dozen lycanfolk, which was quite a gathering of such powerful beings. If you put that many trolls or ogres in the same place World War III would break out, and that would just be over who's the tallest. He relaxed somewhat but still kept his wits about him. Even though he knew that they were in a safe environment, as promised by Count Jocular, he was still slightly on edge. This was new territory for him and he didn't want to let his guard down, especially with his friend behaving like a love sick schoolboy who's got a crush on their maths teacher (Ah, Mrs. Robinson).

"I didn't think there would be many of you guys in tonight, what with the full moon," said Stitches.

A man sitting opposite them leaned forward and spoke. He seemed friendly enough but his eyes looked tired and there was a definite hint of sadness about him. "That's a common misconception, my friend. As lycanthropes we can change our form at will. We're not at the mercy of the lunar cycle, like most people seem to think. We can transform when we feel the need to."

"When you're hungry, you mean," said Ollie.

The man smiled but it was an unenthusiastic effort. "Not really. We do feed, of course, but that's secondary to our desire to be outdoors and roaming the forest at will. Obviously there's a small portion of our time in wolf form that we spend hunting, but there's more to us than mere slaughter. I know it's an old romantic cliché but we feel most at home when we're at one with nature."

"Well, you would be at one with nature if you eat it, I suppose," said Stitches.

"About the disappearances," interrupted Ollie when he noticed a dark and dangerous look pass across the man's face. Stitches' complete lack of tact was liable to get them both stripped and gutted if he wasn't reigned in.

"Ah yes, well, we've lost two far. Isobel and Ross," said Obsidia, a hint of emotion creeping into her voice at the mention of her pack mates. "Were they on their own when they went hunting in the forest?" said Ollie.

Obsidia nodded her head. "Yes, they were. Werewolves always hunt alone. They went out as usual, as they've done a thousand times before, except this time they didn't come back as planned, which is very strange. The transformation is extremely stressful on the individual experiencing the process, so if you combine that with a night spent tracking through the forest, you end up with a being that is intensely tired and in need of rest, which is why a pack member will always, without exception, return to their lair. And to pre-empt your next question, a lycanthrope will never leave a pack once they've been accepted as a member."

"Never?" said Stitches.

"Never. We may spend a lot of our time on individual exploits, but we will always return to the place we call home. To us, it would be like leaving the bosom of a close family."

Stitches, trying desperately to get the word bosom out his head, said, "Isn't it beyond the realms of possibility that the two people you mentioned just got fed up with communal life and decided to leave?

These extraordinary abilities that you all have and the safety of a vampire protected existence wouldn't necessarily stop someone from getting fed up with all of it surely. And whilst I appreciate what you said about the pack mentality, somewhere along the line, someone's going to fancy a change sooner or later so to speak. It's human nature and you can't bury that forever."

"That's a cogent argument that has a lot of merit," replied Obsidia. "But please take this from me as being the absolute and unwavering truth, it does not happen. We're a happy group here and like all other packs, wherever they are, once you're a member you stay a member." Ollie fixed her with a steely glare, but she didn't bat an eyelid under his scrutiny. "Is it by desire or pressure that people choose to stay?" he asked. "I don't wish to cast aspersions on how things are run round here, but it's very easy to extol the virtues of a particular lifestyle that's dear to you and then proclaim disbelief when people become disenchanted and want no more part of it. I'm sorry to bring it up, but please understand that I'm not being accusatory, I just happen to feel that it's a relevant line of enquiry that needs ruling out."

Obsidia smiled at him and her eyes sparkled like a pair of fresh water lagoons in the midday sun. "No apology required. It is indeed a relevant question, but take it from me please, Ollie, no one is pressured to remain. Such are the close relationships that we build within our community and the fealty that comes to us naturally, we can discount that as a possibility straight away. It's nature's law if you like. The way of the fold is an unbreakable as the bond between a parent and child."

"Sounds fair enough to me," said Stitches. "And kind of comforting."

68

He gave Obsidia a wink and then, under the guise of having an itchy eye, pushed his eyelid back up to where it should be.

"Yes, it is, "she replied, oozing a sexuality that threatened to overwhelm the zombie that it was directed at. "Maybe you should stay with us for a short while and learn a bit more about our culture."

Stitches got his mouth half way open to reply, but was interrupted by Ollie, who had neither the intention nor the inclination to find out exactly how these creatures lived. He was very happy to subscribe to the live and let live philosophy but that didn't mean that he wanted to get up close and personal.

"Maybe after we've finished working on the case we could pay you a social visit, but that could be a while considering the lack of information that we've got," he said with a deft, verbal sidestep.

"Mmmm", said Stitches, temporarily diverted from their lustful hostess, "you'd think, bearing in mind who's gone missing, that we'd have more leads."

While Obsidia looked at him and shook her head ever so slightly, and Ollie buried his head in his hands, not believing that the zombie could have made it to two hundred years of age without getting lots of bells and several bags of excrement kicked out of him on a regular basis, the large man that had spoken to them on their arrival left his seat and walked over to where Stitches was sitting. He was enormous, about six feet six and built like a tank. A tank that had spent long hours down the gym and put enough chemicals in its system to kill a donkey built like a tank. Even his hair looked like it was flexing its muscles. He grabbed the zombie by the throat in one massive hand and lifted him clean off the seat and into the air. They were now face to face, but Stitches' feet were dangling eight inches off the floor.

"If you've come here to help us find out what's happened to our friends, that's fine, but one more wise crack like that and I'll snap you in half." He threw the startled zombie back down onto the sofa and stormed out of the room.

"Ooo, someone's tired," said the zombie, rubbing his neck and wincing at the thought of the hand print that was going to remain branded on his flesh until he could get to an iron.

"That'll teach you," scolded Ollie.

Obsidia waved a graceful hand and spoke in a soothing tone as she rubbed Stitches on the shoulder. "It's not his fault. That's Ethan. Isobel is his younger sister, and he's taken her disappearance hard."

Stitches did look genuinely upset. He stared at his feet and spoke quietly. "Maybe I should go and apologise," he offered.

"I wouldn't," replied Obsidia with a flick of her lustrous hair. "Best to let him calm down on his own. He'll be fine. I'll speak to him later." There was silence in the room for a few moments as overwrought emotions settled back down. Ollie left it as long as he thought prudent before deciding to break the palpable tension that had cast a gloom over those assembled. "So when did they actually go missing?" he enquired.

"Last night and the night before," said Obsidia. "As I said they went out as normal but never came back."

"Have any of the other members been out searching for them?" Ollie asked.

Obsidia stood and crossed the room to a coffee table to get herself a drink.

"Anything?" They both shook their heads. "We've all been out at one point or another. We've scoured the forest and been everywhere that they could possibly be. Even with our heightened senses we haven't been able to find a trace. Another member, James, is out there now."

Ollie frowned and watched as she paced elegantly back to the sofa and sat down.

"Isn't that a little foolish bearing in mind what's been happening?" he asked.

"Don't think we didn't try and stop him, but James and Isobel are what you might call something of an item. They've been partners for a while now so it was next to impossible to persuade James that it might not be the wisest course of action."

"I see your point."

"Well," said Stitches, "it looks like we've exhausted all the lines of enquiry here for the moment wouldn't you say, Ollie? Maybe we should move on." As much as he was enjoying Obsidia's company, his run in with Ethan had left him a little shaken and dented his confidence somewhat, as well as his neck and three of his ribs.

Obsidia stroked his knee and blessed him with her most sultry and flirtatious smile.

"Why don't you stay a while longer," she said. "Hopefully James will return soon and he may have some information for you. I'm sure we can find something to keep you occupied in the meantime."

Ollie shrugged his shoulders and relaxed into the soft leather of the sofa. "I suppose it couldn't hurt to stay for a bit. It looks like we're going to need all the help we can get on this one."

———

Flug was bored. Very bored. In fact he'd gone so far beyond the point of terminal boredom that he was currently almost halfway through counting his fingers, an activity that was as alien to the monster as going to the shops, buying what you want and going straight home again was to your wife. Now, I know that's a controversial and somewhat sexist standpoint, but ask any chap who's suffered the indignity of standing forlornly in a clothes shop whilst his good lady is trying on her seventeenth outfit, and see if he agrees. I think you'll find he does. A trek to the North Pole wearing nothing but your pants whilst standing on a sled being pulled by hamsters is less taxing. Quieter, too. To be fair to Flug, he'd been making quite good progress but it wasn't long before his brain had shut down for twenty minutes because of all the information that it had tried to process. The stellar journey from one to four had overloaded a latent synapse or two and caused the dormant organ to spasm, leaving Flug in a comatose trance, sporting a faraway look on his face and playing pendulums with the thin strand of drool running from the corner of his mouth. If you've ever tried to order a meal at McDonald's after nine o'clock at night from a trainee member of staff you can appreciate the state he was in. Flug would have never got a job there anyway. He was far too educated and erudite.

Once his brain had finished sifting of all the advanced mathematical data, Flug once more joined the conscious, if ever so slightly confused world. He gazed at the moon and saw that it had shifted a bit since he'd last looked up.

"Ronnie been gone a long time," he muttered to himself. "He must be havin' fun in dere, but me wish he hurry up and come back."

He inched forward slowly, so as to peer out from his hidey hole. The town square was dead, literally. Not a sound could be heard and there wasn't another being in sight. The odd street light was on here and there and a couple of normal ones too, but other than that it was like being in a ghost town, which it was really, all things considered. Warily he retreated back into the dark confines of his safe place.

Now you might wonder what a creature like Flug had to concern himself about but, in spite of his physical attributes, he was definitely feeling a little spooked by the whole situation, although scaring the massive reanimate didn't take much to be honest. He might very well be as big as a baby dinosaur and able to lift up a horse if one had a blow out and needed to change shoes, but when it came down to it he was, plain and simply, very easily scared. Of lots of things. To clarify further he was scared of just about anything that he didn't understand (which was nearly everything. He still wasn't sure how socks worked) or had never seen before (which was nearly everything. You could show him something two hundred times and on the two hundred and first he'd ask you what it was, what it was for, where do you put it and what it was again), but when you bear in mind that he had the intellectual ability of a bowl of soup this was hardly surprising. He was timid to the point of paranoia and had the constitution of a frightened mouse that's just watched all six seasons of American Horror Story and then realised that he's run out of cheese. Not only would Flug not say BOO to a goose, the goose would turn on him, reduce him to tears after some furious name calling and steal his lunch money. His shadow was a constant source of terror, showing up unexpectedly, following him around and copying everything he did. He was the original big softy, one who had once spent four days hiding in a cellar because he'd heard that the circus was coming to town and they had a massive big top (and no, I can't explain that one either but then what would I know? I'm scared of washing lines, Channel 5 and anything that goes PING, although that might have something to do with watching The Curse of

The Pinging Washing Line one night. I don't know where the Channel 5 thing comes from though, the film was on BBC1).

Girding his loins, and whatever other body-parts he didn't know the name for, Flug tentatively stepped out from the recess and quickly made his way to one of the street lights. Although it only cast a pale glow onto the square, being bathed in its dim radiance made him feel a bit better, but it didn't lift the strange nagging feeling that was turning his stomach over. Something in the back of his mind, and that was a long way back, was telling him that Ronnie was in trouble and should have been back to check on him by now. It would take a while for this information to reach the cognitive part of his brain and afford him the ability to verbalise his concerns, but it was there nonetheless.

"What are you doing out at this time of night, big boy?"

If he hadn't have been expertly tacked together, Flug would have jumped out of his skin and landed in a big wet mess on the floor.

"Feeling lonely?" "All on your own?"

"Need some company?"

Shaking like an Essex girl doing a spelling test, Flug looked down at the three waif like forms that had appeared next to him. They were the Stella triplets, Stella 'a' une, Stella 'a' deux and Stella 'a' trois. They were the towns' resident ladies of the night and prided themselves on the excellence of their service, so much so that they charged pretty much what they wanted. They were *reassuringly* expensive though.

Flug calmed down once he realised that he'd been scared by people that he at least knew, platonically of course. Anything else didn't bear thinking about.

Stitches had once attempted to explain the birds and the bees to an innocent Flug, but it had left him in such a state that he'd locked himself away in his room for the rest of the day, only emerging when Stitches promised that he'd made up the whole story and that par ents collected their little ones from Mother-scare once they'd saved up enough vouchers.

"Hello, ladies," he said. "Have you seen Ronnie? He been gone a long time."

The girls looked at each other and shook their heads.

"Sorry, Flug love," said Stella 'a' trois, "we haven't. Where did he go?"

Flug pointed to the woods. "In dere."

"Why would he go in there at this time of night? It's not safe," said Stella 'a' une.

Flug scratched his head with a Cumberland sausage sized finger. "Me dunno. Me fink he was lookin' for someone."

"I know how he feels," said Stella 'a' deux. "I haven't had a sniff all night."

"Well," said Stella 'a' trois, "you did when Mrs. Skelter's dog ran out of the café and... "

"Yes, thank you very much. Anyway, we're not going to get anywhere if we stand around here all night. Look after yourself, Flug. Don't let the Bogeyman get you."

The three ladies wandered off into the night leaving Flug alone once more. Only he wasn't quite by himself this time. Now he was accompanied by the thought that Stella, whatever number she was, had left implanted in his head. DON'T LET THE BOGEYMAN GET YOU. And so, Flug being Flug, immediately re-entered his obligatory state of panic and ran as fast as he could back to the sanctuary of the office, the one place that he knew was safe.

He needn't have worried though. Nosey the Bogeyman had left for his annual holiday two days previously. He was on a fortnight's get away in Corfu, and judging by the state that he usually arrived home in, there wouldn't be any bogeying going on in Skullenia for quite some time.

———

The beast padded silently through the trees, eyes darting in all directions and ears alert to the slightest sound. Its long, moist tongue licked lips that were pulled back over teeth that wouldn't have looked out of place in Jurassic Park.

All of a sudden the wolf froze, neither a muscle moving nor a fibre twitching. About ten feet ahead, the dense wood gave way to a small clearing, and it was from this oasis that the noise had come. To the creature's senses it was heightened to a loud and distinctive cacophony, but it wasn't reminiscent of any woodland disturbance and the wolf was one hundred percent familiar with every sight and sound of the forest. The creature flared its nostrils and tried to pick up any scent that might be floating on the night air. It only took a microsecond before it registered. Sweat, smoke, artificial fibres and, most importantly, the acrid, pungent stench of fear. The wolf prowled on and prepared to attack.

———

Ronnie was just on the edge of the trees, more or less directly opposite and completely oblivious to the presence of the wolf that was poised to strike. Even if he had have been aware of it he wouldn't have been able to see it though, because his view was obscured by the four soldiers, who were having an ad hoc briefing right in the centre of the treeless glade.

Try as he might, he still couldn't fathom the reason for their presence and hadn't heard anything to give him the slightest clue. Usually, the only people silly enough to enter these woods besides the squad before him and nosey detectives who should know better, were clueless tourists, arty writers and occasionally, well, once, a television crew. Tourists would meander along the forest paths, taking too many photos and making too much noise, writers would explore the leafy domain either for research or use it as somewhere to 'get away from it all and find myself' and, for some inexplicable reason, the television crew filmed a cookery show.

On the whole though, visitors from outside were pretty rare. If they did decide to drop in they'd usually get to the point of entering the wood or sightseeing in the town, and then get no further because they would invariably hear stories from some of the locals that would put them off. "Don't go into the woods," they'd be told. "Dangerous they be, full of vile creatures, spectres, evil doings and hobgoblins with little pointy sticks. Wooooooh." Either that or a sharp "Bugger off," at any rate.

Still, the vile creatures and spectres etc. weren't silly and refrained from devouring strangers and kept to their own. Picking off the odd (very odd) local from time to time was deemed acceptable and was an acknowledged aspect of the culture amongst which such beings existed. After all you couldn't live on the African Savannah without being chased by a lion every now and then, could you? It was just a part of everyday life that people acknowledged had to happen occasionally, no matter how distasteful other people may find it. Kind of like Strictly Come Dancing.

Consequently, the woodland evil was forced to use a little discretion when it came to feeding, and splattering a celebrity chef's internal organs all over the forest floor would have been a bit over the top, although many folk would have seen it as a credible exception and great service to mankind in general. If nothing else, it would be a start. Ronnie was on the point of giving up and going home. He was no closer to getting to the bottom of this, and the protracted length of time that he'd been invisible was taking a toll on his system and making him tired. It wasn't easy keeping every molecule of your body in a constant state of flux, and there was always the ever present danger that he could suddenly become a bit faint, lose concentration and become visible again. Not very good if you were on covert ops, involved in a stakeout or hiding behind a curtain in the shower room after hockey practice at the Scapularian School for Developing Young Ladies. (Damn, maybe I shouldn't have mentioned that last one. Right, let's get this cleared up straight away. Please don't jump to the conclusion that Ronnie is a bit of a perv who uses his physical gift purely to satisfy his own base needs because that's not what I intended at all and couldn't be further from the truth. He quite often puts it to good use and, um... well, sometimes he... uh, no, it's not that either.

Actually, after thinking on it for a bit, he actually doesn't put it to any good use whatsoever. What a perv).

Ronnie made a move to go when something caught his eye. He initially thought it was one of the soldiers, but the slight movement of a leaf on the other side of the clearing started the alarm bells ringing. As he watched, a branch moved forward and down as if some weight were slowly forcing it out of the way, and was that the faint sound of fresh wood splintering that he could hear? It was then that the moonlight reflected off something dark and glossy yet tantalisingly unidentifiable. Now his interest was piqued.

Another couple of seconds later a pair of large oval rubies appeared out of the darkness beyond. They glinted in the lunar glow, fixed and unwavering.

"Oh my goodness," Ronnie muttered to himself as realisation

crashed over him like a tidal wave. "Whatever those guys are hunting isn't playing by the rules."

He watched in rapt fascination as the soldiers continued their discussion in blissful ignorance of the perilous situation they were now in. By now, a foot-long muzzle was protruding from the trees, and a vague wisp of breath condensed into the cold night air. It was unmistakable now. It was a werewolf, and a big one too. The sheer size of the head alone was enough to freeze Ronnie to the spot and render him completely speechless. He obviously knew they existed and he'd heard various tales about them, but he'd never seen one in the flesh.

A flickering notion came to him to call out a warning but any thoughts in that regard were instantly crushed, beaten back by fear and an instinctive sense of self-preservation. Jack booted and standing to rigid attention, Ronnie's brain ordered him to be still and silent. Those poor unfortunate souls in front of him would have to fend for themselves.

Transfixed by the developing tableau, he watched in fascinated horror as the monstrous creature burst forth from the undergrowth with a roar that would have sent a pride of lions to an early grave.

Two of the soldiers dropped to the ground instantly. Whether it was out of shock or due to their training Ronnie couldn't be sure, but for now they were out of the initial fight for survival.

The remaining two reacted equally as quickly, obviously veterans and acutely aware of the position they found themselves in. They split to opposite sides of the clearing, giving the wolf two possible targets, and reducing the chances of them both being taken down in one attack. All of this happened in a split second, but to Ronnie it seemed as if time had slowed, as if the unfolding battle was taking place underwater. He could see that the wolf was making a choice as to which target to attack first, assessing the threat and where any danger to itself was likely to come from. Its eyes darted from one to the other and in an instant, it chose.

The wild side of its psyche would have seen the wolf go into battle without a second thought in a fury of fangs, fur and ferocity, but it's deeply buried human consciousness had made it tactically aware and able to make a choice based on risk and the likely success of the chosen plan of action. It picked the soldier to Ronnie's right, the one that had been giving the orders.

With a speed born of supernatural strength, the beast was on him. Jaws like a steel trap clamped onto the man's head and tightened like a vice. Razor sharp teeth punctured flesh and bone, shattering the skull and sending blood and body fluids in all directions. The soldier's decapitated corpse hit the deck with a wet thud as the wolf turned its attention to its second target. Obviously thinking he would have had more time, the soldier had only just manoeuvred himself to a position just in front of where Ronnie was hiding. As he attempted to ready and deploy his weapon the wolf pounced, barely giving him time to raise his gun. The monster slashed at him with a giant, talon tipped paw, smashing the semi-automatic rifle in half. Vicious claws then slashed into the soldier's torso just below the left armpit and, in one raking movement, ripped through muscle and sinew, exposing bone and internal organs. A second ravaged carcass fell to the forest floor.

SHIT, Ronnie thought as he gazed at the body sprawled before him. Brutal didn't begin to cover it. Gore spread across the ground and formed a bright red pool as the wolf hovered over its kill and steam rose from the spilt innards as it sniffed the freshly rendered meat. As the creature lowered its head, Ronnie saw to his horror that the man's heart was still beating. Surely he couldn't still be alive?

That point very quickly became moot though as in one bite the wolf tore the rich, red organ from the soldiers chest cavity and popped it like an egg yolk between its honed incisors, drenching Ronnie in a shower of warm blood. It was then that he heard a faint thunk, and he would always maintain afterwards that he saw a perplexed look pass over the wolf's frightening features before it toppled sideways, the chewed brawn of the heart still hanging from its jaw. He stared at the immense body, wondering why it had suddenly died, but then noticed that its flank was still moving up and down and a bubble of blood inflating and deflating in one of its nostrils.

"Whoever you are, step forward slowly."

Ronnie snapped back into real time, suddenly remembering the other members of the team. But who was this one talking to? The sight of a gun barrel aimed at his head answered the question for him. But how was it possible?

"Step forward now or I WILL open fire."

Then it dawned on him. It was the blood. The blood from the man killed in front of him. It had sprayed towards him when the wolf attacked. Ronnie put a hand to his face and felt the sticky ooze on his cheek.

Damn it.

When he brought his hand back down he could see the outline of his fingers and even the signet ring that he wore. He clenched his soggy hand into a fist and closed his eyes. To all intents and purposes he was now very, very visible.

Ronnie knew he had no choice; the man was definitely talking to him. Involuntarily, he raised his hands above his head and stepped from his place of safety into the clearing.

"That's far enough." The soldier looked him up and down but kept his weapon fixed at all times. "What the hell are you?"

Ronnie was about to conjure up a vaguely plausible answer when he felt a scratch on his left arm. He glanced down and saw a small, thin dart protruding from his flesh. "What the. . . " The rest of the sentence was cut off as his vision clouded over and his sense of balance started to waver. The last thing he remembered was the soldier's face as he hit the forest floor with a resounding thump, and passed out.

———

Ollie looked at his watch. "This James is taking his time," he said. Obsidia flicked her hair and raised a crescent shaped eyebrow. "Yes, he is. Maybe he's discovered something about the disappearances." "Possibly," agreed Ollie, "but we really do need to get on. If he does have any information for us on his return, maybe you could get in touch and share it with us." He produced a business card and handed it over. "Any time, day or night."

"You can be sure of it," the female lycanthrope oozed, throwing a lascivious glance in the direction of Stitches, who smiled a grey toothed grin right back at her and waved like a coquettish debutante.

Ollie couldn't help but notice the non-verbal interaction between them. "Yes, well, we'll be on our way then. Until we meet again," he said by way of getting the hell out of there before his colleague became completely insensate.

"I can't wait," said Obsidia, rising from her place on the sofa and gesturing towards the front door.

As they got to the exit, Obsidia placed a hand on the zombie's shoulder and turned him to face her. She planted a sensuous kiss on his cheek and whispered in his ear, "Don't be a stranger."

"I'll try not to be," said Stitches. "I've known myself for years and I think I'm great.""

"Rascal. You be safe now and I'll see you soon. Bye."

The door closed and once again the two investigators found themselves on the edge of the primordial forest.

"Right. Now that that's finally over with maybe we can get some work done," Ollie said with an indignant sneer.

"I thought that's what we'd been doing for the last couple of hours," said Stitches, a little confused. "Unless asking questions, probing for clues and engaging in a bit of sleuthery doesn't count."

"Well, I was," Ollie responded with a terse edge to his voice. "You spent most of the time flirting with Morticia Adams in there. And don't think I didn't see you playing footsie under the table."

"I apologised for that. She pushed too hard and, well, my ankle joints aren't what they used to be."

"You're lucky you've still got that foot. Nine times out of ten she'd run outside and bury it," said Ollie.

Stitches frowned. "What's got into you? You don't strike me as the jealous type, mate."

They reached the spot where Egon had left them and stopped to wait for him. Ollie put his hands into this pockets and looked up at the moon.

"No, it's nothing like that. I was just hoping to make a go of. . . " he removed his hands and swept them in a wide arc taking in everything, ". . . this that's all, but all we've done so far is waste our time talking to a sexually uninhibited, female werewolf. I knew taking on this venture was a stupid idea. Not that I had much of a choice of course."

Stitches bumped shoulders with his downhearted friend. "Hey, don't worry. Something'll turn up. You'll see."

A rustle from the trees ahead denoted the return of their erstwhile guide.

"Ah, gentlemen, greetings once more. You've been inside quite a while. I assume your venture proved successful?" asked Egon.

"I wouldn't go that far," answered Ollie, thinking at the same time that this little toad was as nosey as a very nosey person asking for directions to the latest meeting of the Nosey Buggers Society. "Did you have a nice walk whilst we were gone?"

"Yes indeed. Nothing like a night time stroll through the woods to blow away the cobwebs and get back to nature." In fact he did look a bit less dusty when it came down to it.

Egon turned back towards the trees, put two fingers in his mouth and whistled. "PHEEEEEEEEEP. Here boy, come on, One Lump, there's a good fellah."

A faint hint of movement, like a mouse scurrying under a blanket, caught their attention. Stitches cast an unbelieving look at Ollie. "I really have seen it all now," he whispered.

Egon's disembodied appendage crawled out from the undergrowth and obediently joined its master whereupon Egon gave it a loving pat, took a leather lead from his jacket pocket and attached it to the sparkly collar that the pasty, grey chunk of flesh wore around its middle. He then reached across and gave it a tickle under what one would presume to be its chin. Or at least one would *hope* that it was its chin.

"I do hope he's got the right end," muttered the zombie who had clearly read the previous sentence and was wondering exactly the same thing (as were you, dear naughty minded reader).

"Tell me, Egon," asked a curious and, if he was honest, a rather disturbed Ollie as they began their return journey, "why do you call him One Lump?"

Egon instantly became more animated and his excitement level rose several tiers, indicating that talking about his little pet was a subject very close to his heart (as an aside please note that the name of that particular organ is just being used as a frame of reference and not meant to convey ownership of said internal morsel. What with being all supernatural and all, Egon didn't actually have a heart, or anything else recognisable inside him for that matter. His core resembled what's swept up and put into a skip after close of business at an abattoir. It smelt about the same as well).

"Ah, well, let me explain. I have a couple of these delightful creatures as pets, and though they're incredibly loyal and terribly affectionate, the problem is is that they both look the same, so to make things easier I named this little fellah One Lump, and the other one Two. It's quite amusing when I don't know which is which. If one of them is with me I say are you...?"

"One Lump or Two," Ollie and Stitches said in unison, sharing a look similar to that which would have been worn by Mr. and Mrs. Beckham Senior at parent's evening.

Apart from once again fighting off branches from strangely human looking trees, the rest of the trip back to Jocular's castle passed off without incident. On their return, Egon took them to the library where they found His Unholiness poring over a battered copy of a certain novel by one Bram Stoker. As the trio entered, he looked up.

"Ah, velcom back, gentlemen," said Jocular as he placed the book back onto the shelf. He tapped its spine with a long finger. "I don't usually indulge in prose such as zis but I find it's pretentious drivel distracting. Still, vot can vun expect from a drunken Irishman who clearly knew as much about vampires as a troll does personal hygiene. Vhen did you effer see me vandering about in ze middle of ze night like a ghoul, dressed like Jack ze Kipper and generally behaving like ze oddball? Did you manage to gazzer any information on your visit?"
"Not as such, sir," Ollie answered, thinking that Jocular should take a look in the mirror from time to time before he started deriding the habits of fictional vampires. Obviously that would be about as much use as asking someone with St. Vitus Dance to sit still for a portrait and might very well lead to him getting ever so slightly dismembered, but the idea was sound. And the less said about Jack ze Kipper the better. Ollie had learned from others that it was best not to correct Count Jocular if possible on account of him not liking to be told what to do. On one occasion the vampire lord had been entertaining (had strapped to a rack) a guest (prisoner) in dungeon number seven (torture palace that would make Hannibal Lecter queasy) and decided it would be rather fun to use his best cat 'o' nine tails on the chap. Obviously the

poor fellow had vehemently protested his innocence, and quite rightly so because he actually was. "My Lord," he'd pleaded. "You can't do this. It's not right," to which Jocular had replied, "You're qvite correct. Excuse me for a moment vould you," before toddling off and then returning with an axe big enough to dissect a planet. I won't go into what happened next but I'm sure you can guess, suffice to say there was a lot of red involved.

"Zat is a shame," said Jocular.

"But," continued Ollie, "Obsidia informed us that James, one of the pack members, is out searching the woods as we speak, so we're hopeful that he'll be able to shed some light on the matter for us. We'll speak to him as soon as he returns."

"Fery good, but do be careful ven you speak to him. Ven a vulf returns to human form after many hours of transformation, ze after effects can remain for qvite some time. As a drunkard may need a small tipple to counteract ze effects of ze hangover, a lycanthrope may sometimes need a flesh based bonne bouche to, how you say, clear his head. Hair of ze dog, yes?"

Stitches nearly burst a seam.

"To be honest, sir," said Ollie, "I don't think it'd do him any good coming near me anyway. There's not enough meat on my slender bones to feed a werepup." He placed a hand on Stitches' shoulder. "And I don't reckon my friend here needs to concern himself either. It'd be like trying to eat a bowl of pot-pourri."

"Vill you be going back soon?" Jocular added.

"In a while, yes," said Ollie, nodding his head. "But not too soon. I don't want to cause them any undue stress at the moment. They're all feeling the tension up there."

"Yeah," interrupted Stitches, "we don't want to hound them. OW." Jocular raised a pointed eyebrow, crossed his arms and stared at

Ollie, slowly tapping his lips with an index finger. After musing for a while, he spoke to Ollie with a voice that could have split granite.

"Vhy are you alvays striking you colleague, Ollie? It seems zat ze entire time ve have spent togezzer zis evening, you haff been engaged in a relentless attacking spree on Stitches. Vot, may I ask, has he done to incur such wrath?"

Ollie grappled for an answer whilst Stitches stared at him with a 'how are you going to get yourself out of this one' look on his smug face.

"Well, sir," Ollie floundered like a floundering Ollie, "I'm afraid my colleague has the attention span of an autistic halibut, so I give him a little tweak every now and again to keep him on his toes."

Jocular nodded in what Ollie hoped was agreement. The last thing he wanted to do was get on the wrong side of a creature that made Jeffrey Dahmer look like a Brownie (and by that I mean one of the young ladies of that august group and not the small, tasty chocolate square, although that comparison would have served just as well. Unless it was one of Mrs. Ladle's brownies of course in which case facing off against one of the worlds most notorious serial killers was by far the better option. She puts walnuts in them!)

Jocular nodded his head in agreement. "I see your point and must concur zat it can be difficult to keep vuns staff suitably motivated. I usually find zat a few days of rigorous torture accompanied by ze removal of a limb or two vorks vonders."

"Really," said Ollie with as much enthusiasm and interest as he could fake.

"R... really?" asked Stitches in wide eyed terror that was very real. He was now wishing that he'd never made a sarcastic comment in his life and wondering if Mrs. Ladle had a spell in her repertoire that would turn him into a fish, or a pen, or a travel brochure, or. . . oh, let's not beat about the proverbial bush here, he was now on the verge of a very nervous breakdown and his thoughts weren't making any sense at all. "Vhy certainly," the Dark One continued. "In fact, if my memory is correct I had a servant here many years ago who vas just like zat. Chap by ze name off Perry I sink. He vas extremely lazy and unable to complete ze simplest of tasks, so I entertained him down in ze dungeon for a veek before amputating his legs."

"Interesting," said Ollie with an evil glint in his eye.

"Qvite. After zat he couldn't do enough for me, neffer stopped in fact and from zat day on he vas alvays eager to please me at effery available opportunity. He vas constantly rushed off his feet, yes."

A deathly silence blanketed the room. Ollie cast a sidewards glance at Stitches who was rooted to the spot and as still as a corpse, which was logical when you thought about it. Ollie let him suffer for a few more precious seconds before letting him off the giant hook that he was dangling from.

"Although the idea does sound excellent, I think I have things under control for now. And besides, the poor chap's falling to pieces as it is so it'd be a bit unseemly to start lopping bits off at random. Anyway, hoovering up after himself keeps him nice and busy. Rest assured though, if he gets to be too much trouble I'll be sure to call on you for some suitable disciplinary advice."

"Fair enough. I vill bid you goodnight, gentlemen." "Goodnight, sir," said Ollie.

"Mmmm," mumbled Stitches.

As before they followed Egon from the library back through the maze of passages to the front door (they'd never have made it by themselves, not without getting hopelessly lost for a decade or two first anyway. Jocular had suggested that a satellite navigation system might help but as Egon had pointed out you wouldn't get very far when all you heard was, "In a hundred feet turn left at the scary dungeon after which turn right at the scary dungeon and proceed down the scary corridor until you reach the scary dungeon." There was a map but no one knew where it was. He'd sent one of Jocular's flunkies to go and look for it but that had been in 1932 and he still wasn't back).

As the little servant ushered them out he rubbed Stitches on the back in a very friendly fashion. "If you need help sewing anything back on, I'll be more than glad to help," and with a wink and a smile he disappeared inside.

Once outside, Ollie rubbed his hands together and they made their way across the courtyard.

"I hope Bill gets here soon. It's getting a bit cold out."

Silence.

"Lucky though, we seem to have come here on the one night that there isn't any thunder and lightning."

Louder silence.

"That's really unusual, huh. Kind of like waking up in Tokyo and getting through the whole day without Godzilla stomping your house flat."

A silence so loud you could hear it from miles away. "Alright, what's up with you? Cat got your tongue?" "No, but you can have my resignation."

"That's a bit extreme, isn't it?" "Extreme. Really?"

"Well. . . "

"So let me get this straight, it's perfectly alright for you to have a friendly chin wag about removing various parts of my anatomy with a certified nutcase, but when I mention that I'm not very happy about it I'm the one who's being extreme."

Ollie smiled and gave Stitches a companionable punch on the arm. Not too hard of course in case something fell off. "Aw, come on. It was only a bit of fun, and I had to think on my feet, didn't I?"

"If you hadn't I would've been without feet."

"Well, I couldn't very well tell him it's because of all the stupid things he comes out with, could I. He'd have our heads on spikes in one of those horrible rooms of his."

"Suppose."

"I was just pulling your. . . " "Don't say it!"

"Sorry. Here, this'll cheer you up. Did you hear that Jocular and three of his mates got arrested last month for shoplifting some beers?" They were charged with theft on four counts."

The clatter of hooves and the rumble of heavy wooden wheels on cobblestones totally obliterated the distinct lack of laughter echoing around the courtyard. It also heralded the arrival of Bill and their lift back to town. The carriage circled the yard and came to rest next to them.

"Wotcha, me ole shoegobblers 'ow's tricks an all 'at. Did ya see the Guvna?"

"Yes, thank you. All sorted," said Ollie.

"Nice one. Back to the ole rape and pillage, is it?"

"I think so," answered Ollie, wondering when the Viking theme had crept into the conversation.

"Smashballs. I'll 'ave ya there in four slices of a you cow son." Stitches looked up at the driver. "How long is that?"

"Bout' forty minutes give or take" "Wouldn't it be easier if. . . never mind."

They climbed in, shut the door and headed off.

———

It sounded like the tide was coming in. Wave after wave of irresistible water crashing onto a beach. It was as loud as a tumultuous storm and inspired the same sense of wonder, yet at the same time it was strangely distant and out of place.

It must be a dream. But surely dreams shouldn't hurt your head as much as this, with its constant pounding that was like being persistently battered across the back of the skull with a ten pound mallet.

Eventually, but ever so slowly, the darkness began to lift and with it the throb began to decrease, as if the returning light were driving away the insistent noise and pain. Ronnie's eyelids flickered briefly and opened, but then immediately closed again. The sudden influx of light was too much. It seared his retinas to the point that they actually hurt. It was as if tungsten drill bits were boring their way into his skull with the express purpose of causing as much damage as possible. Tears welled in his eyes.

'My God,' he thought, 'did I fall asleep in a lighthouse?' Finally his vision adjusted and acclimatised, and when he was able to fully open his eyes once more he saw.. . something that didn't really make a whole hell of a lot of sense.

The last thing he remembered was being in the forest so why he was lying down and staring at a white ceiling and some fluorescent strip lights was a bit of a mystery. And was that really the faint strains of Barbers Adagio for Strings playing softly in the background? Yes it was.

'Well, this is strange,' he thought. 'Either I'm concussed, or extremely drunk. Or both.'

Thanks to his propensity for imbibing rather large quantities of alcohol, Ronnie had woken up in some weird and wonderful places in his time, but he was damned sure that he hadn't fallen asleep in a dentist's waiting room. A doctor's surgery definitely but this was just silly.

Naturally, as one does upon waking, he tried to rise to better gauge his surroundings, but he was more than a little perturbed to find that he could hardly move. His hands and feet were virtually immobile, strapped down and tied to the table he was lying on. He did manage to raise his head though, the only part of his body that wasn't restricted, and had a look around.

The room was totally and utterly bare apart from one other intriguing item. To his left, about five feet away from him, was another table, seemingly exactly the same as his, and on it was a man. A very large man, who was tied up in the same manner.

"Pssst. Hey," Ronnie called. There was no reply.

"Oi, fellah. Are you awake?"

"He can't hear you. We gave him enough tranquilliser to floor a buffalo."

Ronnie turned his head in the direction of the voice, wondering how this other person had managed to get into the room without him hearing.

"And just who the bloody hell are you?" said Ronnie.

"Direct and to the point, huh. I can appreciate that. I'm Major Buddy Cowan of The United States Army. And now that we have the pleasantries over with, what I'm really interested in is who you are, and how you're able to do what you do?"

Cowan's manner and tone of voice left Ronnie in no doubt that he was confronted with a man used to getting his own way. His entire demeanour gave the impression of one who was unfazed by the methods he used and unperturbed by the consequences of his actions, as long as the results were what he wanted to achieve.

All of that considered though, and despite his less than favourable position, Ronnie was still spectacularly annoyed at the arrogance of the man and decided, all relevant factors taken into consideration, that he was a bit of a knob. He decided to break the ice.

"If you must know, I can't do anything because you've got me trussed up like a Christmas turkey. And if you think for one minute that I'm going to tell you anything when I don't know what the hell is going on here, then you are very much mistaken, my friend. Oh, and one more thing. If my hands were free I'd give you a salute that wasn't strictly military."

A wry grin crowbarred its way onto Cowan's rigid features, but it was as humourless as a funeral director who'd had some really bad news.

"Oh, you'll talk to me," said Cowan. "I promise you'll talk to me."

With that the soldier approached the table and took up a position such that he was hovering right above Ronnie's chest. He reached into a pocket of his dress tunic and pulled out a small silvery object and waved it in Ronnie's face.

"You'd think a medal like this would be quite robust wouldn't you," he said, admiring the shiny piece of metal, "but in actual fact they're quite flimsy and delicate. Ironic really, when you think of what we go through to be awarded one. Take this one for instance. The pin broke just after the President pinned it to my chest. Now bearing in mind what it represents, you'd think they could afford something a bit more resilient, wouldn't you? I mean, you get better pins on a child's birthday card. Still, it's pretty sharp."

With lightning speed he took hold of Ronnie's wrist in a grip of steel and thrust the exposed pin under the nail of the little finger of Ronnie's right hand. The scream he let out reverberated around the stark room, the waves of his shrieks bouncing off the bare walls and coming back to him in a mocking echo as the steel point penetrated the supple, raw tissue of the nail bed. Tears welled up in Ronnie's eyes once more, as bolts of excruciating agony shot through his hand and up his arm.

Cowan remained impassive as he stared down at his prostrate victim.

"Smarts a bit doesn't it? Messy too. Look at all that blood. And just think, there's nine more of those tender little buds to go."

Cowan's blurred figure shimmered and passed in and out of focus as Ronnie tried desperately to cling onto the last vestiges of consciousness. The last thing he wanted to do was pass out. The thought of this raving lunatic let loose on his comatose body didn't bare thinking about.

"You see, son," said Cowan, "I can be a reasonable man, some might say downright friendly, but that's only if I get what I want. If I don't it tends to annoy me and that's when my nasty side takes over. I'm not proud of it and I feel terrible afterwards, but it gets the job done."

Ronnie exhaled long and hard as the pain from his pierced hand began to subside, and try as he might to look on the bright side, he concluded that Cowan had about as much ability to feel guilt and remorse as a serial killer having a really bad day (actually, if a serial killer is having a really bad day does he kill more people or less? If he's in a bad mood and kills lots of people that could be a good day but seeing as he's feeling a bit grumpy it could equally qualify as a bad day. Conversely, if he's feeling rather dandy but doesn't get round to butchering as many people as usual that would still count as a good day because he's such a happy chappy, yet that could still be considered to be a bad day because his numbers are down. Wow that's complicated. I think I'll stick to writing. Not that I was thinking of becoming a serial killer of course. I hate manual labour and can't use power tools to save my life. Anyway, to conclude this wandering digression I was going to have a look at all this from the victims point of view but hey, let's not get maudlin and bring the mood down. I'm having a good day after all.)

The man needed to be placated and stalled so Ronnie could try and figure out how to get out of this place.

"Okay, can I have a minute to relax and gather my thoughts please?" he said.

Cowan placed a large and surprisingly soft hand onto Ronnie's forehead and smoothed the moist hair back from his face. "You take five," he said and left the room.

Ronnie watched him leave, all the while clenching and unclenching his hand as the last of the pain eased off. He had to get out of here, that was certain, but for now the task was quite obviously impossible. His only hope at the moment, such as it was, was that Flug would realise he was taking too long on his sojourn into the woods and raise the alarm. Some choice that was, though. Hope that a uniformed psycho would take pity on him or rely on Flug who, at the moment, was probably still trying to count to ten.

"Urrrrgggghhhh."

The noise came from Ronnie's left. It seemed that his fellow guest had the constitution of something considerably larger than a buffalo. He was a big man, at least six feet four, and had a physique comparable to the bodybuilders you'd see at a Mr Universe contest. His arms were the size of Ronnie's legs. You never know, he thought, with those muscles he might be able to break free of those straps. Let's just hope he's in a good mood.

"Hey, fellah. You okay? Over here."

The big man turned his head and focused on the direction the sound was coming from.

"Where are we?" he asked in a dry, cracked voice.

"Your guess is as good as mine, mate," said Ronnie. "If you want my opinion I'd say it was some sort of military installation. Saying that I've only seen a few blokes in a uniform. It's either that or we've stumbled across a fancy dress party and the entry rules are really strict."

The man offered a wan smile. "Well, as nice as the party idea sounds I think the first option makes more sense based on how they're behaving," he said.

Ronnie looked at him with a puzzled gaze. "Were you out in the forest as well?"

"I was indeed."

"Interesting. I was following them for ages and I didn't see you." "Yes, you did. And I knew you were there because I recognise your scent. It's a little blood tinged now, but it's more or less the same." "Recognise my... oh, I see. In that case I think congratulations are in order. That was quite a fight you and your alter ego put up."

The other man snorted in derision. "If you say so, but if I was that good I wouldn't be tied to this table now would I?" The big man stared at Ronnie more intensely. "I know I said I recognised your scent but I don't recall actually seeing you in the woods, and believe me I don't miss much. Where were you?"

Ronnie wasn't entirely sure about sharing all of the details of his gift with a total stranger, but seeing as he was almost certain that this person had a shape shifting secret of his own, he figured he was in good company, and it wouldn't be too much of a social faux pas if he spilled the beans.

"What's your name by the way? I'm Ronnie."

The door burst open at that point, making them both jump as

Cowan re-entered the room. "Nice to meet you, Ronnie," he growled, an air of superiority and menace in his voice. "Now, if your new friend over there will tell me his name, we can conduct the rest of our business in a more relaxed and peaceful atmosphere."

"If you must know, my name is James," snarled the big man. "And if you think I'm going to cooperate with you, then you are very much mistaken."

Cowan walked over to James' table. "Mistaken, am I? Well, we'll see.

Right, let's get to it. I'd like you to change for me." "What?" said James.

"Come on, don't be shy. I want to see you change. I know you can because we saw you revert to human form after you were drugged so there's no point lying about it. And you don't have to worry about hurting anyone, we've got you strapped down tight enough to cover any eventuality, and Corporal Franks over there has another dose of tranquilliser waiting for you should we, or rather you need it."

Both Ronnie and James looked over to the door and saw a soldier with a weapon pointed directly at James.

James had to admit to himself that he was more than a little worried. The metamorphosis into his wolf form would normally put the fear of God into anyone close enough to witness it. Quite naturally the sight of a grown man suddenly sprouting hair all over his body, dropping onto all fours and howling at the moon would be sufficient to put even the hardiest of souls off their stroke, unless you'd been to an Ozzy Osbourne concert, in which case you were probably used to it. But this guy was not only unafraid, he was actually asking to observe the phenomenon, so by giving him what he wanted the chances were that he would be opening himself up to a whole world of untold suffering. James decided that on this occasion, the best form of attack was ignorance.

"I don't know what you're talking about," he said, his voice steady and confident. "Change position, change my clothes, what?"

Cowan sighed and folded his arms, looking at them both with a stare comparable to what you would see on an angry parent trying to get a truculent child to confess to breaking a window.

"Well, aren't we both modest today? Fair enough. Seems like we're going to have to do this the hard way. Guard."

Through the open door came two men. They were heavily set and dressed in white coats. Without a word they positioned themselves at either end of James' trolley and proceeded to wheel it out.

Cowan approached Ronnie once again and leaned over him in the same threatening manner as before. Ronnie's pulse quickened as phantom pains shot through his arm. It was as if his central nervous system was recalling what had happened the last time this sadistic bastard had gotten this close.

"You get some rest while we talk to your friend because believe me, you're going to need it."

With that, Cowan left once more. Ronnie then heard a faint click and the room was plunged into darkness leaving him all alone in the silence with nothing but his now overactive and colourful imagination for company.

————

Ollie and Stitches waved the black cab off as it thundered away into the distance, leaving behind a whirlwind of dust and litter that Hector Lozenge would be picking up later today.

"Try as I might," said Stitches, "I still can't make out a word that bloke says. There's cockney and there's bloody annoying, and he's managed to transcend even that. No wonder the Luftwaffe bombed the hell out of London. They probably just wanted them to shut up. Maybe that's all the Second World War was about. Hitler didn't like rhyming slang."

Ollie fished in his pocket for his keys. "That's a rather simplistic view of a global conflict isn't it?" He opened the door and stepped into the office.

"Not really. If I live to be two hundred I'll never work out what he's blathering on about."

Ollie raised an eyebrow as he dropped into his chair. "You are two hundred."

"My point exactly," replied the zombie, taking his customary place in

the chair opposite. "So," he continued, "where do we go from here?"
Ollie pondered that for a moment. It was a very good question.

There was no doubt that something peculiar was going on, but finding out what the next step should be towards getting to the bottom of it was the tricky part. Sherlock Holmes and Dr Watson they weren't, and it was going to take a lot more than inspired deduction and detective brilliance to solve this one, and seeing as those two valuable qualities were in rather short supply round here, sheer luck and blundering blindly on regardless of any notable talent would probably have more to do with the final outcome than anything else. Ollie looked at

the clock on his desk. It was getting on for three in the morning, and dawn usually broke early in these parts.

"Sleep, I reckon. Then tomorrow, how's about we ask round the town to see if anyone knows anything?"

Stitches shifted position and rested his chin on his hand.

"Yeah, sounds good to me. I could do with a rest anyway, after all that bleeding walking. I feel like Methuselah's great granddad."

What with being a bit of a zombie, Stitches didn't need to sleep of course, but his aged body did require periods of inactivity on a regular basis just to keep things ticking over rather than falling off. It was more like looking after a classic car than a carcass. The only problem was you couldn't get an MOT inspection for a corpse with a double centuries worth of usage. So that being the case, when the need arose he would sit quietly in his room with the radio on, settle down, relax and drift off into a type of trance for a few hours while his desiccated innards and leathery skin were restored to some semblance of health and, more importantly, functionality. After the process he would feel much refreshed and toddle off to get on with something simple so as not to over tax himself too much. Think about the average day in the life of a member of the House of Lords and you pretty much get the picture.

Ollie was just about to rise from his chair when the office door swung open. This was followed by a loud, dense thud, indicating that Flug was on his way and had forgotten to duck again.

Stitches turned and greeted his hulking friend. "Hi, Stitches," Flug answered. "Where you been?"

"Up to the castle, mate. We had a really lovely time. I haven't had so much fun since Ronnie dropped one of his fags in my trousers."

"Dat good. Why you go dere?"

"Do you remember Jocular?" asked Ollie. "Uh, yeah. Tall man, wear black, smell funny."

Ollie snickered. "Well, yeah, that's him but don't let him ever hear you describe him in that way. We had to go and see him because he

wants us to try and find out why some of his wolf friends have gone missing."

Flug pondered this for a moment, grabbing the bolt in his forehead and giving it a jiggle, as if this action might aid whatever processes were occurring in the dormant organ residing in his skull fall into place and come out with something useful.

"Maybe da ghosts took dem," he said at long last.

Stitches looked at Ollie and shook his head in an 'I don't know what the hell he's talking about' fashion.

"What do you mean ghosts?" Ollie asked patiently, not wanting to rush the monster for fear of him becoming inordinately confused, a common state of affairs that had the potential for him to overload and crash quicker than a ZX81 programmed to have two bouncy balls on the screen instead of one. If that happened there was no telling what sort of nonsense he'd end up coming out with.

Flug raised a finger and pointed at the door, presumably to indicate his general direction of travel this evening. It was either that or he was mesmerised by the magic hole in the wall that allowed him to enter a room. Again.

"Me and Ronnie go for walk and Ronnie and me see sumfing in da woods, and so Ronnie go have a look."

"What did you guys see?" asked Stitches.

"Movin fings in da trees. Dere was more dan one, and dey was shiny. Ronnie not know what dey were, but he say it might be fun to see where dey going and what dey doin', so he follow dem."

"So he was following the ghosts?" asked Ollie. "Yeah, or maybe I fink dem witches."

"Why witches?" said Stitches. "Cos dem all carrying sticks."

95

Stitches pinched the bridge of his nose, being careful not to pull it off, and winced. "So," he said, "Ronnie's gone for a walkabout in the woods after some shiny, stick carrying, ghostly witches?"

"Yup," replied Flug proudly, pleased with himself that he was being so helpful.

The zombie turned to face Ollie once more and saw that he was leaning back on the rear two legs of his chair with his head tilted upwards at the ceiling.

"What do you think?" he asked tentatively.

Ollie dropped his gaze and his chair, shook his head and sighed the sigh of the terminally dumbfounded.

"I'll tell you what I think," he said. "I think that Ronnie has gone off with some drunken mates of his on another glorious bender, and won't be back for a few days. I also think that dear Flug here has finally let go of the tenuous grasp that he had on reality and is away with the fairies."

"So it's not all bad then?" said Stitches.

"It would appear not," said Ollie. "Okay, Flug, it sounds like you've had a busy night. Better be getting off to bed now, alright."

"Okay, Ollie."

"And mind your head on. . . " THUD.

"Wassat, Ollie?" "Never mind."

Stitches chuckled and shook his dusty head as he rose from the chair. "Well, as lovely as this has been it's time for me to get some rest. So as one egg said to the other as they were sitting in the mixing bowl, let's get out of here before we get eaten. I'll see you later."

"Yeah, goodnight."

Once he was on his own, Ollie started to wonder about Flug's story. By itself it didn't add up to much and hardly warranted close scrutiny, but taking into account what'd been happening in the area lately and Ronnie's sudden urge to follow a strange group of people into the forest, there was a distinct, if remote possibility, that Flug just might have witnessed something out of the ordinary. Mmm, maybe not. No doubt they'd get a full report from Ronnie upon his return and that would put the matter to rest. Then, of course, it would be time for him to seriously consider getting Flug's brain replaced with something a little more useful in the thinking department. A potato should do the trick.

You could buy them in ten pound bags and just one would triple the big dope's IQ leaving plenty left over for chips, so everyone was a winner. He tidied up his desk and left the office by the same rear door that led to the laboratory, but rather than turning down to the end of the corridor where Crumble worked, he turned right ten feet before that, which took him into another passageway. This, in turn, steered him to another staircase that descended deeper into the bowels of the building towards the basement. It was here that Ollie slept, in the very same coffin that his uncle and umpteen other forbears had done so before him. Let it not be said that vampires don't have a sense of tradition. Or smell for that matter, if they could all ignore the stench coming from the ancient box. Unfortunately coffins had a tendency to soak up

odours and after a few hundred years they tended to get a bit funky. The coffin itself was absolutely massive and appeared to be constructed from an extremely dark wood that Ollie thought might have been ebony, but he wasn't sure. Stitches maintained that it was fashioned from MDF and that the dingy patina was caused by spilt blood, gallons of which had been abstracted from the countless virgins that had been slaughtered in this room down through the ages. But, all things considered, Ollie was much more comfortable with the dark wood theory. At least that didn't make him feel queasy.

It had been the coffin's width that had really surprised Ollie when he'd seen it for the first time, but he'd been reliably informed that it was that size because some of his more romantic ancestors, including obviously the original owner, had been partial to spending the night with the odd victim or two, a thought that gave Ollie baked bean sized goose bumps. The very idea of waking up to some exsanguinated, lifeless, dreary, slack eyed and toothless simpleton first thing in the evening was enough to make him go weak at the fangs. It would be like living in Norfolk.

Forget what you've seen in Twilight. Being a vampire isn't all about beautiful teenagers swanning about looking gorgeous in designer clothes and feasting on curvaceous, nubile young peasant folk twenty four hours a night, whilst trying to evade some handsome Van

Helsing clone or dashing Peter Cushing wannabe who gets his kicks running around the middle of a forest, dressed like a Victorian fop and waving a slightly threatening crucifix about. The life of a real vampire can be, and very often is, a hard one, especially if your territory is populated by people refused a bit part in Deliverance because they're too weird looking (oh, there's Norfolk again).

Ollie threw back the vast lid, plumped up his pillow and straightened his duvet. Half vampire or not, there were some home comforts that you definitely couldn't do without. His father had even tried to make him sleep on earth 'from the old country' for goodness sake, but Ollie just didn't fancy bedding down for the day on part of someone's allotment thank you very much, so he'd eschewed that as well and gone for a comfy mattress instead.

The adaptations he'd made, whilst not all that traditional, at least went some way to making the place a bit more homey and if his dad didn't like them then that was tough luck. He figured he'd earned these little luxuries. Growing up as a half vampire in a normal town hadn't been easy after all. Being a child is difficult enough what with starting school, feeling socially awkward, attempting to make friends and trying to find out where you fit into everything, but it's ever so slightly more problematic when you have to wear a balaclava in the middle of August, be careful how you smile and carry around a lunchbox that's two feet square and cooled by liquid nitrogen.

That was why throughout his formative years he constantly thanked whoever was in the big chair in the sky for a mother whose chromosome contribution allowed him to bypass some of the more uncivilised aspects of vampire life without any ill effects. Apart from the aforementioned blood drinking of course, which was a constant source of genuine horror.

When he was about eighteen he'd tried going without it for a while claiming it was out of interest rather than as an act of rebellion against his old man. As it turned out he'd lasted about twenty seven hours before the withdrawal symptoms, worse than any drug addict had ever experienced, had forced him to imbibe once more.

Not being the killing type and squeamish to the point of

ridiculousness, Ollie had always relied on his mum to provide his blood, but as much as he hated it, at least he knew where it came from. Mr. Davis, the local butcher, always had plenty and was more than happy to get rid of a couple of pints. Clearly that couldn't happen anymore though and he didn't think DHL would take too kindly to having a few gallons of blood sloshing around in one of their vans, so it was now a duty that Flug had taken over.

On the whole he dealt with the new arrangement admirably but every now and again his thoughts would stray and he'd start to wonder where exactly Flug got hold of the wretched stuff, but he very quickly dismissed such errant ponderings, deciding that being blissfully ignorant of the details was more preferable to actually knowing. The lifeblood of a comely young virgin he might, on a really good night, be able to bolt down, but knowing Flug and his rather skewed view of the world it was more likely to be the fluid from some rancid, meth drinking vagrant who spent his days foraging in rubbish bins and eating decaying rats decaying nether regions.

Ollie shivered at the thought and cast it to the back of his mind to join all the other musings, questions and things you didn't really need to know, but that were so important just as you were drifting off to sleep, like how do blind people know when they're done wiping, why are there so many disabled car parking spaces and why are all the spells used by Harry Potter in Latin when everyone is painfully English?

Ready for a rest he carefully folded his clothes, popped them onto a table, slipped into his jammies, set the alarm and lay down. As he closed the lid he wondered what later today would bring, but the last image that played across his mind as his eyes slowly closed and sleep began to claim him and he entered that strange and wonderful state of semi consciousness where your brain produces drivel of amazing outlandishness and clarity, was of Flug standing behind a bar, looking at him, proffering a glass and saying "Pint of Geldof's Old Tramp, Sir?"

———

Major Cowan sat down at his desk and lifted the telephone receiver. "Cowan," he barked abruptly.

"I think we may have a problem." "Go on."

"I heard talk that some associates of one of your guests are looking into the disappearances of our furry friends."

"I see. And what do you expect me to do about it, may I ask?"

"I'm not sure. I don't think it's too much to worry about at the moment, but I thought you should know just in case."

"And protecting your end of the deal has nothing to do with it, of course?"

"Money is no concern of mine, major. This is a personal issue." "Sure it is. But it is amazing how a personal issue of yours is costing us a couple of million dollars, wouldn't you say?"

Cowan sighed. Why was there always someone who had to stick their nose into things when they were going just fine?

"Okay, thanks for the information. I'll make sure my personnel are kept up to speed."

"Thank you, major. If I hear anymore you'll be the first to know." The line went dead.

———

The shrill shriek of the alarm clock dragged Ollie from the comfort of sleep and deposited him firmly back into the land of the unliving, as it were. Once up he quickly washed, dressed and made his way back up to the office, unusually eager to see what the coming night would bring. He felt a bit more enthusiastic and upbeat, and put it down to the fact that he was well rested and all those inane little things that always seemed so important as you're lying in bed, those annoying niggles that seemed so much worse when it was late and you were tired, had all seemed to lose their urgency and evaporate. It was bizarre how even the most insignificant problem, that wouldn't worry a six year old, became a major issue that even Bruce Willis couldn't have handled if you thought about it whilst trying to sleep.

"Afternoon, Professor," he said as he walked along the corridor. "Ah, hello there, Ollie. Did you sleep well?"

"I did, thanks. So what are you up to today?" he asked, noticing the tangle of miscellaneous items that Crumble had precariously balanced on a large tray.

The Professor looked at the collection in his grasp and shrugged his shoulders, very nearly sending half of it crashing to the floor.

"Oh, nothing specific, these are just some bits and bobs that I found at the back of a cupboard. I Thought I might have a tinker around with them and see what I can conjure up."

About £1.73 at a boot fair if you're lucky, thought Ollie.

"Well, good luck with that," he offered encouragingly. "Let me know if you come up with anything useful."

There wasn't much possibility of that of course. What with the chances of anything that Crumble invented being about as much use as a trampoline on the moon, he concluded that it would be a long time before the old man came a knocking on his door, screaming Eureka and claiming to be the next Leonardo Da Vinci. If Crumble had invented the parachute, his material of choice would probably have been marble. A death trap to be sure, but think of the time you would save on the way down. Still, he was happy in his own insane little way and to be honest, if he was happy in anyone else's way, he'd probably need a straight jacket.

The Professor entered his lab and shut the door. A few seconds later, reassuring crashes, clanks and bangs began to emanate from within. It was comforting really, like a tranquil piece of music but played slightly off kilter and marginally out of tune. Imagine Beethoven's Moonlight Sonata being played by a drunken baboon with an attitude problem and all the musical talent of a Eurovision Song Contest performer, and you'll have some idea of what I'm trying to convey.

It was at this point that Ollie realised his mind was wandering and that he really did have more important things to think about than a mad monkey abusing the keys of a Steinway with its bulbous red backside (obviously it's the monkey that has the bulbous red backside and not the piano. Although amusing to imagine it wouldn't be at all practical. There'd be too many bum notes). "To the office," he said out loud. On entering he bade hello to Stitches, who was occupying his usual place in the chair opposite Ollie's desk. The dry, old leather creaked and groaned as the zombie shifted position but that wasn't surprising as it was getting on a bit. The chair winced a tad as well. Ollie's greeting was returned with a big smile.

"So, what's new?" Ollie asked, settling in behind his desk.

Stitches grinned and gestured in the direction of the waiting room with a nod of his head. "We have a visitor."

"Anyone interesting?"

"Oh, I think so. I'll show her in, shall I?"

The zombie crossed the room and opened the door, which scraped across the plaster remnants of Flug's latest exit miscalculation.

"Would you like to come through?" he called out in what would usually be referred to as a 'telephone voice', that irritating characteristic that seems to afflict every sentient being as soon as they get their lips anywhere near the mouthpiece of any communication device. It usually starts with 'Eeoh helleo' and goes downhill from there until the only people that can understand what they're saying died in 1924. On second thoughts I'm not going to include call centre personnel, because it's difficult to be self-righteous and boorish to members of the public with a plum in your mouth. Not that there would be room for any variety of fruit in there. Their feet would get in the way.

Stitches held the door as Obsidia swept into the office, all style, grace and two inch long, black painted nails. Stitches showed her to his chair and respectfully held the back of it as she lowered herself onto the cushion.

"Hello again, Ollie," she oozed with a voice like liquid velvet. "Did you sleep well?"

Ollie frowned slightly and wondered why everyone was suddenly so interested in his sleeping habits. Maybe he was still looking a bit tired. Or maybe he wasn't, and people were thinking that he was looking well rested. Or maybe he was just being a bit paranoid and those who asked were perhaps just being polite and couldn't really give a flying hoo ha whether he'd slept or not. Anyway, he had breakfast to look forward to. A pint of claret was always guaranteed to put a spring in his step, as well as a stain in his toilet.

"I did. Thank you for asking."

"Slept like the dead, he did," Stitches threw in, starting the day off as usual.

Ollie was on the verge of admonishing his colleague for his uncompromising wit, but seeing Obsidia giggling away to herself like a young girl made him change his mind. For whatever reason, there was a definite attraction between the two of them. The thing was, he could see it from Stitches' point of view, you'd have to be blind not to. Obsidia was a ravishing creature who could no doubt have her choice of partners, but it was the next ingredient of the emerging relationship where Ollie's reasoning failed. What on earth did she see in Stitches that he was evidently missing? Ollie liked him a lot but he was basically a walking Hoover bag, only he split more often. It just went to show that ladies placed a great deal in a good old fashioned sense of humour. You can be as old and decrepit as you like, but if you can make 'em laugh then you'll have women falling at your feet (obviously a flash car, a massive house and a couple of million quid in the bank doesn't do any harm either but that would be doing the elderly gentlemen concerned a disservice. I'm sure Hugh Hefner is a lovely chap who could have his choice of female partner even if he wasn't a multi-millionaire business owner. My god, I can't even believe that and I wrote it. Yuck).

"So, Obsidia. To what do we owe the pleasure?" Ollie asked.

She crossed her shapely legs and flicked a length of hair from her face. She looked upset.

"Business, I'm afraid. James didn't return last night, so I have a horrible feeling that he's fallen foul of the same fate as the others."

"Oh no. I take it he wouldn't normally stay out all night like this?"

"Definitely not. Every member returns to the house after hunting. It's an extremely demanding activity that leaves us weary and ready for rest."

"Puts a whole new twist on getting changed to go out, doesn't it?" said Stitches.

My God, it's relentless, thought Ollie.

"Indeed," replied Obsidia with a tiny smile. "It's not surprising though. It takes a lot of energy to shape shift in the first place so if you factor in a night in the forest as well, you feel like you've run a couple of marathons."

Ollie pondered this new development for a moment before responding.

"I take it you've informed the remainder of your group and told them it would be best to stay put until we've had a chance to sort this out?"

"Oh, yes. It shouldn't be too much of a problem, for a while at least. We do have some stores at the house that we can delve into if necessary."

Ollie didn't want to begin to think what the inside of a werewolf's fridge looked like.

"That's good," he continued, "because our next move has to be a careful one."

"I've got an idea, Ollie," said Stitches. "Go on, then."

"Well, it doesn't take Einstein to work out that someone or something is hunting the wolves, right?"

"Right."

"So, if you and me go into the woods tonight, we should be able to sneak around without too much bother. Whatever's out there won't be looking for us, will it?"

"He makes a good point," offered Obsidia. "No one is going to expect you gentlemen to be there."

Ollie leaned forward, put his elbows on the desk and interlaced his fingers.

"What about Ronnie? Has he come back yet?"

Stitches walked towards the desk. "Not yet. But you said yourself that he probably got drunk and ended up on someone's floor. He'll be back at some point. You never know he may even be half conscious. We'll leave him a note."

"I know what I said, but don't you think it's a bit odd that it's in the midst of all this he chooses to disappear?" said Ollie.

Obsidia rose from the chair and also approached the desk.

"I can see why you're concerned, Ollie, but if Ronnie has indeed become entangled in this plot, then by venturing forth tonight you might very well be coming to his aid."

Ollie nodded his head in agreement. "That's true enough. Okay, tonight it is then. At least this way if Jocular calls I can give him a progress report of sorts. Obsidia, if it's okay with you we'll use your house as a starting point. We'll be there about nine."

"Excellent. Until later, gentlemen. And once again, thank you"

With that she left the office leaving the two detectives to plan the coming night's activities.

"Well," said Stitches, "we've got a couple of hours to kill. Why don't we have a walk round town see if we can pick up any more information that might help."

Ollie thought about it for a moment before deciding that it was a good idea.

"Okay, but you'll have to go by yourself for now. It's still a little early for me and I have a horrible feeling that Flug is going to show up any minute with my breakfast."

Stitches pulled a yuck face. "And we know how much you love that."

Ollie raised an eyebrow and made a disgusted noise that sounded like stagnant air rushing out of a punctured tyre.

"Mmmm. The trouble is, as much as I'm loathe to drink the wretched stuff, I actually need it."

Stitches nodded his head and crossed the room to the door. "No worries. You enjoy and I'll see you later, yeah?"

"Fine. See you around eightish."

Once the zombie had left, Ollie realised that he was alone with no Flug bearing liquid gifts. Quickly he exited the office and rushed back downstairs to his room. He changed and got into his coffin. "Time for a quick nap, I think. It could be a long night."

And do you know what? He was right.

———

Doctor Paul Meredith knocked on Cowan's door, but he didn't bother waiting for an invitation to enter before barging into the Major's office and marching right up to his desk. Cowan looked up impassively from some paperwork that he'd been concentrating on. Seeing that the visitor was a person for whom he had an intense dislike, he blatantly ignored him and returned to his work.

"I have news," said the scientist. Meredith spoke with an air of arrogance and superiority, but there was an underlying waver in his voice indicating that Cowan's dismissive attitude towards him had thrown him off slightly.

After a suitable amount of time, Cowan acknowledged the others presence and looked up once more.

"Could it be that you've invented a cure for rudeness and self-importance?" he said.

"Very droll, major. I meant news about the project if you're interested. We've finally managed to extract the gene and as of now it's still stable. There's been no degradation at all. At least not yet so we're more than hopeful this time."

This was the most enthusiastic that Cowan had ever seen the little man. Compared to his customary demeanour, he was currently bordering on the ecstatic. He was still an impudent little insect though.

"How long has it been?" the soldier asked, leaning back in his chair and forgetting for a moment that he wanted to put a bullet through the man's skull.

"Coming up on two hours. It's looking good."

"Why this time when all of the other attempts have failed so early on?"

Meredith paused for a moment before he replied. He didn't want to get too technical with his answers. Cowan wasn't stupid by any stretch of the gold braid on his shoulders but he wasn't entirely up to speed with all things scientific either and the last thing he wanted was the soldier getting into a mood because he failed to understand what he was being told. He'd no doubt see it as an attempt to belittle him. "Two things, really," said Meredith. "Firstly, we altered the temperature that we kept the sample at, and secondly, I think it had a lot to do with the subject himself. He's by far the most excellent physical specimen we've had to work with; young, fit and incredibly strong and resilient."

"How long before we know for sure that this is it?"

Meredith scratched his head and bounced up and down on the balls of his feet. He was confident, but he didn't want to be definitive in his response in case the worst happened. He was ninety nine percent positive that the sample wouldn't degrade, but it was always just as things were going well that the rug got pulled out from under you. He decided to follow Montgomery Scott's first rule of engineering and scaled up the time factor by two to give himself some leeway.

"I think we need to give it at least another eight hours. If it's still stable by then, I think we can safely move onto Phase 2."

The Major allowed himself a diminutive smile.

"Excellent. Let's just make sure he stays healthy, because as long as he's alive we have an inexhaustible supply of product."

"Fair enough," replied the scientist. "What about the other one?"

Cowan got up from his seat and joined Meredith on the other side of the room.

"I'd suggest you use the same method. If you can isolate the defective gene that activates his particular talent it'll be just as valuable as the shapeshifters. Maybe even more so."

"Okay, I'll get back to it." "You do that."

Meredith left the office and headed back to where the captives were being held. Despite having to deal with the overbearing and aggressive major he was in a very good mood. A lot of people back home, those whose pay grade and position far exceeded his, were going to be extremely pleased with his research, and of course there were the obvious financial benefits of presenting such ground-breaking work to eager and affluent armed forces and corporations across the globe. As far as Cowan was concerned, Meredith put him to the back of his mind. He could take a long walk off a short pier for all he cared and the sooner this was over the better. They'd never got on and their relationship had been fractious from the start. Cowan's disciplined and formal world and the scientist's experimental, 'let's see what happens if we do it like this' way of doing things didn't mix well. That still didn't excuse his behaviour towards him and his staff though, leading Meredith to seriously consider reporting him to his superiors. He couldn't have cared less what the consequences to Cowan might be. He simply didn't like the man.

As he walked along the corridor he saw two orderlies guiding a trolley towards him, but before they crossed paths he noticed that they were returning the lycanthrope to the holding area.

"Has he been a good boy?" he asked sarcastically.

One of the porters grunted and shrugged his shoulders before barging the door open with a meaty forearm.

"Not bad, I suppose," he said disinterestedly. "He's drugged up to the eyeballs now so he's not gonna get up to much."

Meredith held the door for them as they wheeled him in.

"Fair enough. Put him by the wall over there to sleep it off. I need this one now."

This got Ronnie's attention. Initially he'd tried to ignore the men when they came into the room and engaged in a bout of childish, 'if I can't see you then you can't see me' play but, as any four year old, or Flug, would tell you, it didn't work. Well, maybe not Flug. You could actually stand in front of the giant reanimate and claim not be there and he'd go off looking for you. Stitches did it every now and again for a laugh. Not very often of course because that would be mean and the zombie wasn't heartless after all (unless three or four times a day doesn't count as not very often, but that's purely subjective. If you're snowed under at work and the boss brings you reports to be completed three or four times a day that clearly falls under the too often umbrella, but if it's agents and publishers constantly ringing and offering three book deals that easily qualifies as not often enough. Oh hang on, I've got that muddled up. That's wishful thinking).

Ronnie briefly considered confusing the hell out of his captors by going invisible but quickly dismissed the idea because one, he was strapped to a table and two, he knew damn well that that was the very reason why he was strapped to a table. He knew his little DNA quirk was known to them, but that didn't mean that he was going to give it up without a fight, even if that lunatic of a soldier came at him with a whole chest full of medals to threaten him with.

James' trolley was pushed unceremoniously to the far wall and left, the two orderlies taking up positions in front of it.

"Is it my turn for a massage and seaweed body wrap now?" Ronnie asked, trying to inject as much spite and venom into his words as possible.

"Indeed it is," replied Meredith. "And I've got a wonderfully equipped laboratory downstairs that I'm sure you're going to find fascinating."

Ronnie didn't like the look that appeared on the scientist's face. It reminded him of a ravenous lion that had just spotted a baby zebra out for a stroll.

"In what way fascinating?" he asked, the sarcastic tone temporarily put on hold.

Meredith smiled, and with a glance that could only be described as malevolent, approached the trolley.

"Well, I don't want to tell you too much, now do I? That would ruin the surprise. Gentlemen."

The two hefty porters, or henchmen as they were in reality, crossed the room and grabbed a respective side of the trolley each and began to manoeuvre it towards the door.

"I hate surprises," Ronnie commented. "Especially when I don't know anything about them. Can't you tell me where we're going and what's going to happen?"

Meredith patted him affectionately on the shoulder.

"No, but trust me it'll be worth the wait I guarantee it. And look at it this way, at least one of us is going to have a good time."

"I don't like those odds." "Trust me."

"Terrific."

———

Stitches stepped out of the office building and headed off towards the town square. It was getting on for five in the evening so there was plenty of activity. As well as all manner of beings going about their nightly business, Hector Lozenge was busy with his broom near the fountain, the closest he was ever likely to get to running water short of standing in the rain. Mrs. Ladle was getting ready for one of her nightly fly-bys, and old Mrs. Strudel was in the midst of clearing tables outside her café. The zombie reckoned that would be a good place to start. The café was one of busiest places in town so there wasn't likely to be much that happened around here that Mrs. Strudel didn't at least have some idea of.

Now that he thought of it he couldn't recall the place ever being shut, which, when you took into account the eclectic population that she served, kind of made sense. The canteen in Star Wars had nothing on this place, which was why the meals were listed in book form and kept on a shelf. And unlike any other place of dining, you didn't choose a meal here by food category; you flipped to the appropriate species section instead, and dependent on what that was you either asked politely for what you wanted or pointed at a picture and said,

"Me hungry" in a barely understandable, monster like growl (imagine a kebab shop in Hastings after closing time at the Swaggering Tool).

Always remember this though. If you ever come for a meal at Mrs. Strudels you'll need three things, a strong stomach, a couple of hours to look at the menu and a robust set of cutlery (one, to cut the food and two, to fight off any hungry creature who's getting a bit impatient because his troll ribs haven't arrived yet).

It was also rumoured that the old lady had helped Ollie's uncle out with a couple of issues when he'd been resident here, so if nothing else it proved that she was resourceful and wielded considerable influence and power if a vampire approached her for help and advice. There was also the bonus that if she did have any information, Stitches could pass it off as it being the result of his diligent detective work. He was nothing if not resourceful after all.

He traversed the square and was just about to bid good evening to the cafes proprietor when a distinctive and overpowering fragrance assaulted his nasal passages, gave then a damn good thrashing, left them bruised and bleeding on the floor and in dire need of a paramedic. Imagine the smell of rotting fish, old sprouts and fermented cabbage all wrapped up in a tramps sock and you're into the realms of getting close to what Stitches was currently experiencing smell-wise. As the zombie turned round to greet the being that he knew was behind him he pinched his nose in an attempt to ward off the incredible stench.

"Hello, Sweaty," he offered, sounding like he had a really heavy cold. "How are you?"

The phantom hovering next to him shimmered in the early evening twilight. A wide grin spread across his semi-transparent face and in a broad Welsh accent he replied.

"Oh, not so bad thanks, boyo. Yourself?"

"Fine, fine thanks. All the better for seeing you. What are you doing here anyway? I thought Mrs. Strudel banned you for all eternity. Something about making the customers vomit until their insides fell out."

Sweaty affected a hurt look and gazed at the ground.

"Now there's no need to be personal mun, you know I can't help it.

I'd have a bath if I could and deodorant goes straight through me."

"Like those poor sods meals, huh."

"Ah, you're a funny man, Stitches, regular Max Boyce you are. So, do you fancy a sing song then, bach. Calon Lan, Men of Harlech, Cwm Rhondda, what do you say?"

Stitches smiled pleasantly at the apparition, not that he would have appreciated the gesture because the zombie still had his hand clamped over his face tighter than a limpet on a rock. That being said Sweaty was used to this reaction in others and over the years had become very adept in deciphering the hidden expressions and muffled noises that people made when they were in his vicinity, in much the same way that a dentist has no trouble understanding a patient with a mouthful of cotton wool and a tongue that lolls like a dead fish because it's pumped full of anaesthetic.

"No thanks, not right now," said Stitches. "I haven't really got the time and besides, I've already met one racial stereotype recently. Any more and we could be in danger of turning into a Carry On film. All I need is a giggling blond wearing a top four sizes too small and a slightly effeminate doctor and I can start shooting."

Sweaty chuckled, an action that produced a puff of green gas. It was a strange, hollow sound that reverberated through the air like someone laughing at the bottom of a deep well.

"No problem, bud. You do seem preoccupied though. Anything going on that I should know about?"

The zombie thought for a moment. He could kill three bats with one stone here. Not only could he rescue the cafés patrons from the prospect of seeing their lunch for a second time and save his nostrils from permanent damage, he might be able to get this floating rubbish dump to help him out.

"Tell you what," he said, "whilst I'm in there talking to Mrs. Strudel, you could have a scout round and ask if anyone's seen Ronnie since yesterday."

"Gone walkabout, has he?"

"We're not sure. That's what we're trying to find out. You up for it?" "Indeed I am, boyo. I'll find out what I can and get back to you right."

"I'll be busy myself actually. Tell you what, when you're done nip over to the office and see Ollie. You can fill him in if you find out anything and I'm sure he'll be glad of the company." An evil grin hid behind his palm.

"Righto. See you soon."

"Not if I smell you first," Stitches muttered under his breath.

Thanks to his encounter with Sweaty, Mrs. Strudel had finished clearing up outside and was now back in her kitchen so he entered the café. Once inside he stopped for a moment to take in some of the delicious fragrances that were swirling round, each one identifiable by his still active sense of smell (and some by the colour of the smoke they produced. When it came to supernatural cuisine you needed a well trained eye as well as a finely honed appreciation of cooking aromas. The steam off the seared liver of a ghoul, for instance, was so dense that it could almost be classified as a solid. In fact it was only the week before that Jellyroll the dwarf was hospitalised after banging his head on the vapour emanating from an entrail soufflé, not an easy feat when you consider that dwarves craniums regularly come into contact with rocks and he was wearing his helmet at the time. A gas mask wouldn't go amiss either. Not for the dwarves you understand, although they certainly can get a tad pungent. It's not easy keeping a four foot long beard fresh. Well, I say beard. It's more like a hairy lunchbox really. Still, if you ever find yourself with a dwarf, stuck in the middle of nowhere and without sustenance, never fear. Just get him to have a rummage around in his facial fuzz and you'll be eating in no time).

Anyway, in spite of enjoying the smells, being a member of the zombie community quite naturally precluded Stitches from ingesting any type of food stuffs, but being in the cafe took him back to a time when he still could. It was at least a hundred and sixty years since a morsel of food had passed his lips but the memory still remained intact. In fact, for about three years after his original death and subsequent reanimation, Stitches had stubbornly maintained to himself that all was as it had been and that if he wanted to grab a bite to eat and drink, then he bloody well would. The problem was that after a few days of shovelling provisions down his throat, he would start to notice a foetid stench emanating from his midriff and a copious amount of leakage, both liquid and gaseous, escaping from various parts of his anatomy. It wasn't until the time that he was unfortunate enough to fall asleep in a field one evening after a particularly heavy binge, and woke up to find a fox merrily chewing on the rotting food lying dormant in his now defunct innards, that he finally accepted the reality of his situation. Naturally it had taken a lot of adjustment and a fair bit of counselling from a very kind and knowledgeable Caribbean lady to help him come to terms with his new state of being but he'd got there in the end. It had been a tough transition of course but it wasn't long before he was able to pass by or enter any restaurant or cafe without getting an attack of the DT's and wanting to bury his face in the nearest trifle.

Once satiated he made his way through the seating area and into the kitchen beyond.

"Well, hello there, young man. I haven't seen you in here lately."

Mrs. Strudel spoke with a soft West Country accent. It wasn't broad enough to make you think of rosy cheeked bumpkins in smocks with three teeth in their heads doing things to farm animals, but sufficient to give the impression of lazy days tilling the land, freshly mown grass and drinking cold cider. She was plump, silver haired, had bat wing arms that wobbled when she waved goodbye and one of the most pleasant demeanours you could ever wish a person to have. She pretty much reminded everyone she met of their favourite grandmother.

She'd appeared in Skullenia many, many years ago, but no one was quite sure how, or where from. One night the residents had awoken to find a new café slap bang in the middle of the town square, and that was that. The local populous were very accepting of it though, especially because of the food on offer, and as far as unusual occurrences went, it didn't really rank as one of the oddest. A group of inter-dimensional stamp collectors from the future, stopping by to refuel and grab a sandwich on their way to a convention in Bucharest in 2027, was by far the strangest thing to happen in recent memory.

That and Flug getting struck by a bolt of lightning a while back and thinking that he was a member of the Royal Ballet for about three hours. That was bizarre to say the least, and more than a little worrying because he'd taken to it like a duck to being a duck. Now, the more cynical of you out there in readerland might think that an eight foot human jigsaw couldn't possibly have pulled off the frilly pink skirt and dainty shoes look, but he did so with aplomb and as it turned out he was remarkably light on his feet and his bar work was exceptional.

Stitches raised a hand in welcome.

"Hi, Mrs. Strudel. I know it's been a while but we've been busy settling the new guy in." He leaned over and gave her a light peck on the cheek. "How's things been?" he asked casually, straightening back up.

Mrs Strudel took the lid off a pan that would have accommodated a fully grown sea lion and threw in a dash of salt.

"Oh, the same as usual. Busy busy busy. If there's one thing you can rely on round here it's people's appetites. Everyone and everything is constantly hungry. That's why I never close."

"True true," said the zombie. "Still, what with everyone and everything being preoccupied with terrorizing each other all night they haven't really got time to cook for themselves I suppose. I mean, your average modern day demon is probably far too busy to grab a bite to eat during his hectic schedule. And who wants to go to the shops after a long shift scaring and being scared. No wonder you're run off your feet. Mind you, you must be turning a nice profit."

Mrs Strudel raised a grey eyebrow and replaced a man-hole sized lid onto the vast pan.

"Well, I was until the last one complained. He went moaning to the Food Safety Body and told them that the skewers I was using were unclean. Still, I can't complain. I don't mind the hard work, but those poor creatures are shattered when they come in here. That union of theirs has got a lot to answer for."

The zombie nodded in agreement, dismissing the tiny misunderstanding. "Oh, don't I know it. How can you possibly boil down what a ghost does for a living with a time and motion study? It's all targets and performance figures now. How many hauntings per shift, customer satisfaction surveys, warnings if they under achieve. It's a joke, and against their Inhuman Rights I reckon."

Mrs Strudel opened a cave like oven, poured a splash of a thick, green gloop that looked suspiciously like Fairy Liquid over a dubious looking roast, and slammed it shut again. "Ridiculous," she spat, wiping her weather beaten hands on an apron that was a living menu. "Still, they can't touch me in here. One, because I couldn't possibly work any harder and two, the local Fed Rep for the Undead likes eating here."

"He's got his feet nicely under the table then."

"Indeed he has, although they're not strictly speaking his feet. They belonged to the previous rep who had a mysterious accident at a conference last year."

"What happened?"

"Seems he was unfortunate enough to impale himself on a wooden stake while he was asleep. Talk about unlucky."

Just as Stitches was about to offer a retort of the most sarcastic nature, a golem entered the kitchen and picked up a couple of plates of food which he silently and dutifully took out to some patrons in the dining area.

"He's a quiet one," observed Stitches.

"He is, isn't he. He's a lovely lad is our Eugene, and the good thing about having a golem for a waiter is that it doesn't matter how hot the plates are, he can pick them up no problem. Even the ones with molten rock on for the trolls. Also there's the added benefit that he's not too familiar with the concept of money, so all of his tips come my way. I mean what would a seven foot tall lump of clay spend it on?"

"Shrewd."

Mrs Strudel smiled. "That's the mark of a good business woman."

"What. Exploitation?"

"Cheeky. I meant using all available resources to their full extent whilst maintaining a decent profit margin in today's difficult financial climate."

"That's what I said. Exploitation."

"I prefer to look at it as fuelling the local economy and providing those less fortunate and those without viable workplace skills with the chance of gainful employment whilst maintaining a quality establishment that caters to the population in general."

"So still exploitation then really."

"Oh stuff and nonsense, you disrespectful bag of dust." She tried to look serious and hurt, but couldn't help a small smirk travelling across her ruddy features. "What did you come in here for anyway you naughty little imp?"

Stitches put the lid back on a jar, the contents of which smelled wonderful. Not that he was desperate to know what it was, though. That was an illusion that he didn't want to be shattered.

"We seemed to have misplaced one of our colleagues, and I was wondering if you'd seen or heard anything."

"I take it that would be Ronnie." "Yeah. How did you know?"

Mrs. Strudel grinned as she got out a couple of gargantuan serving bowls and placed them onto her hectic work surface. "Well, let's be honest, it's not the first time he's gone missing is it? Ronnie does this quite often, doesn't he? Mind you, when he's gone off in the past he's always left word with someone hasn't he?"

"That's what we thought," agreed Stitches. "This time, though, the only person who seems to know anything about it is Flug and I can't believe for one minute that Ronnie would leave a message with him. You'd be better off telling a paving slab."

"Tricky. What did Flug have to say?"

Stitches shrugged his shoulders "Oh, you know, some nonsense about the forest and witches and God knows what else. I'm tempted to say the big idiot bumped his head and got a concussion but there'd be no discernible difference. There'd probably be an improvement actually."

Mrs. Strudel stopped what she was doing and wiped her hands on the tea towel that was forever draped across her shoulder. "That's odd, " she mused.

"I know," said Stitches. "Last week he thought he was the number seven."

Mrs. Strudel shook her head. "No silly, I didn't mean Flug. I've just remembered something. Hector came in earlier, and besides banging on about litter and the price of beer as per usual, he was saying that on his way home the other night he saw some figures moving around at the edge of the wood."

"That is interesting I suppose, but then again, Hector's in the same league as Flug in the reliability stakes isn't he, and as much as their stories might tally I can't really go on the word of a chronic drunk and someone who needs subtitles for the hard of thinking."

"I can appreciate that, Stitches love, but Hector wasn't rambling on the way he usually does. He seemed pretty clear about the whole thing. It's about the most lucid he's ever been whilst explaining something."

Stitches wasn't convinced but he tried not to let it show in his expression. He remembered the last time that Hector had been 'lucid' about something, but where he'd gotten the notion that Elvis Presley had appeared to him in his morning pint of beer and told him to 'spread the Rock and Roll word' was anybody's guess. Now, the incident should have passed by unnoticed but the entire populace, be they dead, undead or unclassified, did like their music, so notwithstanding the dubious provenance of the tale and disregarding any semblance of common sense whatsoever, the whole town had gone mad. Sales of blue suede everything had been unprecedented, everyone had started talking in an American drawl and saying 'thang you very much' at every available opportunity, and Midriff the ogre, sporting a quiff three feet long and dressed up in a gold lamee suit, had given a rendition of Hound Dog at the top of his voice that was still talked about to this very day. Mostly by Midriff.

A vast pinch of salt was required when it came to the rubbish man's stories. Still, it was an investigators duty to follow all the lines of enquiry and pursue all the leads no matter how tenuous they appeared to be. And of course there was always the possibility that it'd be like an episode of The Midsomer Murders and they'd have it cracked in a hour, including ad breaks.

"What was he saying, exactly?" said Stitches. The café owner stared at her inquisitive visitor.

"He said he saw Ronnie in the town with young Flug. They spoke for a bit and then Hector got on with his cleaning. When he'd finished he decided to go for a walk in the forest, presumably to clear his head after another day's alcohol intake. Well, he reckons he got several hundred yards in when he was stopped in his tracks by some men wearing strange clothes and carrying what he reckoned were guns."

"Guns! Good grief he must have been absolutely trousered."

"Just hear me out. The men, whoever they were, saw him and told him to get out and if he knew what was good for him he wouldn't come back and to not make the mistake of telling anyone what happened."

Stitches though for a moment. "I take it you believed him then?" She plonked her fists onto her vast hips and sighed.

"Do you know what? I did. I know he's come up with some right old tosh in the past, but there was something different about him this time. He just seemed so damn sure of himself."

Stitches mulled over what the old lady had told him. Hector did have a well-deserved reputation for getting through more alcohol than a meeting of the Oliver Reed Appreciation Society, and consequently telling some incredibly tall tales, ranging from being the first man in history to climb The Matterhorn on his hands, to claiming to have seen a decent programme on Channel 5, but it could be a lead nonetheless. Only time would tell.

"Thanks, Mrs. Strudel, you've been a really big help."

She beamed. "Oooh, you're welcome, my dear. Now, are you sure I can't tempt you with anything?"

The zombie smiled as he crossed the kitchen to give her a farewell peck on the cheek. "There's plenty in here to tempt me, but I'm afraid my dried up old innards just couldn't take it. See you soon."

"You take care now."

With a final sniff, Stitches left the cafe.

———

The alarm resounded around the coffin interior, causing a hapless Ollie to wake with a start and crack his head on the dense wooden lid with a reverberating THUD. A few choice expletives bemoaning his lot as a member of the clan of the undead escaped from his mouth as he drew the lid aside. 'How is this natural?' he thought as he extricated himself, 'It's demeaning having to spend half my life in a wooden box. What am I, a tortoise?'

He quickly got out of his jammies and slipped into his evening attire because he wanted to get to the kitchen and line his stomach with a sandwich and a cup of tea before Flug presented him with his evening repast. It was bad enough swallowing a pint of blood on a full stomach, but forcing it down within minutes of getting up and on an empty belly was liable to result in a rather fragrant maroon yawn.

He drew the curtains back and gazed out of the small window that was the only normal thing in his subterranean boudoir. The sun had set, banishing the daylight for another few hours, and an eerie glow had settled over the landscape. It reminded him of the sort of cover that you'd see on the front of a cheap horror novel, one where the taglines boldly stated that you 'shouldn't enter the creepy old building' or 'go out alone after dark', and then within ten pages someone had been hacked to bloody chunks because they'd gone into the creepy old building or gone out alone after dark. All was normal then.

A loud bang from upstairs meant the impending preparation of his breakfast, so he quickly ran out of the room, hurtled up the stairs, tore along the corridor, sprinted across the office and exploded into the kitchen. In a flash he had the kettle on to boil, a cup and tea bag ready, and was almost done buttering a slice of wholemeal bread when Flug came purposefully into the room to join him.

"Hi, Ollie," he droned as he made his way over to the fridge. As the door opened and the little light came on, Ollie heard the distinctive gloopy slap of a chunky liquid connecting with the side of a glass bottle. Although he'd never figured out for sure where Flug got the stuff, he was starting to formulate the theory that Skullenia had, what he could only think of, as a bloodman. Anywhere else on the planet you heard the telltale whine of the milk float, the sound of cheerfully clinking bottles and the tuneful whistle of the milkman to wake up to as he made his rounds, but seeing as he was the only person living (as it were) here that liked a cup of tea on a regular basis, a milkman's round would be a very short lived business venture indeed.

Suddenly a horrible vision invaded Ollie's thoughts. No longer could he picture a rosy cheeked and bemittened fellow carrying frost enshrouded bottles of milky white goodness or hear the happy sounds of a suburban morning as he played his part in the nations break fast ritual. No, that pleasant imagery was gone now, to be replaced by. . . sometime during the dark recesses of the night, the awful hair drier groan of a struggling engine and the ominous knocking of glass as a little vehicle made its way up and down the streets, announc ing the arrival of the day's corpuscle based deliveries. He wondered if the residents put out those miniature cards with the numbers on them, with a red arrow to let the bloodman know how many pints they wanted.

"*How's about a pint of scarlet top today? It's extra thick with plenty of clots. Lovely on a bowl of cereal.*"

'*My God,*' thought Ollie, 'that can't be healthy,' suddenly wondering how much cholesterol was in a pint of blood. Mind you, that would depend on whose blood it was. If it was a drop from an Olympic athlete then you'd be fine and dandy, but if it came from a member of the local branch of 'I can't stop eating and come here to alleviate my guilt and blame everybody else but myself for piling on loads of weight watchers' then you could be on a diet that had the potential to put you in an early grave. Not a pleasant prospect at all. Ollie made a mental note to get it checked out.

He carried on preparing his sandwich and was just about to spread a blob of Marmite on a slice when he caught sight of Flug upending the bottle over his tankard and pouring the liquid out. Although it didn't pour as such. It flowed. Slowly. Like lava from a lazy volcano. He shuddered so much that he put the knife straight through the bread.

"You okay, Ollie?" Flug enquired.

"Fine, thanks," Ollie replied, trying to avert his gaze. "You look a bit pale."

"Really, I wonder why that is?"

Even Flug was capable of working that one out.

"Aw, me sorry. Would it help if me put a little umbrella in it for you?" Ollie grimaced and shook his head. "Flug, mate, it wouldn't help if Christina Hendricks presented it to me wearing nothing but a smile and a swimsuit made of pearls which had next week's winning lottery numbers written on them. Try to understand what I'm saying to you. Listen to the words that I'm using. I don't like drinking blood, never have, never will. Am I getting through to you? Nothing you can say or do is going to make me feel any better about it okay." "Okay, Ollie."

"Good."

"So no umbrella den?" "AAAARRRRGGGGHHHH!"

"Someone seems a little tetchy today. Get out of the grave on the wrong side did we?"

Ollie glanced over at the door. "Ah, Stitches. Thank goodness you're here," he said.

"Nice of you to say so."

"I was just thinking, I wish Stitches were here." "Understandable."

"Talking to Flug and drinking that horrible stuff instead of me." The zombie scowled as he sat down at the kitchen table.

"My oh my, you really are a grumpy bloodsucker today."

Ollie finally got round to finish preparing his tea and sandwich before joining his colleague at the table.

"I'm sorry," he said around a doughy mass of bread, butter and Marmite, "but you know how it is." He indicated the glass on the side.

Stitches pulled a disgusted face. "Enough said, but hey this'll cheer you up. I've done a bit of digging and found out a few things."

"Go on."

He proceeded to tell Ollie about his conversation with Mrs. Strudel. Ollie listened whilst he drank his tea and was so interested that he also managed to get his blood down without too much of a struggle.

"Are you sure this is on the level?" he asked.

Stitches nodded. "Mrs. Strudel seems to think so, and she knows Hector as well as anybody. Anyway, why would she make such a big deal about something he said if she didn't think it had merit? It serves no purpose."

"Fair point. Right, well as much as I'd like to sit here all night drinking tea we better get ready to go."

"Sounds like a plan."

Ollie rose from his chair and put his used dishes into the sink. "Okay, we've got a bit of time before we have to meet Obsidia. I'm going to pop down and see the Professor while you sort out some transport."

"No problem."

"Good. We'll leave in an hour or so." "I'm on it," said Stitches as he left.

Ollie quickly washed up and headed down to the laboratory where he gingerly knocked on the door. The last thing he wanted to do was barge in and disturb Crumble, just in case he was in the middle of some extremely wacky, terminally dangerous and no doubt highly explosive experiment. The laboratory was messy certainly and in need of a good dusting but an unexpected remodelling job wasn't high on the list of things to do. The expense would be prohibitive and he didn't think the Professor would be too pleased either. To be fair to the old boy though he was quite used to powerful detonations going off under his nose as long as he was prepared for them, but a surprise blast out of the blue was liable to do untold damage (especially if he wasn't wearing his Nose Protector 1500, patent pending, which was specifically designed to defend ones olfactory organ from just such eventualities. Obviously it was useless against surprise blasts out of the red, orange, yellow, green, indigo and violet but Crumble was working on those).

"Come in, come in," came a voice from the other side of the reinforced metal.

Ollie opened the door, poked his head round and peered inside. Better safe than sorry after all. Crumbles' idea of health and safety was on a par with a medieval building site. The coast seemed to be clear though. At least Crumble wasn't running for cover with his hands over his ears shouting at everyone to get out, which was a good sign.

"Hi, Prof. Are you busy?"

"Never too busy to see you, my dear. Come through, don't be shy." "Thanks," said the half vampire as he walked into the room, trying not to be too obvious about glancing at the floor. You could step on something unexpected in here at any moment so it paid to keep your eyes open and your wits about you at all times. Conversely, and not surprisingly, the unexpected had been known to creep out from under a table, grab your leg and try and step on you so being watchful of ones foot placement worked on a couple of levels.

"Now then, young man, what can I do for you? Can I help you at all?"

Ollie smiled at the scientist. He liked to maintain the illusion that the Professor was a happy go lucky, older gentleman, who had a passing interest in all things empirical, rather than a moderately senile nearterrorist who was capable of blowing things up just by moving them a few feet across his lab. There was no telling what was stable or unstable in the room, which was why it was best not to touch anything. Even the air could be dangerous.

On the whole though he was rather a lovely chap, and was generally most engaging to be around. Plus, there was always the chance that he might, one day, come up with something vaguely useful (it was a distant hope but then people are still waiting for someone they recognise or didn't think was dead to be on Pointless Celebrities so it's not beyond the limits of credibility).

Ollie thought for a moment about the investigation that was going on.

"I think maybe you can. We do have a bit of a problem at the moment. Some of Count Jocular's werewolves have gone missing and we've been asked by His Lordship to locate them. Oh, and Ronnie's done a disappearing act as well, but we haven't ruled out a drunken binge yet."

"I didn't have werewolves down as heavy drinkers," said Crumble thoughtfully. "They strike me as the healthy, outdoorsy type to be honest."

"No, Professor, it's the werewolves that are missing and Ronnie who we think might be off somewhere drinking himself into oblivion."

"Right. Right. So what's this got to do with Count Jocular again?" Ollie sighed. Very heavily. So heavily that he heard it hit the floor. "No, Professor, not Count Jocular himself. His werewolves have gone astray and we're trying to find them. We think someone may have taken them."

"Oh, fine. I'm with you know." "Good."

"I'd ask Count Jocular where they are. He always seems to know what's going on around here."

Five minutes, two drawings, the first act of newly scripted play entitled 'Some Of My Werewolves Are Missing' and a pseudo game of charades later...

"Oh, I see. Mmmm, well that is a perplexing mystery, "said the Prof, tapping his fingers against his top lip in his best 'trying to look intellectual' stance. "And as luck would have it, I think that I might have something that will help."

He walked over to a battered metal cupboard, the sort that looked like it should be sitting in a school corridor, covered in stickers, awash with lewd graffiti, and emitting a feeble thump from within because the class nerd had been shoved in head first with his pants over his head, after another failed world record, wedgie marathon attempt. The door opened with a loud squeak. Crumble rummaged around inside for thirty seconds or so before pulling from its recesses what looked suspiciously like a television remote control with two bulbs attached to the end.

"There we go," he announced, proudly brandishing the object like a Stone Age man presenting the first wheel with the corners rounded off to his mates.

"What's that?" said Ollie. "It looks like a television remote control with two bulbs attached to the end."

"It's a television remote control with two bulbs attached to the end," said Crumble.

Ollie hadn't felt so underwhelmed since the time that he'd watched the World Rubik's Cube Championships on the TV as a lad, and marvelling as the winner completed the puzzle in one point six seconds, only then to announce that it was a triumph for the visually impaired and that colour blind folk were people too.

He tried not to show his immense disappointment, but it was a feeling that was becoming more and more common around here. It was a never ending catalogue of hopes dashed, promises not kept, dealing with the dross of society and just plain old rubbish. Kind of like the X Factor auditions.

"So what does it actually do, if anything?" he asked with a healthy and robust dose of scepticism.

The Prof smiled. "If you take a look here," he said, taking the back panel off and pointing to a small switch just under the zero button, which in turn was connected by a series of wires to a circuit board on top of the original, "notice how the green light comes on when I flick it."

Ollie was marginally impressed. Indeed one of the lights had come on. A small bulb the size of a pea glowed a very bright shade of green.

"I see it."

"Well, if this is pointed in the right direction at something, the infrared unit, which I've adapted, picks it up and the light turns red."

Ollie had now moved on from being marginally impressed to being reasonably intrigued, and not in a 'what the hell is this deranged pensioner on about now' fashion either. He'd moved on from that and was now in the realms of 'this is interesting, I think I might stick around and not make up feeble excuses to get out of here because he's using his slipper as a mobile phone'.

"So what sort of 'something' will turn the light red then?" said Ollie, having visions of it going off because it had located a piece of toast or a house.

"Something living," said Crumble. "I'd say anything bigger than a cat will set it off. If it passes within a hundred feet of this and the remote picks it up, the light will turn red and you're in business."

"Even if it's hidden?" "Oh, yes."

By way of demonstration, Crumble passed his hand in front of the device and sure enough, the small bulb changed from green to a vibrant red.

Ollie smiled as being reasonably intrigued gave way to being genuinely impressed. "That's very clever. How does it work, exactly?"

The Professor flicked the switch again, turning the unit off and placed it on his workbench.

"That's a very good question. It picks up the electrical field given off by anything with a pulse. If it's got a heartbeat, this little device will find it."

He picked up the instrument again and handed it to Ollie who accepted it gratefully, which was a strange feeling he was not accustomed to experiencing down here. Usually it was a case of get out the door as fast as was decent, lob the proffered item into the garden and hide under a chair until the shock-waves had passed.

"This could come in rather handy if you're trying to find missing lycanthropes, I would imagine."

"I think you might be right there. Thanks, Prof that's really helpful." "No problem, my dear."

Ollie made to leave the lab, but just as he was about to go Crumble grabbed his arm. "Oh and one more thing. Take this; it could also prove to be useful."

He reached into a pocket and pulled out a small packet which he placed into Ollie's outstretched palm.

"It's a Sherbet Stab." "Indeed it is."

"Mmmm, I don't want to be negative, Professor, but how is a fizzy white powder and a liquorice knife going to help me?"

Crumble raised his eyebrows in an expression that said *come on young man, think about it.*

"Just take it," he said, closing Ollie's fingers around the tube. "You never know."

Ollie put the confection into his pocket, safe in the knowledge that he would indeed never know, and almost glad that the moment of clarity and inventiveness had passed, and that things had returned to their normal state of quirky eccentricity.

"Indeed you don't, Professor, indeed you don't."

————

The lights on the ceiling flashed by as the trolley was wheeled along the corridor. It was just like one of those scenes in a film, where the hospital staff are rushing a casualty to accident and emergency so they can get to work on them, and miraculously save their life no matter how severe their injuries. Or, failing that, just in time for them to get their final dying, prophetic words out before they pop their clogs. But, as Ronnie had already concluded, there was nothing miraculous going to occur when he got to wherever it was that he was being taken. If that mentally unstable soldier had seen fit to thrust a needle under his nail, there was no telling what this pompous, uptight little doctor intended to do with him. Ronnie had tried to engage the two porters in a conversation, but it was no use. They were obviously sworn to secrecy and were being as tight lipped as it was possible to be. They wouldn't even look at him as they pushed the trolley like an express train, they just stared blankly ahead, glass eyed and silent as if nothing at all was going on inside their heads.

"So come on guys, tell me," Ronnie tried again as the fluorescent tubes whipped by. "Or at least give me a clue where we're off to. I bet it's a surprise party, isn't it? And there's me thinking you'd forgotten my birthday. Hope there's blancmange and a great big cake."

This riposte at last elicited a response from one of the gown wearing goons. He spoke in a voice that was a deep bass. It was gravelly, as if he'd smoked a few too many cigarettes or recently chewed on a handful of nails.

"Oh, you're gonna get a nice surprise alright, buddy. The Doc is gonna take real good care of you."

Ronnie managed to raise his head enough to be able to see the man properly. His face was a roughly hewn and craggy mask, scarred to the point of immobility, but his countenance, such as it was, was one of stolid unreadability. Here was a man used to seeing nothing and not reacting to anything no matter what it was. No doubt his expression would remain the same whether he was watching an innocent child at play or witnessing the nightmares being perpetrated on some nameless battlefield. What history were those features testament to? What horrors had he seen or been involved in?

His dark eyes stared out from underneath a protruding brow that wouldn't have looked out of place on a simian like throwback. He definitely looked like a man not to be trifled with. If he wasn't here he'd be a professional rugby player, a bouncer or maybe a brick wall. His dazzling conversation and witty comebacks suggested the latter.

"Well, I should hope so," Ronnie shot back, "he's a doctor after all; he's supposed to take *real good care of me*." The last five words were slurred out in a very bad American accent.

"Don't be under the illusion that the Doc here is a friendly neighbourhood MD," the man rumbled in reply. "As far as you're concerned you might as well have a blind trainee butcher looking after you. Make no mistake, he's very good when he needs to be, but with you, let's face it, who cares how much it hurts."

The porter had a sneer on his face when he said the last bit, the first change of expression that Ronnie had seen, and it wasn't pleasant.

It was the sort of predatory look you'd see on a wildlife documentary, just before some poor, dumb herbivore got a first hand look at its insides.

Ronnie quickly reviewed his decision to keep on riling the man and came to the conclusion that on this occasion discretion was by far the better part of valour. In other words, it was time to shut the hell up and stop poking fun at the circus freak.

He rested his head back onto the trolley and concentrated on the ever glowing neon lights. He was still at a bit of a loss as to why he was being held here, wherever here was, but if he was honest it was probably more to do with him not wanting to admit to himself that he knew exactly why he was here. Judging from the little scraps of information that he'd been able to glean from the exchanges in the white room, it appeared to him that not only was this place a military installation, but some type of research facility as well. And being the sort of chap who was able to put two and two together and jump immediately to any conclusions that presented themselves, Ronnie was under the almost certain impression that gene research of some description was going on here. When that sadist Cowan had spoken to him and James earlier, he'd asked them both to 'Do whatever it was that they did'. Presented with those facts and statements, even Flug would have been able to see that Cowan and the Doctor, and therefore the American military, wanted to harness their special talents. Just imagine, Ronnie thought, legions of highly trained soldiers artificially engineered to mutate on the order of a commanding officer. It didn't warrant thinking about. Any army, terrorist group or even a basement rebel with an overzealous dedication to a cause, or a teenager with a grudge against a local shop owner, that got hold of the technology that he feared was be ing manufactured here, would be completely and totally invincible. It would be an army with superhero-like powers, a paranormal fighting force that nobody would be able to resist. There would be no happy ending to this story.

This was the stuff of nightmares and the outside world needed to know what was going on. That being the case all he had to do was free himself, get off the trolley, incapacitate the two fugitives from the zoo, find a way out of the obviously secure and secret facility, and alert the relevant authorities, whomever they may be. Piece of cake really!

"Here we are, buddy," said the porter. "Safely delivered. The Doctor will see you now."

The front of the trolley, and therefore the top of Ronnie's head, connected with a heavy set of double doors that led into yet another stark, colourless room.

Although his field of view was limited, Ronnie could see what he could only assume was scientific equipment, the sort you might see on an in depth documentary on the Discovery Channel, though obviously you had to be viewing at the right time, and not the other twenty three hours of the day when all there is to watch is mating baboons or yet another chronicle about the Nazis (apparently there's eleven people in Northern Alaska who don't know who Adolf Hitler is so they'll keep showing them until they've caught up).

He saw a couple of white coated lab assistants who were busy doing whatever it was that white coated lab assistants do with Petri dishes, glass vials, large beakers full of liquid and bubbling test tubes. He didn't have the first clue what they were doing of course and as curious as he was, he thought he'd leave the questions for now. His initial experiences with the people that he'd met thus far hadn't filled him with confidence about their social skills, and seeing as he was just as likely to get something sharp inserted somewhere painful as he was a sensible answer he decided to keep his own counsel.

He was wheeled to the centre of the room and brought to a stop under an array of lights so bright that Ronnie reckoned he was in danger of getting a half decent tan. Before his shocked eyes could accustom themselves to the extreme luminosity, a blurry and out of focus blob hove into view from above. It got closer and bigger until finally, and thankfully, it totally eclipsed the mini stellar glow.

"Here he is," said the Doctor's already familiar voice. "My second subject of the day. I do hope you're going to be a bit more cooperative than your friend."

"Why should I?" answered Ronnie.

"Well, let me put it this way. The procedures that I'm going to carry out really don't hurt and that's the truth, but your friend got a bit stubborn and chose to fight it. That's when it got painful for him. So you see, how much discomfort you experience is entirely in your hands."

"That's what I like about you sadistic types. You're quite happy to spend a couple of hours torturing me then have the temerity to tell me it's my fault."

"But how could it be anything else?" said Meredith. "It seems perfectly reasonable to me that if you behave like a truculent child then you should be treated as such."

"Really? So ten minutes on the naughty stair and no tea it is then."
"Not quite, but ten minutes sounds about right. You'll be amazed
what can be done to a body in that amount of time."

"What a gracious host you are. Genial, welcoming, jovial. . . " "Why thank you."

"... mad as a box of mad." Meredith smiled "You're too kind."

"But tell me, what's all this for?" said Ronnie, feeling brave. If this was going to hurt he reckoned he might as well get something out of it besides bruises and brain damage. "You're not here on a nature study are you? Someone's gone to a great deal of trouble and expense to set this up haven't they?"

The right corner of Meredith's mouth curled upwards, as if his cheek muscles were attempting a smile but failing miserably. When he spoke there was an edge to his voice. Ronnie couldn't decide what it was but he was sure it wouldn't be good.

"I'm afraid this isn't one of those B movies or second rate novels where the villain suddenly tells the captured hero every detail of his plot for world domination, just before said hero escapes and kills him. I'm going to do what I need to do and that's it. All you need to do is stay still. Got it?"

Ronnie closed his eyes and shook his head. His emotions were hovering between abject despair and acute anger, neither of which were going to be of any use to him whatsoever in his current situation. He breathed out and tried to calm himself.

"I got it."

———

Stitches got back to the office just as Ollie returned from his visit to the lab.

"Oi oi," said the zombie.

"Hiya. Is our lift to the forest sorted out?"

"It is indeed. Bill's going to be here shortly, and I've told him to pick us up from the same place as yesterday."

"Good. I take it he knows we're going to Obsidia's address rather than the castle?"

"Well, I think that's what I said," said Stitches. "Actually, I know that's what I said, but whether Bill understood me speaking plain and clear English is anybody's guess."

"I'm sure he got it. He may use gibberish as a first language, but he always understands what he's being told."

Stitches made to sit in his usual place opposite Ollie's desk, but he was stalled by a waving finger half way there.

"No," said Ollie, "we haven't got time for that. We need to get going. You can do me a quick favour though. Can you nip down to the kitchen and get Flug please."

The zombie huffed moodily and headed for the door.

"Oh, why is he coming? I thought we were going on a covert, nighttime stalking expedition into the woods. How the hell is he going to be any use? We might as well take a pneumatic drill and a steam roller, at least they'll make slightly less noise then he does."

Ollie put his coat on and placed the detection device into a pocket.

He then went to pick up the tube of sherbet, but hesitated. "What's that?" asked Stitches.

Ollie explained briefly about his visit with Crumble and the second unusual offering that he'd been given.

"I don't quite know what to make of that. I suppose it could come in handy if we have to win favour with a difficult diabetic," said Stitches. Ollie hummed in agreement but nevertheless, and despite his misgivings, plucked the packet from the desk and put it in another capacious pocket (that's a nice sentence. I think I'll do it in my best writing and put it on my mum's fridge).

"I tell you what, mate," offered Stitches, "if you can find a use for that other than getting it all over yourself like everyone else does, I'll sew my mouth shut for a whole day."

"Now that's a bet worth taking." Ollie looked at his watch. "Anyway, time's getting on. Come on, go and get Flug."

A couple of minutes later the odd looking trio were standing in the street, awaiting the arrival of the carriage.

"Why we standing in da street?" asked a bewildered Flug, who was still a bit annoyed for being wrenched away from his game of Guess Who. For the very first time he'd been on the verge of winning, and in Flugs world that was something that didn't happen very often, especially when he didn't have a clue how the floor worked and regularly lost battles of wits with coat-hangers (actually that's a tad misleading and just a polite way of saying that he'd tried to eat one once and got it stuck in his throat. It came out easily enough though. It was getting him off the shirt rail that had been the real problem).

I must point out though that Guess Who isn't a particularly tricky game. It essentially involves Flug sitting in front of a mirror trying to determine whom he's looking at by using a cunning set of elimination questions, which, in essence, means him shouting "who are you?" over and over and over again until someone tells him to stop or threatens to remove his head and send it to Mrs. Strudel for a cooking pot.

Ollie turned and spoke to his hulking accomplice.

"As I've already explained about twelve times, we're meeting up with Obsidia and a couple of her friends because we're hoping to find out what's happened to the werewolves that've been going missing." A vacant look passed over the giant's outsize features, much like the slack jawed expression you'd see on a celebrity contestant who was trying to answer a hundred pound question on Who Wants to be a Millionaire.

"Oh." Still the bemused look. "Wot werewolves?" "Uh oh. Time to set phasers to stupid," said Stitches.

Ollie threw his hands up to the heavens in total exasperation. "That's it, I give up. I'd have more luck trying to teach a rhino to play the flute."

Stitches looked at his friend. "Have you been looking at my darknet sites?"

"What!" said Ollie. It was a rhetorical what!, not a what? what. Whatever that was.

"The rhino thing," said the zombie. "It came up during a game we play online?"

"Game?" said Ollie, who was to online tomfoolery what ITV was to a decent sitcom.

"The Useless Gifts Game. A group of friends and me play it on the computer. We go onto Zombie.com and write ideas for rubbish presents to give people. It's a great laugh."

Ollie rubbed his eyes. "I know I'm going to regret this. Like what?" "Well, like a magazine subscription for Blind Arnold, or a slimming club membership for a skeleton."

Ollie couldn't begin to describe how he felt about what Stitches had just said. "You are a sick individual. You know that, don't you?" he offered.

The zombie frowned and looked hurt. "I think that's a bit strong," he whined.

"Well it does sound like a bit of a waste of time doesn't it Surely you must be able to find something a little more productive to occupy your time?"

"Like what?"

"Oh, I don't know. Write your memoirs, decorate the office, start weight training, anything. It's only a short hop from trolling websites to starting your very own blog and feeling the need to update every other no hoper out there what you're up to from one minute to the next."

"I need to go to da blog," rumbled Flug.

"Tiny misunderstanding there, mate," noted Stitches, "but you should have posted before we left. Anyway," he continued, returning to the conversation with Ollie, "that's Twitter you're talking about."

"Really. How remiss of me," said Ollie. "It's still a bit pathetic though, isn't it? Putting your whole life on the darknet for every drooling nobody to gawp at because they've got nothing better to do than gaze in wonder at what you had for lunch. One letter change would describe it a hell of a lot better if you ask me."

Before Stitches could reply and the whole subject turned into a full blown argument about technology, how things were better in the good old days and the state of the modern world in general, Bill and his coach arrived to pick them up.

The trip to the werehouse took longer than previous ones, thanks in part to Flug's massive bulk weighing the carriage down to the extent that the underside kept scraping along the trail every time it passed over anything not as smooth as a snooker table. Another delay of a quarter of an hour was needed for Stitches to locate his right eyeball, which had inadvertently dropped to the floor when he sneezed heavily. They eventually found it under Ollie's seat, but when the zombie put it back in its socket he managed to get a piece of dried grass wedged in behind it that poked out the side of his face, and moved about like an antenna every time he looked at anything. Ollie initially thought it very amusing, but after five minutes the spectacle was making him feel rather nauseous so he pointed it out.

At last they arrived not far from the werehouse. Bill bid them an unintelligible farewell and drove off.

"I wish we could have got off here last time," said Stitches. "It would have saved us slogging through the woods with Egon."

"True, but you'd have missed out on that lovely bonding session with him. Don't be so quick to dismiss what was a very special time

for both of you. And I also think you've now got a friend for life. He'll stick with you through thick and thin."

Stitches look utterly appalled. "So would rising damp. I'd rather bond with a colony of zombie worms to be honest."

"I'm sure. Well here we are again," announced Ollie as they stepped onto the porch.

"Where are we den?" asked Flug, "and how did we get to da trees?" "He's worse than usual tonight," Ollie observed. "Maybe we should get Dr. Zoltan to give him the once over."

Dr. Zoltan was the chief physician at the Skullenian General Hospital and purveyor of medicines and treatments to the sick, the infirm and the downright clumsy, Flug being one of his main charges. I could regale you with his accomplishments and qualifications but I haven't got the time, suffice to say that I became more medically proficient the least time I cut my toe nails.

"What for? It's probably just the cold air affecting him. They told Ronnie at Flug's last check-up that he's got a really slow metabolism so you can't expect too much out of him. His heart rate's only twenty BPM."

"Twenty beats per minute is a bit slow, isn't it?" "Per month."

"Per month what?"

"His heart rate. It's twenty beats per month," Stitches explained. "Are you shi... how can he possibly survive?"

"I'm not sure. The doctor spelled it out using all sorts of medical jargon and surgical technical terms, but what I think he was really saying is that Flug is the almost human equivalent of a cactus that's been kicked about a bit. There's not enough going on inside him to instigate the need for any great speed of movement or thought so his system adjusts accordingly. He's like a mobile statue."

"I still need to go to da blog," stated Flug matter of factly.

Ollie knocked on the door, eager to get the monster inside so he could use a toilet. The thought of him depositing what nature had definitely not intended and destroying a few square yards of woodland and its inhabitants was something that he didn't want on his conscience. Or Obsidia's doorstep for that matter. What Flug produced from his body had a half-life on par with Uranium 238 and was just as potent. A surreptitious anatomical fly tip out in the open had the potential to seriously damage the ozone layer, lay waste to the rainforests and leave polar bears wondering where all the ice had gone. Luckily, Obsidia was quick to answer the door after Ollie's knock.

"Good evening, gentlemen," she gushed.

"Hi there. Look, I'm sorry to be blunt, but can Flug here use your bathroom facilities. He's desperate and the bumpy coach ride has probably shaken things up in there that I really don't want to think about." "Of course." She glanced over her shoulder. "Ethan, could you show our guest to the bathroom please."

They entered the building, whereupon Ethan took hold of Flug's arm and made to guide him in the right direction.

"Flug," called Ollie, "have you got your paper?"

"Oh, it's alright," said Obsidia, placing a hand on Ollie's arm. "There's plenty of the requisite item already in there. We're not completely uncivilised."

"No, I meant his piece of paper with the instructions on it. He gets confused sometimes."

"Oh, I see."

As if to confirm that very thing, Flug reached into a pocket and pulled out a battered notebook and waved it in the air before being led off.

"And don't forget to use the air freshener." "Okay, Ollie."

"Afterwards," added Stitches.

Ollie looked at Obsidia, a vast red look of apology and embarrassment on his face.

"He's like a child, "he explained. "If he doesn't have that book of instructions with him at all times there's no telling what might happen."

"To him?" she asked. "And others."

Stitches, who had been surreptitiously making sure that his eye was facing in the right direction, explained further.

"Even the most mundane, everyday functions have to be spelled out in detail to him. Well, I say spelled out, it's more a series of diagrams and arrows about how to get things done really. It's basically a book of visual aids to get him through the day."

Obsidia tried not to look too bewildered and almost managed it. "Interesting," she said. "So anyway, how are you today, my dusty, little friend?"

"Oh fine, fine thanks. Looking forward to getting stuck into whatever's going on around here. Or out there, anyway."

Between them, Ollie and Stitches spent the next fifteen minutes enlightening Obsidia with what they had discovered thus far.

"So we still have something of a mystery on our hands," she noted. "But hopefully tonight, at the very least, we'll find our missing pack members. I can't tell you what it means to us what you're doing."

"Well, let's hope we get a break, hey," said Stitches encouragingly, "and maybe when this is all over, we could get together or something." "Maybe we could," she replied coyly. "Or perhaps something first." "Well, quite," interjected Ollie. It was at that point that they all heard a toilet flushing, a can of air freshener squirting, a door opening and Ethan exclaiming, "OH MY GOD!" A few seconds later both he and a distinctly more relaxed Flug rejoined them.

"Is that better?" asked Ollie.

"Yeah. Tummy feel better now," Flug replied, a satisfied look on his face.

"Good. At least now there's no danger of you getting caught short in the forest," he said.

"True," said Stitches. "All we have to worry about now is the danger to any offshore shipping."

"Nice," complained Ollie. "Right, shall we get off then? No sense in wasting any more time."

Obsidia picked up a long black coat that was hanging over the back of a chair and slipped it on.

"Very well, gentlemen. Let's begin." "Is Ethan not joining us?" asked Ollie.

"No. I think it'd be best if he stayed here in case of any developments."

With that decided, Ollie, Stitches, Flug and Obsidia left the confines of the werehouse and headed off into the woods.

———

Before stepping out of her front door, Mrs. Ladle adjusted her pointy hat, collected her broomstick and checked that the fuel chamber was loaded up with Professor Crumble's little blue pills. There was no sense in going off half-broomed now was there.

Once outside she locked up and cast a spell over the small building that she called home to protect it from the attentions of the local ne'erdo-wells, of which there were plenty. Then, recalling a few unsavoury incidents that had caused Mr. and Mrs. Sphere a few problems, she wove a more intricate and potent dose of magic about the place just in case. The area had been suffering from a bout of disruptive behaviour of late and she didn't want to fall foul to any naughtiness (it would cause her to lose her temper in a big way and having to explain to Constable Gullett why she was covered in blood, bone and body-parts was a bit of a pain in the backside. The policeman couldn't spell very well and she hated filling in her own charge sheet). The good officer had gone some way to sorting out the matter though and had already issued several ASBO's (Anti Spell Breaking Orders).

Once she was happy she walked a short distance to the small patch of dirt outside her house that she affectionately referred to as the runway and got ready. It was about two feet wide, twenty feet long and was plenty big enough to get her and her broomstick off the ground. She stood at one end and placed the handle between her legs. This she accomplished with ease as there was no faffing about with skirts for your modern airborne witch. Obviously the skirt was her preferred mode of dress when on the ground but for flying she found that a thick pair of woollen leggings was far more comfortable, leaving her plenty of room to manoeuvre, not having to worry about who was looking up and providing somewhere to keep her fags. They also had the added advantage of covering up the road maps that her varicose veins formed. Be warned. Never ask a witch for directions as they're liable to casually raise a hem right in front of you to show you the way in bold, lumpy blue detail. It was like looking at a sock full of Stilton. Anyway, the leggings were also nice and warm and that, if anything, was the best thing about them. There was nothing worse than flying around at seven hundred feet on a chilly winter's night and getting a stiff breeze up your brush every five minutes.

After limbering up and flexing her flying muscles (having a quick smoke) she was poised and ready to go. Normally she'd just take off but what with the trouble she'd been having with the broom of late she began to jog lightly on the spot. Then, after ten seconds or so she moved forward, gaining speed until just before the end of the strip where, with a faint rush of air and a mild KABOOM, she took flight.

She gained altitude rapidly, quickly getting up to about one hundred feet where she levelled out to monitor her speed. The last thing she needed was to be pulled over by The Flying Squad and given a ticket. She'd only just come off a ban for drunk flying and couldn't afford any more points on her license. She hadn't gotten tipsy on purpose of course. Unbeknownst to Mrs. Ladle, a colleague at a coven meeting had laced a batch of snail brownies with whisky, and seeing as she'd eaten fourteen of the things her blood alcohol level had been a teensy weensy bit over the limit (in the same way that Bill Gates has got a bit of spare cash lying around if he fancies a takeaway). She got her own back at the next meeting though. She'd turned her acquaintance into an ashtray and spent the evening stubbing out cigarettes on, what she hoped, were delicate parts of her anatomy.

She turned left and swooped in over the town, just to have a nose at what was going on. There was Hector Lozenge on a late evening stroll, no doubt off to find some booze to throw down his neck. The Stella triplets were out trawling for business and Old Sweaty was flinging himself about all over the place making vapour trails of his own.

Passing over the town square she noticed that Ollie's office was in complete darkness. That's unusual, she thought, as there was normally a light on somewhere in the building, ostensibly for Flug's benefit if nothing else. He was more scared of the night time than a Tour de France winner was of a urine test.

Seeing that there was in fact very little going on in town, Mrs. Ladle decided to take her broomstick for a longer run out over the forest. She did a sharp one hundred and eighty degree turn, ramped up the speed a few notches and climbed another hundred and fifty feet or so.

Half an hour's pleasant cruising later, Mrs. Ladle crossed the threshold of the trees. The forest below her was extraordinarily dark, but thanks to a beautifully clear sky the tops of the trees shimmered in silver as they reflected the light being cast down from the stunning full moon. The night was whisper quiet and thanks to her newly serviced and invigorated mode of transport, she could hear the boughs creaking and even the scurrying of creatures across the forest floor.

(Just in case you were wondering and were surprised that Mrs. Ladle could hear such sounds from over two hundred feet up in the air, keep in mind that a fluffy, scampering woodland creature in Skullenia bears no resemblance to the fluffy, scampering woodland creatures that you might be familiar with. If it were living near you it would probably be in a zoo, locked in a cage, on its own, fed with a fifteen foot pole and watched over by a team of armed guards on twenty four hour rotating shifts. Either that or working for Lidl).

It was while she was trying to locate the source of a particularly exuberant set of running appendages that she noticed, away in the distance, what looked like lights in a building. This struck her as bizarre because the only structures that she knew about out here were Jocular's castle and the werehouse, and both of those were in the other direction.

"I wonder if anyone else knows anything about that?" she said to herself. "Somebody must do, I suppose." She reckoned it was good few miles away, so she slowed down and put the broomstick in park and hovered expertly whilst she had a smoke break. I'm going to have a look at that, she decided, flicking the fag end to the floor below after taking a last lungful. She put the stick into drive and headed off in the direction of the strange lights.

———

Cowan was sitting behind his desk. His chair was pushed back, his legs were stretched out in front of him and his hands were clasped behind his head. A thick black cigar rested between his clenched teeth, its tip glowing brightly and emitting tendrils of wispy smoke that snaked lazily towards the ceiling. He was in a good mood. In fact, he was in a terrific mood after his latest update from Meredith. The diminutive doctor usually enraged the soldier on sight, but as of this moment he was actually feeling pleasantly disposed towards the man. It looked like, at last, that his mission here was drawing to a long overdue but successful conclusion. Not twenty minutes ago, Meredith had come to his office with the news that not only was the werewolf gene stable, but it was looking as if the invisibility specimen was heading in the same direction as well. If that truly was the case then the return trip home would be upon him very soon.

He'd already contacted his superiors and informed them of the glad tidings and they were extremely pleased with what he'd accomplished.

He'd also told them that he'd be travelling with two extra people in tow. Obviously there was no way that he could let the two subjects leave as it was far too risky an option. And, as the doctor had pointed out, disposing of them was equally as perilous and, more importantly, wasteful and counter productive. As he'd said, though harnessing the DNA samples had been an extremely difficult and time consuming process, synthesising a steady supply of it in the laboratory would require decades of research and experimentation. It seemed to him that it made more sense to keep the donors in captivity so that samples could be harvested as and when required. It also meant that they would have a virtually inexhaustible supply of product, and once back home they could begin the human trials straight away.

At first, Cowan had been annoyed at Meredith for being right and for thinking ahead before he did but, ultimately, it was the major who would receive the plaudits for the success and a not inconsiderable boost to his career, whilst the doc would spend the next few years languishing in a lab in some remote location staring at test tubes.

All in all, he thought, the future and his in particular, was looking bright. He chewed heavily on the cigar and pulled the smoke deep into his lungs, relishing the smooth bitterness as it infiltrated his system. He sat forward and pressed the intercom button on his desk.

"Travis."

"Yes, sir."

"Start making arrangements to wrap up here. When everything is set, let me know."

"Yes, sir."

"And allow room for a couple of extra passengers. The meat is coming with us. Nothing too comfortable, though."

"Understood."

"Carry on, Lieutenant." "Yes, sir."

He gazed through the window to the forest outside. God how he hated it here. If he never came back it would be just fine with him. He finished his smoke and stubbed it out. It was time to get organised.

———

For the second time in the last couple of days, Ollie and Stitches, plus companions, found themselves wandering through the Skullenian woods, only this time at least they had more of an idea of what they were supposed to be doing. Of course, that was like giving a five year old a set of crayons and asking them to carry on where Leonardo Da Vinci left off as a homework project, but at least they were trying.

If it was at all possible, the woodland that they were struggling through seemed to be getting denser every couple of minutes. It was a constant battle against whipping branches, coiled tree roots and stinging leaves that all seemed to come at you no matter which direction you were heading in.

Still, when all was said and done, they were nothing if not enthusiastic. Well, three of them were. Stitches was rapidly losing any and all interest in their nocturnal ramble, and groaned inwardly as he stared at the lunar lit forest stretching away before them.

"I don't want to moan or anything," he said, "but how much further are we going?"

Ollie kept on walking but turned his head so he could answer.

"I haven't got a clue. All I know is that something's been going on out here, and other than the solution presenting itself I can't think of a better way of trying to get to the bottom of it than this. And I don't know what you're winging about, this was your idea remember."

"I know it was my idea, but that didn't mean we had to do it."

"Well, if you can come up with a better plan, I'm sure we'll all be willing to give it due consideration," said Ollie.

"Yes, Stitches," added Obsidia, who was off to their left, accompanying Flug. "Do tell."

"Umm, we could. . . umm, no, actually if we, no that won't work... let's see, what about, no, that's far too messy and Flug'll get frightened. . . umm... maybe we could. . . "

"Stitches," interrupted Ollie. "What? I'm thinking."

"Be quiet. This is how it needs to be done so you might as well get on with it."

"Whatever," came the reply in a rather truculent tone.

"Anyway, we've only been out for an hour," Ollie pointed out encouragingly.

"An hour and a quarter actually," said Stitches.

"Oh my. Listen to the chairman of the pedantic society." "Vice chairman, actually."

Obsidia stopped in her tracks and turned to face them both, hands planted firmly on her hips and eyes fixed. Even in the dim light they could see the look of intense displeasure clouding her gorgeous features. She did look beautiful when she was angry though.

"Gentlemen, if I might remind you of why we are undertaking this search. Some of my friends are missing and I'm very keen to see them again or, if the worse comes to the worst, at least discover their fate. Now, whilst I appreciate your help more than you'll ever know, if you can't stop bickering like a disgruntled married couple then I'll just get on with it by myself."

Ollie and Stitches stared at the ground, both thoroughly ashamed of themselves for upsetting Obsidia and possibly making a mockery of the job in hand.

"Sorry," said Ollie. "Sorry," said Stitches. "Sorry," said Flug.

"You don't have anything to be sorry about," said Obsidia when she saw the monsters worried face. "You haven't done anything wrong."

"Oh, okay. Wot pedantic mean?"

"It means being picky over details," she explained. "Ah. And de top hat as well," said Flug.

Obsidia looked slightly confused at this. "Pardon?"

"Dat wot Stitches say when it time for Ollie to go to vampire parties. He get very picky over de top hat and de tails. Stitches say wot he worry 'bout anyway cos he look like a fat penguin dat need a built up shoe and leg brace."

Ollie pursed his pale lips together and stared daggers at the zombie. If looks could kill, then a certified murdering machine had just come into existence.

"That was once, and it wasn't my fault that those shoes were too tight," said the half vampire.

Stitches shook his head, amazed at the fact that of all the snippets of conversation Flug had heard since he'd known him, that was he one that he chose to remember (although to be honest there wasn't really a choice element to it. Flug didn't instigate anything. Things just happened to him).

Stitches was about to respond to the allegation when he caught sight of Obsidia staring right at him. Her eyebrows were raised and she was wagging an insistent index finger at him.

"Just a little joke. I apologise," he said with all the sincerity of a mugger doing community service.

"Okay then," Ollie responded with all the grace of the same mugger executing the very crime that had landed him with community service in the first place.

"Right," Obsidia said, bringing the little episode to a conclusion. She grabbed Flug's hand and headed off once more. "Shall we continue?" A further three quarters of an hour later saw the hardy group of investigators deep in the heart of the forest. The going was now extremely tough, so much so that Flug, with the assurances from the three others that there was definitely nothing to be afraid of, was now leading the way using his tremendous bulk to barge through any herbaceous obstacles that he encountered, thus clearing a path for the others to follow. This did make things a lot easier, but the slow pace and the lack of results had started to get to everyone, apart from Obsidia who was as cheery as ever and seemed intent on keeping the flagging spirits of the group elevated. At one point she'd even given Stitches a hefty slap on the backside after he'd tried to reattach his left foot due to getting it trapped in a contorted tree root without realising and ending up flat on his face when he'd tried to take his next step.

Flug crashed through a particularly large and overgrown bush and stopped in his tracks.

"Dere dey is," he whispered.

"Who?" responded Ollie, straining to see over Flug's beam like shoulder.

"Da witches dat I see de uvver night when me wiv Ronnie."

He pointed a King Kong like finger in the appropriate direction as the others looked on with interest.

About one hundred and fifty yards away a building stood in a clearing. It was three storeys high and about three hundred feet long and, unless you were as close as they were now, you never would have had a clue that it was there. It was painted a khaki green colour and the few windows that it had seemed to reflect the moonlight perfectly, suggesting that they were mirrored to prevent anyone outside seeing what was going on inside. A large silver tank outside suggested that the building had a self-contained power supply for the generator that could be heard faintly humming somewhere in the compound. And there, at what was no doubt the entrance to the facility, was what Flug had been pointing at. Two men dressed in fatigues and carrying weapons were stationed on guard duty at the double steel doors. They were both tall and powerfully built, the uniforms stretched taut over their bulging physiques.

"They're bloody soldiers," gasped Stitches quietly. "What the hell are they doing here?"

Ollie motioned for them all to crouch down and get out of sight. "I'm not one hundred percent sure, but I'd stake my life on the fact

that their being here and the disappearances are connected," he said. "Really?"

"Well, what else. And I'm also guessing that's the reason Ronnie's gone as well. I bet he heard or saw something that he shouldn't have and got picked up to keep him quiet."

"If Ronnie in dere me get 'im," said Flug as he began to rise.

Obsidia placed a hand on his shoulder and coaxed him gently back down to the forest floor. "Not yet Flug, dear. The time will come though, don't you worry." She then addressed all three of them, loud enough to be heard but not by the guards. "Let's not get ahead of ourselves just because we've found something. I'm as keen as you to get in there and find our friends but we need to tread carefully. In the meantime I've got a suggestion."

"Go on," said Ollie.

"If you chaps stay here I'll take an illicit prowl around the perimeter. A reconnaissance mission if you like. Once I've established the layout I'll come back and we can formulate a plan of attack from there. Agreed?"

Ollie was a little reticent about Obsidia going off by herself, but then he remembered that out of all of them she was probably the most capable of taking care of herself. If any problems arose there was no doubt that she could handle them, whether in human form or otherwise.

"Okay, but please be extra careful," Ollie stated, forcefully. "We don't want to have to add your name to the list of the missing."

"Don't concern yourself, Ollie. I'll be fine trust me."

With that she scrambled away, keeping quiet and low to the ground.

Ten seconds later the forest had swallowed her up completely.

Stitches rolled back off of his haunches and down onto his backside.

He looked keenly at the building in front of them. "I hope she knows what she's doing," he mused.

"She'll be fine," said Ollie. "And it makes sense to be honest. And let's face it, it's better than us crashing through the trees like a herd of bison and giving ourselves away."

The zombie nodded in a conciliatory fashion. "I suppose so. Flug is loud enough to shatter a mountain."

"Exactly."

Hidden safely behind the bush they sat in silence with their backs to the compound for another ten minutes until the all-encompassing silence was disturbed by the barely audible rustle of the undergrowth off to the side.

"Hi, boys," whispered Obsidia as she re-joined them at their hiding place.

"That was quick," observed Stitches. "You must have flown round." "Silly boy," she said, smiling and touching him gently on the back of the hand. "It's easy when you know your way around." "So, what's next?" asked Ollie, eager to get on.

"That's simple. The area at the rear isn't very well guarded and there's another door round there. Luckily there's a gap in the fence just opposite, so if we sneak round and creep through I reckon Flug will be able to get us in."

"Mmmm. Sounds a bit dangerous to me,." said Ollie.

"Look, no one said that this was going to be a breeze and totally without risk, but I think it's justified weighed up against what we're trying to accomplish."

"Sounds good to me," said Stitches. "And anyway, who wants to live forever?"

"We don't have any choice in the matter, we're undead. And whilst I don't relish the prospect of nursing a severe injury for all eternity, thank you very much, I can see what you're saying," said Ollie.

Flug raised his hand into the air and looked forlornly at Ollie.

"How many times do I have to tell you," said Ollie, "you don't have to put your hand up every time you want to say something. We're not at nursery school, Flug."

"Just as well, he'd never be able to keep up with the workload," said Stitches.

"Shut up. Go on, Flug."

"Me miss Ronnie. Want him to come home." "I know."

"He my friend. He look after me when we go out. He buy me sweeties."

"*I bloody knew it,*" said Ollie. "I've told that invisible idiot a hundred times not to give him so much sugar. No wonder he gets hyper."

"Me like Chocolate Knobs." "That's. . . "

"And Fruit Bats." "Could you. . . "

"But Wizard's Sleeves are my favourites."

Ollie put a hand over Flug's mouth in a bid to keep him quiet. "Stop naming sweets, Flug. I get the idea."

Stitches also had a hand clasped over his mouth but it was his own and was there in an effort to contain the raucous laugh that was threatening to escape and expose them all. "Whoever heard of Wizards Sleeves?" he got out. "I bet they're on the shelf next to the Clowns Pock.. . "

"It's time to go, gentlemen," said Obsidia, bringing the confectionery based conversation to a conclusion.

It was only then, as he made to follow her into the trees, that Ol lie noticed that the two guards from the front of the building had vanished. He thought that maybe they'd gone for a break, but then thought that it didn't make sense for them both to go at the same time, leaving the entrance insecure. Perhaps that was encouraging. Maybe they didn't have the amount of personnel stationed here that he'd first feared. He stole his gaze away and followed on.

At Obsidia's insistence they stayed low to the ground, almost skirmishing their way through the undergrowth, whilst at the same time trying to maintain total silence, which wasn't easy when every movement meant a pine needle or a splinter of wood tried burying itself into the squidgier parts of their bodies (this is just a fact of life and, like many other little annoyances, completely unavoidable. Go to the sea side, you end up with sand in your pants for a week. Visit the leisure centre, and you'll stink of chlorine and be finding other people's dark, curly hairs in your clothes for ages. Fancy a spot of baking? Fine, but don't moan when flour falls out of your ear three weeks later. This unnatural attraction for bothersome little particles to end up on, in or about your body cannot be explained, rationalised or avoided, it just happens. That's why you never see animals at the beach, in the swimming pool or in the kitchen making a soufflé. Our furry friends are way too clever for that sort of nonsense. You won't ever find a gorilla rubbing a towel furiously between his legs because he's itching like mad after a paddle. They prefer a sauna anyway).

They'd spent about fifteen minutes skirting the periphery of the compound when Obsidia raised a hand, indicating that they should stop. She pointed to her left. When they'd all regrouped, she explained the next stage of the operation.

"We couldn't see it from over the other side, but there's a wire fence encircling the whole complex and lucky for us there just happens to be a handy, Flug sized hole in it."

Stitches nodded in agreement. "Thank God for that. I wouldn't fancy trying to squeeze him through. It'd be like trying to get toothpaste back into the tube."

Ollie stared at the holey fence. For some strange reason he was starting to feel a little uneasy. He couldn't quite put his finger on it, but it revolved around the fact that this all seemed a bit too simple. Not that there was anything particularly wrong with simple. He dealt with it day in and day out, but he could not shake the feeling that something just wasn't right. Nerves maybe, he concluded.

"I'll go through first," said Obsidia, and with that she clambered gracefully through the fence. Stitches was next, followed by Flug, with Ollie bringing up the rear. Once inside the perimeter, Obsidia laid out what they were going to do next.

"We need to make our way round to the other side. That's where the other entrance is. Follow me and stay low and quiet."

They crawled along behind her in a line, in the same order that they'd come through the fence. Stitches was more than happy with this arrangement as he had a lovely view of Obsidia's shapely hindquarters as she stalked silently along like a cat hunting its prey. Ollie, on the other hand, had the pleasure of following Flug, whose rear end wasn't quite as curvaceous as the aforementioned feline-like Obsidia. From Ollie's point of view it was more like being on a small dinghy with a container ship coming right at you.

They'd gone about fifty yards when, all of a sudden and to their great shock and surprise, Obsidia stood up and turned to face them. Instantly, the whole area was bathed in a brilliant white glow as a high powered search light was activated. Ollie was just about to ask what on earth she thought she was doing in some very colourful language, when he noticed that there were two other figures stood behind her. They were both tall and powerfully built, their uniforms stretched taut over their bulging physiques. The exact same description as...

"The guards from the front of the building," he said out loud.

Obsidia smiled, but now accompanying the overt and ever present sexuality, was a smug self-satisfaction.

"That's very observant of you, Ollie. You should do this for a living you know," she said.

Ollie's sense of unease was replaced by a quivering slab of fear as the pieces fell into place.

Obsidia's reconnaissance of the compound was, in hindsight, far too quick, and her comment upon her return about it being easy when you know your way around had totally passed him by. The handy gap in the fence should have been another undead giveaway. Sadly, and to his unending regret, his initial misgivings had proved correct, but there was absolutely nothing that he could do about it now. As one of the soldiers ordered the three of them to their feet, he realised that they had been betrayed.

Stitches had a forlorn look on his face as he spoke dejectedly to Obsidia.

"How could you do this? Not only to us but to your friends. Your family in fact. You've sold them out and you don't give a damn about what's happened to them."

Obsidia didn't look in the least bit bothered. In fact, she appeared rather pleased with herself and the situation that she'd created.

"Well, you know how it is," she said. "If someone dangles enough money in front of you it's hard to say no. Everybody has their price after all, and no one ever got rich by being true to their morals."

"What an absolute load of rubbish," responded Ollie, an edge to his voice. "None of us would ever do anything like that. Guaranteed."

Obsidia shrugged her shoulders. "If that's what you think then I'm happy for you, but seeing how upset you are let me assure you that I'll take plenty of time to consider what you've said and ponder the error of my ways. Obviously I'll be living a life of luxury in some sunny foreign country by then but the sentiment will be just as valid."

"Tell that to James and the others you've deceived. I just hope for your sake that Ronnie's okay," said Ollie.

The soldier who'd ordered them to their feet was now pointing his weapon directly at them. He spoke up.

"Ma'am, we need to get inside now."

"Of course," she responded. "After you, private."

"Alright, ladies," the man shouted, gesturing toward the building with the barrel of his gun. "Let's go. And no talking."

They made their way at gunpoint across the compound towards the mysterious building, Obsidia following up behind with the soldiers. The double doors opened up automatically as they approached and a rush of warm air from within enveloped them. Inside they could see a long corridor stretching away. It was starkly white, devoid of any hint of colour, and was lit by bare neon tubes that buzzed and popped intermittently. Where it led to, and what fate awaited them at its end they didn't know.

"Which way?" asked Stitches.

"Just keep going," replied Obsidia. "We'll let you know where to go." "I bet you will."

"Oh my. Are we a bit upset?" she asked, sarcastically.

"There's no *bit* about it," spat the zombie harshly as they carried on walking. "You've dumped on us good and proper from a great height. And I'm really ticked off with myself for falling for all your rubbish." "Now don't go blaming yourself. I wouldn't be able to resist me and I *am* me."

"Turn right here," one of the soldiers barked.

They were met by the expanse of another austere corridor, which, though slightly shorter than the first, was no less spartan. They hadn't even seen any other personnel yet.

One more passage took them to what appeared at first to be a dead end, but which turned out to have a door. It was only because the door was the same bland hue as its surroundings that it proved difficult to see from any distance.

The soldier who was closest joined them at the door and pressed a series of numbers on the keypad that was situated to its right. With a loud hiss it opened outwards, and before them a flight of stairs was revealed. At the top they went through another keypad locked door and as they exited this they found themselves in, surprise surprise, yet another corridor. This one, however, was a bit more welcoming, if such a thing could be said bearing in mind their current situation. The sides were a soft green and the lights in the ceiling were covered with shades. There was a soft carpet underfoot and even a few landscaped paintings were hanging on the walls. Some of the doors they walked past had glass panels in them, and inside they could see people working feverishly with equipment that none of them had a clue about.

About two thirds of the way down they were ordered to halt outside a rather fancy oak panelled door. Obsidia leaned forward and knocked lightly.

"Come on in," said a voice from the other side (the other side of the door not the other side of existence. Does that mean if there's a door on the other side and someone beckons you in, then they'd be 'on the other side of the door on the other side?' Or would it be simply 'on the other side of the other side?' And what if they're reading a pamphlet and they're looking at the wrong bit? They'd be 'on the other side of the other side and needing to look at the other side.' Wow, I didn't know I could be that interesting. You could say I've discovered a whole other side).

Obsidia opened the door and led them into Cowan's office. As she crossed the room and passed in front of the major she gave him a friendly wink, a gesture not missed by Ollie. She came to a stop by the window and indicated to the three captives that they should stand near the large desk. Then the two guards entered, the last one of whom closed the door.

Cowan stood up but stayed safely ensconced behind his wooden barricade.

"My oh my. What do we have here?" he sneered sarcastically. "Did you guys get lost on the way to a Halloween party, or is this the latest fashion trend in swinging Skullenia?"

"I wouldn't bang on too much about how we look if I were you, pal" Stitches spat back, a trace of anger in his voice. "At least we're not dressed like an out of date action figure topped off by a haircut that went out of fashion forty years ago."

Cowan smiled, but it didn't get any further than his lips. His eyes remained cold and impassive as he put the stub of one of his ever present cigars into his mouth and lit the end. He took a long draw and blew the smoke over the tip, making it glow like a mini sun.

"Don't go getting too feisty, my crumbling friend, or I'll be tempted to find out what the combustion rate is for a zombie. I reckon you'll go up quicker than Dorothy's scarecrow."

"Who Dorothy?" asked Flug.

"Never mind for now," said Ollie in a calm voice. "I'll explain later." Cowan chuckled ever so slightly. "I think you can rule out later to be honest. In fact, I wouldn't go making any plans for, let me see, the rest of your lives, such as they are." He pointed his cigar at Ollie. "You must be Ollie Splint. I gather that you're the leader of this merry band."

"I suppose you could say that yes."

"Excellent." Cowan approached the half vampire until he was within six inches of him. "I just wanted to let you know that you've done a great job. You've saved me a hell of a lot of trouble. There was me thinking that I'd have send out some of my men to bring you in, but you go and have the good grace to do it for me." Cowan leaned in so that their noses were almost touching. "I can't thank you enough."

Ollie stared at the man before him, bitter hatred and utter contempt evident on his usually placid face.

"I'd rather have the softer parts of my body shut in a vice than do anything for you. So what happens now, you egotistical maniac?" he rasped.

Cowan sat down again and placed his feet onto his desk, casting a knowing glance at Obsidia as he did so. She was still at the window but was now leaning against the sill to take the weight off her feet.

"What would you suggest, Miss?" he asked her.

"Well, I think it's relatively simple, major. Find out what they know, which judging by their efforts so far won't be too much, and find out who they've told. Then get rid of them."

Ollie, Stitches and even Flug gasped in unison as the gravity of their situation suddenly increased. Ollie was especially shocked by Obsidia's dismissive attitude toward them. He normally considered himself to be a fair judge of character, but she'd really pulled the cape over his eyes.

Unbeknownst to Ollie though, Cowan had already decided that the three of them would be returning back home with him and the Doctor, but he didn't need to let them know that just yet. Fear was a great provider and, if implemented in just the right way, could be extremely beneficial. He decided to play along with Obsidia's suggestion. He pointed a finger at her.

"Nice to know we're on the same wavelength. Now," he continued to Ollie and the others, "I don't want to come across like a bad guy here but, and let me paraphrase the young lady here, if you're willing to tell me what you know and more importantly who you've told, then I promise that none of you will suffer. And just so we're all clear, please don't be under the mistaken impression that we don't know how to deal with your kind."

Ollie remained silent for a moment. He needed time to think but that was time he didn't have, so he needed to stall this lunatic if they stood any chance of getting out of here.

"How about an exchange of information," he suggested. "You tell me what's been going on around here, just to satisfy my idle curiosity you understand, and I'll reciprocate with the details that you're after. As you've so eloquently hinted, you're going to get rid of us anyway."

It was only Stitches that noticed the intensity with which Ollie was staring at the Major. The half vampire's eyes were as wide as they could possibly be, and his pupils were dilated to the extent that they appeared to be totally black. He had a focussed look on his face but his features remained relaxed as he continued speaking. Stitches was astonished to note, after watching for a good few seconds, that Ollie wasn't even blinking.

'Bugger me,' thought the zombie, as he then cast his gaze at their captor. The soldier was a tad slack jawed and glassy eyed and had a faraway look on his face. 'He's only gone and bloody done it. He's actually put him under.'

This childlike sense of wonder and almost outright disbelief also crossed the portion of Ollie's mind that wasn't engaged in keeping the major under his control. Usually, anyone with a reasonable amount of intelligence and a hint of self-awareness would be impossible for him to ensnare with his rather meagre vampire mind trap but, for whatever reason, the man stood before him was now under his influence. Ollie continued to concentrate because the link was tenuous at best, and any lack of focus on his behalf would shatter it instantly.

To all intents and purposes the major looked perfectly normal. It was only when he started to reply to Ollie's offer of an information exchange that the soldiers on guard and Obsidia realised that something wasn't quite right. Flug, however, had returned to his usual happy state of ignorant bliss and wouldn't have realised that something wasn't quite right if someone was standing in front of him carrying a sign saying 'there's something not quite right'. Being right next to Ollie he'd succumbed to passive mesmerising, but that wasn't surprising when he had the mental agility of an arthritic mollusc.

The major spoke, his voice a grim monotone.

"We're conducting gene research. We needed the wolf specimens to harness the DNA that our scientists required."

"Major, are you sure about this?" asked Obsidia, a worried edge to her voice. Cowan ignored her completely and carried on, his eyes firmly fixed on Ollie's.

"Then we had a lucky break and captured the invisible guy so we got to work on him as well. The whole enterprise has proved incredibly successful."

The soldier who had previously barked sharp orders at Ollie and the others spoke up. "Sir, with respect, you can't tell these civilians the details of our operations here."

The private realised that something was going badly wrong. His superior was usually stoic and not the most talkative of people. He whispered to his colleague to hold his position near the door before walking towards Cowan. He slowed his approach the closer he got though, because he came to see the faraway look on the major's face and the strange way he looked at the vampire. As he got to within six feet, Cowan made a sudden downward motion with his right hand. In a flash it was back up and in it was his service revolver, the barrel of which was pointing directly between the eyes of his encroaching colleague. The private reacted instantaneously and brought his rifle to bear on the major.

"Sir, put your weapon down or I will be forced to fire."

Obsidia had a sudden realisation and admonished herself for not picking up on what was occurring sooner. She glanced at Ollie and at once recognised what was happening. In a flash she was standing next to Cowan where she delivered a powerful and meaty slap to his face.

"SNAP OUT OF IT," she screamed.

Cowan's head whipped violently to the right and his gun fell from his grasp and bounced off his foot. Such was the force of the blow a large wad of spittle flew from his mouth and a large red welt in the shape of Obsidia's hand appeared on his cheek. Cowan shook his head and gazed around the room, a look of puzzlement on his features.

"What in God's name do you think you're doing, private?" he shouted at the soldier who was still in front of him, weapon locked and loaded. "I once had a man shot for pointing a weapon at me."

"But, sir," he spluttered, "you were.. . "

Obsidia raised a hand to him, as much to stop him babbling as it was to stop the major executing him on the spot.

She was just about to open her mouth and explain to Cowan what had happened, when the window exploded inwards sending frame, smoke and lethally sharp shards of glass into the room. The occupants all hit the floor simultaneously as a searing blue light flared above their heads, blinding them all instantly. The ripples of the staggering sound waves pounded into their heads and each and every one of them lay stunned and disorientated, wondering what the hell had happened.

After what seemed like an interminable age, Ollie's senses started to recover. As he lay on the floor he could just make out a vague outline hovering above his face. It was head shaped and blurry, and all he could imagine it to be was, well, a blurry head.

"Oll... are... ight?" "Urrrgggh."

"Don't give... that... ap... ing wake up."

Although his vision was still swimming and his head felt like it'd been given a severe beating by Godzilla's big brother, he was starting to regain his faculties. Whoever the figure was tapped him gently on the cheek and snapped their fingers. At least he could hear that.

"Come on, my lovely. Are you back in the land of the unliving yet? You haven't got time for a nap."

"Mrs. Ladle?" groaned Ollie, gravel voiced and spitting up a grey ball of phlegm that contained at least fifty percent concrete. He blinked rapidly. His vision was finally clear and the dancing stars and circling bluebirds receded as everything came back into focus.

"The very same," she said sympathetically. "How are you, my dear? Feeling better?"

Ollie raised his head and lifted his shoulders from the floor, propping himself up on an elbow.

"I think so. What on earth happened? One minute we were all standing over there and the next, BOOM."

Mrs. Ladle told Ollie about her late night flight. After seeing the lights deep in the forest she'd decided to investigate. Keeping at a safe height she'd flown over the building, trying to work out what it was for, but she'd given up on that when she saw Ollie and the others being led inside at gun point. Realising that all was probably not well and that there were now no guards outside, she'd descended and swooped down low around the perimeter of the building until she saw them in the office.

"When I saw the three of you standing there with an armed guard behind you, I let off a rather powerful detonation spell. Quite effective, wouldn't you agree? Of course, I cast a web of protection around you, Stitches and Flug first, but I didn't realise the effect that Crumble's pills would have on my spell casting. They must have left some residue on my fingers and given me a bit of a boost. Actually, remind me to tell him not to touch them again. The next time he blows his nose his head's liable to go into orbit."

Ollie, now almost fully recovered, got to his feet, albeit a little unsteadily. He looked around the room, which he now could because the dense blue smoke had mostly dissipated. The office had been utterly decimated. There was blast damage everywhere and it seemed that virtually nothing had been left intact, including his nerves which were currently being worked on by a team of paramedics and a priest.

"How are the others?" he asked nervously.

"Don't go worrying yourself. Stitches is over there. He's fine, just a little dustier than normal, and Flug is sleeping it off in the corridor."

Ollie turned round and looked towards the door, or rather where the door had previously been. In its place was a perfectly shaped, Flug sized hole. '*Surely that only happens in Bugs Bunny cartoons,*' he thought randomly. He could hear Flug groaning quietly, which was a relief.

"Where are the soldiers?" he asked.

"Oh, I took care of them," replied Mrs. Ladle, with a wicked look on her face and an evil glint in her eye, which was in keeping with her status as a witch and therefore perfectly normal.

"I don't want to know, do I?" said Ollie. "Not if you ever want to eat again, no."

It was then that Ollie noticed a hand sticking out from underneath the remnants of the desk. He cautiously approached and knelt down next to the shattered piece of furniture.

"Oh no," he said to himself.

Carefully removing some of the larger pieces of wood, he uncovered the figure that was hidden below. Obsidia was on her back. Her eyes were closed, her lustrous hair was unruffled and there was barely a scratch on her beautiful face. If it wasn't for the fact that her chest wasn't moving up and down, anyone looking at her would have been forgiven for thinking that she was fast asleep.

He knew it was a futile gesture at best, but he reached out his hand and placed it gently against her neck. As he touched her flesh he noticed that it was still warm but he knew that was merely due to the time factor. There was no blood coursing through her veins any longer. Obsidia was dead.

As he moved his hand away her head fell to the right, giving away the cause of her demise. A sliver of wood no thicker than a pencil, either from the desk or more probably the window frame, had punctured the back of her neck and severed her spinal column. A thin trickle of blood had run along its length to the exposed end where it dripped off to form a small, coagulating pool on the carpet. Mixed in with the darkening red liquor he could see vague traces of a straw coloured liquid which he knew to be spinal fluid.

In spite of how he should be feeling, Ollie couldn't help but be upset at the sight of the rapidly cooling corpse before him. When all was said and done she was a human being and a supernatural entity, and one who had all the peculiarities and failings inherent with the species. No matter how despicable her behaviour Ollie mourned her loss and would grieve for her. No doubt the others would chastise him for being so soft, but he couldn't help it. Compassion of an extreme nature was something that he was blessed with, or cursed with depending on your point of view and general outlook on life. He felt the insistent prick of salty tears threaten to break free, but was shaken from his reverie when he heard movement behind him. He stood slowly and wiped his eyes with the sleeve of his coat before turning round.

"You okay, Ollie?" asked Stitches, patting himself down in an effort to rid himself of explosion related dust (not that he could tell the difference. He was dusty by nature so it was part of the territory as it were with one speck of airborne detritus looking very much like any other. It would have been easier to tell two chocolate buttons apart. Not that zombies are usually covered in chocolate buttons of course. They'd get all dusty).

"Yeah."

"What are you...? Oh." "I know."

Stitches gazed around the rest of the room, saying hello to Mrs. Ladle as he did so. He knew that Flug was alright and had already given himself a thorough check up. To his relief and utter amazement, all of his body parts were intact. He hadn't lost so much as a fingernail, which was completely mystifying because nine point nine times out of ten if he so much as sneezed something or another would go flying off at just under MACH 1 and disappear.

"What are we going to do now?" he asked Ollie in an attempt to distract his attention from the death and destruction that surrounded them.

"I really don't know," replied the half vampire, his voice subdued. "To be honest, I thought that we would have been overrun by now. That blast must have been heard for miles around."

"Well, Mrs. Ladle took care of the two out there," Stitches said, indicating the corridor.

"I took care of the rest," came a deep voice from a figure stepping through the doorway into the office.

"Ethan!" both Ollie and Stitches exclaimed at precisely the same time and with the same sense of relief.

"But how?" continued Ollie. "We thought you were staying back at the house."

Ethan strode to the centre of the room, nodding politely to Mrs. Ladle as he did so.

"I was going to," he explained, "but I got a sense that I would be better off out here with you chaps rather than hanging around back at the house no use as man nor beast. And I need to know what's happened to Isobel. I got here just as the guards were leading you inside."

Ollie turned towards the body sprawled on the floor behind him and was about to explain, but was cut off by Ethan before a word could pass from his lips.

"You don't have to say a word, Ollie. I saw what happened out there. I've got a good idea what she did, and as much as it pains me to say it, she got what she deserved. Even if she'd lived, no member of a pack could do what she's done and expect to go unpunished. At least it was quick. I know of at least a couple of pack mates that would have wanted her to suffer rather more than she did."

"So what did you get up to out there, my dear?" Mrs. Ladle asked, indicating the rest of the building with a hand that already contained a lit cigarette. She had a pretty good idea what he'd gotten up to but she was a sucker for a few gory details.

Ethan ran his fingers through his thick, luxuriant hair.

"When the explosion went off soldiers came running from all over the place. I thought I might have taken on too much to be honest but they panicked, which surprised me as this seems like such a professional set up. I was still at the fence then so I, how shall I put it, slipped into something more comfortable and took care of them."

"All of them?" asked Ollie.

Ethan nodded his head. "Every one. They were running around like headless chickens so it wasn't hard to pick them off one by one. None of them are running around anymore though, and a lot of them are now rather more headless in the literal sense."

He grinned, showing a set of brilliantly white teeth which Ollie could have sworn had a vague pinkish tint to them.

At that point the assembled company all turned towards the door after hearing a loud THUNK.

"Hey, big stuff, how are you feeling?" asked Stitches.

Flug stomped into the office, a faraway look on his face. Apart from a thin trickle of dark fluid dripping from his left ear and a slight bend in his bolt, he appeared to be okay.

"Me fine, fanks," he replied. "Head hurts a bit dough".

Stitches held a hand up in front of his large friend and extended three digits.

"How many fingers can you see, Flug mate?" "Uh, blue."

"He's fine."

"Where da smoky man?" Flug enquired. "The what?" asked Ollie.

"Da smoky man," repeated Flug. "Da man wiv da smelly cigar."

Ollie and Stitches looked around the office and then looked at each other, the worried expression on their faces mirroring one another's perfectly.

"Damn it," Ollie exclaimed. "In all the turmoil I totally forgot about him. How many soldiers did you say you took care of Mrs..Ladle?"

"Just the two my dear. They were the only ones I could see as I approached the window."

"Okay, mate," Stitches said in exasperation, "we have a problem. He ain't here."

"Who exactly are we talking about?" asked Ethan.

"The guy who was running this whole operation," said Ollie. "He was in here when Mrs. Ladle showed up. Don't ask me how but he's managed to escape."

Ethan thought for a moment. "Maybe he ran outside with the others. If he did the chances are that I dealt with him. What did he look like?"

Ollie described Cowan to Ethan.

"Doesn't ring any bells," replied the lycan. "Sounds like he would have stood out."

"Can you remember individuals when you're in your other form then?" asked Stitches.

"Usually," said Ethan, staring out of the window. "We're not the simple minded killing machines that most people take us for. Believe it or not there is a certain remnant of humanity still intact after we've transformed. We're always aware on a subliminal level of what we're doing and who we're doing it to. It's like a curse within a curse I suppose."

"We're going to have to find him," observed Ollie. "We can't let him get away. If he gets back to wherever it is he came from, there's nothing to stop him from starting all over again, only next time he'll have more weapons and soldiers than any of us can hope to deal with."

"What are we going to do?" asked Stitches.

Ollie shrugged his shoulders in resignation. "The only thing we can do. Find him. We'll start with the facility and if that proves negative, move out into the woods. Ethan, if you can go with Mrs. Ladle and start on the floor above we'll take this one and then move downstairs."

"No problem," said Ethan, gesturing to the witch to follow him. "See you soon. Good luck and be careful." They left.

"Right, let's do it," said Ollie, a grim determination evident in his voice.

The search began.

———

When the blast came through the window Cowan was as surprised and as unprepared for it as everybody else in the room had been. Luckily though the angle of the discharge hadn't been directly at him, but it had still been of sufficient force to knock him clean off his feet and send him clattering into the wall like a rag doll. Amazingly, he hadn't lost consciousness in spite of his head connecting sharply with the floor when he landed in a crumpled heap. Then, with whatever motives that drive certain people on, call it instinct, call it training, he was instantly on his feet and assessing the situation. Without even thinking he used the acrid, choking blue smoke to his advantage. Whoever or whatever had caused the explosion would need to give it time for the smoke to clear, and that was time that he could use. Knowing the office layout he negotiated his way to the door and even though he could barely see his hands in front of his face, within seconds he was out and into the corridor. He wasn't surprised to note that some of the smog had travelled this far.

Fragments of wood and glass crunched under his boots as he

walked on. What was that? There, slumped against the wall opposite. As he approached and the smoke began to clear he saw that it was the big dumb one. He seemed to be alive but out cold. For a moment Cowan contemplated putting a bullet through that big ugly head, but it was only a fleeting consideration. He couldn't afford the time that it would take, or the noise that it would cause, notwithstanding the fact that his trusty side-arm seemed to be missing. Dismissing the eclectic sack of flesh he turned right. About twenty five feet away was something else.

Heaped in a mound was what appeared to be a steaming pile of mincemeat, the only difference being was that he was sure that he could see scraps of uniform amongst the gobbets of seared flesh. Approaching cautiously he got to within a yard or so when his eyes confirmed what he'd initially suspected. Whoever this had been, and he strongly believed it to be the two privates who'd been guarding the prisoners, looked like they had been through an industrial pulping machine. The pieces of cloth were indeed uniform and intermingled with the blood, bone and shredded tissue were hunks of what had been standard US Army issue combat boots. He shook his head. Cowan had been in the military for most of his adult life and during that time he'd seen and, on many occasions, committed acts of violence, but this was something different. For the first time the sight of mangled human bodies and disinterred gore made him wretch. He leaned against the wall, bracing himself with both hands and hung his head as he vomited heavily. When he was done he took a few deep breaths and arched his back to stretch his cramping stomach muscles, all the while being careful not to look again at the carnage on the floor.

Moving on, he made his way to the end of the corridor where he stopped, listening carefully for any hints that might give away what was going on. Yes. There it was. Like a faint shout from a long way off came the shrill call of raised voices and the staccato beat of automatic weapon fire. He opened the door and cautiously descended the stairs to the passageway below. It was deserted, the only clue that anyone had been there recently, a couple of laboratory doors that were open. One of them had been thrust aside with such force that the bottom hinge had detached, leaving the door hanging at an odd angle. The lab inside didn't look too disturbed, just a few shattered test tubes on the floor and a spilled cup of coffee at a work station. Someone had left in a hurry though, that much was clear. He carried on turning left then right until he reached the passageway that led to the double entrance doors. In each one was a twelve inch square pane of reinforced glass. He stuck close to the wall and approached. As he did the noise from outside became louder and louder, the sounds becoming more distinct. Men were shouting at the tops of their voices and Cowan could detect the fear and panic inherent in their exclamations. Heavy footfalls pounded into the ground in quick succession, as if people were running around, but whether they were chasing something or being chased he couldn't be sure. Then another noise assailed his ears and even though he couldn't identify it, it was enough to freeze the breath in his lungs and turn his blood to ice water. It started off as a deep, guttural rumble that was so low that it was almost beyond the range of human hearing, before rising to a ferocious roar that forced him to clamp his hands to the sides of his head because it was so piercing. Whatever the hell had made that noise he didn't have a clue, but it sounded big and extremely angry.

Once at the entrance he ever so slowly leaned his head so that his right eye could look out into the compound beyond.

The footfalls were as he'd expected. His soldiers were charging around, weapons raised and firing brief bursts every few seconds. The shots didn't seem to be aimed at any one point in particular so there were either multiple targets out there or one incredibly fast one. He could see further activities in the tree line beyond the perimeter fence as other soldiers seemed to be firing random shots into the dark woodland beyond. As he was trying to make sense of the chaos before him, he noticed Lieutenant Travis exit from the forest boundary. He was running wildly towards the main gate, every now and again turning the top half of his body around thus enabling him to fire off a few well intentioned, but terribly inaccurate rounds at whatever was behind him. Try as he might, Cowan could not see far enough into the trees to determine what had gotten Travis so spooked. Even the bright light shining into the compound wouldn't stretch that far. Just then, about fifteen yards behind the fleeing Lieutenant, the trees parted as a large form exploded through them and he got his answer. In an instant it had closed the gap and as it leapt and flew through the air, Cowan realised what it was.

Not only was it a werewolf, a creature that he'd become extremely familiar with during the recent past, but it was the biggest one that he'd ever seen. It must have easily weighed in at over two hundred kilos and with barely an ounce of fat on its body, it was one of the most formidable things that he could ever recall seeing. The massive beast slammed into Travis' back, knocking him to the ground and sending up a dust storm of dried mud and leaves and spilling the terrified soldiers' weapon from his grasp. As Travis struck dirt, he rolled over onto his back and tried to scrabble away but it was no use. The wolf was on the struggling marine in a flash, pinning him down by the shoulders with its huge front paws before opening its cavernous jaws and biting into Travis' neck and shoulder. Blood gushed into the air, arcing majestically away from the entwined combatants, some of it splashing down and soaking into the ground whilst still more flowed onto the wolfs muzzle, making its fur glisten in the night. Travis' body twitched spasmodically a couple of times before it went still forever and the wolf bounded from him, already focussed on another target.

Cowan let out the breath that he'd been holding for the duration of the attack on Travis. He'd only stopped breathing for just a few seconds, but the sudden expulsion of air caused him to hyperventilate, his lungs eagerly sucking in oxygen as if he was in the midst of a marathon. Quickly forcing himself to calm down he realised that it was no surprise that none of his personnel had been able to take the beast out. It was lightning fast and moved with a grace and fluidity that belied its tremendous bulk.

It was only now, when he looked carefully, that he noticed the other corpses scattered around the clearing. He could see at least ten, all of them in various states of disarray. A couple had been decapitated whilst others were missing limbs or had deep, jagged lacerations over their exposed torsos. Wide eyed and in danger of going completely over the edge, the major realised that he could no longer see the murderous beast, but then from the left a new figure entered his field of vision. A big, heavily muscled man who was doing up the buttons of a shirt as he surveyed the carnage that surrounded him. Cowan now understood. The beast had reverted to human form and it was he who

Cowan was now staring at. It was at this point that the major was in two minds about what course of action he should take next. He figured escape was probably the best option. He could wait until the attacker outside had finished gloating over the remnants of his bestial rampage and went away, and then find a way out of here, after which he would someday return and with enough firepower to take out this whole god forsaken town and its unholy inhabitants. Or, he could consolidate his position here and stand and fight right now. The second option wasn't the most ideal tactically, considering what he was faced with, but it was the best option emotionally. Nothing would give him greater pleasure than to go Rambo on this lot and destroy them all.

Cowan was still watching out of the small window in the door when his mind was incontrovertibly made up for him. The big man outside had finished perusing his handiwork and was now walking directly towards the door that the major was standing behind. For the first time in his life, the tough, grizzled and battle hardened veteran panicked. A frigid shiver ran down his spine that felt like icy talons being scraped along his very marrow. He tried to swallow but his mouth was too dry, which was in direct opposition to the palms of his hands, which were slippery with sweat. His heart was pounding like a blacksmith's hammer on an anvil, but despite all this his vision remained steady. The man was now within fifty feet of him and striding purposefully. He would be here in just a few seconds. Cowan turned and ran as fast as he could, back down the corridor and away from any chance of escape. At last he came to another door on his right. He forced it open, dashed inside, made sure it was closed properly and ran to the back of the room taking refuge behind a shelving unit in a corner.

"Major?" a timid, whispered voice from behind him said.

Cowan slowly turned his head. There was a steel cabinet roughly three feet high and five feet across. It was highly polished and in its mirrored surface, Cowan could see his own reflected face. The two doors of the cabinet looked to be shut but the one on the right hand side was open about an inch. Peering at it Cowan could see an eye blinking furiously but staring right at him.

"Is that you, major?"

"Meredith?"

The door slid wide open, revealing Dr Meredith who spilled out onto the floor in an untidy heap.

"Major, am I glad to... "

Cowan hushed him with a teacher-like finger to his lips. He glanced back at the door just in time to see the lycanthrope walk past. Thankfully, he didn't stop. Cowan gazed at the door for a good few seconds before he remembered his fellow hider behind him.

"What are we going to do?" Meredith asked, sounding like a frightened child. "What happened out there?"

Cowan didn't answer. His thoughts were elsewhere. He'd realised that in his eagerness to hide from the marauding monster, he'd stumbled into Meredith's lab. A plan was starting to form in his overwrought mind. Where it had come from he didn't know, but if he'd stopped to examine it further he would have realised that it was born out of sheer desperation and a ferocious willingness to survive no matter how high the odds stacked against him were. Above all else of course was revenge, and even though he wasn't capable of rationalising it, the overriding emotion that had taken control of him was the urge to get back at those who had destroyed his chances of completing his mission. The pieces fell into place easily.

Ignoring the whining question from Meredith, Cowan got to his feet and scanned the lab. He knew that he was risking exposure, but he didn't care. His course, his *destiny*, was fixed and set. To his right was a refrigeration unit where he knew that all of the collected samples were stored. Despite the doctors' pleas for him to get out of sight, Cowan walked towards it and slid the door open.

A rush of frigid air escaped. It surrounded him and caused him to gasp in surprise but he ignored the uncomfortable sensation. Inside, there was only one object. It was a hexagonal rack, at each point of which was a frosted steel tube. He grasped it and pulled it closer to him. Each tube had a clasped lid, three of which were open and three of which were secure, and it was these that he was interested in. He popped the lids of the locked tubes and removed the items from within.

The phials were all labelled differently. The first had a capital L on it, the second a capital I and the third a capital C, and it was this third tube that he wanted. The C stood for Combination. It was a mixture of the werewolf and the invisibility genes, a little side project that he'd concocted.

After discarding the two that he didn't require, Cowan took a plunger and attached it to the tube. He stared at the assembled syringe as if it were some ancient relic to be worshipped and revered by all those who laid eyes on it, the keeper of a clandestine secret who's cloistered potency could be the resolution to the dilemma that he found himself in. The golden liquid inside glistened and sparkled like some kind of viscous Christmas decoration, belying the terrible nature of its contents and the awful cost of getting it to this stage. He glanced around to be sure that Meredith wasn't going to interrupt him and once sure that he wouldn't, dismissed him and turned back.

His hand was trembling as if he were freezing cold and he swallowed audibly as the small object nestled against his skin. It felt warm against his palm, but whether this was due to the latent heat of the newly exposed contents or because of his nervous excitement, he wasn't sure. Then, realising that he'd gotten ahead of himself he replaced the syringe on the shelf and took off his dress tunic before rolling up a shirt sleeve. Then, without further hesitation, he exposed the silver point of the needle and plunged it into his arm.

At first, a warm glow seemed to travel along the limb, both towards his hand and upwards towards his shoulder. It felt as if he'd been lying on it for a few minutes and it was now coming back to life. It wasn't an unpleasant sensation, just a little disconcerting, like having a slightly drunken appendage. He withdrew the needle and paused for a few moments with the glistening tip a few inches from his flesh before throwing it to the floor.

'It doesn't seem to be going too badly,' he thought to himself as a fiery, fuzzy sensation spread throughout his entire system. It wasn't a feeling he'd want to experience on a regular basis, but it wasn't altogether objectionable. It was as if someone had turned his thermostat up a couple of degrees. At that point Cowan noticed that his heart rate was rising rapidly. Despite approaching middle age he was a reasonably fit man and was proud of the fact that for a guy of his years he could boast the metabolism of a much younger person, but this new feeling was pushing him to his physical limits extremely quickly. Beads of sweat popped out on his forehead, which now felt cold and clammy to his touch as he wiped them away. His respiration also increased, forcing him to gasp for air in great, big, rattling gulps. Then his vision blurred and an almost euphoric dizziness overcame him as the laboratory and everything in it swam in and out of focus. Then he saw things from a different perspective, almost from a great distance as if he was having an out of body experience. At that precise moment he could have sworn that he was floating above his own head and observing what was happening to his corporeal form which seemed still and redundant. Had he gone into shock? Passed out? Or maybe he'd died and was now some wandering revenant gazing down upon the now empty shell that was his body?

Such morbid thoughts were suddenly banished, however, as in an instant he was back in his own head. Perspiration was now flooding from every pore of his body and the muscle spasms that had recently started were increasing in ferocity and frequency. His hands rose unconsciously and began to tear the remainder of his uniform off, trying to be rid of the now seemingly rough material that was irritating his skin to the extent that it gave him the impression that he was suffering an extreme allergic reaction. It felt like fire breathing insects were burrowing through his flesh and gnawing away at his bones, attempting to gain access to the succulent marrow within. He clawed and dug at his skin until tiny orbs of blood broke the surface. It was whilst scratching his right forearm, eyes wide in fascination and horror, and teeth clenched tightly together with lips curled back in a fierce grimace of pain and wonder, that he noticed the hairs. Thick, black strands of it were erupting over every inch of his body. By now he'd divested himself of every item of clothing, and as he looked down he hollered in abject amazement as the last remnants of his white skin were lost underneath a mat of dark, lustrous fur.

The half beast, half man dropped to the floor, ending up on all fours. It glanced to its left and saw its reflection in the glass of the refrigeration unit. In spite of the changes there was just enough of Cowan left for it to recognise itself, but that last remnant of humanity was quickly fading as it was rapidly usurped by the emerging monster from within. The searing heat in its system had now abated, and as it continued to stare, its body was overtaken by a new sensation. A surge of lactic acid coursed through its innards and the most severe case of the cramps that it had ever experienced assailed every muscle in its body at the same time. The beast had now ceased to watch itself as new pain racked it, as every fibre and sinew went into overdrive as if a massive dose of adrenalin had been pumped directly into its bloodstream. It seemed as if every cell in its body had suddenly become hyperactive, behaving in a way that nature had definitely not intended. It felt as if a million burrowing, stinging ants were biting their way out from within. The beasts' skin rippled and bubbled like grilled cheese and then slowly faded away as the invisibility gene took effect.

With the transformation from man to monster finally complete it let out a low, ominous growl. Major Buddy 'Ironheart' Cowan was no more.

———

Ollie, Stitches and Flug left the office to begin the search but paused in the corridor about fifteen feet from the gross pile of former marines. "Those guys need to pull themselves together," said Stitches. "Look, they haven't even polished their boots."

"Nice," responded Ollie who found himself staring at the grisly mess whilst trying not to look at the grisly mess even though his gaze was inexplicably drawn towards the grisly mess that he was desperately trying not to stare at. "Right, we need to find this chap as soon as possible but I suspect it's not going to be easy. He's going to be rather annoyed, probably in hiding and no doubt armed so I suggest we get on."

"Should we split up or stay together?" asked the zombie, glancing up and down the passageway. "There's quite a lot of rooms."

"Let's stick together. This is a serious situation not an episode of Scooby Doo," said Ollie.

"Shame. This would be over a lot sooner if we just found a caretaker hiding in an abandoned fun fair and pulled his mask off."

"I suppose so."

"I never trusted that Freddie anyway. How come he always got to go off with the two girls? I bet his memoirs would be a good read. I reckon that Velma was a right. . . "

"Can we please get back on track," snapped Ollie, getting ever so slightly miffed.

The three of them then methodically searched every room on the first floor. There was a kitchen area, various offices and storage cupboards and some sleeping quarters, in which Flug found some very exotic magazines that would take a hell of a lot of explaining. Of the major, however, there was no trace.

"Okay, next floor," directed Ollie.

The ground floor seemed to have just as many rooms as the one above, but the majority of these seemed to be dedicated to research. Nearly every one looked like the set of a science fiction film and if it wasn't for Cowan's beguiled confession none of them would have had a clue what any of the equipment was used for.

As they rounded the last corner and entered the first corridor, Flug spoke up and pointed.

"Door moving."

Ollie and Stitches gazed towards the double entrance doors. Both were indeed swinging back and forth about six inches, as if someone had just passed through them.

"I think our friendly host has left the party early," speculated Stitches. "How rude."

"It certainly seems that way," agreed Ollie. "Let's go see."

Neither Ollie nor Stitches could decide who was the most courageous out of the two of them so by mutual agreement Flug went first. As was the norm in situations such as these, Flug didn't have a clue what was going on (not that the situation in and of itself made much of a difference of course. Whatever was happening around him Flug always responded with an air of distracted indifference that one could easily mistake for rudeness when, in fact, his mumbling and drooling simply meant that he was flummoxed yet again. It wouldn't matter if the destruction of the earth was imminent due to an approaching asteroid or the toilet seat had been left up he'd always act the same. Still, he was consistent if nothing else. On a side note, the two examples given above aren't necessarily mutually exclusive. If I leave the toilet seat up my good lady wife acts as if the worlds coming to an end so there you go, everything ties up nicely).

Even though Ollie had explained it to him several times, he was still as confused as a group of German tourists told that they have to queue, and that they didn't, in fact, own the whole of Europe and every sun bed therein. And so, finally fed up with trying to get his point across, Ollie pointed at the door and said, "Out you go, Flug."

He barged through the doors and stomped into the compound, his size eighteen feet loudly announcing their presence to anyone or anything within a hundred meter radius, including down.

"That was stealthy," complained Stitches.

"Flug, mate," implored Ollie, "try and be a bit quieter, please."
"Sorry, Ollie"

The three of them stopped about five feet from the doors. Now that Flug had ceased doing his impression of a herd of angry elephant's tap dancing in lead boots on a slate floor, it was surprising how peaceful and still the night was. There was no wind at all and not a thing was stirring, except that is for Ollie's delicate stomach, which was currently performing a robustly intricate gymnastic routine at the sight of the all the soldiers' bodies littering the compound.

"Wow!" Stitches exclaimed, rubbing a hand across his eyes. "Ethan wasn't kidding when he said he took care of business out here. I haven't seen anything like this since the Great Lawnmower Riots of 1886."

Ollie closed his eyes for a moment in an effort to blank the grisly scene before him, but there are some things that you just can't unsee. "Why don't we save the history lesson for another time. It's pretty grim though, isn't it?" he said.

As he mulled things through he put his hands into his pockets, where his right one bumped into something. He retrieved the remote control that he'd completely forgotten about and flicked it on.

"Wassat?" asked Stitches.

"It's the location device that Crumble gave me. I completely forgot I had it. Maybe it'll help us find Cowan. It's made from an old TV controller but it does work."

"Oooo, TV. Can we watch Herman the Naughty Ghost?" asked Flug, hopefully.

"Not now," rasped Ollie. "Okay then, we'll scan the compound whilst we're moving that way," he pointed towards the forest. "As soon as this thing lights up, at least we'll know that we've found something. Hopefully it'll be our target."

"Makes sense. So what'll we do if we do find him?" said Stitches.

"We can decide on that at the time, but if this does light up at least it'll give us a few moments to figure something out," said Ollie as he stared into the woods. "Although to be honest I'm leaning towards all out attack even if he's wearing pyjamas, tartan booties and carrying a hot water bottle. Right, let's sweep the whole place. Everybody, twenty feet apart and slowly forward."

Flug moved next to Ollie and tapped him on the shoulder. "Ollie."

"What now, Flug?"

"Me can't do twenty feet apart. Me only got dis one and dis one," he said, helpfully lifting up his legs one at a time.

"God Almighty. Go and stand over there and when we move, you follow. Okay?"

"Okay."

When they were finally in place, and with Flug no longer worrying about his apparent lack of limbs, Ollie held the location device out in front of him and walked forward flanked by his colleagues, Stitches to his left and Flug to his right. There was no sound except for the rustle of their feet and the swish of their clothing.

Then the red light flickered hesitantly to life. "Hold it," said Ollie.

"You got something?" replied Stitches, nervously casting glances around the area.

"Maybe. Hang on a sec."

The glow became stronger and more insistent until it stayed on, continuously indicating that something had to be up ahead. Either that or Crumble had stuffed it up completely and the unit was telling Ollie that he was now tuning in to Herman the Naughty Ghost after all. The thing that perplexed him though, was the fact that the light was getting brighter. 'We're not moving,' he thought, 'so the only way that it can be is if...'

He was just about to shout a warning to his companions when all three of them turned at the sound of a loud crash behind them.

A small man in a blood splattered lab coat staggered out of the building. He was as pale as a corpse and was holding his right arm close to his body, probably in an effort to stop it dangling uselessly as he ran. Judging by the slope of his shoulder it was badly dislocated. Blood dripped from his elbow and fell to the ground.

"It's Cowan," he shouted breathlessly, as if the effort was draining the last reserves of the little energy that he had left. "He's injected the sample. He's transformed *and* he's invisible."

"RUN!" Ollie bellowed as loud as he possibly could. Then, for whatever reason, his vampire senses kicked in and he took a step to his left. As he did this he felt a rush of air pass by him and felt something brush his right elbow. It was like standing at the side of the road and having a Land Rover drive past you at sixty miles an hour. The only difference was that Land Rovers don't snarl and leave drool on the floor.

Ollie took off towards the trees but managed a quick look back, just in time to see the man in the lab coat being tossed into the air by the invisible force. He jerked and danced above the ground as if he were performing some sort of grotesque ballet or had fallen into the hands of a sadistic cosmic puppeteer. As the blood flew and the man screamed his last, Ollie turned away and concentrated on the forest that seemed oh so far away.

It was now that he was wishing that the box set of fitness DVDs that he'd been given for his birthday a few years back had been put to their intended use, and not employed as makeshift frisbees, as is the case with all such items designed to improve one's health and well being (although it wouldn't be a good idea to go chucking a rowing machine into the air and expecting your friend to catch it. Try explaining that at the accident and emergency department. It's not that they wouldn't believe it, there just won't be anyone there to tell).

Arms pumping and quadriceps straining for all their worth, Ollie sped towards the forest, and even though he was as breathless as an asthmatic at altitude and panicking like a Grand Wizard on holiday in Harlem, his mind suddenly cleared and he had a moment of clarity.

He pictured himself becoming as light as a feather, able to defy the laws of gravity and the confines of an earthly existence as he soared up into the black night sky. He imagined his clothes getting looser and looser and falling away from his body as he became free of terra firma and gained altitude.

The remarkable thing about Ollie's transformation to bat, apart from it being remarkable that he'd actually managed it at all, was the self-awareness that he retained. Unlike his shape shifting brethren, Ollie's personality remained completely intact so that he was wonderfully cognisant of what he'd achieved.

He gained altitude quickly, his leather wings pushing down on the air as he banked to the right and headed back towards the building. The stranger in the now not so white lab coat lay in a tangled heap not far from the door. Scanning the area now with his heightened batlike senses, he could see Flug once again slumped against a wall. He was dead to the world, but more worrying from Ollie's point of view was the slowly growing pool of blood that was forming on the ground around him as it dripped from the stump of his right leg, which had been ravaged and severed mid-thigh. Ollie grieved for his friend but there was little he could do about it right now, because even with his enhanced sight and hearing he had no idea where the invisible monster was. Luckily though, Stitches seemed to have made something of a getaway. He was hiding behind a large clump of undergrowth about twenty feet into the woods. He must have vaulted over the fence. He was reasonably well concealed but it wouldn't be long before he was certain to be discovered.

Even though Ollie had the advantage of height, he was no match for a rampaging creature charging around the place at high speed. And he was sure that its sense of smell would be far superior to his enhanced faculties.

Ollie flew around, racking his brains trying to come up with a plan that didn't involve flying to the top of the nearest tree, folding his wings around himself and closing his eyes whilst thinking nice thoughts. Anything would do because he had the feeling that he was rapidly running out of time, and any options that he did have were steadily becoming less and less feasible. Banking left and dropping a few feet, he once again traversed the area where he'd started to flee the invisible spectre.

Suddenly, off to his right, he heard a snuffling grunt and saw a puff of earth pop into the air. Looking more closely now, he saw a dent appear in the ground, which was at once flanked at its head by four smaller punctures. Ollie arced round to get a better view when it struck him what the beast was doing. It was tracking wildly about, searching for a scent because it had lost Stitches' trail. The zombie had no functioning metabolism, so the wolf had nothing tangible to lock on to.

As he continued to circumnavigate what he guessed was the wolf's current position, he saw the paw impressions advance towards his discarded clothes, dumped during his own shape shifting episode. The unseen snout prodded at the cloth, nudging it gently, trying to pick up a scent which it inevitably would, but it would be the wrong one. His black coat was flicked over and he noticed something long and yellow fall from out of a pocket. It rolled a few inches then came to rest after rocking back and forth for a moment. In a flash Ollie swooped down, his bat legs outstretched and his claws extended. Diving in, he lost the wolf's position momentarily and, as he targeted the item, his right wing brushed its nose which knocked him off balance temporarily, giving the beast the opportunity to match the scent on the clothes to his own. He felt the whoosh of air as, what he assumed to be a giant paw took a swing at him. Dodging, he came in for one final pass and grabbed the tube and headed upwards once more. As he climbed he chanced a glance down, and even though he couldn't see it he could hear a grunt of effort, quickly followed by a thud as the wolf landed after jumping up at him.

Flying in a tight circle to keep its interest on him, Ollie craned his neck forward and brought his legs up. Opening his mouth he exposed his fangs and bit into the cardboard and ripped it open. He pulled it back as far as it would go until with a final twist, the package burst open and a shower of fine but grainy white particles exploded into the atmosphere before quickly dropping onto the creature below, covering it in a fine, gossamer dust that outlined its head and shoulders.

Another loud crash emanated from the area of the building. Ollie turned and saw Ethan step into the compound. He also noticed the blank look on his face as he scanned the whole area, confused because he couldn't find them.

"Ollie! Stitches! Where are you?" shouted Ethan, his left hand framing his mouth.

Ollie knew that Ethan's voice would distract the wolf and refocus its attention on what it would see as a brand new target. He went to call out but then realised the one limitation of being a bat, wolf or any other shape-shifted creature for that matter. He couldn't warn him, his vocal chords were useless to him now. It appeared that all he was going to be able to do was watch as Ethan was ripped to pieces.

"ETHAN," came a very loud voice from the other side of the compound. "IT'S COVERED IN SHERBET AND IT'S COMING RIGHT AT YOU."

Ethan looked away from the hobbling Stitches after getting the message loud and clear. He took a firm stance and concentrated on what he'd been warned about, as it was in front of him and closing in fast. As if in slow motion the shape coalesced, the white outline becoming more distinct the closer the invisible mass came, until finally he could hear its footfalls pounding into the ground as it thundered towards him like an express train.

"LOOK OUT," screamed Stitches, his voice filled with terror and anguish.

It seemed as if Ethan was too late, but at the very last moment he bent his knees, raised his arms and pulled the trigger of the weapon that was clasped in his hands.

BANG. BANG. BANG. BANG. BANG.

An ear splitting howl of pain was followed by a loud smack as a large mass pounded into the ground and skidded to a stop. Streams of blood oozed, as if from nowhere, as they escaped from the confines of invisibility and pooled on the floor.

Ethan approached the area where the werewolf had come to rest. He could hear a faint hissing noise as clumps of sherbet fell into the congealed blood and fizzed.

"Is it dead?" asked Stitches limping towards him, his right leg trailing behind. He'd caught his foot on the top of the wire fence as he scrambled over it, and in the process had badly dislocated his ankle. It would take more than a needle and thread to put this injury right.

"I'm not sure," replied Ethan, prodding what he assumed was an arm with the toe of his boot.

"Well, I don't care if it is, because I'm going to kill it anyway," said the zombie.

At that point Ollie joined the group. He'd checked on Flug and found to his unending relief and joy that the giant reanimate was still alive. Thankfully, Flug's slow metabolism, which was similar to that of a teapot, meant that it would probably take a week for him to bleed out. Ollie had torn a strip from his coat and bound the wound. He was also grateful that Stitches' timely arrival had offered him the opportunity to get himself together and get dressed unseen.

"That was close," he said to Ethan. "I thought that monstrosity was on you for sure."

"Nah," replied Ethan, amazingly cool under the circumstances. "I had it all under control. Nice work with the sherbet by the way. I wouldn't have thought of that."

"Just one thing, Ollie" observed Stitches, trying to maintain his balance. "The next time you transform, try to leave your clothes somewhere a bit more discrete. I don't want to see that again."

Ollie smiled and shook his head. "Fair enough."

"Still, it's not every day you get to see a naked vampire in the middle of a forest. Where did you get those boxer shorts by the way? I just hope for your sake that any future Mrs. Splint has got a sense of humour."

"Thanks awfully," said Ollie. "And a magnifying glass."

Ollie's exuberant two worded retort was cut off by a groan from the floor as a shimmering light surrounded the reappearing form of Cowan, naked and covered in blood and now back to human form.

"So, not quite dead yet," sneered Ethan. He grabbed the marine under the arms and dragged him to the building where he propped him up against the wall. A torrent of sorrow flooded through him as he remembered Isobel.

He'd loved his sister more than anything else in the world, and finding her body laid out on a slab inside the building had ripped his heart from his chest. It was a good thing for Obsidia that she'd been killed before Ethan had found Isobel.

Summoning all of his self control he forced his emotions to one side. He would grieve for his sister later. For now he needed to deal with Cowan, the person he saw as ultimately responsible for her death, and for that he needed a clear head.

"Right, you bastard. What are we going to do with you, eh?" he said. "Whatever you want," Cowan hissed as pink, frothy drool fell from the corner of his mouth. "I'm dead already."

It appeared that all five of Ethan's shots had hit their target. Two had entered the right shoulder, one had struck the midriff and the last two had hit the chest. If it had been anyone normal, it would have spelled instant death, but the supernatural cells now infesting Cowan's body had increased his constitution a hundred fold and consequently saved him. For now.

"Well, I know exactly what to do as it goes," said Ethan. He removed the handgun from the waistband of his trousers and placed the barrel directly against Cowan's forehead.

The soldier didn't flinch. A tiny, ironic smile played on his lips and he snorted in disgust.

"If that doesn't beat it all. Not only have I been bested by a bunch of undead freaks, one of them is going to kill me with my own gun."

"You've got that right, major," said Ethan, slowly applying pressure to the trigger. As Cowan closed his eyes in preparation for the blast that would end his life, a voice to Ethan's right chimed out, and a gentle hand touched his arm.

"Now you put that down, Ethan dear. We don't go using such uncouth methods of disposal round here, do we?" said Mrs. Ladle.

Ethan would have argued the toss with anyone else and put a bullet straight between Cowan's eyes, but Mrs. Ladle had a certain way with her. When she spoke, you did as you were told.

He looked at her, his eyes brimming and his hand trembling, but he lowered the gun.

Next to exit the building were the now freed Ronnie and James. "Ronnie!" Ollie exclaimed excitedly, rushing over to his friend and embracing him in an all-encompassing bear hug. "How are you doing, mate? Are you okay?"

Ronnie thumped Ollie companionably on the back and reciprocated the squeeze before disentangling himself. He gave Ollie a punch on the shoulder for good measure.

"I'm good, mate, considering what's happened, but I'll tell you one thing."

"What?" asked Stitches, beaming at his rescued companion.

"I am so busting for a cigarette. I haven't had one for ages and I think I lost my baccy somewhere in the woods. Mrs. Ladle, if you please."

As if by magic the cigarettes appeared, and before you could say malignant growth, Ronnie was puffing away contentedly and blowing large plumes of smoke into the air.

Ethan and James also greeted each other, but their reunion was more subdued as they spoke of their lost pack members and quickly shared emotionally charged versions of recent events.

After once again checking on Flug, who was still in the land of nod (a place he was very familiar with, even when he was awake), Ollie once more returned to the group. Ethan and James had resumed watching over Cowan, whilst Ronnie and Stitches exchanged extremely tall tales that even the most gullible of people would have recognised as absolute tosh of the highest order.

"So, Mrs. Ladle," the half vampire said to the witch. "which method of disposal were you thinking about for our friend here? I know you stopped him but I think Ethan would make a very good and extremely painful job of it."

She stubbed her fag out under her foot and dredged up some sticky brown fluid from the depths of her lungs which she then deposited on the door.

"That's not for me to decide, my dear. We can leave that up to the one who tasked you with this venture in the first place."

"Oh yes of course. Now that you mention it I do recall Jocular saying that he very much wanted to meet the person responsible."

"Did you hear that?" Ethan spat at Cowan, nudging his naked thigh rather roughly with his foot. "We're going to let Count Jocular have his way with you. How does that sound? What he doesn't know about inflicting pain isn't worth knowing. I imagine he can come up with tortures that would have seemed unreasonable in the fourteenth century. You'll be praying for death."

Cowan's head lolled lazily from side to side.

"Do what you want," he slurred. He jerked as a spasm of pain shot through his battered and broken body. "I'm just glad I managed to kill a few of you sons of bitches. Just a shame I didn't manage more."

"And you would have got away with it if it wasn't for us pesky kids, huh?" said Stitches revelling in the moment, pleased as punch that he'd managed to use that line no matter how contrived the situation (don't blame me, I didn't write it. Oh, yes I did. Sorry).

"Come on everyone, let's get out of here," said Ollie. "I've just about had enough of this place and I think a few of us need some medical attention and a well-earned rest."

No one disagreed with that.

———

After three days of relaxation and recuperation, the four investigators, Ethan and Mrs. Ladle were gathered in Jocular's castle.

Stitches' ankle had been fixed by Professor Crumble, using a mixture of staples, self-tapping screws, blue tac and a few moderately vulgar expletives involving aspects of paternity and certain parts of a troll. He'd done a good job though and if anything the slight deformity that the zombie now had above his foot seemed to balance him out. Now, when he walked, he didn't look quite so wibbly wobbly. He still wouldn't be able to ice skate at the Olympics or half pipe a skateboard, but then again, who would want to?

Flug's road to recovery had been a tad bumpier though, and filled with the odd pothole. The problem was availability of parts. The leg that had been severed in the attack was completely useless, so Dr. Zoltan had to task his body collection agents with finding a limb of the correct dimensions (they were called Tom, both of them. They ran their own company, 'TomTom, Body Collection Agents of Repute. If you want it, we can find it.' If you needed a head or a leg or even the whole cadaver, they were the guys to get it for you. Their list of clients was as long as your arm or any other arms that they'd pilfered, come to that. It was even rumoured that they donated various items to certain rather well known fast food outlets but that was pure speculation though, and was thought by many to be untrue. After all, nothing they supplied could possibly taste that bad).

After a day and a half search they'd eventually located a suitable subject who was thankfully deceased, which wasn't always the case, and appropriated an acceptable appendage apposite for the aforementioned area. The problem, however, was that the donor had been a semi-professional footballer and it had taken Flug the next twenty four hours to get used to having a rather fit, muscular leg attached to his lower portions.

It would take rather a lot longer for Ollie, Stitches and Ronnie to get used to him swinging said leg at random moments and yelling "GOAL!" at the top of his voice, before throwing himself to the floor, rolling around like he was in a tumble dryer and pleading, "REF!" with his arms outstretched and a feigned look of injustice on his face.

Ollie had satisfied himself with a long rest in the soft interior of his coffin. Ronnie had done the same with the Stella triplets.

At the castle, Egon had shown them to a reception room that looked remarkably like it'd been modelled on a mixture of the IKEA products that even the company owner thought were rubbish, and the under 5's section of the worst toy shop in the entire universe. It didn't matter where you sat or where you stood, it looked really tacky in a subtle, postmodern and 'it'll fall apart after two weeks of use' kind of way. At least when it did, it would be accompanied by bells, whistles and a variety of electronic voices spelling things.

Still, the train set and fantasy wonderland display with matching unicorns and fluffy clouds distracted the eye, and proved to be quite a talking point.

"What a load of old crap," said Stitches, who, surprise surprise, had decided to make a point of talking about it. "I've seen more tasteful displays in the toilets at the Bolt and Jugular during the Helloween Bingefest. At least they've got some artistic merit. Probably last longer, too."

"Keep it down will you, please," said Ollie. "We might very well be Jocular's new bestest buddies, but he's still liable to dismember you ever so slightly if he hears you being rude about his décor."

"God I hope not," said the zombie. "I'd die of shame if he killed me and put me in one of his horror shows."

The door to the room creaked open and Jocular swept in, a big, beaming smile on his face. It wasn't the most pleasant of expressions it has to be said. In fact it was a bit scary and just as scary as his scary face, which was really really scary.

"Velkom, gentleman. Velkom. And lady, of course," he said, bowing to them all. "Congratulations on a job vell done. How can I ever sank you?"

"No need to, sir," smarmed Ollie. "It was a pleasure to be of service, and it was rather pleasant to have the chance to flex our detective muscles, to be honest. Obviously it would've been better if the circumstances hadn't arisen in the first place but at least the outcome was a success."

"Excellent," said Jocular. "Essan, how are sings at ze verehouse after ze recent disruptions?"

"Oh, fine, sir. We were all shocked about Obsidia, of course, but thanks to these good people we've at least had the chance to collect our dead and lay them to rest."

"Indeed. I shall miss Isobel, and Ross also." "Thank you."

"Vell, I do consider vot you haff all done to be a great favour to me. It turned out zat Obsidia vas telling me a pack of lies and shielding me from ze truth about vot vas going on in ze voods. It's sanks to you zat ze mystery has been solved. If any of you effer need anysing, zen please let me know."

"I could do with a new pair of shoes," said Stitches. "Mine got chewed up. I think they're buried in the forest somewhere."

Ollie glared at him.

"Vy not indeed" said Jocular. "New shoes it is. Egon," the door opened, "a nice new pair off shoes for our friend here."

"Yes, Master. Which ones?"

"Let me see. Ah yes. If you pop down to dungeon number four, I believe zat ze current occupant is nearly done. Take his. He von't be needing zem anymore."

Stitches shuddered and wished that he could learn to keep it zipped. Shaking his head in total befuddlement, Ethan spoke up.

"Sir, can I ask what became of the man we captured?"

Jocular got up from the horrendously pink small plastic chair that he'd been sitting in. Strangely it was covered in glittered sequins and coloured crystals.

"Ah, I'm glad you asked. Come viz me."

They followed the vampire lord out of the room and along several passageways until they entered a room that was chock full of stuffed animals. Heads of various beasts, both natural and otherwise, adorned the walls, and glass display cabinets held dead creatures in differing poses designed to reflect their nature. It was like a home shopping channel display for rednecks. All that was missing was a rail of lumberjack shirts and a rack of mullet wigs.

"Over here," the vampire beckoned.

In the centre of the room was a large granite plinth on top of which was an immense aquarium that, with the flick of a switch, was lit up by a series of fluorescent lights. Inside, sealed in a glass bubble of its own was Cowan's head, his eyes wide open and flicking back and forth, watching the fish that swam in front of him. When his gaze fell on the assembled crowd his eyes narrowed, and even though the rest of his face remained waxy and impassive, they could all detect the hatred in them.

"My latest creation," announced Jocular proudly. "And vun zat vill give me great pleasure for many years to come."

He reached down, grabbed a glittering tasselled rope and gave it a tug which opened a pair of black velvet curtains. Once parted they revealed a bronze plaque that had been hidden behind them that was itself attached to the rock. Bright golden capital letters proclaimed the name of the display above. It simply said 'MARINE LIFE'.

———

Later that evening everyone was back in town. Ollie and Stitches were sat in Ollie's office, Ronnie had gone out for a drink on the proviso that he not go wandering off without telling anyone and that he pick up some mobile phones, and Flug was in the kitchen trying to lace up a pair of football boots, an activity that should keep him busy for at least the next two years, provided that he didn't eat them first. Ollie didn't have a clue where he'd got them from, but at least he was happy. Ethan had just left. He'd come back to the office because he wanted to discuss joining the business. He would need a couple of days to sort things out at the werehouse because with the demise of Obsidia he'd become the pack leader and he needed to hand that mantle over. The loss of Isobel had hit him hard and he wanted to get away from the place, and he'd been very impressed with how the investigators had conducted themselves. He'd also particularly enjoyed getting involved in the final scrap and had decided that he needed a little more excitement in his life. That being the case the four of them had discussed the matter (well, three of them had. Flug had been occupied trying to screw some studs into the sole of his foot). The answer had been a resounding yes. It would be good to have some more muscle and brains on the team (*more* was a bit generous. *Some* described it better). "Well," said Stitches, "I'm done in. I think I'll go and have a lie down."

Ollie got up from his chair, walked round to the front of his desk and perched on the edge.

"Haven't you forgotten something?" he asked expectantly. "Huh."

"Don't you have a small debt to settle?" "What are you on about?"

"I seem to remember a certain person saying they would do a certain something if I used a certain item."

"You'd be the worst witness in the world. Have you got a head injury that I don't know about, or am I seeing the early onset of Alzheimer's?"

Ollie reached round and lifted the lid of a petite silver box. He took out a small item and threw it to Stitches.

"An empty Sherbet Stab," said the zombie. "Indeed."

"What the..? Oh, come on. You can't be serious. I didn't mean it!" "A bet's a bet."

Stitches realised that he wasn't going to get out of this one. With a resigned look on his grey features he took a needle out and threaded it. Then, looking at Ollie's impassive face, he slowly and deliberately sewed his mouth shut.

Ollie folded his arms and smiled. Perhaps the next six months weren't going to be too bad after all, but he had a funny feeling that the next twenty four hours were going to be pure bliss.

THE END

CUP AND SORCERY

SKULLENIA BOOK 2

CUP AND SORCERY

T he small dark room crackled and sizzled, as if tiny suspended fireworks were exploding in mid-air, sending particles of myriad colours cascading to the floor. The atmosphere felt alive with electricity, making it feel as if a thousand Van De Graff generators had been turned on at the same time. In the centre of the room was a stone plinth, atop which sat a large marble bowl. Inside the bowl, fluid swirled round and round as if it were being churned by an unseen centrifugal force. In the depths of the liquid, what seemed to be wisps of smoke eddied in the opposite direction, and every now and again a blurred, vague shape tried to form and break through the maelstrom.

The hunched figure sat on a three legged wooden stool, hooded head leaning over the container, eyes unblinking, peering intently into the murky miasma. Hands were raised and sleeves were folded carefully back, before fingers were waved over the bowl in intricate patterns. At the same time, whispered incantations passed from tight, dry lips, attempting to invoke the aid of some otherworldly power.

> *"Demons of darkness come to me*
> *Show me what I long to see*
> *A gift of blood I freely give*

So that you may help me live."

A small knife appeared in the figure's right hand, with which the palm of the left hand was deftly sliced open. Claret beads dripped into the milky mixture as a fist was made and squeezed tight. The liquid turned a light red, and as each drop splashed down it circled faster and faster until a pinkish foam appeared on its surface.

"A sign or clue is all I ask
To aid me in my onerous task
Show me the answer to the text
So I can do that which is next."

The indistinct patterns and swirls moved closer together until they started to mingle and coalesce, until finally they formed one larger mass. As more drops of lifeblood entered the concoction the shape became more and more distinct, recognisable features beginning to appear in the watery pool. Suddenly, the charged atmosphere in the room became thicker, making the air heavy and difficult to breathe. A wispy fog seemed to emanate from the walls, floor and ceiling, as if the very fabric of the building itself were perspiring.

The mixture in the bowl then thickened and stopped moving, and a small bulge appeared in the centre. It rose higher and higher until it was about four feet tall. Two protrusions formed, one on either side, at the ends of which five small buds appeared, wiggling purposefully as they grew. The top of the muddy column was forming a rough sphere which quickly smoothed out, allowing the beginnings of facial features to show through. Under the burgeoning nose a split formed, which widened as if in a yawn, showing a tongue and a set of sharp teeth.

The hooded figure watched in rapt and unadulterated fascination as the outline took on its final form. The wiggling stumps were now fully functional hands and digits that moved languidly, as if the being itself were amazed at its newly found corporeality and was studying it carefully. Pitch black soulless eyes stared out from deep sockets and the lips smacked together, as if the apparition were indicating that it needed a drink. Those lips parted, and when it spoke the voice penetrated the summoner to their very core. It was a deep, rumbling bass that resonated around the room, to the point that the listener could have sworn that they could see sound waves emanating from its mouth.

"WHY HAVE YOU SUMMONED ME, MORTAL?"

"To aid me in my quest," the hooded figure replied in a timid and trembling voice. "To translate the text before me and locate. . . "

"I KNOW OF WHAT YOU SPEAK, MORTAL, BUT I CANNOT HELP YOU WITH THE COMPENDIUM DE MAGICUS TOTALUS."

"May I be permitted to ask why, dark one?"

"THAT BOOK WAS WRITTEN HUNDREDS OF YEARS AGO BY A RENEGADE GOD. IT SHOULD HAVE REMAINED UNSEEN BY HUMAN EYES, BUT IT FELL INTO MORTAL HANDS. THE RESULTING CHAOS WAS CATACLYSMIC."

"In what way?"

"THE MORTAL WHO TRANSLATED THE TEXT USED IT IN AN ATTEMPT TO RULE OVER YOUR WORLD, AND OURS. THAT COULD NOT BE ALLOWED TO HAPPEN, SO HE WAS DESTROYED."

"Why wasn't the book destroyed if it had the capability to cause so much trouble?"

"IT WAS FORMED BY THE GODS THEMSELVES. IT CANNOT BE TORN ASUNDER, SO IT WAS HIDDEN FOR CENTURIES IN PLAIN SIGHT AS AN INTERESTING RELIC."

"But I have no interest in destroying the Gods or attempting to take over their world. My interest is dominion in the mortal realm."

"IF THAT IS THE CASE, THEN PERHAPS WE CAN COME TO ACCEPTABLE TERMS."

"Such as?"

"IF I ASSIST YOU AND YOU ARE SUCCESSFUL IN YOUR QUEST, YOU WILL BE GRANTED RULE OVER YOUR WORLD, BUT YOU WILL BECOME OUR VESSEL. A CONDUIT, THROUGH WHICH OUR BIDDING CAN BE DONE."

"Agreed."

"VERY WELL. FIVE STRANGERS WILL BECOME KNOWN TO YOU, AND IT IS THROUGH THEM THAT THE TEXT WILL BE TRANSLATED. ONE OF THEM WILL DISCOVER THE SECRET, FOR IT MUST BE FOUND BY ONE ABLE TO DECIPHER IT, RATHER

THAN TOLD BY THOSE WHO ALREADY KNOW. THEN IT WILL BE
THESE FIVE WHO COMPLETE THE QUEST."

"Why them and not me?"

"THE WIELDER OF THE ARTEFACT MUST NOT BE THE
DISCOVERER. SO IT IS WRITTEN. THE CHOICE IS YOURS,
MORTAL. DO YOU STILL AGREE?"

There was no hesitation. "Yes, I agree." "VERY WELL. SO IT
SHALL BE."

The representation of the demon disintegrated in an instant,
collapsing back into the marble bowl and leaving nothing but a still,
slightly pink pool. The static charge receded and the room returned to
normal.

Getting up from the stool, the hooded one walked over to a wooden
chest of drawers in which was some salve and a bandage, which would
be used to clean and wrap the injured hand.

All there was to do now was wait.

———

Stitches gripped the arms of the chair and squeezed his hands so
tightly that his skin was in danger of splitting, sending several of his
knuckles flying around the cabin. His eyes were clamped shut and his
lips were pursed tightly together. His feet were involuntarily flexing up
and down, like a drummer hammering the pedals to a pair of bass
drums.

"Why did we have to fly? I hate flying. It's not natural. There's no
way this much weight should be able to get off the ground."

Ollie stopped reading his latest copy of The Moon and rested it on
his lap.

"Well, I'm sure that if a plane can get a load of Americans into the
air, then this one should have no problem. Besides," he continued, a bit
annoyed at having his reading interrupted, "it's the quickest and most
convenient way to travel. It was either this or spend five days on the
ferry, and I don't think that would have been very pleasant, what with
Flug and his seasickness."

"I would have taken that over this," responded the zombie, shifting
in his seat. "At least on a boat he could go outside and throw up into

the water without bothering anyone. If I let rip in this confined space, it'll suddenly seem a hell of a lot smaller."

Ollie picked up his magazine again and flicked it straight.

"The only thing we'd have to worry about if you let rip would be dust clogging up the air vents. Anyway, I don't know what you're worrying about. Statistically speaking, air travel is by far and away the safest mode of transport."

Stitches opened one eye which glared at his half vampire colleague.

"You're kidding me, right?" "No."

"You do know who the pilot is, don't you?"

"I hadn't read the crew list, no. I'm quite happy in the knowledge that they wouldn't let a total stranger into the cockpit because he felt like giving flying a go."

"Well be that as it may, I checked. It's Hamish MacHaggis. When he was alive he was the worst pilot ever to have been in the Royal Air Force. The only thing he ever flew successfully was a toy helicopter, and he's on record as being the only pilot ever to have been shot down before getting into his plane."

"Some kind of aviation expert now, are we?"

"No. I just like to do my research, especially when I know I'm going to be getting on one of these infernal contraptions."

Once again Ollie put his soon-to-be-out-of-date periodical down, resigned to the fact that he wasn't going to be able to finish reading the 'Vampires. Pillaging, Ancient Mythical Beast or Effeminate, OverCompensating Closet Homosexual' article.

"Infernal contraptions?" he laughed. "You sound like a pensioner. You'll be telling me next that things were a lot better before all these new fangled changes. I don't know what you're worried about anyway. Everybody on this flight is undead. If anything happens to us, it'll be of entirely no consequence."

"That's easy for you to say. All you have to do is turn into a flying mouse and flap off into the moonlight, whereas I and poor old Flug here will be scattered over rather a large area. Right, Flug?"

He elbowed his vast travelling companion in the ribs, hoping to elicit some kind of response, but it was a futile gesture. Flug had his headphones on and was caught up in the middle of watching the inflight movie, a remake of a certain space themed film that probably can't be mentioned due to legal reasons. The film that Flug was watching, however, an affectionate and inspired re-imagining of said unmentionable film, can.

It was called The Vampire Bites Back, an uplifting story in which the handsome hero, Puke Piehorder, at the behest of his tutor, the ancient and sagacious Yodel, travels across the galaxy to face his father, the evil and tyrannical Lord Harsh Trader, in a ferocious final battle bidding to deny his destiny in joining Trader running his very successful second hand spacecraft empire. It was a blockbuster of epic proportions that had won four Lecters at the recent Mortuary Awards. Flug didn't actually have a clue what was going on, of course. It was only during their recent trip that he'd discovered that there weren't little people living in the magic TV box and that you didn't have to stand outside looking up at the heavens to watch Sky Sports. Still, at least it was marginally better than the poor excuse for entertainment they'd had to endure on the outward journey. It was about a Mafia Don who was confined to a wheelchair and when all was said and done it didn't matter how convincing the actor or how grisly the torture scenes as he slaughtered his enemies and took control of his territories, there is nothing in the slightest bit intimidating about a character called 'The Quadfather'.

"Anyway," Ollie cut in, "you're only in a bad mood because of what happened at the hotel."

Stitches looked at him with a look of disgust and revulsion on his weathered face.

"Well, wouldn't you be?" he said.

After cracking the difficult, and quite frankly exhausting, case of Jocular's' missing lycanthropes, Ollie had taken some time to sort through some of his Uncle's vast accumulation of paperwork. There was all the usual stuff. Bills for cape cleaning (blood is hell to shift), receipts going back hundreds of years (he found one for a gas powered fang cleaner dated 1756), letters of thanks for work done and some magazine renewal forms (two of which were for publications that Ollie had (a) never heard of and (b) never *wanted* to hear of. They revelled under the headings of 'Bleeders Wives' and 'Double O Positives, How does all that fit in one cup?' Ollie was sure that his Uncle would only peruse these publications for the articles on the latest hansom cabs, but they went in the bin regardless). There was also the odd invitation or two. One of them was asking old Gorge to attend the Antichristening of his Demigodson, so Ollie replied to that one informing the sender of his late Uncle's demise. The second one was an invitation to attend a conference in London where all of the delegates gathered to hear lectures, join in discussion groups and get involved in workshops doing table top exercises and giving presentations. The whole weekend was organised by the BBC (British Bloodletting Corporation) and the RSPCA (Royal Society for the Preservation of Carnal Acts), two charitable bodies whose sole intent was the advancement of the modern day undead. Ollie had figured that not only would it be a chance to get away for a few days to relax and blow away the cobwebs, which in Stitches' case was the literal truth, because his armpits were a constant problem, but he might get some valuable networking done. Not a bad idea, now that he had a computer with darknet access installed in his office.

Also, being the generous soul that he was, he asked his colleagues, the bounty hunters, if they would like to join them. Sadly though, Mr Singh wouldn't shut the shop for anything less than the destruction of the entire planet (bet your life he would still open on Christmas morning, though) and Dr. Jekyll had gone into hiding after an unfortunate incident with a load of fruit, a farmer's daughter and a song by The Tractors, Eastern Europe's premier agricultural band.

So, what with Ronnie being away and Ethan not fancying it one bit ('well he does look dog tired' was Stitches' response. A response which had earned him a hearty smack to the head that had left him looking backwards for an hour or so) it was just the three of them. Stitches was actually looking forward to it, apart from the flying of course, and Flug had come along simply because he could not be left alone. Or to put it another way, he was too simple to be left alone. The last time that Ollie had allowed the giant reanimate to fend for himself had been about a month ago and chaos on a grand scale had, quite naturally, ensued. The resultant remodelling to the kitchen hadn't taken as long as he'd first thought though, but the remodelling of poor old Hector Lozenge was going to take rather a lot longer. He'd knocked on the office door in his usual drunken state, after forgetting where he lived for probably the ninth time that evening. When Flug opened it and saw the poor man standing in the rain and soaking from head to toe, he had picked him up and done the most natural thing that he could think of. Still, the new tumble dryer was a lot better than the old one, especially as it didn't have clumps of bright red but very dry skin stuck to the inside. The only proviso for the trip though was that they had to go incognito. A half vampire, an eight foot monster and a slowly disintegrating zombie couldn't very well wander the streets of England's capital city, scaring every man, woman and child that they came across. Unless it was London fashion week of course, in which case they would have fit right in.

The first person they thought of to help them was Professor Crumble, but on reflection the idea was shelved because the chances were that they would be trying to conceal their identities by wearing market stall quality masks of comedy werewolves, and talking in very unconvincing foreign accents. That being the case they went to see Mrs. Ladle. The witch had been more than happy to help of course, and she'd gotten to work straight away preparing a transformation potion that they could take on the flight over. She concocted it in such a way that not only would it mask their true forms, but it also had the added benefit of allowing the taker, and any other undeads, to still see themselves as they truly are. Only those humans looking at them got the effect. The only thing she didn't mention was the fact that she had absolutely no idea what non-undead form they would take. Still, at least it'd be pleasant to drink. She'd added a bit of flavour because she was nice like that. Chocolate. Lovely. And it would nicely mask the taste of the ground troll shavings that was in it, which is always a bonus, because that tasted worse than anything else, ever. Even kebabs.

As they descended, the three of them had knocked back the liquid and it had worked straight away. Ollie took on the appearance of a rather well dressed city gent complete with briefcase, bowler hat, umbrella and smug, self-satisfied expression. Flug became the member of a death metal band sporting long greasy hair, demonic tattoos that covered most of his body, jeans so filthy that a Hell's Angel would have wanted to put them through the wash, and a t-shirt with the band name, OX STOMPER, emblazoned across the front.

Stitches, however, hadn't been so fortunate, and neither Ollie nor Flug had the heart to tell him what he'd become. It wasn't until they walked through the door of the hotel and the zombie bumped into someone only to hear 'Sorry love, my fault' that Ollie enlightened him. "You know how the Stella girls dress?" he'd said, trying not to laugh.

"Oh my God, yes."

"You make them look rather understated."

"Oh no. So I've got to spend the next two days walking around looking like a high class call girl?"

Ollie shrugged and pursed his lips.

"Not so much high class. More like no class." "Great."

"Oh, and do me a favour. Pull your top up, your boobs are falling out."

After a highly articulate outburst and being asked to watch his/her language or risk getting thrown out, they'd gotten on with the conference.

They'd attended a very informative lecture on 'What not to wear to a summoning' that was presented by a rather flamboyant and extremely well groomed Satanist, who called himself 'The Cloven Poof', before enjoying a workshop on 'Business Relationships. How to end them and where to hide the body'. The only disappointment had been the cancellation of the performance and discussion forum from the GLC (the Goblin Light-theatre Company), after their coach had caught fire on the M4 and they'd all popped.

All in all though, it had been an interesting and productive trip. They'd even managed to get in a bit of sightseeing, but only after they'd convinced Flug that Big Ben was a large bell in a clock-tower, and not a giant monster with four faces and a pointy hat who shouted DONG at unsuspecting passers-by. Stitches, on the other hand, had had three dinner invitations, one proposal of marriage and an offer from a rather unsavoury Eastern European gentleman to 'take him up the back passage in Soho where I have a very interesting selection of bouncy, rubber things'.

The aircraft lurched slightly as it started to descend, causing the nervous zombie to hold onto the armrests even tighter. A light came on in the overhead display showing a buckle and a clip and a voice rattled over the ancient intercom, "Ladies and gentlemen, we are about to start our descent into the airport. Please extinguish your cigarettes, lanterns, joss sticks, fire imps and dragons and fasten your seatbelts." (Airport was a bit wide of the mark to be honest, as no doubt the plane would be. It was more an old field, littered with bits and pieces of animals that hadn't gotten out of the way in time. If ever you see a news report where an aircraft has been downed by cow strike, you'll know where it happened).

"Fasten your seatbelts," muttered Stitches disapprovingly. "What a waste of time that is. If this thing crashes at five hundred miles an hour, I don't think a four foot length of fabric is going to help much. There wouldn't be enough left of me to go in a sick bag."

"If you don't stop moaning, I'll put you in a Hoover bag when we get home," said Ollie.

Half an hour later they'd collected their luggage from the seemingly endless carousel, and were queuing up to go through Customs and Exorcise. Stitches followed Ollie and Flug through the barrier.

"Anything to declare?" asked the officious ghoul at the checkpoint. "Well, those shoes don't go with that shirt for a start, and that tie, where did you, ooof."

Two hours later and with not one part of his body unprobed, Stitches re-joined the other two.

"You'll never learn, will you?" commented Ollie knowingly, throwing his cases on top of the cab and eliciting help from his colleagues with his coffin. "Always have to be a smart arse."

"Funny you should say that," Stitches replied, struggling with the top end of the casket. "My arse is smarting a bit as it goes. Amazing where they think two hundred fags will fit."

"Good job they didn't check in your mouth then, although I doubt they've got the manpower to search such a vast area, especially without helicopters and sea-going search vessels."

"Why would you put a fag up your bottom, Stitches?" asked Flug, a look of confusion on his face usually seen on old people trying to understand how a Blu-ray player works and the younger person trying to explain it to them.

"To keep the tobacco dry." "Oh, okay."

They got into the cab and settled in for the journey home, passing a large overhead sign that read 'Thank you for flying on the Astral Plane,' before hitting the dual dust track home.

———

"I don't understand it at all," said the distinguished looking gentleman, shaking his head in puzzlement. "We're always so careful with our security arrangements. In the four hundred years that this museum has been in existence there has never been an incident such as this. Why it shakes me to the very core thinking that some ne'er-dowell has been wandering about the place unfettered and free to do as they please. It's a dreadful situation, not to mention potentially catastrophic."

A second figure detached itself from the shadows at the back of the room and approached the first.

"What do you mean, Mr. Curator? I'm sorry but I don't see what all the fuss is about, and whilst I don't wish to denigrate what's occurred, I mean a burglary is a burglary after all, it is only a few pages from an old book that have been taken."

"My apologies, Vortex, but I forgot that ancient mythological history isn't your field. I'll explain it all in good time, but for now I think we need to acquire some aid in determining who perpetrated this heinous act."

"A fine suggestion, Mr. Curator."

"Do you have any ideas, Vortex? I wouldn't have the foggiest notion where to begin, and I must say this has left me feeling rather disturbed."

"Don't you worry. I think I know the very people to contact. Very reliable, so I'm told, and they come highly recommended by Count Jocular no less."

Mr. Curator brightened somewhat.

"Really? Well, they must be excellent then. It's only the best for His Royal Darkness, don't you know. Can I leave you to make the necessary arrangements? I think I need a lie down."

Vortex smiled and nodded his head in deference.

"Of course. Leave it to me, I shall contact them at once."

———

When they arrived back at the office, they found that Ronnie had already returned from his sojourn and was now sitting in the kitchen, stirring a pot of tea.

"Ooh, pour us one of those, mate, will you please," asked Ollie as they all piled in. "I'm gasping. The water in London is absolutely disgusting. It tastes like they've dissolved a used urinal cake in it."

"Delightful," said Ronnie. "So, how was the conference?" "Don't ask," said Stitches.

"That bad, huh?" said Ronnie, pouring out a cup of hot, steaming Earl Grey.

"Let's just say I'll never have a sex change operation. I couldn't put up with all the male attention."

"I don't think you'd have to worry too much about that" said Ollie, popping a sweetener into his drink and giving it a stir. "I mean let's face it. It would take a suspension of disbelief of gargantuan proportions, and a potion more powerful than anything that Mrs. Ladle could make, to convince anyone that you were female. Especially an attractive one."

Stitches looked a bit indignant and more than a tad hurt.

"Tell that to Colonel Totherington Bagshot, VC DFC and Bar. He thought I was pretty hot stuff."

"That senile old dinosaur thought that Queen Victoria was still on the throne," said Ollie.

Stitches put his hands on his hips and shot Ollie a look that would have made a Chatham chav proud. "I would have made him very happy actually," he said.

"An Early Learning Centre Activity set and someone to talc his saggy backside would've made him happy."

"Ah well, that's me," Stitches said with a haughty air, doing his best not to look thoroughly dejected. "Always the bridesmaid, never the bride."

"Bride of Frankenstein, maybe," Ronnie added with a sarcastic flourish. He lit the cigarette that was clinging to his lips, puffed on it and sent a vast plume towards the ceiling. "Anyway," he added, "just what on earth are you two banging on about? Sounds like you've been on a stag do in Amsterdam rather than London."

Ollie grinned. "We'll tell you about it sometime. How were your days off?"

Ronnie drained the dregs from his cup and set it back down on the table.

"Yeah, pretty good. I met up with a couple of mates in Humerus, did a bit of sightseeing and then went to that new nightclub, HG's."

"Very nice," said Stitches. "That's supposed to be rather upmarket, isn't it?"

"Well, they do say that if you're invisible, it's the place to be seen."

"My, that is exclusive! Was it any good?" asked Ollie, swallowing another mouthful of tea.

"Yeah it was okay, although I don't think invisible strippers are going to catch on. I know that leaving something to the imagination is said to be alluring, but not everything. And besides that, you don't know what you're tucking your money into. It could have been the seam of some old hag's surgical stocking for all I know."

Stitches experienced an involuntary shudder as some more than disturbing images flashed through his mind. It would have been worse if he could have actually seen them.

"Where, Ethan?" asked Flug, joining in the conversation, late as always but with his usual casual grace and Oscar Wilde type repartee. "He help me go poo."

"Upstairs in the office," Ronnie said after a double take. "He needs to see you actually, Ollie. There's been a few calls while you were away."

Ollie finished his tea, rinsed the cup out and put it on the draining board. "Oh, right. Let's go and see then, shall we?"

He found Ethan sitting behind his desk. The phone was cradled between his shoulder and his ear. He was in the middle of a conversation and was writing notes.

"No problem, Mr. Vortex. I'm sure we can help you. As soon as Mr. Splint returns from his trip, I'll be sure to let him know at once. Thank you. Bye now."

"Anything interesting?" asked Ollie, parking himself in Stitches' usual chair, waving at Ethan to stay seated.

"Could be. There's been a break in at the Fibulan museum. That was the Curator's assistant, Vortex. He didn't say too much, but they'd like us to go over and see what we think."

"Excellent," said Ollie beaming, "we'll attend shortly. Anything else?"

Ethan leafed through several ghost-it notes.

"Uh, nothing really pressing, apart from Professor Crumble blowing up a pig and having to get the cleaners in, and Constable Gullet having to arrest a joy rider who landed on the roof the other night. Usual thing, nicked a broom, under age, no insurance."

"Any damage?"

"A few dented bristles, a couple of loose tiles and the same for three of the young chaps' teeth. The little fellah responsible will be up in front of the Magic State Court in the next couple of days."

"Good," said Ollie. "Hopefully they'll throw the spell book at him." Having the spell book thrown at you was as literal as it sounded. The guilty party, whilst stood in the dock, had a large, black, leather bound tome hurled at them by the prosecuting counsellor. Whichever page the book opened at, after bouncing off said naughty person, was their allotted punishment. This could cover a vast spectrum of penalties ranging from a couple of centuries interred in a marble statue or, as in one very unfortunate case of being caught haunting without a license, the perpetrator spent the whole of August as a youth group leader at an outward bound centre in North Wales. He was still undergoing therapy. Justice in Skullenia is harsh.

"Right," said Ollie, clapping his hands enthusiastically, "let's have the address of the museum and we'll find out what's going on."

––––––––––

The Fibulan museum was a vast stone-built structure nestled at the top of a hill at the end of Digitalis Avenue in Fibular. In the four hundred years of its existence it had amassed supernatural relics and mythological artefacts beyond number and had become known far and wide as a repository for such. For instance, they had on display the fabled Apron of Vomitoria, an item of kitchen apparel that made everything the wearer cooked taste like a Pot Noodle. They also had the hallowed Christmas Lights of Forever, which you were able to switch on for up to ten minutes at a time without one of the green bulbs blowing.

After the cab pulled up outside, Ollie got out and tipped the driver a few pence. Stitches would have tipped him about his cleanliness, but seeing as he was rather a large phantasm who looked like he could pull the top off a steam train, he thought better of it. He liked his body the way it was arranged, thank you very much.

"Impressive," commented the zombie, craning his neck back to take in the massive grey edifice. "You ever been here before?"

"Only the once," Ollie replied, shaking his head and wincing at the memory it conjured up. "Dad brought me here when I was about eight. He thought it would be educational for me to go on the Horror of Terrors Horribly Terrible Tour."

"And was it?"

"It taught me how to hide a wee stain if that's any indication. It took me ages to get over the experience. I had daymares for weeks afterwards."

Ollie lifted the oversized brass knocker and slammed it home.

BOOM. BOOM.

A lock slid across and the immense oak door was opened from within.

"Ah, you must be the gentlemen from the agency. Do come in, please. I'm the Curator's assistant, Vortex. Please allow me to show you the way."

"Thank you very much. I'm Ollie Splint, and this is Stitches."

After seeing them into the building, Vortex closed the door and beckoned them on.

"You might be interested to know, Mr. Stitches, that we have quite an extensive reanimation section on the fourth floor. Some of our zombies date back well over six hundred years. Of course it's only their clothes, a lot of sellotape and a daily spoonful of wishful thinking holding them together these days, but they're still fascinating nonetheless. How old are you, may I ask? You seem to be in remarkable condition, if I may be permitted the observation."

Stitches edged ever so slightly to his left, putting Ollie squarely between himself and the assistant. Vortex, although not a large man by any means, had a certain presence about him that made you take notice. He was of average build, average height, average appearance and, if you checked criminal history, looked like the average serial killer. The only really striking aspect about him were his eyes. They were a bright sky blue, but a sky that had been lightly sprinkled with diamond dust. They actually twinkled as they moved. It was quite attractive in a non-sexual, non-gender specific and non-judgemental about lifestyle choices way, and at the same time a little disconcerting. It felt like no matter in which direction he was facing, he would always be watching you.

"I'm just over two hundred, if you must know, and I do keep myself in good nick, thank you very much," Stitches replied, a little more

forcefully than was probably necessary, "so don't go making room for me on one of your shelves just yet."

"Oh no, perish the thought, dear boy. Here we are."

Vortex showed them into an exhibit room. It was about fifteen feet square and moodily lit, the sort of place where you'd expect to be ruthlessly interrogated to reveal your deepest, darkest secrets, or at the very least asked, 'have you been actively seeking work this last week?'

Uneven slate tiles covered the floor, and the walls looked as if molten lava were flowing down them.

"Amazing what you can do with a bit of artex these days," observed Stitches.

In the centre of the room stood a five foot high plinth, on top of which was a glass cabinet. Inside this, on a small golden lectern, was a red, leather bound book that was closed. On top of the glass case was an arm. Attached to that arm was a tall, thin, kindly looking man with a long white beard and friendly, inviting features. He was dressed in a tweed suit and Hush Puppies, and looked like he would have been right at home either teaching A Level Geography in a Polytechnic, or advanced algebra at three in the morning on BBC2. He approached the two visitors and greeted them warmly, shaking each by the hand. As he spoke though, they could detect a note in his voice, a faint but distinct tremble that told them he was worried about something, and that all was not well.

"Gentlemen, I am Ignacious Starch, curator of the museum. Thank you for coming so quickly. I hope I haven't put you to any trouble."

"None at all," said Ollie pleasantly, trying to put the old boy at ease. "What can we do for you?"

"Well, if I may be permitted to give you a bit of a history lesson, our dilemma should become clearer. This book," he pointed towards the glass case with a shaky hand, "is the Compendium de Magicus Totallus. Basically, gentlemen, it contains within its pages every magic spell, incantation, cantrip, conjuration, charm, jinx and hex known to exist."

"Quite the book of tricks then," said Stitches, wondering where this was going.

"Well indeed. Now, nearly every spell contained within it has been deciphered and used at some point throughout history. However, there is a section at the back that contains a language that has never been translated. Try as we might, we have failed each and every time. Some of the most eminent people in this field and others have attempted it, but to no avail. No one seems to be able to make any sense of it at all. All we do know is that there are five pages of said text, and on the reverse of each there is what appears to be a map, but again, the wording on the diagram is in the same unintelligible code."

"That's all very interesting," said Ollie questioningly, "but what exactly seems to be the problem? ATCHOO! Bless me."

The curator looked downcast, his voice quiet. "The pages in question have been stolen."

"Oh, I see. ATCHOO! I'm ever so sorry; I must have a cold coming, unless it's the dust."

"Well, don't look at me," protested Stitches. "I'm all sewn up nice and tight and gave myself a rigorous hovering last night."

To emphasize the point he slapped himself on the chest, which to Ollie's everlasting disappointment produced nothing except a low, hollow thud.

MEOW. ATCHOO. ATCHOO. MEOW.

Ollie felt a soft, sinuous and very furry body slinking round his legs. "I can't understand why, but it would seem that your cat is setting me off," Ollie said, desperately trying to stem the glutinous flow from his dripping nose.

"Ah, Carter has joined us. My apologies, Mr. Splint. I had no idea he'd snuck in. Vortex, would you please see him out?"

The assistant opened the display room door and ushered the feline out, whilst Ollie blew his nose explosively and tried to equalise the pressure in his cranium by making goldfish faces.

"Right," he said, suitably de-snotted, "where were we? Ah yes, the missing pages."

"Yes indeed," continued the curator. "And we need to get them back before, well, who knows what could happen."

"What could happen?" asked Stitches.

"That's the problem," answered Vortex, appearing from behind the zombie when he still should have been over by the door. "Nobody knows. But it would seem logical that the pages have remained untranslated for a reason, wouldn't you say?"

"Vortex is correct," Starch continued. "History tells us that the only reason secrets stay undiscovered is because they were meant to stay undiscovered. I have a very bad feeling in my water about this, gentlemen, I don't mind telling you."

Stitches, desperately trying to banish the thought of old man's water from his head, spoke up.

"But if a secret is a secret, and no one is meant to discover the secret, what's the point of having a secret in the first place if the secret can never be found?"

"I see your point," said Vortex, "but if we didn't have secrets, whether they were secrets or not, then the world of exploration and discovery would be very dull indeed, if the secrets that we were looking for weren't secrets at all."

"But if all secrets were never discovered and stayed secret, what's the difference between that and this secret, which has stayed secret for so long?"

"Stitches," Ollie interjected. "Yeah".

"Can I have a word?" "In secret?"

Starch coughed audibly and raised his hands. "I think we may be getting a little off the subject. Suffice to say if those pages are translated outside of the protection of this august establishment then, well, as I previously stated, I fear what may occur."

"Quite right too," Ollie agreed. He hadn't been in Skullenia all that long and had already seen what could happen if magic was used irresponsibly. A black eye from a slice of Mrs. Ladle's lemon bastard cake had assured him of that (he'd gone to dip it into his tea but it jumped out of his hand, punched him in the face and returned to the plate where it sat glowering at him) "Who has access to the display?" he continued.

"Just myself, Vortex here, and one other who appears to have gone missing."

"And who would that be?" Ollie enquired.

"Our caretaker, Flange. At the end of each day he does his rounds of the museum, makes sure that everything's in order and locks up. Unfortunately no one has seen or heard from him since the theft."

"And it would seem to me that the person responsible had ready access to the book," observed Ollie, studying the glass case. "This hasn't been tampered with at all has it?"

"No," answered Vortex, "which I'm afraid puts Flange very much in the frame, doesn't it?"

"Potentially," said Stitches. "The only problem that I can foresee is that without the pages, any clues and a place to start, we're pretty much stuck at the first hurdle."

"Maybe not," announced Starch, "This way, gentlemen, if you please."

Starch and Vortex led them out of the display room and into an access passage where an iron, spiral staircase stood. At the bottom of this they traversed a short walkway to a vast steel door. Starch stood in front of the metal barrier and waved a hand whilst muttering a few unintelligible words, after which several large bolts, the size of railway sleepers, slid back, allowing the door to swing silently open.

"The vault, gentlemen," explained Vortex.

It was more than a mere vault. It was a vast warehouse containing aisle after aisle of industrial racking.

"I take it this is all the exhibits that you don't have room for upstairs," Ollie stated.

"Predominantly," replied Starch, "but it also contains the genuine copies of some of our most prized pieces, including the Compendium."

"Oh, I see," said Ollie, understanding what Starch was getting at. "The one upstairs is a fake."

"Yes."

"Very clever," Stitches added. "Fool the people into thinking they're seeing the genuine article, when in fact they're looking at a very convincing copy."

"Precisely," said Starch.

"It's a bit like watching a tribute band isn't it. It's almost the same, but not quite. You could get someone to watch Pynk Floid or Mentallica say, and if they didn't know what was going on they'd be easily fooled wouldn't they." said the zombie.

Surprising everybody in the room, Starch agreed with Stitches' observation and said, "Yes indeed, but I'm more of a Meathead fan myself."

He was the last person you would have expected to be a lover of all things rock, and or, roll. He seemed to be more the 'fall asleep in front of the fire whilst listening to the easiest of easy listening music' type. Either that or he just wanted to appear to be hip, cool and trendy, but then, seeing as it wasn't San Francisco, 1967 it was no doubt genuine. At that point Vortex returned, not that either of the detectives had noticed that he'd gone. He was carrying an iron box and four pairs of latex gloves.

"Here we are, gentlemen," he said. "If you'll follow me to the examination table, we'll have a look."

They stopped in an open area that had a large, flat, metallic table in the centre. Vortex placed the iron box down and took a key from his pocket. He placed it into the ancient lock and turned it slowly, before lifting the lid and revealing the contents.

"Gloves please," he said, passing them round.

He removed the bright red book and placed it carefully onto the spotless surface, and opened it to the appropriate place.

"These, gentlemen," said Starch looking over Vortex's shoulder, "are the missing pages."

Looking at them confirmed to Ollie and Stitches what they'd been told. It was indeed complete and utter gobbledegook. All that was there was line after line of characters that contained no spaces, paragraphs or any punctuation whatsoever. It was five pages of total gibberish that made no sense to man nor beast, undead, mythical or otherwise. If you've ever flicked through the first few pages of a Katie Price novel, then you can appreciate the dilemma facing the four onlookers. "No wonder no one's ever made sense of that," said Ollie, twisting his head at all sorts of angles, trying to get to grips with it and failing.

"It looks so random."

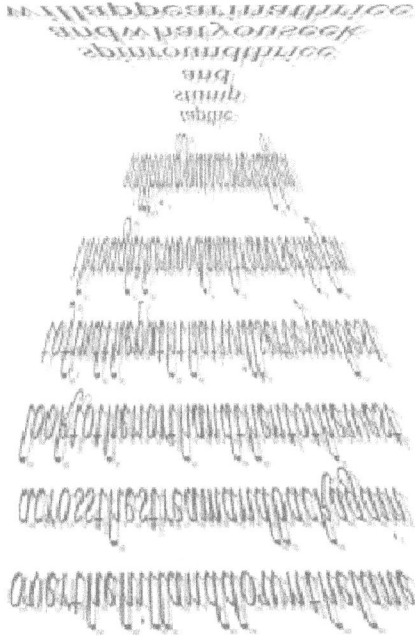

stitches
ginnis,
and

Stitches was standing on the opposite side of the table to the others, observing carefully as the delicate pages were folded over. He watched Vortex lift the first one and place it flat before taking hold of the second. He handled them with as much care as he could muster, lifting them slowly and meticulously so as not to damage their fragile structure. As the page reached the perpendicular and started its journey down, something caught the zombie's eye.

"Hold it there!" he exclaimed loudly.

Vortex stopped dead, afraid to move and wondering why he'd been yelled at.

"Stay perfectly still," Stitches added, resting his hands on the edge of the table and leaning over. He peered intently at the shiny, metallic surface.

"I don't believe it!" he exclaimed.

"What?" asked Starch, a puzzled furrow on his brow. "Come round to me, Mr. Curator, if you wouldn't mind."

The elderly man left Vortex deftly holding the page in position, and joined Stitches.

"What am I looking at, young man?" he asked, a note of excitement tainting his voice.

"Don't look at the page that Vortex is holding. Look at the reflection that it's casting on the table top," said Stitches.

Starch took out a dear little pair of pince-nez, popped them onto the bridge of his nose, and tilted his head.

"Oh, my word. I don't believe it!" he exclaimed. "WHAT?" demanded the other two.

There, plain for all to see, reflected in the mirrored finish of the table, was the page. But it was in English.

"Why, I don't quite know what to say," Starch said, shaking Stitches firmly by the hand, amazed at this sudden and unexpected turn of events. He walked back round to the other side and took over from Vortex, who went and had a look for himself.

"Bugger me backwards," said the assistant, his face lighting up with sheer joy. Realising what he'd said he looked up at the others. "Oh, I am sorry. Please do excuse my profanity."

"No apology necessary, Mr. Vortex," said Ollie. "You're allowed an outburst or two after making a discovery."

"Thank you." Vortex returned his gaze to the reflected passage. "Imagine, after all these years and the massive IQs that have studied this, it turns out the author wrote the passages upside down and back to front."

"Weird, huh," Stitches said. "I used to do the same when I sent notes to Sarah Gilmore in Geography, asking if I could see her rocky outcrops."

Ollie smiled at his colleague, genuinely pleased and, he had to admit, somewhat surprised at his observation skills. If he was perfectly honest with himself, when it came to taking things seriously and getting the job done, Stitches could be a bit lacking due to his steel toe capped boot to the genitals type of humour that spilled out of him with monotonous regularity. Nevertheless, he'd done well.

"Good work, mate ATCHOO!" MEOW.

Carter the cat leaped onto the table and proceeded to rub himself around Ollie's hands as they rested there. Starch quickly shooed him away, with the promise of some chicken and a tickle under the chin later. Not Ollie, you understand. The cat.

"I've never been allergic to any animals," said Ollie, desperately trying to find a dry area on his rapidly stiffening handkerchief. "I even had a cat when I was little."

Starch and Vortex were now enraptured by the book, and not in the slightest bit bothered by the war going on in Ollie's nasal cavity.

"Well, it certainly looks like we've got our work cut out for us for the next few hours at least," the curator said. "First things first though, Vortex. We need to find a mirror."

————

Ollie and Stitches left the two ageing academics pondering the mysteries of the ancient script. They'd decided that it would be a good idea to pay a visit to the home of the absent without leave caretaker, Flange. Seeing as he'd disappeared quicker than a snowman on holiday on Mercury, it seemed a reasonable enough place to start.

"Bit ramshackle, isn't it?" said Stitches as they walked up to the front door of the small, terraced property. "He obviously doesn't take his work ethos home with him."

The front door was warped at the top, and the green paint was peeling across its entire surface. Even the bricks looked tired and forlorn and on the verge of breaking free from the dusty and crumbling cement surrounding them. Ollie knocked lightly but it was enough to push the door open. He wasn't overly surprised. He couldn't imagine anyone wanting to break in. The inside was what you would have expected to see, taking into account the dilapidated exterior.

The hallway was awash with footwear of various styles, and the banister had a large and teetering pile of coats draped over it. Just inside the door was an old school desk, the type with a hinged lid and a stained inkwell. The lewd graffiti and chewing gum stuck to the bottom were optional extras that this model didn't seem to come with. On inspection, the desk contained a goodly supply of cat litter which, judging by the clumps in it, hadn't been changed for a few days.

"I hope that's not muesli," said Stitches, turning his nose up. "The raisins look a bit suspect if you ask me."

At the end of the hallway was the kitchen, which looked cluttered and filthy, a breeding ground for bacteria if ever there was one. They decided not to look. Although they'd agreed to help the two gentlemen of Fibula with their little problem, they didn't want to get food poisoning in the process. They could go for tea at Mrs. Ladle's for that. Two other rooms were off the hallway. The first, which looked like the living room, was sparsely furnished, cold and uninviting and ultimately offered nothing. The back room, however, was a different story. It was chock full of boxes that contained papers, hand written documents and text books that would have taken ages to sift through. The rest of the detritus, that which hadn't found a home as yet, was haphazardly thrown onto various shelves, whilst even more was stacked into lofty, wobbly towers on a large, mahogany dining room table. Some of the books were closed, but they'd obviously been read because they had small bits of paper acting as bookmarks sticking out of them, whilst others had been left open at particular pages. Whether this was random or deliberate, it was impossible to determine. "These are all magic and spell books," said Ollie, glancing over some of the titles in the paper mountain. "Well, nearly all. Some of them are reference volumes about mythology."

"Not looking too good for the old boy, is it?" Stitches said reflectively, gazing around the rest of the room.

His eyes fell (no, not this time) on the mantelpiece which was barely visible under old candles, screwed up receipts and empty, fur covered tea cups, but it wasn't the mess that had drawn the zombie's attention. Behind one of the forgotten cups was an envelope that was crisp and white, making it look totally out of place. On it was written 'Mr Curator'. Stitches picked it up and slid his finger along the seam. He took out the letter that had been contained within, unfolded it and read it out loud.

"Mr. Curator. I'm so sorry about what has happened and what I've done. I don't know if you'll ever be able to forgive me, but I know that I will never be able to forgive myself. Unfortunately, this is something that I simply have to do." It was signed Balthazar Flange.

"That's a bit bleak, isn't it? What do you suppose it means?" asked Stitches.

Ollie pondered over the words that he'd heard. He shook his head. "I don't quite know what to make of it. I suppose the obvious conclusion to come to is that Flange is the thief, and he's off somewhere doing something with the pages. But why would he go to the trouble of writing a confession? Your average burglar doesn't suddenly have an attack of conscience and say sorry, but take the stuff anyway." "Yeah, but he might've had a good reason. I can't think of one off the top of my head, but you never know," said Stitches.

"Mmmm. Maybe, but I think we'll keep the letter to ourselves for the time being. No point in giving everything away, is there? And something's telling me that there's more to this than a rogue caretaker."

With both of them in agreement, the note stayed in Ollie's pocket when they returned to the museum. Once there, he explained what they had discovered, minus the agreed detail.

"That is very perplexing," said the curator, from behind a desk so vast that it made Ollie's look like an occasional table (although what an occasional table does when it's not being a table is a mystery that the great minds of our time have never figured out. And why anyone would have a piece of furniture that only performs its function a small percentage of the time is anyone's guess. You don't get an infrequent chair, an erratic sideboard or an intermittent Welsh Dresser do you, and the only time you ever see a sporadic poof is when Graham Norton gets a new series).

"Yes it is. Have you managed to translate the passages yet?" asked Ollie.

"Indeed we have," said Starch, "and they make for quite interesting, and I must say, somewhat disturbing reading. Mr. Vortex, if you would be so kind."

"Certainly," said the assistant, clearing his throat. "What this chapter, and the pages therein seem to be indicating, is the five hidden locations of a mysterious vessel known as The Cup of All Souls, a legendary artefact only ever previously heard of through word of mouth stories passed down through the generations of a few Scandinavian families. Apparently it was rent asunder many centuries ago and scattered. It's said that once the five pieces are found and brought together, and the Cup is taken to a certain place at a certain time, it will provide the finder with all the knowledge of both the natural and the supernatural worlds, thereby becoming the most powerful being in existence." "It was always thought to be a myth," continued Starch, "or maybe even an urban legend, like the Sofa of Destiny or the Fork of Indecisiveness, but this text and the fact that it may have been stolen by someone believing it to be true, may very well mean that it does actually exist."

"Either that or we're trying to find someone who's madder than a whole family of March hares," said Stitches. "Not that it matters. Whatever their reason for taking it they're no doubt a tad on the mental side."

"What if it does exist?" asked Ollie.

Vortex shook his head solemnly. "If the Cup is indeed real, and I haven't seen anything as of yet to convince me otherwise, and it falls into the wrong hands, then that one individual could wreak untold havoc across the entire world. He would have dominion over everything, and nothing could stop him."

Ollie and Stitches thought on this for a moment before Ollie continued.

"So what would you like from us now, gentlemen? As it's getting late, I'd suggest we continue the search for Flange tomorrow. We can ask around, see if anyone has seen or heard from him, and then do a more thorough search of his house. There may yet be more clues there."

Starch stood up and walked around his desk, an activity that took so long Stitches was convinced that the curator was going to need to take on water at regular intervals, and approached them both.

"If the hunt for this fabled artefact has indeed begun, then we are already at a considerable disadvantage. Mr. Vortex and I are just finishing the last transposition now, and what we would like you to do is follow the trail."

"Follow it!" exclaimed Stitches.

"Yes," said Starch, seriously. "You, my good man, were able to decipher passages unread for centuries after seeing them for only a few moments. You are our best chance. We would like to officially hire you to track down and locate the pieces of the Cup, return them to the safety of the museum, and bring the miscreant to justice."

"I don't know," said Stitches, wandering around the room chewing on a nail that ended up stuck in his gum. "Wandering about god knows where looking for god knows what that was stolen by god knows who or what... "

"We'll do it," Ollie cut in. "Marvellous," replied Starch. "Excellent," replied Vortex. "Bloody hell!" said Stitches.

"We'll talk about it outside," Ollie said in the style of a husband not wanting to have a row with his wife in the middle of a shop when she realises he's bored and has a go at him in front of everyone *because* he's bored but doesn't want to deal with the matter in front of everyone (there's a very simple solution to this most common of retail nightmares, gentlemen. Don't go, stay at home and write stories. It works for me. Unless *I'm* shopping for stationery of course in which case it's a matter of the utmost import and everyone in my family, extended or otherwise, should be suitably interested and want to join in).

"Like you'll let me get a word in." "Leave it."

"It would be nice to be consulted from time to time."

"Not in front of other people, please," Ollie hissed, quietly realising that all that was left to complete their relationship was marriage vows, the lumpy side of the bed and an empty bank account. "Outside."

"Look, all I. . . "

"Excuse me, gentlemen," Ollie said apologetically. With a firm grip and a hefty shove, Ollie manoeuvred his disgruntled colleague out of the office.

"You are so embarrassing," the half-vampire said with a flourish and, for some unknown reason, jazz hands. "Why did you have to show me up like that? Honestly, it's like being with a toddler."

"I just think it would be nice to be asked my opinion once in a while, is all. That's not too much to ask is it?" said Stitches.

"Fine." "Thank you."

"You're welcome. Now, are there any other grievances that I should know about?"

"I don't like your shoes."

Ollie shook his head. "Ladies and gentlemen, my friend the two hundred year old baby."

"Alright, I'm sorry. No there's nothing else," said Stitches.

"Okay. Good. Marvellous," sighed Ollie in as conciliatory a manner as he could muster (which was about as convincing as the school bully telling me he was sorry for stealing my bike, eating my sweets and spending my lunch money on a packet of fags. It wouldn't have been so bad but he'd already given me two hours of homework, split me up from my friend Sean and written a great big 'must try harder' on my school report). "So. What do you think about taking this job on then? It seems like it could be interesting work and we'll get paid."

Stitches smiled, happy to be included in the decision making process.

"Well, if you ask me, and you are. . . " "Splendid. We're doing it."

"You are so frustrating. Trying to use an Ouija board to contact a dyslexic is less taxing." Stitches officially sulked.

An hour and a half later saw them back at their office, with Ollie eagerly telling the others about their new found employment.

"Sounds great," said Ronnie. "Only one problem though." "Which is?" Ollie enquired.

"Well, this is a road trip, isn't it?" "Yes."

"Which means we're going to be away from home for a while, doesn't it?"

"Yes."

Ronnie didn't think he would have to spell it out to Ollie, who was by far the most intelligent member of the group, but it looked like that was going to be the case. Last week whilst playing Scrabble, for instance, Ollie had got two; count them, two six letter words. He would have got a seven, but Ethan pointed out that 'focking' wasn't in fact a word at all, and if it was it certainly wouldn't mean 'the act of sticking a candle up a spectre's backside.' (I know that's a spurious link but hey ho, there must be a reason for it. I can't think of it at the moment but I'm sure there is one. If I remember it, I'll give you a call).

Ronnie carried on. "Well, for one, how are you going to cope with being away from your coffin? Two, if we have to stop every time it starts to get light so you can get your head down, we'll be away for months, and three, where are you going to find fresh blood twice a day if we're not taking the fridge?"

Stitches gazed around the office, trying to avoid Ollie's eyes, but at the same time making the 'if you'd listened to me' look on his face, plain for all to see.

Ollie, impossibly, went as red as a ginger child under a Caribbean sky.

"You don't think for one minute that I hadn't considered any of those things, do you?" said the half vampire weakly.

"Well, no, quite frankly," said Stitches. "You got all excited like a kid on Christmas morning, and jumped in with both feet without thinking about the consequences."

"Didn't."

"Did to."

"I did not."

"Alright then," continued Stitches with a superior air of righteousness. "What had you planned to do about it?" He could sense a rare and somewhat childish victory.

"Umm," whispered Ollie, barely audibly. The zombie almost had him.

"Don't mumble," he ordered. "Crumble!" Ollie exclaimed. "What?"

"Crumble. I was going to ask the Professor to sort something out. I would've told you, but you kept butting in." Ollie breathed a vast sigh of relief.

"You are such a fibber," said Stitches.

"I don't think so," retorted Ollie. "So, if you guys want to get your bits together, I'll go and see the Prof." He opened the door behind his desk and headed to the lab.

"You'll never get him," said Ronnie.

"He's too devious," added Ethan. "When was the last time that you ever heard of a vampire getting caught out, verbally or otherwise?"

"Only once I suppose," said Stitches, resigned to coming off second best again. "There was that incident last year when Splat the Organgrinder fell foul of that get rich quick scam. But he is a bit thick."

"Oh, yeah," said Ronnie. "What happened there then?"

"He bought a share in a jewellery business in Mesotheleoma, except

215

it turned out that he wasn't investing in high quality items and the guy in question was actually a travelling salesman selling cheap crucifixes."

"I take it he didn't get much out of it?" asked Ethan.

"About eight pints I think, by the time he caught up with the bloke," said Stitches.

"Ah well, I'm sure your time will come, mate," said Ronnie. "Come on let's get sorted."

———

A flickering light from the stub of a candle shed its meagre glow across the table, illuminating the pages spread over its surface. They were laid out in order, the jagged edges where they'd been ripped from the book casting sharp, misshapen forms on the wood. Next to each of the pages was a hand written note, detailing the revised versions of the script in legible English. It had taken a while, but the person perusing them had finally decoded the words now that the secret had been revealed to them. Their mouth moved involuntarily as they read the words over and over, savouring each phrase, relishing the implications of what they could mean once all the pieces of the Cup had been found. Eager hands rubbed together and a smile played across lips that would have gone unseen by an observer, the light from the candle was so weak.

"Not long now," a voice spoke from the darkness. It was accompanied by a plume of condensation as hot breath was met by the surrounding frigid air. "Not long."

———

A loud bang and a screech of metal on metal greeted Ollie as he made his way along the corridor towards Crumble's lab. After his verbal battle with Stitches, he had seen the Prof and asked him if he could try and solve the problems that he would face on their trip. He hadn't needed to bother for the journey to London of course. That hadn't been troublesome at all as it was held at night, and he'd had somewhere to sleep during the day. And being a corporate do all the drinks had been on tap twenty four seven. The mini bar had been a veritable blood bank.

Crumble had jumped at the chance to help out once more, and had got to work as soon as Ollie had left. Now, a few short hours later, he was back, eager to see the fruits of Crumble's labours. The time delay had also given him time to cool down from the argument. He was annoyed with Stitches for rowing with him, but at the same time he was disappointed with himself for getting involved in such petty business. The problem was he couldn't help it. He may only have been a half blood vampire and blessed with a good few human characteristics, but verbal and physical confrontations awoke something in his dark half that would not back down or be denied. When it reared its head he would come out all guns blazing from his corner, ready to argue to the death about absolutely anything. It was quite puerile actually, and could at times be very embarrassing. One time when he was about fifteen and had actually managed to secure his first date with a human girl, they'd gone to see The Usual Suspects at the local cinema. It had all been going splendidly and he was even getting to the point of asking said female if she wanted to have a rummage through his pick and mix, when the subject of who Kaiser Soze was raised itself. It had ended up with the pair having a ferocious row in front of everybody, with Ollie bellowing at the top of his voice about why he thought Gabriel Byrne was the bad guy. The girl had stormed out, so he stayed and watched the rest of the film only to be proved wrong. Strangely, he hadn't seen her again.

He knocked on the lab door and went straight in, because there was no way that Crumble would have heard it. He did it out of habit and sheer politeness.

"Ah, dear boy, welcome," the Prof shouted.

Well, he assumed it was the Prof. The voice was coming from a plume of smoke that was taking up about a third of the room. "Come in, come in."

Ollie did so with the usual sense of trepidation and dread that accompanied any visit to Crumble's domain.

"Have you taken up smoking?" he asked.

"Oh no," replied Crumble, appearing from the misty shroud like a contestant on Stars in their Eyes. (Tonight, Matthew, I'm going to be a borderline psychotic pensioner, who enjoys blowing things up more than a member of Al Qaeda who got kicked out of the organisation for being far too extreme). "Just an idea that I had."

"Which would be?" asked Ollie, the spectre of worry ever present on the horizon.

"Well, it seems to me that when you make a cup of tea it takes ages for the flavour to seep from the leaves through the bag and into the water."

"Right."

"So I thought I would add a little explosive to the mixture and then make the tea. The heat from the water reacts with the incendiary compound and sets it off, literally forcing the flavour from the leaves into the cup."

"I see," said Ollie, vowing never again to accept a drink from the Professor unless he was safely hidden behind a blast door and had on a suit of armour. "So how's it going?"

"I'm just having a few problems getting the proportions right. No point in boiling the kettle if you're not going to have a hand to hold the cup, is there?"

"Well, quite. So, assuming you get it sorted out, what will you call them when Twinings come banging on your door?"

"TeaNT Bags."

"Mmmm. I can see there being quite a market for that. Terrorists will love it. No more messing about with Semtex, timers and command wires. All they'll need is a tea pot."

"Indeed. Anyway, how can I help you, dear boy?"

Mad as a particularly insane milliner. "I've come to collect my bits, if you'd had time to conjure something up."

"Oh, of course, of course," said Crumble, walking over to his cupboard. He opened it up and took out three objects which he placed onto the table.

"There we are. Your solar reflecting, ultra violet repelling, protective headgear. Your sod infused, collapsible, nocturnal, encapsulation device and your desiccated, rehydratable, platelet based liquid nourishment."

Ollie rolled his eyes to the ceiling. "And in English please," he said, suddenly wishing that the word a day toilet paper that he'd gotten for Crumble's birthday might not have been such a good idea.

"You hat, your bed and you blood," said Crumble. "Ah. Thank you very much."

Crumble picked up one of the items at a time, and explained how it worked to a rapidly wearying Ollie.

"This first one will keep the harmful rays of the sun off you during the day. It's a balaclava with a hidden inner lining in which I've placed ground up sunglasses. Works a treat."

"How do you know?" said Ollie suspiciously. The last time Crumble had claimed something would 'work a treat', he'd invented mayhem theory, Mount Vesuvius had developed indigestion for the first time since 1944 and David Walliams decided he was so funny that he had to share himself with an unsuspecting public. (To clarify. Mayhem theory is a bit like chaos theory in that minor occurrences in one location may cause major consequences somewhere else. It differs in that the consequences that occur whenever Professor Crumble does anything at all are always major, never good and usually result in something disappearing, being completely destroyed or changed beyond all recognition. There we go, a little bit of science explained for you. David Walliams on the other hand, I can't explain).

"I wrapped a mouse in it and popped it in the microwave for a few minutes. He came out fine."

"Done to a turn, no doubt."

"Yes," said Crumble, quickly and expertly sidestepping the issue of animal cruelty and why he now had a mouse running around the lab with a sun tan. "The second item is very simple indeed."

By way of demonstration he picked it up and spread it across the table.

"It's a foam mattress that I've infused with earth from your coffin, so no matter where you go, you'll be sleeping on your home soil."

"Liking that one," said Ollie, pressing the mattress with a finger to test its springiness. "Memory foam. Nice touch."

Crumble was smiling proudly. A presentation hadn't gone this well since he'd shown the local Neighbourhood Witch Group how to get more miles per twig out of their brooms. They'd loved it and he'd been the toast of the meeting, which was just as well because if it had gone wrong he would've been toasted at the meeting. They were a tough crowd.

"The third thing," he continued, "is very clever, even if I do say so myself. I've dehydrated twenty eight pints of blood down to a very fine powder and placed it in this tin. All you have to do is put a couple of tablespoons full into this shaker and add water." Ollie studied the three inventions and he had to admit he was impressed.

"Well I must say, Crumble, well done. These are just the ticket. They'll do admirably. Thanks a lot, Prof."

"Oh, that's alright, dear boy. And who knows, by the time you get back from your little jaunt, I'll have perfected my latest creation."

"And what would that be?" Ollie asked, even more suspiciously than the last time.

"It's yoghurt that has so much taste that it bursts out of the pot and literally assaults your taste buds."

"I see. And what will this one be called, dare I ask?" "Fromage Affray."

"Black-eye-currant flavour perhaps?" "Pardon me?"

"Never mind. Thanks again, Prof." "Toodles."

———

Dr Jekyll didn't know what to do with himself. (The fact that he'd been languishing in the public domain since 1886 didn't help either, so it was about time he got out and about again. And yes I've checked, yes I can and no it's not stealing. Think of it as a [book] cover version). He was in two minds as to his next course of action. Since the incident with the farmers' daughter, he'd been keeping more of a low profile than a member of the IRA at an SAS Christmas party, and wasn't yet sure if it was safe for him to stick his head above the hay-bale to have a look. Anyway, it had all been a massive misunderstanding, as things often are when there's a nubile, young nymph involved. The lady in question had come to him in secret, telling him that her fiancé had left her with a huge amount of debt, a shed load of work to do at the farm and a growing bump under her dress that didn't get there by accident or divine intervention. Jekyll's enquiries had led him to the small village of Bile, about an hour away from Skullenia, where he'd located the lady's reclusive partner. On strict instructions from the client, he had only gathered evidence, which in this case involved taking photographs of the chap. She'd wanted to see for herself what he was getting up to and who he was getting it up to with before pursuing any course of action.

On his return and due to the need for discretion, he'd met her at midnight in her fathers' barn, where he'd presented her with the documentary proof of her fiancés infidelity. On seeing the photos she'd broken down, wailed like a banshee and attached herself to the surprised bounty hunter like an octopus to a divers mask. Unfortunately, she was so overzealous in her late night fumblings for comfort that she'd toppled over, sending both of them into the packed apple and orange crates below. As they were descending, the cuckolded girl was singing, "The farmers' daughter is a hoe hoe ho," because it was the song that The Tractors had been playing for their first dance in the club where they'd met. Then, in a spectacularly bad piece of timing, her father had come barging in, brandishing a pitchfork that could have easily skewered a Brontosaurus, wearing a face redder than something very red indeed, and yelling, "get your hands off me Grannies."

Jekyll very quickly realised that there was no use trying to explain, because he looked as guilty as a man caught in a barn at midnight in a

compromising position with an angry farmer's daughter (The farmer was angry of course, not the daughter. She was more than happy, having gotten over the bad news about her former beloved not two seconds after getting her leg over Jekyll). So that being the case he'd bolted out the back door like an Olympic sprinter and headed off into the night.

He'd run at top speed for about ten minutes, thinking that this was more than long enough for any man to be annoyed, no matter who'd grabbed their fruit. Sadly for Henry Jekyll though, the farmer in question was not only a disgruntled father who thought the world of his princess, he was a lunatic of epic proportions who'd wasted no time in gathering several of his arable colleagues into a lynch mob.

Just as he'd gotten his breath back (battered, bruised and not containing enough oxygen to keep a lazy sloth going) Jekyll had seen the blazing torches from a good distance away, so at least he had a reasonable head start, and figuring that the farmer hadn't got that much of a good look at him because he'd been tangled up in the daughter's voluminous skirt, a day or so of keeping his head down should do the trick. And it was a far better option than having one of those deranged land tillers taking his head off.

So this was where he now found himself. Hiding in a quarry, worriedly peeking over the rim every now and again and trying to get comfy on a granite mattress (it was bedrock after all).

Presently he realised that it was getting dark and as he hadn't seen the mob for a good long while he decided it was about time to get the hell out of there. Twenty four hours hiding amidst a collection of old rocks was no fun at all no matter which way you sat on it. He could go to a Status Quo concert for that.

Gingerly raising his head above the rim of the quarry once more, he rechecked his surroundings. All clear. Now, if he had his bearings right, he was about six miles north of home, which would put him on the outskirts of Fibula, which was a quiet little town that was usually as dead as daytime TV.

An hour later he arrived at the edge of town. Thankfully he still had the cover of darkness, so when he reached the tiny hamlet he was able to move through it reasonably quickly. As he reached the junction of Main Street and Digitalis Avenue and rounded the corner that would take him up to the museum, he collided with another figure walking quickly in the opposite direction.

"Ouch," he said as his foot was caught under the other person's.

The stranger let out a soft 'ooof' of their own which was followed by the rustle of paper as several sheets of it fell to the ground. Recovering his composure and his balance Jekyll said, "I'm so sorry; I can hardly see a thing in this light."

"Oh, no need to apologise," said the other, bending down to pick up the loose leaves from the pavement, "could have happened to anyone." The person was clearly male, the voice gave it away (unless it was a particularly robust lady of course, but then she wouldn't have been out at this time of night in the first place. Firstly it wasn't at all safe and secondly she'd have been at hockey practice or on a night time exercise with her battalion. Get over it. You were thinking it too).

Pages collected, he stood up. Jekyll stared but he could see hardly anything of the chap, the light from the lamp posts was so dim, but the eyes immediately attracted his attention. They seemed to gather in the meagre illumination and reflect it back tenfold, giving off a steely blue radiance that was at the same time captivating and vaguely frightening.

"Well, I'm sorry all the same," said Jekyll.

As the stranger juggled the pages, one of them flopped over the others into the light, allowing Jekyll to catch a glimpse of the jumbled letters on the page.

"That looks complicated," he offered in a friendly fashion. "Wouldn't fancy trying to sort that lot out. Are you from the museum?"

"Look, I wish I could stop and chat," said blue eyes, rearranging the pages so that none of the writing was visible, "but I really do have to go now. Sorry about your foot."

With that he scurried off towards Main Street, every now and again pausing to make sure that the papers were secure and that no one was watching him.

"Strange little fellow," Jekyll said to himself as he watched the figure recede into the distance before finally getting swallowed up by the cloying darkness. "He seemed a bit nervous."

Jekyll was about to start the final leg of his journey home when his eye was caught by something on the cobbled street. It was lying in the exact spot that the stranger had been standing on. He bent down to see what it was. It glinted in the low light the closer he got, but it wasn't until he picked it up and moved a few yards to his left so that he was under a street lamp, that he could see what it was. It was a small rectangular badge, the type that a school prefect might wear, except this one said 'CARETAKER'.

———

Whilst Ethan and Ronnie paid one last visit to the museum to collect the translated pages from Starch and Vortex, Ollie and Stitches were helping Flug to pack (and by helping Flug to pack I mean that someone else did the work whilst Flug sat in the kitchen, staring at nothing and looking like a hypnotised bullock. They could've got him to help of course but that was fraught with danger, and would've taken three times as long, caused more than a few injuries and involved far more expletives than is reasonable for putting some clothes into a suitcase). Ollie had already packed all of his own stuff a while ago, after he'd emailed Henry Jekyll about their mission. If there was any other information to be had about it, then Mandeep Singh would be able to provide it. He seemed able to collect anything about anything, no matter who it involved or what the subject was.

Stitches was a different matter. Provided that he had enough cotton and needles to deal with any dismemberment style emergencies, he was pretty much good to go as he was. He didn't really need to change his clothes very often, unless environmental conditions caused them to get dirty, and as far as supplies went it was, well, zero. As long as he got a drink of water to lubricate his innards every now and again he was fine.

Flug, on the other hand, was a different kettle of insanity altogether. It would have been less hassle getting ready to go away for a fortnight with twelve month old sextuplets. The number of changes of underwear was similar, though.

"I don't want to be rude or anything," Stitches said, glancing around Flug's room whilst sitting on his vast bed, "but adult nappies?"

"Keep it down," responded Ollie, looking behind him to make sure that Flug hadn't heard what had been said. "You know he's sensitive about it."

"It's not the only thing that'll be sensitive after wandering around in one of those for a couple of days."

"Can't you just be a little more caring for a change? You know he's not that good at going to the toilet yet."

Stitches grimaced and rolled his eyes, always a mistake that required a tap to the side of his head.

"Well I know that," he said. "My room's next to the bathroom, don't forget. Most nights it sounds like an ocean liner's being launched in there. Oh, and if you think for one minute that I'm changing him, then you are very much mistaken."

"Don't panic," said Ollie, placing a cute but well-worn Blue Nosed

Bat in the case. "I had a word with Crumble about it. These ones are self-contained, absorbent, self-cleaning units that can be taken off as easily as a pair of ordinary undies without leaving anything behind."

"There's an image to conjure with."

"So, you don't have to worry. Thanks to these, Flug will be able to sort himself out."

The zombie didn't look entirely convinced.

"And they're biodegradable," Ollie continued, folding up Flug's favourite snuggie blankie, "so there'll be no impact on the environment either."

"If you say so," said the zombie. "But don't forget the last time he went he blocked up the toilet, cracked three pipes and flooded the bathroom. Poor old Hector needed two cups of tea and a lie down, and that was before he went in there to sort it out. It sounded like he was on safari."

"I know, I know," Ollie said, softly popping the lid onto Flug's non drip cup and dropping it into the case. "But he is trying," the wet wipes went in next, "and you've got to remember that in many ways he's still a child."

"You're not kidding. It's getting boring cutting up his food and picking the breadcrumbs off his fish fingers."

"Still," said Ollie, putting a night light into the case, "he is growing up all the time. It won't be long before he can stay up till eight 'o' clock and go to bed in the dark. Anyway, are you going to help me or am I doing this all by myself?"

"Looks like you've pretty much finished," said Stitches getting up from the bed. His hip cracked rather loudly, which caused him to wobble slightly.

"Seems that way, doesn't it?" Ollie replied, fastening the zip on the case. "Right, let's get this out front with the rest and wait for Ronnie and Ethan to get back. I'm quite excited, I must admit," he continued, hefting the case onto the floor. "I reckon this is going to be a really interesting job, out and about hunting for treasure and all that".

"Mmmm, sounds more like an extended ramble to me, but at least it's better than doing nothing."

"Which will make a nice change for you, won't it?" observed Ollie sarcastically, slowly manoeuvring the case to the door.

"Cheeky sod. Here, give us the case. I'll take it outside."

"Thanks," said Ollie gratefully. "And try not to rip an arm off whilst you're carrying it. That thing's heavy."

———

In his haste to get away from the pursuing horde the night before, Dr Jekyll had lost his keys somewhere. He knocked on the door of the converted convenience store that was now his and his partner's place of work, and made sure that he was standing in full view of the spy hole nestling in the wood.

"Yes, who is it please?" came an Indian voice from the other side of the door.

"It's Henry."

"Henry who, please?"

Here we go again, thought Jekyll.

"Henry Jekyll. Come on, Mandeep, open up. Who the hell else is it going to be?"

"One moment please."

The door was unlocked painfully slowly, but finally opened. "Identification please," demanded the diminutive Indian gentleman, standing before him with an outstretched hand.

"What do you mean identification? For goodness sake, put your bloody glasses on, will you. It's me, Henry, your business partner."

Mandeep Singh fumbled in his jacket pocket and extracted his spectacles, and popped them onto his pudgy face.

"Ah, Mr. Jekyll, come in please."

"At last. And how many times have I told you to call me Henry?" said Jekyll, stepping over the threshold.

"Yes, yes of course. Mr. Jekyll, of course."

Jekyll walked along the hallway and into their shared office, which he crossed to get to his desk where he sat down. He switched on his computer and logged on.

"Is everything sorted out with the daughter, please?" asked Singh as he leafed through the contents of a filing cabinet.

"Not quite. Let's just say there could be further developments," replied Jekyll hesitantly.

"How so, please?"

"Put it this way. If anybody comes to the door and they're carrying any farming implements, don't let them in and tell them I've emigrated."

"Very good."

Henry logged on and noticed that he'd received an email from Ollie, which he read at once. He showed it to Mandeep and told him about what the boys were up to, and his incident with the stranger.

"Mandeep," he said, looking up at the hovering Indian, "have we got any files on the Fibulan museum?"

What a silly question that was. His little associate was a consummately professional retailer, a path that he'd taken after spending three decades as a consummately professional hit man. For thirty years Mandeep Singh had worked for the Indian Secret Service, disposing of any and all enemies of the state, human or otherwise that threatened the security of his homeland.

Fearing nothing and willing to take on anything that came his way, he'd been the best in his field and regularly won the Assassin of The Month award and always got his end of year bonus, but an unfortunate encounter with a rogue demon, the likes of which that had never been encountered before, had left him deader than Gandhi's flip flops. Only the unnatural ministrations of a local priest, who'd witnessed the assassins' demise, had brought him back to life. Sadly though, he now hovered in a kind of semi live/dead state, neither one thing nor the other and, due to a clause in his government contract stating that he had to be human at least ninety percent of his working hours, he'd been forced to resign. It made sense though, because every now and then, Singh sort of died all over again. It wasn't actual death as such, and it wasn't a fugue state, a stupor, a blackout or a descent into oblivion either. And he certainly wasn't cataleptic, narcoleptic, catatonic, isotonic, gin and tonic, or anything else with a posh medical name that meant you had to pay more for treatment when you mentioned it to your GP. He quite simply passed away... ish. (n.b. It is a common, if not very well known, medical practice for doctors to base their fees on the length of the name of the condition that their patient has. If you tell him you've got flu for instance, he'll no doubt tell you to rest up for a couple of weeks, drink plenty of fluids and buy a box of paracetamol. You get all smart and tell him you've got influenza brought on by contact with someone carrying the Orthomyxoviridae virus, then you better cancel your holiday, forget about Christmas and take out a bank loan. Or failing that, buy a gun and simply take out the bank).

Dr. Zoltan, Skullenia's physician par excellence, had done quite a lot of research into the matter after Mandeep's last episode and had offered a treatment of his own devising. He'd looked at the semi deadish Indian and declared, "Maybe he needs to get some sleep," which everyone decided was about as much use as Dr. Zoltan's medical qualifications.

The main problem with the condition was that it took at least a couple of hours for the lingering remnants of the priest's spells to rouse Mandeep's system into life once more, and it was no good being in the middle of something important when all of your faculties packed up and left you a useless, brain dead heap on the floor, unless you were auditioning for the antagonist role in Rocky XII or joining The House of Lords of course.

And so, not being able to kill and maim anymore, Mandeep had done what any good, self-respecting Asian gentleman would do. He'd opened a shop and, bearing in mind his experience with the supernatural world, he'd concluded that it would be rather profitable to open up in Skullenia. And it had all gone very well at first, thank you very much, and he'd slowly and steadily began to amass a rather tidy fortune. (So good was his venture that he even thought about applying to appear on Dragon's Den, but then decided against it as they've got enough selfish, blood sucking ghouls on there already, but he would have fit right into the spin off series, 'Yeah We've Done Alright So That Allows Us To Sit And Lord It Over Other Aspiring Business People And Deride Their Life's Work For The Sake Of Ratings And Shameless Self Promotion'. Mind you, the series only lasted for one episode. The entire budget went on the opening credits).

The problems with his business started with the advent of the darknet which allowed people to shop from the comfort of their own coffins, meaning that his turnover had gradually tailed off. Sites like prey.com and evilbay were able to undercut him at every turn. Being an astute sort of a chap he'd seen it coming so he'd sold off the rest of his stock and was in the process of getting ready to head back to India, when a random meeting with the Doctor Jekyll had changed the course of his life.

It transpired that a couple of Singh's customers had neglected to pay off their accounts, and he'd mentioned this in passing to Jekyll during the course of a semi-drunken conversation at the Bolt and Jugular. Jekyll and his alter ego, who tended to put in an appearance when the Doctor was completely bladdered, had both assured the Indian that they could find the missing debtors and secure his missing funds. If Singh could provide the information then Jekyll/Hyde would do the legwork. After all he had four, so to speak.

They'd reached an agreement regarding the matter and the errant shoppers were located twelve hours later and relieved of the majority of their assets. Their money was taken as well.

So what with Singh's talent for information gathering and Jekyll's ability to act on it with the help of his not so silent partner, a relationship was formed, and Hyde and Sikh, Bounty Hunters of Repute, came into existence.

Singh went over to the filing cabinet marked F and rummaged around in it.

"Here we go," he said. "Museum of Fibula. Open since 1621 and said to contain the largest collection of mythological and supernatural artefacts in the known world. The current curator is a Mr. Ignacious Starch, who is aided by his assistant Vortex. The only other employee is a caretaker by the name of Flange."

"Ah, Flange," said Jekyll, tapping his top lip thoughtfully as he recalled the details of Ollie's email. "He's the one that's disappeared, isn't he?"

"Yes indeed. And it would seem from the evidence provided that he is the miscreant who has stolen the pages from the book."

"Mmmm. What about the other two?" Singh flipped to the last quarter of the file.

"Ignacious Starch. One hundred and forty nine years old, human but did have a talent for sorcery in his youth. Studied at Oxford University where he got a first class degree in Ancient History, and some very nice reviews for his performances in the Footlights. He was tipped to become Dean but an incident involving a fellow student being turned to wood put paid to that. He spent many years travelling abroad. In fact many of the exhibits in the museum are ones that he collected himself. It was during his travels that he visited the museum and stayed on as assistant to the previous curator, Fenton Bauble, who was on the verge of retiring. The two became great friends so it was natural for Starch to take over when the old boy left. That was about forty years ago, and he's been there ever since."

"Okay, nice and comprehensive. What about the other one? Vortex wasn't it?"

Singh flicked through the pages until he came to the very last one.

He took it out and studied it before speaking.

"Haven't got a lot on this fellow I'm afraid. For some reason he's been hard to research. No public records, birth, death or undeath certificates. Bit of a mystery, that chap, but based on the description you gave, it certainly does sound like he was the man you bumped into."

"That's fine. I'll try and find out what I can when I go there. Maybe Starch will be able to tell me a bit more."

"Very good," said Singh, replacing the file. "When will you be going please?"

"In a little while. I want to have a surf round the darknet for a bit, see what I can dig up before I go."

He logged onto Wickedpedia, which was always a good place to start.

———

A while later (it was a longish while rather than a shortish one. Flug had been upset because his stuff was missing, and it took a fair bit of time to explain to him that it was in a suitcase and hadn't been stolen by the little orange monsters that he seemed to think lived under his bed. It was errant nonsense of course, but then again Flug wasn't very good with his colours yet), Ollie was sitting at his desk with a steaming hot cup of Earl Grey and a packet of Itinerant Travelling Tinker Folk Creams. (They used to be called Gypsy Creams, but in these days of political correctness and all of its associated flim flammery, that wasn't allowed anymore, in case someone got offended. What was next? Baa

Baa any colour, creed, caste, religion, faith or belief sheep? Snow Could Be Any Colour In Our Diverse And Racially Tolerant Society and The Seven Little People Who Shouldn't Be Judged Because Of Their Stature. Picture the scene outside the theatre:

Mum. "Shall we see a pantomime?" Kids. "Yeah, which one?"

Mum. "How about 'Snow Could Be Any Colour In Our Diverse And Racially Tolerant Society and The Seven Little People Who Shouldn't Be Judged Because Of Their Stature'?"

Kids. "What on earth is that, Mum?"

Mum. "You know. The one with the beautiful girl who falls asleep after eating a poisoned apple, and those little people who work in the diamond mine."

Kids. "Oh yeah. The fit lady and the midgets." Mum. "Yes."

There we are. Conclusive proof that not only is political correctness rather silly, it makes no difference whatsoever as to how people think. A spade will always be a spade. Dig it?)

Ollie switched his computer on, clicked onto his screen name, marmitesarnie@darknet.sk,and perused his emails.

"My God. What a load of old rubbish."

They were having a cape sale at Bela's. Buy one get one half price.

Free blood guarding with every purchase.

Delete.

You have won the Hungarian Lottery. Send your details to General Scamov at uww.hungarianlottery.com (to explain, uww stands for undeadworldweb).

Delete.

Grow your fangs an inch in two weeks with our miracle serum and special exercises. Impress the ladies.

Big delete.

Ollie sighed as he deleted a couple more pointless messages. He wasn't a huge fan of computers, or the darknet for that matter, but he had finally conceded that in the modern business world it was practically indispensable, especially now that word of his agency was beginning to spread. He'd heard that even Count Jocular had invested in one. It was in an office that had been decorated in a style reminiscent of the early Roman Empire, circa 120AD and an allotment damaged by a storm, circa some time last Tuesday.

The last email in the list was from Dr. Jekyll. It was in reply to the one that he'd sent earlier and was only a couple of hours old, so at least it would seem that he'd gotten out of his indelicate situation. (News travelled fast in and around Skullenia, especially if it was bad. When Ollie had tripped on one of Flug's shoes at the top of the stairs for instance, he'd been in the building by himself, but it didn't take long for someone to knock on the door, ask if he was alright and offer to mend his trousers. Spooky).

As he read the message his brow furrowed in consternation. In it Jekyll outlined his encounter with the stranger in Fibula and the fact that he wasn't going to mention it until his conversation with his partner, Mr. Singh indicated the person that Jekyll had stumbled into sounded just like Vortex, although details of the man were scant.

Ollie sat back in his chair and thought about it for a moment. Whilst not overtly strange for the museum assistant to be out at and about in the middle of the night, his furtive behaviour was a little odd, and the fact that he might have been carrying the missing pages from the book wasn't particularly disturbing because he and Starch had been working on the translation. The discarded or dropped caretaker badge was somewhat mysterious, but only up to a point, and a very small point at that. Who was to say that it wasn't already on the ground and just happened to be in the exact spot that the two men had had their encounter? On reflection, he didn't think that it was overtly suspicious, but the fact that Jekyll had seen fit to mention it meant it warranted some consideration. After all, it wasn't that long ago that he'd been totally taken in by the late Obsidia and betrayed. He was starting to learn that not everybody could be trusted.

Still, with all things considered, it wouldn't hurt to do a bit of digging on the parties involved. At the end of the day someone was responsible for stealing the pages, so any information that Jekyll might be able to unearth about Starch, Vortex and Flange might prove useful either way. And what was the use of knowing a couple of bounty hunters if you didn't make use of their services, though not in the way that Flug thought, he mused. He'd assumed that Jekyll and Singh would be able to locate any chocolate bar you'd care to mention. Ollie replied to Jekyll's email confirming that he'd like him to investigate in Fibula further, before logging off and leaning back in his chair.

His train of thought was derailed at that junction by the return of Ronnie and Ethan from the museum.

"Hi, guys," Ollie said enthusiastically, shutting the computer down and filing away the message to the back of his mind. "Have you got the sheets?"

Ronnie placed a leather bound folder onto the desk. "It's all in there," he said.

Ollie flipped it open. Each transcription was in a plastic sheath, and in the one next to it was the accompanying map.

"If you look at the first map," said Ethan, "it actually tells us where to start. The others are a bit more vague, but I reckon a bit of lateral thinking should help us out."

"Mmmm" muttered Ollie as he studied the diagrams. It was the first time that he'd seen them, and he had to admit that they did appear to be, as Ethan said, a bit vague, and about as much use as a pogo stick was to a kangaroo.

All five of them seemed to be bland, featureless pages with one or two lines drawn on them that, depending on which one you were looking at, snaked across the page in seemingly random directions. The only other details were a few words and a small, badly drawn picture.

For the entire world it looked like a four year old had been asked to draw a treasure map. The first one, as Ronnie had pointed out, seemed to be the most straightforward.

"Do we know where this is?" Ollie asked hopefully, pointing at the place name on the map.

"Yes we do, actually," Ronnie said proudly. "It's north east of here, about seventy miles away as the bat flies. It's just over the border into Scapularis. The only thing we can't figure out is the little drawing. I know where Tonboot is though. I went there once on a stag do."

Ollie picked up the map and studied it more closely, holding it a couple of inches from his nose. At first he thought one of the details was a small house, and then a church, but one tiny clue, that was really difficult to see initially, gave it away.

"Oh, I see," he announced triumphantly, placing the map back down onto the desk so that the others could see. "It's a well. If you look close enough you can just make out a little bucket."

Ronnie and Ethan each adopted the look of those missing

something so obvious, a something they obviously shouldn't have missed in the first place such was its complete and utter obviousness. Ollie didn't point it out obviously because it was obvious from the obvious expressions on their faces that they were well aware of their obvious lack of seeing he obvious.

"So the well is where we need to start?" asked Ethan. "Obviously," replied Ronnie.

"Excellent," said Ollie, pleased that they were about to begin and hoping that the rest of the quest would be as easy. He closed the folder and got up from his chair.

"We're off to the Well in Tonboot."

————

"I think the fang belt's gone," said Ethan from under the bonnet. "It's snapped clean in half. It looks older than me." He straightened up and wiped his hand on a greasy rag that Ronnie handed to him. In reality it was actually more of a flannel than a rag. A Gargle the Golem one to be precise. It was one of Flug's, but they could get away with it being dirty by telling Flug that it was night time in the picture and that Gargle was getting ready to go to bed.

"Great," Ollie complained in disappointment. "We get five miles down the road and wallop."

"Could be worse," Ronnie added, encouragingly. "It could've happened in the middle of the day in town. At least this way no one's seen us."

"Hey there, boys. Need a lift?"

A whoosh from above made them all look up. The figure flying over was shrouded in darkness, but the shower of blue sparks and the loud cackle accompanied by a large wad of mottled phlegm hitting the roof of the vehicle kind of gave it away.

"Hello, Mrs. Ladle," they all replied in perfect unison. Well, four of them bade the witch hello. Flug shouted out, "Hi, Santa, can me have a big sack of sweeties for Christmas?"

"Only if he brings you a plunger as well," said Stitches. "Every drainable hole in the building'll get clogged up otherwise."

"Don't you start," said Ollie, levelling his frustration at the zombie. "It's your choice of vehicle that got us here in the first place."

"Well, I thought it would be ideal," protested the zombie. "Plenty of room, rugged bodywork, good mileage and excellent petrol consumption."

"Of course it's good on petrol. The furthest it ever goes is a couple of hundred yards before it breaks down. And did you have to get a hearse? Could you have got anything more sombre?"

"Well it was either this or an ice cream van," Stitches explained, "and I thought this would be better than having to stop every five minutes to tell people that we don't have Sticky Fingers or Yeti Balls."

"Looks like we *are* going to be stopping every five minutes," said Ronnie.

"If I may, boys," Mrs. Ladle cut in from ground level, loud enough to be heard over the slowly rising voices. "But I think I might be able to help."

"Do you know a lot about car engines then?" said Ethan.

"Oh good lord no. I'm afraid my magical abilities don't extend to mechanical devices such as this, I never took the course, but I think that I may have an ideal solution."

With that she alighted from her broom, hoisted up her skirts, and fumbled about in her waistband.

Ollie looked on, the terror on his face plain for all to see. Stitches looked on, the horror of his expression clearly visible.

Ronnie looked on, the fear he felt clearly demonstrated as he took a step back.

Ethan looked on, the dread of the situation forcing him to look away.

Flug looked on, the wonderment at the glistening, gooey mess that he'd just extracted from his nose obvious to one and all.

"Stitches," the monster asked, a worried lilt in his voice. "I fink I pulled my brain out."

Thankful that something had drawn his attention away from the spectacle of the senior striptease going on, he studied the end of Flug's digit.

"I don't think it is, mate. That's far too big. We'd need a police search unit and a forensic team to find your brain. There's more chance of Stephen Hawking winning a game of Twister, to be honest."

"Tada," exclaimed Mrs. Ladle triumphantly, flapping a long, black leather belt around her head. "This should do it." She walked towards the car and stuck her head under the bonnet.

The boys still had the horrified looks on their faces, but it was Stitches who broke the very uncomfortable silence that had descended like a steel blanket.

"Oh my goodness," he said quietly. "I sincerely hope that's not holding anything important up. I really don't think I'm strong enough to handle that."

Ronnie, stunned, nodded in agreement.

"Me either," he said. "The thought of those lower portions being on display would be enough to make the Grim Reaper himself hand his notice in on the grounds of unreasonable working conditions."

"Too right. Still, on the bright side, he would have somewhere to keep his scythe," said Stitches.

"Excuse me, Mrs. Ladle," asked Ollie, trying but failing miserably to tear his eyes away just in case the good witch decided to divest herself of further items of clothing. "What exactly are we supposed to do with that?"

"Well isn't it obvious, my dear boy?" she replied expectantly, her voice echoing from the depths of the engine compartment.

Ollie scratched his head thoughtfully.

"Not really, no. To be honest, if it was I wouldn't be asking, would I?" "Fair point, well presented," the witch admitted.

She took the belt and looped it around itself twice, making a circle roughly eight inches in diameter. She then fiddled around under the bonnet for a couple of minutes, swore a few times, kicked a tire, threw something away that had wires attached to it and finally emerged, slightly grubbier than before.

"There we go, fellahs. All done." She slammed the bonnet into place. "Start her up, Ethan love."

The lycanthrope did as he was told. He climbed in behind the wheel, turned the engine over and pumped the accelerator a little.

"Sounds good in here," he shouted through the hearse window. "How does it sound to you lot?"

The person with the most comprehensive mechanical knowledge answered.

"It's working a treat," said Mrs. Ladle, proud of her handiwork. "That should keep you going for a good few thousand miles, I reckon."

Mrs. Ladle was congratulated and thanked for all her efforts by the formerly stranded travellers. Secretly however, they were all thankful that they hadn't been the discoverers of the age old mystery of what a witch kept under her skirts. That was a puzzle best left to the imagination. Admittedly, that imagination belonged to someone who spent rather a lot of time alone, drew weird shapes with crayons and whose patio needed investigating, but you get the point.

As they all piled back into the car, Ollie called to her from the passenger seat.

"Can we, ATCHOO, ooh bless me, give you a lift anywhere? It's getting a bit late now."

"Oh, no thanks, love," Mrs. Ladle replied, remounting her broomstick and kicking it into action. "I don't trust those mechanical contraptions. They're always breaking down, don't you know? And besides, it's a hearse. I wouldn't be caught dead in one of those. Bye."

She sailed off into the night with an azure whoosh and a shower of sparks.

———

"Idiots," said the hooded figure once more, gazing into the shifting waters of the marble bowl. The current images had unfortunately shown the five so called adventurers pondering over the state of their vehicle. A loud groan elicited from the hood when the witch arrived to help them get moving.

"Is this how i's to be?" a voice ruminated quietly. "The fate of the quest entrusted to these brain dead incompetents. How are they ever going to succeed? What will the Gods do to me if they fail?"

The table began to shake as if a large lorry were rumbling by a few feet away. The figure put hands, palm down on either side of the jiggling bowl in an effort to keep it, and the table, in place. The candles on the mantelpiece spluttered out as a frigid breeze swept through the small room and even though the night was far from cold, there was a distinct chill in the air. Then, a familiar voice boomed from the darkness, but it was still enough of a surprise to cause a start.

"IT WOULD SEEM THAT YOU ARE HAVING DOUBTS, MORTAL."

The voice was everywhere and seemed to come from the same. It was all-encompassing, eternal and not to be denied or ignored. Like being under water there was no escape from its cloying presence, and no matter which direction the figure turned, it seemed to be right there, next to an ear, in front of an eye, penetrating flesh and bone and infiltrating to the wary soul beneath.

"I will admit to being somewhat nervous," came the somewhat timid reply. "I am concerned that the chosen five are not up to the task, and will fail."

"AND WHY IS THAT?"

"Because they can't get more than a few miles down the road without needing help from an old woman."

"BUT THEY HAVE RECOMMENCED THEIR JOURNEY, YES?"

"Well they have, but. . . "

"FEAR NOT. WHILST OUTWARDLY THEY MAY APPEAR TO BE FIVE BUMBLING BUFFOONS, I CAN ASSURE YOU THAT THEY WILL ULTIMATELY BE SUCCESSFUL."

"Are you sure?"

"DO YOU QUESTION THE VALIDITY OF MY WORDS, MORTAL? DO YOU DISBELIEVE WHAT I AM TELLING YOU?"

"No. I apologise profoundly and remain your humble and obedient servant?"

"YOUR SUBSERVIENT GROVELLINGS ARE ACCEPTED. NOW HEED WHAT I SAY. THEY WILL STUMBLE AND THEY WILL HAVE TO OVERCOME MANY PROBLEMS, BUT ULTIMATELY THEY WILL PREVAIL."

"Thank you for putting my mind at ease. I will endeavour to put my trust in what is certain to be."

"VERY WELL. I WILL NOT RETURN UNTIL THE FINAL PIECE IS LOCATED. FAREWELL, MORTAL."

The room returned to normalcy once more, and the only indicator that the demon had visited was the pounding headache that the summoner had crashing through their brain pan. The afflicted area was rubbed between fingers and thumb, as the now still waters of the bowl were studied once more.

"I need to relax or I'm never going to get through this. I need to have faith in what I've been told."

The figure stood, picked up the bowl and walked over to the back door where it was kicked open and the contents of the receptacle thrown outside. It landed with a resounding splash on the ground where it fizzed and bubbled, destroying the surrounding grass. Whilst standing in the doorway, the light from the moon and the intricate constellations cast their glow onto the now dead patch of earth, and the bowed, hooded head hung low, as many rambling thoughts were processed. But the overriding one, the one that would get them through this most testing of times, overrode all of the others. Patience.

———

The hearse shook, rattled and rolled, and any other appropriate fifties rock and roll song genre that you can think of, down the road, the beams from its headlights bouncing up and down all over the place like a cave guide with Parkinson's Disease.

Ethan was firmly in place behind the wheel and as it turned out, he wasn't actually a bad driver. He wasn't a very good one either, but then you can't have everything. Still, he didn't really have a lot of choice in the matter. Seeing as Ollie couldn't drive, Ronnie could but was currently on a twelve month ban for driving under the influence (it was Nosey the Bogeyman's influence, actually. The spectre had convinced Ronnie that it would be a topping wheeze to drive the car whilst invisible, and make everyone think that it was haunted. It turned out to be great fun and had been going swimmingly until he'd run a blood red light and run over Constable Gullet's size fourteen foot. What made the matter worse was that the policeman had dropped his piece of cake, an event which turned what usually would have been a minor occurrence into a full blown incident requiring a cordoned off section of the road, two emergency food trolleys and the attendance of Mrs. Strudel. Sadly the cake couldn't be saved), Stitches wasn't allowed, because there was a very real risk that his arms would pop out at the shoulder at a most inopportune moment, and there was absolutely no use whatsoever in getting Flug to do it. One, he didn't fit in the front seat, (it looked like someone had tried to force a sausage into a thimble), and two, there was no way that he'd be able to get his limited mind around the rudimentary functions required to get the damn thing moving. If we're being perfectly honest, and to put that into some kind of perspective, Flug would have struggled to work out how a hamster wheel went round. Obviously you would have to explain to him what a wheel was first, and possibly a hamster, for that matter, but you get the picture.

So, by a process of elimination and due to the fact that everybody else was either rubbish, unable or disqualified, Ethan had become the quests designated driver.

"Ollie," said Flug from the back seat, his face peering out from between his knees.

"What is it, Flug?" replied Ollie, watching as the scenery literally flashed past at nearly thirty miles an hour.

"It dinner time."

"Pants," said Ollie disgustedly as he felt a soft object nudge him on the right shoulder. He reached over and grabbed the squashy item and placed it into his lap. He undid the lunchbox, for twas such a thing that he now had in his possession, and looked dejectedly at the contents. Even away from home, Flug hadn't neglected his duties. Everything else he forgot in an instant, to the point that it was a good job breathing was involuntary, because if it wasn't he would run out of oxygen faster than a naked climber on top of Mt. Everest, but reminding Ollie about his liquid refreshment was something that he never, ever forgot.

Inside the pack were two containers. One was plastic, almost see through and had a screw top lid. A shaker. The sort that you would normally see permanently attached to the lips of a bodybuilder as he tried to cram in another few grams of protein. The second was more metally and shiny, primarily because it was made of shiny metal. He lifted the plastic one out and tapped at it dispiritedly with his index finger. The red powder inside it sat there like a. . . like a. . . it looked horrendous.

"You put water in it, Ollie," Flug pointed out helpfully. "Yes, thank you, Fulg. I gathered that."

"You not looking forward to your food?" asked Ethan, genuinely interested.

"Is it that obvious?" said Ollie, unscrewing the lid and putting the container between his knees and taking out the second one.

Ethan nodded, casting him a sideways glance. "Pretty much."

Ollie removed the lid from the second container and poured the water it housed into the first. The liquid sat on top of the red powder and flatly refused to seep through.

"I think you're going to have to give that a shake," said Stitches helpfully. "It's mixing about as well as the guests at a Jews and Nazis singles party."

Ollie shook the mixer vigorously for about thirty seconds then checked the contents once more. It frothed and bubbled like a glutinous pink soup, and even had a few lumps in it to add to the look.

"Well, here we go."

He popped the lid and chugged the ghastly concoction down in one go. He then followed that up with the traditional belch and look of extreme disgust that happened naturally as a result of his unnatural repast. He passed the used vessel back to Flug to take care of, before speaking to Ethan.

"So, whereabouts' are we then?" "Hang on a sec."

Ethan wound the window down and leaned out. "How far till we reach Tonboot?" he shouted.

SQUEAK. SQUEAK.

He pulled his head back in and put the window back up. "About twenty miles, according to the Bat Nav."

Ollie turned in his seat and looked at Stitches, who was squashed in the back between Flug and a sleeping Ronnie. He looked like a discarded and thoroughly neglected pillow.

"How reliable is that thing?" he asked, pointing to the roof of the hearse with a thumb.

"Should be fine," the zombie replied. "The guy I got the car from said it was virtually brand new. All we have to do is make sure that it's fully charged before we set off anywhere."

"And how do we do that?"

Stitches pointed to the glove box in front of Ollie's legs. "The charger's in there."

Ollie opened the compartment. There nestled amongst a couple of blank cassettes, some used tissues, an unused car manual, a tin of sweets covered in enough sugar to cause diabetes and a map of Russia, was a small plastic container. He picked it up and had a look. Wiggling away inside were loads of fat, green caterpillars.

"And this is the charger?"

"Yup," answered Stitches. "Before we set off we just pop a couple of those into the Bat Nav, and we're good for about eight hours."

"Fair enough," said Ollie, putting the container back. He settled into his seat. It was surprisingly comfy. "I was thinking," he continued, "once we get to Tonboot, why don't we find somewhere to spend the day and rest up. Then we can start the search nice and fresh tomorrow night."

"Fine by me," said Stitches, who would be glad of the time. It would probably take him most of the day to return his body to its normal width. At the present moment his heart was resting on top of his liver, and he could have crawled through a cat flap with room to spare.

"Sounds good to me," said Ethan. "I need to get out and about anyway."

"That's settled then."

———

On their arrival in Tonboot, the boys parked the hearse and clambered out to stretch their weary, cramped, and in Stitches' case, crinkled and near to snapping off, limbs.

"I think we must have taken a wrong turn somewhere," observed the zombie, looking around. "We seem to have ended up at a genetic dead end."

They spent an hour or so exploring the town, ostensibly trying to find somewhere to stay, but taking in some of the sites as well. There were plenty of places to eat and drink, gift shops where you could buy souvenirs (Flug picked up a snow globe that had a Christmas scene in it. Well, Ollie had assumed it was supposed to be Yuletide based. Santa was on his knees and his neck was resting on a miniature, fully functional guillotine. He wouldn't be going Ho Ho Ho for much longer. Cheery), and an art gallery whose pictures made Dorian Gray's look positively resplendent.

As luck would have it, they found a quaint little bed and breakfast establishment called The Throbbing End, which was run by the very friendly husband and wife team of Mr. and Mrs. Bell. Obviously, when I say quaint, I don't mean in a sleepy hamlet, occupied by persons who live in rose covered thatched cottages, where every day is a summer's day full of ice cold Pimms and cricket on the green way. This was quaint in a noisy, creatures up till all hours, killings, mayhem and long cold winters' nights full of gallons of blood and sacrifices, on what would have actually been a very serviceable cricket pitch if it wasn't soaked with bodily fluids, way. If you think of a major, Middle Eastern war-zone or Southend on a Friday night, you were somewhere close. Still, it was pleasant enough.

Mr. Bell, a retired warlock, and his good lady wife, a former hag, had prepared them a very nice bedtime meal once they'd booked in and then shown them all to their rooms. Much to Stitches' amusement the couple, both being consummate hosts who could spot a guest's traits and habits a mile away, even had one with a bed of straw and a bowl of water for Ethan.

Tired after their days travelling they'd all retired to their rooms and crashed out, with the exception of Ethan, who'd gotten himself changed and gone out.

KNOCK. KNOCK. KNOCK.

"Huh. What?"

KNOCK. KNOCK. KNOCK.

"Jus a mint," Ollie slurred as he tried to get his face to work. He'd been in a lovely, deep and peaceful sleep. Crumble's mattress had turned out to be really rather good and he'd nodded off as soon as his head had touched the pillow.

He stood up and put on his dressing gown before seeing who was responsible for waking him up. Suitably attired (he wasn't going to lower his standards for anything, even if it was having his sleepy time disturbed) he crossed the room and opened the door, determined to give the inconsiderate dolt a piece of his mind. The part of it that was awake anyway.

"Can I help you?" Ollie asked, glancing very obviously at his wrist.

His watch was on the bedside table but the gesture was well inten
tioned, if completely ignored by the person stood before him.

Just as Ollie was about to launch into his tirade about the rights and
wrongs of knocking on peoples doors and the responsibilities that
come with that (which, to be honest would have involved him
halfheartedly moaning a bit, having a glass of water and going back to
bed without solving anything) the figure stuck out a fat little hand,
grabbed Ollie's and pumped it furiously enough to cause the tendons
in his shoulder to complain.

"Och am I glad to meet ye," the little man said in his thick Scots
brogue, still pumping Ollie's hand up and down like he was trying to
draw water from the earthy depths. "It's Ollie Splint, right?"

"Yes. Yes it is. Who are you?"

Finally the digital assault stopped, which was just as well because
Ollie's shoulder ligaments were just about to write a tersely worded
letter of complaint to his brain, enquiring as to why the head organ
hadn't instructed them to revolt and knock this bloke on his wobbly
backside. The visitor beamed proudly, showing an impressive set of
beautifully white teeth and an even more impressive set of fangs.

"Allow me te introduce meself. Ma name is Splat McThroat-Tearer,
but my friends, and I hope to count you among them, call me
Douggie."

Ollie, still in a state of semi-consciousness akin to that seen after a
reasonably serious head injury, still didn't know why this odd little
vampire had woken him up whilst he was resting, and he was keen to
find out so that he could ignore it and get back to sleep.

"That's fine, Douggie, but what exactly can I do for you that
couldn't wait until later?"

"Well, I'm the Mayor o' this wee toon and I must say it's a great
honour for us to have the son of Glut the Bodyripper staying wi' us."
Pleasantly surprised to be known by someone not from Skullenia, Ollie
smiled at his new companion.

"So what I was thenken," continued Douggie, "was that while ye
and yer boys were here, you might like to take part in a wee
tournament that we have organised for tomarra. It'd be great for the
village and a rare treat for the other players."

Ollie furrowed his brow, not knowing what the Mayor meant. "Other players?" he repeated.

"Aye. Every year we have a five a side football competition, and it just so happens that it's later on today. We would be absolutely delighted if your group would join us."

The last thing in the world that Ollie wanted to do was play football. The second to last thing he wanted to do was to be standing here in his pyjamas and talking about football, especially when they were about to embark on their quest, but Douggie was looking at him with such pleading and longing that he didn't have the heart to turn the little guy down. Anyway, it would probably be a bit of fun, and let's face it, the five of them wouldn't exactly pose much of a threat in the sporting arena. If they played anything other than a team of seven year old girls, there was every chance that they'd get knocked out in the first round. Obviously the girls would have to give them a head start and not tackle too hard but they'd have a go at least. And the best part was, it didn't matter how bad they were because they could play for the minimum amount of time and satisfy the local populous. And it wouldn't do his reputation any harm either. He may only have been a half vampire but that didn't mean he wanted people thinking less of him. So, they could effectively join in the tournament and then recommence their journey with virtually no time wasted at all. In other words everyone was a winner, even if they did end up as losers.

"Okay, Douggie, we'll do it," he said, pleased that his affirmative answer had made the little blood sucker's smile even wider and whiter.

"Och that's great news. The villagers will pleased as punch."

He reached down to his left and picked up a large sports bag that he handed to Ollie.

"That'll be yer streps for the games. Everything yer need. See yer at the village green at eleven."

"Look forward to it. See you, Douggie."

———

Jekyll stood on the threshold of Flange's house and peered inside. He'd gotten the address from Starch earlier, when he'd paid a visit to the museum. The curator had been very helpful but hadn't been able to provide him with much more information than he'd either heard from Ollie in the email, gleaned from Mandeep or what he'd looked up on the darknet.

He'd had a look around the museum itself and got to examine the Compendia, which he'd found very interesting, seeing as it had an arcane version of the very potion that he'd concocted to, how shall we say, find himself. The only thing that he found a bit odd was that Vortex wasn't at work. He'd taken the day off but to do what, Starch didn't have a clue.

So here he was, standing at the house of the man who was the number one suspect in the burglary. But, saying that, what he'd seen and heard of Vortex hadn't totally cleared him of any wrongdoing either. In fact, even Starch himself could be considered a suspect. He had the opportunity and the means to perpetrate the act, although his motive could only be guessed at.

As he went through the house he found it exactly as it had been described to him. Sparse was how he would have described it, though. There was virtually nothing in it to signify comfortable human habitation apart from, as Ollie had said, the back room. It was a complete jumble sale that constituted books, papers, books, manuscripts, books and more books. Ollie had mentioned this, but not the extent. Still, at least he had more time to search the place than the others.

As it turned out, it was just as he suspected. A fair few hours leafing through the various tomes scattered around the room had elicited nothing more than a cloud of dust, a tickly throat and a couple of stinging paper cuts. He sat at the table going through the final book, a reference manual about supernatural creatures and their feeding habits. He was halfway through it, perusing an article about golems, when he looked over at the door. His attention was drawn to something that, even in all of the clutter, didn't look quite right. He left the book open on the table and approached the entrance where he got down on his hands and knees to have a closer look.

There were four scratches on the wooden floor about three inches long, and at the end of one of the middle ones was a fingernail. Jekyll took out a hanky from his pocket and wrapped it around his hand. He deftly lifted the nail and turned his hand over, so that it fell onto his cotton covered palm. It was most definitely a nail from a hand and its appearance made him ninety percent sure it was human. He held it up level with his eye line and squinted, because there was something else. Attached to the underside of the clipping were several thin fibres that seemed to be bright red when held in the light.

"Interesting," he muttered to himself, as he folded the hanky around the body part and put it into his pocket.

Twenty minutes later he was back at the museum, sharing his find with Starch.

"I'm pretty certain that Flange never wore anything of that colour," the curator said, studying the fibres closely; his pince-nez perched precariously on the tip of his aquiline nose, "at least definitely not at work. He has a uniform but that's grey, and he's not the sort of man to be seen wearing bright colours. To be frank he's quite a dour individual. I've only seen him outside of work hours a couple of times and his everyday attire is every bit as drab as his work wear."

"And there's no one else that you can think of that would wear clothes of that colour?" Jekyll probed further.

"No, I'm afraid not. Sorry, I can't be of any more help to you, Doctor." "Oh, not to worry. Probably a long shot anyway. Thanks a lot for your time."

Back outside, Jekyll ruminated over the discovery that he'd made in Flange's house. On the face of it, it could be nothing at all, just a random bit of damage and some accumulated bodily detritus but, on the other hand, if you were feeling suspicious and had been watching too many of those endless forensic programmes on the telly, it could indicate that a struggle had taken place in the property. The only thing for sure, was that there was no definite way of knowing until the caretaker turned up or was found. Whatever state he was in would certainly be a big giveaway. All he could do for now was conduct his own enquiries in the town and gather whatever information that he could.

First thing though, he needed to let Ollie know what he'd unearthed in the caretaker's house. He fished around in his pocket and retrieved his mobile phone. That being said, mobile probably wasn't quite the best way to describe the large hunk of black plastic. That would be like saying Nigel Farage didn't have a problem with the odd immigrant or two, enjoyed a spot of multiculturalism and intended to live in an ethnically diverse commune in Brussels when he retired.

With regard to remote communications, Skullenia had been rather slow in getting on board the whole mobile technology merry go round. At present there was only one company operating a mere handful of arrays dotted around the countryside, and trying to get a signal anywhere, any time was a bit of a lottery. You'd probably have more luck trying to send a text to the moon, or using the phone itself to bash out a Morse code message on the nearest wall. The last one that was sent successfully said 'Send help. I'm stuck on a merry go round and my phones knackered.'

Jekyll scrolled through his list of contacts until he found Ollie's, after which he typed out a text and pressed send. With any luck he'd receive it within the next couple of days, a week at the outside which was average to be honest. Alright, so it wasn't much use to you if there was a major emergency, but if you knew you were going to be in serious trouble a week from Tuesday then it was a positive boon. He considered the belt and braces approach and thought about sending a bat as well, but then dismissed the idea as they were notoriously unreliable. Half the time your message would end up in someone's loft covered in poo and protected by some preservation of wildlife act or another. Ah well, at least it was on its way. He put his Shockia 666 back into his pocket and set about rustling up what information he could.

———

"Football!" exclaimed Stitches, a thin dribble of water flowing down his chin and onto the table. "Are you totally and utterly out of your tiny vampire mind?"

They were sitting around a table in the restaurant area of The Throbbing End. It was about eight o'clock in the evening and thus breakfast time, and Ollie had just recounted his conversation with Douggie in the early hours.

"Why?" Ollie protested. "It's not like we'll be at it very long, is it? Look, we'll be complete rubbish and finished in fifteen minutes, less if we get thrashed that badly and the game gets abandoned. The only chance we'll have of winning anything will be if the other teams didn't show up. But notwithstanding that, we get good kudos all round. You know, word of mouth and all that. And don't forget that any publicity is good publicity."

"Tell that to Boris and the Bloodguzzlers, that death metal band from Russia I read about the other week. All it took was one sensationalist story in the paper about all night parties, suspicious disappearances and missing body parts, and they were never heard from again," said Stitches.

"This is slightly different," said Ollie. "Neither was the reporter."

"A pure coincidence, I'm sure," said Ollie. "The paper shut down as well."

"Alright, I get it," Ollie said, raising his voice enough to indicate to his zombie friend that he should be quiet.

"I hate to say it, but I think he's got a point," said Ronnie around a mouthful of greasy, fatty bacon. "We're not fit enough to play football. I'm out of breath just talking about it."

Ronnie did have a point. Being undead or supernaturally gifted didn't automatically make you an athlete, and being a ghoul or a vampire did limit your diet somewhat, notwithstanding the fact there's not much room to jog in a coffin. Even sedate and refined activities were a bit of a problem. The last time that anything had been organised, a darts tournament at The Bolt and Jugular, had been a total disaster requiring the main bar to be forensically cleaned when the competitors decided they couldn't be bothered with all that walking back and forth to the board and so ate each other instead. This lack of fitness of the population is the reason why Skullenia isn't twinned with another town but the accident and emergency department in Colostomy General Hospital. None of them have ever been there of course. It's much too far away.

"Aww, come on guys, it won't be that bad. You're up for it, aren't you Ethan?" Ollie pleaded, expectantly.

The lycanthrope looked up from his rather rare steak. Saying that it was rare wasn't really the best way to describe what he was eating though. It looked more like a cow had wandered into the dining room, sat on his plate and said, "Get stuck in, then."

"Well, I suppose so," he said after swallowing a hefty chunk of blood soaked rarity. "But I tend to find that I'm faster on four legs than two." "Well, at the end of the day I've promised the Mayor that we'll play, so that's that. You'll enjoy it, won't you Flug?"

The hulking mass looked up from his bowl of Burnt Crispies, several of which had attached themselves to his chin. They were now precariously hanging on until they either fell back to the bowl or were licked off.

"Huh?" he said.

"Football," said Ollie. "You'll play won't you?" "Uh, okay. Can I have some sweeties?" "When we're finished, alright," agreed Ollie.

Flug nodded in agreement although he had no idea what football was, what a foot or a ball was, and wouldn't know what to do with a foot and/or a ball if he was given them and told to go and play football. He went back to his cereal.

"Good to see that he's firing on all thrusters this evening. So what are we supposed to be wearing for this sporting spectacular then?" Stitches asked. "Because I left my kit in, ooh let me see now, I don't know because I've never had one because I've never played."

Ollie, a tad perturbed by the slightly negative reaction of his friends, reached under the table and picked up a bag which he plonked onto the table.

"All sorted," he announced. "Kit from Douggie."

Stitches rummaged around in the bag and pulled out a lurid yellow shirt and a pair of bright red shorts.

"Stunning," he continued, turning the items round to see if they looked any better from a different perspective. To be honest they wouldn't have looked any better if seen from a different country. "We're going to look like a chorus line out on that pitch."

"Not one I'd pay to go and see," added Ronnie.

After their respective meals, the guys got changed and made their way through the village to the green. All the way, locals would greet them and thank them in their various ways for agreeing to take part. One old wizard told Ollie what a pleasure it was to have him here. One old woman told Ethan what a pleasure it would be to *have* him here. One young lady told Ronnie that the pleasure was all hers and that she was having it right now, and a toothless crone told Stitches that if he didn't stop dropping dust on the pavement, she would take great pleasure in having him buried here. Flug got some attention as well. It was of the medical kind though, because as they passed through a stone archway near the pitch, he cracked his head and knocked himself senseless for a few minutes, a statement which we are not even going to begin to discuss because it throws up way too many contradictions, oxymoron's, tautologies and whatever other fancy words that I could write here to get my word count up.

"Ach, Ollie," gushed Mayor Douggie when they arrived at the pitch. Once again he grabbed Ollie's hand. "Great to have ye here. Everybody is really excited. I can't tell ye what this means te us all. The players on the other teams are stoked that yer here. And as I mentioned before, Punch is really pleased." He indicated a small person off to their left who had on a pointy, jingly hat and the scariest smile he'd ever seen.

Ollie once again attempted to release his hand from the Mayor's grasp.

"That's splendid, Mr. Mayor. Can I introduce my colleagues to you?" "Och, I'd be delighted."

"This is Stitches." "Hello," said the zombie.

"Aye," came the greeting, accompanied by a vigorous handshake, followed by Douggie wiping some dust off his fingers.

"This is Ronnie." "Wotcha, mate," he said.

"Aye," came the greeting, accompanied by a vigorous handshake, followed by Douggie's strange look as his fingers began to twinkle and start to fade.

"This is Ethan."

"Good evening," he said.

"Aye," came the greeting, accompanied by a vigorous handshake, followed by Douggie's intense scratching due to the lycan's excessively hairy fingers.

"And this is Flug." "."

"Flug, say hello to the Mayor." "."

"My apologies," said Ollie. "I think the blow to his head may have."

"Hello, Mr. Mayor," rumbled Flug, late as usual.

"Aye," no vigorous handshake, due to the fact that Douggie didn't fancy the prospect of entrusting his delicate pinkies to Flug's prehistoric grip.

"Is he always like this?" Douggie asked, staring at Flug's vacant, closed for the season and probably won't open for a good few year's expression.

"Yes, but don't you go worrying about him. He does have trouble with words of more than one letter, but his heart's in the right place. Well, it was the last time I looked," said Ollie.

"Ah, right," continued Douggie. "Right, well we kick off in aboot ten minutes and you lot are up first. You're playing against a team of golems. The Stone Poses."

"Right you are," said Ollie as the Mayor departed to do something Mayorly.

(That's a point. What do mayors actually do that's of any benefit? If you have any idea please let me know, because as far as I can see it seems to involve attending tedious receptions where they get free food, opening coffee shops and café's where they get free food and drink, wearing clothes that a female impersonator wouldn't look twice at even though they're free and showing off your opulent and, oh yeah, free jewellery. Bet their time isn't free. Boom).

"Okay, lads," Ollie said loudly, clapping his hands together, the mark of any good football coach, "quick run around for a few minutes, then we'll get out there, yes?" (He dispensed with the other coaching tenets. Mostly because he didn't know what they were as he didn't really have a clue what he was doing. So not for him chewing gum with his mouth open, spitting whenever someone was looking at him, remonstrating with anyone who had the temerity to disagree with him, standing on the sidelines with his hands in his pockets looking as miserable as sin, wearing a tracksuit two sizes too small and two decades out of date, pointing at the pitch for no discernible reason, telling people fifty years younger than himself how to rubbish they are when he can't sit down without getting winded, being vaguely racist but passing it off as banter and interfering with underage boys).

Twenty five minutes later, amidst the roar of the crowd, the sporting sleuths were sitting on a bench at the side of the pitch and enjoying a post-match refreshment and watching a team of goblins take on a team of warlocks.

"How the hell did that happen?" asked Ollie, incredulously, sipping from a bottle of ice cold water. "Seven one to us."

Stitches looked at him with raised eyebrows and an 'isn't it obvious' expression on his face.

"Well, what did you think was going to happen?" he stated. "As soon as we ran out onto the pitch I thought, hang on they're not moving. They're made of clay, for goodness sake and move about as much as a snail with a limp. The only reason they scored their goal was because the ball ricocheted of one of their player's heads and went in."

"And we had to start scoring some goals," added Ronnie. "There was only so much time we could waste, and even we couldn't justify losing to a team that didn't actually move. At all."

"Yeah, he's right," said Ethan. "The crowd were getting a bit restless for some action. I thought they were going to invade the pitch when Flug stood on the ball and popped it."

"Yeah well, don't forget that was after he tried eating the first one because he thought it was a melon," said Stitches.

"So what or who are we up against next?" asked Ollie of no one in particular.

"A team of spectres. The Ghost Riders. I've heard some of the other players saying that they're supposed to be pretty good," said Stitches helpfully.

"I hope so," said Ronnie. "I think one of my lungs has just had a heart attack."

They beat the Ghost Riders three to two. In the last minute of the game, Ethan was tripped and was awarded a penalty, much to the consternation of the Riders' goalie who was sent off for using some rather colourful language. Seeing as they didn't want to upset the crowd, Ethan had to make a reasonable effort at scoring. He ran up and kicked the ball as hard as he could, straight at the substitute keeper in the hope that he would save it. Unfortunately for his side though, the replacement wasn't as solid as his team mate and he burst on impact, scattering everywhere and allowing the slightly slimy ball to sail into the back of the net.

Another post-match rest saw them discussing the next game, which was the semi-final. They were up against The Sneering Fiends, a fierce looking team who's mascot was a troll with an attitude problem (and such was his towering height he had a bit of an altitude problem as well).

"Right," said Ollie, a determined edge to his voice, "we are definitely going to lose this game. I reckon what we need to do is. . . what's that noise?"

The noise was the sound of the troll mascot's cage being torn asunder as it escaped. After its rampage, which signified to everyone present as to the precise nature of his attitude problem, and which left several spectators needing rearranging, The Sneering Fiends had been forced to forfeit the game as they only had two players left and between them they didn't have the required number of legs to continue. "Absolutely un-freaking-believable!" exclaimed Stitches after the carnage had been cleared away, and the blood soaked up from the pitch (this was thanks to a very helpful wizard and his magic sponge). "We would never have beaten them. Now we're in the bloody final. Do you know what, I haven't had this much fun since. . . since. . . no, can't do it. I can't even take the mick out of the situation. This is absolutely ridiculous."

"Who are we up against?" asked Ethan, tightening his laces.

"A team of demons from the Throbbing End," said Ollie. "They're regulars by all accounts. Call themselves The Djinn and Tonics."

"Hey, guys," said Ronnie, a certain look on his face that indicated that he was about to say a certain something that was certain to cause certain other people cause for concern. And that was certain. "Look, we've come this far, right?"

"Right," voiced the others with a due sense of caution. "Why don't we try and win the damn thing?"

"Are you nuts?" said Stitches, worriedly. "Have you seen the size of those things? They make Ten Feet Teddy look like a four year old. We'll get absolutely marmalised."

"No we won't," Ronnie continued, enthusiastically. "We've got Flug for muscle, and the rest of us will get by on guile, lightning speed and good fortune."

"You can't be serious," said Stitches. "This isn't a light hearted, feel good film, you know, Ron. We're not going to get the brown stuff kicked out of us and then make a remarkable comeback in the final minute and win. What's more likely to happen is that we'll get the brown stuff kicked out of us and then it'll be remarkable if we make a comeback from the comas that we'll all be in."

Ollie stood up and stretched his hamstrings, which were in danger of seizing up quicker than a second hand car. He turned to his assembled colleagues.

"Let's go for it. Are you with me? Come on."

Stitches looked at his friend, a strained and some would say insincere look on his face.

"Well, after a rousing speech like that how can we possibly say no?" he said, sarcastically. "That'd be enough to make anyone charge at an eight foot demigod who looks like he could bench press a house. Henry V couldn't have done it any better."

A quarter of an hour later saw them standing on the pitch and facing their opponents. The smallest one was roughly the size of an ambulance, which was ironic because injuries and long, painful stays in hospital were utmost in their minds as they stood nervously on the field. If they pulled this off it would be the greatest victory since the Women's Institute Invitation Fifteen beat Harlequins 37-10 at Twickenham. Mind you they did have a lot of decent players missing. The Harlequins had fielded a full strength team though.

The doughy form of Douggie jogged to the centre of the pitch. Seeing as this was the final he had elected to officiate, an activity that, judging by the tightness of his shorts, he hadn't performed for many a long and overfed year.

"Good luck to ye, gentlemen," he offered as he reached the centre circle. "May the best team win."

"The biggest would probably be more realistic," said Stitches.

Douggie put his whistle to his pasty lips and prepared to get the game underway, much to the delight of the crowd, who were no doubt looking forward to a fair game, a sterlingly fought contest and the end result looking somewhat like The Somme.

"You want to be buried or cremated?" Stitches asked Ollie. PHEEEP!

For the next ten minutes, absolute bedlam ensued. Ronnie received a blow to the head powerful enough to have floored a rhinoceros wearing a crash helmet, which left him staggering around like a drunk for a few moments. Flug managed a couple of magnificent saves by a rather novel use of the bolt in his forehead (they were currently on ball number four) and Ethan and Ollie, who by some strange twist actually turned out to be quite good players, had managed to score a goal each. Do bear in mind though that the statement 'Ollie and Ethan were quite good players' is relative. That would be like saying that a one armed man was quite good on the guitar simply because he could pick it up. Stitches, all things considered, was doing okay, but he was struggling a bit with the pace of the game (it wasn't anything to do with aerobic fitness as he didn't have a functioning respiratory system, but more that his physical robustness was a tad low. He'd already dislocated his chin calling for the ball and on the one occasion that he headed it, both his eyes flew out of his skull and landed in the water bucket). At one point though he managed to get himself into the opponents' box, where his foot connected with the ball in a spectacular volley, sending it flying into the back of the net. Unfortunately the ball went sailing into the crowd where it clumped a rather large ogre in the unmentionables. Douggie graciously allowed a time out for Stitches to relace his boot. And reattach his foot.

The second half played out much the same as the first with extreme violence, unwarranted aggression, blood, lumps, bumps and bruises. And that was just the queue at the burger van.

With just a minute to go the score was three all.

"Just one more each and they'll be level," the announcer announced helpfully.

With the clock ticking down, the game hanging in the balance and the detectives hanging out of their backsides, Flug made his decisive move. Or rather his left leg did. It was a replacement for the one that had been torn off by a deranged werewolf and had once belonged to a semi-professional footballer (the werewolf hadn't belonged to the footballer of course, the leg had. Petwise the footballer had owned a hamster, a three legged cat and a flock of migrating tortoises. And no his name wasn't Petwise, I forgot to put a comma in).

The Tonics' hulking centre forward, who made the Statue of Liberty look like it had a growth hormone deficiency and in need of a good meal, collected the ball on the halfway line and charged towards Flug like an express train. Except this train was a seething mass of spectral ectoplasm that looked about as friendly as a Dobermann at a cats only disco. It even had steam coming out of its ears.

The memories of hours spent playing football flooded through Flug's system and possessed him completely, turning him into a competitive fiend, who's only real contribution to the game up until this point had been getting in the way.

He charged at the devilish opposition player and took the ball from him with a deftly played and perfectly timed sliding tackle that left a furrow twelve feet long and two deep. Quickly regaining his feet he charged on like a being possessed as he dribbled down the pitch (you can make up your own joke here if you want to. I call it reader participation).

The crowd gasped in amazement.

Ollie, Stitches, Ronnie and Ethan gasped collectively in disbelief.

The ball seemed to be glued to Flug's feet as he beat one, two and then three players, leaving them reeling and confused in his wake. He mesmerised them all with his power and precision, making it seem as if he were created for this very moment. Someone in the crowd even remarked that he seemed to have all the skill and grace of a Brazilian international (and not an international with a Brazilian because that would be a completely different story altogether and somewhat inappropriate for someone with my delicate sensibilities).

He got to within twenty five yards of the opponent's goal when the Djinn and Tonic's goalie rushed out, eager to stop Flug in his tracks.

Seeing him coming Flug slowed down ever so slightly and delicately chipped the ball into the air. It sailed majestically over the goalkeeper's outstretched hands before dipping just under the cross bar and landing in the back of the net.

Douggie blew the final whistle and that was the signal for the crowd to go mad. Well, madder. The pitch was invaded quicker than the Chatham branch of Poundland during its half-price sale, as beings of every description poured on to congratulate the winning team.

Ollie, Stitches, Ronnie and Ethan rushed over to their colleague and hugged him fiercely, congratulating him over and over again.

"Amazing," said Ollie. "Superb," said Stitches. "Blinding," said Ronnie. "Outstanding," said Ethan.

257

Flug looked at his friends and the assembled masses clapping and cheering for him and his teammates.

"Can me have some sweeties now?" he asked.

———

A couple of hours, quite a few drinks and many plaudits and well done's later, the boys were sitting back at the restaurant, a small winners cup sitting in the middle of their table.

"Isn't that amazing," said Ollie proudly.

"Mystifying, more like," answered Stitches. "Who would have thought it? Flug the hero. Good huh, mate?" he added, slapping the monster's shoulder.

Flug didn't reply straight away. He'd slipped back into his own little world of blissful ignorance and was busy working his way through a party size packet of Fizzy Fantoms.

"Mmmm," he said finally, around a multi-coloured, gooey mass of refined sugar. "Did we win at football, Stitches?"

"That we did, Flug. And you were the main man." "Okay."

Douggie came in at some point, they weren't sure of the time, but it was somewhere near dawn. He was gushing congratulations about the game and their overall performances, and offered them the opportunity to defend their title the following year.

"Well, that's a very generous offer," said Ollie, "but we'll have to wait and see what we're up to at the time. Meanwhile, maybe you could answer a question for me?"

"Och aye. Anything. It would be a pleasure."

Ollie reached into a pocket and pulled out the first map, laid it on the table and pointed to the little drawing of the well.

"Do you have any idea where this might be?" he asked innocently. Douggie studied the paper closely and tapped it with his finger. "Aye, I know where that is sure enough. Aboot seven miles outside o' toon is the Tonboot wood. There's a nature trail, you'll see the signs. Follow that and ye'll come right te it."

Ollie stood up and shook Douggie's hand, indicating that not only was he extremely grateful, but that it was time for them to turn in.

They bade the Mayor goodnight and made their separate ways off to bed.

"What time do you want to set off?" asked Stitches as they ascended the stairs. "Early might be best. At least that way we'll avoid the admiring rabble. I'm not sure I like being a celebrity."

"Yeah, we need to get out of here," said Ethan who was following behind them, supporting a rather drunken Ronnie.

"Crack of evening then, I reckon," suggested Ollie. "We'll be up and gone before anyone else is about. See you all later."

———

After a good sleep, a hearty breakfast inside them (or in Ollie's case, a breakfast that had come from inside a heart) and a quiet getaway from the still slumbering town, Ethan brought the hearse to a stop in a small clearing at the edge of a vast forest. The guys piled out of the car and wandered over to a brown information board.

"Not another bloody forest," said Ronnie edgily. "The last time I went in one of these I ended up in a right mess."

"Ah don't worry, mate," said Stitches encouragingly. "You've got us lot to look after you this time."

Ronnie gave him a derisory look that screamed 'and that's supposed to make me feel better, is it?' before retrieving his battered tobacco pouch from his coat pocket and rolling himself a thicker than usual cigarette.

"Looks reasonably straightforward, if this map is anything to go by," said Ollie, tracing a path with his finger through the generic, childlike depiction of the wood. "The nature trail starts over there." He pointed to another, smaller sign that said 'The Nature Trail Starts Here'. "That's where we need to go. Couldn't be simpler."

"The last time you said that, we ended up fighting for our lives," remarked Stitches sullenly.

"He does have a point," agreed Ethan, shrugging into his rucksack. "I don't think we should be taking this too lightly. We really are heading into the unknown."

Ronnie flicked his fag to the ground and squashed it out underfoot. "They're right, Ollie mate. And it's not like we're just outside Skullenia

259

poking around this time. We're miles away from home and pretty much cut off if anything goes wrong."

Ollie considered their various points of view and admitted to himself that he had to agree. And ultimately he was responsible for these guys, who had become his close friends as well as work colleagues. He couldn't and wouldn't be blasé with their safety, or their comradeship when it came to it.

"Okay," he said, hands raised in supplication, "all excellent points and well made. Let's go steady, stay frosty and watch each other's backs. No, not like that, Flug."

Flug removed his nose from between Stitches' shoulder blades. "Sorry, Ollie. Wot you mean?"

"I mean let's be careful, okay?" "Okay."

To all appearances, the nature trail looked like any other that you might find in any area of countryside. The path was nice and wide, enough to fit two abreast, the ground was covered in mushy brown bark chippings and the trees formed a wonderfully lush, verdant canopy overhead. All that aside, the differences between this and any other nature trail that looked like any other you might find in any area of countryside, were more than a little apparent. The night time forest dwellers were making enough noise to drown out a Motörhead concert, and all the crashing and banging made it sound like there was a rugby match going on around them.

"Not so much off the beaten track," commented Stitches, looking around warily. "More like if you get off the track you'll get beaten."

"Yeah, I hear you," responded Ethan. "You get lost out here and you can kiss it all goodbye. Ollie?" he added.

"Yeah."

"I've got a suggestion. How's about I get changed and have a scout ahead, see what we're heading towards?"

"That's a good idea," said the half vampire. "And we might as well make the best use of our resources. What about you, Ronnie? Fancy disappearing and having a look around?"

"I would," answered Ronnie after a moment's consideration, "but I can't mask my odour, and at this time of night that's what most creatures use to track. I'd still be a pretty easy target, especially out on my own."

"Plus the fact that if there was a way of totally eliminating body odour, we would have used it on Flug by now. Well, if there was enough left after they'd deployed it over France first," said Stitches.

Ollie shot him a wry grin but totally ignored the comment, something that he was becoming increasingly adept at. He figured that if he didn't pay any attention to Stitches' joking and mickey taking, he would stop. It was a work in progress that so far had yielded, by his reckoning and based on how much the zombie used to arse about before, compared to how much he arsed about now, absolutely no results whatsoever. He was still as big a pain as ever.

"Just one thing, though," Stitches continued. "Once you're changed, Ethan, will we be safe? No offence."

Ethan chuckled quietly to himself.

"None taken, mate. No, you don't have to worry. You guys have essentially become my pack members, so there's no way I would ever do anything to hurt any of you. Well, most of the time." He winked slyly. "But Obsidia did," the zombie added, still smarting over the memory of the betrayal by the now deceased female lycanthrope. "She got a couple killed, didn't she?"

"She did, but that was a human decision she made, not a wolf one.

Please, don't worry. You'll be perfectly okay."

They all nodded their acquiescence, and watched as Ethan made his way off the path and into the dense foliage.

They all stood as silent and still as statues for five minutes. They could hear the odd snapping sound and stretching noise, as if some unseen person was bending a freshly sawn piece of wood. They also detected yelps of pain from the area that Ethan had gone to.

And then there was quiet. Not just from Ethans' position, but seemingly from the whole forest. It was as if a vast cotton wool blanket had descended and damped down every sound to almost zero. It seemed as if everything living, unliving or whatever had suddenly become aware of the superior creature now in their midst, and whether out of respect or just plain fear, each and every entity had become mute.

The undergrowth parted, and the wolf that Ethan had become rejoined them on the path. He was immense, a mass of undulating, rippling, densely packed and fur-covered muscle. He was the only

TONY LEWIS

thing that they'd ever come across that made Flug look a little on the small side. In its vice-like jaws was the only clue to its former identity. His clothes. He padded over to Ollie, his eyes almost level with the startled half-vampire's, and placed them gently at his feet. Then, with his enormous muzzle, he indicated the rucksack that he'd taken off a few minutes before.

"Oh, I see," said Ollie. "You want me to put your clothes in there and take them with us, don't you?"

Remarkably, the wolf's large head nodded and Stitches could have sworn that he saw Ethan smile, impossible as that must be.

Flug was almost apoplectic with fear. His breath was coming in huge gasps and his eyes were bulging out of his head like Wile. E. Coyote's. "Flug, it's okay" said Ronnie, approaching the petrified monster. "It's Ethan. He's not going to hurt you, okay."

Flug didn't respond, he was that scared. They hadn't seen him like this since the time that he'd seen a meteor shower and had been convinced that aliens were invading, and were going to investigate his nether regions. Stitches hadn't aided the situation when he'd helpfully pointed out that when the little green men landed, they would 'probe Uranus until it turned into a black hole that nothing would ever escape from ever again'.

Ethanwolf must have sensed Flug's fear and discomfort. He approached him and tucked his wet nose under one of Flug's hands and sniffed it before manoeuvring it onto his head, moving it back and forth. Flug looked down into Ethanwolf's shining eyes and in an instant, he visibly relaxed and patted the great creature as you would a family pet.

"Hi, Ethan," said Flug quietly, a smile on his scarred and battered face. "You nice and soft."

Ethanwolf gave a small, almost puppy-like yip, and licked the hand affectionately.

"No," said Flug, "me not scared now." Ethanwolf yipped again.

"Okay. Be careful dough."

Ethanwolf slipped away into the forest, and was gone.

"He goin' ahead now," Flug stated, unconsciously wiping a slick hand on his trousers. "We walk on path. Ethan come back soon."

"Well, bugger me with something long and spiky," said Stitches in total astonishment. "Did that just happen, or did I fall asleep and dream that I was in a Lassie film? Flug, did he tell you that little Johnny has fallen down a mine shaft and we've got to come quickly?"

"That was real, alright," said Ronnie, still bemused. "Flug connected with him."

"That he did," said Ollie, putting Ethans' clothes into the bag and giving it to Stitches. "Flug, were you talking to Ethan in your head?"

"Yeah me fink so," said the giant. "When me look at Ethan's eyes me hear his voice in here," he tapped the side of his skull "and he tell me everyfin' will be okay."

"Remarkable. Something special seems to have been unlocked between those two," said Ollie to Stitches and Ronnie. "It'll be interesting to see whether it's just a one off."

"Well, according to the sign," said Stitches, changing the subject and pointing at the brown board whilst holding a torch in the other, "the well is about three quarters of a mile away along the track. If we take it slow, Ethan will have plenty of time to warn us if anything goes awry."

Twenty minutes later, the trees and bushes started to thin out. "We must be getting close," Ronnie pointed out and, as if to prove him right, Ethanwolf appeared from their left like a vast, hairy shadow. He went straight to Flug and they gazed into each other's eyes.

"Everyfin' okay," Flug rumbled. "Nuffin' bad here. He say wait here while he check da well. It just over dere." He indicated an area that was still out of sight.

A few minutes later, Ethanwolf returned and indicated to Stitches that he wanted his clothes. The zombie did as he was bid, and placed Ethanwolf's attire onto the ground. The creature picked them up in his slathering jaws and returned to the trees. Minutes later, Ethan returned, a big smile on his face.

"That was a turn up for the psychic books," he said, crouching down to tie his laces. "I didn't expect that at all."

"I'll say," commented Stitches. "Try it now, see if it works." Ethan approached Flug and stared into his eyes.

"Hi, Ethan. Wot you doin?"

No matter how hard he concentrated, what had been as easy as a drunk in roller skates falling off a greasy, spinning log now wouldn't happen.

"Nothing," said Ethan. "Maybe it just happens when I'm in wolf form."

"What was it like, mate?" Ollie asked with genuine interest. "Strange, really. I wasn't consciously trying to get through to him, it just happened. Whatever I was thinking, he seemed to pick up on. The weird thing was that whilst we were connected, I got the impression that somewhere in that head of his there's an intellect trying to get out."

"Well it's not trying very hard," observed Stitches ungraciously. "An F for effort there I'm afraid. And the F stands for fu. . ."

"Be that as it may," Ollie cut in. "It's not only quite an amazing thing that we've witnessed, but it also has the potential to be incredibly useful. It saves Ethan having to transform every time he needs to tell us anything."

"That is a fair point that I have to concede," said Stitches happily. "It takes him long enough to get changed to go out as it is."

Ethan emitted a low growl, but the curl of his upper lip couldn't belay the underlying affection that had grown in him for these people over the last couple of months. He'd been close to his pack mates at the werehouse, that was a given, but the creatures standing before him offered something different and filled a gap in his life he hadn't' previously identified. Maybe it came down to choice and the freedom to be more detached from the strict tenets that his lupine brethren adhered to.

Ethan had been born into quite a well to-do family in Esher in Surrey, the sort of people who use a brand new four wheel drive all year round, had their shopping delivered from Fortnum and Mason and never, ever watched anything on ITV unless Sir Derek Jacobi was in it. Young Ethan had had a reasonably happy childhood up until the age of nine that is, when he'd been packed off to boarding school by his workaholic parents. His father was a high flying financial consultant and his mother worked extremely hard at shopping, drinking expensive coffee and spending time with her equally affluent and equally busy friends.

His first term had been an absolute nightmare. A never ending battle against bullies, know-it-alls and smart arses. His fellow students had been even worse. It began to tail off after the first year and a half, but he always felt like his school time was a constant struggle for survival. In his fifth year a new boy had started at St Martins. He was a quiet lad, softly spoken and somewhat effeminate, but Ethan felt a kinship towards him. They'd started spending a lot of time together and it wasn't long before Ethan and Rupert had become the best of friends. One night in a cold, frigid January, Rupert had told Ethan that he was sneaking out of school to meet some friends, and asked if Ethan would like to join him. Ethan had been a tad reticent at first as he liked to think of himself as a model student. There was no particular reason that he behaved that way though. It wasn't as if he wanted to curry favours with his fellow students or become the most thought of member of the class, he simply thought that it was the best way to keep a low profile. To his way of thinking if you shine, you stand out.

If you stand out, it's easier to be shot down and once you've been shot down you had a low profile for a different reason altogether.

Still, he reasoned that a midnight sojourn conducted whilst everybody else was asleep would most probably be alright, and without a doubt the most exciting thing to happen to him in the last five years. And anyway, they would never get caught, and besides that, he didn't want to disappoint Rupert and put their friendship to the test.

And so, in the depths of the night, they'd snuck through the school halls to the kitchen, which in turn led to a small passageway at the end of which was a wooden door that took them into the garden. Rupert had led them through the spartan winter undergrowth to a shaded copse on the other side of a country road. Rupert was confident and assured leaving Ethan with no doubt that he had done this many times before.

As they entered the copse, Ethan was startled to hear voices in the near distance, but Rupert assured him that it was only the people that they had come to meet.

As it turned out, Rupert's friends were very pleasant, although he did find it a bit strange that a fifteen year old boy should have acquaintances in their late twenties and early thirties.

"It's time," a gentleman sitting near Rupert had remarked at some point in the early hours of the morning.

"Time for what?" Ethan had asked, turning to Rupert for clarification.

Ethan was shocked by the look that he now saw on his friends face. Rupert seemed impassive and emotionless, but his eyes were shining brightly, the way a person who was halfway to being drunk would appear.

"This is my real family," said Rupert, a passionate tone in his voice that contradicted the set of his features. "They look after me, and I'll be staying with them when I'm done here. Give me your hand."

It wasn't an order. It didn't even feel like a request. More a statement of fact said in the knowledge that the words spoken would be obeyed without question.

Almost involuntarily Ethan felt his right hand rise, but all the while his gaze never left his friends mesmerising glare.

"Everybody needs a family that loves and supports them," Rupert continued, taking hold of Ethans' hand in his own and raising it to his lips, "and I think you, just like me, need one too."

With that, Rupert bit down on the fleshy pad beneath Ethans' thumb hard enough to draw blood, but he did it with such care and tenderness that Ethan felt absolutely nothing at all. As he withdrew his hand, Ethan saw a thin trickle of blood wend its way down Rupert's chin. It should have felt alien and if it had been anyone else, he would have snatched his hand away and run off screaming. But he didn't. It felt right somehow.

"Welcome, Ethan," Rupert said, now smiling, a greeting that was uttered reverentially by the rest of the group.

Ethan passed out at that point and didn't wake up in his bed until the next morning after having the best sleep of his entire life. How he'd got back to his dormitory he had no idea. He told Rupert about this amazing dream that he'd had, one of those ones that was so vivid that it was almost real.

He'd dreamt of running free through woodlands, unencumbered by his human body and its feeble limitations. On and on he'd gone, never tiring and never wanting to stop. Rupert listened with genuine interest and obvious pleasure.

Rupert had explained to Ethan about his heritage later that night after lights out, and that Ethans' dream wasn't a dream at all. He told Ethan about the life cycle of a lycanthrope and provided him with the information that would guide and protect him for the rest of his days. Ethan listened in rapt wonderment, amazed at everything that he was being told and even more amazed that it all seemed to make perfect sense to him.

The two had remained friends after school had finished, and even to this day stayed in touch and met up whenever they could, but they weren't constrained by the nature of their relationship, which was maybe how living in the confines of the werehouse had made him feel. With Ollie and the others he felt a kinship, a bond of friendship undoubtedly, but he didn't feel tied to them. Of course he would do almost anything for any one of them but it wasn't expected. It was this feeling of freedom within the boundaries of a relationship that ultimately convinced him to remove himself from his pack and move on.

"So," said Ollie, "is the way clear for us?"

"It is," answered Ethan, turning away from Stitches, "and I found the well." he announced proudly.

He led them on for another five minutes or so, until they left the trees behind and entered a large clearing.

"There we go."

About a hundred feet away, there it was. The Tonboot Well.

"Looks like a thatched cottage for a dwarf," said Stitches as he watched Ronnie approach it.

"I think it's dry," said Ronnie, leaning over and peering into the black depths. He took hold of the wooden pulley and turned it slowly for thirty seconds or so, until the ancient bucket appeared.

"Just a bit damp, but I think that's more to do with the rain than anything else."

"Who's got the pages?" asked Ollie keen to get on. Ethan poked around in his backpack and retrieved them. "Right," he said, "here we go."

"Story time," said Stitches.

"Over the hill and down the lane, across the stream and back again. Look to the north and then to the west, to find the path that will serve you best. Through the wood and traverse the fen, will find you near a covered glen. Tap the stump and spin round thrice, and what you seek will appear in a trice."

"Over the hill and down the lane. Well that's simple enough. There's a small knoll just over there," said Ollie.

They crested the shallow incline and saw at once a rocky path leading away from its other side. They followed this new trail until they reached a stream.

"What's next?" asked Stitches.

"Um, across the stream and back again," answered Ethan.

"Ah, I see what they mean," said Ollie, pointing to their left. About twenty feet away was a wooden bridge. Beyond that was a fairly deep chasm that stretched back into the woods, and beyond that still was yet another bridge. "We need to cross this one and then come back over the other one."

Once on the other side of the gorge, Ethan read out the next line of the verse.

"Look to the north and then to the west, to find the path that will serve you best. So do we go north for a bit and then head west?"

"I don't think so," said Ronnie, "otherwise that's what it would tell us to do. I reckon we have to head northwest until we come to the next bit."

All agreed with this reasoning, they set off once more. About five minutes later Flug said, "Ronnie, steps."

He was right. Leading off to their right were three earthen steps that led down into another patch of forest.

"This must be it," said Ethan, directing his torch at the paper. "The next line reads 'through the woods and traverse the fen will find you near a covered glen'. So I'm assuming we go through here until we come to an open area."

Thankfully the wooded area wasn't too extensive, and they were through it in about a quarter of an hour. As they emerged from the forest, they did indeed stumble into a large open area of grassland that looked stunning in the light of the full moon.

"Looks a bit desolate," observed Stitches, straining his eyes in an effort to make out something, anything in fact. "Should we keep going this way?"

"I think so," said Ollie. "We've followed the instructions so far. Let's keep going."

"Dere a building," said Flug, pointing at something that he could see in the distance. Try as they might though, none of the others could see what he was getting at.

"Are you sure?" asked Ethan. "My eyesight's excellent, but I can't make anything out."

"Me sure. It dere," Flug repeated, insistently. Ronnie moved to the front of the group.

"If there's one thing I'm sure of," he stated vehemently, "if Flug says he sees something, then you can be sure that it's there."

"What, like our non-existent cat?" said Stitches. "No," said Ronnie. "That's different."

"Or the dragon he reckons he keeps as a pet at the bottom of the garden?"

"Don't be awkward," said Ollie, joining in Ronnie's defence of their friend. "You know exactly what he means. Flug?"

"Yeah."

"Can you take us to the building, please?"

"Okay, Ollie. But stay wiv me. It dark."

The grassland was damp and overgrown. Thistles and vines covered the ground, making the going tricky, but they eventually made it without too much trouble.

"It's a mausoleum," exclaimed Ollie, shining a light at the marble structure looming before them. "But there's nothing about it in the verse."

"Yes, there is," said Ronnie, chuckling quietly. "Have a look at this." The entrance to the tomb was a large oak door that looked like it weighed about six tonnes. Attached to it was a shiny brass plate, which had what was obviously the family name engraved on it. "GLEN," said Ollie in exasperation. "Would you believe it?"

"Will find you near a covered glen," said Stitches snorting in disbelief and, he admitted silently to himself, a little bit of admiration. "Good job it didn't say you come to a hidden Clive or an out of the way Bob. We'd have been knackered. Well, at least it shows that whoever wrote the text had a sense of humour."

"We'll see," responded Ethan. "I'll make my mind up about that once we're done inside. Okay, everybody look for a stump."

It didn't take long. Round the back of the tomb Stitches came across the stump. Well, came across isn't exactly the right phrase. He fell across it because he didn't see it, and in the process dislocated a knee joint.

"I bet Indiana Jones never had this trouble," he said miserably, trying to manipulate his patella back into place.

"Agreed, but then again, he's not two hundred years old and falling apart," said Ollie.

"Oh, I don't know," responded Stitches after a loud pop. "Did you see The Kingdom of the Crystal Skull? He was older and more decrepit than most of the relics he was looking for. His museum thought that one of its exhibits had escaped."

Ollie reached out a hand and helped his friend back to his feet. "Right," said Ethan, "the last line says tap the stump and spin round thrice and, well, basically something should happen."

"I'll do it," volunteered Ronnie.

He leant over and rapped firmly on the top of the moss covered stump, after which he pirouetted three times on the spot, rather gracefully, it has to be said.

A loud creaking shattered the peaceful silence that covered the landscape, made all the more intense by the stillness of the night. It was the sort of sound that you would hear in one of those old eighties horror films, just before a hapless victim got an axe through their cranium. Let's face it though, they usually deserve it. If you're going to wander around spooky, abandoned buildings because you think that's the most romantic place to take your girlfriend, then good luck to you. Always remember though, if watching horror films has taught society anything, it has to be that you shouldn't visit and then engage in any activity in any place that was a multiple murder scene, a closed insane asylum or a hotel shut for the winter, and the like. Something is bound, nay certain to go badly wrong and you won't be leaving with the same number of limbs that you arrived with. Or with a full compliment of friends. Or anything else for that matter, because you'll probably end up as a lampshade, on a table next to some aged crone in a rocking chair. Then you're dead and gone until your wandering spirit is disturbed by Yvette Fielding, shrieking at you at the top of her voice for you to manifest, which, personally, I bloody well wouldn't if my life depended on it.

Conversely, and maybe any ghost hunters out there should take note, there are many things that a spirit would appear for though. Christina Hendricks in a low cut top, bending over to pick up the glass that's been knocked onto the floor using newly discovered supernatural powers, the chance to watch Reservoir Dogs one more time (the proper one that is, not the director's cut, not the specially extended edition, not the redux version and not the specially extended director's final cut with an extra forty five minutes of footage that you fast forward through anyway, because that's why the director cut it out in the first place, he knew it was rubbish) or to play the Gears of War series again because you never got to finish them on super hard bastard mode. Yes indeed, those are just a few examples on what to do to encourage a spectral form to transcend from their ethereal nether world into ours. DO NOT employ the services of a screaming harpy who prowls around old, abandoned buildings ringing bells, playing with Ouija boards and jumping yards whenever someone so much as breaks wind. It is for that very reason, and no other reason at all so don't try and think of one, that there's no actual documented evidence of ghosts existing. Only complete idiots go looking for them. You wouldn't answer your front door if you knew that a total arse was outside, wanting you to blow out a candle or make a noise on a voice recorder would you. It needs lateral thinking and a different, more radical approach. Send Stephen Fry in. Everybody loves him. QED (Quite Enough of Dat).

The loud creaking sounded just like a mausoleum door opening. "That sounds just like a mausoleum door opening," announced

Ethan to the others (told you).

As they assembled outside the now open tomb, they felt a faint rush of warm air issuing from within. It smelt damp and musty and was tinged with a vague hint of decay, like a fridge that had been switched off for a few days (or mine just after Mrs. Author has decided it's time for liver trifle again).

"I suppose we just go in," suggested Ollie, shining his torch inside. It revealed nothing. The darkness swallowed the light like a black hole.

"Sure, why not? What could possibly go wrong?" mused Stitches.

The gap that the door had left was big enough to allow two of them through at once. Ethan and Ollie stepped up and tentatively made their way in. Slowly.

"This is ridiculous," said Ollie, thrusting his torch forward as if that would encourage the beam to try harder. "It's like the torch is on, but isn't working."

Stitches and Ronnie came in next, with Flug bringing up the rear. As soon as he was over the threshold the door slammed shut, trapping them inside.

Without warning bright lights came on, flooding the whole area and their optic nerves with dazzling intensity.

"And here they are, the Jive plucky adventurers who have chosen to take on this most difficult quest."

The voice was booming and confident but had a subtle hint of insincerity, tucked quietly away in there somewhere. It was a disc jockey's voice, but a disc jockey who was slightly too old to be playing the latest modern music on his early morning show.

"Master Stitches, would you step forward please."

"Huh. What? What's he talking about? Why has my name been called out? How the hell does it know my name anyway? What's going on? Alright, which one of you jokers is pulling my leg?"

The voice from beyond the grave spoke again. Well, it was in the grave, but you get the point. It was a bit spooky.

"No one is pulling your leg, Master Stitches because it would probably come off. HA HA. Excuse my little jest. Would you PLEASE step forward." "I think you'd better do as it says, mate," Ollie said worriedly. "He sounded a bit more serious that time." "Oh, good grief."

Stitches took a tentative step forward. As soon as his foot hit the floor the lights dimmed to a more acceptable level, affording them the luxury of seeing what was going on.

The walls, cracked and covered in cobwebs, had several recesses embedded in them that all appeared to contain coffins or caskets. A large chandelier hung from the ceiling. It was about four feet across and was dripping with sparkling jewels. It was decadent, overly ostentatious and looked totally out of place here. It would have looked more at home hanging somewhere in Jocular's castle, maybe in a library or a torture chamber.

Right in the centre of the open space was a chair that Stitches could have sworn wasn't there a moment ago. It was upholstered in black leather, an office type, high backed, the sort that would be found at desks all over the world.

"*Please sit down, Master Stitches.*"

The zombie looked imploringly back at his friends, a worried expression on his face.

"What do I do now?" he whispered.

"Sit down, mate," answered Ronnie. "After all we're on a quest, aren't we? We're just going to have to get on with it."

"That's easy for you to say when the 'we' you're talking about is me, and not you."

"*Please do not be alarmed, Master Stitches,*" the disembodied voice returned again. "*If you follow the rules, no harm will come to you. Your companions' turns will come in due course.*"

Stitches noticed, with a hint of pleasure he had to admit, four faces suddenly gawping in anguish. He turned away from them and slowly approached the chair. He checked it thoroughly and decided that it was safe to sit down. As soon as his skinny backside touched the leather, the chair spun around so that he was facing away from the others, and a grinding noise from above made them all look up. At least two dozen of the jewels on the light fitting shot downwards and embedded themselves into the stone floor. Connected to each was a shaft of steel running upwards where it came to an end in the chandelier. In effect, Stitches was now trapped in a barred cage.

"Oh, terrific. Now I'm completely stuffed."

Ethan and Ronnie made to move forward to help their friend, but Ollie stopped them.

"I think it's best that we leave well enough alone and let him get on with it by himself," he stated forcefully. "This is happening for a reason, and for the moment he doesn't actually seem to be in any danger. Let's wait and see what occurs."

As a hush descended, a shimmering in the atmosphere about six feet in front of Stitches caught their attention. It looked a bit like the wibbly wobbly visual effect from a TV show when they wanted to denote going back in time. It took a few seconds to stop and when it did, what appeared to be the ghostly apparition of a man was floating before them.

"*Yvette Fielding isn't here, is she?*" asked the figure, looking around nervously.

"No," replied Stitches. "She's off trying to resurrect Amy Winehouse's career. Need to resurrect Miss Winehouse first of course, but hey, it's the thought that counts."

"*Good. In that case, welcome, Master Stitches. My name is Flapper, and I will be your host for this evening's proceedings.*"

"Charmed, I'm sure."

"*Do you know where you are?*" "Sure do. Right in it."

"*This is the first task on your quest for the Cup of All Souls. Each of you in turn will face a challenge, and it is on completion of said challenge that a portion of the Cup will be awarded. Do you wish to continue?*"

"What if I say no?" Stitches asked.

"*Then you will be allowed on your way, but none of you will have any recollection of this encounter.*"

"And if I fail?"

"*Best not to, really, if I'm honest.*"

Stitches turned his head as far as he could and looked at his companions.

"Well," he asked, "what's it going to be?"

Ollie glanced at the others but the only answer he got was the very loud shrugging of shoulders.

"It's your call, mate," he called to the zombie. "You're the one in the chair. If you say let's get out of here, we go."

Stitches sighed heavily and turned back to face the spectre.

"Ah, to hell with it. I'm here now, and anyway, who wants to live forever?"

Ollie called over to his friend again.

"Come on mate, you can do it. Stay alert, stay focussed and listen to what you're being told, okay."

"Okay. What was the second one?" "Does he ever stop?" said Ronnie.

"*Very well,*" said Flapper, who all of a sudden was holding a small stack of cards, *"your challenge is to answer the ten questions that I am going to put to you."*

"That doesn't sound too bad," said Stitches, his mood improving a little.

"However, you must make your answers as entertaining as possible. You see, the challenges that each of you will face are speciJic to the person chosen, based upon personality, temperament, interests etc. In other words, Master Stitches, this should be right up your street."

"Sounds more like a dating show. Well, as long as you don't ask me anything on politics, sport, music, general knowledge or current affairs, I should be fine."

"Excellent. Shall we begin?" asked Flapper, checking his stack of cards.

"Might as well. Oh, by the way, has anyone ever got through the first challenge?"

"Has the Cup been found?" "Bugger."

"Okay. So, here we go. Question one. In the Bible, how did Jesus Christ meet his end?"

"Um, he was run over by a speed boat whilst walking to work." *"Question two. In the game of Monopoly, what is the best way to win*
the game?"

"Uh, by as many properties as you can, then claim you're an immigrant who can't return to your country for political reasons and you'll be given all the houses and hotels for free."

"Question three. Approximately how far does light travel in a light year?"

"About twice as far than it does during a heavy year, on account of it being so busy."

"Question four. In the famous love story, The Hunchback of Notre Dame, what is the name of the eponymous hero who falls in love with Esmeralda?"

"I can't quite put my finger on it, but it certainly does ring a bell."

"Question Jive. What is the name of the item that a Scotsman wears in front of his kilt?"

"A sheep."

"Question six. What was the disastrous move that caused the Nazis to lose the Second World War?"

"One of the Generals didn't wash his hands properly after getting bitten by a small furry animal, and they all caught German Weasels."

"*Question seven. What is a Thesaurus?*" "A dinosaur with a degree in English."

"*Question eight. What is the traditional gift to get someone who has been married for sixty years?*"

"The George Cross."

"*Question nine. What is the worst birthday present ever bought?*" "A set of drums for Anne Frank."

"*And finally, question ten. What is the stupidest thing ever?*"

"The Society of Illiteracy's publication 'How to read in twelve easy to read lessons'. Big print version available."

The moment Stitches gave his final answer, the ghostly questioner before him disappeared with a resounding pop, leaving nothing but sinuous tendrils of smoke that threaded up to the ceiling, where they seeped into the masonry and vanished.

"So, what now?" the zombie asked the empty space.

"Do we go and get him out?" Ronnie asked Ollie as he took a step towards the chandelier cage.

Ollie reached out and put a hand on his friend's arm, stopping him from going any further.

"Best leave it," he said. "Everything else has happened spontaneously. There's no reason to think that anything bad is going to occur now. He did what was asked of him, didn't he?"

As they watched their trapped friend, they saw him reach a hand up. It looked like he was going to grab hold of one of the shafts of metal, but before his fingers could close around it, the whole cage began to shake. The metal whined loudly as it became taut and the jewels that had been driven into the floor rocked back and forth, as if they were being subjected to an invisible force. Then, as quickly as they had shot downwards, the jewels were released. The lengths of steel went flaccid and every one of them raced back up into their original positions. Stitches got up from the chair and walked back across the tomb to his colleagues.

"Well done, mate" said Ollie, taking Stitches by the hand and shaking it. "That was a tough challenge."

"He's right," added Ethan, joining in the hopefully not too premature victory celebrations by giving him a slap on the back. "That was superb, coming up with all that stuff so quickly."

"Ah, it was nothing" replied the dusty one, trying his best to come across as modest.

"So what now, then?" asked Ronnie. "How do we know if we've won the piece? Do we have to look for it? Do we have to wait for Phantomforce to deliver it, what?"

As if in answer to that very question, the leather chair in the centre of the room vanished in a flash and was replaced by a rag. On closer inspection, it seemed to be a tea towel. On even closer inspection it seemed to be a souvenir tea towel from the coastal resort of Sharks Bay.

Flug bent down, picked it up in his giant hand and stood in the middle of the group, the towel resting on his palm.

"It's lumpy. There must be something wrapped up inside it," said Ollie.

"What's your speciality? Stating the bloody obvious? Of course there's something inside it. The question is what?" said Stitches, looking but not touching.

"Well, my guess is that it's the first piece of the Cup," observed Ethan. "It's a good few minutes since the end of the challenge and nothing untoward has happened. It looks like he's done it, even if that is stating the bloody obvious."

Ollie scratched his head thoughtfully.

"I'd like to know for definite though," he said. "Maybe one of us should unwrap it. Away from the others. You know, health and safety and all that. Stitches?"

"Why me?" he protested incredulously. "And what about my health and safety? What about Flug? He's been holding it and nothing's happened to him."

"Me feel a bit strange," Flug announced to the group. "Like me got a headache and my brain hurts."

"You always feel like that, even on a good day," said the zombie. "Come on, it's not fair. I won the damn thing in the first place."

"I know, but I do think that it should be you," said Ollie in as friendly a manner as he could manage, given the situation.

"Why?" said Stitches.

"For two reasons. One, you, as you so rightly said, accomplished the task that made it appear, and two, if I may be permitted the indelicacy, if anything happens, you're easy to put back together again if it goes bang."

Stitches had a look of disgust on his face that would have rivalled anything the Queen could have mustered when told that she was off to visit some poor people.

"Well, seeing as you put it like that, how can I possibly refuse?" God forbid any of you lot lose anything vital."

He snatched the cloth parcel from Flug and stomped to the far end of the necropolis. He placed it on the ground and teased back the corners of the cloth. A glint of shiny metal issued from within.

"I think this is it," he announced proudly to the others. His anticipation overrode his sense of practicality and he quickly removed the rest of the tea towel, faster than a kid on Christmas morning. He picked up the prize and took it to his friends.

"Wassat, Ronnie?" asked Flug.

"It's the base of the Cup, mate. We're on our way, lads. We've got the first piece."

Ollie reached out and took the piece from Stitches and studied it. "Doesn't look like much, does it?" he said. "Still, ATCHOO, excuse me; at least we've got it. Ethan, can you, ATCHOO, for goodness-sake, look after it?"

"Of course," the lycan replied, slipping his rucksack off.

"Right, let's get out of here," suggested Ollie, heading for the now open door. "I think this tomb dust is getting to me."

"I'm with you," agreed Stitches. "It's too cold as well. We're liable to catch our death. Or death is liable to catch hold of us. One or the other." So, with the first challenge completed and the first piece of the Cup safely stowed away in Ethan's bag, they made their way out of the mausoleum and retraced the route back to the car.

———

The hooded figure stared at the swirling misty depths in the bowl. The first task had been completed and now, as the seekers left the ancient tomb, a brief smile played across a mouth seemingly unused to such a gesture.

"Excellent work, my ignorant associates. Outstanding. If only you knew the true nature of what you're engaged in."

Standing up and walking about the dark abode allowed the life to flow back into weary legs. The constant vigil that was being kept was necessary, but also tiresome. The seekers' progress had to be monitored though because the closer they came to completing the quest, the more imperative it was that all was in readiness for the concluding act. This opportunity wasn't going to be missed for anything, even if it meant sitting awake here for days on end.

Leg muscles suitably refreshed, the figure took to the uncomfortable wooden stool once more.

"Onward."

———

As they reached the hearse, the first glimmer of dawn was cast ing its shadowy aura over the countryside. Birds had started singing and the sound of normal daytime woodland creatures could be heard around them.

"Looks like we better get you under cover, Ollie," said Ethan, noticing the rapidly receding gloom. "Do you want to hide up in the back?"

Ollie took off his own backpack and rummaged around in its depths until he found the balaclava that Crumble had made for him.

"Nah. I'll be alright. I'll slip this on. The Prof said it should work a treat. I'll sit on the back seat in the middle. I'll be okay."

Stitches looked at him doubtfully, a hint of concern also on his face. "Are you sure you want to trust your wellbeing to the man who invented an ejector seat for a helicopter? Seems a bit risky to me." "It'll be fine, don't worry," said Ollie, slipping the balaclava onto his head. It covered his bonce completely and even had a fine mesh over the eyes and mouth holes. He stood with his hands on his hips and posed for them, not realising that Crumble had embellished the forehead of the all over hat with a delicately stitched pink bat.

"What do you think?" he asked.

"You look like a gay terrorist," said Stitches, shaking his head. "If I didn't know better, I'd assume you were off to suicide bomb a rather poor production of My Fair Lady."

The sun continued to rise behind them, its heat and light strong and insistent for so early in the morning.

"How does it feel?" asked Ethan.

"Not bad, actually. Bit itchy though, which is a bit odd because I've never had problems with any clothing fibres before," replied Ollie scratching the top of his head. He looked round. "But the sun is well and truly up now and I'm still standing. Any being with vampire blood in it would be a bubbling heap on the floor by now if it weren't under cover. Looks like the Prof has come up trumps for a change."

"Maybe, but I wouldn't go booking your holiday to Majorca or having a session or two on a sunbed just yet," said Ronnie. "It's probably best to be careful with it for now, just to be on the safe side."

"Fair point," said Ollie. "Right, shall we have a look at the next clue?" Ethan retrieved the folder from his backpack. He opened it up and laid it on the bonnet of the hearse, extracting the two required pages. "Right, here we go," he said, passing the text to Ollie whilst he kept hold of the map.

"What does it say?" asked Stitches.

"Travel to the town with a tooth for a name, for here you will find the place for you game. Go to the warehouse where the crowds mass, and speak to the one who'll allow you to pass. His name is important as you will soon see, as he will instruct you on how to proceed. Give all that you have of body and mind, and take home the prize if this you should find." Ollie looked up when he'd finished and shook his head.

"Nicely abstract," said Stitches, taking the piece of paper and looking at it for himself, as if that would help. "Not making it easy for us, are they?"

"I don't suppose they would," commented Ronnie. "It's not like we're popping down the shop and getting some teabags, is it?"

"Here," said Ethan, "have a look at the map." He smoothed it out on the car so they could all have a look.

"Haven't a clue," said Stitches forlornly. "All I'm seeing is a load of straight lines, which I'm assuming are streets, an asterisk and a two tailed fish in a square. Makes no sense to me whatsoever."

"Me neither, I'm afraid," added Ronnie.

"Same as that," said Ethan. "I can't even think of a town with the name of a tooth let alone where it might be."

Ollie scratched his head again, only this time it was in deep thought rather than in deep discomfort. Something was niggling at the back of his mind but he couldn't actually decide if it made sense or not. He told the group to keep studying the pages whilst he wandered off for a few minutes to gather his thoughts.

About ten minutes later and thoughts suitably reined in, he came back to the group.

"What have you been doing?" asked Stitches. "Thinking," he replied.

"What about?"

"Well, it seems to me that this Cup of All Souls, said to be one of the most powerful objects in the world, needs to be found so that it can be used for whatever purpose it was meant for. That being the case, it would make sense for it not to be *too* difficult to find, well, not as difficult as it would first appear, or how difficult and dangerous we may think it is or likely to be. Do you remember when we all looked at the first map back in the office? It made absolutely no sense to any of us except Ronnie. Not only did he work out what the one symbol was when the rest of us were stumped, it turned out that he'd actually been there before."

"So what you're saying," said Ethan trying to understand, "is that although we're still going to have to go through the various challenges, the Cup itself, or whatever forces are guarding it, are in effect giving us a bit of a helping hand."

"More or less, yes. I don't know whether it's preordained or pure luck, or because the clues somehow fit who we are, or who's seeking the Cup at the time, but I suppose what I'm getting at is, it wants to be found. Maybe even needs to be."

"Well, us three have looked at it," said Stitches, indicating himself, Ethan and Ronnie "You try it. And I hope to God that you do recognise something, because the one tiny flaw in your excellent theory is Flug. He wouldn't recognise his own face if it was staring at him. Actually, come to think of it, he can't, which is why Ronnie shaves him. He tried to slice his own nose off once, remember?"

Ollie nodded as he approached the car. "If I'm wrong, then so be it," he said.

Ollie picked up the piece of paper and stared at it. Hard. Then harder still, almost willing it to make sense, hoping that some tiny detail, however insignificant, would spark a glimmer of recognition.

"Nothing," he announced, dejectedly. "Nothing?" Stitches asked, pleadingly. "Nothing," Ollie repeated, disappointedly. "Bugger," said Stitches, angrily.

"Flug," Ronnie called out over his shoulder, attempting to catch the monster's wavering attention.

"Yeah," replied Flug, a stray antennae and silky butterfly wing hanging from his bottom lip.

"Christ. Come here a minute, will you, mate."

Flug thudded over to the group like an ambulatory crane.

"Wassup, Ronnie?"

"I need you to have a look at this pretty picture and tell me what you see, okay."

"Okay."

As Flug studied the map, the other four studied him. It would be polite to say that he looked like a contestant on University Challenge, struggling to answer a particularly taxing question on Theoretical Quantum Physics. It was more realistic, however, to say that he looked like an eight foot slab of meat staring blankly at a piece of paper. It pays to be honest.

"Anything?" asked Ronnie. "Something," pleaded Ethan. "Just one thing," requested Ollie. "Big dumb thing," added Stitches. "Sweeties," announced Flug.

"Yeah, not now, mate," said Ollie. "I need you to concentrate. Do you see anything at all that you've seen before?"

"Sweeties."

"That's it. He's completely gone this time," said Stitches, violently throwing his hands into the air in frustration. Surprisingly, he caught both of them.

"I agree," said Ethan, getting Stitches' sewing kit out of the zombie's pocket, threading a needle and starting to sew. "We'll have to figure this one out from scratch."

"Speaking of which, can you do the end of my nose, please?" the handless one asked.

Ollie was about to reclaim the map when Flug's fist came down on it like a five fingered flesh mallet, slamming it back onto the bonnet of the car, causing a dustbin lid sized dent to appear, (and a round of spontaneous applause from literary critics for such wonderful alliteration! I thank you).

"I get sweeties from dere," he rumbled. "When me little, it was shop." "He's dragging something else up from the depths of his unconscious," said Ronnie. "Must be another buried memory resurfacing."

"Could be," agreed Ollie. "Flug, do you remember where this sweetie shop is?"

The large one removed his fist from the map and scratched his head. "Uh, yeah. Me fink so. It in Molar."

"Oh, I've heard of that," said Ethan, tying off a loop of cotton and finally reattaching Stitches' left hand. "If I remember correctly it's an old industrial town."

"How far away is it?" asked Stitches, taking over the needle and thread.

"About a hundred miles I reckon. I'll make sure the Bat Nav is charged up and give it the details."

"Okay then," said Ollie, climbing into the darkened rear of the hearse and pulling the curtains. "Let's get loaded up and get going."

———

Jekyll was at a dead end. In fact the end that he was at was not only dead, it was in a wooden box six feet under the ground and starting to smell a bit funky.

He'd spent the best part of a day and a half wandering the streets and back alleys of Fibula, trying to gather any information he could about Flange and his mysterious disappearance, but with no luck. Fed up and bored, he was currently sitting in a small café called The Open Wound, on the High Street, nursing his third cup of double strength espresso. The thick, muddy brown liquid was the only thing keeping him awake at the moment.

"Excuse me," came a voice from behind him.

He turned in his seat and was confronted by a woman dressed in a grey suit. She looked to be in her early forties, had long blonde hair, dangly silver earrings and was wearing an understated amount of makeup. She was extremely attractive.

"Can I help you?" asked Jekyll as he stood up to offer her the chair opposite him.

She sat down and rested her hands, fingers interlocked, on the table.

"I think," she said in a quiet voice, "that I may be able to help you.

My name is Scorpio Bytheway."

Jekyll held out a hand, which was accepted. Her skin was warm and soft and she smelled of long, country walks in the morning mist.

"A pleasure to meet you, Miss Bytheway. So, how are you going to help me?"

"I gather you've been asking around town about Mr. Flange." "Have I?"

"Yes you have. And you're interested in why he seems to have gone missing."

"Am I?"

"Yes you are. And part of the reason why you're spending so much time in Fibula is that you don't want any bother with a certain lady's father."

Jekyll sat up straight in his chair and pushed his back into it, as if trying to distance himself from this stranger without her realising that that was what he was doing.

"Alright. Exactly who are you and how do you know so much about me?"

She smiled serenely, but there was no threat there. It was what it was. A genuine smile. She seemed to on the level and, if he was honest with himself, he wasn't getting any bad vibes from her despite his initial reservations.

"I work in the local library," she said, "but in my spare time I practice fortune telling. Every now and again I get flashes on people. I was coming to see you anyway, but when we shook hands I got a hit on you." "I don't suppose you've got next week's lottery numbers to hand, have you, or know exactly which farming implement is going to do me in?"

She chuckled softly and indicated to the waitress that she wanted a cup of tea.

"No, I'm afraid not. I can't control the flashes and they can be quite intermittent. But that's not why I came to see you. Thank you."

She spooned two mounds of sugar into her tea and gave it a vigorous stir before taking a sip.

"A few nights ago I worked late at the library, cataloguing and sorting the books, erasing the comedy genitals in the biology section, the usual stuff, but it meant that I didn't get out of there till about eleven thirty." She sipped more tea. "On my way home I have to walk past Mr. Flange's house, but as I got nearer that night I could hear raised voices, so I stopped to listen. Noise at night is pretty unusual around here. When I realised it was coming from Flange's house I crossed the road and hid in an alleyway. About five minutes later, the front door opened and I saw both Flange and Vortex step outside. They were talking a lot quieter now that they were in the street, but I'm positive they were arguing about something. Anyway, they stayed there for a while, speaking and gesticulating at each other until Vortex wandered off and Flange went back indoors."

"Did you manage to catch any of the conversation?" asked Jekyll. "I'm afraid not, but it certainly didn't look friendly. Vortex was waving his arms wildly about, and Flange was stamping his feet." "Mmmm." Jekyll took a swig of his rapidly cooling and congealing beverage. "What did you do after that?"

"I was going to hang around for a couple of minutes until I was sure that Flange wasn't going to come back out, and that Vortex had definitely gone, but as I was standing in that alley I got scared."

"Scared? Why?"

"The only way I can describe it is that I felt spooked, like someone had just walked over my grave. I felt cold and shivery and a bit nauseous, but I couldn't put my finger on why. Still can't, as a matter of fact. I didn't care who saw me at that point, I just wanted to get out of there and get home."

"Have you seen either of them since? I bumped into Vortex the other night but since then, nothing. No one's seen or heard from him."

"No I haven't" said Scorpio, "which is especially unusual for Flange. He's a regular at the library. He normally comes in three or four times a week. A real bookworm."

"Really," Jekyll said, interestedly. "What sort of books does he usually read?"

"Spell books and magical history in the main. Even some volumes about the dark arts. He loves all that stuff."

Jekyll thanked Scorpio for her help and bade her farewell, as she was due to start work shortly. She promised to stay in touch and let him know if she heard anything else of interest.

He ordered himself another coffee and pondered over what the lady had told him, and how to fit it into what he already knew.

Flange was obviously into wizardry of some sort or another, but for what reason, Jekyll couldn't fathom. Could be a hobby. Could be something more serious. But taken in conjunction with the recent thefts of the pages and his subsequent vanishing act, it firmly put him under the spotlight, centre stage. And did he have an accomplice in Vortex? Maybe Scorpio had seen them arguing about their plans for the pages and ultimately the Cup itself. Or maybe they just didn't get on, but were plotting together as a matter of necessity. That could make sense. Well, it made about as much sense as anything else at the moment. Vortex, as assistant to the curator, would be best placed to get hold of the missing items, maybe even more so than Flange. But it was obviously the caretaker who had the knowledge, if the collection of books in his house were anything to go by. Jekyll did wonder, though. Why, if they'd gone to the effort of arranging the theft, had they not gone after the Cup themselves? Or maybe they had. Perhaps that's why they'd gone missing. Maybe they were on the trail of Ollie and the gang and were going to ambush them once they'd collected all of the pieces. If that was the case, maybe he should follow as well and try to warn them, because there was a good chance that he could track them and locate them before any text message would get through. Or maybe... Jekyll rubbed his eyes. He'd been staring out of the window whilst pondering about how many maybe's he was dealing with, and had just seen something that blew the last half an hour completely out of the water. There, on the other side of the street, walking confidently along without a care in the world, was Vortex. He had a smile on his face and a spring in his step and. . . Jekyll scrunched his eyes and looked closer. There was something else in Vortex's step that caught his attention. Nestled between the tops of his shiny shoes and the bottom of his perfectly creased trousers was a pair of bright red socks.

"You devious so and so," Jekyll muttered to himself.

The thought that struck him on seeing the assistant was that he had obviously set up Flange, and was somehow going to claim the Cup for himself and leave the poor caretaker shouldering the blame. Clearly there was no way he could prove it, but that didn't stop him being able to put the wind up the old boy, in the hope that he slipped up or gave up altogether. He threw some coins down onto the table and rushed out of the café, and along the street.

"Mr. Vortex," he called when he got to within a few feet of the man. "Can I have a word, please?"

Vortex stopped in his tracks and turned to face him. "Haven't we met before?" he asked Jekyll.

"Indeed we have. We bumped into each other a few nights back. You dropped some papers onto the ground."

"Oh yes. I remember now."

Jekyll couldn't detect so much as a twitch on Vortex's face, or any change in his demeanour whatsoever. He decided that the best form of attack was attack.

"I'm going to cut to the chase and get right to the point," he said, lowering his voice and staring at Vortex straight in the eye. "I know what you're up to and I'm going to do everything in my power to put a stop to it."

That got a reaction. Vortex suddenly seemed to shrink into his cloak and he began to breathe heavier.

"Why would you do such a thing?" he asked, his voice trembling. "Because what you're doing is wrong and is liable to upset quite a lot of people. Probably kill a few as well."

"Well, I'm doing my best to make sure that it all goes as smoothly as possible, but I'm afraid I can't please everybody. And I can appreciate that things may get a little raucous, but I don't think anybody's going to die."

"So what do you expect to gain from all this then?" Vortex was silent for a few moments before answering.

"Well. Hopefully I'll take over and become the head of it all afterwards. That would be the logical course to follow, wouldn't you agree? But please don't say anything to anyone. You'll ruin the whole thing. A lot of work has gone into this and I don't want it spoiled at this stage."

"I bet you don't. So where's Flange?"

"I really can't tell you anymore. If I give too much away, I might as well forget the whole thing. I really must be going now. Excuse me."

With that, he turned on his heel and walked away.

Jekyll considered going after him and pressing him further, but realised it would be a wasted effort. Vortex wasn't giving anything away, and without definite proof he was back at the dead end that was now rotten to the core and smelling like an ogres fridge. He could go to Starch, but again he would have the same problem. There was no way he would be able to convince the curator that his trusted assistant was plotting something so insidious. What to do?

After careful consideration, targeted surveillance seemed to be the only option left open to him, the only one with any realistic chance of success anyway. He would have to keep tabs on Vortex and watch his every move, and hope that he gave something away. He was going to have to be patient, but luckily that was a game he knew how to play.

———

"Go on then, Flug. Your turn," said Ronnie.

"Okay. I spy wiv my little eye sumfink beginnin' wiv horse." "What are you doing?" enquired Stitches. "That's not how you play, for goodness sake. You say the first letter of horse, H. Not the whole word, right?"

"Okay."

"Okay. Try again."

"I spy wiv my little eye sumfink beginnin' wiv da H from horse."

"No, just the H of horse, not horse itself, okay. Try again," said Stitches who was running out of patience faster than a history teacher who really hated kids (yes, I remember you, Mrs. Morgan).

"Um. I spy wiv my little eye sumfink beginnin' wiv H." "That's it. Horse?"

"Nope."

"Hearse?"

"Nope."

"Humpbacked bridge?" "Nope."

"Oh I don't know. What is it?" "Tree."

Stitches threw up his hands again but was careful to keep a hold of them this time. "That's it. I give up. I'd get more sense out of a particularly stupid rock. How are we doing, Ethan? Are we nearly there yet?" "We're just on the outskirts of town now," replied the lycan. "Might as well get the map out and give it to Flug. Hopefully something else will jog his memory."

"There's not enough dynamite on the planet to manage that," said Stitches.

Ollie unfolded the piece of paper and handed it to Flug.

"Right," the half vampire said. "I want you to look at this again and tell me if you recognise where we are okay."

"Okay. I spy wiv my little eye. . . "

"No, no, no. We're not doing that now. Look at the place we're driving through and tell Ethan when to stop, yeah?"

"Yeah."

"We're going to end up in the middle of nowhere. You know that, don't you?" said Stitches. "You do recall that he frequently gets lost going to the toilet at home."

"I know, but. . . " "It's en suite."

"Let's just give him a chance, hey," said Ollie. "If he can't figure it out, we'll find another way."

"Dere," said Flug, pointing to a side alley that they were approaching.

Ethan slowed down and brought the hearse to a stop. "Are you sure?" asked Ollie.

"Yeah. Remember walkin' down dere wiv uvver people."

The alley was dark and bleak, and barely touched by the meagre lighting on the main road. The whole area was awash with the litter and detritus of an active town that was now passive and lifeless. It was as if the darkness had sucked all the energy from it. The only sound they could hear was the rustle of stray bits of paper as they swirled endlessly on a soft breeze and occasionally collided with the dank brick walls.

Ollie looked at the map and tried to make sense of where they were, and where they were supposed to be.

"Well," he announced, "if we assume that the alley on the map is this one here, then I think we may have our starting point."

"Seems as good a place to start as any," added Ronnie. "And Flug says he recognises it, so let's go."

Ethan found a place to park and they all got out.

"Is it safe to leave the car here?" Stitches asked. "Seems to be the sort of place where you'd come back to find your wheels gone and four piles of bricks in their place. Then someone nicks the bricks."

"Don't worry," said Ethan locking the doors. "It's insured. Third party spell and disappearance protection. I found the policy under the passenger seat, next to something squidgy."

"Come on, guys," said Ollie from the entrance to the alley, "let's get a move on. Flug, you first."

As they progressed further into the brickwork maze the atmosphere became more oppressive and intimidating, and each turn they took seemed to bring them closer to a vague, distant collection of voices somewhere ahead. In spite of this, Flug strode on with certainty, sometimes making lefts or rights without instructions from Ollie. Obviously he knew where he was going, the strange memory recall that overtook him every now and again once more coming to the fore.

"Can you hear that?" said Ronnie, stopping suddenly and cupping an ear.

"What?" said Ethan.

"I'm sure I can hear singing. Listen."

Straining to hear over the wind that whistled through the tight confines of the alleyway, the group stood still.

"I can just about hear it," said Stitches. "It seems to be coming from where we're supposed to be headed. Looks like we're on the right track then. Or sounds like it anyway."

About ten minutes and several turns later, they came across a figure standing next to a large oil drum that had a fire burning away fiercely on top of it. It cast a warm orange glow that cut through the darkness like the sun, illuminating the little man next to it who was warming his hands, even though they were wrapped in fingerless gloves. (I've never really understood the concept of fingerless gloves. Why would you take an item that is perfect in design and then remove the very aspect that makes it what it is? You wouldn't wear toeless socks or soleless shoes would you, and bottomless pants would just be ridiculous, unless you were in Amsterdam of course, but then the Dutch have always been a bit odd. No one should be that obsessed with the colour orange, and have you ever worn a pair of clogs? Still, flavourless food seems to be a hit on every High Street, so maybe there is something in it. Or not, as the case may be.)

"Ah, good evening, gentlemen. And may I say what a pleasure it is to see five such fine specimens," he said before bending down and putting another couple of bits of wood into the fire. "I hope I find you fit and well."

"With a greeting like that, I don't want him finding us at all," said Stitches quietly. "Sounds like he's getting ready to put an offer in for us."

The stranger was about five feet four, slim, pasty white and didn't have a single hair on his head, not even so much as an eyelash. He looked like a Shaolin monk with a severe case of alopecia. He was smiling broadly, but the adventurers couldn't decide if it was a 'come on over and let's have a chat over the fire' smile or a 'come on over and let's have a chat while I roast you over the fire' smile.

"And who might you be, if I may ask?" said Ollie putting the map away, sensing that it wasn't needed anymore.

"Weird Bald Guy," said the little man.

"That figures," said Stitches. "I bet you've got a couple of mates called Potential Serial Killer and The Stink haven't you."

"How very perceptive of you," replied the little man. He looked at his watch. Ollie noticed that it was drawn on his wrist. "They'll be here in a little while but you won't get to meet them, unfortunately. You've got to be somewhere, I'm guessing."

"You guess right," said Ronnie. "Do we have far to go?"

Weird Bald Guy picked up a long two-pronged fork that had been resting against the oil drum, stuck something white and squishy onto it and placed it into the flames. From a distance it looked like a marshmallow. A closer look would reveal that said alleged sweet treat had an iris, veins and a lens. With it suitably browned to his satisfaction, Weird Bald Guy pulled it off the fork with his teeth and bit down. A disturbing pop echoed around the alley in spite of the wind, and a thin, stringy necklace of goo fell from his mouth and lay across his chin like a stranded jellyfish, before it was recovered with a loud slurp. He smiled that smile again, but this time it was definitely the smile of a psychopath on a roll. Either that or Weird Bald Guy was an estate agent and always looked like this.

"Oh, my dear fellow," he answered after swallowing his unusual snack. "You have a very, very long way to go, but for now, go straight past me to the end, turn right and go to the building. Knock on the door and tell them I sent you."

Not wishing to spend any more time in the company of this malicious and obviously less than sane dwarf, the five of them moved on. Ollie whispered a rushed word of thanks as they passed Weird Bald Guy, but no reply came. He was busy putting something that looked suspiciously like an ear onto the end of his fork.

They took his directions and as they approached the building, Flug pointed at it.

"Made sweeties here. Long time ago," he said.

Ollie nodded, now understanding the monster's obsession with any sweets that he could get his hands on. Ronnie was right; it was another one of his passive memories resurfacing.

"I wonder who's up this time?" pondered Stitches as they got to the door.

Ethan knocked loudly three times.

"We'll soon find out," he said, a hint of trepidation in his voice.

The door was opened straight away by a giant of a being, wearing dirty jeans and a filthy white vest. He had long, black, greasy hair and an untidy, straggly beard that looked capacious enough to house a reasonably sized family of mice. He scratched at it furiously. Obviously the creatures nestling in the dark bristles were a lot smaller than mice and of the jumping variety. He had a rough and ready look about him, the sort of man who would quite happily drive the business end of a hammer through your skull rather than look at you. The type of man who got kicked out of the Hell's Angels for being too antagonistic.

"Oh, hello. And what can I do for you handsome chaps then?" He greeted them in a voice more camp than, well, someone very, very gay who liked to make a point of letting everyone know that he was very, very gay. You know the sort. They're usually comedians who mince about the stage making Eddie Izzard look butch before commenting, 'Before you ask. Yes, I am', as if it's the biggest revelation since we found out who shot JR (Google it). Just so we're clear. Being gay and talking in a high pitched and slightly effeminate voice isn't funny. Telling funny jokes is funny. "Are you looking for someone?"

"Weird Bald Guy sent us," responded Ollie, almost totally unable to accept the sound coming from the doorman. "He said to mention his name."

"Oh that's alright then." The massive man looked them up and down. "He must have liked you boys," he said with a flamboyant flourish of a rather limp wristed hand. "You've all still got your eyeballs."

He opened the door, ushered them inside and then stepped in himself. Once they were safely in, he slammed it shut and locked it.

"Okay. Straight down the hall, then left, right and left again. Got it, honey?" he said with a suggestive wink to Ethan that was accompanied by a gentle squeeze on the shoulder. "Ooh, what firm traps. Do you work out?"

"When I get the chance," said Ethan, smiling uncomfortably. "I'll bet. My name's Denzel."

"Nice to meet you, Denzel, but I think we need to go now." "Okey dokey. Good luck."

They left the doorman to his duties.

"I reckon you were in there," said Stitches, stifling the urge to giggle. "You probably would've hit it off. Do you reckon Denzel likes it doggy...?"

The rest of the less than politically correct verbal insult was cut off, when Ethan's hand closed around the zombie's neck and squeezed ever so slightly.

"You were saying?" he asked. "Nuggghhh."

"As I thought," he said and released Stitches.

The last turn on the left had them at the end of yet another long hallway. At the end was a steel door that was covered in rivets and a gooey brown substance, dribbles of which had run down the door before setting.

"I hope that's toffee," said Ronnie as they approached it.

Once they were within about ten feet, vague sounds started to become audible. It sounded like chanting and shouts of encouragement that were also punctuated by another sound that they couldn't identify.

"What's that?" asked Ronnie of no one in particular.

"I don't know," replied Stitches, "but if I were to take a guess, it sounds like an angry ogre smashing a side of beef with a sledgehammer."

When they got to the door it swung open automatically. Just inside was a set of metal steps that led down onto what would have been the old factory floor. It was dimly lit by bare overhead bulbs that cast their paltry light on old pieces of equipment and empty cardboard boxes. In the middle of the floor was the source of the noise they had heard whilst outside in the hall. It was quiet now though, except for one voice. The owner of that voice was walking around inside a large circle of others, beings of all descriptions, who were listening intently to his every word.

"The first rule of Fright Club is you do not talk about Fright Club. The second rule of Fright Club is, YOU DO NOT TALK ABOUT FRIGHT CLUB... "

"What on earth have we stumbled into this time?" asked Ollie, looking around the dark space.

"God knows, but I don't think it's a reading group," said Stitches, thanking everything that he could think of that his challenge was done and dusted.

As they made their way down the steps, the speaker was coming to the end of his speech.

"And if this is your first night, you have to fright."

He stared straight at the boys, which caused the assembled mass to do likewise. At least two dozen pairs of eyes and a smattering of trios gazed at them sternly.

"Welcome, Ethan," the leader said, a horribly twisted smile on his face. A face that, as he approached and came into the light, was seen to sport a web of scars and damaged knots of thick flesh. "Are you ready for your challenge?"

Ethan visibly tensed, twisting his head from side to side to release the tension in his neck. He stepped forward to meet the leader.

"I am," he said, his voice calm and confident. "What do I have to do?" A ripple of understated laughter came from the gathered crowd.

"I think we've gate crashed a recruitment fair for Ghouls 'R' Us," said Stitches, casting his eyes over them. There were ghouls, spectres, zombies, vampires, wraiths, ghosts and just about every other thesaurus entry for supernatural entities that there was. There were entities as well.

"The local cemetery must be dead, what with this lot being here," he added.

"Either that or it's the final of the world fancy dress championship," said Ronnie.

The leader continued.

"The challenge is as simple as the name of the club. We bring a poor, unsuspecting soul into the combat arena and tie them to that post." He pointed to a post. "A simple spell is then cast over them to keep their eyes open. All you have to do is try and scare them. The winner is the one who scares the victim; excuse me, the *participant*, the most."

"I understand," said Ethan. "What happens if I win?" "You will receive what you came for."

"And if I lose?" "Best not to, really."

"No pressure then," whispered Ronnie.

"Mmmm," agreed Ollie, nodding his head. "Seems the challenges are going to get tougher and tougher, the further we get into this."

"This way, Ethan" said the leader. "Your friends can observe from over there."

Ollie, Stitches, Ronnie and Flug walked over to a small table and made use of the chairs surrounding it.

"Now we begin," said the leader. "Tom," he shouted.

A door on the other side of the factory opened with a bang allowing them to hear high pitched shouts and the odd swear word amidst the sounds of a struggle. Tom, a heavily muscled demon (another thesaurus entry) came into view, dragging something behind him.

"Oh, be quiet," Tom rumbled, struggling to keep control of his squirming charge despite his size and strength. "It won't be that bad." "Why should I, you dense, muscle bound freak. If you hadn't have kidnapped me in the first place I wouldn't have to be shouting at you would I, so don't go blaming me?"

She was slim, blonde and pretty, very feisty and had a mouth like a Martin Scorsese script. She was also bound at the wrist by a length of rope and was currently on the floor on her backside, being dragged unceremoniously along towards the post.

"She giving you a few problems, Tom?" the leader said, a grim leer on his face. "Maybe you should have gotten something a bit smaller, something easier for you to handle. A cat, maybe."

"Yeah, yeah, yeah. Whatever," said Tom, grimly, his face quickly reddening.

He finally managed to negotiate the last few yards and then lifted the young girl to her feet. He undid the rope and pushed her back to the post before retying her hands behind her around the pillar itself.

"Right, that's you sorted," he announced, slightly out of breath. "Tosser," the girl spat.

Tom looked her straight in the eye, brought his hand up in front of her face and clicked his fingers.

"There you go, Brad. The spell's on. She won't be able to close her eyes or turn her head away now."

The leader, Brad, spoke to the group once more, but mostly directed his comments at Ethan.

"Excellent. Okay. This is how it works. Those chosen approach the female one by one. You then do your level best to scare the living daylights out of her. Tom will be watching carefully, and it will be down to him to decide who the winner is. Understand?"

Ethan nodded.

"Marvellous. Gentlemen, let the Fright Club begin."

Tom picked up a steel bucket that had been at his feet. He rummaged around inside it for a few seconds before drawing out a piece of paper.

"Teddy," he called out.

A being stepped forward and walked towards the bound female. He was of average build and height and was dressed in dirty black trousers, a holey, stripy jumper and wore a battered fedora. This wasn't what drew attention to him, though. His face achieved that. It was a mass of livid purple scars and welts, the skin pulled so tight that his mouth was frozen in a permanent rictus grin. It looked like someone had taken a meat tenderiser to a chunk of out of date corned beef and stuck two eyes on it.

"Alright, loser," the girl greeted him.

Teddy stopped about three feet away from her. He flicked his right hand and a sound like metal being drawn across a stone floor broke the air. He raised it then, allowing the four gleaming spoons attached to his fingers to glint in the light. He reached forward and swung his arm, striking the post a couple of inches above the girl's head, sending a shower of glowing sparks down onto her.

"I'm gonna turn you into dessert," he croaked. She wasn't even breathing heavy.

"Next," shouted Brad.

Tom fiddled around in the bucket again. "Jasper."

The next figure that emerged from the throng floated towards the girl a couple of inches off the floor. It was a corpulent, amorphous blob of gelatinous ectoplasm that looked as if it were just about to burst. It looked like someone had taken the skin off a rice pudding, tied it up and filled it with hot air.

"I ain't ever seen an obese ghost before," the girl said disparagingly. "You should try haunting Slimmer's World."

Jasper got up close to her. He opened his mouth and stuck out a tongue that looked like a flaccid sausage skin. Rather than meat though, his tongue was filled with dozens of spiders all scrabbling over each other. The sound of their chitinous legs and carapaces knock ing against each other filled the factory. Their undulations eventually forced the tongue to split, and the arachnids cascaded to the floor where they made a dash towards the girl. She cast her eyes down and without a trace of emotion on her face stamped her feet like a river dancer, squashing every last eight legged runner flat.

"Next," Brad called again. "Terry," said Tom.

A creature stepped from the group and shuffled unsteadily towards the girl. He looked like an eclectic mix of the contents of a deli counter and the tool aisle of a DIY store. Whatever had put him together either had a great sense of humour, or was as blind as a very blind bat wearing a mask in a dark room. As he reached her he brought his hands up and grabbed either side of his head. With a violent jerk he pulled it clean off, leaving a gushing, bloody stump. Drops of blood splattered the girls' cheeks and chin.

"Another time waster," said the girl. "You guys really need to try harder. I've seen scarier Disney films."

"That's a fair point," said Stitches. "Flug can't get through Dumbo without pooing his pants."

Undeterred the creature put its head back on upside down, after which two ectoplasmic tendrils came out from its ears. On the end of each appeared a small mouth which opened, revealing a set of rather sharp teeth. Then, both tubes undulated with a peristalsis-like movement, forcing twin gouts of viscous, chunky vomit to issue forth that splattered over the girl's shins and feet. Whilst this was occurring the atmosphere was punctuated by the most revolting and repugnant retching sounds.

She looked at the creature dispassionately as the steaming, soup like liquid congealed at her feet. She spoke nonchalantly.

"Whatever," she said. "Next," said Brad.

Tom rooted around once more. "Ethan," he barked.

"At last," said Ollie. "Maybe now we'll get somewhere. As soon as he changes and roars in her face, it'll all be over."

"I'm not so sure," said Stitches. "She hasn't been perturbed so far. I had my eyes shut when those spiders were running around, I can tell you."

"Really," said Ronnie. "I didn't know you were afraid of spiders." "Only because they like warm, dry places."

"Which is pretty much all of you, huh," said Ollie.

"Exactly."

"To be fair though, I nearly chucked up my insides when that monster spewed everywhere," admitted Ronnie, still looking a bit pale. "She's tougher than she looks, that one."

Ethan approached the young girl.

"Come on then, handsome," she said, a bored edge to her voice. "Let's see what you've got."

"Here we go," said Ollie watching intently. "Go on, Ethan. You can do it."

The lycan closed in on the young girl.

"As soon as he starts stripping off and changing that'll be that," said Ronnie.

Ethan stopped about a foot in front of her, a broad smile on his face but, his clothes still on.

"He better get undressed soon," said Stitches. "He didn't bring much to change into. He's not the Incredible Hulk. His trousers won't miraculously stay intact even though he gets three times bigger."

Ethan still wasn't undressing. Instead, he leaned in towards the girl and put his mouth next to her ear. The subsequent scream that came from her could have cracked an iceberg, and at one point got so high that only canines would have been capable of hearing it, so it was a blessing that Ethan was still in human form. Tears coursed down her face and rivulets of snot cascaded from her nose. She tried to shake her head from side to side; the tendons in her neck straining with the effort, but the spell in place wouldn't allow it.

"No, no, no," she hollered. "Don't. Please don't."

Ethan had retreated to a distance that took him outside of the arc of the flying spittle that was being blown from the girls' mouth. He looked over his shoulder and winked at his colleagues mischievously. The demon, Tom, produced a tissue from a trouser pocket and cleaned the face of the distraught girl. When that was done, he again snapped his fingers in front of her face. She instantly calmed down, as the horror of the last few moments were erased from her memory.

Brad called out 'next' and Fright Club continued.

An hour later and it was done. A couple of other members of the club had elicited reactions from the girl, but none had managed to reproduce the devastating effects that Ethan had manufactured.

A zombie had tried his luck but had fallen over half way towards her when his hip joint gave out, prompting Ollie to ask Stitches if it was a relative of his, and a ghoul had opened up one of his own veins and drank from it before tearing open his abdominal flesh to display the workings of his internal organs. Clearly that had been a bit over ambitious because he'd passed out and had to be carried off.

The girl had laughed at the first and totally dismissed the second, as a 'pathetic attempt at attention seeking.'

"That's it, gentlemen," announced Brad at the conclusion of the activities. "Tom, would you do the honours, please."

The demon stepped forward, a cardboard box in his hand.

"I don't think this is going to be a great surprise to anyone. Well done, Ethan."

The lycanthrope stepped forward to loud applause and even louder shouts and whoops from his travelling fan club. He shook hands with Tom and gratefully accepted his prize, before re-joining his friends in the viewing area where he was congratulated heartily.

He opened the box and revealed what was within. It was the stem of the Cup. The second piece of their quest was now in their possession. Ethan tucked it away safely into his backpack.

Stitches was about to quiz Ethan about his tactics when Brad called over to them, telling them that they had to leave straight away. So, before even getting a chance to handle the prize, they made their way back to the hearse, on the way saying goodbye to the friendly doorman Denzel and Weird Bald Guy who, thankfully, wasn't eating anything, or anyone.

Once safely back to the vehicle, which to their relief wasn't resting on a pile of masonry, Stitches turned to Ethan and asked him the question that was on everybody's lips. Apart from Flug, obviously, who was still in two minds as to whether he'd been here before and what the things on the ends of his wrists were for.

"What on earth did you say to that poor girl? She looked like she'd seen a ghost, well, a scary one anyway, not the useless articles we saw in there. We were expecting gnashing teeth, hairy knuckles and some rather loud howling from you."

Ethan put the key into the ignition and started the engine. As he pulled away he settled back into his seat and allowed himself a selfsatisfied smile.

"It was relatively simple. I noticed the particular style of the pair of shoes that she was wearing. I told her that I was going to tell all her friends that she shops at Devil's Discounts and put it all over the darknet. It'd be easy to find her on Faceofdeathbook and you know how young girls are about their appearance."

"You sneaky bugger," said Ronnie, shaking his head.

"I never realised you were such a fashion guru," said Ollie. "Still, you do dress well, I suppose."

"That's right," added Stitches. "He never goes out looking like a dog's dinner."

"I'll allow that one on account of my good mood over my recent triumph," said Ethan.

"Very civil," said the zombie.

"But the next one's going to cost you."

Ollie rubbed at his eyes. They had suddenly become itchy and watery.

"You alright, mate?" said Stitches. "There's no need to get emotional."

"No. I've just got something in my eyes, that's all. Ethan, just get us out of town and find somewhere to pull over so we can have a look at the next pages, will you please?"

"No problem."

Molar and its cut price clothing issues receded into the distance.

————

The hooded figure sipped from a cup of steaming hot tea, as once again the visions in the swirling liquids faded away. Pleasure was evident on the shrouded face, now that two fifths of the Cup had been found, and the completion of the quest was drawing ever nearer. At the start it seemed doubtful as to whether the five seekers could find their own backsides, let alone complete the tasks, but as time went on and their ability to accomplish the challenges became ever more apparent, a certain sense of optimism was now felt. Hopefully, it wouldn't be long before they could be done away with, and the rewards of their hard work pilfered. There was no other trace of emotion felt as these thoughts became manifest. After all, you couldn't make an omelette without bumping off a few undead idiots. Still, they would go to their respective makers satisfied in the knowledge that they had participated in something stupendous and world changing. Either that or they would be killed on the spot, leaving them as ignorant as they were now. Time and mood would tell. With tea finished, it was time for a lie down. This questing lark was tiring.

———

Henry Jekyll was sitting in the café once again, nursing yet another cup of thick, black and highly caffeinated coffee. He was flicking through his note book and pondering the observations he'd made over the last couple of days.

He'd spent a lot of time following Vortex around, trying to catch the assistant curator getting up to something that he shouldn't be getting up to. Anything that could give him away would do. Even a visit to Flange's house would have been enough. After all, as law enforcers worldwide will tell you, it is well known criminal behaviour for an offender to revisit the scene of the crime. (Actually, and to provide some semblance of balance to that statement, what a complete load of old rubbish that is. No police force in the world has a Re-attendance Squad, a highly trained group of detectives who waited a couple of hours before springing into action and going back to where the crime had happened.

"Oh, there he is." "Damn, it's the rozzers."

"You're nicked, son."

"How did you know I'd be here?" "Well, it's well known criminal. . ." "Oh, shut up and take me in."

A copper could stand around all day in the aftermath of a crime, and all he'd get is an aching back, cold feet and kids asking, 'can I see your gun?' If criminals did indeed revisit the scene of their misdemeanour, then every crime in the world could be solved by watching Sky News, because they covered everything to death in glorious and monotonous high definition. Especially if it *was* a death).

He'd written down Vortex's activities but to be honest, they made for pretty average reading. Apart from going to work at the museum, the curator's assistant had given a talk at a local school (Jekyll had snuck in masquerading as a salesman, and had done so well that he'd been asked to come back when the new budget was announced), gone to a restaurant for a midday meal, and then done some shopping, taking in a cake shop and a delicatessen.

After work he'd met up with a couple of what Jekyll presumed were friends, and had gone to the local pub for a few hours. Hoping against hope that the two friends were co-conspirators, Jekyll had managed to get hold of Scorpio and persuaded her to join his covert operation to try and identify them, which she did, and it didn't take her long to recognise the nefarious duo. One of them was the Secretary of the Local Council, and the other was Cedric Pie, owner of the town patisserie aptly named Cedric's Pies. Both of them were well known about the town and were respected pillars of the community.

Scorpio had said that she would have been gob-smacked if either of them had any involvement in any shady goings on, and even if they did, he would come up against the same stumbling block that he was having trying to prove that Vortex was involved in something dodgy. Without concrete proof, nobody would believe a word of it.

In an effort to garner some local gossip he'd spent some time talking to the local residents about Vortex, but he hadn't heard a bad word said against the man. The only negative thing that had been reported was that Vortex wasn't running this year's local half marathon for charity because he had a bad ankle. Even this morsel of information was negated, though, by the news that he was going to do a cake bake sale instead, with cakes that he was going to make himself. The man was spotless. It would be easier trying to find dirt on the Virgin Mary, and the more this went on, he reckoned it was going to be easier to unmask her as a master criminal then Vortex.

Fibula was fast becoming a waste of his time. Either Vortex was as angelic as everyone said, or he was the greatest con artist since Wendigo Scatterpants, Chief of The Lower Tribes of The Great Northern Steppe, convinced his armed forces (comprising of two elderly soldiers, a small hand held catapult and a horse older than the surrounding mountains), to invade the United States of America by promising them unbridled opportunity, wealth beyond measure and all the Indians they could eat. It went well until it got a bit drizzly on the morning of their departure, so they had a cup of tea and played backgammon instead.

As he finished his drink he decided to head back home. Maybe someone there might be able to shed some light on the assistant. At least if they did know Vortex, they wouldn't be brainwashed like the residents of Fibula.

———

The hearse was parked in a lay-by at the side of the road. That being said, lay-by was probably too posh a word. It was a dent in a mud bank that passing horses seemed to use as a latrine, leading one to suspect that the mound wasn't entirely made up of soft, moist earth. The flies buzzing in their thousands didn't seem to think so, anyway.

Ollie had retrieved the next two pages, and they were currently trying to decipher the latest clue.

"Makes about as much sense as the last one," said Stitches.

"We'll get it eventually, something will click, you'll see," said Ollie.

He read the verse out loud.

"In this place your foe does live, your life is his to take or give. Use the steel and use it well, or he will send you straight to hell. Use the words that you have gained, to save yourself from being maimed. Be strong in body and in mind, then leave this ghastly place behind."

"Seems like things may be getting more serious," said Ethan. "This is the first one that's mentioned death."

"True," said Ronnie. "But to be fair the other ones have hinted at it, haven't they, so it's not like we don't know that this whole business is entirely without risk."

"Anybody recognise anything on the map yet?" asked Ollie. "Because I don't."

"Pass it here," said Ethan, "let's have a look."

He stared at it for a while, then looked up and snapped his fingers. "I've got it. It's a place called Glans. It's about sixty miles away. The P in the middle there is a car park, and the stuff dotted around the outside is abandoned buildings. I think it used to be an industrial estate, but it's just ruins now."

"How on earth can you tell all that from looking at that map? It's terrible, it doesn't show you anything," said Stitches.

"I really don't know, mate," answered Ethan, shrugging his wide shoulders. "I stared at it and the name just popped into my head. I visited there once a few years ago when I was travelling with a friend.

It's not even as if we did anything exciting there either. It was just a stopover."

"Maybe whatever powers are at work here are actually helping us to get to the various locations," Ollie mused. "They're not going to help us with the challenges of course, but it obviously benefits them to get us there."

"Could be," said Ronnie. "When I saw the first map it was like a little light bulb went on in my head, and all of a sudden without any effort, the memory was there."

"Must have been a supernova that went off in Flug's bonce to trigger a memory," said Stitches. "You can't even remember your own name most of the time can you, mate?"

"Umm." "Never mind."

"Right, let's get going," said Ollie.

Ethan quickly stepped out of the car and charged the Bat Nav, letting it warm up for ten minutes before setting off.

The trip to Glans passed mostly without incident, taking in another liquid lunch break for Ollie, and a twenty minute stop for Flug to get over the worst bout of travel sickness the world has ever seen. When he got back into the car he looked ever so slightly greener than usual and about five pounds lighter, whereas the road surface looked a tad more colourful than usual, and appeared to have gained about five inches in height. Of course after such a violent, projectile explosion, Flug decided that he was hungry, so they stopped at a roadside grease pit called The Devil's Diner, whose neon lit sign bore the legend 'Turn up, eat up, just leave before you throw up'. Nobody could decide whether this was a requirement or a challenge, but as they sat round the table staring at their plates of alleged food, it seemed to be the latter.

"I've never eaten anything like this before," said Ronnie, pushing something grey and unidentifiable around his plate with his fork. "Stepped in it a few times, though."

"It's times like this that being dead is a real bonus," said Stitches, sipping from a glass of water. "You should be alright though, Ethan."

The lycan was staring at his own mysterious plate of brown lumpiness in wonderment.

"Why's that?" he asked.

"Well if that isn't dog food, I don't know what is," said the zombie. The THWACK that came from Ethan's hand connecting with the back of the zombie's head was followed by a PLOP as Stitches' right eye landed in his drink.

As he was fishing around for it, muttering certificate eighteen expletives under his breath, a musical trill came from Ollie's pocket. It was accompanied by a disturbing vibration that tapped insistently against his thigh. It took him a couple of seconds to realise what it was, because it was such a rarity that the item in question did anything. The signal was so bad that if Marconi had turned up with his first primitive radio, his broadcast would have found an audience quicker.

Ollie retrieved his mobile phone from his pocket.

"Bloody hell," said Stitches, "I wonder when that was written. Looks like Starch wasn't the only one trying to decipher ancient texts."

Ollie unlocked the phone and hit the message button.

"It's from Jekyll. He reckons that Vortex is involved in the theft somehow. He doesn't explain too much, but that seems to be the main thrust of the message."

"Wonder why he came to that conclusion?" said Ronnie. "I didn't get the impression that he wasn't to be trusted."

"I sort of know what you mean," added Ethan, "but there was something about him that was a bit strange. I couldn't put my finger on it, but he did make me feel a little uneasy."

Ollie began pressing keys so that he could reply to Jekyll.

"Well, there's not a lot we can do about it if he is," he replied, making an electronic tune with his number pad. "All we can do is carry on doing our best to recover the remaining pieces. Ultimately, it doesn't matter who's embroiled in this. As long as we finish what we've started, everything should be okay."

"If all goes well," said Stitches.

"True. Right, if we're all done, and judging by the amount of pushing around the plates that's going on I'm assuming we are, we can get going."

The only clear plate was Flug's. He'd ordered fish fingers, meaning Ronnie had spent ten minutes picking the breadcrumbs off. Calling them fish fingers was a bit of a leap of the imagination though, he'd suspected on first sight of the greying, rubbery substance. Likening the disgusting matter to anything fish-related was like saying Mrs. Ladle was a beautiful, erudite creature whose face could launch a thousand ships, when in fact she was as attractive as a storm front and could launch any sea going vessel simply by giving it a shove with her chin.

Still, Flug had enjoyed them and wolfed the lot down. How long they would stay down was another matter entirely.

Stitches placed the appropriate amount of money onto the counter top. The waitress counted it and opened up the till.

"What, no tip?" she asked.

"Just one," replied the zombie as he made towards the door. "Try serving edible food. It might liven things up a bit round here."

———

Vortex rushed along the corridor to his office, constantly casting nervous glances over his shoulder to make sure that he wasn't being observed. He had just come up from the store room where he'd been sorting through some new exhibits that had recently arrived, and he didn't want to get caught by Starch wanting to discuss them, which was what usually happened. Starch liked to have the final say on where things went and how they were arranged.

He finally got to his office unnoticed, quickly unlocked the door and slipped in. He went straight over to his desk, pulled out his chair and sat down. He quickly ran through the remaining arrangements in his mind, before picking up the phone and dialling a series of numbers that were written on a small piece of paper that he kept hidden in an inside pocket of his jacket. There were three rings before his call was answered.

"Hello," said a voice that was just about discernible over the static hiss.

"It's me," said Vortex. "I was just checking in to see how the preparations are going."

"It's going very well. The last three are going to be more troublesome than the others, but I'm confident we'll get the result that we want."

"Are you sure?" asked Vortex.

"Everything will be ready at the appropriate time. Don't worry, we're right on schedule."

"I hope so. I don't want this to go awry. This is a once in a lifetime opportunity, and I don't want it to go wrong when we're this close."

"It won't," the voice said reassuringly. "We've put a lot of effort into this and haven't left anything to chance. Don't worry."

"Very well," said Vortex. "Just remember on the day. . . hang on, someone's coming. We'll speak again."

He hung up the phone and busied himself shuffling some papers, when there was a knock at the door.

"Come in."

Starch strode into the office and stood opposite the still seated Vortex.

"Can I help you, Mr. Curator?"

"Oh, I was just wondering how the new exhibits are shaping up. They should make a nice addition to our History of Horror section," said Starch.

"They're marvellous," said Vortex. "We were especially lucky to get hold of Van Helsing's crucifix. I think that should take pride of place." "Oh, most definitely. It was very kind of him to donate it, now that he's retired. I'm not sure what to do with his toilet seat, though. Maybe it should go in the Throne Room. Right, well, I'll leave you to finish up whatever it is that you're doing, and I'll see you downstairs shortly."

With that he left, leaving Vortex alone once again. He gave it a couple of minutes before opening the office door and checking that the hallway was clear. Seeing that it was, he returned to his desk and picked up the phone.

"Hello."

"It's me again," said Vortex, "where were we?"

"Nowhere in particular. I think you were saying something about timing."

"Oh yes. It's vital that this comes together smoothly. We've got one shot to get it right and I don't intend to miss it. How much longer do you need?"

There was a few seconds silence, punctuated by the crackle of interference.

"Judging by how things have gone so far, I'd say three days. That will guarantee that everything is set and in place. And, if I may be so bold, it'll give me some time to get on without being interrupted every half an hour to be told how important this is. I am aware of that you know, so there's no need to keep repeating yourself over and over."

"Fair enough. My apologies. I think it's just nerves. I won't call you again. I shall wait to hear from you."

"That would be better. Goodbye."

The line went dead. As he replaced the receiver, Vortex noticed that his hand was shaking, which was unexpected to say the least. He clenched his fingers into a fist and squeezed it tight. He looked around his office, a strange feeling of self-consciousness suddenly washing over him, which was ludicrous. It wasn't as if he was planning the crime of the century, was it? Sure, he had to keep it a secret. If anyone found out what he was up to it would be a disaster, but that was no reason to feel so nervous. Everything was going to be fine. He gave himself five minutes to relax, and then went to join Starch.

––––––

The sign was bright red, garish and slightly rusty in places. It said simply 'Welcome to Glans. Population fifteen thousand two hundred and forty seven. Have an exciting time'.

"Do you suppose that sign gets bigger when things get *really* exciting round here?" asked Stitches.

The silence in the hearse indicated that none of the other four were going to dignify that last comment with an answer. Not that any of them were particularly keen to open their mouths at the moment. The after effects of their unscheduled stop at The Devil's Diner cum Vomitorium had left them all feeling a tad green around the gills, and none too keen on seeing the putrid mess for a second time.

A short while later, a couple of high-pitched squeaks from the Bat Nav announced their arrival at their intended destination.

"God, I thought Molar was bleak," said Ethan, bringing the hearse to a stop and applying the handbrake. "This place makes it look like a holiday resort."

The area they were looking at did resemble the abandoned industrial site that Ethan had described. There were deserted units everywhere. In their day some had repaired cars; some had offered collection services and at least one had been a coffin renovator (yes, second hand coffins. Those things are expensive, you know). There was even a warehouse that had stocked fancy dress costumes, although the pervading atmosphere wasn't at all party like. Now they were just empty shells, home to rats, bats, insects galore and just about anything else that could creep, crawl or fly through the broken windows.

"I don't remember that," said Ethan, pointing to the very centre of the estate. "That used to be a car park for the workers. I know because we got told off for parking there."

Occupying the once tarmacked area was a large house. A very large house. In fact, if you have a minute, it was a very large, opulent, grandiose and rather stately house. It was the sort of place used to advertise health spas, or where an ambassador might hand out inexpensive but suggestive chocolates, or where you would go on endless school trips year after year, forced to wander from room to room looking at tedious paintings and tapestries whilst some boring tour guide droned on about what life was like in the Middle Ages. Amazingly, it never seemed to occur to these people that kids don't really care what life was like in 1474. If it didn't have Xbox Live and Sponge Bob Squarepants, they weren't in the slightest bit interested.

"Christ Almighty," said Stitches, staring up at the magnificent edifice looming over them, all leaded windows and fancy columns. "I hope whoever's going in there doesn't have to clean the place. That'd be one hell of a challenge."

"There's a note attached to the front door," said Ronnie.

Ethan was closest, so he plucked it from the wood. It was a sealed envelope and it had Ronnie's name written on the front in a fine italic hand. He passed it on.

Ronnie opened it up with a due sense of trepidation and dread, and removed a jet black piece of letter paper from within. On it, in white ink in the same cultured handwriting, was the message, 'Welcome, Ronnie. Please come in'.

"Seems pretty clear," he said, folding up the note and placing it into his trouser pocket. "I gotta go inside."

"Be careful, Ronnie," said Flug, a concerned edge to his deep voice as he placed a giant hand on his friend's shoulder.

"Don't you worry, mate," Ronnie responded as he reached over and patted the heavy extremity, "I'll be ultra-careful. Back before you know it." He offered a smile but it was merely for his friends benefit.

As he approached the door he received good lucks from Ollie and Stitches, and a resounding slap on the back from Ethan.

"Steady, guys. It's not like I've chosen my last meal and I'm heading off down Death Row, is it?"

"I hope not," said Stitches, "because I don't think even the worst inmate should be subject to a last meal from The Devil's Diner."

Ronnie grasped the ornate door handle, gave it a twist and pushed. The door swung open easily, revealing an expansive reception area. It was marble-floored and had several doors leading from it. In the centre there was an enormous staircase that terminated in a seated landing area. More stairs from there led off upwards, left and right. To where, he couldn't make out.

"Pretty fancy," he said, stepping inside. The door slammed shut. He was on his own.

"Well that's not bloody fair," he announced to nobody in particular. "How come I get stuck by myself?"

"That's the nature of the challenge," said a quite frankly, miserable voice that seemed to come from everywhere and nowhere at the same time. He couldn't decide if it was in his head or totally surrounding him. It was a weird sensation. It was like wearing headphones.

"But do not worry," the despondent voice continued. "I'll be with you every step of the way."

"And you are?"

"The spirit of the house."

"More like the house whine, if you'll forgive me," said Ronnie, somewhat apologetically. "You need to cheer up a bit. You'll dampen my mood."

"Oh, I'm sorry. Force of habit. I've been alone so long now, I do tend to get a tiny bit maudlin every couple of centuries."

"Well, if you're staying in my head you can snap out of it, challenge or no challenge. I'm sure you don't want me to ignore you."

"Indeed not," said the voice with renewed vigour and enthusiasm. "And, as things progress, I shall be happy to offer any assistance that I am able, within certain limits of course. They don't just give these things away, you know."

"Pity, but that's very generous of you," said Ronnie.

"Oh, think nothing of it. It's such a pleasure to have some company. This is a big place and when you're on your own, you tend to rattle around a bit."

"I suppose you would at that. What do I call you, by the way?" "Flabbitt."

"Well, Flabbitt, as much as it's very nice to meet you, I'm here now so I might as well get on with it. And I do have four companions waiting for me outside."

"Of course. Okay, down to business. Here comes the formal bit. Welcome, Ronnie. Your goal is to defeat the challenge set before you."

"Defeat? I don't like the sound of that. Solve would have been better."

"As I was saying, defeat the challenge. Your instructions are on the table over there."

"What if I don't complete the challenge?" "Best not to, really," said Flabbitt.

"I've heard that before."

Ronnie's gaze was drawn to a small mahogany table sitting next to the left hand wall of the entranceway. He hadn't realised that it was there when he came in. He inwardly thanked Flabbitt for the unseen helping hand.

Resting on the table was another envelope that on inspection contained another piece of black note paper.

"This better not have another riddle written on it. I'm sick of bloody riddles. That's all we've had so far is stupid bloody riddles," he said.

He read the words in his head. 'Watch out!'

That was it. Just those two words. Nothing else. To say he was confused was an understatement, so in time-honoured tradition, as everybody does when trying to figure something out, he read the words out loud to see if they made more sense. There is no reason to think that this will help, it just seems like the natural thing to do, like turning the radio down in your car when you're lost, or wailing like a town crier when you're having a private conversation on your mobile phone.

"Watch out! What on earth is that supposed to..?" "En garde!"

The shout came from a rather dandy looking chap, standing about twenty feet away from Ronnie. He was all frills, lace and white powder, and was poised nonchalantly, and rather camply, one foot in front of the other. His left hand rested on his hip whilst his right hand clutched a distinctly pointy looking steel blade. The end waved back and forth slightly, the shiny silver metal glinting in the light.

"Are you serious?" asked Ronnie.

"I think he is. Don't you?" said Flabbitt.

"And what am I supposed to use? A butter knife from the kitchen?" "The fireplace," said Flabbitt.

Ronnie looked in that general direction.

"Well, I could throw him in it, I suppose. Or brain him with a log. That should do the trick."

"Above it," said Flabbitt with a sigh. "Oh, right."

Hanging in traditional fashion above the massive stone grate were two crossed swords.

"So I take it I..?"

"You can take whatever you like," said Flabbitt. "Just make sure you take one of those and be quick about it, Ronnie. Our foppish companion seems to be getting a little impatient."

Ronnie unhooked one of the weapons and hefted it, testing its weight and giving it a few practice swipes.

"Seems a bit flimsy," he noted.

"I wouldn't worry too much," said Flabbitt. "Those things were responsible for the deaths of hundreds of toffs in years gone by."

"That's reassuring. So what do I do? Just get on with it and start slashing?"

"Indeed you do, but first the rules." "Of course."

"Okay. Firstly, you have been challenged, so you may choose where to start."

"What do you mean where?" asked Ronnie, slightly confused. "This is a traditional and formal duel," explained Flabbitt. "You have to start somewhere dramatic. You know, one of you on a table, under a piano, hanging from a chandelier. That sort of thing."

Ronnie sighed and raised his eyebrows.

"If I knew I was going to be starring in a second rate Musketeers movie, I would have brought my velvet pants and fancy wig. Okay, what next?"

"Secondly," Flabbitt continued, "any locking of swords that causes the two of you to come face to face, must be accompanied by an appropriate insult. Something like, You offend me, you cankish lean-witted badger's bottom."

Ronnie laughed out loud and shook his head. "You have got to be pulling my leg."

"Not at all. It's the done thing."

"If you say so. What else do I need to know?"

"Only that the winner will be declared on account of first blood being drawn, one of the two parties yielding, or the application of a killing strike."

"Shouldn't a killing strike count double?" asked Ronnie nervously, trying to get himself prepared for the duel.

"Very amusing. The time has come."

"Wherrrre would you laike to begeen, Monsieur?" said his sword wielding opponent in a very cultured French accent.

Ronnie looked around the vast interior, wondering where would be best to start. He didn't really have a clue if he was honest. He did have some fencing experience, but that had been as a child, poncing up and down on blue mats twice a week with a blade so dull it wouldn't have cut the air.

"Just take a stab at it," said Flabbitt.

"That's not even remotely funny," Ronnie shot back. Oh, for a shotgun.

"Sorry. Why don't you try the stairs? That's always a good place to start."

"Why's that?"

"Isn't it obvious? If you put him below you, a few steps down, you'll have the high ground. Best to go into it with an advantage, I would have thought."

"Good point. Thanks, Flabbitt. The stairs," Ronnie announced to his foe.

"Verrry well," he replied, nodding politely. "Afterrr you."

Ronnie walked to the stairs and went about half way up. His opponent followed, coming to a stop four steps below Ronnie.

"I believe this will surrrfice. Arrre you ready, Monsieur?" the fellow asked.

"As I'll ever be. What's your name, by the way?"

"Jean Baptiste Tete de Noeud, Vicomte de Garlic Pompom, First Prince Etranger of the House of La Tour d'Auvergne."

"I had to ask."

"Well, eet ees actually Michel, but I thought that sounded a bit camp. Ironic when I dress like thees yes, but hey, the ladies seem to lov eet."

"Oh, one more thing," said Flabbitt. "What now?"

"You're not allowed to become invisible." "Epic."

"Well, it wouldn't be entirely fair, would it?"

"Oh, no," said Ronnie, barely able to contain his sarcasm. "What could possibly be unfair about an obviously expert swordsman duelling against someone who's only recent experience with sharp objects is cutting a peanut butter sarnie in half. We couldn't be more evenly matched. Good grief, it's going to be like Brazil taking on the Stoke Mandeville wheelchair eleven.

"Exactly. Off you go, then." "You're enjoying this aren't you?"

He heard a quiet chuckle in his head.

"I can't even begin to lie about that," said Flabbitt. "So I suppose the only appropriate answer would be yes."

Ronnie raised his sword in preparation. As quick as a flash, his opponent rushed at him, charging up the stairs straight towards him. Taken by surprise all Ronnie could do was hold his sword up as the man dashed past, slashing as he went. Ronnie turned quickly, now in the disadvantageous lower position. Michel took the initiative and struck downwards with a vicious overhead chop. Ronnie managed to get his sword up in time and blocked it, his own blade coming to a stop a couple of inches from his face. He pushed back causing Michel to stumble up a step.

"So thou dost have some fight in thee, thou mammering, crook paled bum bailey," said Michel in a passable English accent.

"More than enough for you, thou droning, fat headed malignancy," Ronnie answered, not having a clue where that had come from.

Michel struck again, forcing Ronnie down a stair or two and putting him off balance, as his left foot slipped off a carpeted step.

Seeing an opening, Michel pushed forward. He thrust his blade towards Ronnie's midriff, but somehow Ronnie saw it coming. He parried it away just as he completely lost his balance and fell against the wall. Luckily for him though, Michel's momentum continued, and without Ronnie there to stop him he hit the banister, toppled over it and crashed to the floor ten feet below. Seizing the moment, Ronnie vaulted the banister and landed like a cat on the floor, just as Michel regained his feet and his composure.

"Seems that maybe thou ist not as accomplished as ye think you are, thou lumpish, eye offending varlet," Ronnie jibed.

"Even if I am not, it will trouble me little to thrash you to within an inch of thy life, thou puking, wobbly jowled dog fish," came the reply. The blades came together in a series of thrusts, lunges, counter strikes and parries. Ronnie felt that he was doing fine, but he was wishing that he hadn't smoked twenty roll ups an hour for the last fifteen years.

The ring of steel against steel rang out as Michel surged forward yet again, forcing Ronnie back against the opposite stair wall. The blades came together and locked once more, as if they were trying to conjoin without any effort from the two men holding them. Again, their faces were within touching distance as they each struggled to gain the upper hand.

"The sweat upon thy brow tells me that thee is struggling and may soon quit this duel, thou vain, ill nurtured jolt head," said Michel.

"It will take better than thee to put me on my back, thou warped, rump fed maggot pie," responded Ronnie, as he quickly turned Michel round to get himself away from the wall. As he did though, Michel gave him a sharp shove. Ronnie stumbled backwards and crashed into a glass cabinet that he was positive hadn't been there before.

"You're right," said Flabbitt in his head, "it wasn't, but it wouldn't be a sword fight without a few items of handily placed furniture to bump into now would it?"

As he landed on the floor, shattered glass and splintered wood showered down onto him before the main body of the cabinet crashed on top of him, pinning him to the ground. Michel rushed forward and plunged his blade downwards through the fractured frame. Luckily for Ronnie, his sword hand was free and he was able to bat it away and, whilst doing so, he managed to draw his right knee up towards his chest and plant his foot onto the bulky framework. Another thrust from Michel got through though, the point of his blade resting lightly just below Ronnie's Adams apple.

"Looks like victory may be mine sooner than I thought, thou surly, half faced pig nut," said Michel, pressing the blade down another couple of millimetres.

"If quick victories are what thy desire, ye should learn to press home thy advantage, thou hideous, flap mouthed snipe," said Ronnie.

He thrust his leg forward with all the strength he could muster, sending the remains of the cabinet and Michel flying away from him, giving him enough time to extricate himself from the tangled mess and get to his feet. He quickly checked his neck and was relieved to see that his fingers came away free of blood.

They came back together again, slashing, pushing and shoving each other, both now keenly attuned to each other's fighting styles. The sound of their laboured breathing was heavy in the air, punctuated only by the crunch of broken glass under their swiftly moving feet. Both men were beginning to tire now, and as they found themselves either side of the table in the entrance hall, both saw it as a chance for a momentary respite.

Silence descended for a few precious seconds until Michel roused himself once more, kicking the table aside and lunging at Ronnie. Blades locked they came together again, each man so exhausted that they were almost leaning on each other for support.

"I almost have thee vanquished. I can feel the tremor in thy being, thou logger headed, pottle deep, death token," Michel hissed through gritted teeth and a fine spray of spittle.

"Thy feelings are mistaken. Even at my lowest ebb and on my worst day I would still have the beating of you, thou fawning, shag eared, jack-a-nape."

Both of them were visibly shaking and drenched with perspiration. Then suddenly, as if by some mystical pre-arranged signal, both realising that the duel would soon be over, they both pushed at the same time. They each took a step backwards and raised their swords before bringing them sweeping down in fast, tight arcs. The blades crashed together, ringing like a bell, but the combined force proved too great. Both blades shattered, sending shards of metal flying through the air and the reverberations from the collision caused both of them to drop their stunted handles in shock. In a flash Ronnie reacted and punched Michel square on the nose, squashing it into his face and sending a spurt of blood onto his mouth and chin. The Frenchman's backside hit the floor with a resounding THUMP and he sat there dazed and confused, his tongue licking the rapidly drying fluid from his lips.

"Honour is satisfied," announced Flabbitt. "First blood has been drawn. Ronnie, you are victorious."

"Well met, Monsieur Ronnie" said Michel, getting to his feet. "Ah have been bested by the betterrr man." With that he simply vanished.

"So, what now?" asked Ronnie. "Hold your hands out," said Flabbitt.

Ronnie did as he was bid. A quiet pop and a puff of smoke announced the arrival of the second Cup handle.

"Thanks, Flabbitt" said Ronnie. "So I guess that's it. Can I go now?" "Indeed. Unless you want to stay for a bit longer. I've rather enjoyed you being here."

"Well I appreciate the sentiment," said Ronnie, heading for the front door, "but I think it's a bit too hectic round here for my liking."

"Fair enough. Goodbye, Ronnie." "Bye, mate."

The door banged shut, almost catching Ronnie on the backside. "Blimey that was quick," said Ollie. "You've only just gone in." "Really?" said Ronnie disbelievingly.

"Yup," said Stitches. "What did you have to do in there? Spell your name correctly?"

"Not quite."

"Hi, Ronnie," said Flug. "You okay?"

"Couldn't be better, mate," Ronnie said, clapping his large friend on the back.

He regaled them with the tale of his challenge before showing them the third piece of the Cup, which Ethan took and placed into his backpack with the other two.

"Excellent," said Ollie. "Right, let's get working on the next one, shall we?"

Ethan retrieved the fourth map and rhyme from his seemingly infinitely capacious bag.

"Here we go," he said, laying out the sheets on their now usual place on the bonnet of the hearse.

Whilst he did this, Ollie put on his sun blocking fashion accessories due to the fact that the sun was due to rise shortly.

"Here he is," said Stitches. "Ladies and gentlemen, the world's only albino vampire."

"Up yours," said Ollie from beneath his balaclava. "So, how are we doing? Anyth... ooh. I've been there."

"Bloody hell, that was quick," said Ethan.

"Good huh," said Ollie, leaning in to get a closer look at the map. He nodded his head. "Yes. It's a small town called Cornucopia. There's loads of stuff there, it's quite a bustling little place and if I'm right, I think I know exactly where we're going to be."

"And that would be?" Ronnie asked.

"The zoo. Dad used to take me there when I was a kid. Obviously we could only go at night, so all the animals were asleep. For years I thought that all wild animals were invisible. Anyway, let's go over the rhyme. Not that they've been much use so far."

Ethan read it out loud to the group.

"Brawn not brain will see you through. Muscle and sinew will have to do. Gird your loins and don't let go. The prize will then be yours to show."

Stitches looked at the piece of paper and tapped his nose thoughtfully.

"Well, one thing's for sure," he said. "We can pretty much guarantee that Flug is going to be the next one up. The rhyme mentions brawn, not brain. With only him and you left," he pointed at Ollie, "it stands to reason doesn't it. I don't think you have quite as much loin to gird as the big fellah."

"Could be," Ollie replied. "But I'm not without some strength, you know. There are some muscles up these sleeves." As if by way of demonstration, he flexed his arms.

"I'll remember that the next time you ask one of us to take the lid off a Marmite jar," said Ronnie, squeezing Ollie's left bicep.

"Well, it can get sticky," Ollie replied indignantly, rubbing his arm that he was sure would be sporting some bruises tomorrow. "Come on, let's go," he said in a pinched voice as he tried to suppress a sneeze.

———

"Excellent," the figure said, watching the swirling waters. "It's going well now."

———

Jekyll pushed open the doors to the Bolt and Jugular and wandered in, wiping the sticky goo from the handle off his hand as he went. It was a strange place that was always busy, and due to its extremely eclectic clientele, made the cantina at Mos Eisley Spaceport look like a rather normal venue for a sit down, the sort that you might take the kids into for a spot of lunch or treat your favourite with a glass of port, whereas the Bolt and Jugular was the type of establishment where the casual visitor may very well end up *as* a spot of lunch.

As he strode to the bar he acknowledged those that he knew. Hector Lozenge was there, of course, getting to work on his minimum of five a day. Bludger Smith, the district magistrate, was deep in conversation with Constable Gullet, no doubt deciding which local laws and ordinances it would be fun to change or impose this week, ensuring a steady flow of income into the town's coffers. The trouble with Skullenia was that the population may well be a murdering, slaughtering and generally genocidal bunch who made the Nazis look like a sewing circle, but they were, on the whole, a law abiding lot. There were no petty criminals here, so the authorities would never find themselves dealing with a shoplifter or a litter dropper. That being the case, a constantly evolving list of local statutes kept fine money rolling in. Also, Gullet got a perverse pleasure seeing the looks on people's faces when he gave them a ticket for drinking tea on a Wednesday without a reasonable excuse, or laughing without due care and attention.

Jekyll shook hands and exchanged pleasantries with Gareth Hopkins, The Whichfinder General, a magazine fanatic who had the largest collection of consumer publications known to man or beast. It was a well-known fact that before you bought anything it was best to consult with Hopkins, to ensure the best deal was to be had. He had a nice side-line going in bonfire design and construction as well.

At last he saw the person that he had come in to see. Propping up the bar front and centre, talking to Goblet the landlord, was Mrs. Ladle. She was holding a pint of something in one hand and a cigarette in the other. As he approached, she turned towards him and smiled through a misty haze.

"Hello there, Henry. What brings you here on a weekday? Old Singh driving you up the wall, is he?"

"Nah, he's alright. Actually, he's in one of his stupors at the moment so it's nice and quiet. He'll be out for a good few hours yet."

"Can I get you a drink, Doctor?" asked Goblet, whilst engaged in a futile attempt to wipe away some of the viscid resin that had accumulated on the bar over God knew how many years.

"Can I have an orange squash, please?" he asked, not seeing the looks of disgust cast his way. "Mrs. Ladle?"

"Very kind of you, Henry. The usual please, Goblet."

In spite of that particular phrase, no alcoholic beverage served in the Bolt and Jugular could be described as usual. Mrs. Ladle's tipple for instance, a pint of Dangly's Old Codpiece, whilst not the most sinister beverage, was about as near to a regular beer as you were likely to get without growing hair on your tongue. Once you started on the likes of Titley's Bowel Cruncher or Cracknell's Wibbly Wobbly, to name just two, then you were getting into the realms of liquids that had been known to eat through solid rock, although this had never been a problem to the regular drinkers, who had developed stomachs like leather buckets and bowels that could strangle an elephant. One look at the pock marked stone floor of the pub was enough to instantly give someone unaccustomed to such vicious beverages the raging collie wobbles, and make them extremely wary of entrusting their innards to anything coming out of Goblet's pumps. Lead lined pumps, actually, because the drinks flowing through the pipes had a half-life slightly longer than Uranium 238. The toilets were testament to that. They had a permanent greeny glow and an atmosphere so thick that if you dropped a coin you could catch it before it hit the floor, even if you didn't move too quickly. It was the only place in the world outside of Scotland that this phenomenon occurred.

So be warned. Unless you're used to public conveniences such as were installed in the pub, it's wise to take a canary in with you, just in case. (The canary will be carrying a small cage as well by the way. It'll have a fly in it. He's not taking any chances either).

A frothing and disturbingly brown glass of liquid was placed onto the bar in front of Ronnie and then Goblet gave Mrs. Ladle her ale. She blew the foam off the top, which landed with an audible THUMP on the floor akin to dropping curdled milk, and took a long, deep draught. "Ah, that's the stuff," she said, licking her lips and removing the frothy white line clinging to her moustache.

"Don't you ever worry about your liver?" Jekyll asked, sipping at his own drink.

"Not really. It's sitting in a jar on my mantelpiece at home. Pink and lovely, it is."

Jekyll didn't want to get into the mechanics of remote organs, so he shrugged his shoulders and looked nonplussed.

"So are you going to answer my question, Henry? What are you doing here?"

Jekyll nodded his head whilst picking out a couple of clumps of unidentifiable grit from between his teeth that definitely hadn't been there before he took a sip of his 'squash'.

"I was going to ask you about someone."

He told her about the quest that Ollie and the gang were on and what he had been up to in Fibula, in particular his investigation into Vortex.

Mrs. Ladle's eyes lit up at the mention of the curators' assistant. "Oh, I do know him," she said. "We do have a certain amount of history together. When he was a student and I was at Witch College we had, how shall I put it, a bit of a fling."

"So leaving out the gory details, what can you tell me about him?" Mrs. Ladle saw a particular look pass across Jekyll's face.

"Don't be so dismissive about this old exterior you're seeing, Henry. When I was younger I was quite the head turner. And unlike some, I didn't need spells and potions to maintain my looks."

"My apologies."

"Fine. As for me and Vortex, we did have a relationship of sorts, but he was far too wrapped up in his studies to take it too seriously. He was always off on expeditions and digs somewhere or another, sometimes for months at a time." She took a cigarette from the packet on the bar and sparked up, as a wistful and regretful look touched her features.

"Still, I did get to know him quite well, and all I can say is that he never showed any outward signs of leaning towards the dark arts, other than what was required for his work. Still, that was a very long time ago and people can change, I suppose, so who knows what he might have got himself involved in since then. I'd be surprised, though."

"That's the problem I'm having," said Jekyll. "Everyone I've spoken to just sees him as this philanthropic do-gooder, but I'm still convinced he's up to something."

"Well, if that's the case, then I would have thought that he would have done a certain amount of research."

"Agreed," said Jekyll.

"And I dare say that doing such research in the museum under Starch's nose would be rather risky, wouldn't you say?"

"I would."

"So I would suggest you may want to visit somewhere else that said research could be carried out as unobtrusively as possible."

Jekyll slapped the bar, then slapped his head, after which he wiped his head because his hand had picked up something sticky from the bar.

"The library," he announced triumphantly. "Why didn't I think of that before? I've actually spoken to the librarian because she came to me with information. I didn't even think of visiting the place."

"Looks like you need to make another trip, my boy." "I do."

"But not before you buy me another drink for being so helpful. Goblet, a pint of Rigid's Nasty Bastard, please."

———

Cornucopia was, by conventional standards and not those of what is usual in this part of the world, a normal looking town. Very normal. From its car parks and cinema multiplex to the throngs of people wandering up and down its streets looking for a bargain or somewhere to hold up for a drink and a bite to eat it screamed normal.

Ethan followed the signs that took them right through the centre of town and out the other side, until about a quarter of an hour later they picked up directions for the zoo. As they got closer they noticed that the traffic had thinned out considerably, but not to the point that they would be going into the zoo by themselves. It was more like a select group of people that had come out for a specific purpose.

They were third in a line of about eight cars to access the car park, after which they queued up to get into the zoo itself.

"I reckon this challenge might be a bit more public than the others," said Stitches as they got nearer the ticket booth. "I can't for the life of me think what it's going to be, though. Celebrity Safari, maybe? Set a bunch of Z list celebs loose, and the contestants have to hunt them down. I like that actually, might be worth a pitch to a TV company. The public would love it."

"Excuse me, gentlemen," said a voice from a little man who had appeared from nowhere, interrupting Stitches' vision of Amy Bushclimber with an arrow in the back of her head. (Amy Bushclimber was the supernatural world's answer to Pippa Middleton. A complete nobody, bereft of any discernible talent, who had somehow managed to become well known. Amy's one and only claim to fame was that she'd had a fling with a Romanian rockball player; remarkable for the fact that he was over a hundred years old and couldn't have rocked any balls if his life depended on it). "Could I talk to Flug please?"

"You could try," said Stitches, "but I can't guarantee that you're going to get much of a response. He does do a very good impression of a brick for ninety nine percent of the time."

"Who are you?" asked Ronnie.

"Tile, Sir. I've come to escort Flug to where he needs to be, and seeing that you gentlemen are accompanying him, then you had better come too."

"Where are we going then, Tile?" asked Ollie.

"Oh, not far," he pointed round to the left. "Just down there and round the back a bit."

Then, in a rare, insightful understanding of his surroundings, and what was currently going on about him, Flug's brows knitted and, eyes staring skyward, he said, "Is it my turn, Ronnie?"

"Looks that way, mate," Ronnie replied. "And before you ask what you're doing, we'll find out in a minute."

"This way, gentlemen, if you please," said Tile, heading off.

In fact, it wasn't that far at all. About fifty yards along the perimeter was a large steel gate, and it was through this that the little man led them.

"That explains everything," said Ethan, pointing to something ahead.

It appeared that they were in the central region of the zoo where all the various paths and routes converged. It was a reasonably sized open area that was hemmed in on all sides by cages of differing sizes. On inspection it seemed that the only way in or out of the enclosed space was either through the gate that they'd used to come in, or the alleyways between the cages, although you'd be taking your life in your hands if you used the alley between the lion and the zebra enclosures. The cages weren't particularly secure you see, so much so that the local health and safety officer got wind of it and, slave to his job that he was, he'd meandered down there to see what the fuss was about, intending to write a full report and have them shut down on the spot. His colleagues stopped looking for him after a couple of weeks figuring he'd left town, and the zoo staff never worked out why the lion went off his food for a couple of days and had started to collect shoes. There was also a crowd. Quite a reasonable one at that, maybe a hundred or so beings. They were spread out about the whole area, dotted here and there but most, if not all were looking towards the large central sector that was roughly the size of a football pitch.

Upon it were odd pieces of wooden and metallic equipment here and there, but what it would be used for, none of them could fathom. Tile certainly wasn't giving anything away just yet.

As well as the milling crowd, they noticed there were others.

Strange others. Very big others.

"It looks like Ethan's Fright Club on steroids," said Stitches, casting a concerned look around. "That one there's got arms as big as my chest." He was pointing to a massive demon that was sitting on a stool. It was bright red, scaly skinned, had hands the size of shovels and horns that would have shamed a Triceratops. It was eating what appeared to be most of a pig, and was currently receiving a shoulder massage from a grey, stumpy, dwarf-like creature.

"Come on, Tile," said Ollie. "Give us a clue, something that'll help us get ready."

Tile turned to them and smiled in what he no doubt thought was a friendly manner. It wasn't, and only succeeded in making him look like a deranged psychopathic killer of epic proportions.

"If you cast your eyes over there, gentlemen, I think the banner should explain everything."

"Don't know why he's being so shifty," said Ronnie.

"Who knows?" said Ethan. "In fact, who cares? We'll find out in a minute."

The banner looked like any other banner that you might see across a high street, advertising some crappy festival or another, that meant you wouldn't be able to move for Morris Dancers for the next forty eight hours, and would have to listen to the shriek of musical instruments that hadn't seen the light of day since Henry the Eighth was dragging his flaccid backside around Hampton Court Palace. Seriously though, why on earth would you want to listen to a lute being badly plucked while some fat bloke in a beard and white trousers, that are quite frankly far too tight, minces around with bells attached to his ankles. Appreciating history is one thing, but not when it reminds you that throughout the countless aeons of time people have always acted like complete knobs. The passing of five hundred years doesn't make retarded behaviour quaint. If it did we'd still be chucking rocks at the moon and holding gladiatorial tournaments, although I think they still do in Norfolk and certain parts of Chatham. Anyway, all this means is that people in the Middle Ages were weirdos, much as they are now (Why there isn't a Front Age and a Back Age I don't know, but there should be. It rounds things off nicely).

One end of the banner was attached to a lamp post and the other end was half way up a cage, so they were able to read what it said.

"Welcome to the Annual Mr. Cornucopia Strongman Competition." "There you go, Flug," said Ronnie to his friend. "You've got to lift some heavy stuff up." "Okay. Like wot?"

"I don't know. Stones and stuff is the norm, I suppose." Tile had made his way to stand underneath the banner. He had a megaphone in his hand that elicited a loud squeal when he put it to his mouth and switched it on.

"Ladies and gentlemen, boys and girls, gods and goddesses, demons and demonesses... "

"This could take a while," said Stitches, loud enough for Tile to hear. "Why on earth would you use two words when thirty will do?"

"Well, quite," Tile continued, ever so slightly thrown by the zombie's comment. "Welcome, everybody, to this year's Strongman Competition. Would the contestants join me, please?"

And so they emerged from the crowd, thinning it out considerably, and went and stood under the banner with Tile, not that there was a lot of room once they'd all arrived. Just one of them in a room by itself would make it crowded. They were the usual mix of creatures that you might expect to see at any time, but it was the size of them that drew the attention. The demon they had previously seen getting a rub down turned out to be eleven feet tall and five feet wide. The bunched muscles in his arms rippled as he moved, and the veins popping out from his biceps were the width of a grown man's finger. His trapezius muscles were six inches high and his neck could have been used as a normal sized person's waist. And he wasn't the biggest.

"You need to go and stand over there with the others," said Ollie to Flug.

As Flug arrived to join the others, the scale of his task became more apparent. Apart from one scrawny, albeit wiry imp who looked like a two hundred year old schoolboy, Flug was the smallest being there, which, when you remember that he was eight feet tall and forty two stone, was something to behold.

Tile took the opportunity to introduce some of the athletes.

There was amongst others, Lumpy 'I'll lift everything including, well, everything that's put in front of me, really' Truss, Wide Boy Pebble, the aforementioned pig eating demon, Irina Bollokov, an ogress from the Russian steppes who, judging by the size of her boobs, could lift just about anything you'd care to mention, and Thor Finger, an iceman from the frozen North who was the size of a small glacier and the reigning champion.

Some youngsters were wandering through the crowd, handing out leaflets.

"Could be interesting," said Ethan, perusing the timetable. "The first round is the deadlift, then it's the farmers walk, the piggy back carry and so on. About six events in all from the look of things. . . "

The rest of whatever he was going to say was lost, as the remainder of the crowd moved en masse towards the front of one of the cages to their right, and gave a loud cheer. Somehow, Tile had already negotiated his way through the heaving throng and had secured his position out in front to inform everybody of what was about to happen. He was standing in front of a large object that was covered in a tarpaulin sheet. Nobody seemed to be sure what it was, but it certainly seemed to be giving off something of a funky odour.

"Assembled strength fans," shouted Tile. "The famous Cornucopian Deadlift."

With a flourish worthy of a skinny, heavily eyebrowed, statue disappearing magician, Tile grabbed a corner of the tarpaulin and swept it away to gasps of 'Ooh' and 'Ahh' from the crowd. Well, except for four of them.

Ollie, Stitches, Ronnie and Ethan stared wide-eyed at what Tile had revealed, and whether it was in horror, awe, amazement or sheer disbelief, none of them knew. Not that it particularly mattered. It was horrible.

Ronnie rolled himself a cigarette and smoked it silently whilst Ollie and Ethan shook their heads.

"At least that explains why they call it the deadlift," Stitches said without a trace of humour.

What Tile had revealed was an elephant. Or to clarify, two halves of an elephant. It had been neatly severed into a pair of roughly equal sized bipedal portions. They were spaced about ten feet apart, but were joined by what appeared to be a huge scaffold pole the ends of which were buried in the poor deceased creatures' spinal column. The flies that hovered around the massive cadaver and the slightly off red tint of the exposed innards explained the smell.

"At least you know why you never saw any animals here," said Stitches.

"I think you might actually be right," said Ollie, still not quite sure whether what he was seeing was real or not. Half of him was hoping that he was asleep in the back of the hearse and that this was a daymare. Oh for the chance to wake up in a cold sweat and crack his head on the roof of the vehicle.

"I'm definitely going to contact the authorities when this is all over," said Ethan. "People can't go around mistreating dumb animals like that."

Stitches considered a passing comment about the similarities between dumb animals and Flug, but even he couldn't bring himself to do it. He was just as appalled as the others at seeing such a magnificent beast being treated this way. It was shocking, unnecessary and ultimately very sad. What made it worse was the apparent apathy of the locals watching. The sight of the butchered animal didn't seem to bother any of them in the slightest.

"Let's just hope this doesn't drag on for too long," said Ronnie, determinedly puffing away for all his lungs were worth on another rollie. He was thinking that if he smoked enough then he could put a thick, cloudy barrier between himself and the view ahead. "As of now this quest has taken a distinctly nasty turn, and I don't like it."

"I know," said Ollie, "but let's try to look at the bigger picture. This is one small step in a quest to potentially stop something terrible happening, so while it's not right, that elephant's sacrifice will ultimately save lives. It's distasteful, I know, but it'll get us there."

"Contestants," shouted Tile, "will simply lift the bar from the floor as many times as they can." He didn't call anyone because the order had already been sorted out. Each of them had a number attached to his chest. Flug was number six, which was eighty seven higher than his IQ. "I've had an idea," said Ollie. "It's obvious that no one is paying any of us four the slightest bit of attention, so why don't we do what we can to help Flug out and get this thing over with?"

"How are we going to do that?" asked Stitches. "I think we're a bit outnumbered to start a protest, peaceful or otherwise."

"I was thinking about being a bit more subtle than that," continued Ollie. "Essentially, it's going to revolve around you two," he indicated Ronnie and Ethan. "Ronnie, if you can go invisible, I was thinking maybe you could get amongst the other contestants during the events and cause a bit of unseen havoc."

"Liking the sound of that," said Ronnie through the carcinogenic haze.

"Don't forget to clear that lot out of your windpipe first, though," said Stitches. "A wandering column of smoke might raise a few eyebrows."

"What about me?" said Ethan.

"Ah right. If you can find somewhere to change, maybe you could get into Flug's head and mentally help him out, or at the very least let him know that he's not on his own, and that we're doing everything we can to help him."

"I do like the idea," said Ethan enthusiastically, "but where can I go?" "How about over there?" said Stitches. He was pointing to a cage directly opposite the deadlift area, and what with the crowd being so engrossed in what was going on (the imp was doing rather well and was currently on his fifty seventh rep) not a single person was looking their way. "The door looks slightly open. You could easily slip in there." "Gotcha." Ethan quickly and calmly made his way across the green, hopped inside the cage and closed it.

"Okay. Your turn," Ollie said to Ronnie, as he turned back round to face thin air and the back of the person in front of him.

"Already done," a voice whispered in his ear. "See you soon."

"Just one thing slightly off the subject," said Stitches. "Why is it that when invisible people go invisible, their clothes do too? It's a genetic quirk, not a fabric oddity."

"Depends if the story is for kids or adults, I suppose," said Ollie. "But that's something we can discuss later. I'm sure Ronnie will have a reasonable explanation for you."

"Mind you, it shouldn't really matter. If you're invisible, then you don't have to worry about a load of eight year olds seeing your. . . "

"I said later."

"Fair enough. What are we going to do in the meantime?"

"Let's just keep an eye on things here. We can always engage in a spot of crowd disruption and distraction if it's needed," said Ollie.

Stitches nodded. "Good thinking. Hey, look," he pointed at Flug, who had suddenly tensed up with eyes wide and a distinct grin on his face. He nodded ever so slightly.

"Looks like Ethanwolf has made contact," said Ollie, as Flug leaned towards the ghoul next to him and whispered something in his ear. Obviously they had no idea what Flug had said, but the distraught look on said ghoul's face and the slump of his shoulders indicated that it couldn't have been too complimentary. And, as luck would have it, the ghoul was next.

It dragged itself slowly to the event area and stood behind the bar, psyching itself up for a big lift. Unfortunately, it didn't get very far. It bent down to grasp the bar but halfway down it stopped, and instead grasped its head in its hands and let out a tremendous wail before fleeing in a flood of tears.

"Well, I'm not quite sure what happened there or what the problem is," announced Tile, staring in shock at the quivering, sobbing creature not twenty feet away from him, "so if we could have the next contestant please. The current total to beat is seventy four."

"Come on then, mate," said Ethanwolf in Flug's head as he approached the bar, "this is easy, a child could lift it. Remember those rocks you shifted for me at the back of the werehouse?"

"Yeah."

"Most of those were heavier than this and you chucked them around like they were nothing, didn't you?"

"Yeah."

"Okay, so grab hold of that thing and pick it up as many times as you can. I'll tell you when to stop, right?"

"Yeah."

As with most beings of, how shall we put it not so as not to cause offence of a politically incorrect nature, limited intelligence, Flug did as he was told because the person instructing him was someone whom he liked and respected. No distraction, however big, would divert his attention now, and nothing would cause him to deviate from what he had been told to do. He would carry on ad infinitum, until he either collapsed from utter exhaustion, expired or worked out what ad infinitum meant.

Flug lifted. And lifted. And lifted. The crowd was cheering, Ethanwolf was encouraging and Flug was smiling. His expression never changed as the bar went up and down rhythmically, the elephant smacking wetly on the ground and splashing the first couple of rows of clapping spectators with reddish gore. Through all this, Flug kept on smiling.

"Well done, mate. That's seventy five," said Ethanwolf. "But just for good measure, let's get to a hundred."

Flug managed that easily to the unending pleasure of the crowd. Tile announced the result and bade everyone follow him to the next event area.

"He did good, didn't he," said Stitches as they followed the jostling mass. "Did you see the look on his face; he was really enjoying himself up there."

"Of course he was," answered Ollie. "It was a simple, repetitive task. He could do that all day long. Don't forget, he's like a child, always eager to please. And remember, Ethan is in there somewhere as well, tapping into that hidden intelligence he said was in there."

"I've still got my doubts about that, you know," admitted Stitches. "Some things are just too deeply buried to be found. That's if they should be found at all. I'm a bit worried that giving Flug the chance to use his brain power would be like allowing a fatty a trolley dash round a chocolate factory. It'll explode at some point because it's too full."

(So much for being politically incorrect. But don't blame me. I didn't say it).

"The next event, ladies and gentlemen, is the straight arm lift. Contestants must hold this one hundred kilo weight straight out in front of themselves for as long as possible."

Unfortunately, the weight in question, in keeping with the theme so far, was another former resident of the zoo. It was a wild boar that didn't look so wild anymore. In fact it looked a bit pissed off, to be honest.

"This'll be an easy one," said Ollie.

One after another they hoisted the boar, some of them impressively so, which meant that when it came to Flug's turn he was going to have to hold it up for a considerable amount of time. He reached down and with both massive hands took hold of the fold of skin on the boars' neck. He then straightened up and held it out in front and relaxed into it. Now, Flug being the knuckle-dragging, single digit IQ and potential Police Community Support Officer recruit that he was, would normally have had trouble holding onto the boar for long due to the length of his arms, but what Tile, the other competitors and the crowd didn't know was that Ronnie had entered the fray. He'd positioned his shoulders directly under the carcass and tensed up. The combination of his rigid frame and Flug's strength was enough to ensure that after fifteen minutes Tile called a halt, declaring Flug the winner.

Stitches looked around at the crowd and the other athletes. The crowd in particular were showing signs of becoming a little restless and he had no doubt that this was because after the initial enjoyment of the deadlift, the fact that their favourite athletes were being made to look rather ordinary was getting on their nerves. Some of Flug's opponents were definitely giving off signals of being slightly miffed, as well. Wide Boy Pebble was glaring at Flug with a gaze that could melt lead, and Lumpy 'I'll lift everything including, well, everything that's put in front of me really' Truss didn't look too impressed either. "Hey, Ollie," said the zombie, tapping him on the shoulder. "I think it might be an idea to maybe get Flug to lose the next event. This partisan mob would probably appreciate it, and it might be good for our future health."

Ollie had noticed a certain amount of discord himself. Not only were people staring at Flug, but some were gazing in their direction. Although not their fault, they would prove to be an easy and accessible target if tempers flared.

"I concur," he said. "Let's find out what the next event is and we'll sort something out."

"Everybody, the next event will be the piggy back carry," announced Tile.

The contestants had been lined up at the start of a straight run of about two hundred metres. In front of each of them was a zebra, deceased of course.

"Look at all those poor, dead corpses just lying there. It's heartbreaking," said Ollie.

"As opposed to a load of live corpses," replied Stitches, sarcastically. "Oh, you know what I mean, smart arse."

"Hey, if Flug goes out of his lane, will he be disqualified for zebra crossing?"

"You really are a. . . never mind. Right, we need to attract Ronnie's attention without giving too much away, if at all possible."

"RONNIE!" shouted Stitches at the very top (high enough that a flag could have been attached to it) of his voice.

"That was subtle," said Ollie.

"Got him here though, didn't it," said Stitches in response to the invisible tap on his chest.

"Hey, what's up?" said Ronnie's disembodied voice from somewhere in front of them.

"We need you to sabotage the next event," said Ollie in what he thought was Ronnie's general direction. "Flug can't be seen to run away with this thing. The natives are becoming decidedly restless."

"No problem," said Ronnie. "This looks like a straight forward foot race. It shouldn't be too hard to drop a spanner into the works. See ya." The only sign that Ronnie was making his way back through the crowd were the indignant looks that people gave as they were unceremoniously bumped out of the way, and the strange looks on their faces when they saw the same thing happen to someone in front of them without being touched. One guy thought it was the bloke standing next to him, and their argument ended up in a brief but enthusiastic ding dong that was only cut short when Tile announced "On your marks," etc.

A loud bang signified the start of the race, and they were off (both literally and, in some cases, directionally). Each competitor hoisted his or her or its carcass onto either one or both shoulders (or in the case of one shape shifting demon, all three, and in the case of Flug, someone else's until Ethan reminded him that he had to carry it himself) and set off down the course. On first appearances it seemed that everything would be alright and Ronnie wouldn't be needed. Flug dropped his load a couple of metres into the race, causing some gelatinous body fluids to splash onto the carcass itself, meaning that Flug had a spot (or a stripe if you like) of trouble getting it back into position. It looked like he was going to lose this one on his own, but unbeknownst to Ollie and Stitches, Ethanwolf had no idea at all about their scheme to get the monster to fail. He was watching the race closely from the confines of the cage and was presently buried deep in Flug's subconscious mind, urging him on and on. With a massive effort Flug got a grip of the dead zebra and threw it up onto his shoulder as if it were nothing more than a sack of cotton wool, before setting off at a furious pace, rapidly gaining on the others. The crowd, who had been chanting and cheering with renewed vigour and pleasure at Flug's plight, soon began to boo aggressively when they saw the big stranger rapidly gaining on their favourites.

"Ronnie better make his move soon," said Ollie, "otherwise this is going to turn uglier than the athletes."

"Mmmm, they'll tear Flug to pieces if he romps this one as well," agreed Stitches nervously. "My sewing skills won't stretch that far."

"Neither will my neck."

At that point, just as Flug was on the verge of closing the gap between him and the rest of the field, he tripped, stumbled and fell to the ground with all the poise and grace of a Tyrannosaurus Rex trying to put a pair of socks on. With an extremely loud "WAHHHH!" and a BUMP strong enough to knock a spectator off his feet (to be fair to him and his sense of balance, he did only have one 'feet' and had, at that precise moment, put his walking stick down to scratch an itchy left elbow, but it was still an impressive feat nonetheless) Flug crashed down in a tangled heap of arms (2), legs (6), heads (2) and forehead bolts stuck in the ground (1).

The crowd went absolutely wild at the sight and nearly apoplectic when a female ogre crossed the line in first place. She celebrated by eating the zebra that she had been carrying and picking her teeth clean with one if its ribs.

Stitches stifled a laugh at the pathetic sight of his colleague trying in vain to extricate his head from the ground.

"Looks like someone pulled the Flug out from under that zebra," he said.

"Seems so," said Ollie. "Come on, let's go and get him up."

It took both of them and a supreme will of effort to prise Flug's face from the dirt.

"You alright, big fellah?" asked Stitches as Flug rolled onto his back, a stunned look on his face.

"Yeah. Wot 'appened?" he said, spitting a clump of soil out.

"I think you tripped, is all," said Ollie. "Nothing to worry about. You'll win the next one, I'm sure."

He slipped Flug a handful of Sherbet Kneecaps to take his mind off what had happened and to get rid of what, judging by the amount of suspicious brown mounds all over the place, must be a rather horrible taste.

"That went better than expected," came Ronnie's more than slightly amused voice from out of the ether.

"I suppose so," said Ollie. "But did it have to be so blatant?"

"It did look a bit like a mountain toppling over," said Stitches. "I suspect somewhere there's a tsunami gathering speed."

"I had to act fast," said Ronnie defensively. "He was going to win. I had no choice."

With Flug dusted down they ushered him off to the next event. Thankfully, it was one that he had no chance of winning. The idea was to throw as many heavy metal objects over a twenty foot bar as possible, and seeing that one of the participating trolls was fifteen and a half feet tall it was more of a foregone conclusion that he would win than it was that a cyclist on a square wheeled bike would lose the Tour de France. He came second as it happened, but then sadly had to retire due to a nasty case of vibration white buttock (plus the fact that he started in 1956 and finished in 2004).

"Here, fellahs," said Ronnie. "Huddle round so that I can have a smoke will you please."

Stitches wasn't going to huddle with anyone, especially if it meant being subject to smoke making its way through Ronnie's invisible system.

He wandered away from the crowd who were busy watching something or another. He stopped a few feet away from Ethanwolf's hiding place. Six to be precise. He knew his friend was in there somewhere, but he didn't want to find out the hard way that Ethanwolf would have no problem whatsoever in eating some rather stringy, two hundred year old meat. Good job he didn't realise that the cage door was unlocked.

Stitches didn't know which animal had originally been housed there, but he was pretty sure that it wouldn't be here now. If it wasn't currently being used as gym equipment, then it was probably residing in Ethanwolf's stomach, wondering why the world had suddenly become so moist and dark.

A rustle from a bush at the rear of the cage caught his attention. To his surprise, Ethan, back in human form, emerged from the foliage, and in his arms was cradled a fuzzy mass of wispy fluff, about the size of a rugby ball.

"Lunch?" Stitches enquired.

"Not quite. I found it curled up at the back of the cage, over by the wall. I can't say I recognise it but it looks like a cross between a lion cub and an oven glove. I'm surprised it's still here actually."

"Well I don't fancy its chances if you put it back. One of this lot will be using it as a speed-ball before the days out," said Stitches, gently tickling the unidentified little creature under what appeared to be its chin. As it turned out, the zombie didn't touch the animal as gently as he thought he had. Without warning a set of razor sharp teeth emerged from the depths of the fluffy bundle and snagged his probing index finger before giving it a twist and a sideways jerk. Two tiny twinkling eyes gazed up at him and he could have sworn that the cheeky little bugger smirked.

"I'm going to need that back," he said to Ethan, pointing at the creature with his middle finger.

Ethan, with a bit of gentle tugging, eventually managed to free the digit and return it to its rightful owner.

"The holes barely show," he said. "You can always put a bit of filler in."

"You're very kind but I'm not a DIY project, you know," said Stitches, popping the nibbled finger into his pocket. "I don't represent a charming fixer up opportunity. So what do you intend to do with the little charmer, then?"

"Can't leave him," said Ethan, trying to make out that what he was about to say was spontaneous. "Here's a thought. He's small enough to fit into my backpack; I'll look after him when we get home."

"Well, good luck with that." Stitches glanced over his shoulder. "Seems like the throw has finished. I better be getting back."

"Okay, see you in a bit."

"How's it going?" asked Stitches upon his return to the games arena. "Good, mate," said Ollie. "Flug came last but one in the throw so that means the competition has evened up, and as you can see the crowd has mellowed out now. So with only one event left, if Flug

337

comes in the top three, he'll win and we'll get the fourth piece of the Cup." "What's the last event?"

"Looks like we're going to find out now."

"Ladies and gentlemen," shouted Tile. "It's time for the last event in what has been an extremely exciting contest, and the one that you've all been waiting for. The arm wrestling."

"Should be alright here," said Ollie smiling. "Flug's got industrial strength biceps. His forearms are like most people's thighs. I can't see him having too many problems with this one."

And he was right. Blowing the rest of the competitors away without so much as a drop of sweat spilt, the final bout was between Flug and Thor Finger. They were on equal points which meant it was down to this last battle of strength to determine who would be victorious.

The two giant beings sat opposite from each other across a heavy wooden table and grabbed a solid iron rivet with their respective left hands. They then joined right hands with a clap that was as loud as thunder. Ollie and Stitches could see them both squeezing each other's hands as hard as they could, trying to gain the best hold and at the same time trying to convey, without words, that their strength was far greater than the others. As the referee tied their clasped hands together, they stared at each other intently. Thor was attempting to psych out Flug, using his deep scarlet eyes to burrow into Flug's subconscious, trying to unnerve and unsettle him, to delve into his very being to scratch away the exterior and gain access to the weaker and more fallible creature within.

Flug was dribbling from both sides of his mouth at the same time and was wondering what the referee meant by three, two, one, go.

"From the vacant look in his eyes and the length of the spit dangling, I'd say that Ethan has left the building," said Stitches. "We'll just have to hope that. . . "

"Excuse me, gentlemen," interrupted Tile, suddenly appearing next to them, "but is this yours?"

He didn't seem to have a hold of anything, but his right arm was at a right angle to his body. On closer inspection though, his fist did appear to be clasping something.

"Is what ours?" said Ollie, not having the vaguest idea what Tile was banging on about.

"This," Tile explained. "About five feet nine, slim build, giving off a bit of smoke, invisible."

"Hi, guys," said Ronnie.

"Now, I'm not sure what's been going on today," said Tile, the accusatory tone in his voice more than a little obvious, "but I could make a few educated guesses. Not that I would be able to prove anything of course."

"There's nothing to try and prove," said Ollie defensively. "Ronnie here is a bit shy and has a touch of agoraphobia. He normally does this sort of thing if faced with a large crowd. There's nothing sinister or underhand about it, I can assure you, Mr. Tile."

Tile leaned in closer to Ollie and lowered his voice, making him sound all the more menacing.

"I would suggest that when this is all over, you lot get out of here as quickly as possible. Are we clear?"

"About as clear as the cages surrounding us," said Stitches, getting annoyed. "And by clear I mean utterly devoid of anything living. I don't know if you're aware of the concept of how a zoo is supposed to work, but this is not it. I'm sure that certain authorities would be very interested to hear about how the local animal population is being treated for everyone's amusement."

Tile stared at Ollie and Stitches with a fixed and steady steely glare, but some of the bravado had clearly been stripped from his initially arrogant outburst.

"Perhaps we can come to some sort of an arrangement," Tile offered. "Yes we can," said Ollie, "and a very simple one. You let the five of us get on with what we came here to do, and we'll not mention to any animals rights people that we bump into about what's been going on around here."

"Agreed," said Tile who, without another word, wandered off. "What are we going to do now?" said Ronnie. "I can't really go invisible again; there'd be a riot in spite of what we've just sorted out with Tile."

"And Ethan isn't going to be much use at the moment. I'll explain later, but it'll be pretty obvious," said Stitches.

Ollie put his hands on his hips and blew out a heavy breath.

"Looks like he's on his own then," he said. "And there's absolutely nothing that we can do about it."

The referees' voice floated over the crowd. "Three, two, one. . . "

Now, for those of you familiar with the Sylvester Stallone film, Over the Top, you can skip this bit and go straight to the results but, for those of you who haven't seen it, it's about a single dad truck driver who works full time, struggles to see his son, but who still manages to fit in being a world class arm wrestler (time management issues are not covered in the story). He's even got an arm trainer set up in his cab (try explaining that to the CSA when you can't make your payments). At one point Stallone is in a contest and is up against a guy with biceps the size of Bramley apples. They face off, with their hands tied together and the referee says go. Roughly 0.2 seconds later good old Sly smashes his opponent's hand onto the table with the force of a jack-hammer. Transfer the above set of conditions to the present scenario and you have an idea of what Flug did to Thor Finger. It's basically Rocky in a denim shirt.

". . . go."

An instant explosion of shoulder, bicep and forearm power erupted from Flug, and he slammed his opponent's hand down onto the table with a boom that sounded like a cannon being fired. Thor Finger wailed in defeat and a considerable amount of pain as he clutched his damaged hand (please note that there are no jokes relating to sore fingers at this point in the story. Some puns are far too obvious, and no doubt you've thought of one of your own already so don't point the finger at me, Thor or otherwise).

The referee took hold of Flug's free arm and raised it aloft. The giant reanimate had a vague smile on his face, but there was no real indication that he had much of a clue of what he'd done. He'd been asked to do something. That something had now been done so it was of no consequence whatsoever, now that it was over.

Tile looked on with a disappointed and somewhat pissed off expression on his face. Not only had the title been taken by a stranger, but the crowd and even some of the other competitors were shouting and applauding Flug's victory. He took an object from a cloth bag at the side of the event arena and walked towards Flug to give it to him, but he was stopped before he got to him.

"As Flug's representative and manager, I'll take that for him," said Stitches, taking the package from Tile. "He'd only try and eat it."

Stitches quickly retreated and grabbed hold of Flug's arm, and led him from the stage to rejoin the others. Ollie and Ronnie told him well done amidst the back slaps and congratulations from people in the crowd.

"Where's, Ethan?" asked Ollie, glancing round. "I haven't seen him for ages."

"I think he'll meet us at the car," said Stitches. "He had something to take care of."

"Wha... AITCHOO, bless me. What?" "I'm sure he'll fill you in."

When they finally managed to exit the zoo, they did indeed find Ethan waiting for them.

"I take it all went as planned?" he said.

Stitches revealed the second golden handle that he had taken from Tile. "Sure did," he said, passing it across to go with the rest of the pieces.

Ethan rummaged around in his backpack, moving things around to make room.

"Squeak."

"Did you hear something?" asked Ronnie. "Squeak."

"There. You must have heard that."

"I did that time," said Ollie, glancing over at Ethan or more specifically, at his backpack.

"You got something in there you want to tell us about?" he asked the guilty looking lycanthrope.

"Oh, you haven't?" said Stitches.

"I couldn't help it," said Ethan in a pleading tone. "I put it somewhere safe, but it followed me every time I tried to walk away."

He reached into his bag and pulled out the small, furry bundle hiding inside. "So I brought it outside for a drink. He's kind of grown on me and now I haven't got the heart to get rid of him."

"Squeak."

"A compassionate werewolf. What is the world coming to?" said Stitches. "It'll be vampires giving local anaesthetic before sinking their fangs in next."

"I know it's an obvious question," said Ronnie, peering at the creature in Ethan's arms.

"I don't know what it is either," Ethan replied stroking it softly. "But it's so cute that I couldn't stand the thought of one of them lot getting their hands on it."

"Aww soft," said Flug patting it gently, well, as gently as he could. "Can we keep im, Ollie, can we? We'll look after im and love im and walk im every day."

"It's not up to me, mate," said Ollie, "but it looks like it could be here to stay, if the look on Ethan's face is anything to go by."

"You're all heart," said Stitches.

"Not quite, but I try," said Ollie. "Come on, let's get out of here."

———

The hooded figure swept from the room. The last but one piece had been won and won well, it was grudgingly admitted. The end game was close now and preparations needed to be made to ensure that once the final piece was located, all was in readiness to go at a moment's notice. Thanks to the constant monitoring, the figure knew the location of the final piece of the Cup. The seekers had discussed that directly after the previous challenge, as they had with all the others. It was surprising how quickly and efficiently they had proceeded through the quest. A long wait was what had been expected but thankfully, they had proved far more resourceful than had ever been envisaged. It would actually be a bit of a shame to have to do away with them after all their efforts. Still, casualties of war and all that. What was it called? Collateral damage, wasn't it? The conqueror's way of justifying the slaughter of the innocent to assuage a battered and beleaguered conscience, should such a thing exist in a person of that persuasion. Anyway, such trifling matters were of little concern. Not now, not ever. The end was in sight.

———

Jekyll pushed open the old wooden doors and entered the library, and was greeted by a loud creak as the doors closed again. Scorpio looked up from behind her desk and was on the verge of ordering the miscreant to keep quiet, when she recognised who it was. She waved and beckoned Jekyll over.

"Hello again," he whispered. "Hiya. What are you doing here?"

"I need some information, but I can't spend the next fifteen minutes sounding like I've had a tracheotomy. Have you got an office we can go to?"

She nodded and led him off, heading further into the maze of shelves and books until they came to a door.

She knocked, waited for a couple of seconds, then opened it up and went in.

"You can talk normally in here. We're far enough away that no one can hear us. So, what is it that I can do for you? Would you like a cup of tea, by the way?"

"No thanks," replied Jekyll, sitting down in an ancient, wing-backed leather arm chair. "I wanted to ask you a few more questions about Vortex, if that's alright."

"Fire away," said Scorpio, leaning back against an old desk and folding her arms.

"It's quite simple, really. I assume you keep records here of who takes out what, how often and for how long etc.?"

"We do."

"Excellent. What I want is a list of which books Vortex has been lending from here over the last six months, say. Is that something you can do for me?"

"Shouldn't be too difficult," said Scorpio, bumping herself away from her perch. "Won't be long."

Whilst she was away, Jekyll busied himself with making the cup of tea that he had previously declined, but by the time the kettle had boiled and he was about to pour the water, the librarian returned.

"That was quick," said Jekyll, returning the kettle to the desk top after filling the cup. "Where's the milk, please?"

Scorpio pointed to a small cupboard under the half size sink. "Marvellous. So, what did you find out? How many black magic, demon summoning and spell casting books has he had out, then?"

"None," she replied.

"What!" he exclaimed. "None," she repeated. "None!" he protested. "None," she repeated again.

"What do you mean, none?" he asked, not quite sensing the stupidity of the question.

Scorpio raised a finely shaped eyebrow. "I mean none. As in less than one. Nada. Nothing. None."

"Sorry, but that's a bit of a surprise, if I'm honest," said Jekyll, disappointedly. "I was expecting a list as long as, well, as long as a long box of library cards."

"Afraid not. The only books, and by books I mean two, that he's had out in the last year were 'Home baking for the Busy Curators Assistant' and Professor Van Helsing's autobiography 'Don't Get Mad Get Cross'. And that's it."

"Well, Miss Bytheway, it appears that I've not only wasted my time but yours as well. My apologies."

"Don't be so quick to dismiss your trip here," she said encouragingly as she placed a well manicured hand on his arm. "The check on Vortex was so quick that I thought it might be worth compiling a list about another person that you mentioned. This goes back three months." She handed him a piece of paper filled with writing.

"Whose is it?"

"Flange's. For a list of reference books it makes quite interesting reading, if you'll pardon the pun."

It did indeed make for interesting reading. On the list, according to Scorpio, and she should know, were some of the darkest and malevolent volumes ever to have been printed. In fact a couple of them were known to be so maliciously evil that they had written themselves out of sheer bloody mindedness and the need to force themselves into existence to spread their nefarious word.

"That is a veritable Who's That of evil scriptures," she added.

And indeed it was. 'Tipley's Believe It If You Want', a collection of bizarre and possibly true stories from around the world.

'Dante's guide to the Underworld, a Travelling Companion' and 'Spells to Really Mess Someone Up' were just three of them.

"Are they all as nasty as these?" asked Jekyll, shaking the list at Scorpio.

"Pretty much, although you'd need quite a bit of specialist knowledge to get a lot of the stuff in them to work. Some of the rites and rituals need particular places to be visited or certain people to be present, and some of them need specific artefacts or relics, if you get my drift."

Jekyll smacked a hand on his knee.

"Of course. All the time there's me thinking that Vortex is the problem, but as it turns out the chances are that it's Flange. He's the one doing the studying, he's the one who's mysteriously disappeared and hasn't been seen since this whole thing started. And he's got access to anything he wants at the museum."

"Looks like you may have a tangible lead at last. It's quite exciting, this detective business, isn't it?" said Scorpio enthusiastically. "I must admit I always had a hankering to do some law enforcement work, but I never seemed to get round to it. So, what are you going to do now?" "Go to the museum. Starch can show me the maps and clues that the boys are using, so I should be able to work out both where they've been and, more importantly, where they're going. Once we've figured that out, it's just a case of getting there. The least I can do is warn them." "Can't you get in touch by phone?"

"I've tried a couple of times but there's no signal at all trying to call mobile to mobile. I've got Singh on standby outside instead. Once I've finished at the museum, we'll head off. Mandeep is an amazing driver and his car has more horsepower than a budget burger."

Scorpio smiled and raised an eyebrow.

"Can I come with you?" she asked pleasantly.

"Why would you want to do that? We're only heading off to warn them about Flange and, well, whatever may happen. If anything."

"I know, but it's still a little bit of excitement isn't it. It does get a bit boring round here." She came towards him and rubbed the lapel of his coat tenderly. "And besides, I'm rather enjoying your company, if I'm being completely honest."

Jekyll thought for a moment, not sure whether it was a good idea or not. She might be keen, but he didn't want to put her in any danger. And besides, he was beginning to enjoy her company as well.

"I suppose it couldn't hurt," he said once he'd made up his mind.

"Okay then. If you are coming, then we need to leave as soon as possible. I'll meet you outside in five minutes."

Four minutes and thirty seven seconds later they pulled up in front of the museum. Jekyll told Singh to keep the car running whilst he and Scorpio dashed inside to see Starch.

They found him pottering about in his office. (That's a strange activity isn't it. I wonder at what age do you officially start to potter about? When you're a kid you muck about and play around. As a teenager you hang out with your friends and as an adult you go out or even workout if you're feeling particularly energetic. But it isn't until you retire, start wearing beige slacks and comfy, slip on shoes that you bought after seeing them in an advert in a Sunday newspaper supplement, watching Songs of Praise and The Antiques Roadshow and trying to decide which bungalow you want to buy that you have reached the age that you are considered to be one who potters about. A strange point, but one that definitely needed clarifying. Saves me pottering about).

"Ah, Miss Bytheway. Lovely to see you. And Dr. Jekyll, always a pleasure. What can I do for you today?"

Jekyll went on to explain the situation that he found himself in and the fact that, despite his previous misgivings about Vortex, the evidence seemed to be pointing at Flange, which is why he hadn't been seen for a while.

Starch ruminated over what he had heard for a few minutes, carefully considering the available facts before answering.

"Whilst I can see what you're saying, Dr. Jekyll, didn't we cover the same ground when we spoke about Vortex? I don't wish to cast doubts on your investigation methods or the conclusions that you've arrived at, but it would seem to me that you're basing your hypothesis on, what is at best, circumstantial evidence."

"Please, there's no need to apologise," said Jekyll without a trace of anger in his voice, despite what Starch had said. "And don't worry about offending me because I know how it all sounds. To be honest, I think I'm even getting to the point where those shadows I'm chasing are even more insubstantial than I first thought."

Starch sat in his chair and regarded the troubled Doctor.

"Don't forget, though, that we still have the theft to consider. That is something tangible that has occurred, for whatever reason. It doesn't mean that anything terrible is going to arise, but I'm sure that your colleagues have things well in hand. Once they've returned, I'm sure everything will be fine."

"Well, that brings us back to why I came here in the first place. Have you managed to decipher the clues in the last couple of days?" asked Jekyll.

"Oh yes. It proved to be a most interesting exercise and between the two us, Vortex and I figured out the riddles."

So Vortex is keeping abreast of things regarding the Cup, thought Jekyll. Maybe this wasn't such a dead end after all.

"Excellent," said Jekyll. "What were the locations that you came up with?"

Starch went through some of the papers on his desk, found what he was looking for and went through them with Jekyll.

"And this," he said, indicating the final paragraph, "is the last place, and to be frank, this one was ridiculously simple when compared to the others."

"How do you mean?" Jekyll asked.

"Read the clue," he answered, handing it over.

Jekyll looked at the piece of paper and shook his head. "Drive two hours north. Okay, from where?"

"The Cornucopia Zoo. The location itself is the final clue," said Starch.

"Superb," said Jekyll, gathering the various notes together. "We'll start at Tonboot and go from there. We're bound to pick them up at some point."

"Excuse me," said Scorpio, shyly raising a hand as if embarrassed to interrupt the two men. "Can I make a suggestion?"

"Of course, my dear. Any and all input will be greatly appreciated," said Starch.

"How long have they been gone?" she asked, pleased to be involved in the process.

"About five days now," said Jekyll.

"Mmmm," she said, mulling the information over. "So the chances are that this far in they're going to have made quite a bit of progress, and given that the distances between the locations aren't that great, wouldn't it make more sense to start at the last one and work backwards? I think we'd have a much better chance of catching up with them sooner if we head straight to Cornucopia, find the zoo and head north."

"That is an excellent observation, Miss Bytheway. What a sharp mind you have for a young lady," commented Starch with a latent sexism that he was blissfully unaware of.

"I see your point," said Jekyll, "but how on earth are we going to get there in time. It must be a good couple of hundred miles at least."

"What car have you got?" Scorpio asked.

"A three litre fuel injection Ebony Casket. Why?" he replied. "Top speed?"

"A hundred and forty, give or take."

"Good. And how fast does the hearse that the boys are using go?" "We'll, from what I've been led to believe, it's a right hunk of junk.

The guy who sold it to them reckoned thirty, maybe forty. But that's off a cliff with a tail wind."

"Right," she said, "give me a minute." She got a pen and paper from Starch's desk and did some rapid fire calculations.

"Okay, factoring in a bit of time for quests, travelling, etc etc., there's a very real possibility that we could get there and meet up with them, or failing that, stumble across them at some point as we work our way backwards."

"Sounds a bit wafty," said Jekyll, a hint of doubt in his voice. He could see what she was getting at but he wasn't too happy with the wing and a prayer attitude. There was a very real potential for things to go spectacularly, badly wrong.

Scorpio raised her eyebrows and planted her hands on her slender hips. A wry smile played across her lovely face.

"Come on, Henry, work with me a little bit. I know we're somewhat in the dark but it's not like we haven't got any idea what's going on. Have a bit of faith, or if that's too difficult, hell, just go with the flow. At least we get to tear up the countryside in that souped up rocket of yours."

"Quite right, my dear," said Starch. "It always pays to look on the bright side, I feel. If a hundred and seven years of marriage has taught me anything, it's always look on the bright side. And to have an inordinate amount of patience obviously, how to tune out conversations about the WI (Witches Institute), the fact that not moving a piece of plastic ninety degrees drives a woman insane for some reason. . . "

Jekyll and Scorpio crept from the room.

(N.B it is a well-known fact that when a gentleman leaves a toilet seat in the upright position, it is guaranteed to drive his female partner wild, usually culminating in a heavily worded lecture about laziness or, in direct opposition to this, the silent treatment, during which the aforementioned gentleman has to guess what his misdemeanour actually is. No more I say. For generations, men have suffered unjustly for not performing this action. Well, it is time for us to strike back and take the cistern by the chain. Next time you need to pay the bathroom a visit for a number one and you find that the toilet seat is down, call your companion and ask her why, oh why is it that every time I come in here the damn lid is down. Don't you know how hard it is to lift the thing up ninety degrees so that I can go? It's laziness, pure and simple, and it's got to stop. Fellow man, I urge you to reclaim your toilet.

Given time I think that the balance will be redressed, and the inequality of loo seat positioning will become a thing of the past and equality in the water closet will become the norm, as I'm sure my wife would agree. If I was in contact with her of course. I haven't seen her for six months since she kicked me out for being unreasonable, so I've been living in my car. Well, I was. I left the top down and it rained. . . Oh, I see!)

––––––

The hearse rumbled along the road like a dinosaur on wheels.

"Go north for two hours," said Ollie. "That seems fairly easy. A nice straight road, get there, do whatever it is we have to do, and finish. No messing about, go home."

"Hopefully, if all goes well," said Ronnie. "But I reckon that the last test is going to be a right bugger."

"I have to concur with that," said Ethan. "Sorry, Ollie, but it does appear that the challenges have been getting harder and harder. Compared to Flug's, Stitches' one was a doddle."

"Excuse me," said the zombie from his usual place, shoulders pretty much in line with the top of his head and his eyes bulging out a bit, "but I went through a harrowing experience in that crypt I'll have you know. It's not easy being funny all the time."

"That is something that you make abundantly clear on a daily basis," said Ollie. "You should be proud actually. It's hard to achieve that level of consistency."

"Charming. I hope your fangs get mildew."

The road north was indeed as straight as an arrow and, thankfully, free of roadside cafés, which was a major blessing because after all of his exertions in the Strongman competition, Flug announced that he was hungry again. Luckily, Ronnie had a hunk of bread and some Transylvanian cheese left over in a bag (For those of you unfamiliar with Transylvanian cheese, it has the colour of a heart attack victim, the texture of a slab of granite and the fat content of an American fast food restaurant filled to capacity. It's decorated with sets of double punctures as well, which is a nice touch. It's not pleasant stuff though, and you'd probably be better off eating that Icelandic cheese with all the maggots in it. On second thoughts, no you wouldn't. Cheese made from the fungal jam between an ogre's hairy toes would make much better eating than that muck. Still, it all sounds better than anything Subway could knock up).

Flug wolfed down his snack in a couple of bites, uncaring about its taste, smell and general appearance. He actually found it to be quite tasty, but then again, anyone who regularly eats cheese made from the fungal jam between an ogre's hairy toes isn't going to have much of a sense of taste. In London he had even eaten at Wimpy. He threw up straight afterwards of course, but doesn't everyone?

Thankfully, Flug kept his food down and a couple of hours steady travelling saw them nearing their final destination.

"Castle dead ahead," said Ethan, pointing out a road sign. "Which is right on the nose, because there it is."

It was a rather imposing structure that had a passing resemblance to the Tower of London, but only to the point that the designer had possibly seen a postcard of said edifice and thought, I could do that. The main differences on first inspection were that there were more net curtains and no bovine munching guards.

"This must be it," said Ollie "We haven't passed anything else for miles and there's nothing obvious ahead that I can see."

"Let's get it over with, then," said Ronnie.

Ethan turned into the junction and started over the rickety drawbridge. About half way across was another sign that said strictly no vehicles.

"Looks like we're walking," said Ollie. "Everybody out."

They passed under a vast, iron portcullis which every one of them thought was going to come crashing down on their heads at any minute, and into an expansive courtyard in which were carriages, a couple of antiquated cars and some push-bikes.

"Looks like we're not the only ones here," said Stitches, pointing to a man who was skipping his way towards them. He was extremely slim, to the point that you really wanted to take him out for a hearty meal, was as bald as a coot with alopecia and was dressed in Dr. Marten boots, skin tight jeans, a very flamboyant shirt and a dark purple Victorian frock coat. When he got to them he took a mouth organ from a pocket and blasted out a few random notes.

"Welcome, gentlemen," he announced with rather a lot of American style enthusiasm, which sounded a bit daft in his Home Counties accent. "My name is Brian O'Richard and I'll be your guide. Follow me inside and keep up."

He jogged off in the direction that he had originally come from. "Come on," he shouted over his shoulder at the non-moving quintet.

"We better had," said Ethan.

"Great," moaned Stitches, breaking into as much of a jog as he could muster without his hips going on strike.

The strange fellow led them through a massive oak door, which in turn took them into a wide hall. In the centre was an enormous dining table that was all laid out in readiness for a feast of gargantuan proportions and a fire that would have given the Forestry Commission cause for concern was roaring in a voluminous grate. Logs popped and crackled as the intense heat claimed them. Stitches stayed well away from it. He got worried enough when Ronnie stood next to him smoking. He was liable to spontaneously combust if he got within ten feet of that inferno.

Brian stopped at the head of the table and draped his arms across the back rest of a magnificently carved wooden chair. Beads of sweat rolled from the shiny dome of his head and down his face to his pointed chin, where they coalesced and dripped onto the cloth of the seat.

"Ollie," he said, "it's wonderful to have you here and nice to see that you've got some support. Not that they'll be able to help you, of course."

Ollie took a couple of paces towards the genial host.

"I do understand that," he said, "but what exactly is it that I'm going to have to do?"

"Well, first you have to choose." "Choose what?" Ollie asked.

"The sort of game you'd like to play. You can have a skill game, a physical, a mental or a mystery."

"Do I get any clues as to what each of those choices entails?" "Only the title."

"Can I at least confer with my colleagues before making a choice?" Ollie asked.

"Of course," said Brian taking out his mouth organ again. "Take your time."

They huddled together and went over the various options that Ollie had been presented with, and what each might require him to do.

It didn't take too long to decide that a mental challenge was probably the best way to go. Skill and physical you could pretty much group together, and if Ollie was being honest with himself, he was pretty rubbish at anything that required a reasonable level of fitness. He got a cramp a couple of weeks back when coming up the stairs from Crumble's lab, although that might have had something to do with being chased for twenty minutes by a rampant, genetically modified frog armed with a small sword and a croak that could crack glass.

The mystery game sounded a bit too, well, mysterious. That seemed to be just asking for trouble, and they'd had enough of that already.

"Mental, Brian," Ollie announced.

"That's a bit rude," said their host taken aback. "We've only just met.

And anyway I've got the paperwork that says I'm. . . " "No. I mean I'll do a mental game."

"Excellent choice," shouted Brian enthusiastically, instantly forgetting the misunderstanding and running off again. "Let's go," he shouted.

"Do you reckon he works at being that jolly, or it just comes naturally?" asked Ronnie.

"Probably natural," answered Stitches. "No one can be that happy by choice."

"I'm sure I recognise him," said Ethan quietly as they followed Brian. "Didn't he write that musical about the fat transvestite?"

"Oh, I know the one you mean," said Ronnie as they continued through the castle at a steady pace. "The Stocky Horror Picture Show." "Oh I've seen that," said Ollie. "One of the weirdest things ever. A load of wobbly, flaccid old men in dresses playing with their. . ." "We're here," Brian announced, coming to a sudden stop that almost caused a six body pile up that would have been a bloody and messy affair, seeing that the massive juggernaut that was Flug was bringing up the rear.

"Ollie, if you would be so kind as to come and join me at the door please," said Brian, indicating what looked like the entrance to a dungeon type torture chamber. "All you have to do is enter, solve the problem that you're faced with, and collect your prize. Got it?"

"Got it," Ollie replied.

Brian took a large, rusty key from a vast recess in his coat and unlocked the door. He eased it open slowly and with great dramatic effect, making sure that the squeaky hinges made as much squeak as possible.

After what seemed like an eternity, Brian said, "Right, Ollie in you go," after which he slammed the door shut as loudly as was inhumanly possible. "You boys can observe the proceedings if you go round the corner," he added to the others.

Around said corner was a six foot by four foot window that gave then a brilliant view of Ollie inside.

"It is sound proofed and the glass is one way, so you can't help him," said Brian. "Not that I think you'd cheat, but let's face it, you would."

"How long has he got?" asked Ethan.

"Plenty of time," said Brian, "but he shouldn't need it. Anybody with a reasonable amount of intelligence should be able to figure it out. All it requires is a bit of lateral thinking."

He locked the door and returned the key to the vastness of his coat. "What if he can't do it?" asked Stitches.

"Best he does, really," said Brian, mouth organ already in hand.

————

The Ebony Casket was flying down the road so fast that if it went any faster, it would indeed achieve flight. In fact, there were points in the journey that all four wheels of the vehicle had left the road surface at the same time. If Singh drove any more recklessly or any faster, he'd easily qualify as a mini cab driver.

"WOOHOO!" screamed Scorpio as Singh took another hump backed bridge at something slightly under the speed of sound. "This is sooo cool. I didn't think a car could go this fast. I haven't had so much fun since. . . no, I can't top this."

Jekyll looked over his right shoulder at their extremely happy back seat passenger.

"I didn't realise librarians were so easily pleased," he said. "And there's me thinking that nothing could be better than the thrills and spills of book cataloguing and telling people to be quiet. It would appear that you've come down off the shelf."

"Please, Dr. Jekyll," said Singh. "It very much depends on which library you are talking about. The New Delhi Repository of Magic and Myth can be a very dangerous and deadly place. At least a dozen library assistants have been killed in that particular establishment over the years. You see, some of the books therein have a habit of practising what is written in their pages. It can be a most taxing way of making a living."

"I'm sure. It must be hard working in a place where if you don't follow the rulebook, the rulebook kicks the brown stuff out of you," said Jekyll.

"Precisely," said Singh. "And that would take a lot longer on my countrymen than most."

"This looks like it could be it," said Scorpio, pointing to the same road sign that Ethan had seen.

"So it is," agreed Jekyll. "Slow down a bit, Mandeep."

The Cornucopia Zoo had passed them by in a blurry, water colour haze a while back, so given that your average car would have done the trip from there to the castle in about an hour and they had done it in twenty four minutes, Jekyll deduced, using a process of mathematics and elimination, that they had arrived at the final and correct location. He proudly explained his thinking to his two companions.

"That's very impressive," said Scorpio, "but I think the hearse parked on the drawbridge kind of gives it away as well." She winked at him and poked her tongue out.

"Smarty pants," Jekyll retorted, affecting a hurt look. "Okay, Mandeep, pull up behind it and let's get inside. They shouldn't be too hard to find. It doesn't look that big."

They passed under the portcullis and entered the courtyard.

———

Ollie felt and heard the door slam shut behind him. A short breeze ruffled his hair as he took stock of what he was faced with. A mess was what it was. The room was quite large, about thirty feet by fifteen. To his right was a vast mirror so big that an elephant could have used it to check how it looked in its new ball gown. (That is quite obviously a ridiculous analogy. Everyone knows that elephants don't go to balls. They much prefer a rave or a foam party). Somehow, it didn't look quite right. Ollie inspected it more closely. Without a reflection looking back at him, distracting him, he could just make out some vague shapes on the other side. Two way. He waved at whoever was on the other side.

To his left were four tables facing out lengthways from the wall. They looked for the entire world like the roll out mortuary slabs that you see on every police show ever made. The look was made complete by the shrouded figure that lay on top of each of them.

"Creepy," he muttered to himself.

The far wall was floor to ceiling shelves, on each of which was what could only be described as the remnants of a boot fair. They were rammed full of all sorts of crap from old plastic weight training discs and parts of a lawn mower to the mother board of a ZX Spectrum and a battered jigsaw of Big Ben that had more missing pieces than Hadrian's Wall. And even though it wasn't immediately apparent, you could pretty much guarantee that hidden amongst all the detritus would be a battered copy of Stephen King's 'The Stand' that someone had gotten halfway through before slitting their wrists, a model of the Millennium Falcon with the radar dish missing, and a painting that the seller was convinced was by Monet even though he was selling it for fifty pence. Actually a boot fair is not a boot fair without these prerequisite items; in fact, you have to declare that they'll be for sale before you can get a license. All you need then is to throw in an ice cream truck (doesn't matter what time of year it is, it has to be there), a burger van that a starving man wouldn't have eaten from, a doughnut seller who seemed to be selling far more 'sugar' than was needed to cover his deep fried goods, a bloke standing in front of a wallpapering table covered in mystery plastic bags and a couple of prehistoric chemical toilets, and you would be all set.

After taking all this in Ollie had to admit that he was stumped. He didn't have a clue what to do with all of this unconnected stuff.

"Toe tags," came Brian's disembodied voice from over a crackly intercom.

Ollie looked more closely at the shrouded, prostrate figures, and noticed for the first time that the closest one to him did indeed have a yellow toe tag attached to, well, its toe. He removed it and read the message.

"Mr. Hill and his family have been the unfortunate victims of an accidental monstering. Only you can bring them back, using what you see around you."

"What?" shouted Ollie to no one in particular. "I'm a vampire, not a necromancer. I make the dead, not raise them."

He let out a massive breath and turned to face the shelves again. For a moment he was overcome by a sense of panic and impending doom. Was it going to be this way, that after all of their efforts they would fall at the last hurdle, thanks to him? It was whilst musing his inevitable failure, and the fact that the others were no doubt standing at the window, screaming at him to 'do this, this and that' and 'come on man it's bloody obvious' that he had an incidence of clear thought. A light bulb moment if you will (although not an energy saving light bulb moment. If he'd had one of those he'd still be there now waiting for it to warm up. Being ecologically aware and environmentally friendly is all very well but it isn't half slow).

Whilst gazing forlornly at the myriad objects before him, it suddenly became apparent. All but three items blurred into the background and spoke to him. He collected them and put them together. The second went into the back of the first and the third went into the front of the first. This accomplished, he scanned the room until he saw what he needed over in a corner. He carried his bundle over and knelt down in front of the electric socket, and plugged his construction in. He hoped that he'd gotten it right and that his flash of inspiration was going to work, because if it didn't he was well and truly knackered, for he couldn't think of anything else to do apart from reading that damn King book.

Apprehensively, he reached out and hit the play button on the cassette recorder, for twas one of those that he had found and reconstructed. A vague whirring sound came from the machine as the ancient cogs started to turn, which was followed by a few seconds of static during which Ollie was convinced, as is everyone who has ever owned a cassette deck, that the tape was about to be chewed to pieces (it usually happens when you're doing eighty five on the motorway. That's if your bedroom can do eighty five of course).

Fortunately this didn't happen, and the gentle opening chords of 'Floppy Lady's 'I Love You Cos You're Dead' floated across the maudlin dungeon. The surprising clarity of the music and the lilt of the vocals quietly but steadily filled the room, transforming it from a drab and perfunctory space to an F# filled hive of relaxation.

After a few minutes Ollie heard a shuffling noise just behind him. It sounded like a duvet cover being pulled off a bed and then allowed to fall to the floor in a crumpled heap. He turned round, knowing in his heart of hearts that his solution to the puzzle had been the right one. The four figures were not recumbent any longer. All were sitting upright, blinking as the light hit their eyes as if they were waking from a long, deep sleep.

The dungeon door creaked open and at Brian's behest he stepped outside. Their host congratulated him enthusiastically, but his companions were looking rather dumbstruck.

"I think you're going to have to explain it to them," said Brian, retreating a couple of steps before issuing forth with another random burst from his mouth organ.

"So," said Ronnie. "What the hell was that all about?" Ollie smiled and explained.

"It was quite straight forward, once the initial confusion cleared anyway. What you guys didn't know was what was written on the toe tags. They were a family. It was a Mr. Hill, his wife and their two children. The puzzle was to bring them back from the dead, so I figured that the only way, given the stuff that was in there, was to get the tape recorder going."

Ollie paused, wondering if the penny had dropped but unfortunately it was still hovering mid-air, waiting patiently for someone's brain cells to fire up. He was just about to carry on when Stitches snapped his fingers and announced, "Oh, God. I've got it!"

"Go on, then," Ollie invited.

"The Hills came alive to the sound of music," the zombie declared proudly.

"Oh you have got to be kidding me," said Ronnie, incredulously. "After all we've been through, it came down to a very simple bad joke?"

"Obviously not that simple," said Ollie.

"That's a fair one," said Ethan. "None of us got it. Well done, mate.

So when do we get the last piece of the Cup, then?"

Brian reappeared next to them, thankfully mouth organ free this time, but a whirling mass of energy nonetheless.

"The prize awaits, gentlemen. Follow me one last time to the Crystal Globe. Did anyone drop any money, by the way?"

Off he went again in a flurry of velvet, leather and denim. He looked like someone had taken a seventies rock band and put it in a blender, which was ironic because that's how most of them sounded.

This time he didn't lead them too far. Through a double door and into another large open area was the Crystal Globe, a twenty foot high, see through, multi-faceted sphere that sparkled and shone in the light from the torches above.

"That's a hell of a paperweight," said Stitches. "But what do we do now? Ethan will never get that in his backpack."

"Ollie, you have a minute to collect as many black tokens as you can," said Brian. "Place them into the receptacle inside the Globe. If you get enough, the prize will be yours. Clear?"

"Yup," said Ollie.

He walked over to the Globe and stepped inside, after which a door closed, sealing him in and separating him from his colleagues once again. Suddenly, a loud whirring began. He then looked up as another noise, a loud rumble, came from a steel tube that was jutting out from the ceiling. It wobbled slightly, before what seemed like a gout of water gushed from it. But water it was not. It was hundreds upon hundreds of tokens, some black and some blue. They flew around him like paper bats, slapping at his face and making it difficult to see.

"Your time starts now," shouted Brian over the noise of the machines powering the fans under Ollie's feet.

For all he was worth Ollie began frantically collecting all the black tokens that he could get his hands on and stuffing them into the bin. He didn't have a clue how many he needed, but he figured that it would be a reasonable amount to make this last test somewhat challenging. He forced them into the bin, not really paying attention as to what colour he was getting. He reckoned that if he got enough overall, then the odds would be in his favour, and it seemed to be a much better option than trying to sift through them as they whooshed about him. "Time's up," shouted Brian after what seemed considerably less than a minute.

A lid closed over the bin, denying him the last handful. The globe door swung open so he stepped out to rejoin the others. Brian was standing behind what looked like an altar and he was busy speaking to himself, so Ollie let him be for the moment.

"That looked like fun," said Ronnie. "I reckon that's what a load of washing must feel like."

"You were in da pretty rain," said Flug, plucking a stray blue ticket that had wedged itself under Ollie's lapel. "Me keep?"

"Course you can."

Stitches looked on and tutted. "That's him lost for a couple of hours.

Shiny to Flug is like drugs to an addict."

"If I may interrupt," said Brian. "Congratulations, Ollie, you have collected enough black tokens to win the prize. Well done indeed."

He was holding out a black box, the hinged lid of which was open. Nestling on a crushed velvet cushion inside was the last piece of the artefact, the bowl of the Cup of All Souls. Thanking all the deities that he didn't believe in that the quest was finally over, Ollie approached Brian to claim his prize.

"I'll take that, if you don't mind."

All five of them turned to see where and from whom the voice had come from, but the sight that they were met with was one that none of them could possibly have foreseen in their wildest imaginations.

Henry Jekyll stood before them. Sweat was pouring down his forehead and he had an extremely worried look on his face, the sort of look that a bank robber adopts when he realises that not only is the CCTV camera working, but that it's pointed right at him, and the local branch of the Police Firearms Division, Karate and General Hard Bastards Squad, are standing behind him ready to deposit the takings from their latest Kick-the-crap-out-of-anyone-who-thinks-they're-toughenough-to-take-us-on-athon.

What was most disconcerting was the fact that both of his hands were in the air, the reason for which was a small female standing just behind him and to his left, who had the barrel of a gun pointed to his head. A very big gun with a very long and menacing barrel. None of them knew her, and on the strength of this first impression, none of them wanted to get to know her. Ollie was about to say something, but sneezed violently several times.

"Seeing as my colleague is allergically indisposed," said Stitches, "Henry, what the hell is going on here?"

"Oh, that's alright," said Scorpio, edging forward but still keeping the distance between her and Jekyll with a gentle nudge from her weapon. "I can explain that. It's very simple. I wanted the Cup, but due to some ancient red tape I couldn't go looking for it myself, so that's where you guys came in."

Ollie stared at her intently, a very tiny hint of realisation dawning, as well as a hint of redness appearing on his cheeks after his sneezing fit.

"So whilst I obviously don't know the whole story, essentially you've played the five of us from the start?" he surmised.

"I suppose you could put it like that," Scorpio admitted, a smug smile on her face. "But don't be too downhearted, you've played a vital role in something rather spectacular. At the very least, your names will go down in history."

"As the idiots who got taken in by a dodgy woman. Again," said Stitches. "Sometimes I think the Village People had the right idea."

Ethan, seeing that Scorpio was distracted exchanging pleasantries with Ollie, tried to rush her, but she reacted quickly and pulled the trigger.

Ethan stopped dead in his tracks and checked himself for holes.

Thankfully, he wasn't as dead in his tracks as he had first thought. "Look behind you, gentlemen," she said.

They all turned round, just in time to see Brian slump to the ground. He had a look of shock on his face and he was reaching upwards with his right hand. A trickle of blood flowed from the neat entry wound in his forehead. It pooled in a claret puddle when he finally hit the floor. "I mean business, gentlemen, and just to show you that it wasn't a lucky shot." She fired again, this time striking Brian in the chest and piercing his already dying heart. He spasmed once and was still. "Now you," she pointed with her free hand at Flug. "Move that away from there."

"She means shift the body, mate," said Stitches to a very confused and very frightened monster.

"Okay."

Flug thudded over to their ex-host and hoisted him onto his shoulder in a grim re-enactment of his exploits at the Cornucopia Zoo.

"Where he go?" he asked, a tremor in his voice.

"Somewhere over there will do," she said. "Now, back to the matter at hand. Where are the other four pieces?"

"I've got them," Ethan volunteered.

"Excellent. Take the piece from your friend there, and if you'd be a love and put it together for me, I'd be extremely grateful. Once that's done place it onto the altar and back off. And no funny stuff. I don't want to have to demonstrate my shooting prowess again, but I will if I have to. Are we all clear?"

"Clear," answered Ethan, shrugging the backpack off his shoulders. "Good. Now the rest of you, apart from you, Henry, into the globe.

And no talking."

Ollie, Stitches and Ronnie got into the giant crystal as they had been told. The door closed on them, sealing them inside and effectively rendering them useless.

Jekyll turned slightly towards Scorpio, just enough to get her attention but not enough to get himself shot.

"So all that stuff you told me in the coffee shop and the library was just a load of rubbish to get me involved, and get you here?" he asked. "Up to a point," she said. "I did see Vortex and Flange have a discussion in the street, and Flange does have a passing interest in dark magic, but that's as far as it goes. I haven't got a clue what they're up to and to be honest, I don't really care. How's it going, handsome?" Ethan looked up from the altar.

"Alright. I'm nearly done. Don't be getting an itchy finger," he said.

With the Cup finally assembled, Ethan put his backpack onto the ground and gave it a kick.

"I'll show you," he whispered to himself.

In a flash of fur and jagged teeth, his rescued pet from the zoo ran towards Scorpio without being seen and bit her right on the ankle.

"YEEEOWWW," she screamed, taken by complete surprise. "Oh, you little bast. . ."

Still keeping the gun firmly aimed at Jekyll, she glanced down long enough to get a glimpse of the offending creature. Then, with a wellplaced swing of her leg, she booted it twenty feet across the room.

"Little bugger," she said, rubbing her injured ankle with her other foot. "I'm bleeding now. Come on, haven't you finished yet?" she shouted at Ethan.

"All done," he replied.

"Right. The rest of you, into the globe and shut the door. And remember, I've got plenty of bullets and I'm more than willing to share them."

As the door opened, Ollie stood by it, his hands in the air in supplication.

"Can I help you?" Scorpio asked, raising the gun.

"In a way. It seems obvious that you're going to kill us and I would hate to go to my grave without some idea, so I was wondering how this all came about."

Scorpio laughed quietly and shook her head.

"I think you've been watching too many films. There isn't going to be some dramatic last scene where I spill my guts to the hero before he miraculously escapes and foils the whole evil plan. But there is one thing that I will tell you because it gives me pleasure to do so, because it means I'm clever and you're stupid. Remember when you first came to the museum and that cat was in the room, when you and the scarecrow were looking at the clues?"

"Yes."

"It was you, wasn't it?" said Stitches, cutting in. "That's very perceptive," she said.

"Remember you had a sneezing attack?" the zombie said to Ollie. "And every time after that, when we found a piece of the Cup it happened again? I bet she was keeping tabs on us the whole time. You were reacting to her presence."

Ollie nodded in agreement.

"So as you can seen it was all nice and simple really," she said. "And the red tape I was talking about precluded my involvement in finding the pieces, so I used a transforming spell and got into the museum without arousing any suspicion. Everyone loves a cute little cat don't they. Once I knew the layout it was easy to steal the papers and cast aspersions all over the place about Vortex and Flange, and I knew that Starch would call you to look into the matter, especially after he came into the library to get listings for investigators. I just happened to point him in the right direction, which was yours. I then had to make sure I was there when you guys showed up, in case one of you managed to solve any of the clues. Lucky for me, you did. I must admit, at first I thought you were going to royally screw it up, but on the whole you've done rather well. I tell you what, as a reward I'll kill you all quickly. There's no need to make any of you suffer after you've done such a sterling job."

"Don't feel that you've got to do us any favours," said Stitches, still prickling at being called a scarecrow. "I'll be quite happy with walking away and pretending that none of this has ever happened. We won't tell anyone. Honest."

Scorpio shook her head. "That's never going to happen. Right, that's enough talk. Shut the door and get to the back." She fired off one more well placed warning shot.

All they could do was watch as Scorpio went to the altar and stood behind it, in the exact same place that the unfortunate Brian had occupied a few minutes before. She picked up the Cup in both hands and slowly and reverentially lifted it over her head.

"Gods of Darkness hear me. As you can see I am now in possession of The Cup of All Souls. Altrix, Xanthas and Mephisto, prepare to be released."

She returned the Cup to the altar and reached into a hip pocket from which she drew a knife. Closing her eyes, she raised her face to the ceiling before drawing the blade across her palm, which quickly erupted with blood. She placed her hand over the Cup and let the gushing fluid flow into the bowl. In a few seconds it was full enough. Again she clasped it in both hands, wincing this time as the pain from the slash bit deep. She held the Cup a few inches from her lips and spoke once more, but this time in a language that none of the captives understood. It sounded creepy though, and was no doubt hard to spell, but it was roughly:

"Mai drox en vie quettle, son dast monzorp thrux. Breg thuk aklum nol kloz, rew gub breshuq hux."

When she had finished the unintelligible recitation, she put the Cup to her lips and drank the now steaming and bubbling contents straight down.

The atmosphere in the hall changed subtly, almost as if it was suddenly in a bad mood. The light dimmed, not to any great degree, but more as if you were in a room with several bulbs and one suddenly went out. Something was different but you'd be hard pushed to define it.

Shadows started to appear near Scorpio, vague shapes that swirled around her like animated mist. It ebbed and flowed until it finally seemed to thicken and take on form. In front of the altar, three distinct but still wispy figures began to coalesce. Seen from the Globe they were still indefinite, miasmal blobs, but there was no denying that they were going to transform into the three beings that Scorpio had summoned. She smiled as she opened her eyes and wiped a drop of blood from the corner of her mouth. Finally her time had come. The culmination of everything that she had worked for. The reward was about to be hers.

"DO YOU TAKE US FOR FOOLS, MORTAL? WHY DO YOU TRY TO DECEIVE US THIS WAY?"

"Wh... what do you mean?" Scorpio stuttered. "I've done everything that has been asked of me."

"NOT EVERYTHING, PUNY HUMAN. YOU HAVE FAILED."

Before she could utter another word, the three phantoms swept over the altar and totally engulfed her in their thick, foggy greyness. She dropped the Cup and screamed out loud, hands clamped to the side of her head as she shook it back and forth. The mists around her grew more substantial, swirling in cascading torrents until, with an audible thunder-like clap, she completely disappeared. The only clue that she had ever been in the hall were her rapidly fading howls of terror that became fainter and fainter and fainter, until they could be heard no more.

"Typical woman. Can't get her own way so she buggers off to the nether regions of some hell in a mood," said Stitches.

The cloud split once more into the three vaguely humanoid shapes which took up residence at the altar.

"APPROACH," said a booming voice that filled the entire hall.

"I take it they mean us?" said Ronnie, to which Ollie nodded in agreement.

The door of the globe opened and the six of them stepped from it, standing in front of the three hovering phantoms, albeit at a safe distance. Not that you could judge what a decent safe distance was when confronted by the forces of evil. Ollie thought they had it just about right. Stitches thought it was all wrong on many levels. Ronnie didn't care what it was, as long as he could have a fag. Ethan would have liked it to be closer so that he could have gotten his hands on them. Jekyll couldn't decide one way or the other, and Flug was staring mesmerised at his shiny blue ticket, and couldn't have told you what a safe distance was even if his life depended on it and he had a note, written on which was 'you are now at a safe distance.'

"MORTAL, ETHAN. RETURN TO US WHAT IS RIGHTFULLY OURS."

"What on earth does it mean by that?" asked Ollie.

"It's alright," said Ethan, taking his backpack off and rummaging through it. "I know what they're after."

To the disbelief of his colleagues, Ethan produced The Cup of All Souls which he placed reverentially onto the altar. The three gaseous apparitions merged together around it where they became one, spinning faster and faster, forming a small tornado strong enough to tug at their hair and clothing. It spun madly for a few seconds before winking out of existence as quickly as turning off a light switch. The Cup of All Souls was gone.

Ethan turned to look at his companions, who were all doing very passable impressions of goldfish.

"Remember the football tournament in Glans?" he prompted. "We won, didn't we? When Little Ethan bit Scorpio on the ankle, I took advantage of her being distracted and swapped the proper cup for the one we got presented with after the final, so instead of trying to perform the ritual with the solid gold Cup of All Souls, she ended up using a crappy tin one. I thought at the very least it might put the mockers on her little scheme, but I had no idea it would be that dramatic."

"Well, who's a clever boy for saving us and stopping her taking over the world? Good doggie," said Stitches.

"I agree," said Ollie, placing himself between Ethan and the soon to be dismembered zombie if the werewolf got his way. "That was quick thinking."

"So, what was all that business with Vortex and Flange being under suspicion?" said Ronnie to Jekyll.

"That was just bad timing and rumours, put about by Scorpio to her advantage," said Jekyll, examining the altar. "I still don't know exactly what they're up to, but it's certainly not anything underhanded, she just made it look that way. And it all fell neatly into place to point the finger at them, right down to the red fibres that I found in Flange's house that matched Vortexs' socks. It was all coincidence, and when she found out I was helping you lot investigate them and that you were taking on the quest, she simply got on board with me to perpetuate the false leads. She must have even created Flange's dodgy reading list. She must have been planning this for a long time."

"Devious mare," said Stitches shaking his head, thankful it was still on his shoulders. "That'll teach her to call me a scarecrow. So, what now?"

"We go home," said Ollie. "The Cup is back where it belongs, wherever that is, and everyone's safe. There's nothing more for us to do."

"Seems a shame though, doesn't it?" said Ronnie, contemplating the last few days. "After all our efforts and everything we've done, we've got nothing to show for it."

"At least she didn't get hold of the Cup," said Stitches. "The legends about its powers were obviously true. God alone knows what would have happened if Ethan hadn't swapped them over."

"Good point," said Ollie. "Right, I can't think of any good reason to stay here any longer, so if there's no objections, let's get the hell out of here shall we?"

And the hell out of there they got.

When they got back home, a couple of other items of unfinished business were laid to rest. The reason for Vortex's furtiveness and reticence to divulge any information about what he was up to, was because he was arranging a surprise party to celebrate Starches one hundred and fiftieth birthday. That in turn led to the reason for Flange's absence. He had been on a quest of his own, attempting to track down as many of the Curator's old friends and former colleagues as he could. And all credit to him, he hadn't done a bad job. He had even tracked down Miss Fanny Bygaslamp, Starches primary school teacher who was now so incredibly old that when the dinosaurs went extinct, she was pulled in for questioning.

Flange had also taken up a new position as the new part time librarian. His love of old books and the sudden vacancy had been too good an opportunity to pass up.

Starch had been mortified when Ollie relayed the story of the last few days to him, but he was more than happy with the outcome and informed the vampire that the Compendium de Magicus Totallus would no longer be on display at the museum, but would instead be safely sealed away deep within the bowels of the building.

The party had been a pleasant conclusion to the adventure, and it gave them a chance to sample Vortex's culinary skills. As it turned out, he was a dab hand at savoury tartlets, and his chocolate sponge was to undie for.

Back at the office, Ethan headed off to the werehouse to catch up on lycanthrope goings on, and Ronnie did his usual straight out of the office door and into the door of the nearest pub manoeuvre. He had some drinking goings on to catch up on.

Ollie was sitting behind his desk and Stitches was in his usual place, in the soft leather chair opposite. The chair, which when compared to the zombie, looked increasingly healthy and pert of skin.

"Well, that's another interesting case under our belts," he said. "We'll have to be careful though. We'll start getting a reputation as people who are marginally good at getting things done."

"Couldn't hurt," Ollie replied. "The more people that think we're up to it, the more work we'll get. And you have to admit, it is rather enjoyable."

"Absolutely," said Stitches, taking a sip from the glass of water he was holding. "I can't think of anything I'd rather be doing than risking my life for a living."

"Can a zombie make a living?"

"No more than you can, you half-breed bloodsucker."

With that the zombie left the office, leaving Ollie on his own to contemplate another success and to look forward to what might come their way next.

———

Flug walked down the garden path, taking great care not to disturb the furry little bundle in his giant hands. He stroked it gently and smiled at the cute squeaky noises that it made. He had assured Ethan that he would take really good care of Fluffy, after the wolfman had decided that the werehouse wasn't really a suitable place for it to stay. Stitches hadn't been too sure about the idea and had voiced his concerns that Flug would probably eat it, but after several pleading protestations from the eight foot patchwork quilt, Ethan had relented. At the bottom of the garden was an old, disused coal shed. It was warm, dry and, most importantly, safe. Flug opened the door and peered inside.

"Snowy," he called quietly. "Me got a new friend for you to play wiv." The crunch of coal dust heralded the appearance of Fluffy's new roommate. Out from the darkness it came. Three feet long and just under a foot tall, it had bright purple skin and deep red wings, hence Flug naming it Snowy. He tickled it under the chin which caused it to elicit a soft, purr like sound. It was a Skullenian miniature dragon, and it was overjoyed to see its keeper.

"Me fink you two are gonna be really happy togever."

THE END

WUTHERING FRIGHTS

SKULLENIA BOOK 3

For Mum and Dad who let me read horror stories when I was seven

WUTHERING FRIGHTS

F lug was tired. Extremely tired. In fact, he was so tired that the three or four viable brain cells that he had left in his spacious dome had gathered straw and provisions, gone into hibernation, and wouldn't be likely to return to active duty much before the next millennium. Or any other gargantuan time span you'd cared to mention for that matter. Flug functioned on a time scale that made geological epochs seem a bit hasty you see, and the fact that he'd been standing on the office roof with his arms in the air for about five hours now, meant that he'd pretty much had enough when all things were considered (not that he considered many things of course. If asked to chew and walk at the same time he'd probably have a stroke and then have to pick the food off the bottom of his shoes whilst wondering why he had gravel in his mouth).

"Stitches," he said, managing to instil a pleading tone into his deep, bass voice. "Can me stop now?"

The zombie looked down from the chair that he was standing on and pulled a face. Not his actual face of course because that would have come off in his hand. So would his hand.

"Just give it a little while longer, big fellah. I nearly had it then."

The zombie reached up and carefully adjusted the coat hanger that he'd attached to the bolt in Flug's forehead. This, in turn, was

375

connected via a length of wire to a small black and white television that was sat on the floor next to Flug's feet. At that precise moment, the ancient visual device was displaying nothing except a violent snowstorm, although there were probably adverts still being shown for really useful things like food (who'd have thought we needed that?), expensive cars that only a footballer could afford (and drive if he could figure out how to get in it), and Christmas stuff (well, it is July you know).

"Just hold still now," said the zombie. "We're nearly there."

About a week ago Stitches had found the old TV dumped in a bin at the rear of Mrs Strudels café, and he'd come up with the brilliant idea that if Flug was capable of picking up radio waves then logically he should be able to pick up a television signal as well. Unfortunately,

Stitches' grasp of electronics, visual equipment, and how to utilise them and their various applications effectively, was the equivalent of a Roman Catholic priests understanding of the basic concepts of religion. In other words, he didn't have a bloody clue. Consequently, poor old Flug had spent most of the last six days standing on the roof come rain or shine (mostly rain) like a vast meat aerial. He'd also suffered the soul crushing indignity of having various bits of metalwork stuck to his face in a vain attempt to boost his reception capabilities. Forks, spoons, screwdrivers, hammers, and any other item of kitchen or garage paraphernalia that you'd care to mention had ended up stuck to him at some point over the last week or so. The anvil had been particularly hard work, especially when it had fallen off Flug's head, rolled onto Stitches' foot and left three of his toes looking like four-day old porridge.

Despite his best efforts though it was never going to work, because what Stitches had failed to realise was the fact that Skullenia was in something of a sound and vision wave black hole. For some unknown reason signals of any description had trouble getting in or out of the village no matter how hard you, or your equipment tried. It was bad enough trying to send a text message from one side of the square to the other let alone the next village over. In fact, it would have been quicker to use a carrier bat. Even quicker if you used a live one. You might as well be trying to get a signal from the outer reaches of the solar system to be honest. Or on T Mobile, the chances were about the same.

"Stitches me tired. Me want sweeties now."

Just as he was about to plead with Flug for five more minutes, a crackle and a loud whoosh from above distracted the zombie, throwing his delicate coat hanger array awry.

"Stitches," called Mrs. Ladle as she swooped and arced like a demented swallow. "What on earth are you trying to do to that poor boy?"

"Isn't it obvious?" replied the zombie.

"To a mental patient perhaps," she said, deftly landing on the roof and dismounting. "But not to any sane person."

"Well that leaves. . . "

"Easy now, sunshine," said the witch. "Don't you go taking advantage of my good nature there's a good chap." She made a show of checking her pockets. "I know I've got one somewhere, and it wouldn't take kindly to having someone taking the mick out of it. Come to think of it I seem to remember it's on my mantle-piece next to my grandfather's eyes and my mother's sense of decorum."

She helped Flug divest himself of several bits of metal and handed him a packet of sweets.

"Oooh, Fruity Flanges. My faverits. Fanks, Mrs. L."

He lumbered off cramming as many as he could get into his mouth as was inhumanly possible, which was a lot.

"Now, before you start moaning and groaning like a grumpy zombie," said the witch to a disgruntled looking zombie who was just about to start moaning and groaning like a grumpy zombie, "just take a moment or two to think about what you've been doing to that unfortunate lad. You've taken terrible advantage of him as you well know."

"Yeah, but that's the brilliance of it," said Stitches. "He hasn't got a clue about anything so if he doesn't understand what's going on how can I be accused of taking advantage of him? He only knows the sky's above him because it's a slightly different colour to the ground and has fewer buildings in it. Besides, it's a bit of compensation for having to look after him all the time."

Mrs. Ladle took a drag of the cigarette that had appeared in her hand as if by magic, which was ironic because that's exactly what had occurred. She tapped a leather booted foot on the roof and stared at the zombie with nary a blink.

Stitches could tell instantly that she was angry. He was quick on the uptake like that, plus he was more than used to it. There weren't many beings he'd met that he hadn't annoyed at some point or another, and for those that he hadn't, it was only a matter of time before he did.

He looked at the witch and gave her a smile. It didn't work. Even the stream of smoke that she exhaled looked annoyed, and when she spoke it was in a tone of voice that required nay, demanded obedience, oozed command, and left the perceptive listener under no illusion as to what might happen if the speaker was disobeyed. Stitches though, disregarded the danger signals and carried on regardless.

"But surely his innocence and lack of understanding are the very reasons that you shouldn't be doing those things to him in the first place. It's got to stop. Right now. Understand."

"Spose," said the zombie. "Excuse me," said the witch.

"Okay. Okay. I understand," said Stitches, a little more warily than a moment ago. He couldn't be sure but he could have sworn that Mrs. Ladle's exhaled cigarette smoke had formed a noose. It was hanging in the air not two feet from his face and looked very keen to wrap itself around something. Something neck shaped and under his head. "Good. Right. I'm glad that we've reached an agreement. Now don't let me catch you being mean to Flug again or I'll turn you into something nasty."

With that she grabbed her broom and flew off leaving Stitches in her nicotine shrouded wake.

———

Ronnie sat at the kitchen table and drained the last of the tea from the cracked mug that, despite it's off white and slightly grubby appearance was his absolute favourite. It had character, history, and made the tea taste just right. It no doubt had trillions of deadly bacteria and malignant pathogens capable of wiping out entire civilizations in it as well, but that was just by the by as it all added to the flavour. The fact that it had a picture of a cute and fluffy teddy bear on it was neither here nor there either. That's what he told people anyway.

He swallowed his drink with relish, enjoying the burning sensation as the searing liquid flowed down his throat. Ronnie was one of those people that liked his tea ridiculously hot. In fact, the hotter the better, to the point that if you were unlucky enough to spill any of it on yourself, you would be in real danger of having to take a trip to the nearest accident and emergency centre. Stitches, reckoned that Ronnie must have asbestos in his throat, but that had been after he'd gotten some on his left forearm, an incident that had stripped the flesh from the zombie's limb in an instant and left it looking like a bread stick that had fallen on hard times. Ronnie knew different though and that it was from years of dedicated smoking. He might very well have the lung capacity of an asthmatic coal miner, but at least he could get a steaming hot brew down without wincing.

After returning the cup to the table he fished around in a coat pocket and retrieved his leather tobacco pouch because there was no better time to enjoy a nice smoke than after a lovely cup of tea (as well as after waking up, going to the toilet, before breakfast, after breakfast, during the morning, before lunch, during lunch, after lunch, all throughout the afternoon... oh, you get the idea. The only time that Ronnie didn't smoke was when he was in bed, and that was only because he hadn't yet figured out how to keep a steady stream of nicotine flowing into his system while he was asleep).

He flipped the pouch open. "Bugger," he said to himself (which was just as well because there was no one else in the room). Save for a few lonely wisps of brown dust languishing at the bottom, his pouch was devoid of anything suitable for rolling. Usually Ronnie kept a spare with him at all times so that he would never run out, but seeing as he was recovering from a weekend away with a couple of friends during which he'd made a spectacularly heroic effort at drinking and smoking himself to death, it was perfectly understandable that his mind was still a little hazy. He put the bereft pouch back into his pocket, rinsed his mug and made his way to the office. When he got there he met Stitches, who was standing outside. The door was closed.

"Is he in?" Ronnie asked.

"I'm not sure to be honest," replied the zombie, giving the door a gentle knock that wouldn't have roused a very nervous insomniac.

"Well, why don't you just go on in?" said Ronnie. "It's not as if it's off limits".

"I would but when the doors closed it usually means that he's just got up, and you know what he's like about his appearance first thing in the evening. He doesn't like to be seen in a mess does he, but because he hasn't got a reflection, he can't see what he doesn't want us to see, so he just assumes that what he can't see is bound to be something that he wouldn't want us to see, or that we would want to see."

"I see," said Ronnie, ever so slightly confused.

"I can hear you out there you know," came Ollie's voice from the other side of the door. "And I know you're talking about me."

Stitches inclined his head and spoke to Ronnie in a hushed whisper. "When he says, 'I can hear you out there you know', that usually means that he doesn't mind us seeing. . . "

"WILL YOU GET IN HERE YOU DUSTY TW... "

Tired of the verbal badinage that was threatening to turn him into a mass murderer (well, two at any rate), Ronnie flung open the door and marched in, closely followed by Stitches. Ollie was sitting behind his desk and had a 'just got up from a nap and haven't had time to sort myself out properly, you try it when you have the sleeping pattern of a two-year-old' look about him.

"Nice kip?" asked Stitches.

"Yes thank you," replied Ollie, staring in horror at the pint of blood that had been sitting on his desk when he came in. "And to what do I owe the pleasure of a visit so early in the night? And please note that that was directed at Ronnie and not you."

"Well that's just charming," said Stitches, feigning offence quicker than a die hard, soap box, anti-racist who thinks it's disgusting that people of colour still have to ask for black coffee in this day and age. He glanced around the room, desperately trying to find something to talk about in order to lighten the mood. His gaze finally came to rest on the wall above the fireplace.

"How long has that been there?" he asked.

"Only a couple of days," said Ollie, rising from his chair for a leg stretch.

"It's a mirror," said Stitches.

"Indeed it is," said Ollie. "And congratulations on your keen powers of observation. They never cease to amaze me. What do you think of it?"

"Well," Stitches said, "on reflection. . . " "Forget it," snapped Ollie. "What!"

"I asked you a simple question. All I wanted was a simple answer. Is that too much to ask for just once?"

"Alright, calm down, Mister got out of the coffin on the wrong side. I was only. . . hang on. What the hell do you need a mirror for?"

Ollie reached up and adjusted the mirror slightly. Very slightly. So slightly in fact that it was reminiscent of the type of thing that people do when they haven't got the first clue about paintings, portraits or art in general, and the only way that they can convey any artistic knowledge whatsoever is to stand in front of their latest acquisition, with a feigned knowing look on their face whilst they move it by infinitesimal fractions of an inch before spewing forth with drivel such as, 'Isn't it amazing, the eyes seem to follow you around the room', or, 'Of course the artists medium was light don't you know.' You know the sort of pretentious idiot I'm talking about don't you. Everyone has an acquaintance like it, pretending to be all erudite and interesting when they're about as engaging as a sponge. Ask them a real question about proper art like who their favourite impressionist is and just see what happens. 'Well, Jon Culshaw relies too heavily on costume but Robin Williams really nailed the voices and mannerisms.' There is a technical term for them. It starts with knob and ends with head. That's the impression they give anyway.

"Ethan suggested it," explained Ollie. "He reckoned it would give the office the illusion of space."

"You could have used the inside of Flug's head for that," said Stitches, checking his own appearance.

"Funny you should mention him," said Ollie as he returned to his chair. "He walked past it the other day and thought there was an intruder in the place. Obviously, I then had to explain to him what the difference between an intruder and a reflection was and that we didn't actually have one. Then I told him what a reflection was and finally explained to him what a mirror is. He didn't get it of course and then decided that because I don't have a reflection an intruder must have gotten in and stolen it."

"That sounds about right. I'm surprised he didn't attack it actually, that's what he normally does," said Stitches.

Flug did have a tendency to either attack, or flee in terror from things that he didn't understand, and they were legion. It was a long and varied list that's far too extensive to write down here. It's far far simpler, and much much quicker, to note down the things that he *does* understand.

List of things that Flug understands 1.

And that was as far as it went. Still, we live in hope.

Ollie relaxed into his chair and suddenly remembered that Ronnie had come into the office as well.

"Sorry, mate," he said. "What can I do for you?"

Ronnie walked over to the desk and plonked himself heavily down onto the edge. He yawned expansively.

"Dearie me. I didn't notice it before," said the half vampire with a friendly smile before Ronnie could get a word out, "but you don't half look rough. Another few interesting days away with the lads I take it?" "You could say that," answered Ronnie, trying to stifle another epic yawn.

"So, where did you get to this time?" asked Stitches from his usual place in the ancient, cracked, and desiccated leather chair opposite the desk, a chair that he was rapidly coming to resemble. "Because from the looks of you I think we should have an undertaker on standby."

"Tell me about it. I'm wasted," said Ronnie. He shook his head. "I've really got to stop doing this to myself you know. I'm getting too old and it's taking me longer and longer to recover each time." Ollie and Stitches nodded their heads. They'd heard it all before.

Despite his well-intentioned words he didn't mean any of it and sounded as convincing as an alcoholic swearing off the demon drink just as he's opening up a new bottle (not that the actual demon drink would do him any harm. They liked a tall glass of water with a twist of lime or a refreshing pomegranate juice because all that talking in rasping, creepy growls after they've possessed a twelve-year-old girl plays hell with the vocal cords over the years. I should know. My daughter's twelve and she's an absolute monster).

"Still," said Stitches, adjusting his right cheek which had dropped slightly, "look on the bright side. At least when the time comes we won't have to get you embalmed. I reckon you've got enough alcohol in your system to preserve you for centuries. Years from now your perfectly uncorrupted corpse will be on display as an unsolved wonder of nature. You'll be famous."

"Flammable more like," said Ollie. "Anyway, what's up me ole mucker?"

"Mucker?" said Ronnie, with a confused expression.

"Yes. I thought I'd try out a few new terms of endearment for my nearest and dearest," explained Ollie. "I think it'll make me appear more approachable and friendly. You know, not so scary and vampiry."

Stitches raised an eyebrow as a deafening silence descended. "Ollie, I implore you. Don't. It doesn't work and it's kind of weird if I'm honest. It'd be like Mrs. Ladle being polite or Flug saying something vaguely sensible."

"Fair enough," said Ollie. "What about dude? Or maybe bro?"

"Have you banged your head?" said Stitches.

Ollie didn't say any more about it.

"Right, well, now that's cleared up," said Ronnie, glad to be off the subject, "the reason I came in is because I thought we could kill two bats with one stone. I've run out of tobacco and I can't be arsed going to the shop so I was thinking that as we're trying to encourage Flug to take on a little bit more responsibility round here maybe he could pop down there and buy it for me. What do you think?"

"I suppose it might be worth a go," said Ollie, after considering the idea for a few moments. "It's a big step but, to be fair to him he has been making good progress lately."

"And by that he means that the big dope is now able to get to his bed from the door of his bedroom without getting lost and using toilet paper instead of any items of clothing that he happens to find lying around the place," said Stitches with a snort of derision.

Ollie looked at the zombie, his head tilted to one side.

"Now you know that was an accident," said Ollie. "And when I explained it to him he got it."

"Yeah I know but that was my favourite shirt," replied Stitches, indignantly. "I've never seen such a mess. Poor old Ethan felt queasy for days and he eats things that'd make a troll sick. It looked like an explosion in a peanut butter factory."

"Well, thanks for that lovely imagery," said Ronnie, who had gone ever so slightly green.

"And not the smooth kind either."

"Alright alright," said Ollie. "Calm down. It won't happen again."

Ronnie sighed and thought that maybe his regular getaways weren't such a bad idea after all. If it kept him out of the way of dealing with a five-hundred-pound toddler who wasn't quite potty trained then so much the better.

"Flug," called Ollie. "Can you come in here for a moment please?" "Yeah, Ollie. Me comin'."

Flug duly wandered into the office like a confused tower block (as was his wont whether he wanted it or not), but this time his arrival wasn't accompanied by the usual THUD as his head connected with the top of the door frame. The problem was that Flug had a major issue remembering the fact that the doorway was six feet six and that he was over eight feet, so rather than see his insurance premiums go through the roof (Flug had done that as well after he'd indulged in a bout of unsupervised standing up), Ollie had asked Ethan to chisel out an extra twenty-four inches above the frame to give the reanimate some clearance. And it had worked a treat, meaning that Ollie's office had remained intact and plaster free ever since. Obviously that couldn't be said for all of the other doorways and rooms in the building but hey, you can't have everything. Still, progress was progress and as the old saying went, it's all about taking those baby steps (even if the baby in question is roughly the size of a bison with a pituitary problem, and has the IQ of a tree stump).

"Hi, big guy," said Ronnie to the patchwork behemoth. "Hi, Ronnie. Me missed you lots and lots."

"I missed you too, mate. Right, Flug. How do you fancy doing me a favour?"

"And lots and lots." "I get it, mate." "And lots and lots." "Flug."

"Yeah, Ronnie."

"Try and focus now. I need you to do me a favour." "Kay. Me can do dat. Wot is it?"

"I want you go to the shop and get me some tobacco. Is that something you'd like to do?" asked Ronnie, slowly extracting some money from his trouser pocket.

"Yeah, me like to do it. Which one?" asked Flug proudly, pleased beyond measure to be given the chance to perform such an important task.

"Get me a packet of Smouldering Fluff. Not that other stuff he sells, what is it now, Burning Hell or something?"

"Kay. Which shop?" said Flug.

"Come on now, mate think about it," said Ronnie. "It's the same one that we get your sweets from remember?"

Realisation slowly dawned in Flug's mind. It didn't show on his face though. That could take upwards of a fortnight.

"Oh yeah," said Flug as a thin sliver of confectionery inspired drool leaked onto his chin. "Can me get some Corpse Crunchies please, Ronnie?" he added excitedly.

"Of course you can. Now, can you remember what I want?"

"Uh, yeah. Burning Fluff," Flug announced.

"Not quite," said Stitches. "That's what you get if you spend too much time with the Stella triplets."

Ollie shot the zombie the sort of look that the parents of a five-yearold employ when they see said little cherub remove its finger from its nose and attempt to divest it of the glistening, sticky globule it's excavated onto the carpet.

"No," continued Ronnie, patiently. "I want Smouldering Fluff. I do not want Burning Hell. Got it?"

"Kay. Wot difference?" asked Flug.

"Well, not that it really matters, but Burning Hell is pipe tobacco.

It's far too rough for making roll ups," explained Ronnie.

"Kay." Flug paused for a moment then, looking thoughtful as if he wanted to say something else. It was either that or he needed to go to the toilet again. Or worse, already been. Thankfully it was the former. "Um, me no get, Ronnie."

"Think of it like this," said Ollie, seeing that Ronnie was changing colour rather quickly. "It's like cheese. You can have it grated into big pieces or small pieces. Ronnie wants it in small pieces you see."

Outside of any and all sweets, Flug's second favourite food was cheese, so Ollie thought that if he put the tobacco conundrum into the context of something that he was familiar with then Flug would be more likely to understand.

"Ah, me get it now," said Flug, slapping his head in a way that would have stunned an elk.

"Finally," commented Stitches.

Ronnie put the money into Flug's outstretched hand. "And get yourself some sweets with the change."

"Fanks."

"You're welcome." "Ronnie."

"Yes, Flug?"

"Won't da cheese get stuck in your pipe?"

"That's it, I give up," said Ronnie, snatching back the money amidst howls of laughter from Ollie and Stitches. "I'll go myself. Anybody want anything?"

"No thanks," said Stitches, slowly recovering to the point that it was now safe to take his hands away from his rib cage. "I had a couple of slices of tobacco on toast earlier."

Ronnie swore colourfully and walked out.

———

Ten minutes later Ollie was alone in his office once more. Ronnie had gone out to the shop, Flug was doing whatever it was that Flug did in his spare time, and Stitches had left, muttering something about some part of his body that needed ironing.

"What to do?" he said to himself. "I know. Check emails."

He logged onto the Darknet and accessed his account. As usual it was mostly rubbish apart from one that looked quite interesting. It was a link to an information site called Wickedpedia and it had been sent to him by Dr. Jekyll.

'I thought this looked good,' he'd typed. 'It's the place to go if you want to find out anything about anything'.

Being reasonably new to the world of the information super highway (or, with Skullenia's connectivity being what it was, the information off road, dirt track riddled with boulders, stiles, overflowing fords and the occasional cow blocking the way), Ollie and the rest of the residents of Skullenia hadn't quite got to grips with the fact that most of what you read on the intertubes should be taken with a pinch of salt large enough to disable an elephants kidneys, and a very healthy dose of scepticism. Still, as with most things there was a learning curve involved and they'd get to grips with routing out the fact from the fiction soon enough (which would be good because as you, dear reader, and I know from bitter experience it's because most of the information held within a computers flashing innards is usually updated by bored eleven year olds who have nothing better to do after the batteries in their hand-held consoles have run out. God forbid they do something radical like go outside and play. This was the precise reason that a lot of people actually believe that Stephen Hawking celebrated his fortieth birthday on the summit of The Eiger after a particularly challenging ascent of the North Face. This is, of course, utterly ridiculous and anyone believing such patent nonsense would be very silly indeed. The eminent Professor couldn't possibly have achieved this incredible feat because the escalator was closed for repairs. You see, it's all in the details).

Ollie typed in some random subjects just to see how accurate it was. To be fair it wasn't too bad. There was quite a detailed history of Skullenia that contained several references to his Dad, and a nice piece about the Fibulan Museum. Eventually he tired of surfing though; one because he couldn't find anything else of interest, and two, his computer began to throw some very dodgy sites his way that made his eyes itch. That being the case he shut the computer down and went off to the kitchen. Twenty minutes, two cups of Earl Grey, and some Marmite on toast later (who says half vampires aren't afraid to try something different) Ollie decided to pop down to the lab to pay Professor Crumble a visit. What with one thing and another he hadn't seen the old boy for a week, so he thought it best that he check in on him to make sure that he hadn't caused a rift in the space time continuum, caused a massive seismic event, or lost his glasses again. If he was honest with himself though, he rather enjoyed seeing what the mad old duffer had come up with every time he visited.

As he opened the lab door he was greeted by the usual pungent aroma that was a cross between burnt chocolate, and a chemical toilet that had been used a fortnight ago and had no active chemicals of any description in it.

"Hi ho, Prof," Ollie greeted him. "How's it going? Sorry I haven't been down for a while but I've been a bit busy."

The ageing scientist looked up from a mould laden Petri dish and studied Ollie through lenses so thick that in direct sunlight they could easily have started a forest fire a couple of miles away. If there was a forest a couple of miles away of course. Which there was. It wasn't on fire though.

"Ah, young Ollie, lovely to see you. But surely you were here just the other day?" said Crumble.

"That was about a week ago," said Ollie.

"Really! Well, galloping pancakes. That just goes to prove that time certainly does fly when you're having fun I suppose. Conversely if you're not having fun when you're flying then time won't fly at all. Or, if you're timing a flight then you could very well be having fun. Or maybe, if you're in a plane and having fun at the same time, time stops altogether. . . "

"Professor." "Yes, dear boy."

"I came down for a visit, not a lecture on chronology and aeronautics."

"Of course you didn't. Sorry. I do tend to blather on don't I? Would you care to see what I've been working on?"

"That's why I'm here."

Crumble turned to the shelf behind him and grabbed something. Something was as accurate a description as Ollie could come up with anyway. If not that then it could have been anything. The scientist then placed it onto the bench between them and spun it round a hundred and eighty degrees. It was only then that the odd shaped object became recognisable, mostly because of the buttons it had for eyes, and a carrot for a nose.

"A snowman?" asked Ollie, sincerely hoping that he wasn't about to receive a gift-wrapped dwarf.

"Indeed it is. Or a representation of one anyway. This little chap is made of polystyrene. Draw near and observe."

Crumble took hold of the model's head and lifted it, so that the entire thing split about half way down the torso, like a Russian doll. He put that onto the bench and reached into the base from which he pulled a second object. This one was round and about the size of a honeydew melon, and appeared to be covered in poppy plastic, the type that keeps kids entertained for hours at the supermarket whilst their parents get a double hernia pushing overflowing trolleys around. Poppy plastic is the one reason that children never get lost in large shops by the way. You can guarantee that if your little one goes missing you'll find him (or her. Don't want to be accused of being sexist) by the bananas with some poppy plastic in each hand and a piece under each foot doing an excellent impression of a bowl of Rice Crispies (please note that the author strongly advises that potential child kidnappers disregard the last paragraph about supermarkets, bananas, poppy plastic, and the fact that lots of children are to be found in this location. And by child kidnappers I mean adults that kidnap children, not kidnappers who *are* children, because that would be weird).

"Inside this chamber," explained Crumble, "is a high explosive that I've encased in poppy plastic for safety. This all then sits inside the model. The top then goes back on thusly," he put the top back on, "and hey presto, it's ready for deployment."

"Mmmm. And what's this particular wonder called?" asked Ollie, taking a couple of hamstring stretching steps backwards.

"A Bomb in a Bubble Snowman."

Ollie was too dumbfounded to formulate any kind of response, well a rational one at any rate. Perhaps the most terrifying aspect of all this though was what if Crumble ever decided that he'd had enough of living in his lab and wanted to subject the rest of humanity to his strange, wacky and quite frankly extremely dangerous way of thinking. It would make a stay in Baghdad seem like a restful retreat at a monastery with the monks of The Order Of Being Pretty Quiet Really, We Don't Get Up To A Lot And We Don't Go Out Much.

"So how do you envisage this contraption being used then?" Ollie asked, not really sure that he wanted to know, but morbidly curious nonetheless.

"Oh, I don't know," said the Prof, though Ollie suspected he knew damn well what he'd like to do with it but didn't want to let on in case people thought he was mad. Madder anyway. "I suppose it could be utilised to scare children in the winter time when they're being naughty. You could tell them that their snowman committed suicide because they didn't look after him properly. You never know it might instil a sense of responsibility into the little tykes. Actually, it would also be rather handy if the polar bears or the penguins ever decided to rise up and take over the world, which you know is going to happen sooner or later. Imagine armies of these little beauties hidden around the frozen wasteland just in case. They'd never suspect a thing." There was nary a hint of a smile on his face. Professor Crumble was deadly serious.

"Interesting," said Ollie. "Dark certainly, disturbing in the extreme of course, and definitely worthy of an intense psychiatric review, but interesting nonetheless."

"Indeed. Those polar bears aren't to be trusted you know."

In an effort to distract the Professor from formulating any plans for world domination by way of eliminating only the animals at the top and bottom, Ollie pointed at the Petri dish that Crumble had been staring at when he had first come in, which now seemed like a month ago. It still looked like spores flourishing in the bottom.

"What's that?" he asked.

Crumble picked it up and gave it a shake. It turned out to be a fine white powder that had the consistency of baking soda.

"This is one of my best I think," said Crumble, proudly. "An idea that could change the entire world as we know it. It's powdered water."

"You're kidding me, right?"

"Absolutely not," said Crumble, clearly thinking that Ollie was astounded (wow that's amazing!) by the idea and not astounded (you what!) by the idea. "Imagine how beneficial this wonderful invention would be in an area that suffers from perennial drought. All you would have to do is ship in tonnes of my formulation and add water. No one anywhere ever need go thirsty again."

There was absolutely no point whatsoever in trying to explain to Crumble what errant nonsense he had just come out with, no matter how well intentioned. All Ollie could do was what he normally did after a visit to the subterranean nuthouse. He smiled politely, wished him good day and left him to his majestically mad ramblings. And locked him in of course. The world wasn't ready for Professor Rufus Barber Crumble.

Ronnie stepped outside and took a deep breath, trying to get the conversation that he'd just been involved in with Flug out of his head. He loved the big dope to bits but he could be such hard work sometimes. Well, most of the time actually. Still, if nothing else, it gave a group of confirmed bachelors a bit of an insight into what having a child was like. Okay, so the child in question was the evolutionary equivalent of a mushroom and wouldn't be able to point to his nose without poking his eye out, but you couldn't have everything. Beggars can't be choosers after all. (In fact, and in direct contradiction to that statement, they can. They can choose which town to locate themselves in, where to sleep, which is always in the fresh air, who to ask for money from and which train station offers the best earning potential. Then there's which super strength liver destroyer to consume, what breed of scrawny dog to have at your side, and which tune to play endlessly on a mouth organ that sounds like it's been tuned by a tonedeaf moose. In fact beggars have lots of choice so the phrase is now going to be 'People who work for a living forty hours a week and have a family to look after and have to indulge in tasks which include, and aren't limited to shopping, cleaning the house, washing the car, taking the kids to school and hoping there's enough money left over after the monthly bills to take the aforementioned sprogs on an outing that they won't enjoy anyway before the whole thing starts all over again on Monday morning... can't be choosers'. There you go. A bit of social realism for you. It's uncomfortable I know, but necessary nonetheless). Ronnie glanced around and saw that the night was in full swing. In fact, a drunken demon was currently swinging from a lamppost right at that very moment and would no doubt be there all night. It was coming on for one in the morning, which meant that Skullenia was as active as any normal town or village might be in the middle of the day.

Of course, when I say active I don't mean loads of people out shopping for bargains, or kids bunking off school, or office drones dashing round frantically to get their banking business concluded so that they can get back to their places of work before their jobs-worth bosses have a panic attack. No, this was more of a shuffling, staggering, floating and altogether more ethereal and ghostly affair that was punctuated by howls, screeches, screams or a combination of the three.

Spirits and apparitions filled the dark sky, as did witches and warlocks on their various flying thingamajigs, (they ranged from the traditional broomstick and the odd carpet or two, to the not so conventional sofa used by Gadrick the Rotund, a portly chap whose friends called him Three Piece. It wasn't anything to do with the sofa, he didn't like wearing trousers), and bats of every demeanour swooped through the darkness in search of something to drink.

Below the airborne bedlam, creatures that defied any sort of classification wandered slowly about the streets. Some were hungry, some were thirsty, and the rest, who knew. It was certainly an eclectic mix that was for sure. If you're struggling to imagine exactly what it was like, think of a cross between a George A Romero film and a partisan Iron Maiden audience circa 1986. Or, if you live anywhere near Glasgow, open your curtains.

Ronnie crossed the street, passed the fountain and sauntered breezily the couple of hundred yards or so to the 'corner shop.' It wasn't actually on a corner to be honest, but it was the only establishment of its kind in town, and you can't very well have an 'almost on the corner shop' now can you? You'd feel silly saying, 'I'm just off to the shop that's almost on the corner but not quite on the corner'.

Surprisingly though, and going against everything that we've thus far discovered about the fair town of Skullenia, Grendle's was comparatively normal when it came down to it. Obviously you couldn't go in there for a Mars Bar or the latest edition of the Radio Times, and there was always a chance that when you left, your body might have been modified slightly, but it had shelves with stuff on them so there you go.

Narrowly missing a wandering splat of ectoplasm, or Bernard as was more commonly known, with a deft side step, Ronnie entered the shop to the clanging of the little silver bell that hung over the door. Old Grendle had a habit of nipping out the back to check on his various whatever it was that needed checking on and nine times out of nine he wouldn't have had a clue who, or what had entered his establishment. DONG, the bell rang out, announcing for two hundred yards in every direction that Grendle had someone on the premises. Quite how such a tiny object made such an ear-splitting racket was beyond Ronnie, every other customer who entered the shop, and the laws of acoustics. He reckoned that Mrs. Ladle must have had a hand in it. She was quite a compact little creature, but some of the banshee like wails that she was able to create were truly marvellous, especially after she'd had a double helping of curried bat wings and a few pints of Oxfords Thwack. As far as he was aware she was the only person who could shout in high definition.

The door swung shut eliciting another DONG that could have burst an ear drum a couple of time zones away.

"Grendle!" Ronnie called out. "It's Ronnie, mate. I want some baccy." Ronnie's brow furrowed and he absently scratched his cheek. Grendle always came out after the tolling of the first bell. Always. He could have been in another part of town and he would have appeared in the shop before the door shut. It was one of the main tenets of his business vision. The customer always comes first, because he would always want something, and he would always have money to spend.

There was no way that the old boy would let potential profits walk out of the door.

"GRENDLE!" Ronnie called out again, only this time in capital letters. There was still no reply, and no matter how hard he listened he couldn't detect any sounds at all from anywhere in the shop or the back room. All he could hear were the muffled goings on outside. Feeling the hairs rise on the back of his neck, and noticing that his heart was beating ever so slightly faster, Ronnie tentatively stepped forward, all the while carefully listening, but all that he could hear now was the pad of his own footsteps and the rush of blood in his ears. He lifted up the hinged counter that nestled between the sweet racks and the till and crossed over into shop keeper territory.

"Grendle, come on, man. What are you playing at? My lungs are rapidly clearing up."

Ronnie didn't realise but he'd lowered his voice, and a wobbly hint of nervousness had crept into it.

The door to the back room was just to his right, next to the tobacco stand. Without even realising what he was doing, what with listening out for any sort of noise and trying to create any of his own, Ron nie grabbed a pouch of Smouldering Fluff from the shelf and left the money on the counter. He was many things, some of them less than savoury and no doubt against the law (both judicial and natural) in ninety nine percent of the civilised world, but he was no thief.

As he stepped into the back room and was about to call out again, the sight that greeted him stopped the words dead in his throat. Grendle was sprawled out on the floor, flat on his back and out colder than a yeti's fridge. Ronnie rushed over to the elderly shopkeeper and knelt down beside him, checking desperately for any signs of life. Then he remembered that Grendle was a ghoul and that he'd have more chance of finding signs of life on a piece of toast. Just then Grendle's eyes flickered open and he moaned wearily as if he'd just woken up from an extremely long slumber, which was handy because he kind of had. Ronnie grabbed him firmly by the shoulders and shook him gently.

"Grendle. Grendle. Are you alright? What happened? Did you fall or something?"

The shopkeeping ghoul slowly lifted his head of the floor and propped himself up on his elbows.

"I. . . I don't know," he said, voice unsteady. "One minute I was in here getting some Dreaded Wheat to put out and the next. . . I haven't got a clue, Ronnie, really I haven't."

Ronnie looked around the room for anything that might help him in trying to work out what had happened here, but there didn't seem to be a single clue. The place was as neat and tidy as usual and there was no indication that there had been a struggle of any kind.

"Do you remember who was in the shop last?" he asked, helping the old fella into a chair.

"I think I do actually," replied Grendle, a look of concentration on his face, but a faraway look in his eyes. He was obviously still very groggy. "Hector came in for a bottle of Hornswaggler, then after that Mr. Singh arrived to collect the latest copy of Assassins Monthly and then, oh I remember, Ewan Death wanted some cereal, which is what I was getting from out the back." He rubbed a hand across his eyes and shook his head. "And that's it. The next thing I remember is you."

"Hang on a second," said Ronnie. He went back out to the shop and checked the till.

"At least we can rule out theft as the motive," he informed Grendle when he returned. "All the money is still there."

"I'm not so sure about that," said Grendle. "Look." He pointed to a shelf that was to Ronnie's left. It was stacked with glass jars full of sweets (he'd tried selling jars full of glass sweets but they didn't prove to be very popular. Only Flug seemed to like them). There was a gap.

"What was there?" asked Ronnie.

"A jar of Sherbert Demons," replied Grendle.

"Mmm. Is there anybody in particular who buys those on a regular basis?"

"No, actually. I haven't sold any for a long time. That jar must be all of twenty years old. Why on earth would someone want to steal a jar of old sweets? If they'd asked I probably would have let them have them for nothing," said Grendle.

Ronnie nodded his head but he doubted that very much. He knew for a fact that Grendle had a piece of string tied up in the kitchen that had tea bags hanging on it. The tight old so and so would use both sides of the toilet paper if he could.

"Well, be that as it may," said Ronnie, "will you be alright for a few minutes while I go and find Constable Gullett?"

"Is that really necessary?" pleaded Grendle. "I don't want to make a fuss."

"Oh, I think so. We can't have thieves running about the place thinking that they can get away with this sort of naughtiness can we?"

"No. I suppose not."

"Right answer. Now you just take it easy while I'm gone. I'll be back soon."

———

Around about the same time that Ronnie was dealing with the unfortunate Grendle, two figures were walking hand in hand through the Skullenian Cemetery, or as it was more commonly known, The Dead Centre of Town.

"Oh, Noah this is so romantic. I can't remember the last time that I was this happy. Promise me that we'll always be together."

The second, taller figure stopped and turned to face his companion.

He took her three hands in his and kissed each one of them tenderly. Then he looked her lovingly in the eye and smiled, revealing a beautifully maintained set of fangs that a tiger would have been jealous of. "You know you're the only one for me, Gertie. Ever since the night we met I knew that I would never look at another girl. And, if you'll let me, I'll spend the rest of my unnatural life trying to make you happy." "Oh, you do, you do," she gushed before covering Noah in big, sloppy, wet but well intentioned kisses.

Five minutes later they continued their promenade under the pale moonlight.

"Do you think it'll always be like this?" asked Gertie.

"I suppose so, yes" said Noah. "But then cemeteries don't tend to change much do they?"

Gertie detached herself from Noah's clutches and gave him a gentle slap on the arm in feigned shock.

"You know exactly what I mean you naughty bloodsucker. Us." "I'm sorry. Of course it'll always be like this," said Noah, stifling a cheeky snigger. "You'll never get rid of. . . "

Gertie walked on a few more paces before she realised that not only was her hand empty, but so was the space next to her that had previously been occupied by her boyfriend.

"Noah," she called out. "NOAH!" ". . . n . . . re."

"Noah, is that you? You'll have to speak up. I can't hear you properly."

"I. . . wn... ere."

In spite of being more loved up than a very loving person who was in love with a really lovely person who was lovely, Gertie was starting to get a tad miffed.

"Noah Memo, this had better not be one of your silly practical jokes. Remember what happened the last time. The poor cat still can't walk past the bathroom."

"I'M DOWN HERE!"

The voice seemed to come from about ten feet behind her and, strangely, from about six feet below.

Gertie followed the disembodied voice which ultimately led her to the side of an open grave. Luckily the moon light was bright enough for her to see into its depths.

"What on earth are you doing down there?" she asked.

Noah was sat on his backside on top of a coffin looking up at his girlfriend. He had a very hacked off look on his face.

"I'm not on earth. I'm bloody well under it. And my bum hurts."

"Noah."

"Yes, dear."

"You do realise there's no lid on that coffin don't you?"

Noah looked down. There, between his splayed legs was the head of a, well he didn't exactly know who or what it was but that was beside the point quite frankly. Ultimately he was sat on top of a rotting corpse and the remains of its putrefying cranium was staring up at him from between the neatly pressed creases of his trousers.

"Oh terrific," he said as he attempted to wipe himself clean of dirt, dust and various other particles of cadaver related detritus. "I just had this suit laundered as well." He gazed around at the earthly confines of his situation. "Shouldn't this be filled in?" he asked nobody in particular.

"What do you mean?" asked Gertie.

"Isn't it obvious? If there's an occupied coffin down here there should, traditionally, be a couple of tonnes of mud on top of it. You only leave graves open if they're empty, surely."

"I see your point," said Gertie whom, it has to be said, wasn't exactly the sharpest bulb in the box (see, even the analogy is wrong). "But what does it mean?"

Noah got himself to his feet and perched on either side of the coffin. "Well, I'm no expert, but it would appear that maybe someone has come along and, for whatever reason, dug it up."

"Maybe the little man who works here forgot," said Gertie, helpfully. "That's not very likely," answered Noah, testing the earthen walls with a few well-placed slaps. "Grave diggers are usually quite conscientious when it comes to leaving vast, open death-traps in the ground. And I think you'll find that the large mound of soil that you're standing next to is a bit of a giveaway." Being a vampire, Noah was used to the aroma of freshly dug earth. He had to take a suitcase full of the stuff on holiday and couldn't even spend the day at Gertie's unless he had a couple of buckets full just in case he nodded off. "Gertie, love, have a look around to see if

you can find something I can use to get out of here will you please?"
"Okay. Like what?"

"A ladder or some rope should do the trick."

A couple of minutes later, after raiding a small hut that she'd stumbled across, Gertie returned.

"I found this," she announced. "What is it?" asked Noah.

"A rope ladder," she said. "Perfect. Get it down here then."

After explaining to Gertie that she needed to secure one end of the rope ladder topside rather than throwing the whole thing down to him (she did you know), Noah threw it back to her, had her tie it off and climbed out. At last he was reunited with his love.

"What do we do now?" she asked. "We could fill it in I suppose. I have got my best frock on but at least it would stop anyone else having an accident."

Noah rubbed a hand over his face and shook his head.

"That's very community spirited of you, my darling, but I think we need to leave it as it is and inform Constable Gullett. There's definitely something not quite right here."

———

Constable Gullett, the sole embodiment of law and order in Skullenia, was diligently walking his beat. He didn't have a set route as he preferred to leave what might happen to chance, and besides, performing the same task in the same way over and over again had the capacity to become boring beyond measure. If there was one thing that he'd learned over the last forty years of policing it was that spontaneity was the key to effective thief taking. Never give the bad guy a chance to work out your routine was his motto. More importantly he'd also learned that the uniform was a sure-fire way of almost never having to pay for anything, and that people had a habit of reporting the strangest of incidents.

His latest call had been to a dispute on the outskirts of town. A tourist had bought a cuddly toy from an itinerant merchant and then complained when said fluffy purchase had taken off one of his fingers. Whilst he did inform the tourist that shopping in and around Skullenia wasn't quite the same as a trip to Hamleys, he did agree that maybe the proprietor of the mobile jumble sale should reconsider advertising some of his products as 'cuddly toys'. As Gullett had explained, the dictionary definition of a cuddly toy states that it is 'a toy animal made from cloth and filled with a soft material so that it is pleasant to hold' which for the purists of lexicography, was the polar opposite of what the gentleman was actually selling. Nowhere in the description are the words horned, sharp, dangerous, poisonous, or possibility of amputation mentioned. (If you ever get the chance to visit the aforementioned wandering salesman make sure that your clothing is up to scratch or, at the very least, is up to being scratched. Life insurance isn't a bad idea either).

So, with the tourist more culturally aware and the business owner working on a new sign, Gullett had resumed his beat confident in the knowledge that that was probably going to be the highlight of his evening. Although not one to complain, he did after all love his job and its responsibilities, when it came to out and out villainy, Skullenia barely registered on the naughty radar. He never dealt with anything more serious than some of the local youngsters trying to sneak into the Bolt and Jugular for a drink, or Mrs. Ladle and her witchy friends getting tanked up and indulging in a spot of drink flying. One thing was for sure though. At some point during the night he would end up scraping old Hector off the pavement and pouring him through his front door.

Gullett rounded a corner and decided it was time for a well-earned mug of tea and a gargantuan, continent sized piece of cake as an hour and a half of tireless crime busting was thirsty work that literally incinerated the calories. What Gullett got up to didn't qualify as that of course, the average traffic cone used up more energy than the good constable, but he was hungry and thirsty so there.

Weighing up the many options that were open to him he decided to drop in on Ollie. It was warm; the tea was good, there was always something tasty to eat, and seeing as it was about to hammer it down, it was the closest available port of call. Gullett stepped off the pavement and was about to cross the town square when all holy hell broke loose. Or, to put it another way, two people shouted at him at the same time.

"Constable!" "Officer!"

"Someone's broken into. . . "

"I was walking through the cemetery... " ". . . and knocked him out.
. . "

". . . massive great big hole. . . "

". . . the strange thing is. . . "

". . . fell right into it. . . "

". . . all that they've taken. . . "

". . . landed right on my backside. . . " ". . . jar of Sherbet Demons...
"

". . . coffin lid was missing. . . "

". . . Grendle's alright I think. . . "

". . . seems a bit odd of you ask me... " ". . . just got a bit of a
headache... "

Gullett stood resolute and, putting his hands on his not inconsiderable hips, announced, "Quiet please people. I can't make out head nor tail what either of you is rambling on about. All I got was someone's backside is a massive big hole, and that Grendle's sherbet seems a bit odd. Now, decide between the two of you who's going to go first, then hopefully I'll be able to make some sense of what's going on."

Ronnie took his tobacco from his pocket and proceeded to roll a smoke. He nodded his head to the young man and his companion indicating that he should go first.

Noah recounted what had happened to him at the cemetery.

"And it wasn't until I got out and looked down," he continued, "that I noticed that the body had an arm missing. The right one to be precise. Now, I may not know much about the funeral business per se, but I know that Mr. Coffin is very particular about putting the deceased into the ground whole. He buried my dear grandfather last year after his combine harvester accident and you couldn't see a single join."

Caractacus Coffin was Skullenia's undertaker, a business that he had owned for many a decade. He was a diligent practitioner who took great pride in his work and was meticulous to the nth degree when it came to handling the dearly departed, no matter how many times they ended up in his workshop. Due to their nature, not many creatures died just the once you see, meaning that multiple visits were a common theme in the town and his the only undertakers in the world that offered a loyalty card.

Paintpot the ghoul for instance, had been interred at least a dozen times now, although on each occasion there was less and less of him to bury. At the moment he was resting in his plot safely housed in a small, leather suitcase.

"Very well, young Noah. We'll look into this grave of yours," said Gullett, very pleased with the quip even though it was out of place and inappropriate (still, he wouldn't be a proper policeman if he didn't offend at least three or four people every shift). He turned to Ronnie. "Right then, Ronnie. Away you go."

Ronnie told his story next, and seeing as the victim of this potential crime was still above ground (it didn't matter that he was deader than a dead dinosaur), Gullett's keen investigative skills told him that Grendle's was the place to start. Besides, the cemetery didn't have a kettle. "Noah," said the Constable. "I want you to go to Master Splint and tell him everything that you told me, and take him to where it happened alright?"

"Yes, officer," Noah said as he and Gertie trotted off. Ronnie and Gullett made their way to Grendle's.

————

"I know you're lying," said Ollie.

"I am not," said Stitches, cut to the quick. "Whoever heard of someone called Fred Stinks?"

"Be that as it may, it's the truth. He was at my school and that was his name. I sat behind him in geography."

Ollie shook his head and waved a dismissive hand at his colleague. "Go on then, get on with it. Let's hear your story," he said.

"Well, he had a really hard time as you can no doubt appreciate," Stitches explained. "Just imagine going through your formative years with a name like that. No one ever said simply, 'Oi, Fred' or 'Hi, Fred' it was always, 'Oi, Fred Stinks' or 'Who's that? It's Fred Stinks'. Anyway, time went on and we went through primary and junior school and eventually university, and do you know, in all that time it just carried on. Even the professors weren't averse to using the poor chaps name as a punch line. I can still remember seeing him in lectures, head bowed down, resting on his arms, tears dripping onto his text book. Well, as you might expect it all became too much for him."

Ollie leaned forward and put his elbows on his desk. He was quite taken with the story now.

"Oh no," said the half vampire, a hint of concern in his voice. "Don't tell me he went and did something silly."

"No, no. God bless you, no," said Stitches. "Nothing so drastic. He went down to the local council offices and changed his name by deed poll."

"What a good idea," said a relieved Ollie. "What did he change his name to?"

"Harry."

Ollie picked up a rather hefty paperweight, a paperweight that ironically, and in common with paperweights everywhere, wasn't ever used to hold down any paper at all, and launched it at Stitches.

"You total and utter bumhead. Of all the. . ."

Ollie's outburst was cut off by a knock at the door. "Come in," he growled through gritted fangs.

Noah and Gertie entered nervously. Rumours still abounded about the agency premises, a legacy of Gorge's tenure at the helm, and in keeping with every small town or village that has a haunted house that strikes fear into the local youths, Skullenia boasted Ollie's home. It was the sort of place that kids would dare each other to stay overnight in, after telling stories of murder, mutilations, manglings, and any other horrible thing beginning with M that they could think of. It was a testament to Gorge's legend that even in a place such as Skullenia; a single building could inspire such fear.

Noah tentatively introduced himself and Gertie before telling Ollie not only about the events that had transpired earlier that evening to the pair of them, but also what had happened to Grendle.

Whilst he was doing this, Stitches noticed that Gertie was staring at him so, not being one to be impolite, he stared back. Then he saw that Gertie's gaze flickered upwards and hovered for a moment on his forehead. He was just about to enquire as to why she'd started a round of visual ping pong when he suddenly recalled what had happened just before the two visitors had entered. He got up and went over to the mirror.

"Bugger," he said to himself.

The paperweight had left a large paperweight sized dent above his right eye, or to be more correct, where his right eye should have been. The ocular orb was currently resting on his cheek giving him a rather panoramic view of the carpet. He tilted his head and as unobtrusively as he could, if such a thing is possible when reinserting bodily parts into their appropriate vacant space, popped the aforementioned squidgy sphere back into its rightful place. The dent, however, would take a bit more time, effort and steam to sort out.

"Have you seen the divot you've made in my head?" he asked, turning away from the mirror. "It'll take me ages to get rid of that. I'll have to get Crumble to panel beat it out."

"Excuse me for a moment would you, Noah," said Ollie, turning to face his moaning colleague. He stifled a giggle when he saw Stitches concave forehead. "To be fair," he continued, "you kind of asked for it didn't you?"

"I don't think so somehow," said Stitches, sarcastically. "At no point during the conversation do I recall saying to you, 'please chuck that heavy, blunt and quite frankly, rather pointy potential murder weapon at my cranium'. That was out of order as you well know."

"Well possibly," said Ollie, who out of the corner of his eye could see Noah and Gertie looking rather puzzled by the whole display. "But you'll be alright. Anyway, did you hear our young friends' story?"

"I did, yes."

"Excellent. Get hold of Ethan and get him to meet you, Noah and Gertie at the cemetery if you would. It sounds as if something untoward may have gone on, and if that's the case then Ollie and his crew will get to the bottom of it faster than a. . . quickly moving... um... "

"Still haven't come up with a slogan then?" said Stitches. "It's a work in progress. To the graveyard."

"Fine. I'll see what we can dig up. What are you going to do? Batter someone with an ink well?"

"No. I'm going over to Grendle's to meet up with Ronnie and

Gullett. We'll meet back here later to discuss our findings. To the Batmobile."

"I think that one's taken."

———

Stitches, Noah and Gertie met up with Ethan at the entrance to the cemetery after the lycanthrope had finished up his meal at Mrs. Strudel's. Although he was a part time, carnivorous hunting machine and tended to dine alfresco quite a lot, he had developed a taste for Mrs Strudel's rice pudding and tried to avail himself of a gargantuan portion of it at every available opportunity. It was a strange desert that never looked the same twice. Today it might be so runny that you'd need a straw and a bib, whilst tomorrow you might have to hire an angle grinder and have a dentist appointment booked.

Still, however it looked it was the best ricey puddingy type rice pudding ever made, and no matter how much of the thick, gloopy, gelatinous concoction he wolfed down it was never enough. When he'd first tried it he'd quipped to Mrs. Strudel that it was a good job he got regular exercise in the forest a couple of times a week otherwise he would have been busting out of his fur and unable to hunt anything that moved quicker than a tree stump. He could have asked her for the recipe of course but decided against it so that the dish kept its mysterious allure. That was the mistake that Dr. Jekyll had made when he'd enquired what she put into her dwarven chocolate pudding that gave it such a distinctive flavour. Suffice it to say that the details were never made public, she didn't like her recipes spread about, but it was something that had no business whatsoever being in a sweet treat. Dr. Jekyll never ate the choccy dessert again, and for some inexplicable reason he felt nauseous whenever he passed by a cat litter.

"Hi mate," said Stitches as Ethan approached the wrought iron gates. "Enjoy your dinner?"

"Oh, you bet," said the lycanthrope, still able to taste it. "I don't know what she does to it but that rice pudding of hers is amazing."

"I'm sure it is. I've heard it's great at keeping tiles up as well." Stitches was quite often disparaging about people's culinary choices, but that was only because he couldn't indulge himself. Truth be known, he'd give his right arm for a bacon sandwich. Or Flug's at the very least. The zombie pointed to his two companions. "Do you know these two?"

"I do indeed," said Ethan, nodding politely at Noah and Gertie. "So, what's going on here then?"

A brief synopsis, a ten-minute stroll and a couple of stumbles later, the four of them were stood around the offending grave.

"Is this exactly how it was when you left it?" asked Ethan.

"Sure is," answered Noah, peering into the hole from a healthy distance. "We walked along the path and whoosh, down I went."

"The ladder is still there if you want to have a closer look," said Gertie, helpfully. "I got it from the groundsman's shed."

"Was he in there?" asked Stitches.

"I don't know actually," said Gertie. "It was hanging on the wall outside so I didn't bother going in or knocking to ask. I just grabbed it and came straight back because I was worried about my little dumpling."

"Gertie, please," said a horrified Noah. "Not in front of people."

Vampires weren't big on public displays of affection. Apparently it was bad for their image. Go figure.

Stitches suppressed a laugh and indicated to Ethan that he was going to speak to the grounds-keeper, Biddle. He was a forest troll and had been tending to the cemetery for as long as anyone could remember and, as in keeping with most of his kind, he wasn't very bright and about as stimulating as a Puritan stag night, but he was, nevertheless, the ideal candidate for his chosen line of work. The only things that forest trolls care about above all others you see, are wood and earth and seeing as the job involved wood and earth, which are the two things that forest trolls care about above all others (did I mention that?), Biddle was perfectly suited to the job because it involved the two things that he cared about above all others, those being wood and earth (I'm sure I mentioned that). Give him that and he was as happy as a forest troll in wood and earth, the two things they cared about above all others. Unless it was more wood and earth of course, in which case he'd be happy as a pig in shit.

Ethan checked that the rope ladder was still securely fastened and lowered himself down into the grave. He then propped himself up on the sides of the coffin in much the same way as Noah had done (it was exactly the same way actually. Let's face it how many different ways are there of standing on a coffin with no lid when it's at the bottom of a bloody great hole?).

"Throw the torch down would you, Noah," he shouted.

Readily equipped he shone the light into the lidless box and illuminated its grisly contents.

"I know you," said Ethan, more to himself than to anyone else as the beam from the torch fell upon the face of the casket's occupant. "Devlin Floom."

"Ethan," called Stitches from the graveside. "I've spoken to Biddle. He didn't see or hear a thing. He finished his rounds at about eleven and he reckons everything was in order. No one was in the cemetery and all the plots were as they should be. He tidies them up every night before he turns in so he should know. He reckons he was back in his hut by half eleven, sorted out some wood and some earth and was asleep by midnight, so whatever happened must have occurred between then and oneish."

"Seems logical," said Ethan. "Here, have a look at this. Recognise him?"

Stitches leaned forward. "I do. That's Devlin Floom. He died about eighteen months ago. I remember the service, virtually everyone from The Bolt and Jugular turned up."

"I've never heard of him. What did he do?" asked Noah.

"Job wise," said Stitches, "he was a labourer for the council. In his spare time he was the best darts player that the pub team ever had. He was their captain for years."

"Notice anything else?" asked Ethan.

"Indeed I do," said the zombie, leaning over a little more to avail himself a better view. "It's just like you said, Noah. His right arm is missing."

Ethan crouched down to study the body more closely. He lifted a flap of cloth that was draped over where the top of the arm should have been, exposing bare flesh beneath.

"The wounds been sewn up and not clumsily either," he observed. "It looks like whoever or whatever did this knew what they were doing. There's a certain clinical expertise on display here. Not that I'm an expert you understand, but the stitching closely resembles the ones that Dr. Zoltan put into my thigh a couple of months back. This needed medical knowledge, not just to close the wound but to get the arm off in the first place without turning the shoulder joint into mincemeat." "But why on earth would they go to the trouble of sewing the wound up?" pondered Stitches. "It's not like Devlin's going to bleed to death or get a nasty infection is it?"

"Maybe he's got a conscience." suggested Noah. "Not if he's dead, surely," said Gertie.

"Well, quite. Let's go and check the rest of the graves shall we, see if any others have been tampered with," said Stitches.

"What's that?" said Gertie, pointing at something in the hole. "It looks shiny. Is it a coin?"

"Whereabouts?" said Ethan, sweeping the torch beam back and forth.

"Just there," Gertie said, insistently, "on the pillow next to his head." Ethan concentrated the light where she had indicated until it reflected off the object. "What's this?" he said as he plucked the item from its position which was just poking out from between Devlin's head and the silk pillow upon which it rested. He held it up to the light.

"What is it, Ethan?" asked Stitches.

"A sweet wrapper," said the lycan, turning the piece of plastic over. "From a Sherbet Demon."

Three quarters of an hour later they'd checked the rest of the graves in the cemetery and unearthed another four disturbed plots, and with the help of Biddle, whom they had roused from a deep slumber, had identified who they belonged to and established that each and every one had a particular body part missing.

There was Walter Thrice, noted local Rotarian and amateur ballroom dancer, who had died during a rather energetic tango. He was missing both of his feet.

Bodkin Sturdyflaps, a troll, who had worked in the carpet mines of Glans for most of his life, was bereft of both of his elbows.

Next was Cecilia Dragon, a psychic medium who had committed suicide after becoming depressed when she realised that her talents for speaking to the dead were of absolutely no use to anyone in Skullenia.

That's not really surprising though is it? There wouldn't have been a lot of point in asking her to contact the dearly departed when you could go next door, ring the bell and pop in for a cup of tea and a chat yourself. Obviously Cecilia could have moved away and practised her talents elsewhere, but as is well known, a gift for communing with the souls of the dead doesn't necessarily come hand in hand with a particularly high IQ. Have you seen Most Haunted? Anyway, for whatever reason, Cecilia's eyes were missing.

The last desecrated corpse belonged to September Last, a local thief who had perished after a furious chase with Constable Gullett. And by furious chase I mean Gullett had seen Last shoplifting, shouted, "'ere I want a word with you,' before becoming winded after slightly increasing his walking speed and having to mount a rather steep pavement. Luckily for Gullett though, and rather not for Last, Bill the Coachman had chosen just that particular moment to come thundering into town with his coach at full, and terrifying speed. No one really knows exactly what happened next, but according to Bill, "He went over top trumps, all fire dance and giant stones before mooning over like a reapers hound and getting completely slabbed." To reiterate, no one knows exactly what really happened.

For whatever reason, Lasts' thighs were gone.

"This is all a bit strange isn't it?" said Stitches, helping Biddle out of Lasts' final resting place. "And you can't recall anything weird going on?" he asked the groundsman (which, when they'd already been informed that the aged troll had slept through entire incident was, of course, about as insightful a question as asking a resident of 1940's London if he'd had a good night's sleep. Still it pays to be thorough I suppose).

"Nothing at all, Sir. I do my rounds, retire to my hut, sort out the wood and the earth and that's it. Anything untoward I would have reported straight away," explained Biddle.

"Fair enough," said Ethan. He turned to Noah and Gertie. "Right, you two get off home whilst Stitches and I meet up with Ollie back at the office. If either of you, or you Biddle, remember anything else then let us know."

With that they left the cemetery.

Ollie cast his gaze over the room at the rear of Grendles' shop for the umpteenth time, but he still couldn't put it together. Why would someone go to all the trouble of clocking the old boy on the head for the sake of a jar of sweets that cost next to nothing? To be fair if you put most of what was sold here next to nothing then nothing would come out looking pretty darn good.

"Well, I've cast my expert eye over the crime scene," said Gullett, jotting something down in his notebook.

"And," said Ollie.

"And what?" said Gullett. "What do you think happened?"

"Oh, good grief I haven't got a clue, lad. It's all most perplexing indeed. Most perplexing."

More perplexing, and screamingly unclear, was how Gullett had remained an employed officer of the law for the last thirty odd years or so when he couldn't work out the simplest of cases. Good luck, turning a blind eye and slightly irregular paperwork probably had something to do with it. Still, that's what happens everywhere else. Most police statements could top a fiction chart.

Ronnie came into the shop at that point and he had a rather pleased look on his face.

"What are you looking so smug about?" asked Ollie. "I've had a thought," said Ronnie, rolling up a smoke.

"Go on," said Gullett, always keen to appraise someone else's view on a situation (if it was marginally coherent, vaguely sensible and something that he could make stand up in court then he'd have it).

"Well, as we all know, whenever anyone enters the shop the bell emits a clang loud enough to be heard on the moon doesn't it?" said Ronnie.

"It does," said Ollie.

"So it seems to me that whoever attacked Grendle must have already been in the shop or, and this is what my money is on, they didn't come in through the front door at all."

"But that's the only way in, lad," said Gullett. "There isn't another door in the entire place. There aren't even any windows, save the one at the front."

"Mind you," said Ollie, "the door to the shop doesn't let people in one at a time does it? A second person could have come in on one ring of the bell."

"That's a fair point," said Gullett. "But Grendle would have noticed another customer in here surely. He came from the back when Ewan came in and he didn't report seeing anyone else. And there's nowhere to hide out there."

"And to substantiate Constable Gullett's point, I've already spoken to Ewan," added Ronnie. "He confirmed that nobody followed him in and that he was definitely alone in the shop."

"Grendle, are you absolutely sure that the front door is the only way in or out?" asked Ollie.

"Totally positive," said the shopkeeper. "I run a tight ship here. I like to know who's on the premises at all times."

"There's got to be something else," said Ronnie. "Something we've overlooked."

They retreated once more to the back room, and even though they'd been over it already they prepared to do so once again.

"Anyone fancy a cuppa?" said Grendle. "A bit of lubrication before we get going might fire up the old grey matter." (And it just might at that. Grendle's tea was renowned for being hotter than the fiery depths of hell, a raging kiln, or that bit of cheese on toast you ate that's now stuck to the roof of your mouth and making a concerted effort to melt your head from the inside out).

Ollie had his doubts about that particular sentiment though. His grey matter was awfully tired, that was his excuse anyway, Ronnie's was frazzled and wasn't so much grey as beer coloured, and Gullett's was about as much use as a set of brakes on a tortoise.

They all agreed, however, and waited whilst the water warmed up in a kettle that looked like it had been worn by a knight during a rather intense jousting tournament. (Actually the knight in question had been Sir Tentodie, an absent minded sort of a chap who had a habit of walloping his head on the portcullis every time he went back to castle after a hard day's serf bating. Maybe he was an ancestor of Flugs. Which bit of Flug is more of a mystery, but they must be related somehow. Who else would wear a kettle on their head?)

Water suitably boiled, Grendle did the honours and passed round the steaming mugs.

"Be a bit careful with yours, Ronnie," warned the shopkeeper. "The handle is a bit. . ."

SMASH!

"Loose perhaps?" said Ronnie, shaking his head. "Oh look. It's all over my shoes now."

"Hold on a minute," said Ollie, who was also staring in the direction of Ronnie's feet. "Look at that."

The floor of the store room was laid with rough cut slabs approximately two feet square, and it was these that had peaked Ollie's interest. The hot tea that had spilled wasn't resting on the surface of the stones. It was running off to one side and disappearing through what appeared to be a small gap. Ollie knelt down and poured his own drink onto the floor in the same spot. The liquid rushed into the gap and disappeared as if it were being hoovered up from underneath. He held his hand over the area. A faint waft of cold air caressed his palm.

"I've got a feeling this could be it," he said, getting to his feet. "Grendle have you got a crowbar?"

"No, but I've got a ravenstick."

"And the difference would be?" asked Ronnie.

"I haven't the faintest idea," said Grendle, retrieving the long piece of black metal and handing it to Ollie. It looked remarkably like a crowbar. "It does the trick though."

Ollie shoved the business end of the tool into the tea devouring gap and leaned on the other end.

"My goodness it's moving," said Gullett, coming over to help. He placed a meaty hand under the slowly rising slab and started to lift. With a loud grating and a blast of stagnant air the stone was loosed from its place. It toppled over with a loud thunk.

"Well I'll be buggered," said Grendle, taking a tentative step forward. "All the years I've been here and I never had a clue that that was there." The 'that' he was referring to was a hole. And not just any old hole, not just any old hole indeed. It was a hole that had steps going down into it and away into the darkness.

The old man grabbed a lantern off a shelf, lit it and handed it to Ollie, who was now lying flat on his belly trying to make out where the steps went. It was a struggle. Even with his half vampire sight he was having a problem trying to see through the intense blackness.

"Well it would seem that we may have found out how the criminal got in and out," said Gullett. "The question is where does it go?"

"And what to do about it?" added Ronnie. "It could be a little dicey.

There could be anything down there."

"I'm not sure we'll be doing anything about it right this second," said Ollie, bringing the lantern back out of the hole. "There's about ten steps, a short corridor and a door. A very big, heavily riveted, and probably very thick, wooden door to be precise."

"It might be open," said Gullett.

"I somehow doubt that," said Ollie, dusting himself down. "There's a massive lock on it by the looks of things. We'd need a key the size of a ravenstick to open it. Trust me, there's no way we're getting through that door without some serious hardware."

"Well that's all fine and dandy," said a perturbed Grendle, "but what am I supposed to do in the meantime? I don't want to stay here when there's a chance that this, whatever it is, could pop up again unexpectedly. I might get seriously damaged next time."

Gullett approached the old boy and gave him a friendly pat on the back. "Not to worry. I'm sure they'll put you up at the Bolt for a few nights until we can get to the bottom of this."

"Good idea," said Ollie. "We'll drop you off on the way back to the office. We need to meet up with the others and find out what's been going on in the cemetery anyway."

They slid the slab back into place, locked up the shop and left.

———

A pair of beady eyes watched as the stone was replaced. They widened as the light grew dimmer and dimmer until, with a loud THWAP, it settled into its former position. A match was struck lighting up a three feet circle of the underground passageway. The figure holding it came out from behind the stairs, a sigh of relief escaping into the gloom as they offered up a silent thank you. A visit to check on the security of the entrance had almost ended up with them being discovered. Only the heaviness of the slab and the reticence of those who had discovered it to venture down had afforded the watcher the time to get to the steps and hide. More care was needed.

The figure blew out the match, discarded it and then reached into a pocket and retrieved a sweet which was quickly unwrapped. The only sound then that indicated the watcher's presence was a gentle slurping as the Sherbet Demon slowly dissolved.

The figure took a massive key and unlocked the imposing wooden door before disappearing through it into the darkness beyond.

———

With Grendle now safely ensconced in the pub and Noah and Gertie sent home to finish what was left of their evening, Ollie, Ronnie and Gullett met up with Stitches and Ethan back at the office. There they'd discussed their various discoveries and were now desperately trying to figure out what it all meant. They'd been at it for about two hours and hadn't gotten very far, which wasn't all that surprising really. Hercule Poirot like, they were not.

"The only connection that I can see," offered Ethan, "is the sweets. Sherbet Demons go missing from Grendle's and we find a wrapper from one in a grave at the cemetery. It's tenuous and extremely coincidental but it's all we've got so far."

"That's even if anything dodgy has gone on at the cemetery in the first place," said Stitches. "For all we know Biddle forgot to tend the graves and that's how they ended up in that state. He's not going to admit to being negligent is he?"

"I don't think that's very likely," said Ollie. "Some of those people have been dead for a couple of years. That long exposed to the elements would have done untold damage to the corpses. And I don't think Biddle is the sort to go digging them up just to have a look. No, this is something else. Something we haven't thought of yet."

"Nevertheless there are offences to be dealt with," interjected Gullett. "At the very least we have a theft of confectionery, an assault on Grendle and a mysterious hole."

"And speaking of strange things with nothing in them, hi, Flug," said Stitches.

"Hi, Stitches. Hello, Mr. Pleeceman. You need to come wiv me."

"Why's that, Flug?" said Constable Gullett.

"Cos Mrs. L said so. She said get you."

With that Flug took hold of Constable Gullett, threw him over his vast shoulder and headed for the door.

"Flug!" said Ronnie, insistently. "Put him down. He can walk there by himself. You don't need to carry him."

"Oh, okay." He placed Gullett back onto the floor. "Me sorry."

As they made their way outside, Ollie asked Flug if he knew what was going on. His hopes of an intelligent answer weren't high of course because Flug didn't know what was going on ninety-nine-point nine percent of the time, but it was worth a shot. (The other point one percent he was asleep, and he didn't know what that was about either. The fact that he woke up prostrate, dribbling and staring at the ceiling every day was a constant source of terror because he didn't know where he was, how he'd got there, or what he should do next. Ah well, never mind. At least he was qualified to join The House of Lords if nothing else).

The two-word answer that he gave said it all though, and explained rather a lot.

"Maudlin Mandrake."

Wolfgang 'Maudlin' Mandrake was officially the most miserable and depressed person in the entire world. He'd even been awarded a certificate for it in fact, which had cheered him up no end. The problem was he was so depressed that he had developed the habit of trying to end his existence at every available opportunity. There was one tiny sticking point though. He was absolutely rubbish at it. He'd tried overdosing but had ingested oestrogen tablets instead of painkillers. Not only had he not become dead, he'd spent two months sporting a fair-sized pair of boobs and amassing a rather impressive collection of fancy shoes. He'd also tried shooting himself with a starter's pistol, slashing his wrists with a pipe cleaner, bashing his brains in with a sponge, and hanging himself from the branch of a tree that wouldn't have supported the weight of an ant a fortnight into a crash diet.

"I wonder what he's tried this time?" wondered Stitches. "Throwing himself into the path of an oncoming pensioner perhaps?

Or maybe it's something more direct this time. Perhaps he's stabbed himself with a banana."

"It could be anything," said Gullett, who had previous experience with the crestfallen clot. "The last time I dealt with him he was trying to drown himself in the river, but he weighed himself down with three helium balloons and a rubber ring. We found him seventeen miles downstream."

Now, some of you more sympathetic readers may think that Mandrakes continued suicide attempts were a cry for help, whilst others of you out there of a more pragmatic bent may come to the conclusion that he's a consummate show off of epic proportions who loves getting as much attention as he can. Now clearly that's a matter for the individual, their sensibilities and their feelings towards the plight of a fellow human being, so far be if for me to sway you one way or the other. At the end of the day you need to decide for yourself, but bear in mind this. Mandrake once tried to electrocute himself by taking off three woolly jumpers at the same time.

By the time that Gullett and the others reached the town square a large crowd, seemingly comprising of most of the townsfolk, had gathered around the fountain. They were talking in hushed whispers and pointing at something that was obscured by the seething mass of bodies.

"I think he's a goner this time." "Ouch, that looks painful." "Poor chap. So misunderstood."

"When I went on holiday I saw an elephant fall over."

Even most of the regulars from The Bolt and Jugular had left their stools to come and see what all the fuss was about and that was virtually unheard of. As one person was heard to remark, "I've never heard the like." (Told you it was unheard of). Obviously that didn't include Hector Lozenge of course, who wouldn't leave an alcoholic drink behind if you paid him with alcohol.

Others, with well-intentioned words and smiles barely hiding their thinly disguised avarice, had leapt upon the situation and taken the opportunity to earn a little extra cash. The Stella triplets were offering their wares in a buy one get all three special, a travelling salesman had turned up (as they invariably do when a crowd has gathered) and was trying to sell some clothes that would have looked out of date during

The Dark Ages, and Mrs. Strudel was trying to entice those present into purchasing some tasty treats from a mobile oven that looked more like a transient mortuary than a cooking appliance.

"Make way please, make way," shouted Constable Gullett in a booming and authoritative voice as he snow ploughed his large belly through the crowd. "Come on now, people, move along please. I'm sure there's nothing to see here so there's no need to stand around gawking like a bunch of tourists."

Gullett, closely followed by Ollie, Stitches, Ronnie and Ethan, finally made it through the undead mass and saw what everyone was looking at.

"Obviously I was wrong," shouted Gullett, sounding slightly less boomy and not quite as authoritative as before. "There is quite plainly something to see here, but could you please all stand back so I can determine exactly what we're dealing with. I get paid to gawk."

(On a side note why do police officers insist on informing members of the public that 'there's nothing to see here' when there clearly is? Surely that's the precise reason why people gather together in the first place, *because there's clearly something to see*, be it a car crash, a potential suicide or a cat up a tree [this could also be a suicide if the cats feeling a bit down]. A group of people aren't going to stand about in a huddle staring in wonder at something mundane like a crisp packet are they? Unless they're from deepest, darkest Norfolk of course, where the sight of an errant tube of Pringles once brought half the county to a standstill because the locals thought it was the Devil's work. They might have been right though. They were prawn cocktail.

It stands to reason that anything out of the ordinary, or in the slightest bit interesting, and by interesting, I mean having the possibility for people to see internal organs, death, destruction, or a tramp dancing in his pants, is going to attract attention. It's human nature and it's always going to happen. If a copper wants to make best use of that particular phrase in a relevant setting then he should stand in front of a television whenever a reality show comes on. For a start he'd be telling the truth, oh, first time for everything, and he'd be guaranteed a job for life because they're on all the bleeding time).

The fountain, for 'twas that which everyone was interested in, looked the same as usual for the most part. The deep red blood was flowing normally from the demon's mouth, the gargoyles were settling in after a shift change, and Blind Arnold had decided that this was the optimal time for him to have another go at retrieving all of the coins that had been thrown into its crimson depths. Little did he know that it was a futile pursuit though. The dead of the night had been out in the dead of the night and swiped the lot, so creating yet another misdemeanour for Constable Gullett to sort out when he had the time, the inclination, and the opportunity to look up the definition of theft in his Big Book of Crime. Well, he would once he found out who'd nicked it.

The only thing that was out of place in the night time tableau was Maudlin Mandrake, or to be more precise, the position that he was in. At present he was lying sprawled across one of the fountains corner stones, soaking wet, out cold and clutching a piece of paper.

"Oh, not again," said Gullett, approaching the prostrate mess and retrieving the note which, on inspection, was an inky and bloody jumble that was totally indecipherable, although it no doubt contained Mandrakes' usual ramblings about cruel worlds, not being understood, why nobody seemed to like him, and wondering when velvet pan taloons and Afghan coats were going to come back into fashion.

"I think I can pretty much figure out what happened here," said Ollie. "But there's one thing I don't get."

"Go on," said Ethan, who'd come to the same conclusion, in that Mandrake had tried to end his miserable existence by leaping off a ten-foot-high fountain into six inches of blood.

"One of his legs is missing," said Ollie.

"If you crack his head open you'll probably find that his brain's gone AWOL as well," said Stitches. "He'll be able to challenge Flug in next year's densest being competition if he keeps this up." Flug had won this year by being so dense that he'd turned up on the wrong day of the wrong month in the wrong village.

Gullett had given up on the note and was now talking to various people in the crowd. After he'd enquired if any of them had anything to eat he thought he better try to find some witnesses, thus affording Ollie and his colleagues a chance to examine the scene. Even a cursory glance told the story and it quickly became evident what had happened to Mandrake's leg. It was also evident that Gullett would remain a simple village bobby until the end of time because he'd missed not only the vital clue, but the blob of mustard that had taken up residence in his moustache, a testament to his prioritising of actions in the face of such a scene.

"Well look at that," said Stitches, squatting down. "It's gone straight through."

When he landed, Mandrakes left leg had shattered a stone slab and buried itself up to the hip in the earth.

"I didn't think the soil in these parts was so soft," said Ollie, joining the zombie at ground level.

"It isn't," said Ronnie from behind them. "That's why people round here don't have gardens. Not ones they can plant anything in anyway. It's easier to work an allotment in Siberia than it is here."

"You could grow frozen peas I suppose," said Stitches, helpfully.

They both prodded and poked the area where Mandrakes leg had disappeared. Clods of earth fell away from the edge along with small chunks of concrete. After a few moments, they both heard the fragments clatter onto a surface below, where they echoed quietly. They both realised the same thing at the same time, but it was Ollie that voiced it first.

"There's a void down there," he said, manoeuvring Mandrake's flaccid leg out of the hole and resting it gently on the surface next to his other one. The hole it left was roughly a foot square, but other than that it was far too dark to give up any of its secrets.

"Ollie use this," said Ethan, who had borrowed Gullett's torch.

"Who'd have thought I'd be looking into two mysterious holes in the same night?" the half vampire said as he flicked on the torch and guided the beam into the darkness. The light was instantly swallowed by the turgid gloom which was so profound that only a small area was illuminated, but it was just enough to show a certain amount of detail, the most interesting of which was a flight of steps leading down into the unknown.

"Another staircase," said Ollie, sweeping the torch back and forth. "I don't know how far they go but they must be there for a reason."

Ethan held out a hand and helped Ollie and Stitches to their feet. As Ollie wiped the dust from his clothes (Stitches didn't bother.

He couldn't distinguish the difference between his own dust and that which he'd picked up off the floor so it was a futile endeavour at best. It's the same logic that dictates why a smoker shouldn't try and get rid of a lungful on a foggy day), Constable Gullett re-joined them.

"Seems like Mandrake tried to kill himself by leaping from the top of the fountain," said the policeman, whilst helpfully pointing to the top of the fountain just in case anyone was unclear where the top of the fountain was. It was at the top. Of the fountain. The top of the fountain got it. "But in true Mandrake style he made a total arse of it resulting in this nonsense. One witness said as soon as he hit the deck the stone buckled and gave way."

"The witness hit the deck?" asked Stitches. "Buffoon," said Ollie.

"Hang on a sec," said Stitches and walked away.

A short time later he returned carrying a pickaxe and a shovel. "Where did you find them?" asked Ronnie.

"Mrs. Strudel's kitchen. You've seen some of the massive joints that she cooks. She's always got utensils like these lying around. And let's face it any dirt and grime that they pick up won't be half as bad as some of the ingredients she uses. You could find most of the contents of her spice rack in a hospital. Or an undertakers for that matter."

In the interim, with a gentle shake, a kind word, and a hefty smack in the chops, Constable Gullett finally managed to rouse Mandrake, and in good old fashioned copper tradition sent him off with a flea in his ear, the threat of a night in the cells if he didn't stop being a tit, and a size fourteen boot up the backside. (Gullett's style of policing was particular to Skullenia and couldn't be practised anywhere else of course. These days if an officer of the law so much at looks at someone in a funny way it's enough to secure a complaint coming in from one of the great unwashed. The next thing the poor bobby knows he's having to justify why he called a ten-year-old that he'd caught throwing stones at trains a 'naughty boy' to outraged parents, a Home Office Select Committee, and a phalanx of terrified senior officers soiling themselves because a member of the public is ever so slightly miffed, and reckons that the police should engage themselves in far more useful pursuits like 'clearin' up the dog poo', or 'catchin' a murdrer or sumfink').

A solid hours work later and the hole had been expanded to the point that someone of a reasonable size could fit through it and gain access to the steps. Or to be more precise, Flug. Busy as usual, he'd been lured away from his game of staring into the middle distance whilst drooling with the promise of an industrial sized bag of sweets if he would go into the dark hole.

"Wot down dere, Ollie?" he asked.

"I really don't know, Flug," said Ollie, handing him the torch. "That's why we need to have a look."

"Is it safe down dere den?" said Flug, as he looked at the torch and wondered what to do with it.

"Oh, I should think so," said Ollie, taking back the torch, switching it on and returning it to Flugs giant hand. "I mean, if it *wasn't* safe and there *was* something evil or dangerous down there then logic dictates that it would have tried to escape by now and wreak havoc up here wouldn't you say?"

Flug weighed up all the information that he'd been given in response to his query, digested it thoroughly, cogitated for a moment or two, and reached his conclusion. "Dis light pretty," he said, ever so slightly mesmerised by the dancing beam. "It look shiny."

"Well quite," said Ollie. "But don't go worrying yourself about it; the rest of us will be coming as well. If anything happens we'll be right behind you. Which it won't. But if it does, we will."

"Make way please, make way. Press coming through."

"Oh no," said Ethan, putting a hand on Ollie's arm and turning him to face the new arrivals. "Look who's here."

The huffing, puffing shambles that was Excalibur Cross, chief reporter for the Skullenian Times, forced his way through the crowd. He was short, round and so florid of face that his cheeks actually radiated heat and light. He looked like he'd gotten dressed for a bet and already had a notebook and pen in his pudgy little hands. He was closely followed by Ramekin Deadhouse, a tall, gaunt and distinguished looking creature who had a rather large camera round his stick like neck.

"I was wondering when you two would show up," said Gullett, the hint of disdain in his voice evident for all to hear. "Still, I should have known shouldn't I? We lift up a few rocks and out you come."

"Now now, officer," said Cross, all smarm, bluster and ill-fitting waistcoat. "There's no need to be hostile. After all we all have a job to do don't we. Granted there's some that may see mine as less than savoury but, if you think about it, it's not that much different than yours."

"And just how did you arrive at that outlandish conclusion?" said Gullett, already starting to bristle.

"Isn't it obvious?" said the reporter, already jotting something down.

"Not to me," said Gullett.

"Really? Well, seeing as you've asked, I'd say it's mostly because we both strive to gather evidence and get to the truth of whatever we're investigating."

Gullett scratched his chin and eyed Cross.

"There is a slight difference though," said the policeman. "I gather evidence and facts about incidents that have *actually* happened, not what I *think* has happened, or what *might* have happened or, even though I do actually know what happened it's not juicy enough a story so I'll *make up* what happened." Gullett closed the short distance between them and thrust a meaty finger at Cross's rotund chest. "We're oceans apart, Cross and you'd be wise not to forget it."

The reporter swallowed audibly and took an involuntary step back. He tried to smile but failed miserably and there was no mistaking the fear in his eyes. Gullett may have had the outward appearance of an overweight, plodding and sometimes bumbling simpleton, but he possessed the heart of a lion and a fist the size of a shoulder of lamb. It didn't pay to take him lightly.

"Shall-l-l-l I take a few pics-s-s-s?" Deadhouse asked, taking the camera from around his neck and removing the lens cap. "We've gott-t-t a deadline to meet you know-w-w-w, Excalibur."

Ramekin Deadhouse's strange way of speaking was due to the fact that he suffered from a rare form of speech impediment that caused him to stutter at the end of words rather than at the beginning. It wasn't a major issue and no one really noticed it anymore, but it did make him sound like a neurotic kettle if there was an S involved, a letter that seemed to come up more if a certain zombie were nearby. Still, it could have been worse. Ramekin's father had been afflicted with paralysis of the sense of humour, which meant that he looked as if he were constantly miserable and possessing about as much personality as a rhododendron bush (he enjoyed his job at the post office though, not that you'd have been able to tell). Needless to say that he didn't live to a ripe old age. He was killed in a fight after being told a joke by an ogre, and what with ogre's not being very good at comedy in general, but thinking that they are and being overly sensitive if criticised, said ogre had cleaved off the head of his audience.

"I think that's going to depend on the good constable here," said Cross, oozing a newly found charm that he hoped would make Gullett see him in a new light. There was of course more chance of Count Jocular becoming a vegetarian monk, but he was nothing if not an optimist (Cross that is. Not Jocular. Jocular wasn't cross. He was a monk. No, a monk would get Cross with a vegetarian. No no, a monk was Cross at Jocular for eating a vegetarian. Hang on, Cross was a vegetarian and was cross at Jocular's monk. Nope, that's not it. Stand by, I think I've got it now, Jocular was cross at Cross because Cross had gotten cross with a vegetarian monk who had made Jocular cross, which had made... I'm going to stop there I think. I've just had a call from the editor. He's extremely cross, not a monk, and does like a bit of swede and carrot).

"Fine," said the policeman, his begrudging acceptance of the term 'freedom of the press' evident in his body language (he stuck two fingers up at the reporter). "But I don't want either of you getting in the way. Are we clear?"

"Crystal," said Cross and Deadhouse in unison. Well, it was almost in unison. Deadhouse added a few more L's.

Torch in hand, Flug led the way down the steps followed by everybody else. At the bottom, a passageway led off into the oppressive gloom and as far as things went, it wasn't very nice. The atmosphere was heavy with portent, and a cloying moisture shrouded them all with its mote like specks. The walls either side of the steps and passageway were dripping with blood from the fountain above. They glistened with a riot of moss and algae that displayed what seemed to be every colour you could think of. The ground, however, apart from a little moisture here and there was relatively clear, which was surprising because the doughy air indicated that the subterranean void had been hidden for many a year. Clearly no one had used it for an extremely long time.

The clatter and subsequent echo from their footsteps resounded off the walls and took so long to dissipate that it sounded like a Roman legion was marching behind them.

As Flug forged on he swept the torch from side to side and up and down. He wasn't doing it to gauge their surroundings or to make sure that the way forward was safe of course; he was just enjoying the pretty patterns that the light made on the stone but it was helpful nonetheless. On one sweep the beam flashed across something that at first appeared to be the end of the passage. It seemed to be about four feet from the floor, round and made of a silver metal that had glistened when the beam had passed over it. It looked just like a door knob.

"That looks just like a door knob," said Stitches.

"Indeed it does," said Ollie. "Flug, point that thing forward would you."

The monster did as he was told, revealing that not only was the shiny object most definitely a door knob, but that it was attached to, of all things, a door.

"This is weird," said Cross as the pace of the group slowed perceptibly. "Why on earth would anyone construct something like this down here? Seems a bit pointless to me."

"It may very well seem pointless to us," said Ethan, "But there has to be a reason for it. Nobody would go to all this trouble for nothing surely."

Eventually they reached the door. Ollie squeezed his way past Flug, who was doing a reasonable job of blocking the passageway with his immense girth, and geared himself up to face whatever was on the other side. Logic dictated that the biggest and strongest should go first in case things turned nasty, but putting Flug up front would have been about as much use as claiming that having Parkinson's Disease was handy for cleaning your teeth. It was well known throughout Skullenia that Flug was the biggest scaredy cat in the world and liable to panic at just about anything. It wasn't that long ago that he'd been reduced to a quivering, sobbing blob after finding a spider the size of a proton in the bathroom. It wasn't his bathroom of course, and the fact that he'd wandered into Cedric the Decapitators house had passed him by completely.

"Be careful-l-l-l," warned Deadhouse as Ollie reached out with his hand. "There could-d-d-d be something-g-g-g in there."

"I'll be gobsmacked if there's anything in there at all to be honest," said Gullett. "And even if there is I doubt there'll be much of it left."

"Could be a deranged troll gone mad after being locked up for decades," said Cross.

"Or a psychopathic demon just waiting to be released so that he can possess a body and wreak bloody havoc," said Ronnie.

"Or maybe a constipated vampire bat who hasn't realised that he can poo upside down," said Stitches.

"Will you lot please shut up," said Ollie, getting annoyed. "Me done a little bit of wee," said Flug.

Ollie put his hands on his hips and addressed his colleagues and the members of the press.

"See what you've all done now with your silly talk." He turned back to the reanimate. "Don't worry Flug. We'll get you cleaned up later once we get back. . . "

"Sshhh," said Stitches, putting a finger to his lips. "Did anyone else hear that?"

There was a scraping sound coming from the other side of the door. It wasn't particularly loud, and it wasn't particularly insistent, and it almost seemed as if whatever was there was just going through the motions, because it had done the same thing a thousand times before. It sounded like fingernails being dragged down the wood.

"Maybe there is someone or something in there after all," said Cross, making yet more notes in his dog-eared note book.

Ollie reached for the doorknob, blatantly ignoring the staggeringly obvious comment. Then, whilst desperately trying to rid his mind of mad trolls, loopy demons, and bats with skid marks, he closed his trembling fingers around the chunk of metal. He was immediately taken aback by how cold it felt, even for him. Not withstanding the fact that his blood was half human, both he, and vampires in general, had an excellent tolerance for freezing temperatures, so much so that on one famous occasion a vampire spent a whole two-week summer holiday in West Wales without feeling the need to wear a two inch thick duffel coat, astronaut gloves and setting himself on fire just to keep the chill out. Yes indeed vampires are that tough, but then again you have to be if you're visiting a country where you're liable to sustain a dislocated larynx simply by asking the way to the shops.

Ollie gave it a twist clockwise then anti clockwise, then jiggled it a bit to the left, then jiggled it a bit to the right, then pushed it in and pulled it out before finally coming to the conclusion that not only was the door locked but that he'd possibly invented a new dance craze (The Undead Lurch perhaps), the rhythm of which was now stuck in his head thanks to the recalcitrant knob. (There must be something there as well but I can't for the life of me imagine what it could be. It's no doubt on the tip of someone's tongue though).

He pre-empted Cross's obvious observation by announcing the fact himself.

"Well-l-l-l that's-s-s-s a bit of a bugger," said Deadhouse as he twiddled with his lens cap. "I was kind of hoping-g-g-g that this would turn into an interesting story-y-y-y."

"Me too," said Cross, jotting down who knew what. "Things have been a bit slow news wise lately. The last decent bit of copy that we had was when we got that tip off that Ivan the Quite Nasty was planning to invade."

Despite his reservations about the reporter, Gullett let out a chortle as he recalled the incident in question.

Ivan the Quite Nasty, or Derek Crankpipe as he would have been known to his friends if he'd had any, was a full-time logistics supervisor in a cleaning products supply warehouse in neighbouring Berevia, who fancied himself as a bit of a tyrannical dictator on the weekends. That was providing that his manager didn't need him to work overtime of course. "Those pesky containers of 'Shift It' won't move themselves you know," was his favourite quip. Due to his work commitments Ivan/Derek usually confined his despotic activities to ranting at passers-by in the High Street, and producing and distributing highly inflammatory leaflets such as 'Fight Capitalism. Send donations now' and 'Bleach. Why does it always smell like poo?'

One weekend though after finishing early on Friday night with a feigned headache, he decided to put into action a plan that he'd been formulating for at least a fortnight. The invasion of Skullenia. And not being one to go off half cocked, he had everything planned down to the last detail. He knew exactly where and when to strike, where best to deploy his military forces, and what constitutional changes he would implement when he seized power, such as the compulsory issuing of tartan booty slippers to every citizen, the banning of the decimal point, and the removal of those horrible cherries from tins of fruit salad to name but three.

Come Saturday morning he got up early, had a spot of brekkie, said goodbye to his dear old mum, and left his flat full of Vim and Vigour (and any other cleaning products that he'd managed to steal from work) and by ten o'clock all was going swimmingly well until an unfortunate incident scuppered his plans.

Just as he was about to sally forth and blitzkrieg his way across the border, he had a puncture and fell off his tricycle badly grazing his knee and denting his bell. He would have soldiered on but after careful contemplation, and as much as it pained him to do so, he decided that he couldn't very well implement his fiendish plan with a bit of a limp and a muffled dinger. Still, it was probably for the best. He'd already been extremely disappointed that fifty percent of his invasion force, Brian from the canteen, hadn't set his alarm and overslept, so he reluctantly decided to postpone the expansion of his empire (currently Flat B, Hemmy Royd Towers, Back Passage Alley, Berevia) until he was feeling a bit better. Besides he had a backlog of a hundred gross of mops that needed sorting out, so he went home.

"I guess we'll have to break it down," said Ronnie, leaning forward and giving the door an experimental shove with one hand. "It could take a while though. It's a solid chunk of tree."

"Ollie," said Flug, tapping Ollie on the shoulder with a finger that could have split a wind sock. "Maybe dere a key under da mat."

"Of course there is," said Stitches. "And look, there's a little holder for milk, and doilies for cakes, and granny sitting in her rocking chair knitting a warm, woolly jumper. Honestly, I don't know where his head's at sometimes."

The zombie's less than gracious observation was cut off as Flug shone the torchlight at the foot of the door.

"Dere. Look," Flug repeated whilst pointing furiously for emphasis. Astonishingly, there on the floor was a wicker welcome mat. They could tell that it was a wicker welcome mat because it was made of wicker and had welcome written on it. It was also a mat.

"That's quite welcoming really. Well, for a hidden underground labyrinth it is," said Ethan. "Shall we see if granny's in?"

Stitches would have said something rude to the big lycanthrope but he liked his head facing forward.

The supernova that was Deadhouse's flash bulb ignited at that moment making all of them temporarily blind.

"Bloody Hell!" said Ollie, rubbing his eyes. "I'd appreciate it if you'd try and not do that too often if you don't mind. Not unless you issue a warning and hand out goggles at least. I've got a bit of a problem with direct sunlight you know and I think that four-million-watt monstrosity counts."

"Sorry gents-s-s-s," said Deadhouse, apologetically. "But I'm sort-tt-t of used to it."

"I'm sure you are," said Gullett at what he thought was the photographer but was, in actual fact, Flug's left shoulder. "But can't you save it for something other than domestic knick knacks?"

By this time Flug had lifted the mat and was now proudly holding a small silver key in his giant hand.

"Me found it in same place as me keep my key," he announced, smiling a smile that was all puckered scars, cold flesh and dribble.

"You haven't got a key," said Stitches as Ollie took the key from Flug. "You've got a flap remember? You have a bit of a problem with doors."

"Oh yeah. . . Wot doors?"

"Do you mean what are doors, or do you mean what doors do you have trouble with?

"Umm. Me mean... "

"Yes," said Stitches encouragingly, hoping for an answer before New Year's Day. 2051.

"Wot doors?" said Flug.

"Never mind all that rubbish," said Ollie, impatiently. "Flug, point the torch at the knob will you."

(If I could, I'd like to mention a small item at this juncture. I'm sure

427

that you, dear reader, will be pleased to note that the author, me, has chosen to disregard the blatantly obvious, and quite frankly childish, 'willie' joke that could easily have been inserted into the tale at this point. Flug, as you would expect, did point the torch at the appropriate, or inappropriate depending on your point of view, area of his trousers, but in the interests of common decency it's a tiny detail that really isn't worth mentioning. The joke that is, not Flugs nether regions, which as you can imagine... well, you know).

Despite the thickness of the door it was clear that whoever, or whatever, was on the other side of it could hear what was going on, because the scraping on the wood seemed to be becoming more insistent and was now being punctuated by the occasional knock.

Ollie slipped the key into the lock and gave it a turn. It went round as smooth as silk and the sound of a couple of tumblers could be heard clicking into place. It reverberated eerily down the passageway.

"Easy now. Sounds like there could be something very pissed off in there," said Ethan, taking up a defensive position at Ollie's side.

Ollie stood poised with his hand on the knob. Ethan stood poised, rigid and ready for action.

Stitches stood poised trying to stop his joints from popping. Ronnie stood poised trying to roll a fag without rustling.

Gullett stood poised truncheon in hand and ready to smash whatever came through the door.

Cross stood poised notebook in hand and pen at the ready. Deadhouse stood poised camera locked and loaded.

Flug stood poised not because he was ready, but because he was trying to remember what a door was.

Ollie pulled the door open. It creaked so loudly, and at such a high pitch that it hurt their ears. When it was finally open they found that they were confronted with a darkness that was so intense if you had thrown a light bulb into it, it would have stuck.

"Flug," said Ollie. "Point the torch inside."

When he did they all gasped at the sight that greeted them.

It was a laboratory, that was evident from the test tubes, beakers and bubbling liquids, but it was what they saw in the middle of the room that drew their immediate attention. There, on what could only be described as a mortuary slab, was what appeared to be a human jigsaw. It was if someone had poured all the requisite parts out of the box, but had yet to sort them out into edge pieces and middle bits. On first sight it appeared that all of the parts were there, but this was probably due to them being so haphazardly arranged on the cold metal of the table. A closer inspection revealed that there was no head or torso.

"Ethan," said Ollie. "Take Ronnie, Constable Gullett, and Flug and get yourselves topside right now. Whoever was responsible for this seems to have gone but they can't be far away. It must have been them making those noises in here. When they heard us they must have made off."

"Good thinking, Ollie my lad," said Gullett. "That was probably the noises we heard. It was them trying to clear out because they heard us." (He knew what he'd just said was a rehash of what Ollie had just said, but he needed to say something even if it *was* a rehash of what someone else had just said. Besides, if Ollie hadn't have said it, Gullett would have said it anyway, rehashed or not. Nuff said!)

Stitches noticed a cord hanging from the ceiling and gave it a tentative pull. He had all sorts of visions flash through his mind as he did, ranging from a spiked ceiling crashing down on them to a secret door opening up and revealing untold visions of hell and other horrible stuff. Luckily it wasn't anything like that, and a light came on over the table that was bright enough to illuminate not only the whole room but their retreating colleagues, who were now three quarters of the way back to the stairs.

"My goodness-s-s-s. It looks like a butcher's shop-p-p-p," said Deadhouse, merrily snapping away as happy as if he were taking pictures at the seaside. "I haven't-t-t-t seen anything like this-s-s-s since we did that article about Mrs Strudels café."

Stitches gingerly placed a hand on one of the forearms resting on the table. "It's freezing," he said. "But it hasn't started decomposing yet which is a plus. Hang on a minute."

He examined the body parts one by one studying each of them closely.

"Well, I'm no expert," he declared, "but judging by the looks of the suture marks on this lot, these are the bits and pieces missing from the cemetery. You can see where Bodkin Strutdyflaps's elbows have been sewn on."

"But where's the rest of it?" asked Ollie.

"Who knows?" said Cross. "Maybe there's a clue in here somewhere."

"You're absolutely right," said Ollie as he picked up a small, leather bound book off a work bench. "And this could be it. It looks like a diary of sorts."

He flicked through the pages and stopped at random.

"Day 12," he read aloud. "Have started collecting the parts but find I am having trouble keeping them fresh. Note to self, must buy a freezer. Or at least a big bag of peas.

Day 23. Almost got it right today but due to inferior equipment I electrocuted myself after which my shoes started talking to me. They weren't very helpful."

Ollie flicked through to the last entry.

"Day 31. I think I may have found the head and torso that I need to complete the project. They're not the best looking and wouldn't win any beauty contests, but anatomically they're perfect."

Stitches was on the other side of the room and was looking at the various items of equipment on display.

"It looks a lot like Crumble's lab," he said, holding up a test tube at eye level and giving it a shake. "Obviously a tad more sinister I'll grant you." The glass phial clinked subtly as he put it back into place. "Mind you, if you're actually brave enough to go into the mad old duffer's house of horrors in the first place, at least you're not liable to trip over any detached body parts lying on the floor," the zombie continued.

"Not unless he's got a new hobby that we don't know about of course. Hey, you don't think he..?"

"Not for a minute. This is something else entirely. In fact, if I didn't know any better," said Ollie, replacing the notebook, "I'd swear this is how Flug started out. Goodness me, you don't suppose that the mad accountant who created him is at it again do you?"

"I wouldn't have thought so," said Stitches. "He got snapped up by some big company in Vena Cava just after he dragged Flug kicking and screaming into the world. He does all their finances for them as well as a little off the record dismemberment."

"Really?"

"Absolutely. High finance is a cut-throat business you know."

The swoosh of Cross jotting and the click of Deadhouse's camera filled the room as they tried to figure out what was going in this strange and eerie place.

————

Ronnie, Ethan, Flug and Gullett climbed back out of the passageway and into the town square. Thankfully most of the crowd had dispersed which, in the case of the ghosts and the phantoms, was literally the truth. There were a few stragglers left, but they were just finishing the snacks they'd bought off Mrs. Strudel's Travelling Abattoir.

A few quick enquiries established that no one had come out of the hole under the fountain in the time that it had taken for them all to get in and the four of them to get out. Also, Nobody had seen anything out of the ordinary happen topside (Nobody was the nickname given to Wilko Atonement, a resident who'd lost his entire body in a hunting accident in 1765. He'd been hunting a bear when he accidentally fell into its mouth and got eaten).

"What now then?" asked Ronnie, uncertain as to what course of action they should take next.

"Have a look around I suppose," replied Ethan. "See if anything turns up."

Gullett patted his hands on his large belly and flexed his knees. All he need do now was say, 'Evenin' all' in a deep, broad cockney accent, harass a few minorities and he'd have the stereotypical copper done to perfection.

"What I suggest, gentlemen, is that we split up and revisit the crime scenes that we already know about. I'll take Flug and we'll go and check on Grendle's shop, whilst you two go back to the cemetery. Seeing as the underground lab is devoid of a perpetrator, it may very well be the case that he, or she, or it if we're covering all eventualities, is out and about and up to some sort of naughtiness."

"Good idea," said Ethan, mightily impressed with Gullett, whom

431

he'd always assumed had as much idea about crime detection as a Stone Age human had about personal hygiene and good housekeeping (my fault for marrying her I suppose). "Where do you want to meet up when we're done?"

"Back here seems as good a place as any," said the policeman. Twenty minutes later, Ronnie and Ethan passed through the cemetery gates.

"I've got a good mind to go invisible," said Ronnie as he lit up a cigarette.

"Why's that?" asked Ethan, scanning the open expanse before them. "Just a precaution. Judging by the butchered body parts in that room there's a chance we could get waylaid and hacked to pieces."

"I see your point, but I think it'll be a complete waste of time." "How so?"

"Because all our elusive madman will have to do is follow the 'you' shaped cloud of smoke about. You might as well be wearing a luminous donkey jacket covered in bells."

Ronnie surreptitiously dropped his fag onto the ground and stamped it out, whilst trying to look as if he wasn't doing it as a result of Ethan's observation.

"Had enough of that," Ronnie said, with a little bit too much conviction.

They got about forty feet into the cemetery when Ethan stopped completely and stood totally still, to the point that he could have been mistaken for a statue.

"Wh... "

"Sshhh," whispered Ethan, cutting off Ronnie's question.

Ethan was staring off into the distance and he wasn't moving a muscle having come to an instant standstill. Not so much as a twitch or sound came from him. Ronnie couldn't even hear him breathing. After about thirty seconds Ethan blinked and turned his head ever so slightly to the left.

"There," he whispered, imperceptibly nodding in that direction. "What? Where?" said Ronnie, his mouth going dry and his heart rapidly picking up speed. "This way. And quietly."

Like a couple of trained snipers moving into position they picked their way across the ground towards the source of the noise that Ethan had heard. After a minute or so Ronnie found that he was just about able to hear it. It was on the very limits of his sound range but it was definitely there. A vague splat like a trifle falling onto a cold stone floor could be heard every few seconds. This in turn was punctuated by the occasional groan of exertion.

Ethan guided them onwards, but it wasn't until they got to within about ten feet of an open grave that it became clear what exactly the source of the noise was. A clod of earth the size of a football flew out from the hole and landed with a moist thud on the ground. A weary grunt of effort accompanied it.

Swiftly and silently, Ethan and Ronnie covered the remaining distance. They both arrived at the open grave at the same time and shouted in unison.

"What the hell do you think you're doing?"

As quick as a flash the figure in the hole disappeared in a blur of earth and darkness.

"Where'd he go?" asked Ronnie, looking round incredulously. "It's like he winked out of existence."

Ethan leapt into the hole.

"Here," he shouted. "There's a tunnel. Come on."

They plunged into the dark void with Ethan leading the way. Although vision was limited his superior eyesight allowed him to charge on without any particular risk.

Ronnie quickly took out his petrol lighter from his pocket and got it going. At least that was one of the benefits of smoking he thought to himself. You never got stuck in the dark. He stepped into the tunnel holding the lighter out in front.

"Hold up, Ethan," he shouted into the black vacuum.

"S'okay," came the reply. "I'm right on him. You watch yourself."

"Thank God for that," Ronnie muttered to himself. The last thing he wanted to do was head down the tunnel at top speed not knowing what was down there. He could bump into anything. Literally anything. As he progressed he noticed that there were smaller passageways leading off the main one. He investigated one and found that it led straight to a coffin. The others that he checked did the same.

"So that's how you've been getting round is it? Sneaky bugger."

Once back in the main tunnel he could still hear the sound of footsteps up ahead. He also realised that his eyes had grown accustomed to the semi darkness. He picked up his pace and moved on.

———

"Are you sure this is a good idea?" said Stitches, leaning against the table he'd gotten the test tube from.

"I think so," said Ollie, perusing the meat laden slab. "Anyway, who else would you suggest?"

"I suppose you're right," said the zombie. "It's just that Crumble is usually about as much use as a pair of shoes for a snake. I can't see what possible. . . "

"Ooh, this is mysterious. I haven't seen anything like this since that time. . . No forget that. I have never seen anything like this. Except maybe for that time. . . "

"In here, Professor," said Ollie.

Professor Rhubarb Crumble was led into the lab by Deadhouse, who had kindly volunteered to escort him from his den of lunacy to this one. Ollie had concluded that they needed someone with a scientific background to try and make sense of what they had discovered, and seeing that outside of Crumble no one else in Skullenia knew the slightest thing about that particular subject, his choice was pretty limited. To be honest if there'd been a primary school in the vicinity, Ollie would have gone there and would now be chatting to a six-year-old who'd just learned to rub a balloon on his head and stick it to the ceiling about a potential crime scene, and Crumble would still be in his lab defying the laws of nature and sanity with equal measure.

"Hello there, Ollie," said the Professor. "My oh my, what do we have here?"

"That's what we're hoping you can tell us," said Stitches. "All we've determined so far is that someone is harvesting various body parts for some unknown purpose."

Crumble took off his glasses, folded his arms, and cast his gaze across the room. He was clearly deep in thought. He ummed and arred, nodded his head, tapped his finger against his lip and breathed deeply. A hushed quiet descended as his grey matter got to work.

After a couple of minutes Ollie said, "Well?" "Well what, dear boy?" said Crumble.

"What do you think's been going on down here?"

"Oh, I haven't the foggiest idea. I was wondering what to have for tea."

"Snake. Shoes," said Stitches.

"Why don't you show the professor the diary," said Cross, as his pen moved across a page. "Maybe that'll help."

"Here, Prof. Have a read of this," said Ollie, handing him the book. "I thought this whole set up might have something to do with the chap who created Flug, but Stitches said he's not around anymore."

"Indeed he isn't," said Crumble, leafing through the pages of the diary. "But that wouldn't preclude someone else from following the same path now would it? You can get any number of books on the subject. I've got one myself actually. It's entitled, 'How to make friends and imitate people'."

"Please don't tell me that you've started tinkering around with this sort of stuff," said Stitches.

"Oh good lord no," said Crumble, continuing to peruse the diary. "Far too involved a business. It's costly, time consuming and causes havoc with the carpets. Well, I would conclude, based on these entries and the fact that there's a pile of flesh on that table that by rights should be connected together, that someone or something is definitely trying to create a human being of sorts."

"Well, this one hasn't got a brain yet so it should at least be as intelligent as Flug," said Stitches.

"So who do you think would be responsible for this," asked Cross. "Anybody you know or have heard about?"

"Oh I don't think so, my good man. I did meet Dr. Frankenstein once though. Strange fellow who seemed a bit disjointed to me. I always had the impression that he wasn't put together quite right."

Just then they heard footsteps behind them. Gullett had returned, but he was on his own.

"I've left Flug with Mrs. Ladle for the time being," he announced. "He didn't want to come down here again."

"Fair enough," said Ollie. "Did you manage to find out anything else?"

"Nope. You?"

"Not really. Someone's collecting body parts. That's about it."

"Maybe we should stake-e-e-e the place out-t-t-t," said Deadhouse.

"You know-w-w-w. Lie in wait to catch-h-h-h the fellow, or fellows, red handed-d-d-d."

"Seems like that's our only option at the moment," said Stitches, watching as Crumble fiddled about with bits of lab equipment that wouldn't have looked out of place in a medieval torture chamber, or one of Count Jocular's sitting rooms. "And whatever happens, there's enough of us here to take on whoever comes back."

It was at that precise moment that every one of them heard footsteps. Quick ones as if someone was running flat out. Before anyone could ask, Gullett turned and checked the entryway.

"Not coming from there," he said.

"Then where on earth is it coming from?" said Cross, his constant jotting for the moment interrupted.

They all stood as still as they could to try and pinpoint the sound. Even Crumble managed not to move and he usually fidgeted more than a Tourette's sufferer having an epileptic fit whilst being attacked by wasps covered in itching powder.

The seconds ticked slowly by. Not only did the metronomic thump of the footsteps get louder and louder but they were also getting closer and closer.

"I do believe, dear boy," said Crumble, pointing behind Ollie, "that it's coming from beyond that wall."

Ollie turned round and faced the cabinet that he'd been propped up against. He leaned forward and inclined is head.

"He's right you know," he whispered. He gave the cabinet a wobble. "Give me a hand with this somebody."

Between them Ollie and Gullett manoeuvred the piece of furniture away from the wall.

"Well, that explains how they're getting in and out unseen," said Gullett.

Hidden behind it was a small wooden door about three feet high. There was a handle on it, but it didn't appear to have any sort of locking mechanism so it was obviously open. It was clearly used as well, and recently, because there was an arc on the floor where the bottom of it scraped through the dirt.

The footsteps sounded perilously close now and they could also hear vague noises that almost definitely sounded like voices.

Cross, realising that he might actually have an honest to goodness story on his hands rather than a witch's cat stuck up a tree, or Flug getting his finger stuck up his nose (again), made a suggestion.

"Gentlemen. What with there being five of us here why don't we, as my colleague already stated, lie in wait? If we turn the light off and take up positions near the entrance, we will have the element of surprise firmly on our side."

"I don't like surprises," said Stitches, backing up ever so slightly without trying to look as if he were backing up ever so slightly. "The last time I had one it took me three days to get my face back to normal. My nose didn't look quite right on my forehead."

"Let's get ready, chaps," said Gullett. Stitches hesitantly turned off the light.

———

"Do you want another biscuit, Flug love?" "Yes please."

Mrs. Ladle took another one of the warm goodies off the griddle and handed it to the smiling behemoth.

"Fanks, Mrs. L."

"You're welcome, love. But take your time with that one. You're not having any more because that's your seventh."

"Okay." CRUNCH!

Mrs. Ladle's Ghouls Goitres were a rare treat that subtly combined two very distinct traits. Not only did each of them have the sweetness of a five-pound bag of sugar, they also possessed the consistency of quick drying cement, so much so that the mixture had been used in the past as a replacement concrete overcoat by one or two notorious crime families. Not only was it denser, it set quicker, sunk faster, and there was usually enough left over for a tasty post whacking nibble.

"Mrs. L."

"Yes, dear,"

"How many is sevenf?"

"Well, it's seven isn't it," said the witch, pouring a smidgeon of lizard milk into her tea.

"Okay. How many is seven?"

Mrs. Ladle took a sip of a brew that was hot enough to boil the skin off a rhinoceros and rolled her eyes. She loved Flug to bits (all of them) but he really was as thick as an elephant milk shake.

"Why don't we leave advanced mathematics to one side for a bit," she said, plonking herself down at the kitchen table opposite Flug. "Counting can be such hard work can't it." (A statement you'd know to be true if you ever ate anything she cooked). "So. What shall we talk about instead?"

The aim of the question was an attempt to get Flug involved in a normal bit of everyday chit chat, one that might increase his IQ, broaden his horizons and stop him drooling all the time and looking like a tasered camel. Ollie, Stitches, Ronnie, Ethan, and Mrs. Ladle all took turns, but it was hard work that required dedication, tact and the patience of a saint (although the saint in question was Barry Saint of Oswestry, who diligently pushed past old age pensioners in queues, kicked homeless people if they didn't get out of his way and thought nothing of, well, anything really).

"Dunno," said the monster, around a mouthful of half chewed biccie. "Okay. What sort of things do you like?"

"Sweeties."

"Apart from sweeties."

"More sweeties. Me like Wolf Willies, Minty Mint Mints and Chocolate Ghoulies."

"I tell you what, let's forget about sweets for a moment," she said, lighting a cigarette. "Tell me what do you like to do?"

". . . . ."

"For fun." "."

"Good grief, there really is very little going on upstairs isn't there. Tell you what, let's try something simple. Do you like colouring in?"

"Wot, like pic.tures?"

"Yes, that's right. If I get you a book would you like to do that for a bit?"

"Yes please, Mrs. L. Me like colours," said Flug, exuding more childlike excitement than a person with a body the size of small building had the right to.

"Alright then," she said as she got up. "Back in a mo. Maybe when you're done Ollie will let you put a drawing up on the fridge."

Flug watched Mrs. Ladle leave the kitchen. Normally, in a circumstance such as this, the 'this' being left on his own, Flug would go into a sort of stasis mode. With no outside stimulation, his prehistoric brain wasn't really capable of too much other than keeping him breathing, although sometimes it even forgot to do that. On quite a few occa sions, Ollie or Stitches had had to beat him severely on the chest with a sledgehammer to get his heart going again. And that wasn't fun. It was like trying to jump start a beluga whale.

Mrs. Ladle's kitchen was a different kettle of fish though as there was always plenty to look at, including a kettle of fish (she used them in chocolate pudding).

His eyes flickered involuntarily around the room taking in all of the various items, none of which meant much to him, but stopped when they came to rest on something that got a few atrophied synapses firing. He got up and walked over to the larder. It was quite snug but he managed to squeeze his massive body inside.

"Colours," he said to himself reaching out.

About twenty-five minutes later Mrs. Ladle returned bearing a colouring book entitled, 'Depraved Demons, Demigods and other Dark Nasties.' If the truth be told she'd stuck together a few pieces of paper that she'd drawn some very bad doodles on. It didn't really make any difference that she had the artistic ability of a brick though; it would keep Flug happy for ages.

"Right, Fl. . . "

She stared worriedly. Flug was sat just where she'd left him, but the items on the table had most definitely not been there when she left to go and get the book.

"Flug. Where did you get those bottles from?" she asked, sitting down opposite him once more.

"In dere," he replied, pointing with an out-sized finger. "Me saw pretty colours."

She picked up one of the bottles and read the label. Monkey Juice.

She looked at another. Essence of Despair. "Oh no," she groaned.

As a witch, Mrs. Ladle kept potions. Lots of them. It was a rigorously enforced job requirement actually. You couldn't very well claim to be a mistress of the dark arts if you didn't have a few vials of innocuous looking liquids stashed in your pants drawer (although just to clarify, your pants draw wasn't strictly necessary, you could keep them where you liked. Mrs. Ladle kept some of hers in someone else's pants draw. She wasn't having Chambers Distillation of Evil in her house. That stuff was nasty. Smelled nice though).

The ones she did have she kept all over the house, in jars, in containers, and in bottles of various sizes and colours. Most of them contained your more common or garden substances such as Hound Dust, Crippled Dick and Soulmantle. They were the type of things that she would use in ordinary spells like turning someone into a vegetable or predicting the future (especially if it was someone who had pissed her off. Predicting someone's impending future as a swede was a piece of cake. As was turning them into a piece of cake). They also made very nice cookies.

Her more exotic liquors and ointments she kept in her larder which, under normal circumstances she kept locked. It was evident though, judging by the dozen or so containers on the kitchen table, that she had forgotten. Even more worrying however, was the empty glass that she noticed in Flugs hand.

"Flug, what did you do?"

The big one smiled and held up the worryingly arid container. "Played wiv da colours," he said. "Dey lully."

"Which ones did you play with?" "All me fink."

"I see. Be a dear and show me your tongue would you."

Flug poked out the massive slab of flesh. It rippled and glistened like a ripe slug and nestled on his chin, looking for all the world as if a butcher had hung it there. It had taken on a purpley, bluey, greeny hue and was smoking ever so slightly. It looked like an outraged gorilla had gone to work on it with a ten-pound meat tenderiser and chucked it on a barbecue.

"When you say all," she said, picking up a bottle that contained Spirit of Haunted Dragon, "did you use any of this blue one?"

Flug thought for a moment. A strange look passed over his outsize features, and it almost seemed that he was actually processing information other than sweets, or getting to the nearest toilet before he had an accident. It was a look that Mrs. Ladle wasn't using to seeing on the creature's features.

"Why, yes I did. But it's not so much blue as more a subtle, yet dazzling shade of azure, wouldn't you agree, Mrs. Ladle?"

For a few seconds Mrs. Ladle was lost for words. A rare occurrence that hadn't happened since she was in her third year at Witch School and had misread a transmogrification spell and turned her teeth into a fourth dimensional being that could only understand the complex language of the Transparent Jovian Steamfly. She'd had to retake that exam.

She was also wondering when she had banged her head and how long the concussion would last.

"What did you say?" she asked quietly.

Flug put the glass onto the table, leaned back in his chair and folded his arms. He smiled serenely and there was a definite sparkle in his eyes.

"Oh, nothing really. I was just commenting on the shade of the liquid in the container. By the way, did you know that the Azure Damselfly is easily distinguished from the Common Blue Damselfly because it has less blue colouring on its thorax and abdomen?"

"Is that a fact?"

"Indeed it is. Do you mind if I have a glass of water please, Mrs. Ladle? I think I'm a little dehydrated."

Well, she thought to herself, it was pretty obvious what had happened. Flug had mixed up her potions, drank whatever concoction that had been the result of said mixing, and boosted his IQ by about a thousand percent. Lord alone knew how long it would last or what the side effects might be, but he seemed alright for now. It would have to run its course though, because there was no way that she could replicate what he'd done as it had been completely random, therefore producing a counter spell was out of the question. Not only that, but without knowing what the dosages should be it could prove harmful to Flug's health. Of course there was always the possibility that the effects were permanent but, however amazing the discovery, it would take a hundred lifetimes to repeat it. A certain group of primates would have the complete works of the Immortal Bard knocked out before that.

"Ah, that's better," said Flug, after downing his drink. "Nothing like a glass of sweet, fresh water to cleanse the pallet."

"Well, quite," said Mrs Ladle, sparking up another nicotine stick with slightly trembling hands.

"Oh, by the way," said Flug. "I seem to be having a spot of bother trying to remember how I got here. My head's a little fuzzy to be honest." "Um. You've been asleep (brain in permanent hibernation) for quite a while (since the day you were created) because you caught a virus (Stupidus Eternium). It'll probably take a while (god only knows) for everything to come back to you," (you could turn stupid again at any moment).

It was a bit of a fib but it was vaguely tinged with an element of truth. Flugs brain had pretty much been as active as a bowl of muesli since he was 'born'.

Mrs Ladle stubbed her fag out and stood up. She could handle just about anything on her own but this situation was, to say the least, a little bit odd. She needed help and advice. This was a burden that she couldn't shoulder by herself.

"Come on, Flug love. Let's get going." "Okey dokey. Where are we off to, Mrs. L?"

"The Town Square I think," she said as she adjusted her pointy hat and opened the back door. "I need to talk to Ollie."

———

It was dark. Extremely dark. In fact it was so dark that it was almost a physical object with texture and mass. It was darker than a black hole having a power cut. It was darker than the deepest, darkest corner of the deepest, darkest cave in the deepest, darkest dark bit of the world. It was even darker than Adolf Hitler's ill-fated venture, Auschwitz the Musical.

"Dark isn't it?" said Crumble, his voice carrying an almost supernatural quality.

"Thanks for that, Prof," said Stitches. "And there was me thinking that I'd put my eyes in the wrong way round."

"I hate to be a bore and state the bleeding obvious," said Ollie, in a barely audible whisper, "but there's absolutely no point whatsoever in us continuously talking whilst we're hiding in the dark trying not to be discovered. We might as well put a sign on the door saying, 'Please tread carefully. Lynch mob waiting inside'."

"So, absolute silence it is then, yes?" said Stitches. "Correct," replied Ollie.

"So 'shut up' or 'be quiet' would have done really wouldn't it?" Ollie swore silently.

The pounding footsteps could still be heard but for some reason they didn't seem to be getting any closer. In fact, every now and again they even sounded further away. Crumble was just about to point out the disadvantages of lying in wait in a subterranean cavern with less than ideal acoustics when the small door burst open. Glass shattered, equipment fell to the floor, voices shouted all at once and, wouldn't you just know it, the light bulb blew the moment Stitches tried to turn it on.

"Get your hands off me." "Grab that bit."

"Ouch!"

"Cross?"

"Yes."

"Sorry."

"How did you get in here?" "The Constable brought me."

"All of you I meant. Ow! There's no need for hair pulling." "Ollie." "What?"

"I've got a hand." "I'll get the cuffs on." FLASH.

"For God's sake will you quit it with that bloody camera?" CLINK.

"I think I've got them on." "That's my ankle."

"Oh."

"And my wrist."

"You lot are rubbish." THWACK.

"Ooofff!"

"I say, that's not playing fair." "Aww, who's dropped one?" "Not me."

"Or me."

"Whoever smelt it. . . " "Oh, grow up."

"I think I've scratched my helmet." "Sorry, my nails need cutting." CLICK.

The underground lab was once again bathed in light. Ethan had crossed from the door and fixed the switch. He was surveying the scene before him.

Ramekin Deadhouse was flat on his back with a lens cap stuffed up his left nostril. Excalibur Cross was sat on his backside (his, not Deadhouse's. Don't make up your own jokes) looking dazed and confused,

and wondering why his right wrist was handcuffed to Ollie's left leg. Stitches had a hand around Crumble's throat and was doing a sterling job of trying to throttle the professor. Unfortunately he wasn't attached to said appendage. He was lying in a heap six feet away with his head at a funny angle (we'll go with 54 degrees. That's quite a funny one. Funnier than 45 degrees anyway. Phew, what a misery he is).

"Please tell me he's under there somewhere," said Ethan, approaching the flesh based collision.

"Mmmmmpppppphhhhhfffff."

"Where did that come from?" said Ollie. Gullett rolled over onto his back.

"Thought that was a bit uncomfortable," said the policeman. "Anybody recognise him?" said Ollie, pointing at the unconscious figure.

Nobody did.

"Well, whoever he is, he put up a hell of a fight" said Stitches, retrieving his hand from Crumble's neck.

"You're not wrong," said Ollie, rubbing his trouser area delicately. "He caught me a blinder right in the unmentionables. I hope it was him anyway."

"Right," said Gullett, hoisting his enormous bulk back to vertical. "I'll get our friend here into a nice, cosy cell until he wakes up. Then I'll question him. I'm sure I can get to the bottom of all this."

"That sounds like a plan," said Ollie, now able to brush himself down after releasing himself from Cross. He gazed around the lab and the mess the scuffle had caused. "We might as well leave this lot in situ so that he can explain himself."

Ethan helped Crumble up.

"Has Ronnie come through yet?" he asked. "I thought he was right behind me."

"Here I am, boys," said Ronnie, coming through the door. "No need to panic. It's all under control now."

"And thank goodness for that," said Stitches, with just the vaguest soupçon of sarcasm. "How would we have coped without you?"

"What kept you anyway? I though you right on my tail?" said Ethan. "I was but I stopped a few times."

"Ah, out of breath eh? I told you that smoking all those fags was bad for you."

"Well, that's where you're wrong," said Ronnie, producing a cigarette and lighting it. "I found a load of side tunnels off the main one so I went and had a look."

He told them that they led to other coffins scattered around the cemetery.

Cross made a note of Ronnie's story before turning to Deadhouse and suggesting that they make their way to the cemetery to get some snaps for the next edition of the paper. The photographer agreed so they made their way back along the tunnel that Ethan and Ronnie had just exited from.

Gullett, keen to get to interrogating, hoisted his captive over his shoulder and headed off to his station.

"Well, I guess that's it for now," said Stitches. "Until our friend wakes up and gives Gullett some answers we can't really move forward."

"Agreed," said Ollie. "Anyway, I need to get back to the office. It's coming up for tea time and Flug will have my drink ready."

"Gorgeous. Well, you enjoy that, mate. I'm off to Mrs. Strudels for something to eat. You coming, Ethan?" said Ronnie.

"Yeah, I will actually. I'm famished. We'll see you guys later then." They all left the lab.

———

"Uhhhhhmmmmmmmmmm." "Doctor."

"Ow. It hurts."

"DOCTOR!"

"Yes, Nurse Parsnip."

"Our new arrival is coming round. He's moaning and says it hurts."

"Thank you, Nurse. It's hardly a remarkable occurrence though, seeing as he threw himself off the fountain onto a concrete block."

"Has he broken anything?" asked Nurse Parsnip, handing her colleague a medical chart.

Dr. Zoltan took the board and quickly scanned the information on it. "Only the world record for the number of times that a single person has successfully been stupid in one month. How many times is it now, Mandrake? Eight. Nine. I'm beginning to lose track." He replaced the medical chart onto a hook at the end of the bed, and then thinking better of it, took it off and gave it back to Nurse Parsnip. Mandrake would only try and batter himself over the head with it causing extremely minor injuries. He took the hook off as well.

Dr. Roman Zoltan was the Chief Medical Officer at the Skullenian General Hospital. It wasn't a large establishment and usually managed to get by on a skeleton staff (ha ha) comprising of himself, three nurses and a mortician. It wasn't the busiest of places either because almost the entire population of Skullenia were already dead, dying or somewhere in between. That being said it did make for some rather interesting and unusual cases coming through the doors. Zombies with rising damp, werewolves with mange and trolls with grazed knuckles were to name but a few. Add to that more obscure conditions such as Booby Syndrome, and Carpet Disease and it usually worked out that no two days were the same. Three or four were exactly the same, however, but even the most interesting jobs can get a bit samey can't they. All in all though it was a happy place, despite all the pain, suffering, discomfort, misery, and torment (the canteen staff did their best with what they had though).

The only patients that Dr. Zoltan and his staff didn't really relish treating on a regular basis were vampires i.e. the biggest hypochondriacs since Mr. Münchhausen decided he quite liked going into hospitals pretending to be sick. There was rarely a night went by that some moaning bloodsucker didn't come in complaining of this or that. If it wasn't a wobbly fang or a bruised finger from a coffin lid accident, it was 'can you check my cholesterol I've just savaged a slimmer's group' or 'I think I'm looking a bit pale. Can you give me something to put some colour back into my cheeks?' The absolute very worst offender was Count Jocular. Zoltan had lost count of the number of times that he'd had to administer to that particular fiend. His last house call had been because Jocular was complaining of a constant ringing in his ears that just wouldn't go away (Jocular wouldn't come to the hospital. Germs don't you know, which was a bit silly seeing as how he was a full blood vampire lord and had about as much chance of catching a human disease as he did of winning The Nobel Peace Prize for his humanitarian work. Still, it's a fair point for the mere mortals amongst us. At least with a house call you actually get to see a doctor. You could hang around a hospital for a couple of weeks without seeing a member of the medical profession. You're more likely to see a tap dancing giraffe).

After a brief examination the problem was alleviated when Zoltan had taken down the industrial sized wind chime that the vampire had put up outside his bedroom window.

On the whole though, Zoltan didn't have cause to complain about his position. It wasn't as if he had to deal with drunken teenagers and snotty kids with bits of Lego stuck up their noses on a regular basis (Flug had managed it seventeen times with a house brick mind you). And when a golem came in because he'd chipped something off, it was surprising the fun you could have with a handful of quick drying cement and a rude thought or two.

"So, come on then," the Doctor continued. "What was it this time?"

"I don't know what you mean," said Mandrake, propping himself up.

"Why, your latest effort to self-destruct of course." The word 'attempt' was laden with sarcastic emphasis, and for good reason. Mandrake's suicide attempts were notoriously lacklustre and displayed about as much effort and tenacity as someone turning up to assist at a major flood with a sponge, a plastic jug, and a pair of armbands.

"I feel lonely, unloved and misunderstood," said Mandrake, all sad and stuff.

"But you have a loving wife and two wonderful children," said Zoltan. "What more could you ask for?"

"Noggin doesn't like me."

"Whose Noggin?" "Our cat."

Nurse Parsnip tried to stifle an unprofessional giggle.

Dr. Zoltan took out a pen light and flicked it across Mandrakes eyes. (On a side note, it is a well-known fact that, despite all claims to

447

the contrary, this 'procedure' is a total and utter nonsense. The only time that doctors do it is when they have a patient who is a complete and utter lolly-gagger that has nothing wrong with them at all. It makes them feel that they haven't entirely wasted their trip and that they've received at least some modicum of medical treatment before being sent on their way as healthy as can be. That's until the infection they picked up at the hospital takes hold of course, no doubt caught by having a filthy pen light shoved in their face).

"Why should it be so important that your cat loves you?" asked Zoltan, popping his pen light away. That needs a clean, he thought.

"Because I look after him and feed him," said Mandrake, sounding more than a little pathetic, needy and just like someone trying to claim benefits (which they'd no doubt get after saying they can't work because they've got a bit of a limp and look after an elderly relative who died in 1974). "I raised him from a kitten you know."

"Oh, I shouldn't worry about it too much if I were you," said Zoltan. "Pets will always love you unconditionally. What makes you think otherwise?"

"He chewed up my slippers." "That's not so bad."

"Whilst I was wearing them." "I see."

"I couldn't walk for a week. My feet looked like they'd been through a mincer."

Mandrake's cat, Noggin, for all his furry feline features, was not your ordinary, everyday, friendly, domestic moggy. He was a psychotic black mass of seething hairiness that could scare the hyenas off a zebra carcass and wouldn't look out of place in Jurassic Park IV. Forget coming down in the morning to find a dead bird or a mouse on your back doorstep. The last present that Noggin had left was a cow.

"Well, be that as it may, you've been thoroughly checked over, Mandrake and apart from a bruised thigh there's nothing wrong with you (physically anyway, Zoltan thought to himself). "Consequently, and thankfully, there's no real reason to keep you here."

"But I need to stay here," Mandrake protested. "I'm in a highly volatile mental state and a danger to myself and others."

Dr. Zoltan asked Nurse Parsnip to collect some pills from the pharmacy. Sugar pills that is. At least if Mandrake tried overdosing on them the only side effects would be a sleepless night and a furry tongue.

"Mandrake, you're no more of a danger to anyone else than I am. I could cause more injuries by dropping a load of helium filled balloons on a school assembly."

"Who's going to look after me then?" asked Mandrake. "What about your family? Surely they'll take care of you."

"The kids are away at school and my wife's away on business. There's only me and Noggin." Mandrake had asked his wife what business she was going away for and had been told that the business that she was engaged in was none of his business.

Dr. Zoltan thought for a moment. Whilst it was true that Mandrake was as liable to succeed in killing himself as the Rugby World Cup being won by a team of meerkats (still more chance than the Scots though), his attempts did cause a certain amount of disruption, like the time that he had tried to end it all by sitting on the steps of the Bolt and Jugular, covering himself with water and trying to ignite himself (the matches had been in his pocket and wouldn't have ignited if he'd struck them on the sun). He'd brought the whole town to a standstill and interrupted some serious drinking. If for no other reason than the preservation of peace and order, Dr. Zoltan thought that it might be reasonable for Mandrake to spend some time in good company. And he had just the fellows in mind.

"How do you fancy spending a bit of time with Ollie Splint and his friends? There's always something or another going on over there so you wouldn't be bored or lonely. You can even take Noggin with you. Flug loves animals."

Mandrake thought about it for a moment. He had to admit that the idea was quite appealing, and anyway it was preferable to spending the next few days on his own with a cat that Satan couldn't control.

"Do you think they'll mind me hanging around?" he asked, wondering if he'd find the opportunity to hang himself whist he was around. "Of course not," said Zoltan cheerily, moving away from the bed whilst surreptitiously crossing his fingers behind his back. "It'll be a nice change for them having a new face about the place. Leave it with me."

As Dr. Zoltan and Nurse Parsnip walked away, Mandrake rested his head on his pillow and smiled as he looked up at the ceiling, all thoughts of suicide very much in the forefront of his mind (Oh come on. This isn't a Disney story).

———

Constable Gullett took a set of keys the size of a very large set of keys off his hip and clanged them along the bars of the cell. It was extremely loud and sounded like someone had dropped King Kong's cutlery onto a metal floor.

"Come on, sunshine," he shouted, leaning in toward the iron gate. "Up and at 'em. You've got some explaining to do."

"Alright, alright I'm coming."

"At a boy. Now, let's start off with an easy one. Who the hell are you?"

"Golden Kilo."

"And where are you from?" "Here, there and everywhere."

"So, no fixed abode is it? Right then." Gullett unlocked the cell. "Come with me, young man."

Gullett escorted Kilo to the interview room in an armlock that was designed to convey authority whilst still allowing the blood to flow, albeit rather more slowly than usual.

The room was a dark, dripping, moisture laden space that housed a battered wooden table and a couple of rickety chairs.

"Sit yourself down then, lad" said the Constable. He opened a draw on his side of the table and took out a stack of lined paper. He wrote his prisoners name onto the first sheet.

"Okay," he said. "This is a formal interview during which I'm going to ask you a series of questions that I want you to answer truthfully. And don't go thinking that you can pull the wool over my eyes. I've dealt with your type before."

"And what's, 'my type?' " said Kilo.

"Guilty. Look, I know you snuck into Grendle's and knocked the poor old boy out. I know you swiped a jar of sweets because we found the wrappers in the graves and in your lab, and I know it was you that stole all those body parts."

"Constable," said Kilo.

"Hang on, lad. This is a legal procedure. Let me do my bit first."
"But. . . "

"Wait for it. You'll get your turn. Now, I need to caution you. You do not have to say anything, but it may harm your defence when I find out that you've told me a complete pack of lies and I tell the judge what a naughty boy you've been. Do you want a solicitor?"

"Nope," said Kilo, looking strangely at ease. It was probably just as well that he didn't require legal representation. The last solicitor who had tried to practice in Skullenia was last seen entering Jocular's castle about fifteen years ago to discuss suing the vampire lord for a bit of a slaughter that happened somewhere just outside Hemp. There were rumours that bits of him had been seen since, but no one could be sure.

"Why's that?" asked Gullett. "Don't need one."

"How do you figure that out?"

"I haven't done anything wrong."

"Um, as I think I pointed out a few seconds ago, your secret lair was found to contain various, disconnected body parts. I'd class that as being a little on the naughty side wouldn't you?"

Kilo leaned back in his chair and smiled confidently.

"I do admit that I surreptitiously went into Grendle's store and took the sweets. They're my favourites."

"So why not go in via the front door and buy them like a normal person?" said Gullett, realising that his use of the word normal was wide of the mark by at least a couple of psychiatric disorders.

"I found myself temporarily void in the pecuniary department rendering me unable to purchase the requisite comestibles."

"Which means?" said Gullett, who hated fancy words. They took up far too much room in his pocket book and wasted ink. And he didn't understand them of course.

"I haven't got any money, Constable." "So why didn't you say so. Carry on."

"It was whilst I was in the back room that Grendle came in. I startled him and he jumped and fell over. I didn't hit him. I even checked on him before I left to make sure that he was alright. I'm not a monster. As for the other stuff, have you checked the statute books?"

"Not lately no," said Gullett. "But I think I know the law well enough." (And what he didn't know he made up. He'd once arrested someone for being 'overtly horizontal in a built-up area').

"I think you should," said Kilo.

Five minutes later, Gullett was sat in his office and Kilo was back in his cell. The Constable was going through the latest edition of Skullenia's laws and by-laws (circa 1682). They didn't get updated very often because four-hundred-year-old justice seemed to work quite nicely thank you very much. Alright, so no one had been prosecuted for turnip rustling or assaulting a pig for a while, but it was still reasonably fit for purpose.

It was a tricky read because the text was a trifle archaic, but about half way through the weighty tome he found a small section relating to reanimation.

'The Raife the Dead Act 1564. Whofoever fhall be found in poffeffion of variouf partf of human anatomy for the purpofe of reanimation fhall not be guilty of a crime if he can prove beyond reafonable doubt that the faid partf of the body in hif poffeffion come from the dead and not of the living, and that being the cafe providing that the deceafed had been paffed from thif mortal coil for a peiod of time of no leff the twelve monthf, the accufed fhall not be guilty of grave robbing. Ftated cafe, Puddle vf Fkullenia 1536. Jebediah Puddle amaffed a collection of fome four and a half thoufand body partf, all of which proved to be from thofe departed for more than a year. He therefore fuccefffully argued that he had not committed any crimef. He waf of courfe locked up for the reft of hif life for being a complete looney of the firft water.' "Bugger," said Gullett, slamming the book shut and tossing it back onto the desk. He grabbed hold of his keys again and went back down to the cell thinking, 'What a load of old fhit.'

———

Ollie sat at his desk. His brow was furrowed and he was gazing about distractedly.

"You alright there, Ollie?" said Stitches, easing himself into the leather chair. "You seem to be miles away."

"I was just wondering where Flug was. It's time for my glass of blood and he's never late."

"Maybe he's still at Mrs. Ladle's," offered Ronnie. "You know what he's like when he gets into her biscuits. He could be munching away for days."

Stitches suppressed a shudder. "I dread to think what goes into one of her biccies. Her recipes are a cross between a primordial swamp."

"And?" said Ollie.

"Nothing else," said the zombie.

"So, did Crumble have any other useful information about what we found under the fountain?" asked Ronnie.

"Not really," said Ollie. "He went straight back to his lab mumbling something about a shirt that he was working on."

"Oh, I know the one," said Stitches. "He's designed the ultimate camouflage shirt. It can blend in with just about any background that you care to mention. I think he wants to sell it to the military."

"Oh, right. How's it coming on?" asked Ollie. "Not sure really. He can't find it."

Just then Mrs. Ladles head popped through the door; quickly followed by the rest of her. (She did have a habit of occasionally sticking her head through a door whilst her body came in through a different entrance entirely but only if she felt up to it. It was most disconcerting though).

She had Flug in tow. At least they thought it was Flug. He was smiling, standing up straight, had a distinct glint in his eye and wasn't dribbling like a teenage boy at the Playboy Mansion's Smallest Bikini Competition.

"Hello, boys," she said.

They all greeted her at once.

"Hello, everyone," said Flug. "How are we all doing on this resplendent day?"

Ollie got up from his desk and went and stood next to the leather chair occupied by Stitches. Stitches stood up and stood next to Ollie. Ronnie stayed where he was. He wasn't sure that his legs were going to work properly. All three of them had odd looks on their faces.

"I think I've got a bit of explaining to do," said Mrs. Ladle. "Flug, love, why don't you toddle off and get Ollie's drink for him."

"Certainly, Mrs. L. One Bloody Mary coming right up for the man in black. Incidentally, did you know that some people think that the name of the drink refers to Queen Mary I of England, whose persecution of the Protestants in the sixteenth century earned her the nickname." With that he left for the kitchen.

Mrs. Ladle explained what had happened to three very gobsmacked beings.

"So, based on what you've just told us," said Ollie, "Flug is now as intelligent as the rest of us?" (To be fair that wasn't saying an awful lot. The average bath sponge was more capable of reasoned thought than most of the residents of Skullenia. It also had a nicer personality, a sunnier disposition and wasn't liable to bite your face off if it got a bit miffed).

"Actually," said the witch, "judging by the stuff that he's been coming out with since it happened, I'd say that he's cleverer than the rest of us put together."

"My God," said Stitches, running a hand down his face, inadvertently leaving an eyebrow on his cheek. "It's the end of everything I hold dear. I like things to have a certain order and consistency. I like routine. The moon rising every night. Ronnie rolling a fag every four and a half minutes (which he was), and Flug being as dense as a neutron star. I'm pretty sure that the world isn't ready for a clever Flug, but I'm damned sure that I'm not."

"Come on now, mate be honest," said Ronnie. "You're only annoyed because you won't be able to take the mick out of him until it wears off."

"Well, there is that as well, yes," said Stitches.

"That's if it wears of at all don't forget," said Mrs. Ladle. "But remember he doesn't know anything about this so not a word. He'd be really upset if he found out."

"Who'd be really upset if they found out what?" said Flug, reentering the office carrying Ollie's blood filled tankard.

"Oh, Stitches," said Ollie, accepting his liquid lunch.

"What is it that perturbs you so, Stitches, old chap?" asked Flug, a look of concern on his face. Even his scars had taken on a softer more sympathetic look.

"Um," said the zombie, struggling to come up with a plausible answer and cursing Ollie for dropping him in it yet again. "Oh, it's nothing really I. . . I lost a finger in a door this morning and I was saying to the guys that I'd be really upset if something fell off and I couldn't find it again. Give it a few months and I'd be nothing but an eyebrow in a pair of shoes."

"I tell you what might work," said Flug. "Cat gut." "Cat gut?" said Ollie.

"Indeed," said Flug. "It's much stronger than cotton and far more versatile." He looked at Stitches. "If you repaired yourself with that then your various joints and tendons would last a lot longer I can assure you."

"I can supply you with some," said Mrs. Ladle, helpful as ever. "I use it all the time when I'm cooking."

"Thanks," said a dumbfounded Stitches, trying desperately not to think of what dish might necessitate the use of cat related body parts. "On a side note, and to put to rest what you're all now thinking," continued Flug, "were you aware that cat gut doesn't actually come from cats? No? Well, it's usually made from the fibres found in the intestines of sheep or goats. Sometimes though, cows were used which is where the term 'cat gut' may have come from. It's an abbreviation of cattle gut."

"Well," said Stitches. "To be honest, once you start inserting bits of animal into yourself it doesn't really matter where it comes from does it? Personally, I don't care whether it's cat, sheep, goat or Tyrannosaurus Rex. I think I'll stick with the cotton if it's all the same to you."

By now Ollie had finished his drink, and it had gone down without too much trouble, but that was only because he found it marginally easier to digest than what had happened to Flug. As nice as it was for all concerned he sort of understood where Stitches was coming from. Life in Skullenia, as weird as it was, wasn't all that bad, but like everything else it thrived on routine and Flug's extreme thickness was an ever-present part of that. The way he behaved and the things that he did were comforting in a way. Like how he fled in terror every time he flushed the toilet, his abject wonder at the fridge lighting up whenever he opened the door, and his utter conviction that there was a creature called Michael McIntyre who some people thought was a very funny comedian. (None of them had heard the name before so they were convinced that he'd made it up. We know though don't we. Sadly).

There was a knock at the door then that disturbed Ollie's musings. "Come in," he called out.

Doctor Zoltan appeared, and trailing behind him like a lost puppy was Mandrake looking rather drier and considerably more conscious than the last time that they'd seen him. Mandrake was carrying a metal box in his right hand. He seemed to be having trouble keeping it still and faint hisses and scratches seemed to be coming from inside it.

"Ah, Dr. Zoltan, my eminent medical friend," said Flug, grasping the physicians hand and giving it a shake that could have toppled a crane. "Marvellous to see you."

Zoltan stared at his swamped hand and then at everyone else in the room. Needless to say he was lost for words. (I've never understood the benefit of the word 'needless' when used in such a way. If to say something is needless then why say it? The use of the word is *always* followed by the very thing that is needless to say, so why bother in the first place. It's like other redundant phrases such as 'I shouldn't tell you this but. . . ' and 'don't look now but. . . ' Needless to say I shan't be using such nonsensical wordage during this particular tale. Oh bugger).

"Don't worry about it, Doc," said Stitches, quietly, out of Flug's earshot. "That was our reaction as well. We're still trying to get our heads round it."

"I'll bet," whispered the doctor. He didn't press the matter any further because Mrs. Ladle had gestured to him in no uncertain terms to curb his curiosity there and then. Her nonverbal method of delivery sent a shiver up his spine leaving him in no doubt as to what would happen if he enquired any more. God help anyone deaf who bumped into her. Her sign language was a cross between Makaton's, the subtle use of lip reading, understated facial gestures, and Brazilian street fighting.

"So what can we do for you, Doctor?" asked Ollie, wondering why he had Mandrake with him.

"Well," said the physician, "I suppose you're wondering why I've got Mandrake with me?"

"The thought had crossed my mind, yes."

Zoltan related the conversation that he and his patient had had in the hospital, conveniently leaving out the fact that Mandrake had tried to end it all again twice on the way over to the office. Firstly, he had tried to jump out of a ground floor window at the hospital thereby landing on some dense and very soft moss, and then by lying on a railway track that hadn't been used since Methuselah had a paper round. "So, I take it you can assure me then, Doctor, that he's of no risk to himself or anybody else whatsoever?" said Ollie.

"Absolutely," said Zoltan, who still had his fingers crossed. They were getting a bit sore now.

"So what are we going to do with him then?" said Ronnie. "He can't just kick about here all day every day."

"I'm sure we can find him something to do. Right, Mandrake?" said Ollie.

"Oh, yes indeed. I'm more than happy to muck in with anything you want," Mandrake replied, wondering if he could suffocate himself by placing a blanket over Ollie's desk and getting under it.

"I'll look after him," said Flug, draping an arm over Mandrake's shoulder and causing him to droop by six inches. "He'll be fine as long as he's with me."

Stitches rolled his eyes and raised his eyebrows at Ollie. The look said, 'you know he's going to try and kill himself at every available opportunity, and be a complete pain in the rear end don't you?'

Ollie shook his head because he didn't have a clue what Stitches was trying to impart to him. Not that it would have mattered. Ordinarily he would never agree to a request like the doctors, but he was such a pleasant chap and did so much for the community that he felt that he couldn't really refuse him. And he was awfully helpful when Ollie went to see him with his medical complaints. The ointment that Zoltan had given him for his cape rash had worked wonders.

PHHHHSSSSSSHHHHHTTTTT.

"What was that?" said Stitches, looking round the room. "What was what?" answered Ronnie.

"That noise. It sounded like a tractor tyre being let down." PHHHHSSSSSSHHHHHTTTTT.

"It's coming from that box of yours," said the zombie, approaching Mandrake who was trying to secrete said box behind his legs, which was proving to be as successful as trying to hide an elephant in a rabbit hutch. As he got closer the noise got louder. "What on earth have you got in there because it doesn't sound very happy?"

"That's Noggin," said Mandrake. "And Noggin would be?"

"My cat."

Stitches knelt down and peered into the cage. "I know this may sound like a dumb question, but why would a cat need a steel box that looks strong enough to hold a werewolf with anger management issues who hasn't eaten for a week?"

"He's a little feisty," said Mandrake, who was getting cramp in his hand trying to keep the cage under control. The sinews in his forearm were bulging like wire cords.

"But he's just a cat," said Stitches, putting a finger up to the grill and tapping it gently. "How dangerous can a moggy be for goodness sake? I think you're over reacting a bit. Here puss."

Just then a fur covered javelin shot out from the cage and attached itself to Stitches' left nostril.

"YEOWWWW!" screamed the zombie, as his nose was deftly removed from his face. It was left dangling on a set of claws that wouldn't have looked out of place on Elm Street.

"Maybe that's something I should have mentioned," said Dr. Zoltan, helping the stricken zombie to his feet. "I told Mandrake to bring Noggin along so that they can bond."

"Sorry about that," said Mandrake, amidst the general amusement rippling through the room. He extricated the disembodied appendage from the clutches of Noggin and handed it back to its owner. "I told you he was a bit feisty."

"FEISTY!" shouted Stitches, rather more nasally than usual. "That's not a cat, that's a hairy killing machine. What on earth does it eat?"

"Zombie jerky by the looks of things," said Ronnie. "I reckon you better watch out Stitches, mate. Noggin seems to be rather attached to you."

Dr. Zoltan apologised once more, thanked them all profusely for their help and took his leave, ostensibly because he had patients to see to, but more realistically it was before Ollie changed his mind and he got stuck with Mandrake and his mad moggy.

As soon as he'd gone, Gullett came in followed closely by Golden

Kilo who was unfettered and not quite as in custody as he was before. "Is that normal procedure?" enquired Ollie, wondering which bit of him the one-time prisoner would use in his fleshy collage. "Because I was under the impression that it was common judicial practice to keep offenders locked up."

"He's not an offender," said Gullett. "What!" they said collectively.

Gullett explained the findings of his legal research.

"That's interesting," said Stitches, half way through putting his nose back on. "I didn't realise that corpses had a use by date."

"Well, be that as it may," said Gullett, "Mr Kilo here hasn't committed any offences so he's free to go."

"So, can I assume that you intend to carry on with your work?" said Ollie, beginning to wish that he was lying in his coffin all snuggled up and flollopy.

"Why, yes of course," replied Kilo. "But I do seem to have come to a bit of a sticking point that's hampering my progress somewhat."

"I'd call a body not having a head a bit more than a sticking point, mate," said Ronnie. "It's more like, 'I've got two hundred pounds of meat on my slab and it doesn't work.' "

"Well, I suppose you could put it like that," said Kilo. "But I actually do have a head down there."

"Whereabouts?" asked Ollie. "I didn't see it."

"It's in a mini fridge under the work bench. I just haven't had time to put it on yet."

"Remind me not to have a sandwich that you've made," said Stitches, tying off a loop of cotton.

Kilo smiled. It was a friendly one. Genuine and welcoming. On first impression he seemed to be quite a decent chap, even if he was a bit of a head-case. He explained his problem.

"If where to keep my packed lunch were my only issue I'd be fine and dandy trust me. The problem I'm having," he continued, waving his hands in the air, "is the electricity supply round here. It's absolutely useless. I'd generate more power rubbing a balloon on my head and shocking the corpse with that. I just can't create enough voltage to get things going."

A short debate ensued during which no useful comments or ideas arose because no one had the slightest clue on how to help Kilo with his problem. Even Flug with his newly discovered intellect wasn't able to come up with anything vaguely usable. He did point out though that it was a little known fact that a bolt of lightning carried about three million volts of charge, and lasted less than a second.

"Excuse me, boys."

All eyes turned to the fireplace where Mrs. Ladle stood in a cloud of grey smoke. Ninety percent of it was coming from her lungs. She'd trim the burnt bit off her skirt later.

"I really am most dreadfully sorry, Mrs. L," said Flug. "What with everything else going on I totally forgot that you were here. I do hope you'll accept my most sincere apologies."

"Don't worry about it, Flug love," she said. "I like blending into the background. It lends me a certain air of mystery. Now, it seems to me that there's someone in the building who should be able to help, if any of you bothered to ask him."

Ollie knew exactly who she was talking about.

"But we've already taken the Professor down to the lab," said the half vampire. "And not to be indelicate, he was about as much use as a season ticket for Skullenia United." (An ill-fated football team that had only lasted one season. Well, one game to be precise. They'd gotten into the changing room and proceeded to slaughter each other without even seeing a ball. All that was left was a boot, a torn shirt, a couple of toes, and a knife and fork)

"When he's caught on the hop I would entirely agree with you," said the witch, knowing full well that Crumble needed at least a fortnights notice before making a cup of tea. "But if you acquaint him with all the relevant facts and let him think about it for a while, there's a very good chance that he'll come up with a practical solution."

Stitches sighed and shook his head. His nose held. "What, like that idea he had to cure smelly feet by wearing your socks over your shoes. Look, I am usually quite optimistic about things, Mrs. Ladle but when it comes to Crumble I don't care how many facts you make available to him it'll end badly. Or be totally worse. Usually both."

"I'm afraid I'm going to have to disagree with your observations, Stitches," said Flug, still clamped firmly to an ever shrinking Mandrake. "Given the right circumstances he can be very inventive. And don't forget that some of sciences most important discoveries were made by accident and that many of those poor intellectuals were derided for their work and, in many cases, persecuted. I think we should give him a chance."

Unbeknownst to those assembled in Ollie's office the door behind his desk was open a crack. It was just enough to allow all the conversation to be heard but not enough to be noticed. On the other side of it, ensconced in the dark confines of the secret passageway, Crumble listened and inwardly digested. On the whole, what he'd heard had been quite encouraging but he had to disagree with Stitches regarding the socks and shoes issue. Crumble himself had tried it and it had been very successful. Obviously he'd developed blisters on his feet the size of jam tarts, but at least they hadn't stunk, once the infection had cleared up anyway. He pushed the door all the way open and entered the office.

"Hello, Prof," said Stitches. "Locked yourself out again? Glasses gone walkabout? Created a fourth dimension?"

"Oh no, dear boy. I gave up on the whole fourth dimension thing quite a while back. It was all rather dull if you must know. I'm hoping the fifth will be much more interesting."

"So what can we do for you?" asked Ollie.

"Well, as a matter of fact, it's more a case of what I can do for you, or in particular, Mr. Kilo here."

Now he had their attention.

"Go on, Professor," said Kilo, approaching Crumble. "What are you thinking about?"

Looking like a wise and vaguely deranged old owl, Crumble perched on the edge of Ollie's desk and addressed his audience. He hadn't had this many people pay attention to him since the time that he'd put a self-made air freshener into Mrs. Strudel's café. The theory had been sound but he'd slightly over estimated the amount of neutraliser needed and consequently rendered every single customer comatose for a day and a half. Mrs. Strudel hadn't minded though. She charged every single one of them for five meals that they hadn't actually eaten. She was nothing if not opportunistic. And a bit of a crook.

"Well" said the professor. "Your problem seems to be with the electric current correct?"

Kilo nodded.

"So, what we need to do is ramp up the power somewhat. Now, in my laboratory I have a dynamo that's powered by bats that I suspect might prove rather useful."

"I've seen that in action," Ollie cut in. "It was okay but it won't be powerful enough by a long chalk. It only just got one small light bulb going."

"And the bats needed a week off afterwards," said Stitches. "Indeed. And you're right of course," Crumble continued. "But imagine the power we could generate if we scaled everything up a tad." Flug smiled and nodded his head knowingly. "Jocular," he said. "Exactly," said Crumble, who hadn't noticed Flug's evolutionary leap.

"I don't think the Count will take very kindly to being strapped to a wheel and told to flap about," said Ronnie. "Not unless he's allowed to decorate it first at any rate."

"I think you're going to have to enlighten them, Rufus," said Mrs. Ladle, who also knew what was being suggested. "They'll never get it on their own. They're slower on the uptake than a brain-dead troll."

"She's right," said Stitches. "You're going to have to tell us."

"It's really rather simple actually," Crumble continued. "As I said it's all a matter of scale. If a tiny wheel and a dozen small bats can power a light bulb, think of the power that we could generate with a much larger wheel and. . . "

"Jocular's giant vampire bats," said Ollie, triumphantly. "That's brilliant, Prof."

"Thank you. And don't forget the thunderstorms of course. Jocular's castle wouldn't be a credible vampire's lair if there wasn't a violent electrical storm every night."

Golden Kilo grabbed the Professor by the hand and shook it vigorously. "Thank you," he said, a trace of emotion in his voice.

"Not at all, dear boy," said Crumble, patting the man on the shoulder. "Glad to be of service."

"How high is the castle exactly?" asked Mandrake. He didn't get a response.

Fifteen minutes later Ollie finally had his office back to himself. Crumble was in his lab with Kilo getting to work on the design for the upgraded dynamo, and the others were somewhere or another doing something or another. He picked up the phone and dialled Jocular's number. It was all very well coming up with a plan to help Kilo but it would be for naught if His Royal Darkness decided to say no.

As he held the handset to his ear he noticed that even the dialling tone had an eerie, malevolent quality to it. After six rings it was answered.

"His Royal Darkness Count Jocular, Black Knight of the Realms of Fury, Keeper of the Unholy Seal of Instability, Grand Protector of the Wristwatch of Doom, Overseer of the Undead lands of Skullenia and Winner of Best Decorated Dungeon, September 1947's residence."

"Hello, Egon," said Ollie, trying to stay focussed in the face of the overblown welcome.

"Ah, Master Splint, what a pleasure to speak to you. How are you?" "Oh, fine fine thanks. Bearing up you know."

"Of course. And how is that delightful colleague of yours?" "I take it you mean Stitches?"

"I do indeed. He does make me chuckle. So, are you intending on dropping in? It's been a while since you've visited and I do enjoy it when you come up."

I'll bet you do, thought Ollie. He and Stitches had taken a trip up to the castle a couple of months ago because Jocular wanted Ollie's opinion on some wallpaper that he was thinking of putting up on the outside walls of the ancient building. Ollie had diplomatically pointed out that not only would it be a massively awkward task that would take ages to complete, but that wallpaper paste would have a bit of a problem sticking to centuries old stone. He less than diplomatically thought to himself that it was the worst idea since the dawn of time, and that his host was a complete loon of a magnitude not seen since Leyton The Brainless tried to row to Shark's Bay in a tea cup dressed in nothing but a pair of flip flops and a deranged grin.

That was until Jocular suggested using fresh blood to get the job done, however, another off the scale idea that made Ollie squirm and wonder about His Lordship's mental health. (It has been said that there's a fine line between artistic genius and madness, but it's more clear cut than that. Van Gogh was a genius, so to Leonardo Da Vinci, both giants of creation and innovation whose works still inspire awe to this very day. Count Jocular, on the other hand, was an undead loon whose idea of fine décor was internal organs and velvet cushions strewn haphazardly about a room. So, as you can see, it's not actually a fine line at all. It's a dirty great, thick black one that art critics and snobs choose to ignore lest they be seen as less than Bohemian and as uncultured as a clean Petri dish. Unless it costs over a hundred grand or so of course, in which case they drool over it like a demented llama). Anyway, during Ollie's artistic deliberations with the Count, Stitches had the dubious pleasure of Egon's company. This incorporated a visit to the well-equipped torture chamber, (wailing victims included), a roof top walk in the worst storm since Noah built his floating zoo, and a detailed study of Egon's collection of bath plugs, which was ironic because the zombie was convinced that Egon hadn't immersed himself in soap and water for at least three hundred years. Add to that the spectacle of feeding time for One Lump and Two, and Stitches had left the castle on the verge of a nervous breakdown, vowing never to return until Flug was able to have a conversation of more than two sentences without fainting. Irony. Don't you just love it?

"Well, it does get busy down here, but we stop by when we can. Anyway, can I have a word with the Count please, Egon?" asked Ollie, eager to end his chat with the dwarf. He didn't mind talking to Egon he just didn't want to listen to any more of Jocular's titles being rattled off. That could go on for hours. "If he's not too busy of course."

"Certainly, Master Splint. I shall go and fetch him directly. I believe that he's in the atbrom... the arbormat... the greenhouse. Shan't be a mo."

The 'mo' turned out to be about five minutes during which Ollie wondered what on earth a vampire would want, or need, with a greenhouse. It's not as if he could pop out there at midday to check on his sunflowers and water his tomatoes.

"Sunflowers prosper very vell in zis climate, Ollie," said Jocular down the phone. "It's all a matter off creatiff cultiffation you see."

A sense of ice cold foreboding swept over Ollie like a freezing tsunami. It was bad enough that Jocular's voice alone was enough to shrink the softer parts of your anatomy and stop your heart mid beat, but to be able to pick up on the fact that he'd been thinking about particular items of flora was taking things a bit too far. He made a mental note to be more careful with his mental notes in future.

"Do they really?" he said, trying to keep his voice, and his bladder, on an even keel. "How very interesting."

"Indeed it is. So, vot can I do for you, Ollie?" asked Jocular.

The half vampire gave his immediate superior a rundown of the series of events leading up to his making the phone call. He tried to keep it as precise and as factual as possible because Jocular did have a tendency to lose his concentration sometimes, forget what you were talking about and kill you ever so slightly.

"So, Professor Crumble sinks zat vith ze aid off my bats and a decent storm, he and Mr. Kilo can reanimate ze corpse?"

"That's about the size of it yes, Sir."

"Vell, I must say zat it does sound like a very interesting project, Ollie. Anozer chapter to add to your ever increasing body of vork yes?"

"Absolutely."

"So, it is agreed zen. Ven shall I tell Egon to be expecting you?" "Probably a couple of days, My Lord, but I'll call ahead and give you plenty of notice if that's alright."

"Excellent. I shall haf Egon prepare some rooms for you and your colleagues."

"That's very kind of you, Sir."

"Not at all. Sink nussing of it. And now I must go. I'm helping vun off my staff members recuperate from a hop operation."

"Don't you mean a hip operation, My Lord?" "No. I had vun off his legs removed. Farevell."

———

Two days, four hospital visits, and thirty seven explosions (one of which made a tourist in Budapest say to his friend, "Did you feel that?") later, Crumble proudly announced that all was ready for them to travel to Jocular's castle to proceed with the full scale version of Kilo's experiment. That being the case he, Kilo, Flug and Mandrake made their way there first, taking all of the equipment and body parts with them. That left Ollie, Stitches and Ethan to bring up the rear and take any items the others had forgotten. Ronnie had volunteered to stay behind to take care of any business at the office. A couple of days shacked up at the vampire lord's palace of pain wasn't his idea of a good time. Ronnie's idea of a good time involved, well, you must have some idea by now.

A cold, dark evening saw the three of them boarding Bill the Coachman's carriage to make the trip.

"Flip flop, gents. 'Ow the out 'o' date chicken are ya? Wobble an' tripe awright?"

"Good grief, he's worse than usual tonight," observed Stitches, as he clambered onto the carriage. "Ordinarily I'd be able to glean some meaning from what he's saying but that was total and utter nonsense. It'd be easier to understand a drunk Russian with a speech impediment."

"What are you talking about?" countered Ethan, taking a seat opposite the zombie. "It makes perfect sense. Well, it does to me anyway." "How do you figure that out?" said Ollie. "Because I have to admit I struggle understanding Bill these days."

"It's simple. Flip flop, open shoe, exposed toe, hello," said Ethan. Both Ollie and Stitches stared at the lycan dumbfounded.

He continued. "And so it goes with, 'how the out of date chicken are you?' Out of date chicken, gone off a bit, rotten smell, hell."

"You're putting me on," said Stitches. "Not at all," said Ethan.

Stitches shook his head. "So, what you're essentially saying is that you take a phrase that has no bearing whatsoever on what you're trying to say, chuck in a few tenuous links and slap what you really mean on the end?"

"Precisely," said Ethan.

"Okay then," said Ollie, mischievously. "Let's take 'Wobble and tripe alright,' for instance. Wobble and tripe, jelly and meat, Sunday dinner, day of rest, work tomorrow, get up early, alarm bell ring, everything." "There you go," said Ethan with a big smile on his face. "Not bad for a beginner but you got there in the end."

"I don't know how," admitted Ollie, flabbergasted. "I was taking the mick if I'm honest."

"But that's the beauty of this type of slang. It kind of comes naturally," said Ethan.

"I think I'll stick to good old English thanks very much," said Stitches, relaxing into the soft velvet of his seat. "I can't say I fancy getting involved in a conversation that takes twice as long as it should because I have to use forty-seven words instead of one. Might as well be a politician."

"Almost there, gents," Bill shouted through his view flap. "Anuvver ten mins and we'll be right sorted aht." (Bill had heard the chat regarding his colourful verbalisations so he decided to tone it down a bit from Cockney BowBellend to Eastend stereotype.)

"That was bloody quick," said Stitches, sadly realising that he would be bumping into Egon rather sooner than he had hoped. "It seems like we only just got in."

And indeed they had but it wasn't just pleasant company and a bit of convivial chat that made the journey fly by. The remarkable thing about Bill's set up was that he operated on the fringes of time and space, and whilst certainly not alive he was by no means completely dead. This meant that he occupied a shadowy netherworld where the normal laws of physics had a bit of trouble making themselves heard. Up wasn't necessarily up, down was arbitrary at best, and time had a few problems travelling in a straight line. In fact, it wasn't unheard of for passengers to arrive at their destinations a few minutes before they'd actually gotten on board, which could be a teensy weensy bit disconcerting if you weren't prepared for it, as in the case of one poor soul who had boarded the carriage in the midst of a particularly robust cosmic flux. He'd been on his way to a surprise birthday party for his dear old mum the next day but had actually arrived just as she was preparing to get married. To his Father. Naturally he'd had to think quickly to explain why a young man looking a lot like her future husband had suddenly appeared, which took some doing because not everyone has bright purple hair and three nostrils. He got out of it by claiming that he was a distant cousin several dozen times removed and had travelled to the celebration from his mud hut on the side of a mountain. This also conveniently explained why one of his legs was eight inches shorter than the other one. Another family trait you see. After all, legs do run in families, ha ha.

It does make you wonder though, what on earth his poor mum saw in his dad to be honest. Mind you she was a cave dwelling mud ogre so she couldn't afford to be too choosy. Anyway, the young chap had a great time at the reception and even managed to suggest to his mum that should she have a son in the future, she should get him the Grim Reaper costume that he would no doubt want for his ninth birthday, and not the hand knitted bobble hat and glove combo that she would first think of because three of the gloves would be too small and not have enough finger and ear holes. As you've no doubt already imagined they weren't a particularly attractive family, but then inbreeding and genetic mutations are a common factor amongst the royals.

(Authors note. Any issues that the reader may have with paradoxes, time travel, quantum mechanics and the like please write to Professor Brian Cox at whichever highbrow university he's knocking about in these days or courtesy of the BBC. He can explain it because I sure as hell can't).

"Ere we go, peeps," said Bill, his red eyes glowing like the fires of Hell from the depths of his hood. "Safe as arses."

Ollie, Stitches and Ethan disembarked and said farewell to the coachman, thankful that their 'arses' had been in good hands.

"Ah well," said the zombie, trailing the other two to the front door. "Here goes another entertaining few days trying to avoid that mentally disturbed oompah loompah."

"Hopefully it won't be as bad for you this time," said Ollie, who was using both hands to raise the new door knocker. It was jet black and etched with variously coloured flecks of paint and was in the shape of what seemed to be Santa Claus (If he was in a really bad mood, had taken a wheelbarrow full of steroids and carrying a meat cleaver that had suspiciously looking meaty globs along it's sharp edge.)

Ollie let it go and a crash like two planets colliding resounded throughout the valley, as well as in their heads. It was so loud that people twenty five miles away answered their front doors before shouting at non-existent kids to stop mucking about.

Very slowly but very surely, the door to Jocular's castle opened revealing the magnificent entrance hall, exquisite artistry and one extremely ugly dwarf type thing.

"Hello, Egon," said Ollie. "How are you?"

"Oh, splendid thank you. And all the better for having a few visitors it has to be said. Good evening, Ethan."

"Egon."

"And a very warm welcome to you, Master Stitches," oozed Egon as he ushered the trio inside. "I trust you're keeping well?"

"Indeed I am," replied the zombie in a strictly formal and businesslike manner. "Couldn't be better. And yes, everything is in working order and where it should be thank you very much. And that's how I expect it to be when we leave."

"Well isn't that smashing," said a smiling Egon, not picking up on the hint.

"As long as we're clear," said Stitches, being careful not to step on Egon's hump and not picking up on the fact that Egon hadn't picked up on his hint.

"Wasn't that thing a different colour the last time we were here?" asked Ollie, looking at the disturbing, gelatinous splat of flesh before him, after which he returned his gaze to the hump.

"It was, yes. How observant of you. Both One Lump and Two used to be flesh coloured, but I was starting to have some trouble telling them apart so I painted this one red."

"That makes sense," said Ethan. "What colour is the other one?"
"Red," said Egon, matter of factly.

"I don't want to state the obvious but I think I'm going to have to," said Stitches. "Tell me, Egon. Are you still having problems telling them apart by any chance?"

"Funnily enough yes," said Egon, a perplexed look on his misshapen, pumpkin like head. "You would've thought that marking them would have made it easier. I really can't understand it."

"Maybe you should try painting them a different colour," said Ollie, wondering if Skullenia was on the verge of crowning a brand new Thickie of the Year champion.

"What a splendid idea," said Egon, closing the enormous front door. "I'll do that as soon as my duties are over for the night. This way please, gentlemen."

"Where are the others, Egon?" asked Ethan, as they traversed the innards of the castle. He hadn't been killed in an explosion yet so they couldn't be that close. Then again. . .

"They're in the laboratory on the top floor. I haven't been up there since this morning but I've heard a lot of banging and crashing and swearing so I assume that they're hard at work."

"It's not the banging and crashing that you need to worry about," said Stitches. "It's the unexpected detonations that you need to be wary of."

"Really?"

"Yup, because they're usually the precursor to buildings and people going missing, more damage than an earthquake in a third world country, and expensive repair bills. And that's just when he's making a glass of squash."

"I shouldn't overly concern yourself with that too much if I were you," said Egon after a moments consideration. He placed a stubby figured hand on Stitches' arm. "The castle is quite resilient you know. It's survived all sorts of disasters, both manmade and natural, including the Master's extensive remodelling. Ah, here we are."

Egon raised his hand to knock but as always he was pre-empted by a chilling voice from within.

"Enter."

"Our visitors, My Lord," Egon announced as he led them into the room. It was comparatively smaller than any of the other rooms that they'd previously visited and by far and away the most normal. There were no outlandish pieces of furniture, no wallpaper so dazzling that it would give a blind person double vision, and not a single disturbing sculpture, lurid painting, or torture victim in sight.

His Royal Darkness was sat at a table fiddling with a small black box. Well it looked small in Jocular's gigantic mitts. If any normal person was messing around with it you might have thought that they were interfering with a microwave.

"Ah, good effening, gentlemen. I vill be viz you shortly. I seem to be haffing a spot of bozzer viz my new item."

There were buttons on it, wires sticking out of it, and a distinct crackle coming from somewhere inside it.

"What is it, Sir, if you don't mind me asking?" said Ethan.

"It is an AM PM radio," said Jocular, untangling a red wire from a blue one. "I purchased it from a travelling fendor."

"Sorry. Did you say an AM PM radio?" said the lycan.

"I did indeed. Ze fellow said it produces high qvality music in ze

470

morning and in ze afternoon, but I don't seem to be able to get a sing out of it."

Stitches wandered over and cast a glance over the electronic jumble that the vampire lord was wrestling with. Despite the enormous size of his hands Jocular was quite dexterous as it turned out and he seemed to be rummaging through the mess with all the consummate ease of a seasoned watch-smith. He supposed that made sense though. You couldn't very well survive for centuries as a vampire Lord without being fairly nimble of digit. Virgins needed handling very delicately, and silk shirts and cravats snagged and tore very easily. Jocular was also surprisingly adept at the Rubiks Cube, threading needles, and assembling those fiddly little models that come inside chocolate eggs. Of course it also helped to be a bloodthirsty, homicidal maniac, but then everyone has a softer side don't they.

The zombie, as per usual, was about to make a subtly sarcastic comment, but the sight of fingers that had biceps put him off ever so slightly, which was just as well. Jocular could easily strangle him with one hand and have enough overlap at the back to snap his fingers to a funky salsa beat (one of his favourites apparently.) So what with discretion being the better part of not wanting to get shredded, and the fact that they couldn't be more terrified of The Count if he put on a scary clown mask, went 'Mwahahahahaha', and whipped out a balloon in the shape of a battleaxe, Ollie and Ethan kept their witty comments and observations to themselves as well. It was better to be undead than completely dead after all.

"Maybe you should have a word with the chap," said Ollie. "I'm sure he'd oblige if you asked him for a refund."

"Oh, zere's no need for zat," said Jocular, pushing the useless box away from him. "He von't be knocking on my door again."

"Disappeared has he?" asked Ethan.

"Not exactly no. He is currently hanging upside down in my cellar. I am hoping zat a head full of blood and getting an attack off ze dizzies vill make him see ze sense. I haff found zat some time taken out in ze qviet allows vun to contemplate ze error off vuns vays. I belief it is called cognitive behaffioural therapy."

"Oh, that's a good idea. I must say that's very forward thinking of you. It's not many people that go to the trouble of getting to the root causes of peoples actions and understanding them, rather than indulging in knee jerk reactions of retribution," said Stitches, genuinely impressed. "So what'll happen when he's had his time?"

Jocular stood up and stretched. It was like watching a pylon being straightened out.

"Oh, I shall kill him off course, and fery messily, but at least he vill go to his final resting place knowing how fery naughty he has been. And about eight pints drier I suspect, no?"

Not even the smallest of titters broke through.

'So much for that', thought the zombie, taking an involuntary step back.

"Anyvay, enough off such trifling triffia," Jocular continued. "I vould imagine zat you're qvite keen to check on ze progress off your colleagues, yes? From vot Egon tells me zey are getting on splendidly."

"Have you not seen it for yourself, My Lord?" asked Ollie, thinking that seeing the others wasn't the only reason that he was keen to get to the lab.

Jocular shook his head and knitted his eyebrows. It was like watching two mutant, but very well turned out caterpillars running toward each other.

"No. It is fery high up and exposed to ze elements. Zere's not enough glass up zere you see, and I do haff a bit of a problem viz ze heights sometimes. Effry now and again it makes me feel a bit like a voozy."

(Now it might seem a bit strange that a vampire, and in particular one of Jocular's elevated status, should suffer from acrophobia, but it is quite common. Although able to tolerate flying around in bat form, a lot of vampires like to stay fairly close to the ground once they take flight for fear of going all wibbly wobbly and crashing into something. And it does make sense if you think about it. If they were happy to go up any higher then evolution would have created such creatures as vampire eagles, blood sucking albatrosses and flocks of marauding starlings swooping down and getting up to all sorts of nonsense. Plus there'd be a hell of a lot more vampires out there with a pilot's license). "Egon vill show you ze vay," said Jocular. "I must check on my guest anyvay. I don't vont to leave him hanging around forever."

Once dismissed from Jocular's quite frankly terrifying presence, they made their way up what seemed like an infinite number of steps before reaching laboratory level. As they approached the door they could hear clangs, crashes, smashes and bangs coming from inside. It was reminiscent of standing outside Crumble's lab at home, only much louder and, no doubt, decidedly more dangerous.

"Sounds like the Prof is having a whale of a time in there," said Stitches. "Can you imagine what he's getting up to with all that equipment. I'm genuinely shocked that the planet's still in one piece."

"To be fair," said Egon, who was well aware of Crumble's reputation for being more destructive than a troop of river dancers in an active minefield, "it hasn't gone too badly. We've only lost two benches, one wall, and a cat."

He bent down and picked up One Lump and Two. The other one, (whichever one it was, it was nigh on impossible to tell. It was like trying to tell the difference between a chair), having joined them at some point between Jocular's room and the lab. He turned to Stitches. "Would you mind? It's quite dangerous in there and I wouldn't want one of the little chaps getting hurt."

'Can you tell if a lump gets a lump', thought Stitches as one of the fleshy sacks manoeuvred its way onto his arm and nestled there. It didn't have legs or any other obvious form of locomotion so heaven knew how it moved about.

"Surely if one of them takes a knock you could just put an ice pack on it couldn't you?" he said. "Or pop it into the freezer." The incorporeal dollop wriggled next to his bicep. "Which one is this by the way?"

"One Lump I think," said Egon, looking carefully. "But I'm not a hundred percent sure. I really must take up Master Splint's suggestion and paint them different colours."

Fed up with lump talk, Ethan opened up the door and they all entered the lab.

"Wow!" exclaimed the lycan.

The laboratory was immense and it seemed as if every available space within its cavernous interior was taken up with some bit of equipment or another. Some of it was humming quietly whilst other items had sparks and mini bolts of lightning coursing round them. There were spinning copper coils, variously coloured diodes and switches, levers all over the place, and two eight feet tall glass tanks that seemed to be full of a cloudy, transparent liquid. Wooden crates lay scattered about the place, some of them open, some not, and hundreds of feet of wire curled around the walls and ceiling. In the rafters was a large silver sphere covered in a golden mesh. It swung lazily back and forth like a massive chrome pendulum. It whispered quietly through the air as it moved.

SWOOSH. SWOOSH. SWOOSH.

In the centre of all this technological madness was a mortuary table. On it lay Kilo's body parts (not his own obviously. He was using those), and he, Crumble and Flug were gathered around it. It was Flug who spotted them first.

"Ah, greetings friends," he boomed. "Welcome to our humble work place. As you can see we've been rather busy."

"I'll say," said Ollie, taking it all in. "Who'd have thought that you needed this lot for a bit of reanimation."

"You got that right," Stitches agreed. "There must be enough electricity flowing through here to get Godzilla up and running."

Crumble looked up from the slab and smiled.

"I think you may be a little confused," he said, gesturing to the myriad mechanical madness. "We had nothing to do with this lot."

"What's it all for then?" asked Ethan.

"It runs the central heating," said Egon. "That's why it's so big. You'd be surprised how hard it is to warm up a castle this size. The stonework haemorrhages heat like a colander." He looked at a misted gauge and gave it a flick. The dial beneath the glass jumped slightly then settled back to its original position. "It's not the best though. It's been here for decades and I have a feeling its badly in need of a service. Even when its at full capacity the hot water can be extremely temperamental. Sometimes I can make tea with it."

Ollie instantly went from being really excited to downright disappointed faster than a lottery winner who's just found out that his winning ticket is currently residing in the digestive system of the cat, and won't be making a reappearance until the next day in Mrs. Spire's garden at number 56.

"So what exactly are you doing here then?" asked Ethan. "And where's all your stuff?"

"It's round the back but we're doing the main bulk of the work here because the floor back there isn't that robust. There's no way it would have taken this table as it's made of marble, but seeing as it cleans up easily we decided to use it," said Kilo, who was holding a bloodstained scalpel in his bloodstained hand. "Once the body's reassembled we'll transfer it to a light weight trolley and take it through."

Ollie, Stitches and Ethan, led by Crumble, went and had a look 'round the back.' To be honest it wasn't quite as impressive as the area that they'd just come from. It was like comparing Buckingham Palace to a rain soaked cardboard box that hadn't had a decent tidy up since the Victorian era. There was a single bench that had scientific odds and ends on it, a couple of chairs, and a fair smattering of discarded sweet wrappers (even with an enhanced IQ Flug still craved confectionery every thirty-seven seconds.) What did look marginally decent though was the large wooden wheel attached to the farthest wall. It was about thirty feet in diameter and roughly six feet off the floor. A wad of thick wires protruded from behind it, snaking across the floor before stopping just behind Crumble's feet.

"So as you can see," said the Professor, "once Mr. Kilo has finished with his knife and needle we can bring the body in here and get set up. We hook up the wires, ask Count Jocular to summon his bats and away we go."

There were indeed at least three dozen leather harnesses attached to the wheel at regular intervals along its circumference.

"And then we just open up a window and hope a passing bolt of lightning pops in?" said Stitches.

"Oh no, my dear boy," said Crumble, suppressing a smile. "I think you've been reading too much Shelley. This isn't the Dark Ages you know. Once the bats get moving they'll provide more than enough power."

(To be honest, Skullenia does reside in an evolutionary time frame that could quite easily be compared to life in the Dark Ages. There's pseudo barbarians wandering about killing and maiming anything they lay their eyes on, barely functioning peasants whose brains are about as much use as a slimming club in a concentration camp, and a ruler who oversees his lands with an iron fist and who has no qualms whatsoever in rendering to grisly chunks anyone who gets on his nerves. Don't let that sully your image of Skullenia though. It could be worse. It could be like Glasgow).

Ollie walked over to the wheel and gave it a shake.

"Sturdy," he said, not really having any idea how fixtures and fittings were fixed and fitted. "How did you get it built so quickly?"

"We didn't actually," said Crumble, tidying up the wires on the floor. "There's an old mill on the castle grounds. It's not used any more so we borrowed it. It saved us a lot of time."

"How on earth did you get it up here?" asked Ethan, who was as powerful as an Olympic weightlifter, but under no illusions that if he tried to lift it he'd get a hernia the size of a mattress. "It must weigh a ton."

"Flug and Egon brought it up," said Crumble. "That little chap is a lot stronger then he looks."

They all stared back at the diminutive domestic who had a smug, self-satisfied grin on his squashy chops.

"It was nothing really," he said, waving a dismissive hand. "I've always been blessed with a certain amount of natural strength."

"There's nothing natural about being able to shift that," said Stitches, suddenly remembering that he was carrying a wandering cyst. "Can you take this back by the way? It seems to be getting a bit restless," he added, sounding like a single man forced into holding a baby.

"Actually it's their bedtime. Would you like to help me put them down for the night?" said Egon.

Just them Flug came round the corner.

"Professor Crumble," he said. "Mr. Kilo is ready to attach the head and he requires your. . . um... sweets."

"Righto," said Crumble, as if Flug's statement were the most normal thing ever uttered.

Ollie looked at Stitches and ever so slightly shook his head.

"Not a word," whispered the half vampire, a warning note in his voice. "We knew this might happen at some point, just not when. Let it go please."

"Fair enough," said the disgruntled zombie, who was fit to burst after such an extended period of not being able to chastise Flug.

"I tell you what. Why don't you go with Egon," Ollie suggested, figuring Flug's transition from esteemed intellectual back to gibbering imbecile would be a damned sight easier if Stitches wasn't around. Unfortunately for the zombie, Ollie had heard Egon's offer a few minutes before.

Stitches, well aware of the sensitivity of Egon's hearing, motioned Ollie to a far corner of the room.

"You know how I feel about him," he protested quietly. "He's weird and makes me feel uncomfortable."

"Then a little bit of time with him will do you good," said Ollie. "But he's got the grooming habits of a chimpanzee," the zombie complained bitterly.

"I won't be argued with," insisted Ollie, folding his arms defiantly.

"And have you seen him eat? It's like watching a cement mixer." "I want you to go with Egon."

"He'll chop me up limb from limb, you know that don't you? I'll be a headline in the paper. Handsome zombie comes apart at the seams."

"Stitches." "Yes."

"Go away."

"Fine. But if I get dismembered I'll. . . " "What?"

"£$%&*+? % $£*& ?%$£&... and then pull it out again."

"Charming^. See yo^u later."

———

Excalibur Cross and Ramekin Deadhouse were sitting at their respective desks in their office at the headquarters of the Skullenian Times. Actually headquarters was a bit of a grand title to be honest. It was more of an oversized shed on the outskirts of town that got so cold during the winter that it was enough to freeze the icicles off a penguin. Also, to continue with the description, their office was so small that Cross had to be careful with the arm of his typewriter, lest it break the window, and their desks were a couple of upturned crates snaffled from somewhere or another. These paltry surroundings however, did nothing to diminish their enthusiasm for reporting the news, and despite the primitive nature of their work environment they managed to put out a reasonably decent paper sometimes up to twice a fortnight (or once a week depending on how busy they were.)

Past successes had included an expose into the illegal trade in zombie worms, where had the postman gone, and a stunning piece of investigative journalism into what actually goes into a witch's apple pie. As it turned out it was nothing out of the ordinary. It was simply spider's eggs, worm dribble, ant sweat, fractured hamster feet, tincture of bat dust, 125 grammes of flour and sugar to taste. Their findings had totally negated the claim that one had been made containing Bramley apples which was, quite frankly, disgusting. As of now though they were struggling for their latest headline.

Cross threw down his pen, closed his notebook, and leaned back in his chair (another upturned crate with a plank nailed to the back).

"Nothing," he said, exasperated. "I can't think of a single thing that's happened that's worthy of a story."

After taking a load of snaps at the cemetery they'd spoken to Constable Gullett who'd informed them of the outcome of his interview with Kilo, and that had killed the story stone dead, because reanimation wasn't exactly something new. It was *creating* something new, but that was old hat. In fact they'd reported on it only last year when Jethro Rockbuster, a visiting dimwit of some renown, had tried to breathe life into Skullenia's flagging tourism trade. Despite some criticism (I mean who wants to go all the way to the desolate wastes of a spooky village in Eastern Europe and get brutally murdered and eaten by a drooling, half witted, preternatural monster when you can get the bus to Millwall), he did have a small amount of success with his venture. A mob of villagers had visited from the next village and caught up with him at his room at The Bolt and Jugular. After some robust discussions involving a length of rope, a chair, and a blunt machete, they'd left him in rather more pieces than usual. It was something to do with a time share scam apparently. Mind you, when the mob left the pub they'd stolen some towels, half a dozen light bulbs, and a shower head, so it was kind of touristy.

"What-t-t-t about the Fibulan-n-n-n library scandal-l-l-l?" said Deadhouse, fiddling about with his camera. "We could do a piece on that-t-t-t."

"It's slightly out of our area, but at the moment I'm willing to go with anything. Go on then. What's the big scoop?"

"Well-l-l-l, Aubrey Tombjumper heard from Mrs. Crackpot that her friend-d-d-d, Captain Von Schitenhausen's cousins-s-s-s housekeeper's younger brother-r-r-r, forgot to take his book-k-k-k back and got quite a hefty-y-y-y fine."

Cross pinched the bridge of his nose extremely tightly, not because it helped, but because it was slightly more painful than what he'd just listened to, and may go some way to making hearing it slightly less arduous. Why he asked his next question was beyond him. Maybe it was a measure of how bored and fed up he actually was.

"Well, I can't deny it, Ramekin old chap, you've got me hooked. Don't leave me hanging now."

"As it turned out-t-t-t," continued Deadhouse, totally oblivious of Cross's sarcastic demeanour, "the book, Rowling's Guide to the Tedious-s-s-s, was three days late and he was fined-d-d-d sixpence. It was the talk-k-k-k of the town."

"So was the Black Death and nobody bothered to write about that either. Although that's probably because they were all dead, and nobody noticed any discernible difference, but that's beside the point. There has to be something we can print."

"We could-d-d-d do what we've done before-e-e-e," suggested Deadhouse. "We could make up a story-y-y-y or two."

Cross furrowed his brow and shook his head.

"I have considered it believe me. But after the confrontation with Gullett the other day I'm not sure that's such a good idea. He'd probably lock me up. I know there's a certain amount of freedom to our press but I don't want to push it too far."

Deadhouse left his chair and made them both a cup of tea which they sat drinking in silence. Ten minutes passed before Cross suddenly sat bolt upright, seized his notebook and exclaimed, "Yes!" excitedly.

"What-t-t-t," said Deadhouse, picking his camera up off the floor. "Jocular. No one has ever done an interview with Jocular. We could go up to the castle, I could do an in-depth interview with him and you can get some piccies of the place. If he agrees and we print it, we'll sell more copies than we've ever sold before."

"Twenty-six-x-x-x!" exclaimed Deadhouse.

"Maybe even more than that. I'll nip down to the village and use Mrs. Strudel's phone."

"Just bear-r-r-r in mind that this was tried-d-d-d once before," said Deadhouse, a warning tone to his voice.

"I know, I know," said Cross, putting his coat on. "Whatever happened to old Humpy anyway? The last anyone saw of him he was getting into Bill's coach."

"You know-w-w-w the larger of the two gargoyles-s-s-s above Jocular's front door?"

"I've heard about it yes."

Deadhouse didn't need to say another word. His meaning was clear. "Ah, but there's one thing you've got to remember, Ramekin old chap," said Cross as he opened the door. "What-t-t-t?"

"It's me."

That's exactly what I'm afraid of, Deadhouse thought to himself as Cross headed into the night.

———

Stitches paced up and down the corridor nervously. He'd been doing so for about ten minutes but it felt more like a century and a half. After leaving the lab, Egon had told him to wait here because he needed to attend to a small task. No doubt it was something innocuous, but of course the zombie's imagination had run wild on the strength of that ambiguous open ended statement. He was thinking of everything from thumb screws and the rack to hanging, drawing, and quartering with instruments ranging from red hot pokers to teaspoons. 'I should have stood up to Ollie,' he thought. 'I'm definitely going to get him back for this'.

"Ah, Master Stitches," came the dulcet tones of Egon as he rejoined his guest. "I seem to have encountered a slight problem."

Apart from all the ones that Mother Nature had given him, Stitches couldn't immediately see what he was talking about.

Egon lifted up a wicker basket that he was holding and opened a flap in the top.

"I tried Master Splint's suggestion," he said, disconsolately, "but I'm afraid I still can't tell them apart."

"Did you paint them a different colour?" asked Stitches. "Indeed I did. See for yourself."

Stitches gazed into the basket. Inside, the two amorphous blobs lay side by side on a bed of fresh hay. At least it looked like hay. It was probably human hair ripped from a witless victim that Egon had kidnapped in the depths of the night who was even now shackled in a subterranean pit whilst he waited for a grisly and messy death. Not that Stitches had any preconceived ideas about the creepy, serial killing dwarf though.

"Egon."

"Yes, Master."

"When Ollie said to paint them a different colour I think he meant to paint one of them blue and one of them red. You've painted them both blue."

"Oh I see," said Egon, slapping his forehead and making a sound reminiscent of a dead catfish flopping onto the surface of a stagnant pond. "That does make more sense. I'll sort it out tomorrow."

"So where do the little darlings sleep?" asked Stitches, trying to inject as much enthusiasm into the question as he was able, which was precisely none.

"In a little cubby hole in my bedroom," said Egon, removing a large key from a trouser pocket. "I have a suite of rooms off the main dungeon complex."

Stitches shuddered at the thought of what Egon's suite of rooms must look like. The set of the latest Saw movie sprang immediately to mind.

A short walk along the corridor led to a side door which Egon opened.

"This way, Master."

Cold stone steps led down, down, and further down until the only light that was left was the meagre glow from a candle that Egon had produced from somewhere. Their footsteps echoed in the dark passage as their shoes clicked eerily on the frigid rock.

After what seemed like the concluding portion of the second century that he'd already been in Egon's company had passed and made it into a nice round double, Stitches noticed something that could be described of as a 'bit weird' (our sort of weird that is, not his. A lot of people would find the cat not coming in on time, or the bins not being collected, 'a bit weird'. The average Skullenian resident's idea of something 'a bit weird' would be the postman having not as many legs as usual, which was normally about five and a half, or going out at night and not being attacked by all manner of, quite frankly, odd looking thingies that squirt ectoplasm like a haunted fire hose, and want to eat your face. Now that's quite a sweeping statement so just for balance, and acknowledging the fact that you can't pigeon-hole people, if you live in the wilds of The Outer Hebrides you can disregard that last bit. No one wants to know what you lot find weird. Chances are it's not a very long list).

"Egon, it's getting warm." (Told you it was weird).

"Indeed it is, Master. Just a few more steps and we'll be at my humble abode."

Stitches had already decided that the increase in temperature was due to the fact that Egon had a rusty spit above a large fire that he would be slowly roasted over. Maybe he should just cut his losses and bolt, admit to Ollie that he was a big wuss, and emigrate somewhere safer like down-town Mali.

"Here we are, Master." Too late.

Egon opened the door onto. . . hang on. . . that's unexpected.

It was a sitting room, he realised, noting that it was thankfully bereft of any torture chamber like fixtures and fittings. On closer inspection, there didn't appear to be anything abnormal or creepy or other worldly present, and nothing sharp, pointy, or overtly tortury seemed to be immediately obvious. It was just a normal room. For sitting in.

A sitting room. The heat was coming from a coal fire nestled in the far wall.

"Well, this is rather pleasant," said the zombie, pleasantly taken aback somewhat. "More homey and less homeycidal than I imagined." "Mmm. Do sit down won't you," said Egon, not quite sure what Stitches was on about. "Cup of tea?" "Just water thanks."

Whilst Egon was away getting the drinks, Stitches took the opportunity to have a proper look around from the confines of his, quite frankly, extremely comfy arm chair. At least that's what his opinion of it would be until it suddenly turned into a shuddering, metal spike extruding, body slicing contraption that would give Edgar Allen Poe the heebie jeebies. Still, he wasn't judging. Much.

There were a couple of landscape paintings hanging on the wall, a charming ornament on the mantle-piece depicting an entwined couple, and an antique wooden stand on top of which was an old-style gramophone. Next to the fireplace was a bookshelf. Stitches got up to have a look. 'Loves Errand' by Doris Doorknocker, 'I've Had it Up To Here With Being Short' by Little John 'O' Jonjon, and 'Everything You Wanted To Know About Vampires But Were Afraid To Ask Because You Were Worried About Getting Your Throat Torn Out' by Bleeders Digest, were just three of the titles that he read to himself.

"I see you're admiring my collection," said Egon upon his return. He handed Stitches a glass of water and they both sat down. "Something of a hobby of mine, old books," he continued, after taking a sip of tea. He pointed at the bookcase. "Some of them are extremely rare. My copy of Fotheringay's 'Wibbles, Wobbles and Wonky Things' is one of only two in existence."

"That's interesting," said Stitches, genuinely curious much to his surprise. "Must be worth quite a bit too. Who's got the other one?"

"Me. It's in a box under my bed." "I see. What's that one?"

"Which one, Master?"

"The one on the table next to you. Is that what you're reading at the moment?"

"Not as such no," said Egon, picking up the leather bound tome and flicking through it. "These are my memoirs."

"Really. How long have you been writing those?"

"About forty years now I think. It's quite the undertaking though. I've been in His Lordships service since 1583, about lunchtime on January 29th to be precise, so there's quite a lot to get through. I'm up the early 1900's at present. I think I'll probably be done within the next five years or so, give or take the odd decorating mishap or unscheduled genocide."

"So what then? Get it published? I reckon there could be quite a market for a book like that. You could make a fortune and get yourself out of here."

"Oh no. I couldn't ever do that," said Egon, putting the book back onto the table. "I could never leave Count Jocular's employ. No, if I ever come into any money I'll put it to use around the castle. Anyway, it's about time I put the boys down. Would you like to bring them through?"

Stitches, feeling a lot more relaxed and well disposed towards the tiny domestic on account of the fact that he hadn't come at him with any farming implements or items of sharpened cutlery, grabbed the wicker basket from the floor and followed Egon into his bedroom. As the zombie passed through the doorway he nearly fell over. The last thing he ever expected to see in Egon's bedroom was a massive four poster bed, the posts of which were intricately carved mahogany. The bed spread was eclectically flamboyant as well. It was a patch work quilt that, up until a few hours ago, Stitches would have assumed to be made of human skin. It seemed to comprise silk and velvet and looked so inviting that it was all that Stitches could do not to dive onto it and have a lie down.

"I bet you made that, didn't you?" he said, giving it a plump with his free hand.

"Most certainly. I find needlework very relaxing after a long night."

Stitches handed the basket over to Egon.

"But how do find the time? Jocular must keep you busy from dusk till dawn. If he's not entertaining someone in one of his spiky guest rooms he's decorating something or another."

Egon opened up a wardrobe and placed the wicker basket containing its lumpy inhabitants onto a large purple pillow. Then he opened the side flap and waited until both of them had crawled out and settled down. (Try as he might Stitches still couldn't figure out how they moved).

"I just seem to," said Egon, removing the basket and closing the door. "No matter how time consuming my duties are I always seem to have enough left over to do all the little extra things I must, and all of the things I want. Anyway," he whispered, "let's go back to the sitting room. The boys are light sleepers."

Contemplating the fact that the last half an hour had been bizarre to say the least, Stitches quietly tiptoed out of the bedroom.

———

Ollie had been watching Kilo work with rapt attention, marvelling at the chap's dextrous skill. He really was a master at his craft, and bearing in mind how minuscule some of the internal capillaries and nerves were, it was truly amazing that such an operation as this were possible at all, especially as most of the beings that he'd met in Skullenia had trouble tying their shoes up (which in the case of some was nigh on impossible because they'd eaten them).

As he observed Kilo putting the final sutures into some part of the liver, the sudden lack of a presence caught his attention. It was kind of like the Force in reverse, just with less light sabres and fewer scantily clad princesses (Unfortunately. I could have put one in I suppose, but I would have had terrible trouble fitting it into the story. The same goes for the princess). He looked up and gazed round the laboratory.

"Flug," he said.

Nothing.

"FLUG!" he said again, a bit louder.

"Yeah, Ollie." "Where's Mandrake?" "Uh. . . who?"

"Mandrake. The chap we brought with us. Six feet, slim build, got a cat called Noggin, always trying to top himself. Mandrake that is, not the cat."

"Uh, me don't know, Ollie." "Terrific."

"Ollie."

"Yes, Flug." "Where are we?"

Ollie realised that Flug had finally returned to abnormal. Gone were the stratospheric intellect and the dazzling insights to the amazing world around him. He had come back to earth with a resoundingly dull sounding thump. Straight onto his head. It was quite comforting in a way he supposed, and he had to admit, he wouldn't miss the detailed snippets of information that had been tagged onto the end of every conversation.

"We're at Count Jocular's castle, remember?"

The bemused look on the monster's face was ample testimony to his understanding of the current situation.

"Why don't you just sit on that crate over there okay, mate." "Okay."

'Right', thought Ollie, after showing Flug what a crate was, where it was and how to sit on it. 'Where are you, you deranged lunatic?'

By reputation alone it was obvious that Mandrake wasn't going to be anywhere unsafe and doing anything remotely dangerous. Flug would have more chance of receiving a serious injury from a sweet wrapper than Mandrake had of actually hurting himself during one of his end of life escapades. Actually, scratch that thought he mused. On one memorable occasion Flug had conspired to damage himself with a washing up sponge. Okay so he was cleaning moss off the roof tiles at the time (Stitches' idea), forgot where he was, and stepped off, but the principal was the same. Not that Marmaduke Thesaurus was likely to ascribe to that train of thought. No doubt he hadn't gotten up that day with the intention of being flattened by a falling monster coming towards him at roughly the same speed as the meteor that did for the dinosaurs. To say that he wasn't very happy about the incident was a bit of an understatement. He said, and I quote, "Can't you keep control of that big lumbering, heavy footed, blundering, and ungainly, maladroit ox. I was lucky not to be killed, terminated, dispatched, liquidated, and butchered." Conversations with Marmaduke could take a very, very long time.

Ollie was walking passed a particularly large bundle of copper wire when he heard a muffled noise.

"Mmmppffhh." "Hello," he called out.

"MMMPPFFHH," came the sound again. It was followed by a clink as if someone had wrapped a knuckle on a window.

Ollie cautiously made his way to the rear of the pile of wire. "Oh, you absolute arse head."

Hidden away behind the copper was a large glass cabinet very similar to the ones on the other side of the lab. This one though was empty, covered in cobwebs, and cracked in several places. The only other subtle difference was that the other ones in the main part of the lab didn't have a forlorn looking Mandrake hiding inside them looking as if he was about to burst into tears.

"Hang on a minute," said Ollie, exasperatedly. He quickly located the step ladder that Mandrake had no doubt used to climb in and propped it up against the tank.

"Thanks," said Mandrake, extricating himself and climbing down. "What on earth were you trying this time?" asked Ollie, helping him down the last few rungs.

"I thought I'd have a go at suffocating myself but I panicked," said Mandrake, looking thoroughly ashamed of himself. "I've got a bit of a problem with small spaces."

Ollie studied the glass tank in more detail. Not only were there so many cracks in it that it couldn't have held a solid let alone a liquid, a grill ran around the top ensuring an ever constant flow of air.

"You'd have had more chance suffocating yourself standing in the street," said the vampire, clearly a bit miffed.

"Sorry, Ollie," said Mandrake.

Ollie decided enough was enough. He had plenty to do without having to babysit a walking organ donor twenty-four hours a day. It was time to be cruel to be kind and employ a touch of reverse psychology. Ollie approached the prospective suicide victim (seventy-four attempts so far and counting), and went into full scale demon mode. He seemed to grow six inches in height and suddenly took on the stature of a lifelong power lifter. Then, as if in tandem with the emerging beast, the atmosphere in their immediate vicinity darkened and became more oppressive and threatening. All extraneous noise dissipated so that all that could be heard was the rapidly increasing rate of Mandrake's breathing. As he stared in mounting terror at Ollie he saw his face begin to change. The half vampire's cheeks seemed to sink inwards causing his lips to draw back from his gums revealing a pair of perfectly white fangs that grew longer and sharper as he watched. Ollie's eyes widened to twice their normal size and blazed a hellish red. Blood red. Their gaze seemed to bore into Mandrake's very being and he felt as if an icy, clawed hand had taken hold of his soul and was slowly, but irrevocably, choking it out of existence.

Ollie took a step forward so that he was now towering over the trembling figure of Mandrake.

"I DON'T DO THIS LIGHTLY," he said, his voice a full octave lower than usual, "BUT YOUR CONSTANT, PATHETIC EFFORTS TO END YOURSELF ARE TESTING MY PATIENCE TO ITS LIMITS. AT PRESENT, MY HUMAN SIDE IS THE ONLY THING PREVENTING ME TEARING YOU LIMB FROM BLOODY LIMB. IF YOU REALLY WISH TO DIE THEN I CAN ASSIST YOU. IT WILL BE QUICK, BUT IT WILL FINALLY BE DONE. SO, MANDRAKE, SPEAK. WHAT IS IT THAT YOU WANT? LIVE OR DIE. THE CHOICE IS YOURS."

Mandrake stood perfectly still, his eyes agog and his breath coming in ragged, shallow gasps. He had the look of a springbok staring at a river that it needed to cross, realising that it contained more crocodiles than water. Like a drowning man his whole life flashed before his eyes, and the numerous attempts he had made to bring it to a premature conclusion flooded his mind. His subconscious self decided to join in at that point and began to hammer away at its conscious counterpart. Unbidden words popped into his head as he watched Ollie's eyes grow redder and redder.

'Here's your chance. If you want to die this is it. You can have it all ended here and now so stop being such a baby and get on with it.' (The subconscious is quite adept at mind games).

Other images coalesced in his mind. His wife, his children, and yes even dear, fluffy, homicidal Noggin. A sudden rush of emotion swept over him. His subconscious tutted subconsciously.

Mandrake let out a wail and threw his arms around Ollie. "I want to live," he cried, as tears coursed down his cheeks.

"I know you do," said Ollie, returning to normal. He patted Mandrake on the back and gave him a squeeze. "But remember, my offer still stands."

"Oh no," said Mandrake, whose face now looked as if it had been dipped in wallpaper paste. "I've reached a turning point." He let go of Ollie and wiped his face. "The prospect of actually dying scared me to death."

"Well, you hold onto that thought and everything will be fine," said Ollie, making a mental note to get his top steam cleaned.

"Thanks."

"Ollie, dear boy," called Crumble from somewhere behind him. "Mr. Kilo is almost ready to attach the head."

"Righto. I'll be there shortly." He clapped Mandrake on the shoulder and led him away from the empty tank. "Stitches wanted to be here for the last part of the experiment. Can you go and find him for me, bring him up?"

"Of course," said Mandrake, "then we can move on full steam ahead eh?"

"Well, quite," said Ollie, wondering if it was acceptable to kill someone for telling a stupid joke.

———

Cross and Deadhouse stood in the fog laden courtyard of Castle Jocular and watched as Bill's coach disappeared into the gloom.

"I suppose we could interview him at some point," Cross said, pointing at the retreating vehicle. "We'd have to give away a free translation booklet with every copy of the paper of course, but it might be interesting."

"I take it-t-t-t Jocular knows we're coming," said Deadhouse, gazing at his feet, or where his feet should have been. The fog was half way up his calves now. It almost seemed to have a life of its own, and when he wasn't looking it would surreptitiously creep further up his body. He felt like he was being probed, and not in a good way. "Something just moved past my leg," he said, not alluding at all to a line from a war film about stars.

"That's just your imagination," said Cross, wishing he had a good blaster at his side.

"Only if-f-f-f my imagination has six-x-x-x legs and fur."

"Just take it easy," said Cross. "And to answer your question, yes, The Count knows we're coming."

"Definitely?"

"Yes. Well, I left a message on the answer machine. That's good enough."

Deadhouse began to face the very real possibility that he might die here. Or worse. Jocular was notoriously fickle. One minute he was painting butterflies on a woodland backdrop, the next he was using your jugular vein as dental floss.

"Don't look like that," said Cross, wielding the mighty door knocker. "It'll be alright you'll see."

As the knocker connected with the door it moved. The door, not the knocker. The knocker had finished moving. Unlike the door. Which was. Moving that is.

"That's unusual. I thought he was really security conscious," said Cross.

"He is-s-s-s," said Deadhouse, starting to feel a little unwell. "It must just mean he's left it open for us then. Come on."

Displaying slightly more confidence than he actually felt, Cross pushed the giant slab of wood away from him and stepped inside.

"It's warm-m-m-m in here isn't it-t-t-t," observed Deadhouse. "Not really what you'd-d-d-d expect."

Cross ignored him. Something on a small side table had caught his attention. He picked it up.

"What's that-t-t-t?" asked Deadhouse, as his colleague looked at it. "An envelope addressed to me," said Cross. He tore it open. Inside was a note written in red. He prayed it was ink but his hopes weren't high. In his long journalistic career he didn't recall ink ever being that lumpy. "It's from The Count," he announced.

"It's probably-y-y-y a couple of death-h-h-h warrants." Cross didn't reply.

"Well. What does-s-s-s it say?"

"Dear, Mr. Cross," read Mr. Cross. "Sorry zere voz novone to meet you. Both Egon and I are busy. Please make your vay to ze Post Modern Torture Chamber. Sird floor, sixth door on ze left after ze toilet. Zere ve can conduct our business in prifate. Yours truly. CJ."

"There you go," said Cross, pocketing the note. "Nothing at all to worry about. And what a scoop. We could probably go inter-town with this."

"Maybe-e-e-e," said Deadhouse. "But why invite us to a torture chamber? Why not a drawing room-m-m-m or a nice conservatory? We're going to end up-p-p-p tied to a rack dangling-g-g-g by our articles, you know-w-w-w that don't-t-t-t you."

Cross took into account what his colleague had said, and seeing as he was feeling a little jittery, he tried to make him feel more at ease.

"Oh, don't be such a big girl, Ramekin. Just make sure your cameras ready."

They reached the appropriate room twenty-five minutes later. This included a ten-minute loo break for Deadhouse who was now so nervous that he'd lost about a third of his bodyweight. (Ironically the next person to use the toilet after him would lose roughly a third of their sense of smell).

As ever with Jocular a knock on the door wasn't required. "Enter," he boomed, his voice like a vocal cannon.

As they walked in, Deadhouse caught sight of a rather interesting piece of furniture in the middle of the room and wondered, 'are those real legs on that table?'

The door slammed shut behind them.

————

Stitches and Mandrake returned to the laboratory. Egon hadn't joined them. He was off doing something dwarfy or butlery, or a combination of the two at any rate. They made their way quietly 'round the back'.

> *"Me am a chocolate frog,*
> *Sat on a chocolate log,*
> *Eatin' some scrummy chocolate flies,*
> *Yum Yum Yum,*
> *One flew into my mouf,*
> *Now it is heading Souf,*
> *Soon it will come out of my,*
> *Bum Bum Bum."*

"I see things are back to normal then," said Stitches, waving at Flug. "Nice song, mate."

"Fanks," said Flug from his position perched upon his crate (although 'perched' wasn't the most apt word to use for Flug's current position. It was like a news reporter saying, 'The five-hundred-pound bomb went off with a bit of a pop, sending shock waves that tickled their way through the crowd causing some of their clothing to become slightly crumpled. A police spokesman said that five minutes with a dustpan and brush should sort out the mess').

"Indeed they have," said Ollie. "In fact, I think he might be even more dense than before."

"Is that possible? Any denser and he'll collapse in on himself," said Stitches.

"I'm not sure," responded Ollie, "but ten minutes ago he tried picking his nose with an electric prod. He shorted out three batteries and had steam coming out of his ears."

"He seems alright now," said Mandrake.

"Maybe," said Ollie, pointing at Flug's face. "But his eyes have changed places. The green one's on the left now."

"Okay, gentlemen," announced Kilo. "I'm all set to attach the head." As he walked over to the mini fridge, Stitches gazed at the shrouded mound lying on the table. It had a couple of funny lumps on it that he couldn't identify.

"What are those?" he asked Crumble, pointing at the points. "Is that where you attach the electric connections?"

"Not quite, dear boy," said the Professor. "I believe the technical term for those items is boobies."

"Boobies," said Stitches, confused. "Why on earth would a reanimated man need boobies? Where do you plan on taking him? Thailand?"

"It's because he's a she," said Kilo, approaching the table. "I couldn't find a suitable male cadaver, but on balance I'm glad it turned out this way. This one has been an absolute delight to work on."

Stitches nodded his head, pleased that he hadn't given said lumps a little tweak when posing his original question. He didn't really want to be lambasted for interfering with a corpse, which was ironic considering what they were up to.

"I assume the head is female as well?" asked Mandrake.

"I do hope so," said Stitches. "I'm sure Kilo doesn't want to go down in history as the man who created the first reanimate pantomime dame."

Kilo placed the covered cranium onto the table. He then shifted uneasily on the balls of his feet and pulled a, 'There's something I haven't mentioned yet,' sort of a face.

"There's something I haven't mentioned yet," he said. "What's that?" said Ollie.

"She's. . . how can I put it. . . not that attractive."

By now everyone was stood around the table awaiting the big reveal. They weren't that worried. There were some hideous creatures in town, and Ollie and the boys had seen a picture of Katie Hopkins on the darknet so they were pretty much ready for anything.

"Ready everyone?" said Kilo. "Ready," they said.

He whipped off the towel and revealed the head lying beneath it. Contrary to the previous statement, they weren't ready for anything.

"Oh my," said Crumble. "Good Lord," said Mandrake.

"That's, er, interesting," said Ollie.

"At least she won't have to buy a mask at Halloween," said Stitches. "My goodness, she could scare the maggots off one of Mrs. Ladle's cupcakes."

"What's going on then, chaps?" said Ethan joining them. He'd been up on the roof securing some extra cables that ran to the underside of the reanimation table. They were in case a backup electricity supply was needed if the bats should struggle to provide enough power. "Oh, I see we're at the head stage. Let's have a. . . eeewww. Did you drop it in a fire or something?"

"Alright, alright," said Kilo, chucking the towel away. "I know she's not going to win any beauty contests, but. . . "

"She wouldn't win at a county show either," said Stitches.

". . . BUT, this was the one that was most compatible with the corpse so I didn't really have a lot of choice. You'll get used to it."

"Only in the same way you'd get used to a tumour," said Ollie. "She beautiful."

They all turned round and stared at Flug and tried to work out what he was going on about, but if the expression on his chops was anything to go by, it was glaringly obvious.

Imagine the look on the face of the first man ever to see a sunrise, or the serene glow of a first-time parent as they gazed lovingly at their newborn child. This was almost like that, only it was a stapled together bag of bits with the IQ of a deckchair staring at, well, who knew what at the moment.

"What was that, Flug?" said Ollie.

"She lovely. Me fink she da prettiest fing me ever ever seen ever." "Which bearing in mind his only frames of reference are Mrs. Ladle and some of the sexually ambiguous creatures in town, you can sort of see where he's coming from I suppose," said Ethan, who really couldn't but thought it best if he said something reassuring. "Still, in the right light, I'm sure she's nice enough to look at."

"Only if you're blind," said Stitches.

"She ever so pretty," continued Flug, gushing like a teenage boy. "Can me give her a name, Ollie?"

"Oh, Lordy," said Ollie.

"That's alright," said Kilo. "He can do that. It saves us calling her thingy, or whatserface."

"Go on then, Flug. What are you going to call her?" asked Ollie. "Oboe."

"Why Oboe?"

"Cos dat my favourite flower."

You can imagine the silence and the looks on their faces.

"If I may," said Kilo, a little anxiously. "We really need to begin the process before it starts to go off."

"How on earth would you know?" said Stitches. "It's already more shades of green than a frog disco where the dress code is wear something green."

Kilo got to work. He was fast, and with Crumble's help and the others chipping in, he fair rattled through the procedure. Flug wasn't much help of course. What with being all loved up and all that he was mooning about the place like the front row of a Little Mix concert (apologies for the pathetic attempt at 'street talk'. I thought it would be down with the kids. Revolting isn't it. I thought Little Mix was a child's cookery toy).

Four and a half hours later the operation was complete, with the head now sitting in its rightful place atop the neck (actually its rightful place was at the local tip where the seagulls could pick it to pieces, but you can't have everything your own way. And it's my story so there). "That's impressive work," said Mandrake, admiring the suturing and stitching. "Where did you learn to do that?"

"I don't know really. I used to work in a factory."

"Talent such as this is a natural gift," said Crumble. "You can either do it or you can't. Well, Mr Kilo, are you ready to engage the power?"

"Oh, yes. Ethan, if you would please."

The lycan took a small golden tube from his trouser pocket and walked over to the exposed balcony.

"What's he doing?" asked Stitches.

"Calling the bats," said Ollie. "Jocular lent Kilo his bat whistle. It takes a lot of puff to get it going, and seeing as Ethan is the fittest one here it made sense to get him to do it."

"Just one thing before he does," said Crumble. "You might want to cover your ears."

"Why's that?" said Mandrake. "Is it one of those high pitched ones that feels like a mosquito..?"

PHHAAARRRRPPPPP!

The noise from the whistle howled like a thousand banshees in a spectacularly bad mood. Dust was shaken from the rafters, the floor shook violently, and the very stones of the building themselves rattled in their fixings. Kilo stumbled and struggled to stay on his feet. Ollie's face was screwed up in agony due to his sensitive hearing, and Stitches right eye popped out of its socket due to the sonic waves bouncing round the lab.

"That wasn't a mosquito," said the zombie as the relentless uproar started to decline. "That was a jumbo jet. Every bat in the Northern hemisphere's likely to turn up at this rate."

Just as they began to gather themselves, a fluttering sound could be heard outside. Faint at first it rose rapidly until it sounded like an audience clapping furiously. Ethan ran from the balcony and joined the others.

"Here they come," he said.

"I hope they're not hungry," said Mandrake, thinking it would be just typical that a few short hours after discovering a new zest for life, he would end up as an entrée for a flock of ravenous, blood sucking sky rats.

All of a sudden, the noise reached a cataclysmic crescendo as dozens of enormous vampire bats swarmed into the lab. Like a giant, black swirling curtain they flew round and round, in and out of the beams, around the equipment and circled the watching group. It was a dizzying display but then, as quickly as it had started, it was over. The mad flapping ceased as all of the velvety creatures arced gracefully towards the large wheel and settled themselves into the harnesses. Silence once again descended as the bats rested in place ready for their next command.

"I can honestly say that I've never seen anything quite like that," said Mandrake in amazement. "They're incredibly well trained aren't they." "Very misunderstood little things actually," said Crumble, checking a few connections that had come loose during the whistle inspired tumult. "And rather intelligent."

"Really?" said Ollie, not entirely convinced.

"Yes indeed. Your average Desmodus Draculae is far more intellectually capable than a rabbit for instance, and may even be as perceptive as a pig."

"That's something to put on your CV, mate," Stitches said to Ollie as he popped his eye back into place. "Ollie Splint. Business owner, self-made being, half vampire, and almost as intelligent as a bacon sandwich."

"Alright then," said Kilo, cutting off a florid retort from Ollie. "All the bats are nicely in place; every connection has been checked and the body is stitched up and leak free. Shall we... Ollie."

"Yup."

"Stop him doing that will you please. He's liable to snap something off."

Without anyone noticing, Flug had snuck up to the table. (Quite how he'd managed it was beyond anybody's guess. It was the equivalent of standing in a totally flat and barren desert on your own, only to turn round and discover that Nelson's Column had crept up on you). Then he'd lifted up Oboe, who was now dressed thankfully, and was cradling her in one massive arm. With his other hand he was tenderly stroking her face and hair.

As Ollie approached he could hear Flug whispering.

"I will love you and look after you and make sure dat you always safe. You more special dan any bag of sweeties."

Ollie put a hand on Flug's shoulder. He wasn't going to be harsh with him because, all things considered, it was rather touching. He actually had a lump in his throat.

"Flug, mate. We've got to leave her alone now because Kilo wants to try and wake her up."

"She been sleepy for long time hasn't she?" said the monster.

"Yes, she has. So think how happy she's going to be when she wakes up and sees you smiling at her and saying hello."

"Okay," said Flug. He gently laid her back down and pulled the sheet back up to her neck.

"Now, we all need to stand well back," said Crumble, indicating what he considered to be a safe distance, which in this case turned out to be about twenty feet. (If the others had their way, and based on past experience, any procedure that had any hint whatsoever of

Crumble's involvement would have normally required a safe distance of approximately seventeen and a half miles, but seeing as that was a little impractical, they backed off as far as they could and trusted to luck). "There'll be lots of electricity flying round shortly. Not the sort of thing we want to get caught in the middle of."

They all moved away from the table apart from Ethan who was standing next to the wheel.

"Please don't tell me he's going to let loose with that bloody foghorn again," said Stitches, looking round for something to plug his ears with. "No, not this time," said Golden Kilo. "All that's needed for this bit is a click of the fingers. When you're ready, Ethan." The lycanthrope gave a thumbs up.

SNAP.

Unlike the demented, leather winged, flapping madness they'd indulged in when they entered the lab, this time the vampire bats started slowly and with measured purpose. With gentle flaps of their coriaceous wings beating in unison, the heavy wooden wheel began to turn. As it did so, an electric charge began to throb, infusing the atmosphere with a faint blue, green glow. As the bats picked up speed the static buzz became louder and louder and the air started to feel as if a thunder storm were readying to unleash itself. Ollie looked at Stitches and was amazed to see that his hair was standing straight up like wheat stalks swaying in a summer breeze.

"I wouldn't laugh too much if I were you," said the zombie, trying to flatten down his unruly mop. "You look like a frightened raccoon."

The clamour of the electricity in the air was now so loud that they had to shout to make themselves heard over it.

"How's it going in there?" bellowed Ethan. He was studying the wheel as it spun at incredible speed.

"Excellent," said Kilo. "The charge is building up nicely."

Round and round went the wheel, faster and faster as the bats urged it ever onwards.

"How much longer do you need?" shouted Ethan at the top of his voice. "The structure's holding together okay, but the bracket holding it to the wall is a bit insecure." As if to confirm this, the large bolts buried in the stone shifted a little, causing the wheel to tilt outwards ever so slightly.

"Not too much longer. Surely it can last. It must. IT HAS TO!" shouted Kilo amidst a shower of sparks that shot from the underside of the table. He looked at the figure resting on top. There, Oboe's as yet, still lifeless body bucked and jumped as surge after surge of elemental power coursed through her dormant system. "We need just a bit more," Kilo implored quietly, almost as if he were speaking to the corpse itself. He nodded at Crumble as the professor adjusted a couple of switches on a flashing control panel. "I think we're nearly there. A couple more decent jolts should do it."

The bats, as if understanding what was required, urged themselves to even greater velocity. The wheel was now a wooden blur, so much so that the aroma of burning tree began to intermingle with the acrid tang of ozone.

"This bracket isn't going to last much longer," roared Ethan. "It's going to have to be now or never."

Kilo gave Crumble an anxious hand signal. Nodding in understanding, the Professor took a step to his left and took hold of the largest lever on the control panel. He braced himself for a moment before yanking it down with all of his might.

Surpassing all of the other explosions, crashes, and electrical bangs that had come before, it seemed as if Crumble, by this one simple action, had unleashed hell on earth. An ear-splitting boom that made the bat whistle seem like a whispering child battered through the laboratory, knocking them all clean off their feet. The lights dimmed to a barely perceptible glow and then, an instant later, grew so bright that temporary loss of sight was a distinct possibility.

Excited by the environmental fury going on around them the vampire bats flew as if the slavering beasts of the underworld themselves were in manic pursuit. Faster and faster they pushed themselves until, with an almighty kaboom, the table upon which Oboe lay exploded in a shower of sparks, wires and shroud. Untethered, her inert body was catapulted through the air in a graceful swan dive before coming to rest about fifteen feet away.

Professor Crumble picked himself up off the floor and took hold of the levers one by one throwing them into neutral. A silence, just as loud as the riot of noise that it replaced, descended instantly. Glancing around, he could see that everyone was more or less alright. Flug had a gash on his neck that would have proved fatal to any normal person, and Stitches had lost an arm, but apart from that they seemed to have been incredibly fortuitous.

"Kilo," Crumble called out, suddenly realising that the scientist was unaccounted for. "Are you okay?"

"Look," said a dazed Ollie, pointing towards the wheel.

"What's he doing?" said Mandrake, extracting himself from a large tangle of silver wiring. "Is he alive?"

Ethan, who wasn't too far away from Kilo, shook his head free of dust and debris and nodded.

"I think he's fine but you need to come over here," he said.

All of them had already pretty much fully recovered, and not having any injuries that a simple patch up job wouldn't fix, joined the lycan. Instantly it became clear that Kilo was in fact alright. In fact he was more than alright. He was overjoyed as the broad grin on his face indicated.

"She's alive. SHE'S ALIVE!" he shouted in triumph.

And indeed she was. There in the middle of the floor surrounded by fragments of lab equipment sat Oboe. Her eyes were open and she was looking inquisitively round the room whilst scratching her head. Flug was mesmerised, although that was no great achievement seeing as how he could be brought to a virtual standstill by a bladder on a stick, but he was awestruck nonetheless. (Stitches had found the stick/bladder combo in the fountain one morning. The stick on its own had scared Flug to the point of immobility and the bladder took some explaining but he'd eventually calmed down. They never did find out who the bladder belonged to though, but a resident of the town lived the rest of his life never having to go for a number one again. He didn't question it. He put it down to luck).

Flug wanted to approach her but he was far too wary. Just looking at her made him feel, well, even if he'd still had his intellect he wouldn't have been able to describe it. His heart skipped a beat, (meaning it would be about another eight hours until the next one), so he just stood there smiling.

Oboe suddenly realised that she was the subject of some attention.

A tentative smile spread across her features. "Hello," she said.

"H. . . hello, Oboe," stuttered Kilo, taking a hesitant step towards her. "I was just. . . "

At that precise moment, a bolt of lightning the size of which hadn't been seen since the formation of the earth four and a half billion years ago (or last Thursday afternoon if you're a Creationist) ploughed through the atmosphere and through the open balcony where its white hot tip struck the bracket holding the giant wheel to the wall. The metal was blasted into tiny fragments with an ear pounding wallop, rendering all those watching useless and staring in horror as the the wooden structure began to topple and fall.

Unlike most situations of an extreme nature, here there was no, 'time seemed to slow down,' or, 'it was as if time stood still,' nonsense. The extreme weight of the wheel was such that it went over in an instant. It just missed Oboe who had turned round to see where the noise had come from. She looked on helplessly as gravity took over. The top of the wheel smashed into the floor barely two feet behind her, rending it to matchsticks and, a microsecond later, both it and Oboe went down through the gaping hole that it had rent in the floor.

"NOOOOOOO!" screamed Kilo, running to the cavernous opening. As he gazed down into the darkness he heard a distant cry before silence once again covered the laboratory like a funeral shroud.

"Oboe," whispered Flug to himself, as a single tear fell from his bright green eye.

———

"Vot on earth vas zat?" said Jocular, a perplexed look on his face. He sent out a mental command to Egon, telling him to 'get his arse up here pretty damn sharpish'. "I hope ze boiler hasn't exploded again. It took days to scrub ze skin off ze valls ze last time it happened. I didn't do it off course, Egon did. Four sack loads he got."

Cross had no idea how to respond to something so gross, which was just as well because he didn't want Jocular to embellish the story any further.

Deadhouse occupied himself by taking a few more pictures. (Now you might think that this was a pointless venture because vampires don't appear on film in the same way that they don't have a reflection.

This, however, is an urban myth and has no basis in fact whatsoever. If it did, how would they have made all those horror movies?)

Mere seconds later the door burst open and Egon skidded into the room.

"Yes, Master," he puffed, slightly out of breath after his mad dash from the bowels of the castle, or to put it another way, he had received Jocular's message whilst relaxing on his toilet (you can make up your own joke about dashing and bowels).

"I take it you heard zat rarzer loud bang?" asked Jocular.

"I did, Almighty One. I just assumed the boiler was playing up again.

I'll go and give it a kick." "Excellent."

Five minutes later Egon, considerably more flustered and significantly more bereft of oxygen than last time, returned.

"Vell?" said Jocular.

"I think you had better come and see for yourself, O Dark One." "Can you not just fill me in as it vere?"

"It really would be much quicker if you came and had a look, O Lord of the Night and all the Naughty Things Residing Therein."

Jocular sighed and got up from his chair.

"Oh, fery vell. You had better not be vasting my time, Egon. You know how I feel about zat don't you?"

"I do, O Great and Powerful Overseer of all Things Nasty and Bitey, but this is the real deal."

Ten minutes later they arrived at what Egon had been alluding to. (It would have been five if Jocular hadn't fannied about trying to get Egon to explain things. Amusingly the next sentence would be here by now if I hadn't fannied about writing the last few lines about Jocular fannying about. Oh, well, you live and learn. Ah, here it comes).

"I see vot you mean, Egon," said Jocular, gazing upwards. They hadn't gone to the top floor to the laboratory. They were on the ground floor, standing amidst the detritus that had cascaded from the many floors above. The weight of the wheel had been such that not only had it smashed through the third story's floorboards, but it had barrelled through the two below as well, straight into the entrance hall.

Putting aside his annoyance for a moment, Jocular noticed two things. One, that everyone was very quiet and melancholy and two, the front door was wide open. The only voices he could hear were coming from outside. Kilo and Flug were bellowing for something called Oboe until their lungs heaved.

"I take it all did not qvite go to plan," he said, putting a heavy and claustrophobia inducing arm around Ollie's shoulders.

"If you'll forgive me the indelicacy, Sir, that's qvite, excuse me, quite an understatement of gargantuan proportions."

Ollie explained to their host what had happened right up to the point that they had rushed down and discovered the front door wide open.

"And zere vas no sign off her at all?" said Jocular, genuinely concerned, his anger at the damage to his home temporarily put on the back burner, which is where Ollie had assumed he would end up once Jocular saw the wreckage.

"None," said Ethan. "We got down here within moments but she was gone."

"If nothing else," said Stitches, who had already asked his new-found friend Egon to reattach his arm, "it shows that Kilo's work is up to scratch. Her joints must be in pretty good order to get out of here that quick."

MEEOOWW.

"Uh oh," said Mandrake. "Noggin?" said Ollie. "Noggin," said Mandrake. "Noggin?" said Jocular. "Noggin," said Stitches.

"I see." The vampire lord pause for a moment. "In fact, I do not see.

Vot, if you do not mind me asking, is a Noggin?" said Jocular.

An explanation wasn't required as an exploding ball of bristling fur and claws like scythes burst forth from underneath a pile of wood and attached itself to Mandrake's leg.

"YEEOWWW!" he hollerred, dancing around like a man on a hot tin roof.

Jocular looked on interestedly for a few moments, seeming to find the spectacle rather amusing. Then he put two fingers into his mouth and gave a soft whistle.

In an instant, Noggin calmed down, retracted his claws, leaving a fair few puncture wounds in Mandrake's flesh, bounded over to Jocular like he didn't have a care in the world, and started rubbing around the vampire Lord's legs.

"How did you do that?" said Mandrake, noting the blood seeping through his trousers. "I haven't seen him that docile since. . . Well I haven't actually. He bites me when he's asleep."

Jocular bent down and stroked Noggin with an enormous hand. "It is very simple," he said, as Noggin purred and dribbled everywhere. "Your feline is off a fery rare breed. I haff only effer seen vun of his kind before. Noggin here is a fampire cat."

"I've heard it all now," said Stitches. He was sitting on the floor as Egon worked on his shoulder joint. "What next? A zombie hamster? A wereguineapig?"

Ollie cast him a 'shut the hell up or Jocular will turn you into a sofa' look.

"You may haf noticed," continued Jocular, "zat Noggin's hunting and eating habits are slightly more unusual zan vat you might expect."

"I'll say," concurred Mandrake. "One time I found him chewing on a leg."

"That doesn't sound too weird," said Ethan, who wasn't averse to chewing on the odd bone or three.

"Maybe not but this one was still attached to the postman. He wasn't very amused I can tell you. So, My Lord, what do I do with him?"

"You just need to alter his diet a smidge. Make it high in rich, gamey meats and, rarzer zan milk or vater, giff him fresh blood to drink."

Unconsciously Mandrake covered the gouges in his legs just in case Noggin decided it was time for a snack.

"Thank you, Sir that's very helpful."

At that point Kilo came back inside closely followed by a very depressed looking Flug.

"Any sign?" asked Ollie, sort of knowing the answer.

"None at all," said the scientist. "There's a few footprints out there by the door but after that, nothing."

Excalibur Cross, who had been busy writing away furiously in his notebook, piped up.

"Seems like some sort of search is in order. Might I suggest we split up?"

"It seems zat Stitches has already done zat yes. Ha ha ha," said

Jocular. He was met by an absence of noise only matched by the audience's reaction to the first ever showing of the controversial, Taliban funded comedy film, 'Planes, Trains and Kill the Infidels', during which a couple of Islamic misfits have hilarious adventures trying to find a suitable mode of transport to destroy a building owned by the western capitalist devils.

"Very droll, Sir," said Ollie. "Anyway, I think Mr. Cross makes a good point. Stitches, you Flug and Mandrake come with me. Ethan, you go with Professor Crumble and Kilo."

"Egon and I vill stay here in case ze lady decides to return yes," said Jocular, making the suggestion sound very much like a command, which it was.

"That's fine, My Lord." Ollie gestured to the others. "Well then, people. Let's get moving."

———

Oboe wandered through the dark, oppressive forest. She didn't know who Oboe was, or that she actually in a forest, however, and wouldn't start to assimilate such basic facts for a little while yet. The reanimation process was peculiar in that those brought back to life were more or less like new born babies. It took time, teaching, and patience to bring them up to being a fully functional and sentient individual. (What had happened to Flug was anybody's guess though. Either he'd been hit in the head with a seven-tonne mallet or his creator got his brain from a bin at the back of an abattoir).

On the whole though, reanimates usually coped well with their second bite at life's cherry and became reasonably normal members of society. Obviously not to the point that you wouldn't stop and stare if you saw one pushing a shopping trolley round the local supermarket of course, but enough that they could go out at night without scaring Mr. and Mrs. Average out of several years of life. None of them could ever claim to be geniuses either, but at least the majority were selfaware enough to know how their legs worked and which way was up. The next time you're out have a look around. You'll see them. Check out the vacant eyed chap standing outside the toy store proudly showing passers-by how to use a hoola hoop, the lady asking you to sponsor a tree, or the slack jawed bloke holding up a sign promoting a golf sale. If you study them closely enough you'll see the stitches and slightly mismatched body-parts.

When she'd initially gained consciousness at the laboratory it was only pure, motorised instinct that had gotten her upright, and it was only when one of the creatures there said 'hello' to her, that the word, and its meaning, had been dredged up from the deepest recesses of her mind causing long dead synapses to trigger a vague memory. And then she was falling, falling amongst a torrent of metal and wooden debris, down and down until she'd landed with a colossal thump. Although she didn't know it her fall had been broken by half a dozen leather harnesses that had been vacated by escaping vampire bats. She hadn't lost consciousness, but when she landed, a large chunk of stone had dealt her a hefty blow on the head, rendering her newly activated brain somewhat dazed and confused.

She stumbled onwards unaware of what she was doing or where she was going, just driven on by some mysterious inner force. Tough, sinewy branches whipped the exposed flesh of her arms, raising welts and scratches, some of which dripped blood onto the forest floor.

Strange noises came out of the darkness that made her jump, and eerie shadows cast by the light of the moon shifted like ghostly apparitions on the periphery of her vision.

On and on she went, unaware of the passage of time, a concept that would have been as alien to her as the process by which she had come to be. At one point she plunged into a small stream that came up to her chest. As she waded through the water a strange sensation crawled over her skin. At first it was extremely unpleasant as the cold began to bite, but it quickly became more comfortable as the frigid fluid soothed her wounds.

Once onto the bank on the other side, Oboe collapsed in an exhausted, sodden heap. The gnawing, bitter chill of the fast flowing water had seeped into her leg muscles, seizing them to the point that they locked up in protest, refusing to carry her any further. She didn't know what was going on. Confusion reigned as the automatic internal systems, those that a short while ago had propelled her along so effortlessly, no longer obeyed her commands. Her stiff fingers clawed ineffectually at the leaf strewn ground, desperately trying to gain purchase, but it was no use. The encroaching gelidity had laid waste to her deepest muscle fibres and sinews, rendering her virtually immobile.

"Mmmm," was the only sound that she was able to produce, and that was more from natural exhalation than conscious effort.

"Who's there?" came a voice from the distant, gloomy, bleak wilderness. (Actually it was more like twenty feet if we're being accurate, but that just wouldn't sound as good, and surely as authors we have to be allowed to get a bit flowery with the wordage from time to time. If we didn't, think of all those literary masterpieces that you love so much and how they might have turned out if the writers hadn't got a bit wordy. Would you have remembered, 'It was awesome for a bit and then it got a bit crap?' No you wouldn't, because Mr. Dickens used his imagination and came up with, 'It was the best of times, it was the worst of times.' And who would have been moved by, 'Hiya, my name's Bernard,' instead of, 'Call me Ishmael.' Alright, so the rest of Moby Dick is heavier going than an obese whale swimming through treacle but the point's valid).

Again, all that Oboe could summon was a dispirited moan into the loamy earth.

"I can hear you," came the voice again, closer now.

Oboe could just about make out shuffling footsteps and a strange tapping sound edging closer and closer. Then she felt hands on her shoulders and neck, probing her arms, legs and back. Strangely she wasn't frightened. The hands were gentle, soothing, and offered no threat that she could discern.

"You seem to be fine on the whole," said the man's voice. It was assuasive and friendly, almost grandfatherly, "but those cuts and bumps are going to need seeing to. Are you able to stand up?"

Oboe craned her neck and looked up into the good Samaritans face. He was old, bearded, and wrinkled, and had crooked, yellowing teeth behind a warm, welcoming smile. His nose was contorted and out of shape, indicating that it been badly broken at some point. His breath smelt vaguely of mint and coffee but it was his eyes that drew her attention. They were as white and sightless as marble. As she stared at him, dormant synapses began to fire in her brain. Cells in her language centre sparked into activity as they deciphered the sounds entering her ears.

"I. . . I. . . I think so," she said quietly. "But I am a bit. . . stiff."

"Let me help you," said the man, putting his hands underneath her arms and heaving. Slowly he got her upright. She wobbled at first as wave after wave of dizziness washed over her bringing on a rush of nausea. If she'd had any food in her stomach it would have made a very swift and messy exit. As her balance returned, the sick feeling passed and she began to feel better.

"Thank you," she said.

"You're very welcome," responded her benefactor. "Well, allow me to introduce myself. I'm Royston, but my friends call me No See Norman. I've never figured out why to be honest. There's never been a Norman in my family. What's your name, my dear?" He held out a gnarled, thick fingered hand, the type that had spent most of its time tilling the earth.

"I don't know," said Oboe. "I can't seem to remember anything at the moment."

"Ah well, never mind," said No See Norman, taking her by the arm. "My goodness you're as cold as the grave. We need to get you warmed up. I would imagine that you're famished as well."

"What is famished?" said Oboe, as No See Norman led her away from the stream and further into the forest.

"Hungry, my dear. Do you want something to eat?"

"Food," she said. The mere mention of the word set her long out of use digestive system rumbling like an angry ogre. Her tummy gurgled and groaned with a life of its own.

"As is often reported, the benefit of being blind is the enhancement of the other senses," said No See Norman, tapping away with his stick as he moved effortlessly passed, around, and over any obstacle in his path. "And judging by the noises that your stomach is making I would say that the answer to my question is a resounding yes."

Whoever this person was, Oboe felt no fear in his presence. Her overriding impression was that he would look after her no matter what. She was already holding his hand because she'd taken a couple of stumbles, but now she squeezed it. It felt warm.

———

Mrs. Ladle stopped what she was doing and stared off into the distance, which in this case was the wall behind her stove. She put the wooden spoon she'd been holding down and plonked herself into a chair. She was in the middle of making a batch of strawberry jelly and was about to weigh up the pro's and con's of replacing the hundreds and thousands (werewolf ticks dried out and ground into a fine powder) with Tincture of Daggerwort, when a strange feeling had overwhelmed her. It was like a shift in the fabric of space as if something had just happened. We're not talking full on Jedi here, just a little niggle at the back of her mind.

"Must be old age creeping up on me," she muttered to herself as she lit a cigarette (the ash was a vital ingredient to the jelly). She sat quietly for a few moments carefully collecting the ash in the palm of her hand. When she finished, she dropped it into the mixture and then, for good measure, threw the fag butt in as well. After all you can't have too much of a good thing can you. (That statement is actually rather silly isn't it? Fire is quite a good thing but too much of it and you won't have anything else left to have too much of. Socks. Too many of those can be disastrous. Not only are they a nightmare to pair up but when you lose one, oh the humanity. About the only thing you can't have too much of is money. Unfortunately this is not something that I, the author of this fine narrative, is going to experience any time soon because this story isn't about a witheringly dull boy wizard and his dreary adventures, written by some Z list celebrity famous for absolutely sod all, or penned by a sportsmen who suddenly thinks he's a competent wordsmith because he can ride a bike quite fast and won a few gold medals. NB. There's a fine line between plugging and begging and I'm not going to debate the various pros and cons of either but, whichever way you look at it, you bought my book so thanks).

Whilst she squashed the spent butt of the cigarette with her spoon to squeeze all of the tar out of it, a fluttering at the window caught her attention. At first she thought that some joker had hung a pair of curtains to the outside of the window, but she quickly realised that curtains, with the rare exception of the odd pair at the castle, didn't have eyes, ears and a mouth full of needle like teeth that could plunge into flesh as easy as if it were, well, flesh really. It is rather squidgy after all.

No. This was one of Jocular's vampire bats. They were huge, leathery blood fiends that were relentless in their pursuit of prey, famed for their brutality, and feared by all those that came into contact with them, especially when they made house calls. They were more terrifying than any Jehovah's Witness.

"Aw, how sweet," said Mrs. Ladle, opening the window. Said bat flew in and settled onto her kitchen table, taking up the whole of its expansive surface.

"SQUEAKY SQUEAKY SQUEAK SQUEAK."

"Come again," said the witch.

"SQUEAKY SQUEAKY SQUEAK SQUEAK!"

"Little Johnny's fallen down the well and broken his leg?" "SQUEAK!!!"

"Alright, calm down. That's what it usually means. Go on but just a bit slower."

"SQUEAK... SQUEAK... SQUEAKITY... "

"Not that slow you furry little imp. I'm old not senile."

The next set of squeaks implied that Mrs. Ladle was playing it fast and loose with the term, 'not senile,' but she didn't pick up on it. If she had she would've punched the bat right in the squeaks.

"SQUEAKITY SQUEAK SQUEAK SQUEAKY SQUEAK."

"Oh I see. Is there a lot of damage?" "SQUEAK."

"So what does he want me to do?"

"SQUEAK SQUEAKY SQUEAK SQUEAK SQUEAKITY SQUEAK."

"Well, I'll have a look but I haven't used that spell since I remodelled the bathroom." (The result of an unfortunate exploding amphibian incident. She'd been making toad in the hole, but the toad, not all that keen on being roasted and not a big fan of Yorkshire Pudding, had escaped from the oven and finished cooking in the bathroom. Sadly its sticky and rather violent expansion hadn't been contained by the batter, which left the walls dripping with greeny, red ichor, the ceiling looking like the inside of Ted Bundy's van, and her toilet three doors down).

"SQUEAK."

"Fine. I'll find it. Tell His Royal Bossiness I'll be there as soon as I can."

"SQUEAKITY SQUEAK SQUEAKITY SQUEAKY."

"Oh does he now? Well, he's in luck. I made a fresh batch this morning. Go on then. Off you go."

The bat hopped to the window sill and took off.

"Now," said Mrs. Ladle, tapping her crinkled lips with an index finger. "Where did I put that bloody spell book?"

———

Oboe sat quietly on a small, three-legged wooden stool in No See Norman's hut. It was a simple, open plan affair with a rudimentary kitchen in one corner, a table and chair in the middle, and a cot like bed in another corner. Not so much open plan actually, more no space for any more than one room.

On their arrival, No See Norman had told Oboe that he had a hearty vegetable stew on the go and a fresh loaf of bread that was just the thing for mopping up all the juices. If he'd been able to see Oboe's face he would've realised that she didn't have the slightest idea what he was talking about other than it was regarding food.

She watched No See Norman as he pottered around his shack. Something deep in the recesses of her mind marvelled at how adept he was despite his disability. It was no surprise though. After living here for more than sixty years he could have told you where everything was and how to get around it with his eyes closed (I know. But it's only a little joke).

He deftly ladled the thick broth into two wooden bowls and carried them to the table without spilling a drop.

"There you go, my dear. Tuck in. We don't stand on ceremony round here. I'll cut you a nice thick slice of bread."

The gorgeous aroma from the cooked food assailed her nostrils and aroused her sense of smell, giving it a much needed kick start. In response her stomach growled louder than ever as if urging her to partake of the sustenance offered. She wasn't quite sure what to do at first, confused as to how to get the fragrant, lumpy liquid into her mouth. She waited until No See Norman had sliced two large hunks of bread and watched as he picked up a spoon and used it to eat.

With a hand still trembling from cold and hunger, Oboe copied what he was doing. The soup was hot but not uncomfortably so, but it wouldn't have mattered if it had been molten lava. To Oboe's underused senses it was the most amazing experience that she had been a part of thus far. The textures, tastes and smells were almost overwhelming. She downed one mouthful after another barely pausing for breath.

"How is it, my dear?" asked No See Norman, only halfway through his own repast when Oboe was swallowing her last piece of bread.

"It is, um, lovely. Thank you."

"You're very welcome. Oh, would you like something to drink? A refreshing brew to wash the food down is always so civilised, don't you agree. I can offer you water, coffee or tea. Actually I have a rather nice beer as well. That'd do the trick even on such a cold night as this. It's a robust beverage perfect for these long winter evenings."

Oboe didn't know the difference between any of the drinks that he'd mentioned so she opted for beer, mainly because her host had alluded to the fact that it would warm her up, and that was what he was having.

Once the drink was placed in front of her she again waited to see what No See Norman would do with it. Watching then copying his actions, she lifted the tankard to her lips and drank. The bubbles tickled her nose and throat and once she'd finished swallowing she issued forth with rather an impressive belch.

"Better out than in I always say," said No See Norman. "Unless the werewolves are out hunting of course." He chuckled to himself. "Then it's much better to be in because if you do go out you'll end up in a wolf's tummy. More beer, my dear?"

"Please," said Oboe, proffering her empty vessel. Whatever it was she liked it and he was right, it was making her warm, especially on the inside.

No See Norman refilled her tankard to the brim with the dark, frothy liquid.

"So what's your story, my dear? Where do you come from and how did you manage to end up in the forest? We don't tend to get too many people wanderering out this far."

"I don't know," replied Oboe, the alcohol rapidly relaxing her. Strangely it allowed her struggling brain to process the information it was receiving and offer a response. (Obviously this isn't the normal effect of alcohol, but then your average Friday night binge drinker, staggering around a town centre with a traffic cone on his head and a suspicious stain on the front of his trousers, has an IQ far lower than any reanimated corpse. Or an inanimate one for that matter). "I remember waking up and it felt as if I had been asleep for a very long time," said Oboe. "I was in a big room with open windows."

"Was anybody else there?"

Oboe took another long draught of beer.

"Yes, there were others, but I don't know who they were." "Perhaps they're your friends. Maybe they'll be looking for you because they're worried about you." "What are 'friends'?" asked Oboe.

No See Norman poured her more beer.

"A friend is a person whom you trust. Someone to share things with, both good and bad. It's someone who'll listen, and take care of you when times are tough."

"So," said Oboe, "you are my friend?"

"Well, yes I suppose I am. And an honour it is to be called that." "I am your friend too," said Oboe.

No See Norman reached across the table and took hold of Oboe's hand and gave it a loving squeeze.

"Good," he said.

"Where are you from?" asked Oboe.

No See Norman sipped his beer and rubbed a hand over his long, white beard.

"Oddly, I'm a bit like you. I don't know where I was born or who my parents were. My earliest memories start right here, living in this hut. I've always been here by myself. It's never been a problem though. I'm more than self-reliant as you can see, but it is nice to have some company though."

Oboe nodded her head in understanding but there were concepts that she still didn't get.

"What are parents?" she asked.

"Oh, you poor thing. Ultimately you will have, or would have had some somewhere. Your parents are you mother and father. A man and a woman who fell in love and created you."

The words mother and father conjured up emotions in Oboe. Warm, happy feelings that, although made her feel good, had no memories attached to them.

"I understand," she said, a sudden melancholy temporarily overtaking her good mood. She stared at her friend and tried to process the emotions building within. "I can feel them but I don't remember them." "Not to worry, my dear," said No See Norman, his voice subdued but laced with parental kindness. "I'm sure it'll all come back to you eventually. Happy memories have a habit of doing that and the bad ones will ebb away as if they never existed." "Will they. Really?"

"Why certainly. Whenever you're feeling a bit low all you have to do is recall a time that you were happy and you'll cheer right up."

Oboe reached across the table and stroked the old man's cheek. "I shall always remember now," she said.

Ollie, Stitches, Flug and Mandrake trudged through the forest. It was dark, eerie, quiet, and wouldn't you just know it, it was raining.

"Terrific," said Stitches. "Once again I find myself tramping through the woods in the middle of the night and for what? To go and fetch a transvestite Flug lookalike that's decided to wander off. There really needs to be some sort of quality control for reanimations. I mean, God forbid someone should bring something back to life that's got a modicum of intelligence. It's all wrong."

Ollie was as hacked off as his colleague if the truth be known, but it didn't help having a disgruntled zombie along for the ride moaning about absolutely everything.

"I tell you what," he said, "if you're that fed up, turn round and go back to the castle. It's not that far."

Stitches vehemently shook his head.

"You're having a laugh aren't you? Walk back there. On my own. In the dark. Through the forest. On my own. During a full moon. With all those monsters out there. ON MY OWN?"

"Looks like you're stuck with us then doesn't it?" said Ollie.

Flug, who'd been trailing along behind, forlornly calling out every now and then, quickened his pace and caught up with Stitches. He put an arm around the zombie's shoulder. Luckily he didn't squeeze otherwise they'd have been treated to the zombies impression of a tube of toothpaste.

"Me know you sad, Stitches" he said, "but me sad too. Me want find Oboe as well."

Stitches reached up and patted his friend's hand.

"I know," he said. "And I'm sorry. Look, don't you go worrying your big self about it. We'll find her."

"Fanks, Stitches."

Mandrake stopped suddenly and looked around. "You see something?" asked Ollie.

"No. It's just that this place looks familiar. I could swear that I've been here before."

"Well, there's plenty of places for you to hang around I suppose," said Stitches.

"No, it's not that," said Mandrake. "I wouldn't have wandered this far to end it all. My legs would've been killing me the next day. Anyway, I'm better now." He cast a knowing glance at Ollie then looked back to the forest. "It was a long time ago, when I first met Davina. I'm positive we came here for a picnic."

"You came out here for a picnic? You're braver than I gave you credit for," said Ollie.

"I'll say," added Stitches. "I'd rather put on a meat suit and go for a swim in a croc infested swamp. Or eat one of Mrs. Ladle's cakes. The chances of survival are about the same."

"I take it you do actually recognise something then, Mandrake?" said Ollie.

"Mmm. I think so."

Stitches wasn't so sure. Most forests looked the same even when compared to the prehistoric domain that he was standing in now. In fact, now he thought about it, it looked just like the woods and forests that he remembered from his youth near the New Forest, and subsequently his time spent in the Caribbean.

Phillip Meeup, as he was known, had been born in 1805, the same year in which Nelson had kicked Napoleon's backside at Trafalgar, and saw the opening of Thomas Telford's Pontcysyllte Aqueduct, carrying the Llangollen Canal over the River Dee (I know that second fact is dull, but at least you've learned something new).

His family had been rather well to do. Mother stayed at home and tended house whilst Father ran a very successful import business, bringing in everything from apples to something beginning with z. (Thank goodness it wasn't zebras or I'd have to put in a terrible joke about them crossing). On a side note, due to the lack of health and safety, customs, and any sort of rules and regulations regarding what you could and couldn't bring in, his ships also managed to smuggle in as many diseases as you could count on one hand (unless you picked up the virulent Portuguese Fingers Falling From The Right Hand Syndrome, in which case you'd have to use the left one. There was also Indonesian Left Wrist Rot which if caught meant you couldn't count at all. Unless you used your toes. Of course if you contracted Shepton Mallet Toe Fungus... anyway, you get the picture and I do hate to digress).

As was usual in those bygone days, after finishing a long and boring apprenticeship, and managing to reach the age of twenty-five without catching something horrible and dying as so many of the lower classes did, (or as his father described them, lazy work-shy fops who'd do anything to get off doing an honest day's work), Phillip took up a position helping to run his father's firm. He travelled all over Europe securing new business and even got as far as Moscow where he brokered a deal to import top quality vodka (what the Russians had left anyway, which at that time was about three dozen bottles in a merchant's cellar).

In 1839, when Phillip was thirty-four, his father, whose health wasn't the best, asked him to travel to the West Indies, as he'd heard that all sorts of exotic items were up for grabs, and seeing as the locals judged how prosperous a person was by how many bananas he had, there was quite a profit to be made.

Excited by this new prospect for travel and adventure, Phillip jumped at the chance. He'd never married or had any children and therefore had no ties to hold him back. And so on a bright summer's morning in 1840, Phillip Meeup set foot on Haitian soil.

To cut a long story short, (paper doesn't grow on trees you know), he settled in very well. He got a thriving export business up and running that sent out all sorts of stuff back home. He also met a lovely young lady and, as befitting a gentleman of his standing, he had a rather decadent house built for them. (It appeared decadent to the islanders at any rate. To be honest they'd have been impressed by a dwelling not made of mud and reeds, had a door, and didn't reek of goat).

All was going swimmingly until completely out of the blue, a man claiming to be the husband of his lady friend showed up. Quite naturally a fierce confrontation ensued involving all three of them. Ultimately, Phillip got the better of the interloper and threw him out, and not being one to be being taken for a fool, the young lass, after admitting that she'd been rather economical with the truth when it came to any previous relationships, followed swiftly behind.

Phillip, never one to dwell on the past, put the unfortunate incident to the back of his mind and carried on with expanding his rapidly growing business.

It wasn't until about a week later that he started to feel a bit funny. His head ached as if he was in the midst of the worst hangover since alcohol had been invented, his teeth had begun to throb, and his gums were bleeding when he brushed them. He was also off his food, unusual for someone with such a healthy appetite as his. After a fortnight he started to panic. His skin was turning grey and papery to the point that patches of it were flaking off, and if that wasn't bad enough he wasn't sleeping too well either. When he did manage to snatch a few hours, disturbing nightmares plagued him. In them he was dead, but not dead, condemned to spend the rest of eternity as neither man nor spirit. A wandering wraith of no earthly purpose, destined to live out the rest of his days on the fringes of society, shunned and abused by those he encountered and forever alone. (Shame Burger King hadn't been around back then. He'd have got onto their management programme).

Three days later he passed away. His housekeeper, a wonderfully eccentric black woman with the biggest hips you've ever seen outside of a Tom and Jerry cartoon, found him in bed as stiff and as dead as a post. The doctor diagnosed a viral infection, (what a surprise. It's two hundred years later and they still use that tired old rubbish), adding that he was surprised that someone with a 'feeble Western constitution managed to survive out here so long.'

Phillip Meeup was buried the next day without much ceremony, in a dusty, ramshackle plot in the local cemetery.

When he woke up, to say that he was confused was the biggest understatement since the Mayor of New Orleans sent a message to the President of the USA saying, 'It's been a bit breezy here. Any chance of a couple of tents and a mop?'

As he tried to sit up he cracked his head a belter on what sounded like a piece of wood. A very long piece of wood. It went from above his head to beyond his feet. He reached out to his sides and an inferno of panic blazed through him as his knuckles rapped on solid walls. He was totally enclosed. But where and why? He managed to get his arms up so that they rested on his chest and pushed upwards. Whatever it was, it wouldn't budge so much as an inch. So there he was, trapped and alone in the dark without any inkling as to what had occurred. He remembered feeling a bit under the weather but that was about it. Everything after that was a bit of a blur. If he didn't know any better, and if it wasn't a completely outlandish conclusion, he might have thought that he was in a coffin. It was about the right size but. . . no, it couldn't be. He was being paranoid wasn't he?

Time passed slowly. Eventually boredom set in and niggly little things began to prey on his mind. 'Why aren't I hungry or thirsty?' 'How come I don't need to go to the loo?' 'How come I haven't run out of air yet?' 'And why, oh why can't someone invent some sort of bag to put tea leaves into to stop them getting everywhere? You could call them leaf cases. No, that would never catch on.'

It could have been hours, days or weeks, he wasn't sure, but at some point he was disturbed by a scrabbling sound from above. It sounded like an animal digging through the earth. It was insistent, rapidly increasing in speed and coming ever closer.

BANG BANG BANG.

"Phillip, can you hear me?"

He was so shocked at first that he couldn't get a word out of his parched throat no matter how hard he tried.

BANG BANG.

"Answer me, dammit?"

"I'm here," he eventually managed to croak. "It's me." "Mind out."

With a splintering thud the head of an axe sliced through the wood stopping just short of his nose. Fingers, then hands probed the gap, took hold of the ragged edges and pulled. Then, amidst a flurry of chunks of wood and dry soil he was grabbed by the lapels and hauled upwards.

It was pitch black and he couldn't see his hands in front of his face.

He shook his head to clear it of detritus. "Are you alright?"

Finally he recognised the voice of his saviour. "Deborah?" he said.

"Yes, Phillip it's me," she said, giving him a hug.

"What's happened to me?" he asked, pushing her away, still confused. "How did I end up here?" He pointed to the hole in the ground. "Or should I say there?"

She paused for a moment and he could hear her swallowing. Whatever it was it wasn't good.

"It was Dubois," she said quietly. "After you threw him out he wanted revenge. He crept back to the house one night and laced your wine with a certain. . . concoction."

"Not the twenty-six. That's my favourite, it cost. . . Hang on. What do you mean by concoction? And exactly how long have I been down there?"

"A month."

"A MONTH!" he shouted. "But how? Why haven't I starved to death? Or dehydrated? It's not possible."

"I'm so sorry but it's true," she said. "My family?"

"They've been informed of your demise," she said, matter of factly. "Go on then. Tell me what happened."

"Dubois got drunk a few nights ago and shot his mouth off about what he'd done. He gave you a mixture of local herbs and frog poison. It causes your body to shut down so to all outside appearances you appear to be, well, dead."

"But obviously I'm not," he said, incredulously.

"Not quite. Not to put too fine a point on it, you've been zombiefied." "Zombie what?"

"The herbs that he administered have basically killed you. . . "
"Wha... "

". . . but you're not entirely dead."

Phillip was now as mystified as a person told that they had died, but not quite, been buried for a month, which was stupid, and had come back to life. Sort of.

Although she couldn't see him, Deborah could sense his fear and anxiety.

"Look, I know none of this makes sense and I'll try and explain it more and as best as I can, but for now I need to get you out of here and back to my house. I don't think it's wise for me to be seen having a midnight chat with a dead man in the middle of a graveyard."

"Oh, of course not. What will the neighbours think?" "I'm only trying to help."

"I know. I'm sorry. Anyway, what's wrong with my house?" "It's been sold off I'm afraid."

"Good grief. This just keeps getting better and better."

Unfortunately it didn't. Once back at Deborah's he got a chance to see himself in a mirror.

"I look like three-day old gruel," he said, dejectedly. "And not the expensive stuff either. I mean the filth they serve prisoners in gaol. And even they'd send it back."

If he had any moisture left in his system he would have shed some tears. Instead he was only able to produce dry, heaving sobs that left him curled up in a foetal position on the bathroom floor.

"So how long..?" he started, but trailed off once he'd calmed down somewhat.

Deborah didn't need to hear the rest of the question.

"Forever, as long as you look after yourself. As you get older there will be a certain amount of wear and tear, but zombiefied bodies are usually fairly resilient."

"Makes me sound like a traction engine," he said. "So why did that lunatic feel it necessary to do this to me? I'd never heard of him until you mentioned him, let alone did him any harm."

The silence issuing forth from Deborah told him everything he needed to know. All of it.

"He's your ex isn't he?" "Yes."

"You ended the relationship didn't you?" "Yes."

"He couldn't accept it could he?" "No."

"Came back for you didn't he?" "Yes."

"Didn't know about me did he?" "No."

"Bit of a lunatic isn't he?" "Yes."

"I'm stuffed aren't I?"

"Yes. No. Not really. Oh, I don't know. Look, at least you're alive." "Alive! Well, let's examine that shall we. I don't need to eat, sleep, drink, or go to the toilet apparently, so aside from saving me, oh let me see now, one hundred percent on my grocery bill, I'm not seeing all the major benefits of this sudden shift in lifestyle."

"I'm sorry, Phillip."

"Oh yeah, and not forgetting the fact that I'll get the chance to see in a new millennium or three. Of course that's if I don't fall apart at the seams first."

"I said I'm sorry," she said, crying openly. "I know. Come here."

He wrapped his arms around her and gave her a squeeze. As he did his knuckles cracked like walnuts and his shoulders moved too far in their drying joints.

"Oh good lord," he muttered to himself as he held Deborah and watched the sun begin to rise. "It's going to be a long century."

"Stitches. STITCHES!" shouted Ollie. "Wake up. Stop nightdreaming will you."

"Sorry about that. I was miles away. So, do you recognise it then, Mandrake?"

"Nah. My mistake. I must have been thinking of somewhere else." They moved on.

———

Mrs. Ladle flew round and round and round and round the roof of Jocular's castle. She didn't need to she just wanted to. Also it gave her broom a good run, allowed her to hone her cornering skills plus, bonus, she got to chase the bats that lived under the eaves of the topmost tower. (And before you say anything I know you can't technically corner whilst going round, but it's all I could think of in the time available. If you can come up with a better term then feel free).

Eventually she tired of terrorising the bats though and decided that she better go and see Jocular to find out what he wanted her to do. Obviously it was something decorating related otherwise he wouldn't have asked her to bring her 'WITCH GUIDE TO RENOVATION AND RESTORATION: MODERN LIVING IN A SUPERNATURAL WORLD' spell book. Actually it was more a serial magazine than a book, one of those that starts off as a 'fascinating week by week insight into something extremely dull' that ends up extending to so many editions landing on your doormat that your great, great, great grandchildren will only be a third of the way through the entire series when they inherit the massive collection of heaving 'handy binders' that you felt compelled to buy via the 'special one time only offer' in issue three. Mrs Ladle's periodical had started in 1167. She kept them all in a shoebox thanks to a handy shrinking spell revealed in issue 21,438.

It contained everything within its millions of pages, from how to keep skin moist and pliable (for lampshades, cushion covers etc), to a hundred and one things to do with a vase (a hundred and two if you put flowers in it).

She'd used it up at the castle a couple of times before. The first occasion was when Jocular wanted every wooden stair in the castle to say 'OOF' whenever they were stepped on, and the second time was when he decided it would be a grand idea to turn all of the water supply yellow. Now, Mrs. Ladle was no great respecter of the Vampire Lords lofty station, and in particular his decorative skills, and had wasted no time at all in letting him know that the stair idea was just plain odd and that no one, resident or visitor, dead or alive, or into whatever fetish you could think of, would want to drink water that looked like wee wee, especially when some of The Children of The Night weren't quite castle trained as yet and it was handy to have water coloured water so that if it suddenly turned yellow in hue it was reasonable to assume that some of them had been relieving themselves in the water tanks again. And if you think that's disgusting, you should see what they do in the gutters.

God alone knew what he wanted her to do this time. He probably wanted the statues to sing greetings to anyone walking along the corridors and passageways, or have a musical trap door opening over the basement.

She swooped down in a tricky, and quite frankly, hazardous manoeuvre, and landed outside the front door. Or where she thought the front door should be. Or, to be more precise, where the front door used to be. All that was there now was a large hole, a pile of assorted debris, and a very sullen looking Egon who was standing there with a door knob in his hand.

"I coughed and it fell off," he said, indicating the vast slab of wood at his feet.

"I see," said Mrs. Ladle, putting her broom in park and dismounting. "Well, that explains the door but what happened to the entrance hall? His Royal Dimness decided the castle needed a sunroof did he? Hello, Humpy."

"Not exactly," said Egon, readjusting his comb over so that it didn't resemble a wandering shag pile carpet. "We had a close encounter of the absurd kind."

"Do tell," said the witch, although she did have a sneaking suspicion about what had happened though. All the signs were here. And there, and everywhere else as well.

Egon gave her a brief rundown of the night's events thus far. "And that's how the door broke," he concluded.

Mrs. Ladle shook her head, sighed, and sparked up immediately, instantly giving off more smoke than a steam train going up the side of Mount Etna when it was in a really foul mood.

"I knew it would go wrong," she said, shaking her head. "It always does. I'll never understand why beings of limited intellect insist on meddling with forces beyond the grasp of their single celled brains."

"Because zey strife to furzer zere knowledge of ze frontiers of science in an attempt to improof zere vorld," said Jocular, appearing behind her like a seven-foot vampire. "Also it is tremendous fun into ze bargain ven zey are doing ze messing up on it."

"That's another way of looking at it if you're feeling charitable," said Mrs. Ladle. "Anyway, let's get on with cleaning this mess up so I can go and help the boys find this missing monster. Lord alone knows what trouble they'll get into by themselves."

———

Professor Crumble, lending credence to the rumour that witches had an uncanny idea about what was going to happen in the future, was in trouble. In fact, it had bugger all to do with Mrs. Ladles powers of prognostication, and more to do with the fact that Crumble and crew were about as much use as a Braille copy of Lord of the Rings was to a double arm amputee who didn't know Braille.

At present, the Professor was hanging upside down by his ankle and swinging back and forth like a wrinkly, white haired pendulum.

"How did you manage that?" said Ethan, looking at Crumble going forwards and backwards like a tennis ball. "I would've thought that me saying, 'be careful of the trap, Professor,' would have given you some sort of a clue to be careful of the trap, Professor."

"Yes yes, you're quite right, Ethan. Good point, well presented. My fault entirely I'm afraid," said Crumble, his face starting to turn an impressive shade of crimson. "I noticed that it was tied with a Rhinos Twist and seeing as how I haven't seen one used in this capacity before, I got a bit curious, unfortunately."

Amongst his many hobbies, (tinkering with machinery, trying various teas from all over the world, knitting multicoloured mittens, and causing the near destruction of the planet earth and everything on it on an hourly basis), Professor Crumble liked to collect knots. He had a load in a drawer back at the lab. He had everything from the more common types such as Dudley's Elbow and the Parson's Tangle, to rarities like Appleyard's Möbius Three Rope Nightmare, and Ironfist's Thump. Such was his knowledge on the subject that in knotty circles he was known as something of a guru. In not knotty circles he was known as a crazy old duffer who had an unhealthy attraction to bits of string. Knot quite all there if you like.

Ethan followed the rope to where it was looped around the trunk of a large tree.

"Brace yourself," he said as he cut the line.

Crumble tumbled to the ground with a loud crash. Luckily he landed on his head so he didn't damage anything vital.

As they were helping him up Golden Kilo stopped and said, "Shush a minute."

"What?" said Ethan.

"I thought I heard a rustle over there in those trees."

"I don't know anyone called Russell," said Crumble, divesting himself of leaves, twigs and other forest detritus, some of which had legs and sharp pincers.

"Is he serious?" said Kilo, noting the serious look on the Professor's face.

"Oh yes," answered Ethan. "You'll know when he's trying to be humorous. A pig will fly past a blue moon on a day that's got a Z in it."

"So never then." "Well, once actually."

"How on earth did that happen?"

"Some kind of time and space type accident. I think it had something to do with quarks, neutrinos, positive destabilisers, the discovery of anti-matter, and a jar of mixed fruit jam if I remember rightly."

"Excuse me," said Crumble, gloriously unaware of the conversation going on between the other two. "I don't wish to be rude but shouldn't we go and see if Russell's alright?"

The trio followed the noise. It led them about fifteen yards into a dense clump of trees and undergrowth. As they pushed through the branches a small furry, lumpy thing jumped up and ran off.

"Skullenian Forest Devil," said Kilo.

"Agreed," said Ethan, "and look." He pointed at a patch of dark liquid on the ground.

"Looks like tomato sauce," said Crumble. Ethan raised his nose into the air and sniffed.

"It's blood," he said. "Fresh too. Not more than three or four hours old I'd say."

"You can tell all that from just one sniff?" asked Kilo. "Of course."

"That's Impressive. It's unusual for a person to have such a strong sense of smell."

Ethan smiled. "A normal person yes. But I'm fortunate to have the help of a rather special alter ego."

Kilo looked incredulous, almost as if he didn't have a clue what Ethan was talking about.

"I haven't got a clue what you're talking about, Ethan," he said. (Told you so).

"Werewolf," said Ethan, pointing to his chest. "Over there I think," said Crumble.

"Oh I see," said Kilo, rather overawed but internally vowing never to be around the big fellah when he got peckish. "So can you follow the trail?"

"Most assuredly. The tang is still in the air and seeing as it hasn't been too windy it's very easy to pick it up. It heads off in that direction.

It's certainly Oboe. Her scent is all over the place." He pointed at the heading that he was alluding to.

"Let's get going then," said Kilo. "If it's that fresh then she can't be too far away."

"Come on, Prof," said Ethan, noting that the scientist had slipped the knot into his pocket. "We've got a trail to follow."

Crumble followed on obediently, lost in his own little world as per normal. He was watching carefully where he put his feet, glad to be on the move again, and wondering why a werewolf called Russell was hiding in a bush.

———

Mind numbingly bright colours, strange creatures that had no business existing in any realm, and noises the like of which should never be heard by earthly beings pummelled her mind relentlessly. She tossed and turned, thrashing her limbs wildly, trying desperately in vain to escape the shadowy phantoms that stalked her in the darkness. There was no rhyme or reason as to why these denizens of the abyss wanted to hunt her down, but she knew that if they did she would be rendered asunder, suffering unimaginable torment in the process. She tried to flee but it was as if something were holding her back, an unseen but powerful force willing her to fail and fall prey to the screeching demons of the pit. Hot. She was so hot. A granite melting, volcanic core of molten agony seemed to be writhing within her belly, battering her with its unmerciful heat, searching for a way out. Then cold. A bone chilling, soul crushing cold the likes of which could only be found in the farthest reaches of the frozen North. It crept into her at a cellular level, making her very organs gelid and non-functioning. Need to get away. Need to get away. Need to get. . .

"ou. . . right? . . . u hear me? . . . ke up."

Her eyes flew open in an instant and focused on the figure hovering over her like a malevolent puppet. She cried out in utter terror not knowing who this was, what she was doing here, or why this aberration was leering down at her.

Firm hands gripped her shoulders and forced her down making it difficult for her to move.

"You need to calm down and lie still," the voice said. "You had a nightmare."

She heard the words but they didn't mean anything to her. All they registered as were random sounds, nonsensical enunciations generated by an unknown being that seemed intent on restraining her. Whatever its dread purpose was she did not know, and had no intention of finding out.

A wave of supercharged adrenalin rushed through her system, and with a mighty effort she took a hold of her erstwhile captor's head and sat up. It looked like its mouth was moving but if it made any noise, she now couldn't hear it such was the fervour of the all-consuming terror that had her in its maleficent clutches. Flexing muscles that had, until now, laid long dormant, she squeezed as hard as she could and launched the interloper across the room. With a crash it landed on the kitchen table, the splintering of the wood intermingling with the crack of aged, desiccated bones.

She stood up and took in her surroundings. She didn't recognise anything, an absence of information that heightened her anxiety to almost tangible levels. By now she was in a near blind panic.

"Urrghh."

The creature on the floor stirred, moaning in agony as it tried to move its shattered, useless limbs.

"Help me," it said, managing to raise an imploring hand towards her. Ancient impulses bent on survival at all costs completely disregarded the other sentient beings call for help. The strangled cries for mercy and the outstretched fingers meant only one thing to her addled mind. Danger.

The need for self-preservation and a fear born of instinct took control and consumed her absolutely. Subsumed by forces beyond her comprehension she crossed the room with a steely and determined spark in her eye. Purposeful of movement, and with only one intention in mind she swiftly closed in on her perceived enemy giving it little or no chance to attack her once more.

"Please," it pleaded. Blood dripped from its lips and its breath rattled in its broken chest. "I tried to help you."

Once again the words fell on deaf and uncaring, non-understanding ears. As he struggled to breathe, No See Norman felt hands around his throat. Strong, determined hands that tightened like a vice, choking the very life from him.

"Why?" he managed to force out through his constricted vocal cords. "Why?"

She squeezed tighter and tighter until eventually, when her strength was all but spent; she felt the body go limp. She relaxed her grip and allowed the lifeless, blue tinged head to fall to the floor. It fell with a dull thud and was still.

Angry, red finger marks stared at her as if in admonishment, and the dead things eyes, although glazed over and motionless, seemed to mock her, damning and chastising her for what she had done.

She rose slowly, surveying the aftermath of her outburst. Unbidden a tear broke free and trickled down her face as a torrent of emotion threatened to sweep her away. Suddenly, she bolted for the door, crashing through it and into the harsh, uncaring night-time world of the forest.

"NOOOOOOOOO!" she cried, the enormity of what she had done hitting her straight between her misty, bleary eyes. Hands clasped to her temples she shook her head back and forth, whimpering, as if the action would shake free the images plaguing her, releasing her from the shackles of responsibility.

Oboe took off at full speed into the welcoming blackness that the woods afforded, aiming to put as much distance between herself and her foul deed as possible.

As she ran, she cried.

"Did you hear that?" said Mandrake, waving at the others to stop. "I've never heard anything like it. It sounded awful."

"Was Oboe," said Flug. "She very sad."

"Do you really think it was her?" said Ollie, to no one in particular.

He was listening out in case the sound came again.

"I suppose it could've been," said Stitches, trying to ascertain where it had come from. "But there are a lot of weird things out here especially at this time of night. It could be anything from mating swamp toads to a pissed off ghost."

"Well, whatever it was," said Mandrake, "I think it came from that direction."

"Okay, well we definitely need to check it out," said Ollie. "It might be nothing but you never know. If Oboe's in trouble we really should get there as quick as we can."

"Tis, Oboe," said Flug adamantly, striding forth into the trees. "She sad. Me goin' to help her."

A good (or bad depending on your point of view) fifteen minutes later, Flug stumbled down an incline and landed boots first in a freezing cold stream.

"It cold," he said, tramping through it to the other bank. Once there he stamped his feet causing a minor landslide and releasing about four gallons of water from each of his comedy sized footwear. "Noise comin' from dis way," he continued, pointing determinedly.

"He seems pretty sure," said Ollie, tiptoeing through the water like a ballet dancer. "Good grief that's freezing." (Only full blood vampires have a problem with water. It makes them bubble and squirm and go all squidgy, and leaves them rather melty looking. It was similar to putting a frog in a kettle. Ollie's human DNA though allowed him the luxury of being able to enjoy all of the wonders that $H2O$ had to offer, the highlight of which was a bubble bath every Friday night. His favourite at the moment was Jasmine infused honey with a hint of Asian Lily and Dragonfruit).

"I reckon he's right," said Mandrake. "That's certainly where I thought the noise came from." He was next to immerse his lower portions into the frigid stream. "Bloody Hell! I think that's the coldest thing I've ever felt. And I'm married."

Stitches reached the other side of the stream, not a single drop of water on his feet.

"Losers," he mocked. "You should have used the stepping stones." He started to laugh. Unfortunately his merriment distracted him and he didn't see the large branch lying on the floor directly in his path. As he stepped on its leading edge it shot upright and clunked him on the head with a resounding THWACK. He stumbled backwards, arms spinning like a windmill in a hurricane, legs going up and down like a crazy sprinter, and mouth going like the world swearing champion.

SPLASH!

"Well, I think that's six point two for execution, three for difficultly, but only point seven for presentation. You should have worn your rubber ring," said Ollie.

A very wet and soggy zombie clambered onto the bank. He didn't look his usual self. In fact he looked twice his usual self.

"Oh no," he wailed, as his clothes expanded and threatened to burst at the seams. "I've soaked it all up."

He tried to walk but only managed a couple of heavy steps before he fell forward in a bloated, squishy heap.

"I suppose you think this is funny?" his muffled voice said. "Course not," said Mandrake, stuffing a fist into his mouth.

"Oh good Lord no," said Ollie, knowing now what a fluid filled balloon would look like if it had legs.

"Flug. Stitches needs a hug before we go any further."

(The big monster knew exactly what was required of him. He'd had to do the very same thing a couple of months ago when the zombie had annoyed Mrs. Ladle by banging on about her being 'a little wide in the broom' to be flying around like a lunatic at all the hours of the day and night. The kindly witch had responded by conjuring up a storm cloud that had followed Stitches around for the next twelve hours. By the time the mini Nimbo Stratus had emptied itself, Stitches was stranded in the town square unable to move and sounding like a urinal after a rock festival).

Flug bent down and lifted Stitches off the forest floor. Even for the big guy it was a bit of a struggle. Not because of the weight but because of the awkwardness of it. It was like trying to manoeuvre a water filled mattress.

Flug got him upright and moved Stitches until he had him face to face in a bear hug. Then, flexing his massive muscles, he squeezed. Hard.

A torrent of fresh stream water pooled in the zombie's feet, swelling them to four or five times their normal size. His shoes popped off and landed near Mandrake, and his socks split and fell to the floor where they lay like deflated slugs. Then, with a loud gush, the pores in the soles of his feet expanded releasing all of the water that had soaked into his system.

"Oh my God," moaned Stitches. "That feels sooooo good. Now I know why elephants look so happy all the time."

Flug put him down again. He looked at Stitches strangely. "Your tummy gone funny," he said. "Look."

Stitches gazed down at his midriff.

"Oh for goodness sake," he moaned. His waist had been reduced to about half of what it had been thanks to being rammed into the vice that was Flugs arms. He quickly took hold of his belt to stop his trousers falling down.

"Do you think you could have squeezed me any harder?" he said to Flug, realising that his belly button was touching his spine.

"Me can do," said Flug, making to pick up Stitches again. "You still got water?"

"Get out of it," said the zombie, taking a step back. "I don't want to be crushed out of existence."

"How long will that take to pop back to normal?" asked Ollie, convinced that Stitches's head was bigger than it had been a few moments ago.

"Don't know. I think it was a couple of hours last time."

"He looks like a kid's bendy toy," said Mandrake.

"I'm so glad you're not suicidal anymore, sunshine. What would I do without you?" said Stitches, poking a new hole in his belt with one of his larger needles. It was now so small that it could've held a pea plant to a stake. Ollie wouldn't have liked that though as he had a bit of a thing about those (the stakes that is not the peas. Vampire movies would have been a whole lot different, and definitely a lot more rubbish if, after capturing the naughty bloodsucker, the hero smacked him on the chest with a two-pound bag of frozen petits pois. 'Dracula Has Risen From The Allotment Just Behind The Cabbages', just doesn't have quite the same ring somehow).

"Come on," said Ollie. "Let's find out where that wail came from. If it was Oboe we might not be too far behind her."

They forged on through the forest until not too far ahead they caught sight of No See Norman's ramshackle hut.

"I'll bet that's where she is," said Stitches. "If I was scared, lost and alone in the woods I'd try to find somewhere warm and safe."

"I agree," said Mandrake. "HELLO!" he called out. "IS ANYBODY THERE!?"

"HELLO THERE!" shouted Ollie as well as they approached. "OBOE!!!" bellowed Flug, loud enough to rattle the trees.

There was no reply from inside the hut or the surrounding woodland.

"What ho, chaps. Looks like we've all managed to follow the trail here," announced Crumble as he, Ethan and Kilo exited the forest.

"How did you find it?" said Ollie. "We heard a loud shout."

"Ethan picked up a fresh blood spoor so it was easy really," said Kilo. "We just followed his nose."

"Well he has got a great sense of smell for that sort of thing," said Stitches. "He can find bones that have been buried for years. In fact I think he found a Tyrannosaurus last week."

"No one'll find you when I'm done with your saggy backside," snarled the lycan, showing a dazzling set of gnashers.

Ollie disregarded what they were banging on about and walked up to the front door. It was only when he got up close that he noticed the topmost hinge had been knocked out and the door itself was hanging at an angle.

"Guys," he said. "Something's not quite right here."

Ethan joined him at the entrance and unobtrusively placed himself in front of Ollie, who just as unobtrusively gave way. He wasn't a coward by any stretch of the imagination but Ethan was bigger, stronger, and faster than him so it made sense that he should venture into this particular unknown first.

"Where, Oboe?" said Flug.

"That's what we're trying to find out," said Mandrake, patting the monster affectionately on the back. He wasn't sure if Flug felt it because it was like slapping his hand against a tower block.

Ethan eased the door open slowly and stepped inside.

It was dark but not to the point that you couldn't see. A couple of candles still burned inside, casting flickering shadows as their flames dancing gently, moved by the breeze coming through the open door.

Furniture, what little of it there was, lay scattered about the floor, some of it broken, the rest overturned.

Ethan raised his head up and tested the air. The unmistakable tang of blood assailed his nostrils once again. He was just about to turn to Ollie and say so when something over in a far corner caught his eye. A pair of feet were protruding from behind the upturned kitchen table. He couldn't see anything else but you didn't have to be a genius or a great detective to realise that there was a body attached to those feet. A very still body.

"Professor," he called out.

Within moments Crumble had entered the hut and been guided to the prostrate figure on the ground.

It wasn't pretty. The old man, whoever he was none of them knew, had taken quite a ferocious beating. His head was positioned at an acute angle and one of his eyes was swollen completely shut. His bottom lip was split and there were traces of bubbled blood on his teeth indicating possible internal injuries. Several of his fingers appeared to be broken and his left shoulder was badly dislocated. Crumble put two fingers to the old man's neck just to be sure. He gave it a moment before turning to the others and shaking his head sadly.

"Who could do this?" said Mandrake. "And to a defenceless old man." "I've got a horrible feeling. . . " said Ollie.

Ethan nodded in agreement. "It's not just a feeling," he said, confirming Ollie's worst fears. "You know that blood type that led us here? I'm picking up traces of it all over this hut, but in particular over by the bed and next to the body."

Kilo sank down to the floor, the realisation of what they were talking about suddenly hitting him like a thunderbolt. He put his head in his hands and sobbed pathetically.

"What have I done?" he said to himself, but loud enough for the others to hear. "Oh my God what have I done?" He was desolate, forlorn, and now forever tainted by what his creation had wrought in this quiet and peaceful home.

Crumble covered up the old man's corpse with the blood-stained table cloth lying next to it, and went over to the distraught Kilo. He squatted down beside him and put an arm around his heaving shoulders. The professor then leaned in and whispered something into his ear. The others didn't hear what he said but Kilo looked up and nodded his head.

"So what do we do now?" said Stitches, staring at the shape un der the cloth. It reminded him of how Oboe had looked underneath her shroud. This one though would never move again, and the only thing that would rise from under it would be the inevitable stench of death and decay. "Because this sort of puts a different slant on things doesn't it?"

"It does," said Ollie, quietly. "And it seems fairly obvious to me what the solution is. She has to be caught and. . . you know."

The rest silently nodded their heads in agreement, knowing precisely what he meant.

Flug, who'd been waiting outside due to the restricted room, squeezed through the doorway. He saw the others crowded around the body.

"Who dat?" he asked.

"We don't know," said Ollie. "Why him sleeping on da floor?"

"He's not asleep, Flug mate. He's dead."

"Aw. Me give him sweetie. Make him feel better."

"I don't think that's going to work, big fellah," said Stitches. "Oboe did a pretty good job. . . "

Ollie and Ethan shot the zombie a warning look but it was too late. Despite having a brain that was the evolutionary equivalent of a wilted salad, Flug somehow knew exactly what his colleague was referring to.

"Oboe done dis?" he said.

"It looks that way," said Ollie, giving Stitches a glare that could have withered a Giant Redwood. Stitches shrugged his shoulders and stared back with a, 'how was I supposed to know we were going to keep it a secret from Flug to protect his feelings. You really should keep me in the loop if you don't want things to go wrong,' look.

"But why? She not naughty," said Flug.

"I know, mate but she's sick. There's something wrong in her head that made her do this," said Ollie.

Mandrake was keeping a close eye on Flug. The monster was tensing up and the bolt in his forehead was pulsing up and down.

"I think. . . " said Mandrake.

"Way ahead of you," said Ethan. "The trail will still be fresh. Come on, Flug. Let's go and find Oboe."

It was clear that Kilo was in no fit state to join them so Crumble volunteered to stay in the shack to look after him.

Once more, following Ethan's lead, the remainder of the group headed off into the night once more.

On and on she forged through the woods, aware now of the immensity of the evil deed that she had perpetrated. Even the trees that she pushed past seemed to lean in towards her in an accusatory manner, cursing and condemning, distraught at her flagrant disregard for the sanctity of life. An image of the old man's bruised and broken body forced itself into her mind and the whispered cry of his pleas for clemency never left her.

Tears streaked down her face as she ventured further and further into the cold embrace of the night, not caring in the slightest where she may end up.

"I'm sorry," she muttered breathlessly to the encroaching darkness. "I'm so sorry."

It was strange that in the short time since she'd been reanimated, the one act that had finally awakened her self-awareness more than any other had been the taking of the old man's life. Not for her the joy of waking and being welcomed into the arms of companions, or the wonders of the natural world that surrounded her, or the unconditional kindness of a fellow being. No, for her it was a violent, unnecessary killing that had roused her sentience to its full capacity. Oboe could not and would never justify the act to herself.

As she plunged deeper and deeper into the woods, she'd unconsciously come to the inevitable conclusion that a creature such as herself must not be allowed to carry on its existence. Her brief time in this world had to come to an end in order to protect those around her, both those that she didn't know and those that she had already met. An old saying sprang to mind; maybe it was from her past life, but she wasn't sure. 'Strangers are just friends that you haven't met yet'. From whence it came she did not know but it rang true. And what of those new friends whoever they may be? How long would they enjoy their time on earth before she rendered them asunder as she had the old man?

"*But the people from before can help you,*" said a voice from the darkness. "*Trust them. They have the potential to become the friends that you so desperately seek.*"

She recalled their faces gathered around her as she sat on the floor in the big building. Kind, benevolent and eager to assist.

"But that's what happened with the old man," she retorted. "He was all of those things and more, and look what I did to him."

"*That was a one off I'm sure,*" the voice continued like a determined defence counsellor. "*An aberration brought on by confusion, alcohol, and maybe a bump to the head. You can't blame yourself.*"

"No," she said angrily. "There are no excuses. No bargaining with myself in the hope that I can feel better and brush it all to one side. Confusion may well have reigned in my mind when I acted as I did, but that doesn't justify the actions that it caused. Where does that lead? How far can you take justification? Before long you'd have everyone committing all sorts of unspeakable acts and using their own twisted rationale as to why it was alright to do it. It won't work. It can not work. Wrong is wrong no matter what the circumstances. No mitigation. No diminishing of responsibility. No aberration."

The voice from the gloom did not respond. It appeared that it couldn't argue in the face of such logic and fierce determination.

Oboe was finally left with her own thoughts. As unpalatable as they were they spurred her on and made her even more committed to seek out her own destruction. How she would achieve her aim she didn't know, but she was absolutely steadfast in the knowledge that she would not be leaving the forest alive.

————

Mrs. Ladle skimmed over treetops, skirted by branches, swooped round rocky outcrops, and performed every other flying activity that you can think of beginning with S. (Except skydiving though, because that would just be silly. And besides, she didn't have her big skirt on so would have plummeted to the forest floor like a silly, old woman who'd fallen off her broom). Despite all this she still couldn't find Ollie, any of his crew, or the missing monster.

"Bloody forest," she said to herself. "They should cut the whole lot down and build a massive multiplex cinema."

Witches, as highlighted by Mrs. Ladle's views on what the future of the woodland below her should be, are not the most ecologically or environmentally friendly of creatures. Forget green issues and the preservation of the Earth's natural, and rapidly decreasing resources, it wasn't unheard of for Mrs. Ladle to use her broom to get from one room to the next in her own house. And as for recycling, forget it. All that meant to her was peddling round the same place that you had the day before. Neither the plight of the Polar Bear, the worries of the greenhouse effect, nor the rapidly increasing size of the hole in the ozone layer held any interest for those of the pointy hat brigade. If she had her way there'd be an airport in every town, and petrol would be free and contain more lead per litre than the roof at Notre Dame.

On and on she flew in seemingly endless and ever increasing circles until, "What was that?" she said, coming to a stop and putting her broom into hover. She looked around and absently flicked a spent cigarette butt to the ground far below. (Don't worry, it was out, although that wasn't always the case, and if you'll allow me the indulgence to take you on a little wander back through the history books, I'll explain why. You'll no doubt have noticed they tell us that the Great Fire of London started in a bakery on Pudding Lane, but that's not entirely true. It did start in a bakery in Pudding Lane, most certainly burnt most of London to the ground, and made for a very interesting entry in Samuel Pepys' diary, but it had nothing to do with super-heated flour. A passing witch, who'd been on a three-day bender with her coven, was flying back from Stonehenge when she decided to knock her pipe out. The burning cinders had slowly, and majestically drifted down onto, yes indeed, you've guessed it, the roof of the very dry and very wooden food emporium previously mentioned. The witch in question was totally unaware of what she'd done of course, but for days afterwards she couldn't get the stench of freshly baked humans out of her nose).

Mrs. Ladle was sure that the strange sound had come from somewhere behind her. Not that there wasn't a plethora of weird noises emanating from the forest at any given time of course, but like everything else you get used to it, and anything that doesn't sound familiar raises alarm bells, especially if it's an alarm bell.

It sounded to her like someone sobbing and proper going at it as well. They were throat shredding, snot river inducing, red eye causing gasps of emotion.

She angled the nose of her broomstick down a few degrees and began to descend to where she thought it was coming from. She hoped that it wasn't someone too upset. She wasn't big on sympathy, understanding, and getting to the root cause of someone's problems. She was more of the, 'pull yourself together and snap out of it or I'll give you something to cry about,' type of person.

There it was again, except this time the crying was punctuated by howls of anguish.

As she closed in on the sound she noticed that the trees had begun to thin out to the point that she could see down to the forest floor where a stony path wended its way through the undergrowth.

She followed it casually at first, until it became more than obvious that whatever was making all the racket had traversed it as well. A sudden wave of panic rose within her as she remembered where it led to.

"Oh no," she said to herself as she turned right and picked up speed. "Of all the places."

The path, not used for many, many decades as far as she knew, led to Percy's Precipice, a sharp outcrop of granite that looked out over the whole of Skullenia. It was beautifully picturesque and a perfect spot for viewing the sweeping vistas of the valley below. Its only major drawback was that there were only two ways off it. You either took the same path, only in reverse, or took the more direct route, which in this case was four and a half thousand feet straight down onto the jagged rocks below.

The venue had been named after Percy Froglicker, a young man who had thrown himself into the abyss after being spurned in love. Some folk spoke of his spirit still haunting the area, constantly prowling around and ever eager to coax other unwitting souls to their doom.

The rest of the folks spoke about the weather, what they'd had for dinner, and why did some folks have to talk such utter rubbish about bedevilled cliffs.

Coming in low, Mrs. Ladle caught sight of the source of the all the noise. It was a misshapen and deformed aberration; a throwback to more primitive times when evolutionary chaos still reigned and mortal man didn't have wit enough or curiosity sufficient to meddle with nature or supernature. It was either that or Flug had decided on a major lifestyle change, stolen one of Mrs. Strudels voluminous bras and gotten lost. Maybe not, although that would have been absolutely hilarious.

The creature, clearly the one that had gone missing, (and let's face it, how many mindless, psychotic and borderline proto-human misanthropes are you likely to find out and about in the middle of the night? Well, there's always Essex I suppose, but that depends on how badly you want your mobile phone stolen and your car turned into a house/toilet/funeral pyre), was stood precariously on the very edge of the drop. It literally couldn't go any further forward without plunging into oblivion. At this point a strong gust of wind would have sent it toppling over.

"Just wait," hollered the witch. "Please don't give up. Help is on its way."

The figure looked up and stared directly at Mrs. Ladle, who'd taken up a position about six feet in front of it. The broomstick hummed and spluttered quietly as it hovered in place. She didn't want to get too close in case the thing made a sudden grab for her. (Although she didn't know what had occurred with No See Norman, Mrs. Ladle recognised the signs of someone wanting to end it all. The tangible fear, overtly extreme emotion, clearly some sort of anger or guilt, and possibly some mental health issues told her intuitive and logical mind exactly what was happening. The fact that it was standing on a cliff top and maybe going to jump a half mile straight down was a bit of a giveaway as well).

She stayed back because a lot of potential suicides had a nasty habit of wanting a bit of companionship on their journey into the afterlife because after all, misery does love company, (as well as office parties, work outings, traffic jams, Eastenders, homework, that medicine you have to take that tastes like poo, updates on Facebook about dead relatives, Grease 2, and sprouts).

"It doesn't matter," the figure said. "I've done something terrible so I deserve to die. Nothing you say is going to sway me."

Disregarding the obvious comment she could have made about swaying at the top of a mountain as inappropriate, Mrs. Ladle weighed up her options, not that there were many. She didn't recall there being a lesson at Witch College about dealing with this sort of incident.

The creature was clearly far too heavy for her to carry on her broomstick, and she hadn't quite mastered the 'Floatation of Organic Material' spell yet (issue 14,236). She'd only tried it once and the poor victim had never been seen again, except by disbelieving astronauts who put it down to space sickness and too much additive laden, dehydrated food. 'And what was the fate of this poor, unfortunate soul?' I hear you cry. Well, I'll tell you. He's currently in a geostationary orbit about two hundred miles above the earth and due to splash down off the coast of Australia some time in the late twenty third century. I think it's a Tuesday.

She suddenly realised that Ethan was with the group and if he was as good at tracking as most werewolves were, then hopefully they shouldn't be too far away.

"Don't do anything hasty," she said. "I'll be back."

As fast as the woodland allowed, she followed the path down the mountain.

———

"Why don't they understand?" Oboe said to herself. "Do they not realise what I've done? Can they not accept the fact that I can't go on? I mustn't go on. It must finish here."

Was she expecting answers? Guidance? Affirmation? She gazed at the stunning panorama before her but took in none of its tranquil beauty. The majesty of the natural world was as dead to her as the blackened core of her being.

She shuffled forward a couple of millimetres until she could feel a subtle shift in her centre of gravity. As she looked down, the impenetrable darkness seemed to beckon to her, calling her to join it in a passionate and everlasting embrace that would take away her pain and her suffering. It was as if it were calling her home.

Bits of stone and dusty shale cascaded down as her feet moved unconsciously, attempting to gain purchase.

"*What are you doing?*" the voice from the forest said, returning to plague her once more. *"I told you that you'd get away with it. There's any number of excuses you could use."*

"I'm not listening to you," she said, vehemently. "In fact there's no one there. You're an illusion, an intruder in my head, and I won't bow to the will of a voice from the ether. I will NOT allow myself to be dissuaded from this course of action. And if I were to change my mind, it would be at my behest, not yours."

"But. . ."

"NO! No more."

She made to move forward.

"And if you can't be quiet of your own accord, perhaps I can do it for you."

Oboe took a deep breath and leaned over.

———

"Ollie," shouted Mrs. Ladle, closing in like an Exocet missile on a tight schedule. "I've found her."

Ollie, closely followed by the others, picked himself up off the floor and checked that his head was still attached to his shoulders.

"That was bit close you mad old mare," shouted Stitches, spitting out a dried leaf. "You'll have someone's eye out with that bloody thing."

"Where is she?" said Mandrake.

"Percy's Precipice, and not to put too fine a point on it, I don't think you've got long, so if you intend to rescue her you better hurry up."

"Can you help, Mrs. L?" asked Flug, hopefully.

"I could, Flug love, but I don't think turning her into a turnip is going to help all that much. She'd roll off."

Thinking about it for a moment, Ollie considered keeping everybody back. If Oboe was at the top of the mountain then she clearly only had one thing in mind, which would ultimately save them from performing the onerous task that they all knew was the outcome of all this should they catch up with her. He turned to address the group when he heard Mrs. Ladle say, "Follow me."

So much for that idea, he thought.

Flug pushed his way past them all and strode towards Mrs. Ladle. "Me go. Me help, Oboe," he announced.

"Okay, mate," said Stitches to his friend's back. "We'll go with you to make sure she's alright."

"No," said the monster. "Just me. Me love Oboe. Me save her." "But. . ." started Ollie.

Flug thrust a finger at his own chest, a gesture that would've sent any of them flying backwards at a rate of knots. "Just me or me be angry," he said matter of factly, and with such conviction that Ollie actually took a step back. The reanimate might very well be a gentle giant normally, but the prospect, however unlikely, of Flug losing his temper wasn't a pleasant one. It would like be trying to calm down an outraged Brontosaurus with a smile, a kind word and a pea shooter.

"Let him go," said Ethan. "I suspect he won't be able to do much anyway. We'll follow on discretely in a few minutes."

"But if he does rescue her, how are we going to get her away from him?" said Mandrake. "He's not going to give her up, and I suspect even Ethan here wouldn't relish the thought of taking on an outraged Flug."

"I wouldn't overly concern yourself," said Stitches. "We can always distract him with a bag of sweets, or a piece of silver foil, or something." Although it may have sounded sarcastic, the zombie felt for his big friend and turned away sadly.

As it turned out following Flug at a 'discrete distance' proved to be rather easier than they'd anticipated. They were, in fact, only about ten feet behind the big fellah, who was so intent on rescuing Oboe that he didn't even notice when a Shrieking Bush Hamster attached itself to Mandrakes leg in a rather romantic fashion.

Disregarding, or totally unaware of all that was going on around him, Flug strode purposefully along the steep path.

"Oboe," he called out. "Me coming. Me look after you."

"Keep going, Flug love," shouted Mrs. Ladle from above. "Not too far to go now."

Flug quickened his pace to the point that he began to out distance his colleagues. It was one of those rare occasions that his virtually immobile metabolism proved to be an advantage. He had the resting pulse of a block of concrete so he could go for hours at a fair old speed without getting out of breath. Stitches could have achieved the same thing due to his innate zombieness, but he wouldn't because he was so lazy that he got worn out putting his shoes on (and they were slip ons for goodness sake).

Flug topped a small knoll and came to a complete stop.

"Oboe," he said, managing to infuse his voice with relief, affection and concern all at the same time. "You need to come away from dere it dangerous."

She turned, wobbling ever so slightly as she did. It was as if gravity had one heavy hand on her already.

"You need to go," she said, recognising Flug from before. "I can't stay here."

"But you must," said Flug, moving closer. "Me love you, Oboe. Everyfing will be okay."

"Who's Oboe?" she asked.

"You is, silly. Me chose your name. It because you pretty. Please come wiv me."

She shook her head, wary now of the monster who was slowly but surely getting nearer and nearer.

"That's very sweet of you to say so but I'm not. Not really. Especially on the inside. I've been really bad and I need to go away now."

"Oh, dat okay," said Flug, now within a few feet of her. "When me naughty, Ollie stop me havin' sweeties for a bit."

That did actually raise a wan smile on her sad, battered face. She seemed to be like him in a lot of ways, and under different circumstances maybe she would have liked to get to know him better. But his innocence was his undoing. He was clearly totally unaware of the gravity of her predicament, and judging by his adoring and pleading demeanour, it wouldn't make one iota of difference to him if he was. But still she couldn't stay, and even if there'd have been a hint of doubt in her mind, Flug's simple minded view of the world would've confirmed that her decision was the right one.

She was about to speak again when she saw other figures approaching along the path. In that same instant Flug noticed that her attention was distracted, so with a burst of speed born of desperation he lunged forward. When he landed, a loud crack was heard by everyone, including Mrs. Ladle hovering helplessly nearby.

The rocky outcrop on which both Flug and Oboe now stood split as an unseen fissure, unable to deal with the weight of the two of them, broke wide open sending them and half a ton of rock over the edge.

"OH GOD NO!" shouted Ollie, leading the charge to the new edge of the cliff. "We've lost them," he choked. "Not even Flug could survive that."

As they arrived, Mrs. Ladle was gesticulating wildly.

"They're just there," she shouted. "Both of them are hanging on by their fingertips."

A tightness in her throat made her words seem thicker and more resonant than usual, and she felt a stinging in her eyes. "I'm sorry," she croaked, her voice laden with emotion. "There's nothing I can do for them."

By now Ollie and Ethan, held in place thanks to Mandrake straining and holding on to their legs for all he was worth, were face down in the dirt and hanging over the precipice. It was pitch black and as scary as hell, but they could just about make out the two figures below them. Ethan stretched out an arm but it was no use, he was a good four feet short. There was no way that any of them would be able to reach down far enough.

"MRS LADLE!" shouted Ollie. "GET OFF THAT DAMN THING AND BRING IT HERE. IF WE CAN LOWER IT DOWN MAYBE FLUG CAN GRAB ONTO IT!"

The witch acknowledged, flew over their heads and landed about fifteen feet behind them.

———

With the departure of Mrs Ladle, Flug and Oboe were completely alone. It was a desperate situation and both of them knew what the probable outcome would be.

Flug had managed to get both hands onto a thin lip of rock, but Oboe was hanging by her right wrist. It was wedged in a narrow gap and was the only thing keeping her in place. A thin trickle of blood flowed down her arm, staining her top.

"Why did you do it you silly man?" she said. "I told you I had to leave."

"But me love you," said Flug.

"No you don't. You only think that you do. You don't even know me, and if you did I don't think you'd be quite so eager to save me."

Flug was confused. He thought that Oboe would be happy to be rescued. He knew he would.

"But me was finkin. . . "

Before he could finish his sentence the massive, corded muscles in his left forearm could take no more and he lost his grip. As his arm dropped free his weight shifted, pulling him further down. The thumb and little finger of his right hand slipped from the ledge leaving him dangling by three straining digits.

"Me can't hold on," he said sadly. "Fingers hurtin'."

Oboe was beside herself with grief. Not only had she killed the old man but she was now responsible for the demise of this being. She couldn't even summon the words to thank him for his sacrifice or to comfort him in what would no doubt prove to be his final moments.

Then, without warning, a green glow came from under their feet and surrounded them in its eerie embrace. They were both overcome with a sudden and intense feeling of calm, almost as if whilst shrouded in its warm clutches they were safe from harm. The tension in Flug's fingers lessened slightly.

Between them a spectral figure of a man appeared. When he spoke, his voice was soothing and comforting.

> *"I am the ghost of this here rock*
> *And I say to one and all*
> *It gets quite lonely out here in the dark*
> *So those who come must fall."*

Flug didn't have the slightest inkling about what was going on. He couldn't understand how someone could be floating in mid air let alone discern the meaning of his rhyming words, but seeing as Flug didn't even comprehend the difference between up and down this was no great surprise. Many was the time that he would be halfway up a flight of stairs and have his internal compass go haywire. You'd usually find him a couple of hours later, sitting disconsolately on a step saying that he'd gotten lost again.

Oboe, on the other hand, grasped the concept immediately.

> *"But wait one moment, it's not all bad*
> *For I'm not a black hearted knave*
> *I have the power within my grasp*
> *And one soul I can save."*

That was all she needed to know. This phantom, whoever he was, had not only offered her a way out but also the opportunity to save her rescuer.

> *"Percy's my name and for many a year*
> *I've waited for someone to come*
> *A likeminded spirit too sad to go on*
> *Then to rest as two and not one."*

She wouldn't be alone. She could go to her maker in the company of someone who seemed to be as melancholy as she was. She didn't know his reasons but she would have eternity to find out.

"Wot goin' on, Oboe?" asked Flug. "Who dat?"

"He's a friend," she said, "and he's going to take you back." "Wot about you?"

"I'm going with him. He's lonely. And so am I."

"But me be lonely if you gone," said Flug, his voice cracking. "Please come wiv me."

"I can't," she said.

The buoyant nature of the ebbing green cloud allowed her to rise up ever so slightly so that with her free hand she was able to stroke his cheek.

"And I think, deep down, you know why."

"The time has come," said Percy. "We must go now. My power is not limitless."

Oboe leaned towards Flug and kissed him tenderly on the lips. "Goodbye," she said. "And thank you."

A signal way, way down in the depths of Flug's permanently

unconscious subconscious fired off a message. It said that this was how things should end. This was right. The correct balance was established. This didn't mean an awful lot to Flug, but he did know one thing. If Oboe was happy then he was happy.

The ethereal figure that was Percy dissipated into the green mist, which in turn left Flug and amassed around Oboe. Slowly and gracefully she drifted downwards, all the while staring back at him with a smile on her face.

A tear dripped from the end of his nose, fell through the air, and landed softly on the misty surface. It caused a series of concentric ripples to form, like a stone dropped onto the still waters of an emerald lake.

"Bye, Oboe," said Flug, as she finally disappeared into the endless black. "Me love you."

———

"What on earth is going on down there?" said Mrs. Ladle, handing her broomstick to Ethan. "The last time I saw that much green was after I made that dodgy batch of toad pudding."

Stitches recalled the incident in question. The local branch of the Neighbourhood Witch had held a charity bake sale. The bake had been provided by Mrs. Ladle and several of her crone like cronies, and the charity was to offer support for 'Elderly Practitioners of the Ancient Arts of Magic, Mystery and Mayhem' (otherwise known as Mrs. Ladle and several of her crone like cronies).

Unfortunately one of the aforementioned crone like cronies (Mrs. Ladle. She didn't like to be left out) had used out of date Cave Toad juice in her recipe. Even more unfortunately, she made rather a lot of toad pudding using the out of date Cave Toad juice. Still more unfortunately she'd sold every last glutinous globule of the toad pudding, containing the out of date Cave Toad juice. The resulting vomit storm had turned into a lumpy jade river that was so potent that it had eaten through several paving slabs, two trolls and a golem who had fallen asleep in its viscous path. To this day some buildings still had faded green stains on them. So did quite a few a pairs of pants.

"I'm not sure," said Ollie. "We couldn't see very much because of the cloud, but the green glow's disappearing now, or to be more precise, it's moving away."

"Where's Flug and Oboe?" said Mandrake, desperately trying to stop his shoulders from taking a short, painful holiday from their sockets.

"I can't tell," said Ethan, who was just about to lower the broomstick, "but. . . oh, hang on." He shuffled about. "Quick, get back."

Like a phoenix from the flames (only he wasn't a bird, or on fire. Or a bird on fire for that matter), Flug rose up towards them. No one could see how it was happening; only that it was, as inexplicable as that may be.

Slowly he ascended to the top of the cliff, travelled over their heads and came to rest just behind them. They rushed to join him.

"Flug, love," said Mrs. Ladle, putting a hand on his arm. "What happened down there?"

"Me met nice man. He help me come back."

"What about, Oboe?" said Ollie. "Where's she gone? Is she still hanging on?"

Flug smiled and shook his head.

"No. She go wiv da nice man. Dey friends now so Oboe not sad and lonely anymore. But it okay. She happy so me happy."

And that was it. He didn't say another word about it, and it didn't seem to be upsetting him at all. In fact he was calm and accepting about the loss of Oboe.

As they turned and began the long walk back to the castle Mandrake looked at Flug, or to be more exact, his hand.

"What's that you're carrying?" he asked. Flug raised his arm and showed him. "Oh good grief," said Stitches.

———

After stopping at the old man's hut to lay him to rest and collect Crumble and Kilo, they all returned to Jocular's Castle which, thanks to Mrs. Ladle and her handy magazine, had been restored to its former, if somewhat gaudy appearance.

Egon, covered in dust as usual (not from the redecorating though.

This was how he usually looked) answered the door and showed them to the Dark Lords current whereabouts.

He was in the Mexican room, a straw donkey, piñata strewn, la Cucaracha inducing slice of Latino nastiness that smelt vaguely of chilli and sweaty sombreros.

Jocular was sitting in a flesh coloured reclining chair and had Noggin on his lap. He was purring contentedly and rubbing himself on the leather surface (the cat that is. Vampire lords didn't tend to go around rubbing themselves on random pieces of furniture).

"Ah, I'fe been expecting you, Ollie," said Jocular, smiling and stroking his furry menace. (I know that sounds a bit rude, but I'm going to leave it in because it pleases me to do so. If you happen to be one of my younger readers though and you don't know why it sounds a bit rude, go and ask a parent to explain what a euphemism is. It's in the same part of the dictionary as embarrassment if that helps).

Ollie filled him in about what had happened and expressed his happiness that the castle had been put to rights. To his unending relief Jocular harboured no grudges or thoughts of retribution against those who had torn his home asunder, because it had given him the excuse to put up some new curtains and the cherry wood banisters that he'd wanted for ages.

"So where are Cross and Deadhouse?" asked Stitches, noting the very skin like tone of Jocular's seat. Egon had informed him that the journalists had visited, and knowing that The Count wasn't averse to a bit of living art, or dead art as the case may be, he wondered if they'd been permanently added to the vampire's collection (as a couple of columns perhaps, ha ha).

"Oh, zey left a short vile ago to prepare ze next issue of ze paper. It's going to haff my interfiew in it."

"We'll have to get a copy, my Lord," said Ollie. "It should be an interesting read."

"You can count on it, yes," said Jocular, smiling.

A couple of hours later they were back at the office. Ethan was escorting Kilo home, (the scientist had decided to retire from his current line of research and was thinking that maybe flower arranging would be a more practical and ultimately safer pursuit. Sadly, he was killed three months later when the seven foot Neptune Bat Trap that he'd grown had gotten fed up with its diet and decided to try something with a few more calories in it. All that was found in Kilo's greenhouse was a fingernail, some sweet wrappers, an empty bottle of Country Bob's Rapid Flower Growth Formula and a very fat plant with indigestion), Crumble was safely ensconced in his lab once more, and Ollie and Stitches, with Mandrake in tow, were filling Ronnie in on recent events.

"So you've no idea where she went?" asked Ronnie.

"None at all," said Ollie. "There was a green light that came and went and then Flug floated back up to us safe and sound."

"And he's not saying anything?" "Not a word."

The familiar seismic thump in the corridor indicated to all those present (and to some a good few hundred metres away) that the monster in question was on his way.

"Hi, Ronnie," said Flug.

"Hiya, mate. How are. . . oh my goodness whatever the heck is that?" Secured by a length of chain around his neck, Flug was proudly wearing Oboe's right hand. When she had descended with Percy it hadn't worked loose and Kilo's stitching had parted at the wrist leaving the five-fingered pendant behind.

"Tis a minto.. . um, a meneto... uh, sumfink to remember Oboe," said Flug, tenderly stroking it and dislodging a couple of flies in the process. "That's lovely," said Ollie, "but I think you might want to keep it somewhere safe. You don't want to lose it."

"Okay, Ollie. Me keep it in bedroom." He trundled off with a spring in his step.

"I've heard of fiddlers elbow but Oboe's hand is taking it a bit too far if you ask me," said Stitches. "It's going to start smelling you know." "Don't worry. I'll get Crumble to preserve it," said Ollie. "If it works for his raspberries then it should work on body-parts."

"Right," said Ronnie. "I'm off to the shop. Anybody want anything?"

THE END

549

EXTRACT FROM THE SKULLENIAN TIMES

JOB ADVERTS

Mortician required at the Glans Forensic Institute. No experience necessary but must be able to work to tight deadlines.

Mr. Underdown, Fibulas long serving grave digger is retiring, leaving an opening. If you think you can fill it, send your CV to Third grave from the left, The Cemetery, Fibula (own spade preferred).

LOST AND FOUND

Hector Lozenge, town cleaner and drunk has gone missing again. If found please return to The Bolt and Jugular. His beer is getting warm.

Found. One cat, no collar, madder than a Viking with a personality disorder. If you can offer him a home, and the horse that he's attached to, contact the editorial team.

FEATURE BY EXCALIBUR CROSS

In the first of our celebrity interviews we were honoured to be invited to the home of our resident Vampire Lord, Count Jocular. What follows is an account of the conversation that took place.

"Firstly, may I say thank you for inviting us into your home?" "Off course you may."

" . . . . . . "

" . . . . . . "

"Oh I see. Thank you for inviting us into your home." "You are most velkom, indeed."

"If I may, how do you prefer to be addressed?"

"Usually in a brown enfelope and a little stamp, but how is zat important, Mr. Cross? I didn't realise ve vere going to discuss my postal arrangements."

"Um, you'd be surprised what our readers like to know, Sir." "Vell, qvite. Please continue."

"So, what is life like for a vampire lord in a modern, technological world?"

"Vell, pretty much ze same as it has alvays been. Ze only real difference is zat viz ze adfent of more advanced methods of trafel, I don't haff to go out off my vay for foreign food. I am particularly fond of Indians at ze moment."

"Don't you mean fond of an Indian?" "No. I do not."

"I see. So, the castle itself. It's rather spacious. How do you manage to keep it running?"

"Vell, it is not easy let me tell you, especially viz ze dodgy central heating. Luckily I haf many helpers who keep it going for me, ze most important of vhich is Egon. I truly could not do vizout him you know."

"How many staff do you have?" "Zat depends."

"On what, Sir?"

"On how vell zey perform zeir duties. Some days zere are more zan others. For example zere are two less today zan zere vere yesterday."

"Uh huh. And where are they now?"

"Vun is lighting up vun of my dungeons, he is about sixty vatts at ze moment I sink, and ze uzzer vun is underneath you."

"Sorry I don't understand."

"Your feet are resting on him. He is lying down on ze job yes."

"Right. Excellent. Moving on then. What is your relationship with the inhabitants of Skullenia like and how do you view your position within the community?"

"If I can answer ze first part of zat qvestion. I get on fery vell viz all of ze people in my kingdom. My doors are alvays open and I'm very happy to listen to zose liffing in ze local area. Of course disagreements do arise from time to time but zey are always resolved."

"Meaning?"

"Meaning zat zey generally see sings from my point of fiew eventually. Obviously zere's ze odd disappearance or sree but hey, zat is life yes?"

"Indeed it is. And your position here?"

"Zat all depends on ze time of night. Sometimes I am sitting down, sometimes I am standing up, and sometimes I am flying. You do ask some fery odd qvestions, Mr. Cross."

"All part of the job, My Lord. Now, about your interior designs.

Where do you get your ideas from?"

"Zat is a tricky vun. You might as vell ask a musician vhere he gets his songs from, or vhere a writer finds his stories. I sink it is a natural gift zat I am blessed viz. Zat and a subscription to Dream Castle magazine, a handy publication zat comes in veekly editions."

"Interesting."

"And ze binders are fery useful. Stops zem getting in a mess you see." "Indeed I do."

"And now it is time for you to go."

"Oh that's a shame. Can I ask why, My Lord?" "Off course you can ask."

" . . . . . . "

" . . . . . . "

"Oh, that again. Why do we have to leave, Sir?"

"Because I am hungry and I kind off like you just ze vay you are, Mr. Cross. Egon vill show you ze vay out."

We hope you enjoyed this small insight into our Vampire Lords world. Next week we speak to Mrs. Strudel and ask her, apart from broccoli, is there anything that an ogre won't eat?

ABOUT THE AUTHOR

I was born in Cardiff, South Wales in 1967. After finishing school I, like many authors, have had a series of differing and varied jobs including working in a warehouse, a bailiff and as a police officer. Obviously I'll never settle anywhere because all I want to do is write for a living so work is just something that I have to do between chapters (although I do sneak off whenever I can with my notebook and pen. Most of my first novel was written whilst parked up out in the sticks in a police car).

I'm extremely happily married to Sharon, an ex nurse, who designs and paints all of my book covers. I have a son, who works at a games developement company and two stepchildren and live in Kent, UK.

My novels are a mixture of the supernatural combined with a healthy dose of extreme silliness. In short I write what makes me laugh.

If you've been kind enough to read any of my books and enjoyed them, then a review would be great.

———

To learn more about Tony Lewis and discover more Next Chapter authors, visit our website at www.nextchapter.pub

Skullenia Collection - Books 1-3
ISBN: 978-4-82417-352-2
Hardcover Edition

Published by
Next Chapter
2-5-6 SANNO
SANNO BRIDGE
143-0023 Ota-Ku, Tokyo
+818035793528

24th July 2024

Milton Keynes UK
Ingram Content Group UK Ltd.
UKHW040256291024
450401UK00006B/88

9 784824 173522